The Tattered Heart

The Tattered Heart

A Historical Fiction Biography
of
Mother St. Andrew Feltin, CDP
Foundress
of the
Sisters of Divine Providence
of San Antonio, Texas

Mary Diane Langford, CDP

iUniverse, Inc.
New York Lincoln Shanghai

The Tattered Heart
A Historical Fiction Biography of Mother St. Andrew Feltin, CDP
Foundress of the Sisters of Divine Providence
of San Antonio, Texas

iUniverse books may be ordered through booksellers or by contacting:

iUniverse
2021 Pine Lake Road, Suite 100
Lincoln, NE 68512
www.iuniverse.com
1-800-Authors (1-800-288-4677)

ISBN: 978-0-595-43639-2 (pbk)
ISBN: 978-0-595-87964-9 (ebk)

Printed in the United States of America

Information on Cover Design

"The Tattered, But Holy, Pioneer" (based on "The Tattered Pioneer"
design) quilt, crafted by Regina Langford Decker in 2006, provides
the background for the cover. In her documentation, Regina notes
that the quilt is in honor of "all of the Sisters of Divine Providence of
San Antonio, especially Mother St. Andrew Feltin, their founder, who
pioneered the spiritual terrain of Texas … with a holy perseverance."
Her documentation concludes: "With gratitude to all the Sisters who
taught and cared for many people while working with scraps and
producing beautiful quilts." This quilt inspired the title for this book.
Thank you, Regina!

Cover design: original idea of Andrew Garrett Cross of Chanute, KS

Graphic design work: Catherine T. Maule, Our Lady of the Lake
University, San Antonio, Texas

To the Mothers and Sisters
in my life,
living here on Earth
and living in the Communion of Saints,
who inspired and encouraged this work.
You are the "tattered but holy pioneers"!

TABLE OF CONTENTS

FOREWORD

Genealogical studies have become quite common in recent years. Families delight in stories about their forebears of strong and heroic character. They celebrate their ancestors whose lives witnessed to bravery, fortitude, resilience, resourcefulness—to mention just a few of the virtues and traits held in esteem. Many families have designated one or several family members to do the research required to produce the lineage and descriptors of their ancestors. Success in this truly demanding endeavor is determined by the ingenuity, resourcefulness, perseverance, and, in the main, the love and dedication of the researcher for the subject of his/her study.

Though this historical fiction account of Mother St. Andrew Feltin's life by Sister Diane Langford, CDP, is not in essence a genealogical study, it is in fact a poignant story that we Sisters of Divine Providence of San Antonio (CDP) have longed for; and our Sisters' interest in the life of Mother St. Andrew has grown over the years. This is a book that examines the trials, reversals, and heroic endeavors that make up the threads in the fabric of our Texas foundress' life. Since we have precious little in our Congregational archives on her life and background, we were waiting for "just the right person" to take on the formidable task of extensive research and of capturing in words the life of this remarkable woman. We wanted this story for ourselves, for the challenge and motivation that Mother St. Andrew's life and struggles offer us. It was our own Sister Diane Langford, with her devotion and admiration for Mother St. Andrew, who stepped forward to do the extensive research and to write the story. This "moment of Providence" occurred in the summer of 2005 when Sister Diane, having completed a six-year term as a General Councilor of the Texas CDPs, asked for time to write Mother St.

Andrew's story. We were delighted! Sister Diane, with striking ingenuity and persistence in the discovery of heretofore-unknown facts,
has spent the last two years in writing this intriguing story of a "tattered heart."

This book is a well-stated piece of research told in a fascinating
historical fiction account with endnotes documenting the basic facts.
The book traces both the setbacks and the joys of success, the virtues and strengths to go on with total trust in a provident God. It
is an excursion into a soul-searching of one dauntless individual;
but it is not only Mother St. Andrew's story, it is every Texas Divine
Providence Sister's story as we try, even now, to live the legacy of
this strong and holy woman.

We celebrate Sister Diane and her compelling narrative. We thank
Sister Diane for taking on this labor of love.

> Sister Jane Ann Slater, CDP
> Superior General
> Congregation of Divine
> Providence
> San Antonio, Texas
> May 2007

PREFACE

Mother St. Andrew Feltin, an extremely courageous woman of her time who bore with grace the physical, spiritual, and psychological hardships of her life now is accepted by her daughters, the Sisters of Divine Providence of San Antonio, Texas. However, for the most part, Sisters who entered the Congregation in the twentieth century seldom learned anything about her. At times, certain episodes of her life story were even points of shame for our Community.

Although both Sister Mary Joseph Neeb's *Memoirs of Fifty Years* (1916) and Sister Generosa Callahan's *The History of the Sisters of Divine Providence* (1955), present a great deal about Mother St. Andrew, until this writing her story has not been told in its fullest in part due to a lack of primary source material. For undocumented reasons the Congregation of Divine Providence has a dearth of primary source material from the first fifty years of our history as the Texas branch of the Sisters of Divine Providence of St. Jean-de-Bassel, France (Germany). Because of the dearth of primary source material (e.g., letters of Mother St. Andrew, her writings), I have chosen to write a work of historical fiction. However, to satisfy those who will ask, "What is true?" documented material upon which the fiction is based, along with notations of sources appear in the "Endnotes" to each chapter. To the best of my ability, the information in the chapter endnotes is correct. (Readers may wish to read the "Endnotes" first!)

On occasion a character will reference the words of our European founder, Father Jean-Martin Moye. These quotations are from the 1983 edition of *The Directory of the Sisters of Providence of Portieux (France)* which holds Father Moye's letters to and writings about the Sisters of Providence whom he founded in the 1760's.

Given the style of education in the nineteenth century, I presume that Mother St. Andrew studied selections from **The Directory** during her novitiate training (1849-1851), committing portions to memory. It is also likely that Mother St. Andrew brought with her to Texas a copy of parts of the 1858 text of **The Directory of the Sisters of Providence of Portieux** which was held at St. Jean-de-Bassel at the time Mother St. Andrew emigrated in 1866.

Though descriptors of characters are largely fiction, their names, if known, have not been altered. I acknowledge that my imagination has filled in the gaps and expanded upon that which can be documented with primary and secondary sources.

Words cannot express my gratitude to Sister Jane Coles and Sister Margaret Riché who edited the manuscript. Their work made the book so much better than my poor efforts could ever have done!

In the process of writing this book, I grew to love Mother St. Andrew, to accept her faults, and to be inspired by her virtue. She is an outstanding example of the resilience of the human spirit who trusts deeply in a Provident God to bring her to salvation despite the vicissitudes of her life and the limitations of her personality. Her "tattered heart" is truly a "Providence heart." I offer her my sincere apology if I have taken undue liberties to depict her experiences or have misrepresented her in any way. In addition, I take full responsibility for any error that is present in the chapters or endnotes due to my speculation or lack of insight.

Mary Diane Langford, CDP

FRANCE

Clarksville

·Austin

Fredericksburg·

·New
Braunfels
· San Antonio

·Frelsburg
Houston

Castroville

Galveston

MAP OF TEXAS

Descendants of Jean-Claude Isidore Feltin

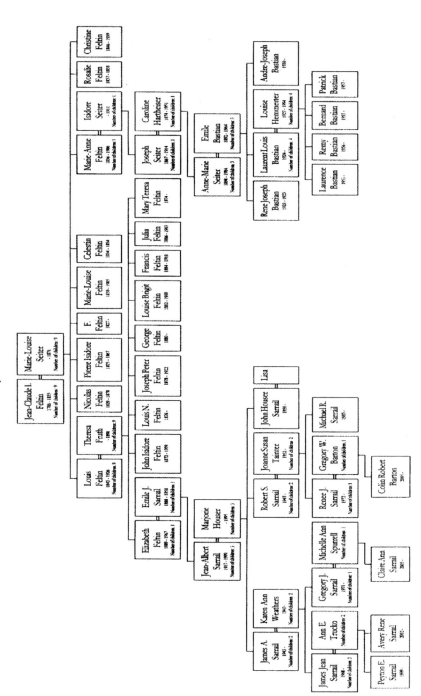

THE SEVEN CONGREGATIONS OF THE DAUGHTERS OF FATHER JEAN-MARTIN MOYE

Father Jean-Martin Moye (1730-1793)

Marguerite Lecomte
(1st Sister; opened 1st school at Befy in 1762)

Marie Morel
(1st Superior of the Sisters of the Christian Schools Consecrated to the Infant Jesus [c.1765])

Novitiate at St. Die (1768)
(French-speaking)

Novitiate at Haut-Clocher (1770)
(French-speaking)

Novitiate at Hommarting
(German-speaking)

Novitiate at Siersthal
(German-speaking)

Novitiate at Cutting
(under Fr. Moye--1784)

Novitiate at Essegney
(under Fr. Galland – 1785)

Novitiate at Portieux (1806)
(under Fr. E. Feys)

Novitiate at St. Jean-de-Bassel (1827)
(under Fr. Jean Decker)

Now: **Congregation of Divine Providence of Portieux, France**

Novitiate at Vitrolles, France

1838: Became the **Sisters of Providence of Gap**, France under the Bishop of Gap

1837: Novitiate at **Champion (near Namur), Belgium** under the Bishop of Namur

Now: **Congregation of Divine Providence of St. Jean-de-Bassel, France**

1866: Branch established in Texas under Mother St. Andrew Feltin (became independent in 1886, under Bishop John Neraz of San Antonio, Texas; became a Congregation of "pontifical right", the **Congregation of Divine Providence of San Antonio, Texas** in 1912

1930: **Missionary Catechists of Divine Providence** established by Sister Benetia Vermeersch, CDP. -Texas (Became independent of CDP-Texas in 1989?)

Also: **Sisters of Divine Providence of Ribeauville, France**. Founded by Father Louis Krempp. Adopted the spirituality of Father Jean-Martin Moye. In 2000, at their tri-annual meeting, the Daughters of Father Moye embraced the Sisters of Divine Providence of Ribeauville, as "Daughters of Father Moye."

CHRONOLOGY

1763—Father Jean-Martin Moye, a priest of the Diocese of Metz, France, sends Marguerite LeComte, a factory worker in Metz, to the village of Befey, north of Metz, in order to begin a school, the first venture of the project that eventually became the Sisters of Providence.

1794—Father Jean-Martin Moye died in Triers, Germany.

March 1812—A second, German-speaking, novitiate (the first novitiate at Portieux being French-speaking) established at Hommarting, France.

1815—Both German-speaking novitiates, Siersthal and Hommarting merged.

1826—The novitiate at Hommarting moved to St. Jean-de-Bassel in Lorraine, France.

December 27, 1830—Louise Feltin was born in Geispolsheim, Alsace, France.

1836—The Sisters of Providence of Ribeauvillé (Alsace) [founded by Father Louis Krempp, but based on the spirituality of Father Jean-Martin Moye] started a school for girls in Geispolsheim.

1838—The Bishop of Die separated the community at St. Jean-de-Bassel from the community at Portieux, making St. Jean-de-Bassel canonically independent.

1840—The Feltin family moved to LaWalck, Alsace, France.

1845—Sister Basilisse Gand named first official Superior General at St. Jean-de-Bassel (serving until 1864)

1845—Louise Feltin began her life in the Sisters of Divine Providence of St. Jean-de-Bassel. As a Candidate she was sent to teach at Krautergersheim in Alsace.

November 8, 1849—Louise Feltin entrance into the Congregation of Divine Providence at St.Jean-de-Bassel, Lorraine, France is recorded in the Book of Entrants.

September 20, 1851—Louise Feltin received into the novitiate of the Congregation of Divine Providence and given the name *Sœur* (Sister) St. André.

March 16, 1852—St. Jean-de-Bassel established as a legally independent diocesan congregation, separate from the Sisters of Providence of Portieux, France.

September 21, 1852—Sister St. Andrew made promises of obedience, poverty, and chastity.

September 1852—1853—Sister St. Andrew was missioned to the village school in Epfig, Alsace, France (St. Georges Parish).

1853-1859—Sister St. Andrew was missioned to the village of Heiligenberg, Alsace, France, the Parish of St. Vincent. It is presumed that she opened the school for this village.

1855—Sister St. Andrew made her profession of vows. [This was the vow of chastity; perpetual profession of vows was not the custom at St. Jean-de-Bassel at this time.]

1859-1866—Sister St. Andrew was missioned to the village school of Batzendorf, Alsace, France (St. Abrogast Parish).

1864—Sister Adrienne Frache was elected Superior General when Mother Basilisse Gand stepped aside due to failing health.

Summer 1866—Bishop Claude Dubuis visits St. Jean-de-Bassel in hopes of getting Sisters for Texas.

October 1866—Sister St. Andrew and Sister Alphonse Boëgler accompanied Bishop Claude-Marie Dubuis to the United States, arriving in Galveston, Texas, on October 25, 1866.

November 27, 1866—Carolyn Spann Rice of Corpus Christi was received as a novice into the Congregation of Divine Providence in Galveston and receives the name Sister St. Joseph; Sister St. Andrew (now known as Mother St. Andrew) made perpetual vows under Bishop Dubuis; Sister Alphonse Boëgler made perpetual vows and changed her name to Sister St. Claude.

November 1867—Mother St. Andrew, Sister St. Claude and Sister St. Joseph go to Austin, Texas, to start a school at St. Mary's Parish which was pastored by Father Nicolas Feltin, Mother St. Andrew's brother, a priest of the Diocese of Galveston.

1867—Sister Constantine Eck was elected Superior General due to the death of Mother Adrienne Frache. Mother Constantine served until her death on September 18, 1885.

September 1, 1868—Mother St. Andrew was directed by Bishop Dubuis to move to Castroville where her motherhouse would be established. Sister St. Joseph remained at St. Mary's School; Sister St. Claude was sent to Corpus Christi to teach at the parish school there. A new vocation, Sister Agnes Wolf of Bastrop County, accompanied Mother St. Andrew to Castroville. A school for St. Louis Parish was started immediately. Father Peter Richard, pastor of St. Louis Parish, was appointed Ecclesiastical Superior of the fledgling Congregation.

1870-1871—Franco-Prussian War. After this war, Alsace and Lorraine became states or departments in Germany. Those living in Alsace and Lorraine were German citizens until after World War I in 1918.

1871—A new Motherhouse building is erected in Castroville on property given to the Sisters of Divine Providence by Bishop Dubuis.

1871—Sister Mary Pierre Bader (novice) died in New Braunfels, Texas at age eighteen.

October 29, 1871—Sister St. Claude Boëgler left the Congregation of Divine Providence and joined the Sisters of the Incarnate Word and Blessed Sacrament in Victoria, Texas.

1872—1875—Controversy over the ownership of the property at St. Mary's School in Austin.

1874—Sisters of the Holy Cross from Indiana took over St. Mary's School in Austin; Holy Cross Fathers took over the parish.

February 5, 1875—Sister St. Joseph Rice left the Sisters of Divine Providence and returned to Corpus Christi where she joined the Sisters of the Incarnate Word and Blessed Sacrament.

1874—The Diocese of Texas was divided and Bishop Anthony Pellicer was consecrated Bishop of San Antonio; Bishop Dubuis remained the Ordinary of the Diocese of Galveston. Pellicer died on April 14, 1880.

1875—A school at the German parish of St. Joseph in downtown San Antonio was opened. Father Nicolas Feltin had been appointed the pastor of St. Joseph's in January 1875.

June 1878—Mother St. Andrew returned to St. Jean-de-Bassel for more Sisters. Mother Constantine Eck missioned eight professed Sisters, all experienced teachers, to Texas.

November 30, 1878—Father Nicolas Feltin died suddenly at St. Joseph Church in San Antonio.

1880-Mother St. Andrew returns again to St. Jean-de-Bassel for more Sisters for Texas.

1881—Mother St. Andrew and Bishop Dubuis agree to set up a second novitiate in the Diocese of Galveston at Frelsburg, Texas.

1881—Bishop John C. Neraz was named Bishop of San Antonio.

1882—Mother St. Andrew visited St. Jean-de-Bassel and asked for more assistance. Mother Constantine sent novices and postulants. Other young women from Germany and Ireland also came to Texas.

1883—Mother St. Andrew made her final trip to St. Jean-de-Bassel to recruit more vocations. She brought back fifty-two candidates from Germany, Poland, and Ireland.

September 1883—Bishop John Neraz visited St. Jean-de-Bassel and inquired of Mother Constantine about the future relationship between the St. Jean-de-Bassel Motherhouse and the Texas branch.

August 1884—Under the new Constitution of St. Jean-de-Bassel, Mother St. Andrew is elected Superior of the Texas Sisters.

September 18, 1885—Mother Constantine Eck died.

1885—Sister Anna Houlné was elected Superior General at St. Jean-de-Bassel and served until her death in 1903.

Spring 1886—Sister Florence Walter and Sister Berthilde Thiel were sent to St. Jean-de-Bassel for more Sisters.

July 1886—Father Henry Pefferkorn pastor of St. Joseph's German Parish in downtown San Antonio, and other priests accused Mother St. Andrew of turning the Sisters against the priests.

August 1886—Bishop Neraz insisted that the Texas Congregation be independent of St. Jean-de-Bassel and elect a new Superior. Bishop Neraz refused to allow the Sister-electors to re-elect Mother St. Andrew

August 26, 1886—Sister Florence Walter, then en route from Europe, was elected Superior General and confirmed by Bishop Neraz.

September 1886—Sister St. Andrew was sent to St. Joseph School in Galveston. Sister St. Andrew submitted her resignation to Bishop Neraz with the intention of establishing herself in a new novitiate under the Diocese of Galveston at Frelsburg. Bishop Gallagher, Bishop of Galveston agreed to accept her and move forward with plans for the novitiate that had been begun under Bishop Dubuis, but Bishop Neraz would not release her from her relationship with the Congregation in Castroville and Gallagher rescinded his offer.

October 1886—Sister St. Andrew and Sister Arsene Schaff went to Anaheim, California, to investigate opening a school at St. Boniface Parish there. Bishop Neraz ex-communicated both Sister St. Andrew and Sister Arsene and would not approve a California school.

November 1886—Sister St. Andrew was sent to teach at Clarksville, Texas.

March 1887—Sister St. Andrew left Clarksville without permission and returned to St. Boniface Parish in Anaheim, California. Sister Arsene followed with permission from Mother Florence.

Bishop Neraz required Mother Florence to denounce Sister St. Andrew.

July 1887—Both Sister St. Andrew and Sister Arsene returned to Castroville. Mother Florence was instructed by Bishop Neraz to send them away from the Motherhouse. Sister Arsene chose to return to St. Jean-de-Bassel and Sister St. Andrew lived in a house in Castroville, estranged from the Congregation.

February 14, 1890—Theresa Fruth Feltin, Louis Feltin's wife, Sister St. Andrew's sister-in-law committed suicide.

April 1890—The Louis Feltin Family moved to San Jose, California; Sister St. Andrew, estranged from the Congregation, accompanied her brother and his children.

October 1900—Sister St. Andrew returned to Castroville

February 1, 1905—Mother St. Andrew Feltin died in Castroville at age seventy-five.

CHAPTER I

LETTERS

Louise Feltin sat on the porch swing looking off into her mountains, so much like the Vosges Mountains of her childhood in France. Five years ago she would never had had to take a break from work in the store. With increasing heart problems, she felt tired all the time. The days now seemed long, and increasingly empty. So incredibly painful, the surgery to remove her appendix at O'Connor Sanatorium had taken its toll. Strangely, she welcomed the physical suffering. The Lord knew that she had sins to atone for and her sufferings in this world might assuage punishment in the next. But, she feared, from now on she would be only a burden to her family. The time had come to write to the Motherhouse in San Antonio.

Perhaps the nagging loneliness was the worst part of her situation. Her original intention had been to accompany her younger brother Louis and his seven children from Castroville, Texas, to San Jose, California, in 1890 staying only long enough to help him with his youngest children. Ten years had passed. Louise had remained hopeful that Mamie, her eldest niece, would be able to assume the duties of a mother to this motherless family. Certain now that Mamie who was in her mid-twenties, would never be mentally strong enough to manage the household alone, Louise had begun to think differently about her own future.

When Mamie graduated from high school, Louise had encouraged her to attend the California State Normal School right there in San Jose, but the girl always had a number of excuses why she couldn't matriculate. Recently, Louise had abandoned hope that Mamie could

Mother St. Andrew (Louise Feltin) while estranged from the Congregation. Circa 1890 (Courtesy of Mr. Laurent Bastian, LaWalck, France)

be a teacher. Now, she thought, I can't keep putting off my future hoping that past wounds will magically heal.

The mountains seemed to embrace her and the words of the Psalmist filled her heart: *I will lift up mine eyes to the mountains from whence comes my help.*

Two years had turned into four and four into eight and eight into ten. Next month, the youngest of Louis' children, Lizette, would be eleven years old. She was smart, doing well in school, and very helpful in the family-run grocery store. Between Julia, now nearly thirteen; young Louise, who had been named for her aunt but had always been called Lou-Lou, almost eighteen; and Mamie, the family's little grocery store was running smoothly. Now twenty-two, Joe was holding down a full-time job at a fruit-packing warehouse not too far from their house. The two other boys, Louis Nicolas and James—well—they were boys. Louise had hoped that Louis Nicolas would be more goal-oriented but he did not yet have firm plans for what he wanted to do with his life. James was just too young yet.

In recent months, their aunt Louise had been spending more and more time reflecting on her unplanned-for move to California ten years ago. The entire venture had proven to be very costly. Moving to San Jose with her brother Louis had required setting aside her identity as a Sister of Divine Providence and leaving behind her beloved village of Castroville. Raising children at age sixty, a task she had never thought suited her, especially caring for the youngest who were just babies in the spring of 1890, had been exhausting.

Though she had done her best to tend these children, she never felt particularly successful at mothering.

Deeply depressed following the birth of Lizette in the summer of 1889, dear Theresa, Louis Feltin's wife of nearly twenty years and the mother of his eight children, hanged herself in their barn on February 14, 1890. Abject with grief, and feeling like a total failure at life, husbanding, and fatherhood, Louis, she remembered, had been near suicide himself. He was desperate to get away from all that reminded him of his wife's action.

How often during these past ten years had she asked herself whether she had made the right decision during the Lent of 1890? She had packed away her beloved habit, resumed her Christian name, and left the ghost of "Sister St. Andrew Feltin" in Castroville. Miss Louise Feltin, wearing a simple housedress borrowed from a friend in Castroville, had made that interminable train ride with her brother and seven of his eight children. Her neighbors here in San Jose knew her only by her given name and she had confided her past to no one except the pastor at St. Patrick's Church and the chaplain at O'Connor Sanatorium.

Once Louis had made up his mind to leave Castroville, Louise had tried to convince him that they should go to Anaheim where she at least knew the people at St. Boniface Parish. Had they gone there, she would have been able to work in the parish, preparing children for the sacraments and perhaps starting a school. But Louis, barely thinking straight, was adamant about their destination. He had wanted a completely fresh—and anonymous—start. So their destination had been San Jose, a bustling town with plenty of work in the orchards and fruit-packing companies.

Lents and Easters had come and gone for the last decade, but in recent years Louise had experienced very few resurrections.

In San Jose the Feltin family had actually done well. After seven years in business in San Jose, their grocery store was practically running itself. Relying on her memories of her father's grocery story in LaWalck, Alsace, Louise had started with only a small inventory:

The store that Louise Feltin operated as it appeared in 2006.
(Photo by Sister Diane Langford, CDP, 2006.)

eggs, milk, butter, dried meat, tinned vegetables, flour, sugar, and a few dry goods. The building was a long one-story structure with a door that opened directly onto the corner of Ninth and Empire. It was relatively new, but filthy when the owner of their rented house agreed to lease to her. Hard work and her good business sense had developed a thriving business over the past seven years. It was the kind of little store that her neighbors would send their children to for those items that they had forgotten to buy in their regular shopping trips to the markets ten blocks away on Santa Clara Street. Her neighbor ladies, when they came themselves, seemed to enjoy lingering there, chatting over the neighborhood gossip, fashion prospects of the day, and the future of local crops.

Following her father's example, and relying on God's providential care for her family, Louise had extended credit to anyone who needed it. During fruit-picking season and canning season when most people had cash, her patrons paid off their bills, but many found themselves in her debt during the off-season. It was always the proverbial feast or famine.

The building was in a growing neighborhood of mostly Italian, Mexican, and German immigrants on the north end of San Jose. The surrounding houses were predominantly two-story Victorians, neatly painted in varied colors. Their own home, a real find, was one of the last houses on the northern edge of San Jose. What became known as "418 Empire," was a large two-story clapboard house with a small front porch and plenty of room for Louis, his three boys and four girls, and Louise herself.

Down the street was Grant Elementary School where the younger children had gone to school. The autobus ran to the corner of Tenth and Julian Streets, three blocks away so, one by one, as the children got older, they went downtown to the high school. Joe had finished two years of high school, as had Louis Nicolas, and it looked like James might finish all four years.

When Lou-Lou had been asked if she wanted to go to the Normal School after graduation at the end of the month, Louise was surprised that her niece wanted to help in the store. The education of her nephews and nieces had been their aunt's major focus over the past ten years and, with lots of prodding and some nagging, Aunt Louise's goal had prevailed. Lou-Lou's decision was now her hope.

Louise had always been glad that they were within walking distance of St. Patrick's Church, which was ten blocks away at Ninth and Santa Clara Streets. When they had first moved to San Jose, that ten blocks was a pleasant stroll, an opportunity to chat with neighbors and enjoy the usually crisp, fresh air. Now, however, she noticed that pains in her chest left her out of breath before arriving for Sunday Mass. That worried her.

A bustling little town, San Jose had a metropolitan feel to it. Expanding orchards and canneries contributed to its growth, which meant that orders at the millwright company where Louis worked as a carpenter were not seasonal. For the first time in his life, Louise's brother had kept a steady job.

Having spent her young years helping her father in the family store in LaWalck before entering the convent, Louise knew "the tricks of the trade." She regularly reminded the girls: "the customer is always right," and "make friends with your vendors." Though Mamie wasn't interested in acquiring a profession, she was somewhat helpful in the store. The future of the business, however, was going to depend on young Lou-Lou. Having become really good at the business end of the enterprise, Lou-Lou, now that she had finished high school, was anxious to take over the management. Before long, she would be a grocer in her own right. Their aunt had spent the last five years teaching the younger girls all she knew about operating their store; and now they could order merchandise from vendors, handle arrangements with local orchards for deliveries of fresh fruit, and contract with growers for seasonal vegetables. Dairy Hill Farm supplied the dairy products, and a neighbor woman always had eggs. Louise was needed less and less. With each passing year, she had missed her Sisters more and more. Yes, it was time to go home.

During the past twelve years while estranged from her Congregation, Louise Feltin had never turned her back on her convent training. With the grocery store closed on Sunday and the children now older, she had plenty of time for prayer and reflection. Today, Pentecost Sunday, offered a day to reflect on the presence of the Holy Ghost in new beginnings. Prayer calmed her heart as she gathered her courage to write her letter to Mother Florence, her successor as Mother Superior.

Taking a last glance at the surrounding mountains, Louise rose slowly from the porch swing and opened the front door. With the children gone to nearby parks to spend Sunday afternoon with their friends, she had their small, sparsely furnished parlor all to herself. The quiet was soothing—so reminiscent of her convent Sundays. The desk where she had often worked late into the night on the store's ledgers was in front of an east window and Louise once again drank in the majesty of the distant, unchanging mountains. While so much of her life had seemed to drift over the past decade, those mountains remained a symbol of God's strong, enduring providential care. A peace settled over her even now as she let their grandeur wash over her.

During those lonesome years, while she had straightened shelves in the grocery store or prepared a meal for the children, Louise's mind often wandered back to Castroville, to Mother Florence, to the Sisters there. In her mind's eye she could always see her beloved Providence Motherhouse, the little boarders who needed motherly attention from the nuns, the people of the village of Castroville who would bring fresh meat or a special Alsatian pastry for "their" nuns. Though Louise had set her own desires aside hundreds of times during her years as Superior, her spirit now called her homeward.

On this quiet Sunday afternoon, alone with her memories, Louise took plenty of time to think of just what she wanted to say in her letter to Mother Florence. Her words must be clear and must reveal her heart's desire to return to her beloved Sisters, to the home of her heart. Should she express her fears, she asked herself. Perhaps her words in the letter should ask forgiveness again. Trepidation over how to express her deepest yearnings edged out the loneliness. Maybe she wouldn't write the letter after all.

From her apron pocket, Louise drew two letters that Mother Florence had written her. The first, written five years ago in early 1895, told her of the death of Bishop Neraz and mentioned her plans to move the Motherhouse to the outskirts of San Antonio. The second, written just last year in 1899, contained the news that Father Pefferkorn, another old nemesis, would be retiring to his native France. The last letter was short, revealing in a few paragraphs how competent Mother Florence had become in administering the Congregation during her years as Superior General. During her tenure as Superior General, Mother Florence had learned to work with Bishop Neraz. That was more than Louise could say about herself!

Though Mother Florence hadn't exactly invited her to come home, the tone in each of the letters was open as though Mother considered the reader to be an old friend.

When Louise had received the first letter in 1895, she was simply too busy raising children and starting her grocery store to consider returning to Castroville, although the death of Bishop Neraz made the possibility of returning to her convent quite alluring. The content of the second letter, however, had drawn her heart homeward. With Father Pefferkorn gone from San Antonio, perhaps she ought to think about going home. That letter had come just after that treacherous surgery at O'Connor Sanatorium. Was it offering her a sign from Providence that now was the time to consider returning to her former identity?

Tears came to Louise's dark brown eyes and rolled down her sunbrowned cheeks as she recalled her own failures with the second Bishop of San Antonio. She knew that her Alsatian stubbornness had been provoked only the more by his attempt to separate her beloved community from its Motherhouse in St. Jean-de-Bassel in Lorraine, now a German state. As Bishop Neraz had seemed to wrestle her for more and more control over her administrative decisions, she had fought harder. Even thinking of all that had happened those dozen years ago made her weary and anxious. She knew that a part of her would always be angry with the dead bishop—and herself—for all that had happened. The memories of all that had transpired would never dim. Sorrow for her failures still weighed upon her spirit and her chest tightened. Leaning heavily on the desk, Louise covered her face with her hands, giving way to a private, lonely grief.

Setting aside the letters from Mother Florence, she resolutely took up a new pen, dipped the tip into the ink, and began to write in French. Strong and steady, her even penmanship belied her seventy years.

> *9th and Empire*
> *San Jose, California*
> *Pentecost Sunday*
> *June 3, 1900*

> ### *Ma Très Chère Mère*

> *I am writing to thank you for the letters that you sent me during these last years. I can see that you are doing well as Mother Superior and it warms my heart to know of your successes, especially with the building of the new Academy and Motherhouse in San Antonio.*

In addition, I am writing to ask you if I can please return to the Congregation. Your kind letters have sustained me during these last years. As you know, I have continued to live my vows of poverty, chastity, and obedience while raising the children and helping Louis as best I can. But, my health is going down. My heart is failing and I have diabetes.

In asking to return to the Congregation, I assure you that I will live anywhere you choose to send me. I also assure you that I will never interfere with your administration of the Congregation. Those days for me are past. I want only to live in quiet and solitude, pray with my Sisters, and be of service in the community for whatever days God will allow me to have.

I await your kind response.

Your obedient daughter,
Sœur St. André

She read over her words one more time. Having paused several times as she wrote, Louise wanted to be sure that her letter expressed her true feelings. As she signed her name—her <u>true</u> name—she breathed a sigh of relief. She had been Aunt Louise and Miss Feltin long enough. It was time now to return to her deepest identity: Sister St. André, CDP.

She found an envelope and addressed it to Mother Florence who now lived in the new Motherhouse in San Antonio. She wondered what Our Lady of the Lake Convent and Academy looked like. The few descriptions that Mother Florence had put in her letters only piqued her curiosity. Her mind's eye could see a tall, light-colored brick building with castle-like turrets surrounded by a wooded acreage similar to the forest that surrounded St. Jean-de-Bassel. And, all on the banks of a lovely lake!

What a wonderful environment for the contemplation needed by young women learning to live their vocation during the days of the novitiate. The solitude of St. Jean-de-Bassel had been the perfect setting to prepare her for her mission years in remote French villages. Later, that same training in contemplation had supported her through the many challenges she faced as Superior of her little Congregation in Texas.

So many memories. Now, if she could go home to Castroville—or wherever Mother Florence would send her—she would have time to sort through those memories and find a place in her heart and soul for each one.

She had always thought that memories were like the pieces of a quilt: when stitched together they reveal our tattered hearts where the Providence of God alone understands all that our lives mean. Wanting time now to prepare to see what God had done with all those events and people in her life, all those patches and stitches, Louise longed for quiet and solitude. She needed to relish her good memories and to come to peace with the sad ones.

Thinking of returning to Texas was daunting. Louise realized that her stomach had begun to feel queasy. Perhaps it was too much to ask for, to hope for. Over the years, Mother Florence's letters were always polite, even warm at times, and she had written as soon as Bishop Neraz had died five years ago. An old woman now, Louise had been gone from Castroville for ten years, and estranged from the Congregation for longer than that! Perhaps the other Sisters wouldn't want her. She would only be a burden.

Truth be told, while living alone in Castroville, away from the Motherhouse, Louise knew that she had been a point of scandal in Castroville and perhaps the Sisters would find her return an embarrassment. She slipped the newly written letter into her apron pocket, not sure whether she really should mail it. But just thinking of remaining here in California, far from her dear Sisters forever, brought more tears to her eyes. She was so very lonely.

She found her black shawl, the shawl that every Sister of Divine Providence had to protect her from the winter wind, and settled it on her thin shoulders. Though it was the cusp of summer and a mild 70 degrees, Louise felt chilled in the unheated house, her arthritic bones now feeling the cold more and more. Laying aside her spectacles, she moved to her rocker that sat near the big west window. A few minutes of basking in the warm June sun coming through the windowpanes would take away the chill.

The slam of the back screen door and the sound of happy, young voices drifting through the kitchen and into the parlor startled the weary old woman who had nodded off.

"*Ma tante*, are you here?" Julia shouted as she and her sisters Lizette and Lou-Lou raced into the parlor.

"*Oui, mes infantes, je suis ici!*" She had insisted that the younger children learn both French and Alsatian and they all easily went back and forth in both languages.

Louise Feltin, her brother Louis, and their other sisters and brothers had grown up in Alsace when it was a state in France. They had spoken the Alsatian at home and in the village; French was the language of school and church. Hoping that their family heritage would continue in her family's second generation of Alsatian-Americans, she usually spoke in French or Alsatian to the younger children. Having grown up in Castroville, an Alsatian-speaking Texas village, the older children were at ease in the mother tongue of their father and aunt. And then, of course, doing business in their San Jose grocery store had served to strengthen their English.

"What did you do all afternoon, *ma tante*?" Lizette asked as she bent over to kiss her aunt on the cheek. Not waiting for an answer, Lizette rushed on: "We went to the park and played with our friends. Julia and I learned a new rhyme for jumping rope and I won some marbles from Johnny Parker. We had so much fun!"

"I'm so glad, *liebchen**! I had a good afternoon as well." This was not the time to tell the girls about her hopes. If Mother Florence refused her request, it would be unnecessary for them to know that she had planned to leave them. On the other hand, if Mother Florence accepted her request, goodbyes would come soon enough and she didn't want to upset them. Since she was the only mother these youngest three had ever known, she had always felt that in some ways they were emotionally fragile.

Their mother's suicide, now over a decade past, had damaged them all. Though Mamie had found their mother in the barn, the ordeal had etched sorrowful images on the minds of all but the youngest two girls. Louise always feared that the six older children might never truly recover.

For nearly three years after her departure from the Congregation in the summer of 1887, Sister St. Andrew—St. André in the French—had lived alone in a poorly built rock house a few blocks from Providence Motherhouse in Castroville. Her brother Louis' home had been nearby to the southwest. During the fall and winter months of 1889 and 1890, after the birth of Lizette, Louise had done as much as she could for her sister-in-law, going to the Feltin house several times a week to help Theresa with cleaning, cooking, washing, and ironing.

Louis and his wife Theresa and their four eldest children had moved to Castroville from Austin in 1878. The Motherhouse of the Congregation of Divine Providence in Castroville needed enlarging to accommodate new postulants, novices, and professed Sisters who were coming from Germany; and Louis, a carpenter, was willing to take on the work. Except for the work on the Motherhouse and some carpentry work for St. Louis Parish, Louis Feltin had seldom kept a job for more than a few months.

Though shocking, Theresa Feltin's suicide was not altogether a surprise. At the time of Theresa's death, Lizette had been a babe in arms; Julia had been barely two; James was six; Lou-Lou, eight;

*   **a term of endearment in Alsatian: dear little one**

Joe, twelve; Louis Nicholas, fourteen; and Mamie, the eldest daughter, seventeen. John Isidore, the eldest son, then a young man of eighteen, had not come with the family to California, retreating to Austin to live with his mother's sister, Elizabeth. Louise always suspected that John Isidore had blamed his father for his mother's suicide. They heard from John occasionally, but his decision to remain behind had wounded Louis.

Not particularly strong in character, Louis Feltin had been shattered by his wife's tragic death. Sister St. Andrew, then living alone in Castroville, convinced Father Brücklin, the pastor at St. Louis Church, to bury her sister-in-law in blessed ground. The usual type of small town, Castroville was filled with rumor and gossip, and Louis was ashamed. Sister St. Andrew's scandalous exile from the Convent in the summer of 1887 had been hard enough for Louis to deal with. Even though the people of Castroville loved Sister St. Andrew and saw to it that she had adequate food, firewood, and water, Louis had been rankled by the remarks about his sister that he had heard at Mann's Store. His wife's death was the last straw. Seeing no alternative but to take his whole family and leave town, Louis left Castroville to start over in California.

Sister St. Andrew, believing that she had no future in Castroville and recognizing that she would never be considered to be a Sister of Divine Providence as long as Bishop Neraz was alive, decided that Providence meant for her to accompany Louis and his children.

Hoping that Father Stöters could help them start over, she had written to the pastor with whom she had worked at St. Boniface Parish in Anaheim. Though Father Stöters was willing to help, Louis was adamant. Refusing to consider Anaheim, he had decided to go to northern California where the family and its bizarre history would be unknown.

By late April 1890 Louis had sold his house and they had packed up their few belongings. Sister St. Andrew had nothing but a few books, her habit, borrowed dresses, and her *prie-dieu*, which she had brought to Texas from France. The *prie-dieu* had been hers at the

Motherhouse and she had spent hours in prayer on it in her sad little house in Castroville. Leaving it behind was out of the question. Neighbors helped her crate it with Louis' few furnishings and take everything to the train station in Hondo. Nothing else in her house was worth keeping.

Before leaving town, the motherless family had gathered around the fresh unmarked graves of their mother and their baby brother George near the entry gate to St. Louis Cemetery. Tears filling their eyes had drowned any words that they might have wanted to say on that cold and windy April day as they bade a silent farewell to the mother who had loved them.

Louis, seven of his eight children, and Sister St. Andrew had then piled into the buckboards and headed to Hondo. Boarding the westbound Southern Pacific, they had joined hundreds of thousands of Americans who believed that they might find their fortune in golden California.

"So, what did you do while we were at the park, *ma tante?*" Breaking her aunt's reverie, Lou-Lou went back to Lizette's unanswered question.

"Oh, I prayed and wrote a letter and took a little nap," was their aunt's simple reply. "Let's get some supper and then you girls had better get to bed early. We have much to do in the store tomorrow. Now that you are out of school, we need to do a thorough cleaning!"

After supper, the girls prepared for bed and then came into their aunt's room to get their hair brushed and to say the rosary, their nightly ritual. Their brothers and their papa weren't home. Joe and young Louis Nicolas who liked to be called "Nick" worked extra shifts at the fruit-packing warehouse and the earliest summer crop was just coming in. James would be out with his friends now that they were all on summer vacation. Their lonely papa often stayed out late.

The grocery store paid for basic necessities, but the money that the boys brought home afforded Lizette's music lessons, the girls' schoolbooks, and other extras. James had promised he would look for a summer job and was bound to find something. At sixteen he was tall and a good worker in spurts. His aunt was very proud of him, but she also knew that James would always have grand ambitions but never the "stick-to-it-tive-ness" that would give him a solid future. Following the example of his older brothers, James would probably end up working in the canneries or in the orchards.

"*Ma tante*, can you tell us some family stories tonight?" Julia asked.

"Not tonight, child. I'm very tired and need to get a good night's sleep if we're going to make progress in the store tomorrow. But I promise that we'll have a good long story time soon." Over the last ten years, Louise had woven the tale of the Feltin family, its French roots, and the lives of her brothers and sisters for her nieces and nephews. Before she returned to her Congregation, God willing that Mother Florence would take her back, she wanted to tell the whole story one more time.

"Come, now, let's get your hair brushed and pray the rosary and then get right to bed. Tonight we pray the Glorious Mysteries. Let us remember in our prayers your brothers at work, that God will keep them safe; your papa; my Sisters in San Antonio; and the repose of your dear mother's soul. In the name of the Father, and of the Son, and of the Holy Ghost. I believe in God ...*"*

Auntie Louise rose early on Monday morning and was pleased that it would be another beautiful day in San Jose. She called the girls and heard them begin to stir. The kitchen had always been her domain, but now she recognized that the girls had to be prepared for her absence.

"Jule, after you're dressed, come and help me with breakfast! And Lou-Lou, I need you to begin to prepare for dinner. Lizette, come and prepare lunches for your papa and brothers to take to work." Her voice was light and she sounded happy. Though she remained anxious about the possibility of returning to her Congregation, she wanted to sound calm and peaceful. Maintaining a calm, prayerful home had been her objective over these ten years. Louis seldom added much to family life, and Mamie and the older children might never get over their mother's horrible death; but the younger ones deserved a good home. She prayed often that they would have happy memories of their childhood in San Jose.

Lizette was the first to arrive in the kitchen. "What do I do first, *ma tante?*" she asked.

"First, you take this letter and put it out for the postman. Take care with it now. It is important to me." She had spent a restless night, waking often to the question of whether or not she should send her letter. Her directive to Lizette seemed to come out of her mouth by itself, sealing the decision.

Lizette looked at the envelope. *"Ma tante,* are you writing again to your friend Mother Florence? What did you tell her?"

"Never mind now, *ma chèrie.* Just put it out for the postman. We've got to get breakfast, start dinner, and pack lunches for your father and brothers. The boys are still working the late shifts at the warehouse. And 7:30 will be here before we know it. Dairy Hill Farm will deliver milk soon, too. Let's hurry!"

When Julia arrived in the kitchen she was put in charge of making oatmeal and toasting bread. Their aunt had already built the fire in the stove. She watched as Lou-Lou prepared the chops that would be for dinner. Then, without being coached, the young girl quickly peeled potatoes and had them ready to boil. Her aunt was proud of how competent Lou-Lou had become. Louise watched carefully as each of her nieces moved quickly through her assigned tasks. She realized that she had nothing to worry about. Under her tutelage, her girls had become quite proficient in the kitchen. They wouldn't starve for lack of knowing how to cook, she thought.

Promptly at 7:30 that morning, as on every day of the week except Sunday, Louise Feltin unlocked the door of the grocery store and stepped into the dark interior, taking a deep breath. She loved the mixture of odors that wafted from the cases and shelves. The earthy smell of newly dug potatoes mingled with the sharp citrus of fresh oranges and lemons and the pungent aroma of dried sausages and coffee beans. Just like her father's store those many years ago in her home village of LaWalck. The blend of aromas always reminded her of her youth. She would have to remember to tell her nieces about Papa's store and their little village beside the river.

The days of June passed quickly and as Louise continued to be intentional about preparing the family for her absence, she also began to be caught up in thinking about her future in the Congregation. Hoping that Mother Florence would receive her back, she began to re-read her *Constitution,* now worn from years of study. Ever faithful to saying the Little Office of the Blessed Virgin daily, she renewed her vowed commitment as part of her devotional prayers. She spent hours every night on her precious *prie-dieu* praying the rosary with her arms extended, a Congregational practice of repentance and humility.

Each day, after the postman handed her the mail, Louise carefully organized the bills and flyers. Days came and went but no letter arrived from San Antonio.

"Tomorrow is Independence Day, *ma tante*. We won't open the store, will we?" Lou-Lou asked hopefully. She wanted to join her friends in the park for the Independence Day picnic.

"I had forgotten. I guess I never think much about July 4. Bastille Day is the day of independence we celebrated as children. But, no, we won't be open tomorrow. It won't interrupt business as everyone will be in the park. We won't have any customers. Go on and plan to join your friends. There's plenty of ham if you want to take sandwiches."

"*Merci beaucoup, ma tante*! You are so good to us."

Independence Day dawned with San Jose's usual perfect weather—cloudless blue skies and cool temperatures. Lizette and Julia would spend the day playing with friends in the park nearer their home; while Joe, Louis Nicholas, and James took off early with their friends. Lou-Lou and Mamie went to Almaden Park for the festivities there.

Hoping with all her heart that Mother Florence would welcome her, Louise began to make the lists that would guide her preparations for returning to Texas. As soon as the letter came, she would need to move quickly. So much needed to be done. The leases to the house and the store needed to be put in either Joe's name or Mamie's name. Leaving it only in her brother Louis' name might jeopardize the future of the younger girls if Louis got behind in his bills and couldn't pay the rent or, God forbid, had to declare bankruptcy. It had happened before. A complete inventory of the store had to be made and the value recorded. She wanted no loose ends. She must leave the children with economic security. Her leaving would be sad, but she must not expose them to financial peril.

Though the children were exhausted from too much fun on their Fourth of July holiday, the next day, Thursday, was a regular workday. The morning began in the kitchen as usual, and then all trooped next door to begin the day in their small store. There were so many customers that no one even noticed the postman who didn't get so much as a nod as he laid the mail on the counter. It was noon before Louise picked up the stack of bills and ads and went back to the house to put dinner on the table.

Lou-Lou had done a nice job of getting most of the food ready before going to the store and, in between helping customers she had finished the preparations throughout the morning. They were having one of the favorite meals at the Castroville Motherhouse: baked chops, boiled potatoes with fresh butter and boiled cabbage. The savory menu items took Louise back to the dining table in the convent motherhouse where as many as fifty Sisters might be gathered for dinner during the summer in years gone by. How many times had Sister Gabriel prepared this same menu in Castroville? It all tasted as good today as it ever had years ago.

Only after dinner was finished and dishes were put away did she sort the mail. Buried in the stack of bills was a small off-white envelope. Louise recognized the handwriting immediately and noted the postmark: San Antonio, Texas. The date on the postmark indicated that the letter had taken ten days to reach San Jose. She pushed a loose strand of her graying brown hair back from her face and wiped her hands on a dishtowel before she picked up a table knife and slit the envelope. As she carefully removed the single sheet of heavy linen paper, her hands shook a bit. The chops and cabbage seemed to sit at the pit of her stomach. Perhaps Mother Florence would say no, she thought fearfully. She read with hesitation.

> **Our Lady of the Lake Convent**
> **515 Southwest 24th Street**
> **San Antonio, Texas**

> **June 25, 1900**

> **Ma Chère Fille!**

> *I was so pleased to receive your letter and I hope that the children are all well. I am happy for you to return to us. Please inform us of your travel plans. I suggest that you disembark in Hondo. I myself will meet your train. After consultation with the Council, I am asking you to live at Castroville where you will assist with household duties as your health permits. I will announce your return when the Sisters are gathered for the Feast of St. Anne.*

> *Our Constitution was translated into English in 1897. I will send you a copy under separate cover.*

> *I eagerly await your homecoming. We have so much to say to one another.*

> **In Providence I remain,**
> **Mother Florence**

Her eyes filled with tears as she read and re-read the words. Mother Florence's kind words made the words of the Founder, Jean-Martin Moye, leap to her mind.

> *You can see the visible proof of God's goodness toward you. You see how Providence governs all things, provides for everything, arranges everything, turns everything to good.* *

Soon she must sit down with Mamie and Joe and talk over her plans. She was going home at last.

---

* **The Directory, p. 246 ff.**

CHAPTER II

OLD FRIENDS

The Sunday after she had received Mother Florence's letter, Louise sent the girls to the park so that she would be able to have some peace and quiet. Mamie was in the girls' room, reading, she supposed. Mamie seldom went out and was timid about meeting new people. The older two boys, Joe and Louis Nicolas, were at the cannery on the afternoon shift. Having worked an extra shift at the mill, her brother Louis was asleep; and James was out with his pals. No one would need her attention for several hours.

She slowly climbed the steps up to the attic. Her rheumatism made the exertion painful and she was short of breath as she opened the attic door. The one window let in a shaft of light that did little more than illumine the particles of dust that hung in the air. She hadn't been up here in a couple of years. There were only some odd boxes of clothes that no one would wear again and a few pieces of broken-down furniture that had made the trip with them from Castroville to California. Though the furniture was no longer usable, Louis couldn't seem to part with it. It was all he had to remind him of Theresa. His life had been so sad after Theresa's death. He seemed to wander aimlessly, and would have lost one job after another without her constant encouragement. He probably wouldn't be working now, but San Jose was booming and millwork was abundant. No longer young, Louis had lost his spirit. In his youth, he had been full of life. Louise recalled how excited he had been when he had arrived in Austin in 1868. At twenty-six he had been full of dreams and seemed to have talent enough to make most of them come true.

A blond, blue-eyed, Bavarian, his wife, Theresa Fruth, had been a beautiful girl. Her parents had come to Austin after the European revolutions of the 1840s and '50s had closed doors there for people without land. Fearing that he would be drawn into France's inevitable war with Prussia, Louis had said goodbye to their mother, their brother Pierre's family, and their sister Anne-Marie, all of whom still lived in their home village at the time, and left France to come to Texas. Louis and Theresa had met at Father Nicolas Feltin's parish, St. Mary's in Austin, where the Fruth family was well known. Father Nicolas had assured his younger brother that Theresa Fruth would be a good solid mate. With Father Nicolas officiating, they had married two days after Christmas in 1870. Louise—then Mother St. Andrew—had heard about the wedding festivities from Nicolas when he had visited her in the following spring. Her own duties as Superior of her Congregation in Castroville precluded her attending.

In those early years in Austin, as Theresa birthed a child about every two years, Louis worked hard at building a new school building for his brother's parish. Then, after Father Nicolas was no longer the pastor at St. Mary's, Mother St. Andrew had invited her brother to move his family to Castroville to work on the Motherhouse that needed to be enlarged to accommodate more vocations. Hoping that Father Richard, the pastor at St. Louis Parish, might have a part-time job for him as parish caretaker as well, Mother St. Andrew had believed that her brother's move to Castroville would provide him with a secure future for his family.

As she herself was sometimes overwhelmed with the responsibilities of raising her brother's children, Louise now recalled Theresa's struggles with the births of their five children who were born in Castroville. Louis had worked to find and keep part-time jobs in addition to his work on the Motherhouse. But, with his growing family, he never seemed to make ends meet.

California had not provided the prosperity that tales had promised, and if she hadn't been along to help with the children and start their grocery store, she was sure the family would have foundered.

Each piece of old furniture brought back a specific memory of days gone by. She laid her hand reverently on the old table and memories of that fateful morning when young Mamie had found her mother's body hanging in the barn flooded back. Louis had gotten her down somehow, brought her into the kitchen, and laid her on that very table. Louise remembered the sad yet sacred washing to prepare the thin, limp body for its burial. She had been so grateful to her good friend Tillie Christilles who had helped her.

The old rocker, now with the one arm missing. She gave it a push. How many hours had she rocked Lizette in that rocker? With such an upsetting beginning to her life, Lizette had been a very colicky baby who needed constant attention. Oh, my. Louise's breathing became more and more shallow as the memories washed over her.

Finally, her eyes found her old black trunk, which had been shoved into a corner. Louise used her apron to wipe away the dust and then opened the lid. The top tray held the few mementos that she had acquired over the last ten years. For a moment she couldn't decide where to start. And then, as though it were detached from her body, her hand reached for a small stack of letters tied with a thin blue ribbon.

She had kept the letters in the order of their arrival. The one on top had come two years earlier from her nephew John Isidore. Though they seldom heard from him, he seemed to be getting along all right as an assistant at a dairy in Austin. His aunt and uncle were very good to him. Then the one behind that had come in 1896 from Mother Florence. The next one … she paused, cradling it in her hands, holding it as one would hold a holy object. She had read it so many times. She didn't have to open the envelope to recall how worn the pages were, nearly torn where the creased folds were. There were two more envelopes in the same crisp, neat handwriting.

She took these three letters and set them aside. "I wonder if that old rocker will still hold me," she muttered to herself. Drawing it away from the rest of the furniture into the shaft of sunlight, and giving the seat a wipe with her apron, Louise cautiously sat down. She settled back, resting her head on the high back.

Reshuffling the three letters into the order in which she had received them, she picked out the first one. What a surprise on that summer day in 1888! She had been working in her small garden in Castroville when Alton Tschirhart, the postmaster, had driven his buggy up into her yard on his way home for lunch. She let her mind return to that day.

"*Ma mère* André," Alton called. "How are you?"

"Just fine, Alton. How are you? What brings you this way?"

"You got a letter this morning. I just thought I would drop it by— save you the walk into town."

"Bless you, Alton. You are so thoughtful." The postmaster handed her the white envelope. She recognized the handwriting immediately. There was a catch in her voice as she said, "Thank you so much, Alton. I'll remember you in my prayers."

"Thank *you, ma mère*. Your prayers are worth more than money! Is there anything that you need?"

"No, thank you. People are so good. Mary Suehs sent me a dozen eggs just this morning!"

"I'll see you then," Alton had said. "God bless you!"

"And you, too. Remember me to your dear wife!"

As Alton turned his horse around, she had hurried back into her house.

Arsene, dear Arsene. Never had any one person been so faithful to another in time trial. She carefully slit the envelope, seated herself at her small table, and lit the oil lamp so that she could read without difficulty.

St.Jean-de-Bassel, Lorraine, Germany
June 21, 1888
Feast of St. Aloysius Gonzaga

Ma Chère Sœur!

Even as I begin this letter I realize that I do not know where you are. So, I am sending this to the Castroville post office, presuming that the good postmaster will find you. So much has happened in the last months, I scarce know where to begin, so I will begin with today, the feast of St.Aloysius, patron of novices. In celebration, we were given permission to write letters. The younger novices are all writing to their parents, but as my dear mother and father are in heaven, I choose to write to you. Our blessed Founder, Jean-Martin, says that the Sisters may write to one another in order to maintain mutual union and to encourage one another to practice virtue. I still consider you to be our dear Sister. As my year in the novitiate comes to an end, I am writing to assure you that I am well and hope that this letter finds you in good health.

When I arrived at St. Jean last August, Mother Anna welcomed me warmly, but she insisted that the past had to be put completely behind me and I must begin again. Therefore, I became a novice and received the name Sister Camille. At first, I was very angry, thinking that being treated like an infant in religious life was a punishment. But, as the year wore on, as we studied again our dear Founder's writings, I began to accept the designs of Providence for me. Going to Holy

Mass each day and receiving our Blessed Lord in communion healed my soul of the deprivations imposed upon us by His Lordship in Texas.

Sister Camille (Arsene) Schaff
(Courtesy of the Sisters of Divine Providence of Melbourne, KY. Date unknown.)

Louise's fingers, now knarled with arthritis, moved slowly over the penned words, pausing at the splotched marks where the ink had run. Her tears of those many years ago when she had first read the letter came back to her mind. When she had read that letter for the first time, she had still been under the interdict of excommunication. Bishop Neraz had really never relented and the priest at St. Louis Parish in Castroville, fearing repercussion, had told her not to present herself at the communion rail. "The Bishop has spoken," he had said. Oh, how she had missed the Holy Sacrament.

Sister Camille's letter went on:

I am sad to report to you that l'abbé Nicolas Michel has died. He was so kind to our Congregation for these many years. Though he lived in Metz, his death brought a pall of sadness over the Motherhouse. Mother Anna seems to be at loose ends. She depended on him, as did Mother Constantine of happy memory. God rest her soul.

The talk in the Motherhouse is that the Germans will continue to press our Sisters for more and more certificates in order to be able to teach here in Lorraine and in Alsace. I am planning to return to teaching, but I am fearful that I will not be able to pass the mandatory examinations which will be given in August. We will have to go to Fenetrange to sit for the examination and all who take it speak of it as 'horrible.' Pray for me.

Another rumor in the house is that Mother is looking for an opportunity to send more Sisters to the United States missions. We have many, many vocations here in Lorraine and she wants to be able to do the most good for our loving God. If she allows, I will volunteer. With my English surely I could do some good in America once again. Perhaps we will come to a place near you!

We seem to have no word from Mother Florence. At least, she is never mentioned. It is as though Mother Anna is hurt by what happened and cannot bear to speak of it. I, for one, feel as though a part of me has been ripped away. The pain is less after these months, but the feelings run deep. The younger novices usually stay at a distance from me. They simply do not have the life experience to understand me.

The tears ran down Louise's wrinkled cheeks once again as she read the last sentence.

I fear that now you are the only one who could possibly know what I am feeling. Perhaps you might say the same about me.

I remain your dear Sister,
Sœur Camille

Though the light in the attic had begun to dim, Louise wanted to remain in her solitary reverie. Twilight might last only another hour, but remembering her response to Sister Arsene's first letter could be done in the coming darkness. She had waited until fall to write back. If her calculations were correct, she had thought, Sister Camille would have finished her novitiate in August. Those many years ago, she had wanted to wait until she was sure that her letter would not be compromised by inspection by Sister Camille's Novice Mistress. September 14, the Feast of the Holy Cross, had been a day when she had meditated on the words of their holy Founder: **"The cross, the cross, the cross! That is the way to heaven."**[*]After her prayer, weighed down by the cross of her exile, alone in her poor, little house, she had taken pen in hand to write to Sister Camille.

Writing that first letter to her old friend had been Sister St. Andrew's first opportunity to reveal her feelings about those troubling two years since August of 1886 when Bishop Neraz had insisted that she step down from her position of Superior of the Texas foundation.

There had been no doubt that the Sisters wanted her to continue to guide them, but the Bishop had insisted, and so she had directed them to elect Sister Florence on that fateful August day in 1886. She remembered how Bishop Neraz had closeted himself with Mother Florence after her election and how different Mother Florence had seemed afterwards. She supposed she would never know how deeply the Bishop's injunctions impacted the young Superior.

---

[*]   **The Directory, p. 183.**

Louise recalled that hot, still night after the election of Mother Florence. Feeling almost physically ill, Louise had lain awake contemplating her future. Mother Florence had made it very clear to her that she could not remain in Castroville, but that she could go wherever she felt most needed.

Though she had chosen to go to St. Joseph's School in Galveston, the month spent there had proven disastrous. The weather was terrible—hot, humid, and rainy, with the constant threat of a hurricane. Her arthritic bones had ached day and night and she had been plagued by a constant headache, no doubt from the tensions of her situation since none of her plans had worked. Writing that 1888 letter to Sister Camille had allowed her to reflect on the fateful fall of 1886—and her stubbornness. She realized that she had acted impetuously, once again allowing her Alsatian temperament to be a stumbling block.

As she poured out her feelings in that first letter, Louise, then still Sister St. Andrew, had been certain that Sister Camille would be the one person who would understand. While serving as administrative assistant to Mother Florence, Sister Camille, then Sister Arsene, had endeared herself to Louise forever by resigning her position on the council and coming to Galveston to support her. In some ways, Louise had written, she felt that she had lost her rudder during those months between the fall of 1886 and the fall of 1888. Threats to her identity as a missionary for the gospel overshadowed her usual rationality. Acting too quickly out of anger and frustration, she had allowed her unbridled feelings to lead to rash behaviors. If only she had heeded Father Moye's wise advice to his daughters:

> *Watch over all your emotions so that there will be in you no feeling of spite, revenge, irritation, or indignation against anyone, but that your heart will always be full of peace, charity, and*

kindness toward everyone, even your enemies and opponents. [V]

If only Bishop Gallagher of Galveston had agreed to establish a branch house of the Castroville Motherhouse at Frelsburg in the Galveston Diocese as she and Bishop Dubuis had planned. Thinking that a novitiate in the Galveston Diocese would attract vocations from the area, Mother St. Andrew and Bishop Dubuis had contracted to make the Frelsburg convent a branch of the Castroville Motherhouse. But she and Bishop Dubuis had never acted on their agreement. Then, in the summer of 1881, Bishop Dubuis, in poor health, had returned to his home in France, leaving Texas forever

Louise supposed that it had been her own restless spirit that had drawn her to investigate the needs at St. Boniface Parish in Anaheim, California. She had known that His Lordship Bishop Neraz would never allow her to go if she had asked, so she simply made the decision to go to Anaheim by herself. After all, she had thought, earlier consultations with her own council while she was superior general had indicated that the Sisters, including Sister Florence, were positive toward venturing outside of Texas. While she was superior general, her on-going correspondence with Father Stöters of St. Boniface Parish had convinced her of the great need of the German immigrants who were coming by droves to southern California to work in the vineyards.

Perhaps she had been foolish. Now she was left with "if only." If only Bishop Dubuis had returned from France; if only Mother Florence had approved of the California mission; if only the Congregation had opened a mission in Anaheim before she had been deposed; if only she had not been disobedient; if only … if only … if only.

As Louise recalled those disastrous months which had led to her exile from the Castroville Motherhouse in August of 1887, and her words to Sister Camille a year later in that letter of the fall of 1888, the "if onlys" tumbled over and over in her mind.

V   **The Directory, p. 229.**

Though Sister Camille couldn't have known when she had written her first letter, the news of the death of *l'abbé* Michel had slammed the door to Mother's return to the German Congregation at St. Jean-de-Bassel.

In her response to Sister Camille's letter, Louise had written about her own letter to *l'abbé* Michel—and his disappointing response written just a month before his death. It had been her last hope of finding a path to be able to serve God once again as a religious teacher. Learning that he was dead had required a final surrender to her plight, to her failure. Now there would be no recourse, she had written to Camille; now her fate was sealed.

As she re-read Sister Camille's letter, she was struck again by the costly sacrifice that her friend had made in remaining loyal to her during those bleak months. She, too, had lost everything. Her return to Germany, though understood at the time, left a permanent hole in Louise's heart. Camille's first letter and Louise's many-paged response had been the beginning of healing.

Louise looked out the window and noticed that the gas street lamps were beginning to come on. She had heard the girls come in from the park earlier but she had needed time for herself and had remained in the attic.

She felt so tired. Going back over that painful time and recalling the losses she had incurred was exhausting. She stood slowly, tucked all three of Sister Camille's letters into her apron pocket, wiped her eyes once more, and descended the attic steps into the hallway.

The hustle and bustle of preparing supper and hearing from the children about their day were distracting, but once the house was quiet again and she had retired to her small bedroom her thoughts returned to those three letters. Before taking off her apron, she removed them carefully from the pocket and laid them on the small bureau. After she had finished preparing for bed, while she brushed her long, gray-brown hair, Louise scrutinized herself in the mirror.

How she had changed! Wearing the bandeau for those nearly forty years had left her with a tanned face and a permanently lighter-colored forehead. Though exposure to the California sun these last ten years had darkened it a bit, the contrast was still evident. Her hair was now long, much longer than she had ever kept it while it was covered with the coif those many years. And it had become so much grayer. Even her heavy eyebrows were flecked with gray.

But her brown eyes seemed to be the same. Perhaps now they were softer. The Sisters had occasionally complained that she had "piercing" eyes that seemed to look right into their hearts. She smiled as she recalled those comments, remembering that she had cultivated that "look" as a young teacher. She had used "the look" rarely but effectively as superior general when she had needed the postulants, novices, and young Sisters to believe that she saw everything. Her firmness with them as she tried to shape them into the type of religious who could withstand the rigors of life in small villages with few comforts of any kind had brought forth positive results. Her Sisters were strong women.

But over a dozen years of suffering and a different "motherhood" of sorts had softened her features. The wrinkles at the corners of her eyes and mouth had deepened and her skin seemed more leathery. She had never been one to use creams or lotions and she guessed that this was the result. But, just because she didn't wear her habit didn't mean that her way of life as a religious had been altered. Carrying her habit within her tattered heart for the last ten years, Louise had remained faithful to her vows and to a prayerful life.

Those two years after Sister Camille had left Texas to return to St. Jean-de-Bassel were written in her soul forever. That first letter to Sister Camille could only scratch the surface of what was happening to her. She had written of her true poverty—how she had had literally nothing. The days in the convent had seemed luxurious by comparison. During those two years, the wonderful people of Castroville had the habit of dropping food items off for her. One woman down the road brought her eggs every other day or so; another friend would give her an occasional chicken; and when the Suehses butchered, she received a share in their salted pork and sausage. Most of her benefactors were former students from St. Louis School whom she had taught some twenty years before. Now they took their opportunity to repay her sacrifices for them. And, Wilhelm Tondre insisted that she take things from his new store that he knew she would never pay for. So at least she always had coffee and beans. The writings of *l'abbé* Jean-Martin came to her, as they had those many years ago, sustaining her and encouraging her: ***"You will expect everything from God: food, clothing, health and strength, talents, and in a word, everything."****

His words were true.

Louise wrote of all that to Sister Camille. But she had held back on her living situation. She simply couldn't tell her about that terrible little house that had such big chinks out of the mortar in the walls that the temperature inside and outside was nearly the same—no matter what the season. Tillie Christelles' husband had had to completely rebuild the privy. As a result, it was the more reliable of the two structures!

Her few pieces of furniture had been Convent cast offs with the exception of the *prie-dieu*. Her pride and joy. Made of dark cherry wood, with a red brocade upholstered kneeling bench, this piece had come from France. Father Nicolas had asked her get it for him on her 1878 trip to the German Motherhouse. She had found just the right piece at a furniture maker's shop in Lyons, France. But Nicolas never got to use it. His untimely death in the fall of that year left her with the *prie-dieu*. She had used it every single day since her brother's death. And, now it graced her near hovel of a house, speaking to her of days gone by, of her own family's triumphs and tragedies as well as her personal sins and successes as a religious. She recalled that she had not taken it with her when she left the Convent and went to reside in Louis' home while her friends in Castroville looked for a place for her. Only a few days after finding the little, tumbled-down house—what a mess it had been!—the Convent caretaker had arrived unexpectedly with a wagonload of furniture.

---

* **The Directory, p. 78**

Nothing had been of consequence: an old table, a couple of kitchen chairs, some rusted pots, a small table, an old, wing-back chair, a bed and a small chest of drawers. The caretaker had brought everything into the house and placed it where she had asked. Then, he had said, "They sent one more thing, but it's wrapped up."

"What is it?" she remembered asking.

"I have no idea, *Mère* André." He had brought it in and just left it in the small room that served as both kitchen and parlor. He had rushed on to other chores and left her to take care of unwrapping the piece.

She had wept when she had gotten the brown paper off and realized that the Sisters had sent her dear *prie-dieu*. From then on, it had stood in a place of prominence in her bedroom. On that *prie-dieu*, over the last dozen years, she had prayed countless rosaries, begged God for forgiveness for all her failings, and had learned to accept the unfathomable designs of Providence.

Finished now with her reverie, her hair falling over her shoulders, she wrapped her black shawl around her shoulders and knelt on her beloved *prie-dieu* before retiring. Her night prayers were always the same: begging God's blessing on her dear Congregation and on her little family, and asking for the grace to trust in God's forgiving mercy for herself.

Over the next few days, Louise was able to steal more time away from the grocery store since now all three girls were working there. She read and re-read her old letters from Sister Camille.

Postmarked in Newport, Kentucky, across the Ohio River from Cincinnati, the second letter had come unexpectedly in early 1891, just a little over a year since she and her family had moved to San Jose from Castroville. Sister Camille wrote that she and two others had been in Kentucky since August of 1889. This letter was full of reflections on their crossing of the Atlantic which had reminded Sister Camille of her first crossing in 1878. The three Sisters of Divine Providence had come to Kentucky at the invitation of the

Bishop of Covington who had visited St. Jean-de-Bassel in the autumn of 1888. Sister Camille had told Louise how her return to America had developed. But, she had admitted that she had not been hopeful about being chosen to go since over forty Sisters had volunteered for this mission to Kentucky. English classes for the volunteers had begun at once. Her fluency in English was, Sister Camille had admitted in her letter, the reason that she had been chosen.

After receiving that second letter, Louise had read one paragraph of it so many times that she nearly had it memorized:

> ***Before we left, Mother Anna told us that she would not allow what had happened in Texas to happen with this Kentucky mission. She asked us to take an oath of allegiance to our Congregation; and when we renewed our vows before leaving, she added a phrase to the formula that meant we were making our vows 'in this Congregation.' I can still see the sadness in Mother Anna's eyes as she talked with us before we left. She assured us of her support for our mission and said she would visit us as soon as she could and never abandon us.***

Oh, how Louise wished now that she had encouraged Mother Constantine to come to Texas. The many concerns at the St. Jean-de-Bassel Motherhouse: the takeover of Lorraine by the Germans, the building of the new chapel, the draining of the marshes around the motherhouse seemed to require Mother Constantine's attention. Mother Constantine's own physical ailments made traveling almost impossible for her. And, Louise blamed herself as well. If only she had written more frequently; if only she had not been so independent; if only she had asked for money or help more often. If only ... if only ... if only.

Louise wished that she could review once again that letter that Mother Constantine had written to her shortly before she had returned to Germany in 1878. The cryptic message had been so puzzling. Mother had alluded to the new laws taking place under the Reich. She had indicated that her letters would be few and that letters from Texas might not be necessary, as though she were afraid for their future if it appeared that the now-German congregation had a missionary branch in the United States. She had so carefully guarded those precious letters from Mother Constantine over the twenty years that she had been the Superior. Gone in a puff of smoke.

Over the last dozen years Louise had humbly recognized that her pride had driven certain decisions. As Superior she had attempted to cover all expenses with monies earned by the Sisters or with donations from their benefactors in Castroville. Believing that her frugalities would only enhance the possibilities of improvements at the Lorraine Motherhouse, she had never imagined that her actions would have distanced the Texas foundation from Mother Constantine to the degree that Mother would accept Bishop Neraz' plan to assume control of the Texas Sisters as his own Congregation! If only ...

But, she had to begin putting all of that firmly behind her as she prepared herself to return to Texas. The fate of her Congregation had been sealed with Mother Florence's election, and Louise had learned long ago that God truly did write straight with crooked lines. She had to believe that good would triumph.

What had happened to Sister Camille was another proof of God's all-knowing design. Her second letter to Louise had spoken of their humble start in Kentucky, the purchase of an old mansion overlooking the Ohio River that had become their Motherhouse in Newport, and Sister Camille's own work of beginning two schools single-handedly. What had thrilled Louise, however, was that Sister Camille was enjoying her community life there in West Covington, Kentucky so much.

Mount St. Martin, Newport, KY, Original Provincial House of the Sisters of Divine Providence of St. Jean-de-Bassel, circa 1900.
(Courtesy, Congregation of Divine Providence, St. Jean-de-Bassel, France.)

The third letter had served to further confirm God's loving guidance of all that happens. Sister Camille had written in 1898 from Washington, DC, where she and seven other Sisters had begun a ministry of domestic service at Catholic University of America at a student residence named Caldwell Hall. She had sounded so happy.

Louise had so enjoyed reading and re-reading that third letter. Now, preparing to put it away, perhaps forever, she lingered over a few of the lines:

> *... and, I never thought I could enjoy housekeeping, but the students who live here at Caldwell Hall are so lively that they make our day-to-day existence quite interesting. They come from all over the country for a Catholic education. Many are seminarians from various dioceses. I feel as though we are in some small way helping the future of the Church through our quiet service. And, I guess I didn't realize how tired I had become of the task of starting up schools and trying to get them on their feet. That is best left to younger Sisters now!*

After receiving that letter, she had never worried about Sister Camille again. Anything that had seemed lost in 1886 had been returned a hundredfold. She knew that her dear friend was exactly where God had wanted her to be. Her letter in response, she recalled, had noted that. But, confiding to her old friend, Louise had also been frank about her own growing loneliness and restlessness in San Jose. Though Sister Camille had found a place where she could do God's work, Louise's health deterioration and her heart that yearned for her Sisters only added to her need to come to the same peace that Sister Camille had found. Her decision to return to Texas, she hoped, would bring her the peace that doing God's will can give.

Before the next Sunday, Louise asked Joe to bring her old trunk down from the attic. She needed to do so much with its contents that having it the attic was inconvenient. Joe had found time on Saturday night to bring the trunk down and had asked her why she wanted it in her bedroom.

"*Ma tante,* your room is so small. It will take up half the room," he had argued.

"I need it, Joe," she had responded. "I'll tell you why after you get it down here."

Joe was not very tall, but his muscular frame was a result of hours of lifting crates of fruit. It had taken Joe only a few minutes to drag it down, and he was right. It took up the entire middle part of her bedroom. There was literally no way to get it out of the way.

"There's barely room to get around it in there, *ma tante,*" Joe had protested, washing the dust off his hands at the kitchen sink and pushing his long brown hair out of his eyes.

"Sit down a minute, Joe. I need to tell you something."

After Joe had settled in a kitchen chair, his aunt took off her spectacles and rubbed her face with her hands, taking time to calm herself so that she could say what was needed without tears.

"I'm planning to go back to Texas, Joe," she began. "I never intended to stay with you children for ten years. I don't know where the time has gone! But, now I am old and I don't feel well much of the time."

**418 Empire: the home of the Feltins in
San Jose from 1892 until 1922
(Photo by Sister Diane Langford, CDP, 2006)**

Joe started to pro-test, but she held up her hand to stop him. She continued. "No, no, don't stop me. The girls are doing well. Now that Lou-Lou has finished high school, she'll be able to run the store. And, Julia is coming along right after her. Lizette is a good little girl and she won't give you all any trouble." She stopped to catch her breath, but Joe knew better than to interject again. He simply sat there quietly, his chin resting on his chest.

"I do worry about Mamie. She seems to be doing all right now, but she is fragile, Joe. She may never be able to stand up to stress and I don't think she can handle the business end of the store. But Lou-Lou can if you will only help her a little. Just give her advice now and then. And don't criticize her too much, lest she lose heart. She actually has a knack for the business. I guess she gets that from your grandfather. He did so well with his little grocery in LaWalck."

She paused to think. She had to be sure that she covered all her details about her future and the security of her little family. Joe seemed sullen about this news but she had to believe that he would come through for her and take care of his younger sisters.

"You're right about Mamie, *ma tante*. That's why I don't think you should go. Do you really think Lou-Lou and Jule can handle the store? What about James? He's a smart boy. But he doesn't listen to me or Papa. And you know Louis Nicholas!

"Yes, I know they won't help much. I'm sorry about that. Please just try to encourage them, Joe. I know you don't want to go to school, but you'll always keep a good job. I know you will. Please, Joe," she begged.

"All right, *ma tante*. Don't worry. I'll do my best. But I've got to keep working. This store won't support us completely! And you know we can't depend on Papa. He's starting to be old now, too."

"No, your Papa won't be much help." She said this with sadness. Her brother Louis was twelve years younger than she was and should have ten more good working years. It was too bad that he just couldn't manage to do better. The children would always suffer because of his disabilities.

Joe had a dozen questions. But finally, he asked the one she did not have a firm answer for. "When are you going to leave us, *ma tante*?"

"I don't know," she said honestly. "I have written to Mother Florence and she has answered saying that I may return to Castroville."

Joe sputtered, "I don't see why you want to go back there, *ma tante*. I remember how it was for you. I was twelve years old. Those nuns let you live in that hovel of a house. You had nothing! How can you want to go back? They were so mean to you!" His tone of voice escalated with every sentence. His aunt had never seen this anger in him.

"Now, now, Joe. You're right. Those were terrible years for me, and I thank you for your sense of care for me. But, for better or for worse, those are my Sisters. I am a religious. You see those days from your point of view. I, on the other hand, know that I, too, carry responsibility for how things turned out.

"When I came with you children to California, that was God's plan for me at the time; but now I must follow another plan. Please, please try to understand. I am so lonely here. You children are growing up and will have a bright future. I have nothing. One day you will all leave home and you know that I simply cannot live with your Papa. I want to go home. I need to go home." The last sentence was nearly a whisper.

Joe did understand and he knew that she was right. The future without her scared him, though. She had done so much for them.

"*Oui, ma tante.*" He reverted to the language of his boyhood as he pledged to her that he would take care of everything as she wished.

Relieved that he would help her, Louise spoke again. "I think that I will plan to return to Castroville in the fall. Lizette and Julie will be back in school; Lou-Lou will be running the store with Mamie's help. And, perhaps it won't be so warm in Texas by then." She said that last sentence with a chuckle. She had become accustomed to the mild California weather and she did not look forward to the hot summers and rainy winters of south Texas. She knew, however, that she would accept any climate as long as she could return to her full life as a religious but she knew that her old bones would not enjoy the damp Texas winter.

CHAPTER III

ROOTS

The summer days seemed to speed by. It was already the middle of August. After receiving Mother Florence's letter, Louise Feltin had begun making her plans to return to Castroville in October; but since there were so many details to see to before leaving, she had decided not to share her plans with the rest of her family just yet. Reading over Arsene's (she'd never get accustomed to her dear friend being called 'Sister Camille') letters had brought back such tragic memories—memories that she knew would never fade, no matter what happened to her—that she had begun to have second thoughts about returning to the Congregation.

With each day's passing, Louise began to experience more deeply the bittersweet feelings of sorrow at leaving her family and neighbors in San Jose and joy at thinking of returning to her beloved Sisters. She knew that her decision to go back to her Congregation was of God, yet her heart had begun to yield to maternal instincts. Celebrating little Lizette's eleventh birthday at the end of July had only deepened the cleft in her heart that her decision had opened. She loved Louis' children as though she herself had given them birth. And perhaps she had, in a way. She alone had accompanied them down the dark channel from their mother's tragic death to the lighter days of their lives now in San Jose. Her brother Louis had focused his time on earning a living and, with her prodding, had taken every extra shift at the nearby millworks in those first years. She had been the one to get the children into school, wash and iron their clothes, cook their meals, listen to their lessons, wipe their tears, and give them a mother's love as they adjusted to a new home and a motherless future. In her musings during her prayer Louise allowed only God to know the depths of her hopes and fears for them.

Now nearly thirty years old, Mamie was still so fragile emotionally. Finding the limp body of her mother hanging in their barn had scarred her for life. Louise doubted that she would ever be truly strong enough to deal with the vicissitudes that life would throw at her. The girl had valiantly taken up the lion's share of the work in their little grocery store when they finally opened in 1893; but, as the years passed, Mamie leaned more and more on Joe for support and affirmation. Her education had ended with their departure from Castroville and now she struggled with the subtleties of running a business.

Joe had truly become the man of the family. Louise was so proud of him. He alone seemed to have the ambition to seek employment that would provide him and the family with security. Her brother Louis, now almost sixty, was showing the wear and tear of the sadness and hardships of his life and would not be able to keep up his carpenter's job for much longer. Joe was learning a trade in machinery and manufacturing in the canning business. In his twenty-one years he had learned many of life's hard lessons and had developed broad shoulders. His aunt believed that he would accept the necessary responsibilities to see the family through. She only hoped that somehow, in the midst of all that swirled around him, Joe might find time to meet a woman who would comfort him and draw him out of his shyness.

Louise wished that James was more like his older brother Joe, but James' temperament so often got him into fights that she doubted he would ever be more than a laborer. Her prayer included gratitude to God that there was never a shortage of work in San Jose. Between jobs in the canneries, the livery stables, the construction sites, and the farms and orchards, James would always have work even though he had not finished high school. But he would never have security. Louise accepted that she would always worry about him.

When she wasn't worrying about James, she knew she'd be worrying about Louis Nicholas. Nick, as he like to be called, had been nearly fourteen years old when the family had gotten on that train to the west. Too much like the father for whom he was named, now at age twenty-four, he seemed to drift from one job to another. Having long since given up trying to influence this nephew, Louise knew that her motherly prayers would have to suffice.

Her own namesake, Louise Briget, known fondly as Lou-Lou since she was a toddler, had always been a plucky girl and was now growing into a lovely young woman. She could have gone on to the Normal School, but never seemed to desire further study after high school. Lou-Lou spent a lot of time in the grocery store and without Lou-Lou Mamie would never be able to keep her head above water. Lou-Lou was the businesswoman. After spending hours teaching her niece how to keep the ledgers, order to merchandise, rotate the stock, and work with customers, Louise was gratified that Lou-Lou seemed to love the challenge. Lou-Lou would be the mainstay; if she would stay in the business, it would thrive.

Louise supposed that Julia—fondly known as "Jule"—and dear little Lizette would always be her darlings. As the only mother they had ever known, she had watched them grow up. Jule had been confirmed at St. Patrick's in the spring and Lizette would be confirmed in the spring to come; but they were still children. Louise placed her hope in these two youngest girls, feeling sure that they would carry her legacy. Jule had a popular personality and could marry well, while Lizette talked about being a teacher when she grew up. Her prayer for them would always be that they would hold fast to their faith and trust in the dear Lord to carry them through any trial until they would all meet again in the heavenly realm. "I'll write to them," Louise said to herself over and over again. "I love them so." Tears often filled her eyes these days as she pondered leaving them.

She knew that her motherly heart would never forget them if she left; but maybe she shouldn't leave them.

"Ma petite tata-Maman, you promised that you would tell us family stories," Lizette addressed her aunt with their intimate name for her. The youngest children had developed this unique name for her: a combination of her identity as their aunt with the French word for "Mama." Lizette added, in her most endearing, little-girl voice, "You promised!"

"And so I did, *liebchen.* Shall we start tonight?"

Saturday nights were usually special nights for the Feltin family. Always tired from a busy day in the grocery store, Louise had long ago started the custom of having a casual, light supper. Cold ham, sausage and cheese, sliced tongue, and boiled eggs would be laid out with bread and milk. Fruit from the local trees was always abundant and provided a good dessert. Each one took what he or she pleased; and since there was little to clean up, they would often stay at the table playing dominoes or cards, relaxing after a hard day in the store.

"Yes, *tata,*" Lizette begged. "Please. Please. I love to hear you talk about the old country."

"I do, too! I do, too!" Jule added. "Start with *Meémeé et Pépé* and tell about everyone."

Louise was always so surprised at how hungry these younger children were for stories of their family. Living so far from their mother's family and only knowing herself from their father's family had left them with an orphan's curiosity about where they came from.

"All right. Let's put away the food and then we'll go into the parlor for stories."

By the time Louise had put up her apron and joined the children in the parlor, they had closed the shutters on the front window and drawn the drapes. The oil lamp cast a yellow glow on the faces of the three young girls who sat on the floor around the old rocker, waiting impatiently.

Settling into her chair and gazing lovingly into the sparkling young eyes of her dear children, so eager to know more about who they were and where they were from, Louise cleared her throat, beginning as she always did. "Once upon a time long ago in faraway France in a village by the River Moder lived a young girl named Marie-Louise …"

"Like your name, *ma petite tata!*" Lizette interrupted. The children had heard these stories before, but each time their response was as though they were fresh and new.

"Yes, like my name—and Lou-Lou's! Now you must not interrupt or I'll never get the story told." Her words were scolding, but her tone was patient and amused.

Louise continued. "Marie-Louise was a beautiful girl of almost twenty. She had light brown hair—about the same color as yours, Lou-Lou—and dark brown eyes. Jule, you and Lou-Lou have your grandmother's eyes; Lizette," she said, lowering her voice, "yours are your mother's. Your great-grandfather had a grocery store in their little village of LaWalck and he had wanted his beautiful daughter to marry a prince. But, of course, there were no princes in that area any longer since the French Revolution had sent them all into hiding or to the guillotine many years before. It was the year 1825 and France was having a little peace from the uproar following the Revolution. Marie-Louise had been asking God to send her a beau, a man who would take care of her and provide her with a good home and many children. Although there were a couple of young men in the village who would have given anything to have the hand of Marie-Louise in marriage, your grandmother knew that God would send her someone special.

"One day, shortly after New Year's while Marie-Louise was helping her papa in the store, a lieutenant from the *Ordre des Douanes*, the Customs Service, came into the store for some tobacco for his pipe. When his eyes fell on Marie-Louise, he was startled by her beauty and found himself speechless. And Lt. Jean-Claude Feltin, accustomed to giving orders, was never speechless! Marie-Louise looked into his tanned face and saw that his blue eyes were clear and honest. She fell in love immediately.

"The lieutenant was stationed in Mertzviller, about five miles away, but after that day he spent many evenings in LaWalck, courting the beautiful Marie-Louise. One thing led to another and Lt. Feltin asked my Grandfather Seiter for Marie-Louise's hand in marriage. The ceremony took place in the middle of the summer in our family parish, Sts. Peter and Paul, just across the River Moder in Pfaffenhoffen. It took your grandfather a few months to find a home for his young wife. Since he was so much older than she, he was a little afraid that she would become homesick for her mother so it was a while before they moved to Mertzviller. Your uncle Pierre Isidore was born there in LaWalck. While they lived in Mertzviller, *Maman*, your *grand-mère*, had two more sons, your uncles Nicolas and François-Joseph. John Isidore is named for your uncle Pierre, Nick is named for your uncle Nicolas, and James Frank is named for your uncle François-Joseph. It is good to keep names in the family."

Though she had told this story many times before, somehow Louise knew that this telling was different. It would be the last telling and tonight's story must carry more than just facts. Tonight's story must carry meaning as well.

When speaking the names of her dear brothers and parents, Louise more carefully used the French pronunciations; and Lizette and Jule often spoke the names softly after her, letting the lilting French roll off their tongues in imitation.

"*Maman* and Papa didn't stay in Mertzviller too long because Papa was transferred to the area of Strasbourg about sixty miles away. Papa thought that Strasbourg was too big for them to live there and that *Maman* would be afraid without her family nearby, so he found a house in a small village called Geispolsheim, just to the south of Strasbourg. Now that name means 'House of Geis' and in the Alsatian we would always say ..."

"*Gaispitze!*" The girls interjected.

"That's right! And, your accent is very good," their aunt smiled good-humoredly. "Now, let me continue." The teacher in her knew that their participation in the storytelling would better insure their remembering the details.

"Now Geispolsheim was a pretty large village—about 2,000 people! LaWalck and Mertzviller were much smaller—only about 800 people each, so *Maman* was afraid at first because she didn't know anybody and everything was new to her. Soon she met her neighbors and the parishioners at St. Marguerite Church and so she began to feel at home. And taking care of her three baby boys kept her very busy.

"Papa was gone much of the time since he would have to stay on patrol for several days when it was his turn to guard the German border along the big Rhine River which was very near. Soon after they moved to Geispolsheim *Maman* began to prepare for a new baby, and Jesus gave the Feltins an early Epiphany gift—their baby Louise."

"That's you, *tata-Maman!*" Lizette chimed in. "You were the special gift!"

"Yes, I was, but my *Maman* and Papa were always the good God's gift to me! My *Maman* was a special woman. Though she had much to do taking care of us, she asked our priest, *l'abbé* Laroche, for a very special favor. *Maman* had studied in Haguenau with the Sisters and she wanted her daughter to be able to go to school. Our village had a school for boys, but there was no school for girls. So, *l'abbé* Laroche found some Sisters who came to Geispolsheim just before I was ready to start school, and they opened a school for girls. The Sisters of Divine Providence—not my Sisters from St. Jean-de-Bassel, but the ones from Ribeauvillé—were my first teachers. They were so kind and gentle. I learned to read and write, and I learned to love God from them. Now that I think about it, I wonder why I didn't join that group of Sisters at Ribeauvillé. Surely if I had, my life would have turned out so differently! And," she touched Lizette's blond curly hair, "my dear ones, perhaps I would not have had the privilege of being your mother!"

**Sisters of Divine Providence of
Ribeauvillé, France
(Date unknown)**

Jule, now aged fourteen—and not unlike most girls of her age—had been giving much thought to the experiences of her life. She did not remember her mother and wondered if she was like her mother in any way. Being raised by their aunt really didn't make them all that different from other children her age, but *Tante* Louise was different. Now seemed like a good time to say aloud some of her thoughts.

"*Tata-Maman*, are you sorry that you came with us from Texas? You could have stayed there," Jule asked timidly.

"Perhaps I could have stayed in Castroville. The people there were very good to me at a hard time in my life, but your papa was so distraught when your dear mother died. I truly felt that God was leading me to trust in Him in new ways and to step into the unknown. I certainly did not know how to be a mother. I was a schoolteacher. And when I was the Superior of my Sisters, I don't think they thought of me as 'motherly.' In fact, I was rather hard on them sometimes because I thought they could always do better—both as teachers and as nuns. I've had to learn how to be a mother, how to be more gentle. I have prayed to God and to the Blessed Virgin to help me. Your own dear mother was so loving and she wanted only the best for each one of you. I have tried to be as good a mother to you as my mother was to me, as good as your mother. When my brothers and sisters and I were little children, our dear *Maman* taught us to pray, and she reminded us often to depend on our loving God who cares for us each and every day. To always have hope—even when times are hard. That was a lesson I never forgot—and a lesson that I have tried to teach you girls. Promise me that you will always trust in the goodness of God, especially if hard times come."

"We promise, *tata*. We won't forget!" the young voices chorused.

"I think that another important reality for our family during our time in Geispolsheim was that the people there were mostly farmers. They owned the land surrounding the village. In France people who own land are more likely to have a better living standard. The poorer people, since they don't own any land, are forced to tend animals. Did you know that they let the animals live in the house with them? Or at least in a shed built onto the house. Lou-Lou, do you remember how some of the houses in Castroville were, with slanting roofs and a barn attached to the house? How you could hear the cow mooing from the kitchen?"

Lou-Lou nodded and the girls laughed out loud.

"Wouldn't our neighbors laugh if they knew how we lived in Castroville? I'm not going to tell anyone or they will make fun of me," Lizette noted with seriousness.

Typical Alsatian house of the 19th century. (From Geispolsheim—Entre Tradition et Modernisme. (Used with permission)

Louise looked at Lizette and smiled. "A very practical thought, Lizette. Well, that is how the houses of the poor are in France. But, Geispolsheim had people with more wealth. I am sure that is why we had such a good school for the girls as well as a school for the boys. The school for the boys was very good also even though they didn't have religious or priests as teachers when we lived there. Pierre and Nicolas would often say how good their teachers were in the Geispolsheim school. Of course, both of your uncles did very well because they had a good education. Your uncle Pierre eventually became the mayor of LaWalck and you know that your uncle Nicolas became a priest of God.

"I remember how Papa used to look in his uniform. He was tall with broad shoulders and a big black mustache, which tickled when he kissed me. His navy blue uniform had beautiful gold buttons with lots of braid and he had a tall hat that had a strap that went under his chin. But he had a hard job and *Maman* was home by herself with us children much of the time. After I was born, along came another brother, Celestin; and then I finally got a sister, Marie-Anne! I was six when Marie-Anne was born and to me she was like a real live doll. Though I had to go to school, *Maman* would let me play with her as much as I wanted. But mostly I played with the boys. *Maman* used to scold me because I would get my dresses dirty in the mud and I always had a dirty face."

"It's hard to imagine you with a dirty face, *ma petite tata!*" Lou-Lou quipped. "You are always after us to clean up and wash our faces and hands."

"It's true," Louise said, "I have to admit I liked playing with the boys. They seemed to have games that were more fun and they could always stay out later than girls could." She paused and became more serious. "And then we had a very sad occurrence. I was almost seven and I still remember it quite well. *Maman* had a new baby, Rosalie, on Christmas Day, two days before my seventh birthday. However, Rosalie was not strong and I think *Maman* must have been sick as well."

Unexpectedly, tears welled in her eyes. Louise had never truly mourned the deaths of any of her family members. She had been in her second teaching assignment when she had received the letter from Nicolas telling her of Celestin's death in America. Then Pierre had died shortly after she had come to Texas and she was so busy working on the school in Austin that she had not taken even a moment to give in to sorrow. Even when her own dear mother had died just before Christmas in 1871, she had set her grief aside as she concentrate on her many duties at Providence House in Castroville. Her priest-brother Nicolas had died so suddenly in 1878, just after her return from Germany with her first new postulants, novices, and professed Sisters. Being so busy with all the new members of the struggling Texas Congregation and burden with her duties as Superior General, Louise had, she now realized, buried her feelings about that death as well. She paused in her story to rummage in her pocket for her handkerchief.

"*Ma petite tata-Maman,* you are crying!" Lou-Lou said with surprise. "You never cry. Why are you so sad tonight?"

"I wonder myself, *ma chèrie.* Perhaps I am just realizing that most of my dear brothers and my dear parents are with God, and I know that I will never see your aunt Marie-Anne again—or your aunt Christine. These are old tears that have never been shed. I must let them fall now."

Louise knew that that explanation was too complicated for these young girls. She hoped that one day they would understand. Though her eyes were still moist, she took a deep breath, continuing her saga.

"Each day after Rosalie's birth the house became more and more quiet. Papa seemed so anxious. He would stay in their bedroom for hours with *Maman* and Baby Rosalie. We were never allowed in and a neighbor came to take care of us. One day, just at sunset, Papa came out to the parlor and told us that little Rosalie had gone home to God. He took Marie-Anne up on his lap and I tucked under his arm. We sat like that before the fire for a long while.

"The next day was very cold. Shortly after breakfast, a man came with a small box and we all took Baby Rosalie to the church where *Monsieur l'abbé* Laroche said the Mass of the Angels. As we walked to the cemetery, snow began to fall. We all cried, even Pierre, when the box was put into the ground in the cemetery behind the church.

Ste. Marguerite Church, Geispolsheim
(from <u>Geispolsheim—Entre Tradition</u>
<u>et Modernisme</u>; Courtesy, Marie-Jeanne
Schneider, Co-author)

Maman was sad for a very long time.

"Whenever we went to Sunday Mass she would cry and cry. Many neighbors came to help us. I think Papa didn't know what to do so he just stayed at the barracks more. We didn't see him very much. I remember feeling sad, and a little afraid. I was so glad that I could go to school because the Sisters were kind to me, just like mothers. And the boys watched out for me and Marie-Anne. I always felt safe walking with them to school. They would never go so fast that I couldn't keep up, especially Nicolas.

"The School for Girls was on one side of the church and the School for Boys was on the other side. My brothers and I walked to school each morning—about the same distance as from here to our parish church."

"Oh, *ma petite tata*," Lizette interrupted, "that is so much farther than I have to go. My school is just across the street. You were so little. Didn't you get tired everyday with that long walk? I get tired when we walk to St. Patrick's for Mass."

"I don't remember being tired. Other children joined us along the way. On the way home, we would often go a different route to pass by the *pâtisserie* for some lovely pastry or buns. We lived on *Rue des Moines*. I remember thinking that that was a funny name because no one ever spoke of any monks living there.

"Most of the houses in Alsatian villages are the same. Every house has a statue of a stork with its nest on the roof. That's a symbol of good luck! Some of the houses even have real storks, too! The houses in LaWalck were similar. Our house in LaWalck had two bedrooms downstairs and a big room upstairs where the boys slept. Marie-Anne and I shared one bedroom downstairs and *Maman* and Papa had the other one. The babies were always in a crib in their room."

"That's not fair, *ma tante*! I have to share my room with three sisters," protested Lou-Lou.

"Be grateful that you have three sisters, *ma chérie*. I had only Marie-Anne growing up. And then I left her behind when I went to the convent and later came to America. I miss her still. Christine was only three years old when I went to the convent—just a baby. I really hardly knew her at all."

Fearing that her aunt was going to cry again, Jule broke in. *"Tata-Maman*, you didn't tell us about the processions! We love to hear all about those. Don't forget!"

The reverie was broken for the moment. "Oh, yes, my darlings. The processions. I didn't know you liked to hear about those! In both Geispolsheim and in LaWalck the parishes had several processions each year, to celebrate the big feasts or the Ember Days. I suppose I will never forget the procession in Geispolsheim in honor of Ste. Marguerite, the town's patroness. The entire town would take part. First would come all the school children carrying flowers that we had picked in the fields. Then would come all the women. They would wear their long black dresses but with their special Alsatian headdresses of black taffeta and silk ribbons.

"Maman always had the freshest bonnet and the widest skirt. We were so proud of her. On those day she was light-hearted and happy. Rosalie's death seemed to leave her with a heaviness that would not go away.

"Papa's battalion would be in the parade as well. They would all march with their swords drawn and lifted high toward the beautiful statue of Ste. Marguerite from the church. The young men of the parish carried the statue high on a wooden platform, and the choir would follow behind singing wonderful hymns.

Procession in Geispolsheim

(From <u>Geispolsheim—Entre Tradition et Modernism</u>.
Courtesy, Marie-Jeanne Schneider, Co-author)

"I think the young girls just used those processions as an excuse to look over the young men and to pick out the ones they thought they would like to marry! Girls always wanted to walk near Pierre as he was handsome and strong. The priest walked ahead of the statue, but facing Ste. Marguerite, swinging the incense. I remember a young priest once who would swing the incense way over his head in such a high arc that Marie-Anne and I thought the coals would fling out! But that never happened. The procession would go all through the town and at each home, the bearers paused so that Ste. Marguerite could bless each house. It really was grand.

"And then on the night of the procession we would all gather in the town square for a big party for the whole village. There would be music and dancing and singing. And the food! We feasted on wonderful Alsatian sausages and cheeses and lots of new wine and delicious pastries! I used to love it! So did Marie-Anne. We would eat all we wanted. *Maman* never scolded us even though we did misbehave by teasing the boys from the Boys' School."

The girls loved hearing their aunt speak about her girlhood days this way. She was always happy when she was remembering her family and its celebrations. These memories were like a smoldering ember in her soul that was fanned into flame when she told the stories of her youth. Even her face changed as she spoke. Her eyes twinkled and her usually straight lips turned up into a genuine smile. She looked so pretty when she smiled. They liked that.

Louise went on. "When we would come home from the feast day celebration, it would be late and Papa would light a fire in the kitchen fireplace. He would take out his pipe and tell us stories of how he met *Maman* and how he always thought she was the most beautiful woman in the village. *Maman* would smile in a special way. I suppose that the kitchen was our favorite room both in Geispolsheim and in LaWalck, but the house in LaWalck had a much bigger brick fireplace and a brick floor. *Maman* insisted that the kitchen be spotless. She would never let us get away with our casual ways if she were here with us today!"

Louise could tell by the look in the eyes of her nieces that they loved a grandmother they had never known who had now been with the Lord for nearly thirty years.

"Tell us more about LaWalck, *tata-Maman*," said Jule. "I like that part the best."

"All right. But I'm growing a little tired. After this part, I'll have to go to bed. Today was a hard day in the grocery store." Louise readjusted her shawl and resettled herself in her rocker, taking a deep breath as she readied herself to launch into the conclusion to this part of the family story.

"We moved back to LaWalck when I was just ten. Because *Maman* had been so sad for so long in Geispolsheim, Papa decided to resign his commission in the *Ordre des Douanes*. But he had to have a way to earn a living. We were a large family and Papa didn't have any land. *Meémeé* Seiter, *Maman*'s mother—*votre arriére-grand-mère!*—sent us a letter to tell us that *Pépère* was ill and *Meémère* needed help in the store. *Maman* begged Papa to take us back to LaWalck to help. I think now that Papa was reluctant to take on the store. He had always worked out of doors and knew nothing about running a store. *Maman* promised him that she would help; finally he agreed. I remember the long trip back to LaWalck. We packed our things in barrels and loaded a wagon. Then Maman and we children went on the stagecoach while Papa and Pierre went with the wagon.

"One of the hardest things for me was saying goodbye to the Sisters who had been so kind to me. In LaWalck we did not have a school run by the Sisters, so it was a double loss to me.

"As I said before, LaWalck is much smaller than Geispolsheim and, in many ways, much prettier. There are more trees and the streets are shady. It is on the north bank of the River Moder while Pfaffenhoffen is on the south bank. The Moder is a small river. I don't think you've seen a river that small. You can walk over it on a small footbridge. We had to use the footbridge to go to Mass each Sunday because our church, Sts. Peter and Paul, is in Pfaffenhoffen. Our church there is beautiful, made of pink stone from the Vosges Mountains. Inside it is sort of dark with a big high altar and a high pulpit where the priest would preach. Our church here is nothing like that one. Papa's store was on *Rue de l'Eglise* and the school I went to was on *Rue des Bois*. We lived on *Rue de Kinderwiller*, near the store.

"So many things happened to our family in LaWalck. The first thing was that your papa was born. I was not quite twelve years old. *Maman* loved your papa so much. She was so happy that he wasn't sick like Rosalie had been. We probably spoiled him, Marie-Anne and myself. We held him all the time so he never cried. Your papa was a happy little boy. Then a few years later along came your aunt Christine. She was such a beautiful child. When I said goodbye to her when I left for the convent, I cried so much. I knew it would be a long time before I saw her again. And, your papa was just a little boy.

"Your uncle Nicolas was the first one to leave home. To be honest I remember being glad when he left." Realizing that she had never admitted this before, she chuckled. "He was always bossing me around. He was only one year older than I and yet he always acted like he knew everything."

"Didn't you like Uncle Nicolas, *ma tante*?" Jule was always the insightful one.

"I understand just what *ma petite tata* means," Lizette piped up. "I get so tired of James bossing me around. He thinks he knows everything!" Lizette's voice held a child's sympathy.

"I suppose we were just too Alsatian, Julie. Alsatians are very stubborn people with a single-minded nature and sometimes a short temper. Alsatian brothers and sisters, especially when they are adults, are often very critical of each other. It was like that with Nicolas and myself after we grew up and came to America. But that is for another story. Nicolas went to the minor seminary in Molsheim and studied with the Jesuits. He always said he wanted to be a priest and so he went when he was sixteen. I was fifteen and I had begun to think about being a Sister so that I could be a teacher like the Sisters in Geispolsheim. I knew that I would miss Nicolas, but I wouldn't miss being bossed around!"

The girls laughed. Seldom did they hear their aunt speak so frankly and with such humor. These stories tonight were a little different. The facts were the same, but Auntie Louise seemed more touched by them somehow.

Louise continued. "Our village was surrounded by a forest where I would go on long walks to think and to pray. Sometimes Marie-Anne would go with me. Also, I would help Papa in the store just like you girls help me! He taught me how to rotate the stock so that it would be fresh, how to gauge how much to order, how to deal with customers who were in a bad mood; just like I've taught you. When I went to the convent, I never thought I would need to know what Papa spent hours teaching me. However, through the Providence of God, we got our grocery store here in San Jose, and I was so grateful to Papa for everything he taught me. You know, he treated me just as he treated the boys. That was very important to my life. I've tried to teach you girls to be on your own, too. Do you understand?"

"Yes, *ma tante*. I do." Lou-Lou's response was reflective. "You want us to be able to take care of things when we become adults." She said this thoughtfully, deliberately, as though somehow she sensed that things might be changing.

"I'm very tired now, *mes filles*. Tomorrow is another day. It is the Lord's Day—and Lizette, you have your class for Confirmation and First Communion. We will go to the 7:30 Mass as usual and then I will fix us a special dinner. It will be a surprise!"

The girls went upstairs to their room, but Louise stayed downstairs, wanting to spend some quiet time on the front porch for a few minutes before going to her bedroom. Even on this summer night, the air was cool and crisp. Empire Street was nothing more than a dirt path on the north edge of San Jose and seldom did a wagon or buggy come down it. She knew that the town was growing this way, and it would be only a matter of time before nearby orchards and pastures would be filled with houses for the waves of people moving into this beautiful valley. Fond of standing on her front porch to gaze out to the mountains that surrounded San Jose, Louise knew that she would miss so many things that had become part of her life in the last ten years. *Her* home with her—yes, *her*—children; *her* store; *her* neighbors; St. Patrick's Church; the mountains; the weather that was so similar to that of France; the groves and groves of fruit trees, especially the wonderful prunes that reminded her so much of her dear, dear homeland. Tears filled her eyes once again and she let them spill over until her cheeks were wet. All she had now was hope that her decision to return to Castroville was the right one. All she had was hope.

Sunday morning dawned bright with a cloudless sky like so many of the days in San Jose. The Feltin family attended the 7:30 Mass at St. Patrick's Church and then Lizette went to her class to prepare for Confirmation while the others found friends to walk home with. Louise and her brother Louis walked the ten blocks home by themselves. The walk home gave Louise an opportunity to discuss with Louis her plans for returning to Castroville. In his own way Louis seemed to be sorry to see Louise go. They hadn't always gotten along, but he knew he owed her a debt of gratitude for coming with them to California when he had no one to help him. And, she had been a good mother to his youngest daughters. Louise told her brother that she had decided to return to Castroville in October with hopes that the killing heat of the Texas summer would be over and she might not have such a challenging adjustment. Louis agreed with her plan. The children would be settled in school and Lou-Lou would be well-oriented to her work in the grocery store. He agreed that it would be sensible to return in October. And, he agreed to pay the $57.00 fare on the Southern Pacific. He owed her that much. They further agreed that she should take the $700 that she had saved over the years. The store did fairly well, both he and Joe made pretty good money, and Nick and James brought in a bit. If she took the money with her, she wouldn't feel like a beggar, he insisted. When Louis had proposed that, she knew that he had strong feelings about her being put out of the Sisterhood under, in his words, "that power-hungry bishop." He hadn't really said much during those trying years, but Louise surmised that what had befallen her had rankled him for these dozen or so years.

Louise and her brother were home by mid-morning and Louise announced that she was making chicken with noodles for dinner, which would be served about two o'clock. The meal was a special treat, one that they all enjoyed but that she seldom took the time to prepare. As she rolled the dough for the noodles while the chicken boiled, she wondered if she would ever be able to cook at the school in Castroville. Probably not.

Thickening thunderclouds rolled in from the west by early afternoon, and as they were finishing dinner, rain began to fall. While washing the dishes, Lizette ventured the question that her two older sisters had put her up to.

"*Ma petite tata-Maman*, don't you think it's a good afternoon to finish your story. We'll just be stuck in the house because of the rain. Please, *ma tata*," Lizette wheedled.

"Yes, darling, it is a good afternoon for the rest of the story. Would you mind if I took a short nap first and then we'll have coffee and talk."

"Oh, no, *tata-Maman*. Take a nap and then we'll be ready!" Lizette and the other two girls could hardly believe how easy it had been to get their aunt to continue the family story.

When they assembled in the parlor later in the afternoon, it was still raining and the atmosphere seemed perfect for the weaving of the final chapters in the saga of the Family Feltin. Louise began with her own story.

"When I was almost fifteen, I told my mother and father that I wanted to go to the convent. The only Sisters I knew about, of course, were the ones from Ribeauvillé. I thought about going there, but I knew that it was very far from LaWalck. I talked with our priest and he said he knew of a similar group of Sisters in a place called St. Jean-de-Bassel, in Lorraine. After I talked to Papa, he talked with the priest as well. The priest told him that the Sisters at that convent were German- and Alsatian-speaking and that they had schools in some villages near LaWalck. When he told Papa that the convent was about forty miles away, Papa agreed that I could go. Since it was all right with *Maman* and Papa, it was all right with me; and *l'abbé* Vincent helped me to write the letter asking for admittance. *Maman* and Papa thought that maybe, in time, I would be sent to a nearby village to teach.

"Your uncle Pierre had worked in the grocery store since he was a young man, and as Papa got older Pierre began to take over the business. In France, by law, the oldest son inherited all the property. The other boys would receive nothing since the store went to Pierre and there was no other land. François moved to Paris, joining the Customs Service, and Celestin and your Papa had to seek their fortune elsewhere.

"Dear Papa went to heaven in 1855 while I was teaching in Heiligenberg. That was too far away and I wasn't able to go to Papa's funeral. I had been home to see Papa just before I went to teach. I knew that he was sick, and he was so sad about Celestin's death. I was sad when Papa died. Your uncle Pierre died in 1867, just after I came to Texas." Louise held her voice in check as she re-visited these three deaths. Only the tears streaming down her cheeks betrayed the deep grief that washed over her.

"Nicolas had been ready to prepare for ordination when the Bishop of Texas came to Alsace to recruit seminarians and priests for the missions there. Nicolas talked to Papa but he had already made up his mind to go to Texas. I was in the convent. I remember when he came to tell me goodbye. He was so excited! His letters from America were filled with the needs of the Texas frontier. There were few churches, no schools, no Sisters like us, more and more Catholics, and very few priests. But, he loved his work there. The Bishop of Texas ordained him in 1853 and he was made a pastor in just a few years.

"Your uncle Celestin was only eighteen when he went to Texas to be with Father Nicolas. He had learned to lay bricks in LaWalck, and your uncle Nicolas had promised that there was no end to work for a bricklayer in Texas. But, alas, Celestin died only a short time after arriving in Houston where Uncle Nicolas was a priest. He's buried there in St. Vincent de Paul Parish Cemetery."

Remembering the shock of her mother's letter and recalling the visit she had made to Celestin's grave after she had come to America, Louise stopped at that point. She had been teaching in Heiligenberg for just a year when *Maman* wrote in 1854 that Celestin had gotten yellow fever and died in Nicolas' arms in Houston. Nicolas had said the Requiem Mass. In one part of the letter, the ink had been blotched, the stain of her dear mother's tears. The blotches had brought to mind those winter days in Geispolsheim when their house had been so sad and cold after Baby Rosalie's death. Louise now wondered if Celestin's death at such a young age and so far away had contributed to Papa's death. When only a year later she had received another letter from *Maman* telling her that dear Papa had gone home to God, she had never even considered the effect of Celestin's death on their Papa. How self-centered I have been, she thought now.

The girls were patient as she sat with a faraway look in her eyes.

Before her own tears began again, taking a deep breath, she continued. "As I said, your uncle François went to Paris and entered the *Ordre des Douanes*. I know Papa was proud of him, but then the men in the Customs Service were called into the regular army to defend France against the Prussians. *Maman* wrote to me just before she died telling me of her fear for François.

"Marie-Anne had the sad task of writing to Nicolas, your papa, and myself telling us that *Maman* had died of cancer just two weeks before Christmas in 1871. We knew that she was in heaven with Papa, Celestin, Pierre, and Baby Rosalie, so we weren't too sad. Then, in a few months, another letter came from Marie-Anne telling us that François had been killed in a late battle of a war that was basically over. Poor Marie-Anne! Such a hard task!

"As I remember, I was so glad to know that *Maman* had already gone to heaven. At least with François she could welcome him into God's eternal kingdom and not have to think of him in an unknown grave. Poor Marie-Anne! Such a hard task to write to us about our losses!" Louise's sad tone brought a hush to her audience and her nieces remained silent as the grief of these deaths engulfed her once again.

As an afterthought, Louise added with the same sadness, "That's when our dear homeland became part of the Reich."

Taking a deep breath, Louise plunged back into the story. "In those years France was building its army to try to stand up against the Prussians and your own Papa was afraid he might be called into service. Since he had no property, he decided to come to Texas to be with Father Nicolas and myself. Father Nicolas helped him get started by hiring him to build the convent and school at St. Mary's Parish in Austin. Of course, that's where he met your dear, beautiful Mama and married her. I only wish that you knew your Mama's family better. They are so wonderful. They were a prominent family in the small town of Austin, Texas. I'm sorry I don't know their story, but you can be proud of your ancestors on both sides!"

The physical distance between the Fruths and her own nephews and nieces had been a heartache for Louise. She knew that Louis' decision to go to California meant that Theresa's family would be lost to their children. Travel and communication were just too hard. Louise wished she had some words of comfort for her nieces, but nothing she could say would change that they were basically alone in the world.

The story was almost finished. "Your aunt Marie-Anne married one of our distant cousins, Joseph Seiter, who lived in LaWalck. The marriage took place just before I came to America and I really didn't have an opportunity to know him. On my trips back to Germany while I was still the Superior, I met their son Joseph. It would be wonderful if you could meet him some day."

Jule was the first to ask the question the others held. "Do we have any other cousins, *ma tante?*"

"One other. Your Uncle Pierre had one daughter. She still lives in LaWalck. So the grandchildren of *Maman* and Papa are ten, counting you three, Mamie, and your brothers. If you never meet your cousins in this life, I pray that you will be good girls and meet them in the next."

"We will, we will, *tata-Maman*," the three girls assured her with enthusiasm. "You'll be proud of us!"

Telling the story had worn Louise out. And even so, she had left so much unsaid. She realized that she knew so very little about her youngest sister, Christine. Louise had left a toddler behind in LaWalck when she had entered the convent. She had met her grown sister only a handful of times over the years. Though she and Christine had maintained a correspondence and Louise had always made it a point to visit with her when she returned to St. Jean-de-Bassel, the distance and age difference had dampened their relationship as sisters. All she had been able to tell the girls was that their *Tante* Christine had never married and had become a schoolteacher. Once in a while Christine had written about wanting to come to America, but Louise never really thought she would. Now that she herself was planning to return to Texas maybe she ought to write to Christine and encourage her to come to California. She would give that some thought, but Providence would have to work it all out.

The girls scattered to find a little supper and then to do the things they loved: Jule would most likely spend the evening drawing; Lizette would play the piano; Lou-Lou would look over the grocery store's books, preparing for the next day's business.

The rain had stopped now, and Louise decided to spend some time on the front porch before going to bed. She was always so tired at night now. No doubt a combination of the effects of her bad heart and the diabetes that the doctor had discovered when she had had her appendix removed at O'Conner Sanitarium.

She wasn't sure why her memories of the operation had suddenly and vividly come to mind as she sat on the porch swing looking off to the mountains. She placed her hand on her side where the rough scar could be felt through her thin summer dress. The remnant of that horrible surgery, it was a constant reminder of the unimaginable pain.

Living for years on the Texas frontier had accustomed Louise to pain of all sorts, but the pains in her side had become agonizing on that night two years ago. No amount of home remedies would diminish them. Finally, Louis and Mamie had insisted that she be taken to the newly opened O'Connor Sanatorium, which was quite some distance away. She supposed now that it was her encounter with the Sisters of Charity there that made her think seriously about returning to her Congregation. The solitude during those two weeks in the quiet environment at the hospital, the crisp clean sheets on the cot-like beds, the sparkling floors, the nursing care by the Sisters reminded her in a strange way of her dear Motherhouse in Castroville. That convent-like atmosphere had made her heart long for her own convent.

While she was at the hospital, she had taken time to confide her story to the priest-chaplain who had encouraged her to let God forgive the past and guide the future. He had suggested that Mother

Florence would welcome her return to the Texas Congregation
and that by not writing for re-admission she was denying Mother
Florence the opportunity that she too needed for reconciliation.
Perhaps she had allowed herself to be bereft of hope, he had challenged gently.

Due to a shortage of anesthetic, the operation to remove her
appendix had been still more agony. Noting that perhaps the doctor's scalpel should be seen as God's own cleansing sword, the priest
had assured her that her sins were now atoned.

In her prayer on that summer night she found again her resolve
to rejoin her Sisters. God had been guiding this process for months
now and He would not abandon her. Words of *l 'abbé* Moye came to
her mind: ***Be assured that the more you abandon yourselves
without anxiety to God, the more He will take care of you.***[*]

---

[*] **The Directory, p.225.**

CHAPTER IV

A NEW LIFE

"*Maman,* I need to talk with you about something very important."
Today was the day. Now fifteen years old, Louise Feltin had waited
for the store to empty on that July afternoon in 1845. Indicating that
he would be gone for most of the afternoon, her father had left her
mother and herself alone in the store. The small hamlet of LaWalck
still did not have a schoolteacher for the upcoming term and the
mayor had called a meeting of town leaders to see what could be
done.

Louise's voice was both firm and tentative at the same time. She
had grown into a young woman in the past couple of years and her
mother suspected that this tone of voice underpinned a life-changing topic. Louise had talked with *l'abbé* Kübler, the pastor at Sts.
Peter and Paul Church in next-door Pfaffenhoffen, more than once.
He believed that her intentions were of God and had urged her to
talk frankly with her mother and father.

"What is it, *ma chérie?*" Madame Feltin asked.

Having thought and prayed about this moment for months, perhaps even years, Louise was calm. She tucked a stray tendril of
curling brown hair back behind her ear and began. "*Maman,* I have
been thinking and praying for months. I have spoken with *Monsieur
l'abbé* Kübler. I want to go to the convent and become a religious in
one of those groups that provide schoolteachers to small villages—
like the Sisters of Ribeauvillé." The words tumbled out, leaving her
breathless. She was so afraid that her mother would ask her to stay
at home. Nicolas had just gone to the seminary two years earlier and

67

Louise did not think her mother wanted another child to leave home so soon. Papa always said he needed help in the store. Lately, Papa had been saying that she might be needed to teach in the village school.

"Oh, Louise, *ma chérie, ma fille*! I always suspected that you would be thinking of this type of life. But what does *Monsieur l'abbé* Kübler say?"

At that, Louise sighed. She knew that her mother, a truly devout Catholic, would follow whatever her priest indicated. "He says that he thinks God is calling me and that he will help me find a group that will take me." Louise said this shyly, with her head down. It sounded like she was bragging and she was not that type of girl.

"*Maman*, I will be sixteen in just a few months. I am old enough." This last comment came as an assertion and was not spoken rebelliously.

"Yes, *ma fille*, I know. Are you sure?" Having watched this child, her eldest daughter, very carefully, Madame Feltin was not surprised at Louise's request. She remembered how much Louise admired the Sisters of Divine Providence of Ribeauvillé in Geispolsheim, how often she went to church to pray, how helpful she was to her papa in their store, and how Nicolas' decision to go to the seminary had affected her.

"Yes, *Maman*. I am sure," Louise replied confidently. "I believe God is asking me to do this."

"We don't have any Sisters here, Louise. Where would you go? To a convent in Paris or Metz or Strasbourg?"

"No, *Maman*. I want to be like the Sisters in Geispolsheim. *Monsieur l'abbé* knows of a group near Sarrebourg in Lorraine. He thinks I should go there and he says that he will write to them for me. May I tell him that you and Papa will allow me to go?"

"When Baby Rosalie died," her mother began, "I was so lost in my pain—in our loss." She was taken back in time to that house in Geispolsheim that had grown so cold in those winter months in 1838. She shivered now, even though the warmth of a summer afternoon filled their store in LaWalck. "I could hardly believe that God would take my child. Over the years I began to understand that each one of you is only on loan to your papa and me by *le Bon Dieu*. You came from *le Bon Dieu* ... and you belong to Him. When Nicolas asked us to go to the seminary, I thought my heart would break to say good-bye to another child. But God is good. I believe that. If God is asking me to give up my dear daughter, then, I surrender to His holy will. I surrender to His Providence."

These last words revealed the foundation of Madame Feltin's spirituality. In hearing these words, Louise knew that she had received her mother's blessing. She couldn't count the number of times she had heard her mother say, "I surrender to His Providence." When times were good, when times were hard, when her own father had died, and when Nicolas left home, the words "I surrender to His Providence" were on Madame Feltin's lips as surely as they were in her heart.

"Will you speak to Papa for me?" Louise asked timidly.

"*Non, ma chérie*. You will speak to your papa yourself!" Madame Feltin had never spoken to Jean-Claude on behalf of her children. She believed that the girls especially needed to learn how to stand up to men. Practicing on their father would be good for them!

"Though he may be disappointed that you will not be the school-teacher here until the mayor finds one," Madame Feltin continued, "your papa will be proud of you. He thinks you are very smart. Many times he has said that you are more help in the store than all the boys combined!" Madame Feltin had walked a thin line with each of her children. Wanting her children to know their strengths, this wise mother knew that they must always take opportunities to grow stronger. For Louise, to speak to her papa herself would make her stronger. "Tonight, after supper, I will leave you alone with Papa. Take coffee with him and tell him of your hopes."

"Thank you, *Maman*," Louise said, somewhat shyly.

With the late-afternoon customers now coming into the small village store, Louise and her mother were both occupied with filling orders and stocking and straightening shelves for the next day's trade until closing time. At six o'clock they closed the store and walked down the block to the family home for the night.

Pierre Isidore and François-Joseph had come home from the fields where they were working and Marie-Anne had begun to set out boiled ham, bread, and cheese for the family supper. Monsieur Feltin came in just as Madame Feltin was lighting the lamps. Though his dark hair had gone gray over the years, his erect military bearing still commanded a special respect from anyone who saw him. He immediately came forth with news of his meeting.

"There seems no hope for finding a teacher for our school. If Pfaffenhoffen weren't a Lutheran village, we could send our children to their school, but I simply will not jeopardize the faith of our children that way. We must have a school with a Catholic teacher! I wish we had pursued finding some Sisters earlier. The mayor says that the Congregations of Sisters who take small village schools are already committed for this year and they have no one to send out. We are simply too small to attract another lay teacher. "Louise," he turned to his eldest daughter who was slicing the ham, "I would like to talk with you after supper." All those years as a lieutenant in the customs service had given Jean-Claude Feltin much practice at giving orders and he easily fell into that mode of relating. His children were accustomed to his brusque ways; but when he spoke with such command, they knew better than to question or to falter against the order.

Louise replied simply, "Yes, Papa." She was fairly certain that her father wanted to ask her to teach in the village school after the harvest was over. She was no longer sure that now would be best time to ask him about her own future plans. Her heart told her to leave it in the hands of God and that everything would be all right.

After the supper was over, the boys all went outside. Though exhausted from a long day of cutting and stacking hay, the older boys were never too tired to enjoy a smoke and to talk about the village girls with their friends. The youngest, Louis, went out to find his pals to continue their afternoon games into the long summer twilight. There was plenty of time to have more fun. To give Louise privacy with her father, Madame Feltin took Marie-Anne in tow to help with baby Christine.

"Papa, would you like a cup of coffee?" Louise asked her father after he was settled with his Bible. Noticing dark circles under his eyes, she realized that he was beginning to look his sixty-two years. Each night, after supper, *Monsieur* Feltin read from the Bible. During the regular school term, he would require that the entire family gather as he read aloud for not less than half an hour.

"Yes, *ma fille*. And, we must have our talk."

Louise brought his coffee, strong and black, and brought a cup of *café au lait* for herself. "I put in one lump of sugar, Papa. Just like you like it."

"Thank you, *ma chérie*. Now, I will come to my subject. Our small village cannot find a Catholic teacher for the primary school. Since you can read, write, and cipher, I suggested to the mayor that you could run the school until we can find some Sisters who will come to take it over. Will you?"

Louise was a bit surprised that he ended with the question. She had almost expected him to say that he had volunteered her! She took a deep breath and began.

"*Non, Papa*." Louise was not sure why, but her voice was steady and she spoke clearly. "I spoke with *Maman* this afternoon and I want to speak with you now. I believe that God is calling me to be a Sister—one who teaches in small villages like ours. I know that our village needs a teacher now, but I must do what God asks of me." She could hardly believe the strength of her words! She hoped that her papa would not think her defiant.

Monsieur Feltin was not surprised at the content of his daughter's short speech, but he was surprised at her confidence.

"Well! Though I have been expecting this conversation for some time, I have to admit that you are more confident than I imagined!

He looked straight into her dark brown eyes, pausing before he asked his short question.

"Are you sure? You are not even sixteen years old." *Monsieur* Feltin's voice was cautious.

"Yes, Papa," she said simply. "I am sure."

Her papa abandoned his own agenda and continued to explore his daughter's hopes. "What does *l' abbé* Kübler say?" *Monsieur* Feltin was always direct with his children and he would not even bother to continue the conversation if Louise had not consulted the priest at Sts. Peter and Paul in Pfaffenhoffen.

"*Monsieur l' Abbé* says that he thinks God is calling me. He says that he knows of a Congregation in Lorraine, near Sarrebourg, and that he will write to them to inquire for me. They accept girls my age and send them to their schools to see if they have a vocation. He thinks they will take me."

"So." He began slowly. "You've thought of everything?"

"*Non, Papa*. I've only gone this far. I wanted to talk with you and *Maman* before I pursued further with *Monsieur l'Abbé*."

"That's good." He sat back, sipped his coffee, and rested his head on the back of his chair. Louise didn't know what "good" referred to, but she knew not to ask. With her papa, it was simply best to let him mull over new information and then follow his lead with the remainder of the conversation. She, too, leaned back in her chair and sipped her *café au lait*. She remembered her mother's adage, "I will surrender to Divine Providence," and she adopted it for herself at that moment, placing all in the hands of God.

After what seemed an eternity, *Monsieur* Feltin finally came out of his reverie, returning to his military-like control. "Tell *Monsieur l' Abbé* to write the letter. I myself want to talk with him about these Sisters."

Louise knew the conversation was over. She got up, took her father's coffee cup and, in silence, bent to kiss him on the forehead, realizing that no more words were necessary.

Louise thought of that conversation with her father as the coach pulled away from the way station in Sarrebourg, leaving her alone to await transportation to St. Jean-de-Bassel. The journey had been a long and exhausting two days by stagecoach over mountainous terrain to Sarrebourg, the largest town nearby the motherhouse of the Congregation of Divine Providence. The wintry November weather was daunting and Louise knew that she would have been really cold in the stagecoach except that she was packed in with four other people. Though she might not have enjoyed the proximity of the other passengers if she were traveling in the summer months, she was glad for the snug accommodations in November. She was so glad that her papa had come with her to Sarrebourg. He had bade her farewell there.

"This last part you must do on your own, *ma fille*," he said with a smile. "The Sisters will not want to receive a little girl on her father's arm. And I must get back to the store." With that he had awaited the return stagecoach for Haguenau.

Her feelings during the long journey had been mixed with sorrow at leaving her family, especially baby Christine, anxiety at going to a completely unknown place, and fear that she might not measure up to the standards the Sisters had for new candidates. *Monsieur l' Abbé's* letter to the Sisters had been very complimentary and the reply was welcoming; but, still, Louise was anxious and fearful. This was such a life-changing step for her. Would she measure up? Her face was wet with tears for most of the two days in the coach. If asked, she would have been hard put to tell the inquirer exactly what was causing those particular tears.

The man from the convent who came to pick her up seemed kind, but she was so tired that she really wasn't concentrating on his conversation. He said that his name was Jean-Pierre and that he had met various coaches at Sarrebourg almost daily for a month. Louise could tell by his remarks that she would not be alone as she began this first step into the unknown world of the convent. The ten-mile trip from Sarrebourg to St. Jean-de-Bassel took just under two hours but Jean-Pierre had picked up various supplies in Sarrebourg so the long trip had had more than one purpose. He spoke less and less as he drove along and was completely silent as he turned off the main road and entered the tree-lined lane that led to the front door of the convent.

Main Entrance St. Jean-de-Bassel Convent
(Courtesy: Congregation of Divine Providence, St. Jean-de-Bassel, France)

The view caused Louise to gasp. She never dreamed that the convent would be so enormous! The huge three-story gray-stone convent looked like a castle. The main building's double front door was flanked by large windows. The four windows on the second floor were shuttered against the cold as were the third-floor dormer windows on the roof. Another building, taller still, rose behind the main building. She could tell that there were uncountable nooks and crannies to the convent and wondered if she would ever learn where everything was. As the wagon went around to the back Louise saw that the buildings were clustered around a courtyard.

Several Sisters clothed in brown dresses, black capes and bonnets that fit tightly over some type of linen headcoverings came to greet her. Jean-Pierre stopped the wagon near the stables and jumped down. Then he helped her step from the high seat to the wagon wheel and then to the ground. Her black valise was handed to her and he said that her small trunk would be taken to the trunk storage room. Since she didn't know where that was, she merely nodded.

The Sister-greeters gave their names, but she was so tired that she knew she would forget. And, in their identical dresses and headcoverings, they all looked alike!* The Sisters who welcomed her were all talking at once, a couple in French and one in Alsatian. Looking from one to the other in confusion, Louise decided to respond to their questions in Alsatian. Someone who seemed about her age yet wore the full brown habit with white bonnet said, "My name is *Sœur* Marie Reine. As your guardian angel, I will be helping you find your way. Come with me now and I'll show you where you can put your valise and where you will sleep. Supper will be at six o'clock after we pray the Office of Divine Providence at five-thirty. You don't have to go to prayers today if you want to clean up after your trip. I'll go to prayers and then I'll come back to get you for supper." She spoke fast in a mixture of French and Alsatian. Louise was so tired; she realized that she wasn't quite sure what she had been told. If only I can wash my face and comb my hair, she thought, I know I'll feel better.

True to her word, *Sœur* Marie Reine took Louise into *la Maison Ste. Marie*, the largest building in the complex. Three stories high and longer than any barn Louise had ever seen, the building seemed to be very new. After climbing stairs to the third floor, they entered an enormous room where all the candidates and novices slept. Cots with white

---

* **Wanting his Sisters to work among the people of the village as teachers and spiritual companions, not as traditional nuns, Father Moye had not designed a habit for his Sisters at the beginning of "The Project" in the mid-1700's. While Father Moye was in China (1772-1784), Father Antoine Raulin, another priest-leader of the fledgling congregation, designed a simple habit believing that it was needed to protect the Sisters from the uncertain effects of the unrest that preceded the French Revolution. Even still, the earliest versions of the habit remained simple and very much like the dress of the women of the day. By the time Louise entered, however, the habit, consisting of a brown dress, a black cape and a headpiece which at that time consisted of a linen coif (or cap) which covered the hair, a piece of starched linen that covered the forehead, and a tight-fitting bonnet-like piece that covered the above. At some time between 1830 and 1865 a white *"guimpe"* or starched collar was added. The photo of Sister St. André shows her in this habit.**

Maison Ste. Marie at St. Jean-de-Bassel Convent.
(Courtesy: Congregation of Divine Providence, St. Jean-de-Bassel, France)

coverlets lined either side of a center aisle. A wooden chair and a small cabinet with a basin and pitcher stood next to each bed. There were no pillows. *Sœur* Marie Reine took her to a bed next to a cabinet where the basin was upside down.

"Here, no one has this bed yet. You can have it. The novices all sleep at the other end. You candidates sleep at this end. I think there are about eighteen of you now. You're the last one to arrive this week and I don't know if more are coming next week. Usually everyone in the group is here by now. I'll get you some water from the barrel in the hallway. You may want to wash your face and hands and put your clothes away in your cabinet. I must run to prayers but then I will be returning to get you for supper."

Before Louise could say a word, the young, energetic novice had gotten the water and was out the door. Louise could hear her footfall on the stairs. She had no idea where *Sœur* Marie Reine was going—and she really didn't know exactly where she was either. After brushing her skirt, which had collected some dirt during her journey, Louise bent over the porcelain basin to wash her face. Using the small clean towel hanging on a nearby peg, she wiped the two-day's dust from her forehead, cheeks, and neck. Without benefit of a mirror, Louise smoothed her hair as best she could and pinned up the locks that had escaped with the jostling of the coach. Everything seemed both unfamiliar and familiar at the same time. A strange paradox. In some way she felt like she had come home. The year was 1845.

After supper Louise had spoken briefly to two other girls, sisters, who had been at St. Jean-de-Bassel since last spring. They said they were going to become novices the next September. She liked these two, Marie Therese and Marie Catherine, very much. They were quick to help her hang up her uniform-like dresses and tell her of the schedules for classes. Happy but exhausted, Louise welcomed the silence which fell over the dormitory at eight o'clock as everyone began to prepare for bed. By nine o'clock everyone was sound asleep.

A clanging bell woke Louise from a sound sleep at five o'clock the next morning and the dormitory came to life. Someone intoned the first prayer of the day and some forty young voices responded with words that were not yet familiar to Louise. After the prayer was recited, water was poured into basins, mattresses were turned, and beds completely remade. No one spoke a word. Faces were washed, black dresses replaced white night gowns, black stocks were drawn up, and black shoes were buttoned. Hair was rolled into a knot at the base of the neck and pinned into place; and a simple veil for chapel covered the head and draped over the shoulders of each girl. Louise followed along, hoping that she was doing everything correctly. Dressing had been completed without a single glance into a mirror!

Then, precisely at five-twenty, the bell rang again and forty young girls and novices lined up by two's to process to St. Jean Baptiste Church, the village church across the yard, for morning prayers and Mass.

Morning prayers began with a recitation of the Litany of the Child Jesus for Students, a traditional prayer of the Congregation prescribed by the founder, Father Moye. The Office of the Virgin, sung choir to choir* in a high-pitched chant followed the Litany. Louise felt lost most of the time since she did not know the chant nor did she know when to bow or sit or stand. Holy Mass followed. This familiar Latin ritual was a welcome relief after the previous unfamiliar prayers.

After Holy Mass a Sister read the subject for that day's meditation and silence descended over the small church for the next half hour. Louise, noticing that each candidate and novice sat ramrod straight, their backs not touching the pews, copied that posture. The few older Sisters who were seated on the other side of the room appeared more relaxed; some even nodded, their chins dropping onto their *guimpes*. At the end of the mediation period, the ringing of a bell brought all those present to their knees for an examination of conscience and homage to the Blessed Sacrament. A Prayer to St. Anne said in unison concluded the service. A second ringing of the bell announced the permission to leave; and each Sister, novice, and candidate stood, genuflected at her place, and moved in silent procession to other destinations.

The Sisters had been in prayer for not less than an hour and a half before the day even began. Louise was in awe! She would learn as the day went on that prayers of some type peppered the day causing all to focus constantly on the presence of God in their midst.

Following her companions in procession as they left the church, Louise found herself back in the large dining room for breakfast. Only bareheaded girls like herself and a very few Sisters in bonnets sat at the long tables, heads bowed. Since the novices were not in the dining room, she hoped that someone would find her after the meal was over to tell her where to go next. To this point no one had spoken except in prayer.

Shifting her eyes to the left and right, Louise tried to take in the room. Countless baguettes filled baskets placed along the long tables, and large pitchers with steaming coffee waiting to be poured

---

* **The right and left sides of the assembly alternating verses of Psalms or prayers**

lined a nearby cupboard. After the blessing, the bread was passed and Louise was glad she had time to watch before the basket came to her. Each girl broke off a large piece of bread from a baguette and put it into her bowl. Next came the coffee, which each person poured onto her bread. Finally came hot milk, which was poured into the coffee and bread mixture. Sugar bowls were then handed from one girl to another. A spoon was used to consume the sopping bread-coffee-milk-sugar pudding-like mixture. Louise had not had this breakfast menu before, but she presumed she could become accustomed to it. The clatter of spoons clinking against china bowls filled the otherwise silent room.

After breakfast, everyone proceeded to take care of personal needs and Louise began to shiver as she stood in line for the privy. It wasn't even eight o'clock in the morning and so much had already been accomplished. As she followed her companions back into *la Maison Ste. Marie*, everyone seemed to know what to do next except Louise. A tall, thin Sister approached her and said without emotion, "Come with me." Louise followed obediently in silence. Without a word or a smile, the tall Sister, took Louise to a closet filled with brooms, mops, and rags. Opening a can stuffed with rags, the Sister handed Louise a large oily one. "Your job after breakfast for the next few days will be to dust the wainscoting in this hallway. Go down the hallway that way, staying to the left and return along the opposite wall. That way you will always be facing the Sisters as they walk the hallway. We are accustomed to walking to the right with our eyes cast down. If you dust in this manner, you will not be an obstacle. Do you understand?" She said all of this crisply and simply, not expecting to repeat herself.

"*Oui, ma sœur*. Yes, Sister," Louise said timidly. She took the rag and began her task. Just as she came to the end of her job, her guardian angel, *Sœur* Marie Reine, came to her and said, "Here you are! I've been out in the barn. The novices take care of milking and barn chores while everyone else is at breakfast; we eat afterwards. Within a few days you will begin to work outside with the other candidates, working the gardens, mucking out the barns, or other such chores. For these first days, you will have this inside job until you get used to the house. Now come with me and I will take you to your classroom. You will have two weeks of school before you go to your mission assignment."

Louise was struck by how happy this novice seemed. She all but glowed with enthusiasm for what she had been doing. The attitude was catching and Louise followed with a lively step. Again they were in silence. Louise hoped that she might have an opportunity to ask *Sœur* Marie Reine some questions but obviously there would not be time now. Though she had been at St. Jean-de-Bassel for fewer than twenty-four hours, it was apparent to Louise that most of the day in the convent was lived in silence. As they climbed the stairs to the second floor of *la Maison Ste. Marie*, other young girls began to appear, walking two by two down the corridor, always to the right— toward a very large classroom.

"Just do what they do today," *Sœur* Marie Reine said. "I'm not sure I'll see you again until we go to Vespers, but you will sit with me in church until you learn how to chant the Office of the Blessed Virgin. Don't worry about it, though. You will have plenty of time to learn on the mission. God bless you. Praised be Divine Providence. When someone says that to you, you answer, 'Now and forever. Amen.' and nod your head ever-so-slightly."

Louise repeated, nodding: "Now and forever. Amen."

Lowering her voice to a whisper, the novice, to Louise's relief, said, "We'll have more time to talk tonight at recreation after supper." As she left, *Sœur* Marie Reine said, "Praised be Divine Providence."

Louise responded, with a nod of her head, "Now and forever. Amen." Then she joined her class of candidates in their classroom.

"Girls," began *Sœur* Adelaïde, "please answer 'Here' in either French or German when you hear your name." Names were called and when Louise heard "*Mademoiselle* Louise Feltin," she quickly responded, "*Présente*." After the roll call, *Sœur* Adelaïde said, "*Je suis Sœur Adelaïde*. I am Sister Adelaïde. I prefer that you respond to me in French. I want to caution you girls against loud conversation, too much talking, and explosive laughter. Just because you are young does not give you leave to run and jump about, bumping into each other, and elbowing each other. These boisterous behaviors are contrary to religious decorum." *Sœur* Adelaïde paused to take a breath and Louise was certain that the pall that had fallen over the room indicated that most of the nearly fifty girls dressed in simple black two-piece uniforms had heard this speech before, and that it had gone unheeded more than once.

Sœur Adelaïde continued. "Those of you who are new to our convent have been introduced to our morning schedule: The Office of the Virgin, Holy Mass, meditation time, breakfast, small chores, and then our class. You have seen that we remain in silence in order to give our Blessed Lord an opportunity to speak with us and so as to not distract one another from God's voice. Listening to God is the first step toward realizing your vocation, whatever it is. Not all of you are truly called to religious life. Either while you are here or when you go to your assigned school, you may come to understand that God is directing you elsewhere and you will return to your home. Or, if you are uncertain, I will help you to understand God's holy will for you. Today we will continue where we left off yesterday. Those who have not had an opportunity to read aloud in French and German will do so. Please begin, *Mademoiselle* Huver. Take the Holy Bible from the shelf and turn to Psalm 121 and begin reading. This morning we will read aloud in German. Tomorrow morning we will read aloud in French. If you cannot read, please stand now."

A few girls stood up.

"Draw your chairs up next to another girl and read with her as her turn comes. If you cannot read, you will begin reading lessons in Salon A at one o'clock. Should you be unable to read the Psalms within one month, you will return to your home. Do you understand?" With that she paused and glanced directly at each girl standing.

In one voice, the girls standing replied, "*Oui, ma sœur.* Yes, Sister."

Mademoiselle Huver took the Bible carefully from the shelf, fumbled until she found Psalm 121 and began reading aloud in halting German.

Sœur Adelaïde interrupted her before she finished the Psalm. "*Mademoiselle*, you will need to take the German class in Salon B that begins at one o'clock."

"*Oui, ma sœur*," Mademoiselle Huver said shyly.

The lesson proceeded until each candidate was assessed. Louise had been able to read satisfactorily in German, so she was told to go to Salon C at one o'clock for a beginning lesson in basic arithmetic. *Sœur* Adelaïde marked the end of the class session by saying, "Praised be Jesus Christ." Eighteen young voices responded in unison, "Now and forever. Amen." This time, Louise knew what to say.

After two days, Louise understood that on Tuesdays, Thursdays, and Saturdays lessons were in German while Mondays, Wednesdays, and Fridays lessons were in French. The obvious goal was to prepare the girls to be teachers' aides in the school to which they would be assigned. True success depended on competency in both French and German. Relieved that she was well-prepared in both German and French, Louise often said a prayer of gratitude for the Sisters at Geispolsheim and her teachers in LaWalck. Since her father had expected her to be able to cipher in order to help in the store, she was able to proceed satisfactorily in those classes as well.

Actually, the daily class at ten o'clock was Louise's favorite. *Sœur* Irène who taught the novices came to the candidates' classroom to teach them about *Père* Moye and the beginnings of "The Project." She spoke with such devotion for the Holy Founder, recalling his commitment to provide schools for girls who lived in the small hamlets throughout Lorraine and Alsace. *Sœur* Irène's lessons were so vivid that Louise could easily imagine *le Père* Moye walking from village to village, giving retreats and calling young women to join in his Project. She decided that he must have been very charismatic and that people no doubt listened to him with rapt attention.

Sœur Irène was especially animated as she told stories of *le Père* Moye's ten-year adventure in China as a missionary. She read to the girls directly from copies of his letters to the Sisters, making the tales of China even more interesting.

After an introductory week of evaluation, the girls were eventually given assignments. Louise Feltin was sent to Krautergersheim, "house of cabbage growers," a village in the heart of Alsace, south of Saverne. The journey would take nearly three days. Several girls were going in the same area and a professed Sister from Epfig had come to accompany them. Once at Krautergersheim, the candidate would be put to work assisting in the classroom, cleaning the house, and caring for their chickens and gardens. After several years of hard work, a determination would be made as to the candidate's suitability for religious life.

The few weeks before Christmas in 1845 flew by and Louise Feltin found that she had a strange mix of emotions. Part of her missed her mother and father so much that she usually felt like crying. Part of her loved the life of a teacher in a small hamlet. Each day had its own problems and promises.

One day, just before Christmas, the Superior took Louise aside.

"My dear," she began, "I will be going to Haguenau just after Christmas Day. If you wish to travel with me to LaWalck, I believe it will work out." The Superior had seldom said more than two words at a time to the young candidate and so the invitation took Louise by surprise.

"I hardly know what to say, Sister. Do you think it will be all right?"

"A visit to your family will be a good test of your vocation. If you come back with me after you have seen your parents and brothers and sisters, then perhaps God will have some use for you."

"Yes, Sister," Louise said, "I would like to go with you." She had not been too sure about the Superior's meaning of the home visit being a "test of her vocation," but when the day came for Louise to meet the Superior at Brouxwiller to return to Krautergersheim, the words came back to haunt her. The second leave-taking was so much harder than the first. Her mother's tears simply would not stop as Louise and her father climbed into their wagon. The biting wind and gloomy day only served to underscore the sadness felt by the whole family.

Marie-Anne whispered to her sister just before Louise climbed up onto the seat beside her father: "Please come back again soon. I am so lonely without you!"

Those words struck at Louise's heart. She would never forget that the cost of her vocation was borne by so many others.

The seasons of early 1846 passed quickly and soon it was time for the Sisters in Krautergersheim to close their school and travel back to the Motherhouse at St. Jean-de-Bassel. This was the time that girls were often dismissed because their work or temperaments had revealed that they were unsuited to religious life. Each day of May Louise started whenever the Superior spoke to her, expecting the conversation to be the one that would send her home.

Eventually, the Superior asked her to take a walk with her. As they walked through the cobbled streets of the small village and out into the cabbage patches which gave the village its name, the Superior said, "Are you happy, Louise?"

"Why, yes, Sister. Very happy."

"Good. Then when we get to St. Jean, I will report that I would like for you to return here next year."

The rest of the walk was in silence, revealing nothing more of the Superior's thoughts about her young subject. Louise was ecstatic!

Three more years like her first passed swiftly. Several more visits to her home village of LaWalck continued to offer Louise one heart-wrenching good-bye after another, and by the time the fall of 1849 came, the young woman knew that she would never become accustomed to saying good-bye to those whom she loved.

The younger children were in school and since she was not returning to Krautergersheim, Louise had remained in LaWalck until her father was able to escort her to St. Jean. Taking coffee together in the mornings at the family table gave the mother and daughter time for a personal exchange.

"*Ma fille*, are you certain that this is the way of life that God wants for you? There are young men in the village …," and then Marie-Louise Feltin laughed. "How silly of me. You are so well suited to the life of a Sister-teacher. Besides, I dare say there's not a single young man in this village who could handle you!" Her comment revealed how well she knew her strong-willed daughter.

"Oh, *Maman*," Louise blushed. "You know me too well. I know I probably wouldn't make a very good wife or mother. But do you think I'll make a good nun?"

"The Sisters of Providence are fortunate to receive you, daughter. You will do very well in that type of community. But I would not say the same thing if you were leaving us to become an Ursuline!" At that both women laughed. Louise Feltin could never survive the cloister and both of them knew it!

"I wish you well, *ma fille*! And you know that your father and I will pray a rosary for you each and every day."

"Thank you, *Maman*. I love you. I will pray for you as well."

Early in November, *Monsieur* Feltin escorted his daughter once again through the forest to Sarrebourg and left her in the able hands of Jean-Pierre who again met the stagecoach.

On November 8, 1849, Louise Feltin shed her traveling dress and donned the black Postulant's uniform of the Sisters of Providence of St. Jean-de-Bassel. Tried and proven by four years of hard work in Krautergersheim, Louise easily settled into life at the Motherhouse. Each week was filled with lessons and chores, and chores and lessons. Prayer and silence permeated everything. When the Sisters and postulants met one another in the hallway, they merely nodded and said, "Praised be Divine Providence" or "Praised be Jesus Christ." The other would answer in a similar whisper, "Now and forever. Amen." Every afternoon at 3:00 the entire house became still as each Sister knelt for fifteen minutes to pray the rosary with arms outstretched in remembrance of the agonies of Jesus on the cross.

An hour each evening was set aside for recreation. During the winter months, the young hands of novices and postulants, grown rough from hard work on the farm, in the kitchen, and in the laundry, took up fancy work: tatting, embroidery, and knitting. Oftentimes, young voices grew louder than the Mistresses preferred and occasional bursts of laughter filled the large room.

In the warmer summer months, recreation might include looking for the special mushrooms that grew in their forest, or picking berries in the twilight hours.

Occasionally, a missionary priest returning from a far-away land would speak to the whole community, regaling the soon-to-be religious with enticing tales of natives who had never even heard of Jesus.

During their training, the novices and postulants got to know each other as friends. Those who remained to profess their vows would later serve with one another in lonely villages, making these relationships important to their perseverance in the life to which God had called them. As they matured in religious life, missioned in rustic villages with primitive schools, sometimes living in ramshackle, ill-repaired dwellings with inadequate food and heat, they would look back at these formative days of intense prayer, study and backbreaking physical work as a more-than-adequate foundation for the hard life that had lain ahead.

On occasion, all the Sisters, novices, and postulants would gather together in the largest dining room for a party to celebrate a feast of the Church or a feast of the Congregation. Louise first experienced how much the Congregation loved a community party on December 6, St. Nicolas Day, just a month after her entrance into the postulancy. In accordance with the customs of both France and Germany, the feast of this beloved saint brings a pre-Christmas treat for children who have been good or the threat of switches and lumps of coal for children who are behaving badly. After placing an empty shoe next to his or her bed, each child dreams hopefully of treats from St. Nicolas and his companion *Pierre Noir*, Black Peter, who are said to go from household to household filling shoes with oranges and candies for the good children—or the dreaded switch or lump of coal for those who had misbehaved.

The Feltin household loved this feast, and *Père* Noël was always generous to the Feltin children. Thinking that she had left this childhood custom behind upon entering St. Jean-de-Bassel, Louise was completely surprised when one of the novices came to the postulants on December 4 to tell them to prepare their shoes for St. Nicolas' visit the next night.

High spirits spilled over into whisperings about hoped-for goodies as the postulants prepared for bed the next night. By the time the lamp was extinguished and all were in bed, a readied shoe, freshly polished, stood at the end of each cot, just waiting for St. Nicolas to fill it with a surprise.

On the morning of December 6, the usual silence gave way to squeals of smothered laughter as each girl found her shoe filled with an orange, a new writing pen, and a small packet of sweets. It would be only after they were professed that the young Sisters would learn that it was the Reverend Mother herself who went from bed to bed filling the shoes. *Mère* Basilisse had begun the custom, insisting from the beginning that no one know the true identity of "St. Nicolas." Her years as *econome** had taught her how uplifting a small surprise could be to the spirits of young girls who were accepting unfamiliar deprivations as they offered their lives to God completely.

Mère Basilisse delighted in the celebration of St. Nicolas Day, never skimping on those festivities, even when funds were short. Continuing the celebration at the noonday meal, the community

---

*   **In the St. Jean-de-Bassel leadership structure, the *econome*, or treasurer was the assistant to the priest who had been named ecclesiastical superior by the bishop. The 1852 legal independence of St. Jean-de-Bassel changed the structure and a Sister Superior was elected from then on. A priest remained the ecclesiastical superior; *the econome* became the general treasurer.**

feasted on venison from their forest, small roasted potatoes, and rich gravy. Later that night after supper, a special recreation for the whole house was held in the largest classroom. Transformed into a multi-colored wonderland by the creativity of the novices who had hung streamers and ribbons of all types from the ceiling, the usually drab classroom had become a magical setting for the party. Chairs and desks were pushed to the sides and the Sisters who played instruments came forward with all present joining in the traditional folk dances of Alsace and Lorraine. Cookies and little cakes of all types filled platters on long tables at the back of the room and each one could enjoy as much as she wished. Laughter spilled out of the room, filling the entire building as young and old alike enjoyed the dancing and the sweets.

Sitting in her chair near the door and having as much fun as the youngest postulant, *Mère* Basilisse allowed the party to continue until nine o'clock. Just at nine, she stood and nodded ever so imperceptively to her assistant, *Sœur* Constantine, who rang a tiny bell signaling the end of the celebration. The music stopped and fifty pairs of feet came to a standstill in the middle of a *schottische* dance. The assistant intoned: "*Salve, Regina, mater misericordiae, vita dulcedo, et spes nostra, salve* ... Hail, Mother and Queen of tender mercy, our life, our comfort, and our hope, hail ..." in the ancient notes of Gregorian chant, and all voices joined in. St. Nicolas Day was over.

The weeks of candidacy sped by as winter snows gave way to spring rains. Louise wrote weekly to her mother and father, and her mother wrote back just as faithfully with page after page of news of her brothers and sisters. Marie-Anne was now giving more time in the store and helping *Maman* with baby Christine. Though it seemed paradoxical since she was surrounded by dozens of "Sisters", Louise knew that it was Marie-Anne that she missed the most. They had been close ever since the death of little Rosalie so many years ago, and Louise hoped that Marie-Anne would find the path that God wanted her to follow in life just as she had.

On the Feast of the Annunciation in March* of 1850, Louise Feltin and nearly thirty of her companions received the short cape, which was worn over the black blouse of the postulant's uniform. Receiving this simple piece of the holy habit marked the postulant's formal entrance into the first of three distinct phases for preparation for religious life. For Louise, the postulancy stage would last until September of 1851, when, God willing, the young religious-to-be would receive the rest of the holy habit and begin the year-long novitiate phase for more intensive religious training and study.

The two years of postulancy, filled with lessons, farm work, housekeeping, kitchen and laundry chores, and especially prayer, moved slowly and it seemed to Louise that the day she would enter the novitiate would never arrive. She knew that she was being scrutinized constantly and, as other girls were sent home or left of their own accord, she hoped that she would not be found wanting.

Summer brought enormous adjustments at St. Jean-de-Bassel as nearly two hundred and fifty Sisters from the missions came home for study and spiritual renewal. The summer homecoming of 1850, Louise's first summer at St. Jean-de-Bassel, had been both overwhelming and exhilarating for her. The mission Sisters, each one exhausted from her year of service, had come home to be both physically and spiritually rejuvenated. Dormitories were filled to capacity, and those who could not be accommodated in the village Church for Holy Mass gathered in the community room where they prayed in silence until someone came to get them for Holy Communion.

Postulants and novices took on the extra duties of serving the professed Sisters in the dining rooms where several seatings were required to accommodate everyone. Fresh produce from the convent gardens provided abundant meals for Sisters who had, for the most part, been completely dependent on the good will of the parents of their students for their food during the academic year.

---

* **March 25**

Summer recreation centered on renewal of friendships and celebrations for the entire community. Daily at four o'clock, with *Mère* Basilisse presiding, a special spiritual reading offered a review of *Père* Moye's writings along with the works of other spiritual writers of the day. The Sisters spent their time in renewing friendships, study, prayer, repair of their habits, and rest.

The summer homecoming came to a close with an eight-day retreat, which concluded on the Feast of St. Anne, July 26. In the days following the retreat the Sisters received their mission assignments for the coming year. It was a time of great excitement and great anxiety with many a tear shed when a change of mission was unexpected or unwanted.

When assignments were completed, the Sisters from the missions were given time for visits with their families or further rest. By the middle of August, St. Jean-de-Bassel resumed its normal *horarium.*^{V} The postulants prepared for entrance into the novitiate; the candidates who would be received into the novitiate the next year studied; the novices prepared for profession of obedience and poverty. With only a few professed Sisters remaining at the Motherhouse, the last days of summer and the early autumn required all in residence at St. Jean to take on extra duties until new candidates began to arrive after the fall harvest.

By the spring of 1851, Louise began to carefully observe the novices who would make their consecration of promises at the end of their canonical year in September. She watched how they walked, how they prayed, how they looked in their habits. It was clear to her that their prayer lives were deepening and Louise longed for the same depth in her growing relationship with God.

Louise and her twenty-eight companions who would enter the novitiate in September of 1851 began to imagine what religious names they would receive, hoping that their new names would be both pronounceable and somewhat familiar.

---

^{V} **daily schedule**

September 20, 1851, the day chosen by the Superior for the ceremony of entrance into the novitiate dawned bright and clear—a perfect last-day of summer, a perfect first-day in the novitiate with a new name and a new identity on the road to being a religious.

The community gathered in St. Jean Baptiste Church for a ceremony, now familiar to the hundreds of women who had chosen this life in order to be of service to the uneducated poor. The ceremony had always been, on the advice of *Père* Moye, a simple one. Twenty-eight postulants processed into the church, taking their places on the front rows. *L' abbé* Larvette, the ecclesiastical superior of the Congregation, began the prayer service in his deep resonant voice: *In nomine Patris, et Filiis, et Spirituis Sancti.* Amen. Louise felt the knot in her stomach tighten as she realized anew the importance of this step.

After a sermon, each postulant, called by her baptismal name, entered the sanctuary and lay prostrate before *l' abbé* Larvette. Sister-assistants, one for each novice-to-be, entered with the brown dresses which were folded into perfect squares, and stood in front of each prostrate girl. The priest went from Sister-assistant to Sister-assistant blessing each garment with holy water. After prayers were said for the future novices, each one stood and accepted her habit from *l' abbé* Larvette's hands. Cradling the sacred habit in her hands, Louise walked down the long aisle with her companions, realizing that, with the acceptance of this garment, she was bidding goodbye to a secular identity that would forever belong to her past. Led by the Sister-assistants, the young women processed across the courtyard and into *Maison Ste. Marie.* In their third-floor dormitory the assistants cut their hair and dressed them in the new and unfamiliar garb. The heavier brown dress with long, full sleeves replaced the simple postulant's uniform; a snugly fitting white linen *coif** was pulled over the new novice's shorter hair and neck. Another piece of heavily starched linen, the white *bandeau,** covered the forehead

---

* **These parts of the headpiece of the Sisters of Divine Providence, with modifications, were used throughout the next 125 years.**

and was then tied at the back of the head. The cape was then draped over the new novice's shoulders, covering the top of the dress from neck to waist, and a white starched collar or *guimpe** encircled the neck. Finally, the white bonnet with long sides, reminiscent of the bonnets of country workingwomen, was pulled tightly over the *coif* and *bandeau.*

Sœur St. André
(Courtesy of the Congregation of Divine Providence, St. Jean-de-Bassel, France)

The Sister-assistants, after long years of dressing themselves in the dark dormitory morning after morning, moved quickly through their chore, and it seemed to Louise that it was no time at all before they were all ready to return to the church. She was not alone in wondering whether or not she could repeat this process the next morning in time for prayer! Two-by two the newly dressed novices returned to the village church where each one knelt before *l' abbé* Larvette to receive her name in religion.

"Madeleine Bertin, in religion you will be known as *Sœur* Romuald. Marie Catherine Clementz, in religion you will be known as *Sœur* Remi."

Each new novice responded with *"Deo gratias,"* "Thanks be to God," no matter how unfamiliar or strange her new name seemed.

Though a very few Sisters continue to wear a modified headpiece, in keeping with Father Moye's original plan that the Sisters should dress simply and in the general style of women of the time, the vast majority of Sisters of Divine Providence (St. Jean-de-Bassel, Texas, Ribeauvillé, Gap, Portieux) throughout the world discontinued wearing a headpiece in the years following the Second Vatican Council.

As her turn to be renamed approached, Louise, feeling clumsy in the complicated habit, moved ever so slowly closer to *l'abbé* Larvette. Finally, she knelt and listened.

"Louise Feltin, in religion you will be known as *Sœur* St. André."

With relief that she had received a familiar and pronounceable name, Louise bowed her veiled head and replied in a steady, and truly grateful, voice, *"Deo gratias."*

Louise thought: I will never be called Louise Feltin again. She now had a new name, a strong name that would meld with her strong Alsatian personality until she wore it as one would a comfortable dress. The habit she had received would cover her body for the rest of her life, and in time would also become so internalized that it would become more than clothing. It would be a signal to all of her consecration to Jesus and her religious promises.

She didn't know on that September day in 1851 that there would be a time nearly fifty years later when her religious habit was so at one with her personal identity that even when she no longer wore it, people who met her would recognize instantly that Louise Feltin was much more than the small little lady with the French accent who ran the corner store.

Novitiate days were more challenging than the postulancy. Meeting lofty spiritual goals demanded more introspection, more self-discipline, more deprivation, harder physical work, and more intense study and prayer. The twenty-eight novices had only one year to learn the entire Holy Rule by heart, to become absolutely certain of the curriculum required by the State in the schools, to pass the examination for teachers, and to become confident enough to take on whatever tasks might lie ahead in the rustic hamlets that needed the Sisters for their schools.

Each day included hard work on the convent farm. The wheat harvest took up the rest of September and the early days of October. Gardens had to be hoed and the apple crop would need picking in late October. Until more candidates arrived, pre-dawn chores of mucking out the barn and milking the cows also fell on the shoulders of the new novices. In addition, for the few months between September and November, nearly all of the housework and kitchen chores were done by the new novices and the remaining postulants. It would be these few months of hard work and study that would prove the mettle of the young women who so wanted to be Sisters.

The Mistress of Novices was *Sœur* Irène, a wise woman who had held this esteemed position for a number of years. Her sole ministry was to scrutinize and train the novices, and she had taken as a personal mandate the words of *Père* Moye: ***"In our society we want only persons who are good and who are able to bring and to maintain peace, union, and concord."****

Though her anticipation was mixed with anxiety, *Sœur* St. André actually had looked forward to her days in the novitiate with *Sœur* Irène despite *Sœur* Irène's reputation in the Congregation as a strict Mistress. During the postulate, the Mistress's vivid stories of *Père* Moye's life had immediately captured *Sœur* St. André's imagination, making her hungry for more about the Founder's life and teachings.

In the novitiate, a daily lesson on the four fundamental virtues of simplicity, poverty, abandonment to Divine Providence, and charity, grounded the young novices in an understanding of the virtues that *Père* Moye had insisted would guide their lives as Sisters of Divine Providence. Their acceptance of any and all deprivations would, *Sœur* Irène taught, serve to immerse them into the poverty of our Lord Himself who was born in a stable in order to show God's special love for those who lived impoverished of this world's goods. Living the virtue of poverty at St. Jean-de-Bassel prepared the novices for crude housing; inconsistent, and sometimes insufficient, food for their meals; and primitive schoolrooms with few of the items needed to conduct lessons.

Sœur Irène especially emphasized the virtue of simplicity because to her this virtue was key to the particular life that Sisters of Divine Providence led. Since they would always live among the villagers

---

* **The Directory, p. 270.**

and often alone, their personal character would have to be beyond reproach. *Sœur* Irène constantly reminded her novices, "Sisters, our dear Lord said, 'Say yes when you mean yes, and no when you mean no.' Forthrightness is one of the key aspects of our virtue of simplicity which assists us to be straightforward with others and honest at all times with them and especially with ourselves. This honesty will serve you well. You will never have to try to remember what you have said to whom in the small villages where you will serve. You come from these types of villages and you know how mired down the people can become in falsely representing themselves to one another and in gossiping about one another. You must refrain from this at every turn. In addition, this very virtue of simplicity will guard you against entanglements with the village priests. You must never forget that the priests are only men underneath their cassocks. Your simplicity will strengthen you to act only forthrightly with them, never acquiescing to any duplicitous advances, thus protecting your vocation. Pray for this virtue, my dear Sisters."

The young novice *Sœur* St. André took this lesson to heart. She prayed for this virtue of simplicity each and every day for the rest of her life. Her straightforward speech and behavior would forge in her a trustworthiness, especially during those years that she worked alone in Heiligenberg and Batzendorf. Likely, this same straight-arrow demeanor would encourage a bishop from Texas some years into the future to risk inviting her to come to Texas to begin schools in small towns there.

"*Sœur* St. André," *Sœur* Irène interrupted the young novice as she pored over the Holy Rule, trying to commit the entire work to memory.

"Yes, Mistress?"

"You have a visitor in the parlor. You may take thirty minutes to see your brother."

Nicolas was now in the last months of his preparation for the priesthood in the Diocese of Strasbourg. Her mother's recent letters had given *Sœur* St. André indication that he had been in touch with

Rev. Nicolas Feltin, circa 1855
(Courtesy, Catholic Archives of
Texas, Austin, TX)

the Bishop of Texas, Jean-Marie Odin, who constantly recruited in French seminaries for his vast diocese, which had so many critical needs. Madame Feltin's letters had sounded both proud and sorrowful at the prospect of her son embracing the tenuous life of a missionary in a foreign land. If Nicolas were coming to see her, a decision must have been made.

"Nicolas, how are you?" *Sœur* St. André said as she kissed her brother on both cheeks. He looked so handsome in his cassock and collar, though his long curly hair had its usual wild look, betraying his mere twenty-two years and giving him a boyish appearance. Nicolas had not yet seen *Sœur* St. André in her habit.

"Oh, my!" he stammered. "You look like a real nun!"

"I'm trying to become a 'real nun', " his younger sister retorted. "Why are you here? I only have about thirty minutes to visit."

"Then I'll get right to my point. I'm going to America! To the Diocese of New Orleans—to serve in a place called Texas."

"No! When will you leave?"

"About eighteen other seminarians and myself will sail with Bishop Odin, the Bishop of Texas, from LeHavre on March 18. I have no idea when or if I will return to France. After a short period to study English with the Vincentian priests in a place called Missouri, I will be ordained a priest for Texas." Nicolas was breathless with the excitement of his missionary future. In many ways his plans to leave France were not surprising to his sister. He had always spoken with admiration of the many French missionaries who had taken the faith to China or Japan.

John Odin, First Bishop of Texas
(Courtesy, Catholic Archives of Texas, Austin, Texas)

"Oh, Nicolas! Have you spoken with *Maman*? Is she all right with your decision?" *Sœur* St. André did not want to dampen her brother's enthusiasm, but her heart went out to their dear mother who was being asked to give up so much.

"You know dear *Maman*. When I spoke with her and Papa, after I had pretty much made up my mind and spoken with our Bishop here, she had only one thing to say: I surrender to the will of Divine Providence."

"That is not a surprise. *Maman* is so good. She is very generous with *Le Bon Dieu*." *Sœur* St. André would not say so to Nicolas, but she suspected that her mother's heart felt pierced through when Nicolas had told their parents of his plans.

The next twenty minutes flew by as Nicolas tried to impress his sister with what he knew about Texas. Some of his comments seemed so outrageous that she hardly knew if she should believe him. Both young religious were exuberant about their futures; and, as *Sœur* St. André hugged her brother at the door, their parting words contained no sadness.

Each month *Sœur* Irène met the novices individually with the intent of speaking frankly to them about her observations of their character and progress in the religious life. Just under six months into the novitiate year, *Sœur* Irène called *Sœur* St. André to her office.

"Sit down, *ma sœur*." As she had been taught, *Sœur* St. André sat on the edge of the chair with her back board-straight. *Sœur* Irène continued immediately. "Are you feeling well, *ma sœur?*"

"Yes, Mistress. I feel very well."

"Good. I have come to the decision that I must bring something to your attention." *Sœur* St. André's mouth went dry and her breathing became shallow. Had she not been in the presence of her novice mistress, she would have pulled at the collar of her *guimpe* as she felt as though she were choking. Was *Sœur* Irène going to tell her that she did not have a vocation; that she must return to LaWalck? Two other novices had left the convent just before Christmas. Would she be next? As the Mistress began to talk, her heart pounded so hard that she was certain *Sœur* Irène could hear it. The pounding was so distracting that she missed the first few words of *Sœur* Irène's message.

"… and you must try to shift your behavior and live more fully our virtue of charity. You often appear haughty and aloof with your novice companions. Do you not see the look of disdain in their eyes when you always approach them from a position of strength? That fault will not bode you well as you get older. I suspect that you will not understand this admonition. When you constantly relate to others from a posture of superiority, even if you are correct, they respond with hostility, no matter how subtle. In fact, you might not even realize that they have been offended. But, they will not forget your overbearing way and will eventually find a way to retaliate. If you don't change this, you will have a great deal of trouble both in the classroom and with your superiors."

Sœur St. André was taken aback. She had no idea that this comportment belonged to her and she was confused. Wasn't it preferable, according to the virtue of simplicity, to always be straightforward and, if necessary, even blunt? She timidly asked this question.

"Actually, *non, ma chére*. By no accident our Holy Founder placed the virtues of simplicity and charity as 'the bookends' when he noted these virtues in his writings. One balances the other. Oftentimes, charity requires that we step back from an encounter and say nothing. At other times, simplicity demands that we speak firmly and without fear of the feelings of another. It is important to constantly pray for the wisdom to know what each situation requires. Think of the two virtues as on a scale. They must balance, neither of them 'lording it over' the other. Simplicity tempered with kindness; charity tempered with forthrightness. This is our goal in order that we might be holy as God is holy. You see, don't you, that our Founder was extremely wise. He placed poverty and abandonment to Divine Providence between the 'bookends' of simplicity and charity in order that those virtues might be the very center of our lives. Without abandonment to God's Providence we could never authentically live our poverty and without true poverty, abandonment to Divine Providence is empty."

The wise Mistress paused for a moment to allow her words to take hold.

"Now, think over what I have said. Simplicity and charity must be held in a certain tension for holiness to blossom. Pray over this. I am certainly not sure at this time what our *Bon Dieu* has in mind for you. But, whatever it is, our virtues will need to be firmly in place or you will founder. Go now, my child. Pray about all this."

With these last words, *Sœur* St. André knew that she was being dismissed. Since a few minutes remained before she had to be at her next chore, she went straight to the novice's chapel room and began to pray for the "balance" that *Sœur* Irène had described. In the springtime of her religious life the young novice had no way of knowing that the imbalance described by her wise novice mistress would result in future spiritual winters and disastrous consequences. She would commit to memory *Père* Moye's directive: ***"The Sisters of Providence will often ask God for the four fundamental virtues of their institute: simplicity, poverty, abandonment to Providence, and charity. They will continually practice these virtues."****

---

*   **The Directory**, p. 311

And she would never compromise the order in which *Père* Moye had listed the four fundamental virtues: **simplicity, poverty, abandonment to Divine Providence, charity.** That order now had meaning.

CHAPTER V

EARLY MISSIONS

In 1850, the Sisters at St. Jean-de-Bassel had welcomed *Père* Christophe Larvette as ecclesiastical superior, replacing *Père* Grusy who had been transferred to a small parish. *Père* Larvette, being somewhat unfamiliar with the writings of the Founder, *Père* Moye, waited until he was more steeped in the Founder's writings before presenting the annual retreat. However, feeling ready in July of 1852, he took his first opportunity to speak to the entire Congregation on the works of their Founder. By then *Père* Larvette had immersed himself into the writings of *Père* Moye. His retreat lectures were filled with the Founder's insight into the spiritual life.

Though she had heard *Père* Larvette speak on spiritual matters many times during her novitiate year, *Sœur* St. André nevertheless listened intently to each lecture, realizing that the nourishment received would have to carry her through her first year on the mission. Having no idea where they might be sent, *Sœur* St. André and her twenty-three companions were trying to wait patiently for their assignments, but the eight days of the retreat seemed to crawl by.

Once the retreat was over the process of assignments would begin. The large black slate board outside *Mère* Basilisse's office would be filled with the names of Sisters and their specific appointment times—nine o'clock, nine-fifteen, nine-thirty, nine-forty-five, ten o'clock, ten-fifteen and so on throughout the days following the retreat until *Mère* Basilisse had personally spoken with each Sister. Though ten-thirty would be skipped and two-hours would be allowed for lunch, the schedule was grueling for the Superior. Believing that she herself was responsible for the welfare of each Sister receiving a new assignment or re-committing to last year's mission, *Mère* Basilisse hoped that her motherly interest would encourage the Sisters who might find a particular assignment distasteful or fearsome.

The names of Sisters with appointments for a given day were posted at four-thirty the day before and word spread like wildfire to those being summoned, informing each one of her time to see the Superior to receive her assignment. It would take a full two weeks for the Superior to meet with two hundred and fifty Sisters. The novices would be scheduled for the last days. Everything would be finished in time for the annual community celebration of the Feast of St. Anne on July 26 which included a special high Mass* and festive dinner to close the summer homecoming.

Sœur St. André was thinking about these upcoming days during *Père* Larvette's last conference. His deep, resonant voice squeezed into her thoughts.

"Your Holy Founder wanted only one thing for his daughters: your own holiness. His letters from China are filled with this call. In 1776 he wrote: *'Refer everything to God. Desire above all the greater glory of God, even infinitely more than your eternal happiness which you must refer, like everything else to the greater glory of God. For this is the doctrine of theologians who hold with St. Thomas that when the precept of charity obliges, we must suffer everything, sacrifice everything, direct everything—even our eternal happiness—to the glory and the love of God. All the virtues are beautiful, holy, and praiseworthy and very desirable. Let us practice them all—faith, hope, etc. But the most sublime is charity to which St. Paul exhorts us above all.'"*[∇]

---

*   Before the Second Vatican Council, a "high Mass" was one during which all the service music was sung in addition to a number of hymns or anthems, usually by a choir.

∇   The Directory, p. 207.

There it was again: charity. Deep within herself, the young novice knew that the virtue of charity would always be her most serious stumbling block in the spiritual life. "I must try harder," she said to herself. "I know I will falter and I will fail, but I will humbly ask forgiveness of those whom I might hurt and immediately renew my commitment to be charitable."

Since novices were always sent to a mission that would help them in their first year as a teacher, *Sœur* St. André was certain that she would be sent to a school with several Sisters. In many ways, serving on the mission would be different from the novitiate. Her novitiate companions were all about her same age and in their early development in religious life. Living with Sisters who were older, more seasoned, and mission-oriented, would be less challenging, she hoped.

Le père Larvette was concluding his conference. "I am so edified by your holy Founder. Though I did not know his writings before coming to St. Jean-de-Bassel, I now think that they leave behind a vivid picture of his virtue and his vision. I am humbled to serve you as your ecclesiastical superior and pledge myself to continue to work with *Mère* Basilisse and her successors to provide your—or, now that I have been with you for nearly two years, may I say 'our'—Congregation with every resource necessary for its endurance. *Père* Grusy has left us with magnificent buildings and a strong spiritual identity which will serve you well for decades to come. I have spent the last eighteen months reviewing what still needs to be done; and at this time, I want us to concentrate on spiritual growth and unity. We will see what else needs to be done to secure our properties, but I hope to build up the living stones of the community—yourselves. It is my hope to visit each house over the next few years.

"*Mère* Basilisse is an extraordinary person who has a great love for you, her Sisters. She will continue to guide me as I find my way in this position. I ask that each of you pray for me this year, as I will for you. And now, please spend the final hour of our retreat in silent prayer relishing the graces you have received in these last eight days and asking for the grace to live conscientiously the vision of your Founder. Please rejoin me at the church at four o'clock for the closing benediction."

The crowd of Sisters that filled the community room in *Maison Ste. Marie* moved slowly and in silence out into the corridor. Many of the Sisters went on to the village church, but a number chose to spend the last quiet hour outside in the warm sunshine. For her final meditation, *Sœur* St. André hoped to find her favorite bench near an old apple tree in the large, garden-filled park. The bench was waiting for her. As she sat down, she allowed her eyes to wander, almost caressingly, over the three buildings that surrounded the gardens and orchards. The main building of gray stone formed the east side of the quadrangle. She remembered her first day at St. Jean and could still smell the oil on the rags that she had used to dust the wainscoting in the main hallway. Straight ahead of her was *la Maison Ste. Marie.*

The large airy salons had provided a cheerful environment for her group as they studied French and German literature, read some of the classic Latin texts, studied history and geography, and acquired the basics of ciphering. Their education had been broad and thorough. Each novice was prepared to teach children in any of the primary grades on the day she left the novitiate.

From Ste. Anne Hall, the building directly east of *la Maison Ste. Marie*, the aroma of that evening's soup wafted from the big kitchen, making her mouth water. Supper was always simple; cold ham, cheese, and bread were the staples. But a hot, fresh soup made of garden vegetables and meat stock was also usual fare.

Behind the buildings, to the west, was the big barn where a dozen or more milk cows were tended and plow horses were curried and fed.

In her nearly three years at St. Jean-de-Bassel, Louise Feltin, now *Sœur* St. André, had put down roots. She sat on her bench, allowing God's loving Providence to wash over her. Such a deep sense of gratitude filled her that tears came to her eyes. She kept repeating the four fundamental virtues—simplicity, poverty, abandonment to Divine Providence, charity—until she believed she could actually feel them taking up residence deep within her soul. They would be both breastplate and sword as she accepted her first assignment, wherever that would be.

Sœur St. André was among those who had dining room duty for that summer. They gathered in the large dining room adjacent to the kitchen and filled fifty glasses with water, put out the bread and cold foods, and readied the room for the evening meal. The oldest sisters ate with the superiors in the dining room, while the rest of the Congregation—about two hundred—carried their plates to one of the classrooms, making each summer meal a picnic-style event. On this day, *l'abbé* Larvette announced *"Deo gratias"* after the prayer of blessing, the signal that this meal would not be taken in the usual silence, but that the Sisters, novices and postulants were free to visit with whomever they wished. To further add to the festivities, *Mère* Basilisse invited those who wished to enjoy the meal outside on the lawns.

The next days crept by. It seemed to the novices as though the Feast of Ste. Anne which would bring the summer homecoming to a close would never come. Anxiety over their impending assignments heightened. Even their classes could not totally distract the novices from imagining their unknown futures. *Sœur* Irène, their Mistress, exacted final reviews of the writings of *Père* Moye and gave examinations in every subject they had studied as a pre-test to the State exams that they would take in late August. The professed Sisters busily mended their habits and repacked their trunks, preparing to return to last year's mission assignments or to take on the adventure of a new place. Many Sisters were facing their first experience of serving alone in small hamlets. They used this time with their friends to bank against the days when they would have no Sister-companion to talk with, no one with whom to share their spiritual life, with its ups and downs, joys and sorrows. The Sisters in the kitchen prepared the best meals and served special dishes so that the lean days that many would face would seem less harsh. A rich

Alsatian pastry, *kugelhopf*, made with flour, butter, eggs, sweetened milk, almonds, and raisins, appeared more than once.

Finally, on the last possible day of the assignment process, *Mère* Basilisse interviewed the novices. One by one they entered and left her office on the first floor of the main building. *Sœur* St. André had the three o'clock appointment, wondering if that were a bad omen. Three o'clock was the time that Our Lord had died on the cross. Would she receive an assignment that would be a crucifixion? As she stood in the corridor outside the Superior's office, waiting her turn, the professed Sisters who passed by gave her a knowing and sympathetic look. Their fresh memories of recent anxieties as they awaited their own assignments lent an immediate sympathy for this young novice as she stood, quiet and straight, waiting to see *Mère* Basilisse.

"Praised be Jesus Christ," *Mère* Basilisse began after *Sœur* St. André had entered her office.

"Now and forever. Amen," replied *Sœur* St. André with a nod of her head.

"*Sœur* St. André. Please be seated," *Mère* Basilisse began. "Are you well, my child?"

Sœur St. André sat still and erect in the hard-backed chair across the desk from *Mère* Basilisse. "*Oui, ma mère*," she replied in a quiet voice.

"*Bon*. Good. I have your file here. I see that you are proficient in German and do fairly well in French. You are Alsatian, are you not?"

"*Oui, ma mère*. I was born in Geispolsheim, but I lived in LaWalck, near Pfaffenhoffen, since I was ten years old. We spoke Alsatian at home, but we had both German- and French-speaking teachers." When she finished, she knew she had offered too much information. Another character flaw, but typically Alsatian.

"*Bon*. I have decided to send you to Epfig, to the Parish of St. Georges. The school is large and you will be with three other Sisters. The superior of the house will contact you to assist you with travel arrangements. You will leave for Epfig the day after your novitiate year ends." She had said these or similar words to a dozen other novices so by now they were beginning to sound automatic.

"*Merci beaucoup, ma mère.*" This was the standard reply, no matter what *Mère* Basilisse had said. There would be no questions, no showing of emotion, neither pleasure at an assignment that seemed positive nor disappointment at one that was feared to be hard. The novices had been coached well by *Sœur* Irène.

"Please see *Sœur* Constantine in the next office. She wants to review your academic strengths."

"*Oui, ma mère. Merci.*"

"Praised be Divine Providence," *Mère* Basilisse concluded.

"Now and forever. Amen." *Sœur* St. André's voice was sure and steady. As she left *Mère* Basilisse's office and turned toward *Sœur* Constantine's office, the words that she had heard her mother say countless times, "I will surrender to the will of Providence," echoed in her mind.

She knocked at *Sœur* Constantine's door and heard the First Assistant's voice on the other side say, "*Entréz.* Come in."

"Praised be Jesus Christ," *Sœur* Constantine initiated.

"Now and forever. Amen," came the automatic reply.

"Sit down, my child. I want to go over your records."

"*Oui, ma sœur.*" Actually, *Sœur* St. André was unprepared for this interview. She didn't anticipate it, as *Sœur* Irène had said nothing about an interview with *Sœur* Constantine. She waited while *Sœur* Constantine perused the papers in front of her. In addition to being *Mère* Basilisse's assistant, *Sœur* Constantine was Mistress of Studies. Her work included reviewing each Sister's file annually to ascertain that her certifications were current. All the Sisters knew that her advice to *Mère* Basilisse determined where Sisters would be moved. Sisters with better French went certain places; Sisters with better German went other places. Sisters with more skills in numbers were sent to schools with older children; Sisters who struggled with ciphering were sent to teach primary.

**Mother Constantine Eck
(Date: after 1875; Courtesy
of Congregation of Divine
Providence,
St. Jean-de-Bassel)**

"You seem to have done quite well with your studies over the last three years," *Sœur* Constantine began. "And, your German seems excellent. We want your French to match your German, thus Epfig. The village, though Alsatian, is French-speaking and large enough to afford a variety of people, some, better educated. They are stubborn like all of us who are Alsatian." With the last comment, *Sœur* Constantine smiled and gave the novice a knowing look. *Sœur* St. Andre was surprised at *Sœur* Constantine's familiarity in addressing her as a fellow Alsatian.

Sœur Constantine continued. "Epfig is not far from Krautergersheim, in the heart of wine country. Some of the people are vintners, others are involved in commerce and thus somewhat cosmopolitan. We ordinarily send novices there who need to solidify their French, but who will be excellent teachers without too much supervision. The school is large and each Sister has two grade levels to work with. *Sœur* Catherine will supervise you, but she both teaches and directs the school. She is also superior of the house. You must be able to stand on your own. Our observations over the last three years and reports on your years in Krautergersheim indicate that this is possible."

She paused just long enough for *Sœur* St. André to say, "I will try."

"I know you will," *Sœur* Constantine continued. "I've watched you carefully and I see a certain spirit in you. I caution you, however. Take your time; listen to what others are saying first before you come to a conclusion or decision. Our Alsatian temperament can lead one to be impatient and obstinate. Guard yourself against these character flaws. Instead, use the positive aspect of these qualities: fervor for the good and the ability to stay with a project."

With that she seemed finished. She took another moment to review her papers once more and then said, "Praised be Divine Providence," dismissing the young novice with a nod.

"Now and forever. Amen," *Sœur* St. André replied. From there she went straight to the St. Jean Baptiste Church to review in detail the words that *Sœur* Constantine had uttered. *Sœur* Irène had cautioned her about her temperament similarly, but somehow, *Sœur* Constantine's advice showed her a positive way to look at what had before only been viewed as character flaws. At times she wished she weren't an Alsatian. Lorrainians seemed so much more docile. They got along nicely with everyone and never acted stubbornly. But, now, she was beginning to see positive aspects to the Alsatian character. Perhaps more would be revealed as she observed the people of Epfig.

As a young girl in LaWalck, she hadn't the maturity to observe others in a way that would promote her own spiritual growth. Her novitiate year, especially *Père* Moye's writings, had given her such profound insight into human nature. For the first time she began to think of all there would be to learn in Epfig. She promised the Lord that she would be open; that she would take the mind and heart of a missionary into the Vosges Mountains and try to embrace the people there as *Père* Moye had accepted the people of China. Because of her three o'clock appointment, she had missed reciting the rosary with arms extended and reflecting on the five wounds of Jesus. Kneeling on the wood floor of St. Jean Baptiste Church, the mission-minded novice found her rosary in her pocket. As *Sœur* St. André extended her arms to imitate the position of Our Lord on the cross, her thoughts turned to the life of Jesus. He had accepted the failures of his apostles and the tortures of his agony and crucifixion. She vowed in her prayers, with the help of Jesus' passion, to be more self-accepting and, hopefully, more accepting of others.

The August examination for the Certificate of Obedience, the state license for teachers, was grueling. The novices had studied hard; however, in general, they did not feel confident as the two-day examination wore on. *Sœur* St. André believed that she had passed, but, remembering *Sœur* Irène's observations, chose to take a more tentative posture in solidarity with her companions. When two weeks later the examination results arrived by messenger, *Sœur* Irène called them all into the novitiate classroom to give them the results.

Every novice had passed! Each one of them would be taking the mission assignment she had been given. *Sœur* St. André was going to Epfig! After the announcement, *Mère* Basilisse came into the salon to congratulate them on their achievement. Speaking to them about their future as instructors of children, the Superior recalled for them their Founder's insistence that they receive each child as Jesus would.

"*Père* Moye's exact words are challenging," *Mère* Basilisse reminded them.

> ***The Sisters will have the same zeal and charity for all children without giving in to the natural aversion that some of them could arouse. On the contrary, they will take greater pains with those who have nothing attractive, who are stubborn, who have uncouth manners and appearance, who are poor, badly dressed, dirty, because they are the ones with whom the best results can be achieved ...****

After quoting the Founder, *Mère* Basilisse concluded. "We are so pleased that you have all completed your studies and have passed the State examination. But you must remember: imparting a particular subject is not your main goal. Any good lay teacher can do that. Your

---

* **The Directory, p. 143**

goal, as a Sister of Divine Providence, is to live fully the four fundamental virtues of simplicity, poverty, abandonment to Providence, and
charity. I know that *Sœur* Irène has imbued you with their meaning
and that you fully intend to be guided by them. It will be living these
virtues, not your Certificate of Obedience, that will make you a true
daughter of *Père* Moye. Never forget that our holy Founder believed
that by keeping these virtues we will remain close to our Lord and
that our holiness will be the glory of God. May God bless each of you in
these last days here at St. Jean's. In less than a month we will gather
here in this room again and you will profess your obedience to me and
to our Holy Rule. Praised be Divine Providence."

Twenty-four young and eager voices responded, "Now and forever.
Amen."

For the first time in three years, *Sœur* St. André climbed into
the wagon with Jean-Pierre to leave St. Jean-de-Bassel. Her world
had been limited to the confines of the convent, its forest, and pastures during her postulancy and novitiate. Now, clothed in the simple habit of her institute, fortified by the four fundamental virtues
bequeathed to his daughters by their Founder and certified as a
teacher by the State of France, she was setting off, at age twenty-one,
for her first mission, Epfig. Her small traveling trunk was hoisted
into the back of the wagon along with her valise. Everything she
owned in the world was in her baggage. Two other newly professed
climbed aboard and sat among the trunks and cases with *Sœur* St.
André. Jean-Pierre flicked the reins over the backs of the two horses
and the wagon lurched forward. *Sœur* Irène, *Mère* Basilisse, *Sœur*
Constantine, and a number of others had gathered for their departure as they had every day for the leave-takings of scores of other
Sisters over the past two weeks.

Jean-Pierre, who knew all the convent gossip, said, "Let's see.
Sœur Marie Ange, you are traveling to La Wantzenau? *Oui*? And,
Sœur Anne Virginie, you are going to Surbourg? And *Sœur* St. André,
you to Epfig? *Oui*?"

"*Oui, monsieur.* Yes, sir," replied the three young teachers in unison. There was a fall wind and each had to hold onto her bonnet as Jean-Pierre had the horses pick up their speed on the road. In excited voices they talked enthusiastically about their futures. The ten miles to Sarrebourg passed quickly and all three had a wait for their coach after they arrived at the station. The coach would take them to Saverne where they would separate, each taking other coaches to their destinations. Their life as missionaries had begun.

The journey from Saverne to Molsheim had taken two days. Two long, dusty days. The coach had been full most of the time and, though the shoulder-to-shoulder accommodations lessened the impact of the rutted roads on the passengers, *Sœur* St. André was very glad to come to the end of this part of the trip. At Molsheim she changed coaches again, to a smaller one this time, and proceeded on to Epfig. By the time the coach pulled into the small station near the post office, her *guimpe* was soiled, her new bonnet was filled with dust, and the skirt of her brown wool dress was splattered with mud. She was afraid she would not make a very favorable impression on her waiting companions. *Sœur* Catherine was at the station and laughed as she gave her a warm embrace.

"You look just like I did when I arrived in August! Isn't that a terrible journey? You must be exhausted. We've only two blocks to walk before we come to our house. There you can take off these filthy clothes and rest. Come now, let's get you home! I've made arrangements for your trunk to be picked up later by *Monsieur* Starck, one of our parishioners. We have his children in our school. He lives near us and is always happy to help us."

Sœur St. André did not know *Sœur* Catherine but instantly she felt comfortable with her. She was so lively, so friendly!

"*Merci, Sœur Supérieure,*" *Sœur* St. André said shyly.

"Oh, we're not that formal out here in the wilds of the Vosges Mountains. Please call me *Sœur* Catherine. There are times when I have to be the superior, but I much prefer being one of the Sisters."

"*Oui, Sœur* Catherine," *Soeur* St. André corrected herself.

"The other two Sisters are at home. They returned last week after visiting their families."

The two blocks were short so the walk took less than ten minutes.

"Here is our house. Come in!" *Sœur* Catherine said proudly.

The attractive house constructed of brown-colored stucco and exterior wooden traces was typical of Alsatian homes. *Sœur* St. André remembered that the Sisters in Geispolsheim had lived in a neighborhood house, but her three years in the large institution-like convent at St. Jean-de-Bassel had all but erased her memories of living in a regular house. *Sœur* Octavie and *Sœur* Alphonse were just inside the front door, both talking at once as they greeted the new arrival.

"Come now! Give *Sœur* St. André a chance to breathe," laughed *Sœur* Catherine. "I'll show you to the room which you will share with *Sœur* Alphonse. You can take off these dusty clothes and put on your nightclothes while we give these a good brushing and cleaning. When you're ready, come downstairs to the kitchen. We are going to have a party to welcome you!"

Sœur St. André was so surprised. The formality of her life at St. Jean instantly gave way here to a familiar camaraderie. The Sisters, too, seemed so friendly! Her anxieties that had heightened the closer the small coach had come to Epfig fell away, and she felt that her year here would be a good one.

After she had taken off her habit, *guimpe*, cape, bonnet, and *bandeau*, she donned her nightgown and nightrobe and came downstairs with only her *coif* covering her short brown hair.

"That looks better!" *Sœur* Octavie said. "Give me your dress and cape. It will take me only a few minutes to get them back into a wearable state."

"Sit here," *Sœur* Alphonse motioned to a place at the simple wooden table in the middle of the kitchen. "This will be your place. Would you like your coffee with or without milk and sugar?"

"With milk, please, but no sugar," *Sœur* St. André replied. She hardly knew what to say. At the convent there had never been a choice!

"*Bon*. We begin school in one week. Enjoy these moments while they last. Soon we will all be too busy and there won't be time to breathe much less to have parties in the middle of the afternoon!" *Sœur* Catherine laughed as she spoke, preparing them for the hard work ahead, but suggesting that there might be a few other parties in their future.

Preparing for the first day of school took every minute of the next week. After the Sunday Mass, the Sisters registered the students for the upcoming year. Two hundred and eighty students were registered into four divisions: primers, second year, middle level, and advanced. Each teacher would have over sixty children and so the four classrooms in the school building next to the Church of St. Georges had to be thoroughly cleaned after being empty through the summer months. Desks and benches needed to be washed and arranged, and an inventory of supplies taken. Each year more children were registered, requiring *Sœur* Catherine to present the mayor with a list of items that would be needed: ten new slates, fifteen new pens, ink, and paper. Many of the families owned vineyards and had the means to provide their children with supplies, but some few families were poor and required assistance. Though the mayor was usually good about buying what was needed, *Sœur* Catherine reminded the other Sisters frequently that no waste of any type would be tolerated.

The day after registration, *Sœur* Catherine called her Sisters together to receive their assignments. "*Sœur* Alphonse, please take the second year students. You had them last year as primers and should be able to start them without losing too much ground. *Sœur* Octavie, can you manage the middle section? They will need to focus on reading and ciphering. You will handle that well. Of course, with your proficiency on the violin, you will also take the music classes. *Sœur* St. André, you will take the primers. That is a good place to start your teaching career. You have the opportunity to enter into the world of these children and grow with them. You will also strengthen your French as you teach them their mother country's tongue. We have more little ones than ever this year—nearly seventy-five! Many of them will come speaking only Alsatian. You will conduct all lessons in French and shape their language skills as they learn their lessons. I will take the advanced students. We will probably have no more than fifty of the older students, but other duties will take up my time."

After the term started, the days were long and filled with activities. Classes began at eight o'clock in the morning, but the Sisters rose at five o'clock in order to pray, to attend Holy Mass, to do a few chores in their house before arriving at the school by seven-thirty. Classes in French filled the first part of the morning followed by ciphering classes until eleven o'clock. The school children then had various music lessons for an hour. After dinner, lessons resumed at one-thirty with instructions in religion, prayers, and the catechism filling the time until two-thirty. After a short recess, more French lessons for the older children and lessons in penmanship for the younger children took the next hour and a half. The day was brought to a close with a general lesson in French for the whole school, making order, and saying end-of-day prayers.

One cold wintry day, *Sœur* Alphonse confided to *Sœur* St. André. "Last year I worked with *Sœur* Octavie on the Christmas pageant. I suspect that *Sœur* Catherine will give that unpleasant chore to you and me this year. She will probably be speaking with us in the near future. I can't tell you how demanding the project will be! All the children in the school have to participate. All two hundred and eighty! Of course, most of them can be in the chorus, but we have to involve as many as we can in the presentation of the Christmas story. It will be a real challenge. Let's pray for inspiration and rely on God's Providence!"

Sœur Alphonse and *Sœur* St. André had become good friends. They shared a tiny room above the kitchen and laughed together when they realized that only one of them could get out of bed at a time. There wasn't room for both of them to stand at once! Their novice mistress, *Sœur* Irène, had constantly recited an adage: A place for everything and everything in its place. Never was this axiom more carefully practiced than in their small bedroom filled with two small cot-like beds, two tiny desks, a washstand, and an armoire. They had fallen into a routine each morning in order to be able to get dressed and wash their faces. But sometimes, one or the other would take an unexpected turn and they would literally run into each other. Laughter always followed.

True to *Sœur* Alphonse's prediction, *Sœur* Catherine used the high spirits that prevailed at their little St. Nicolas party in their home on December 6 to buffer her announcement that *Sœur* Alphonse and *Sœur* St. André would be in charge of the annual Christmas pageant. *Sœur* Alphonse looked at *Sœur* St. André knowingly and sighed audibly.

"I heard that, *Sœur* Alphonse," *Sœur* Catherine said good-naturedly. "I know that this is not your favorite event. But perhaps the two of you will have a good time plotting the pageant together."

At their first opportunity, the two young religious got busy with plans for the pageant. Within a week they had finalized the plans for the pageant now scheduled for the last day before the break between Christmas and Epiphany. They had barely two weeks to pull the entire event together, but *Sœur* Alphonse assured *Sœur* St. André that more time would not necessarily yield a better play.

Between the two energetic young women, a short play based on the Nativity story was put together. But, since there was really no time to teach parts to the older children who always took the roles of the principal characters, they decided to simply soak the youngest children in the story and let them play the parts of Mary, Joseph, shepherds, angels, and three kings with "free" presentations. The children's "creative" presentations might get out of hand; but at least, the two of them agreed, the play would be memorable. The older divisions took on the various parts of the angels and the shepherds. *Sœur* Octavie, thrilled at not having to work on the play itself, gladly agreed to play the violin and prepare the chorus to sing familiar Christmas hymns. It was agreed that all the hymns would be in French with the exception of *Stille Nacht*. The German language was the only appropriate setting for Franz Gruber's hymn that had become so popular. The final hymn of the play would be *Il Est Né, Le Divine Enfant* and all the audience would be invited to join in.

After only a few days of rehearsals, *Sœur* St. André agreed wholeheartedly with *Sœur* Alphonse: the project was very burdensome. They both worked with the little ones to drill them on the age-old story of the birth of the Savior, but each time they let the children act out the story, they changed it! Their performance often bore no resemblance to the events chronicled in either Matthew's or Luke's gospels.

When *Sœur* Catherine frequently asked them how the pageant was coming along, they both would say, in unison, "*Trés bien, ma sœur*. Very well, Sister." But neither of them felt that their response was truthful. Realizing their superior's heavy schedule, the two young nuns agreed not to burden *Sœur* Catherine with their innovative plan for the play.

The last two weeks of the school term seemed to speed by. Both *Sœur* Alphonse and *Sœur* St. André were certain that *Sœur* Octavie had the music well prepared. They were equally certain that the play itself was in complete disarray.

Eventually the day of the performance came. Parents and grandparents, eagerly awaiting their children's performance, filled the large baroque-styled church. The hundred and seventy-five children in the upper divisions filled the areas on either side of the sanctuary while the children of the primary grade took their places on the steps leading up to the altar railing. With *Sœur* Octavie leading the older children in familiar Christmas hymns and anthems on her violin, the music began.

Eventually, the primers who played Mary and Joseph began to speak. *Sœurs* Alphonse and St. André held their breath as the tiny voices piped out in rudimentary French the story of how salvation began.

"Joseph" had been instructed to begin. "You are so good, Mary, and I am not. But we must go far away so that I can pay my taxes. If you don't want to go, I will understand. I have not always been nice to you."

"Don't worry about that, Joseph," 'Mary'said cheerily. "If I don't go with you, I cannot have my baby in a stable. And the story would be ruined," she ended brightly.

"*Bon*! Then let's go! It may take us a long time to get to the Bread House. I think that's where we are going!" The bright-eyed boy, proud of his part but unsure of his words, turned to *Sœur* St. André. "Is that right, *ma sœur*?" The audience chuckled audibly. As he went on, the small 'boy-Joseph' grew in courage. "I had a donkey, Mary, but I lost him. We'll have to walk."

The audience laughed frequently, totally enjoying the simplicity of the children. The story continued to unfold through the fresh eyes and limited vocabulary of the village's smallest children. *Sœur* Alphonse was kept busy prompting the children with their parts while *Sœur* St. André, her assistant, often had to physically guide children to the place of their performance.

The play concluded with the pre-arranged singing and *Sœur* Catherine rose to close the event.

"My dear parents, I was not aware that such liberties would be taken with the holy story of our dear Savior's birth, and I personally apologize if any of you were offended by the lightness of the play. We have simply seen the story through the eyes of your dear children who were wonderful in their portrayal of Mary, Joseph, the angels, the shepherds, the innkeepers, the townspeople, and the wise men. I believe that we have witnessed a performance that we shall never forget. May each of you have a Blessed Christmas, and may the coming of the Magi teach us the deepest truths about who has been born to us. *Bon soir!* Good night!"

She glowered at *Sœur* Alphonse and *Sœur* St. André as she moved into the crowd.

After they had returned to their home, *Sœur* Catherine called the two young nuns to the kitchen and asked *Sœur* Octavie to leave them.

Her voice was somewhere between scolding and exasperation as she reviewed with the two how their creative work might have turned out a failure. But, she also admitted that the play had been memorable—and in a good way. In the end, *Sœur* St. André and *Sœur* Alphonse weren't really sure how *Sœur* Catherine felt about the pageant.

Later, breaking Sacred Silence, they whispered together about their experience.

"I'd do it all over again," *Sœur* St. André said with conviction.

"So would I," *Sœur* Alphonse said. "And, if we had asked permission, we would probably have been told to do the traditional play with lines we had written."

"True. One day we will both be alone in some remote hamlet. We won't have much to work with and yet the children will be hungry for the truths of the faith. Only through ingenuity can we make the gospel come alive for them. Let's remember that."

"*Oui,*" *Sœur* Alphonse agreed. "I'd work with you again—anytime," she added.

"*Moi aussi*! Me, too!" *Sœur* St. André finished in a whisper.

The next five months in Epfig passed all too quickly. *Sœur* St. André learned how to run a school and work with the mayor of a village and the pastor of a parish by watching *Sœur* Catherine who was an excellent model.

By the middle of June, the four companions had cleaned the school, closed their house, and taken the coach back to St. Jean-de-Bassel for the traditional summer homecoming. They were exhausted. Sleeping most of the way, they barely noticed the jolting, uncomfortable ride that had been so jarring only nine months earlier.

With reunions with novitiate companions taking precedence over their own relationships, the four sisters did not expect to see one another regularly in the summer months. Each one had different classes of study, and only after the annual retreat did they meet again for conversation on the day that *Sœur* Alphonse learned that she was returning to Epfig with *Sœur* Octavie who had been named director of the school. *Sœur* Catherine had learned that she was being assigned to Haguenau; *Sœur* St. André still did not know her placement.

On the fourth day of appointments, *Sœur* St. Andre's name was listed for the eleven o'clock appointment on the slate board outside *Mère* Basilisse's office. Certain that she would return to Epfig, she felt at ease as she awaited the appointment. The morning of the appointment, however, there was a rustle throughout the house. *Mère* Basilisse was ill and would not be seeing those with appointments today. Instead, *Sœur* Constantine, who now served as both General Councilor and Mistress of Novices, would continue conducting the scheduled appointments. In some ways, *Sœur* St. Andre welcomed that news. She felt comfortable with *Sœur* Constantine. *Sœur* Constantine had often spoken to her novitiate group on the spirit of the Congregation, especially the importance of having the attitude of a missionary no matter where one was sent; and *Sœur* St. André admired her very much. As the morning wore on, she found herself anticipating her appointment without anxiety.

At precisely eleven o'clock, *Sœur* St. André knocked at the door to *Sœur* Constantine's office.

"*Entréz!* Come in," was the response.

Sœur Constantine initiated the usual greeting. "Praised be Jesus Christ."

And *Sœur* St. André replied, "Now and forever. Amen."

"Please sit down. How are you? How was your year in Epfig?"

"Thank you, *ma sœur*. I am very well. I enjoyed my year very much. The teaching was very challenging, but *Sœur* Catherine and the others were most helpful. Our community was very nice."

"I am glad that you had a good year. I have spoken with *Sœur* Catherine about you. She tells me that you have a creative streak?"

At first, *Sœur* St. André did not readily understand the meaning of *Sœur* Constantine's remark. Then it dawned on her: the Christmas pageant! Oh, no! What had *Sœur* Catherine said about that?

"Are you referring to the Christmas pageant, *ma sœur?*"

"As a matter of fact, yes. Did you and *Sœur* Alphonse both have the idea about not having a planned script?"

"Well, not exactly. I take responsibility for that. *Sœur* Alphonse had had the primers the year before and had said how hard it was to get them to participate in the play as part of the chorus. So, I suggested we turn it around, allowing the older children to be the chorus and the youngest to do the roles of Mary and Joseph and the others. I really didn't think the little ones could learn lines. However, if they knew the story, they could take the parts and say the story in their own little ways. Was I wrong to do that, *ma sœur?*"

"No, not completely. Many of us, and *Sœur* Catherine is typical, prefer to remain informed about happenings, especially when we have the ultimate responsibility. Personally, I enjoy watching others take initiative and come up with new ways to do things. For others, that is disconcerting. Your failure to inform her of your change from the traditional presentation was basically uncharitable. She was the one who had to defend you to the mayor, the pastor and the parents. Remember the words of our Founder: *'The Sisters will also maintain a community spirit, that is to say, they will have among themselves the union, charity, and community love that binds them to one another by the same spirit, the same views, the same intentions to educate the young well.'* In leaving *Sœur* Catherine out of your plans, even though she might have challenged your ideas, you failed our union as Sisters and the charity that we must have for one another. From here on you might want simply to be more conscious of others' needs."

"I understand." Failure in charity again, she thought to herself. She would speak to *Sœur* Catherine as soon as possible, offering her a deep apology for her thoughtlessness.

"Now. After reviewing the notes from *Sœur* Catherine on your work in Epfig and analyzing the needs of the Congregation, we have decided to send you to Heiligenberg to open a small school in that little hamlet. The school will begin with fewer than fifty students, we're sure, but the pastor and mayor are very enthusiastic about our Congregation. They have begged us to send someone, and we are certain that they will be very supportive. We will try to find another Sister to go with you, but I really cannot give you hope about that. We were not prepared to begin this school this year and right now we have no one else to send. Both the mayor and the pastor are willing to accept an unseasoned teacher. We believe that you will be able to manage the situation. *Sœur* Catherine concurs. Are you willing?"

Since their life presupposed that a Sister would go wherever she was sent, it was unusual for a Sister to be asked if she were "willing." But it also was unusual to send such a young teacher to begin a school.

"I am willing if you believe I can do this."

"I personally look for Sisters who will take initiative for these types of assignments. But, I warn you: this mission will be hard.

* **The Directory, p. 145**

None of us knows how living alone will affect our vocation. There are Sisters nearby in Mutzig and I suggest that you visit them often, weekly if possible. The director of the school there, *Sœur* Elise, has agreed to assist you as you need it."

Sœur St. André, of course, had never lived alone in her life. The news came as a shock. She was barely out of the novitiate! Would her vocation be strong enough? Where would she live and where would the school be?

"The village has had a lay teacher for some years; but because the village is poor and so small, it cannot afford to pay an attractive salary and the present teacher must find a position which will pay more. The pastor and the mayor have begged us to send someone," *Sœur* Constantine continued. "They will accept you because you are Alsatian but they need someone who can teach them well in French and German. You have these abilities."

"*Merci beaucoup, ma sœur*," Sœur St. André replied shyly. She was not used to being complimented so.

"We will make arrangements for your travel but you will need to arrive by the end of August so that you will have time to prepare for school's opening on October 15. This hamlet is in the mountains and because people do not have large vineyards, they are not directly involved in the harvest. However, there is little use trying to begin before the middle of October."

"I understand. Where is the school located?"

"The letter says that it is in a room next to the mayor's office across the street from St. Vincent's Church."

"Does it say where I will live?" *Sœur* St. André asked this question timidly. She did not want to give the impression that her living quarters were of any importance. She would accept this assignment with an open heart regardless of where she was housed.

"Yes. *Le prêtre* says that the former teacher boarded with a family. The mayor and the pastor hope that this arrangement can continue. We have agreed to allow this since many of us live this way."

"Very well."

"Thank you for taking this mission. I will pray for you, as will *Mère* Basilisse and *Père* Larvette. We are all depending upon you to represent us well to the people and pastor of Heiligenberg. Praised be Jesus Christ." With that *Sœur* Constantine concluded the interview.

Sœur St. André's head was reeling as she left *Sœur* Constantine's office. She went straight to the church, thinking that she must have some time alone to reflect on this great change. Then she would need to find *Sœur* Catherine and *Sœur* Alphonse. Since *Sœur* Alphonse had already had her appointment with *Mère* Basilisse, she knew that she was returning to Epfig. *Sœur* St. André wanted to be the one to tell her good friend that she had been given another assignment. Both friends understood that the welfare of the schools came first. They would accept their separation without disappointment.

Upon departing St. Jean, *Sœur* St. André took the same route to Heiligenberg that she had traveled to and from Epfig, but since Heiligenberg was closer, the journey took only two days. The pastor, *Le père* Kirst, met the coach in Molsheim and on the way to Heiligenberg he was very animated about the parish, the school, and the small village. *Le père* Kirst acknowledged that many people were poor and had few possibilities for their livelihood; but they were good, he assured her, and she would like them.

"Now, about your housing," he interjected after he had told her about the beautiful gothic church.

Sœur St. André fully expected him to describe a parish family who would share their home with her. Instead he cleared his throat.

"Now, the letter I received from *Mère* Basilisse said that you would be able to have the same arrangement that we had for the lay teacher." He posed this statement almost as though it were a question.

"Yes, I understood the same thing."

"*Bien!* Well! Our last teacher lived with the Rohlmans. They are a very nice family. *Monsieur* Rohlman runs the small bank."

"Do they attend St. Vincent's?"

"Not exactly. They are Jewish." The priest waited for this comment to take hold; then he quickly went on. "Madame Rohlman has a very clean house and prepares good meals. She and *Monsieur* Rohlman are observant Jews. They attend synagogue. The Jews here—there are about a dozen families—meet in one another's homes on Saturday mornings to read from the Old Testament and to sing the Psalms. They are somewhat educated and their children are well behaved. I think you will find this arrangement to be a happy one." He said this last sentence with great hope.

Sœur St. André was speechless. After a moment, she said, "Does *Mère* Basilisse know this?"

"*Ma sœur*, we were so desperate." He sounded sorrowful. "Can you manage? I will assist in every way that I can, as will our mayor." The pastor sounded anxious.

"Before I entered the convent, my own village of LaWalck found itself in exactly these same circumstances. When the schoolteacher did not return, they, too, were desperate to find another. My father had hoped that I would take the school; but instead, I asked his permission to enter the convent. When he relinquished his plans in favor of the dreams in my heart, I felt that I had disappointed him. Perhaps this assignment will serve to assuage my guilt. Do not have concern, *mon père*. Everything will work out according to the designs of Providence. This is what our holy Founder teaches us."

"*Merci beaucoup, ma sœur. Merci beaucoup,*" the young pastor said with relief.

In truth, all did work well. *Sœur* St. André was well loved in Heiligenberg and she was reassigned there until 1859. Having lived with the Rohlmans for the entire six years, she all but became a member of the family. Her experiences during these years made her strong and independent. Summer studies at St. Jean-de-Bassel developed her skills as a teacher and director of a school, while being with the community at the motherhouse offset the loneliness

126   The Tattered Heart

of living alone in Heiligenberg. The summer months also gave *Sœur* St. André the opportunity to continue her friendship with *Sœur* Alphonse and her novitiate companions.

At the end of her first year at St. Vincent's parish school in Heiligenberg, her appointment with *Mère* Basilisse included a positive review of her teaching and other duties. In the interview *la mère superieure* asked unexpectedly, "*Ma chére sœur*, my dear sister, are you happy in your vocation?"

"*Oui, ma mère!* I have many opportunities to live our virtues and I feel a deep love for our community, even though I see our sisters only as the weather permits traveling to Mutzig. The road up to Heiligenberg is steep; snow makes it impassable. The Mutzig Sisters have been very good to me this year, welcoming me into their community as often as I can go there. I feel that I am following *Père* Moye's vision when he said, '**We should rely so much on Providence that we do not know and do not even want to know what will happen to us in the future, nor how our life will end, nor what means God will eventually use to provide for our needs.**'* I try to do this. The Rohlmans with whom I live provide me with a true home though they do not know Jesus as our savior. I am challenged to respect their beliefs as well as to live in such a way as to bring them to Jesus if that is God's will. The balance needed for this experience is good for my Alsatian temperament! I remain over-zealous and Madame Rohlman often rebukes me when I work on my lessons on Sunday instead of taking rest. I try to live each and every virtue, especially charity."

"*Bon!* Will you choose to take the Vow of Chastity next summer when you return from Heiligenberg?"

"*Mais oui, ma mère.* If you believe I am suited."

"*Oui!* We will celebrate the vows on the Feast of the Sacred Heart, June 22. I will be pleased to receive yours."

---

* **The Directory**, p. 354.

The second year in Heiligenberg began with a few more students in the school. Some mothers of the youngest children generously helped with various school events and *Sœur* St. André grew as she realized that dependence on Providence begins with the ability to depend on others.

Letters from her priest-brother Nicolas in Texas were prized diversions that stretched her world past the boundaries of the small hamlet, giving her pause as she considered the tremendous needs of the Church outside Europe. But it was with deep sadness that she opened a letter from Nicolas just after she had returned to Heiligenberg in the fall of 1857. His letters usually were so enthusiastic about his work in the ecclesiastical region of Texas since his ordination in 1853. He had quickly learned English and now served in St. Vincent de Paul Parish in Houston. *Sœur* St. André had believed it ironic that both she and her brother were in parishes named for that fatherly French saint who was so devoted to love of the poor.

The 1857 letter was brief, telling her of their younger brother Celestin's untimely death. Barely five years younger than Nicolas, Celestin had always admired his older brother and needed very little encouragement to join him in Texas. Nicolas' letters to the family had described Houston as a growing town; since Celestin had learned to lay bricks in LaWalck, Nicolas had been certain that his younger brother would find work. Celestin had begged their parents to let him go. To be struck down by yellow fever, a vicious disease that took the lives of so many young people, seemed so unfair. *Sœur* St. André wept bitter tears as she read and re-read the letter. What must her poor dear mother feel, having lost another child forever? A permanent good-bye. And her dear Papa! To have to accept the death of a son that he would not even be able to bury! Where was the good God in the tragedies of people's lives? Alone in her room in the Rohlman's home in Heiligenberg, *Sœur* St. André struggled with her first faith doubts.

As she sat with Nicolas' letter on her lap on that late Friday afternoon, shadows began to fall, and she could hear Madame Rohlman bustling in the kitchen below trying to finish supper preparations before sundown. The last light of day slipped from her room, as *Sœur* St. André lit her lamp. Hearing Madame Rohlman intone the Sabbath prayer in Hebrew, she imagined Madame Rohlman lighting the Sabbath candles in her silver candlesticks. Engulfed anew by loneliness, she opened her Office Book and found the *De Profundis* Psalm.*

"Out of the depths I cry to thee, O Lord," she began in a whisper. With tears streaming down her cheeks and falling in wet blotches on her *guimpe*, she momentarily allowed herself to feel the pain of loss: the finality of the loss of her brother Celestin, the loss of Nicolas who was suffering alone so far away, the loss of her family whom she so seldom saw, the loss of her community as she lived alone in this tiny hamlet, and every other loss that had permeated her life in recent years. Then she realized: it wasn't merely the loss, but it was being alone in the loss that was so devastating. On this lonely night, as on many similar nights in years to come, she would realize that only the Psalmist seemed to truly understand. Only his age-old words would be a comfort to her now and in the future when other persons would desert her in other lands stranger than a Jewish house in Heiligenberg. With the help of the Psalmist, she tried to set her grief aside and continued to pray,

> **Lord, hear my voice! Let thine ears be attentive to my voice in supplication:**
> **If Thee, O Lord, mark iniquities, Lord, who can stand? But with Thee is forgiveness, that we might revere Thee.**
> **I trust in the Lord; my soul trusts in His word.**
> **My soul waits for the Lord, more than watchers wait for the dawn.**

---

* **Psalm 130. Traditionally recited by Sisters of Divine Providence upon hearing of the death of one of their Sisters**

More than watchers wait for the dawn, let Israel
  wait for the Lord,
For with the Lord is kindness and with Him
  is plenteous redemption.
And He will redeem Israel from all their iniquities. Amen.

CHAPTER VI

CHANGES

"*Ma trés chère sœur, comment allez-vous?* How are you?" *Mère* Basilisse's greeting to *Sœur* St. André was effusive. *Mère* Basilisse genuinely loved her daughters and during her fifteen years as Superior, the time of summer assignments was her favorite for she had the opportunity to visit personally with each Sister.

"*Je vais bien, ma mère,*" *Sœur* St. André replied. Her voice displayed a tentative quality. Rumor in the Motherhouse was that she was being changed this year. While loving her work in Heiligenberg, she would be the first to admit that her talents had been nearly exhausted in the six years that she had been there. Starting up projects was more interesting to her than maintaining them. Though the opening of the small school at St. Vincent Parish in Heiligenberg had been challenging, keeping it going, facing the same problems year after year, had proved to be less stimulating. Living alone had served to deepen and strengthen her vocation, and in many ways she enjoyed the relationships and freedoms not afforded her while living with other Sisters, but she would readily acknowledge that it was probably time for her to receive another assignment.

"We have another Sister whom we can now send to Heiligenberg and you have put St. Vincent's school on such a solid footing that we feel certain that it will continue to thrive!"

"*Merci, ma mère.*" *Sœur* St. André had worked hard at St. Vincent. Her relationship with the people had been the mainstay of her success. Being the only Sister in the village had taught her to be self-reliant; but involving the parents in the school was also imperative for its success. Working with a pastor had posed a challenge all its own. She had been forever grateful to the Sisters in nearby Mutzig who had mentored her and supported her.

Living with the Rohlman family for those six years had been a delight. *Sœur* St. André would never forget the look on *l'abbé* Larvette's face when he visited her during that first year and learned that she was living with a Jewish family! Her annual interview with *Mère* Basilisse at the end of that first year had not been routine! Mother, furious that the pastor had not been forthcoming about the planned for living arrangement, had all but grilled her about the situation. *Sœur* St. André was not the first Sister of Providence to live with a Jewish family, and *Mère* Basilisse had acknowledged that she probably wouldn't be the last!

"Are you ready for a change, *ma sœur?*" *Mère* Basilisse asked cautiously. Though the council had been certain that a change was necessary, they had been concerned that *Sœur* St. André would find it upsetting.

"*Oui, ma mère.* I have done my best in Heiligenberg. It is time to go somewhere else; six years are enough."

"*Bon!*" *Mère* Basilisse's response was both relieved and enthusiastic. She deeply appreciated her daughters' desire to serve and to be flexible so that re-assignments could be a joy rather than a cause for sadness. "We have given this serious thought. *Sœur* Constantine has followed your professional growth over the years. She has told us that you have taken advantage of our academic offerings each summer and has assured us that you could take on a new challenge. We want you to go to Batzendorf, a small, poor village. Actually you may know it since it is near LaWalck." *Sœur* St. André did know the village in question but before she could respond, *Mère* Basilisse went on. "The parish is St. Abrogast. *Sœur* Polycarpe has been alone there for several years and has done very well at beginning the school and developing it. Without any resources, I might add! Her health is not good now, but she does not feel ready to come home. We're sending you to assist her. She will remain in charge. I warn you: this arrangement may be difficult. *Sœur* Polycarpe does not want to let go. You will want to take over: that is your nature." This last sentence was said lovingly, and with a smile. *Mère* Basilisse knew her daughters! "Do you think that you can take this assignment?" *Mère* Basilisse knew that her last question could elicit any number of answers, depending on which word in the question she emphasized.

"I will try, *ma mère*," *Sœur* St. André answered. She, too, knew the implications of this assignment and she was unsure. An Alsatian temperament did not lend itself to the subtleties needed. She would have to pray!

"*Merci, ma sœur*," *Mère* Basilisse said simply. As though reading *Sœur* St. André's mind, she added, "Let us both pray about this!"

Having been a Sister of Providence now for nearly a decade, *Sœur* St. André found the years rewarding and satisfying. Never had she regretted her decision to enter the convent, though some experiences had been hard and others had been exasperating. As she prepared for her move to Batzendorf, she wondered how this mission would be categorized.

How would she deal with *Sœur* Polycarpe? She did not know her soon-to-be companion and believed that meeting her as soon as possible would be positive for the future of their relationship. "Dear God, please don't let her reject me outright! With your assistance, I pray that things will work out! Help me to be patient!" That was her first of hundreds of prayers on this subject!

Before going to her new mission, *Sœur* St. André spent a short time at home in LaWalck. Finding her mother more and more frail each time she visited LaWalck had begun to worry her and she was relieved that she would now be fairly close to her home village. Her sister Marie-Anne took very good care of their mother, but their father's death had taken its toll. Being in Batzendorf would be a great grace.

Sœur Polycarpe and *Sœur* St. André had a hesitant first meeting just a few days before the annual retreat began. It was clear to *Sœur* St. André that *Sœur* Polycarpe was not pleased with having a companion. But she seemed resigned—as a good religious should be. In their very short conversation, *Sœur* St. André learned that *Sœur* Polycarpe was ill, more from her appearance than from a verbal acknowledgement. Her black eyes were clouded and her sallow complexion belied the residual effects of yellow fever. Her too thin frame was racked by a constant cough and she was stooped and slow. Though she was only thirty-five years old, her demeanor was already that of a very old woman. Disease and hard work had taken their toll, as they did on many Sisters of Providence. Theirs was a strenuous life.

Their first year together was relatively uneventful for the two Sisters. *Sœur* Polycarpe had established a good school; the villagers were friendly and grateful that the Sisters were teaching their children; the pastor at St. Abrogast was congenial.

By late spring, however, after being worn down by a bad winter cold, *Sœur* Polycarpe grew tired and somewhat irritable.

"*Sœur* St. André!" *Sœur* Polycarpe's shrill voice broke the early morning silence. Once again, as on so many mornings now, the day began with uncertainty. *Sœur* St. André raised herself from her cot in the room over the kitchen and descended the ladder to the kitchen. Due to an unusually cold and rainy spring, the house was freezing and she went straight to the stove to start a fire to take the chill off their small home. The house was typical of those in the village: two downstairs rooms and a sort of loft reached by a ladder as a third room over the kitchen. An outside wall was shared with a shed that housed the neighbor's cow and pig. The smell of manure wafted through the front door each time it was opened. *Sœur* Polycarpe slept in the second downstairs room as she no longer had the physical strength to go up the ladder to the loft. The kitchen now served doubly as dining area and sitting room.

"What is it, *ma sœur?*" *Sœur* St. André answered after she had the fire going.

"I simply cannot go to school today. I am chilled to the bone and believe I had better remain at home. Can you manage the students?"

"*Oui, ma sœur.* I am so sorry that you feel badly …" She was going to add "again today," but realized before the words came out that they arose from her frustrations and would be construed as such. The element of unpredictability in the entire arrangement tried *Sœur* St. André's patience more and more as the school term wore on. She was certain that she could persevere until the summer break, but each day was more of a challenge due to *Sœur* Polycarpe's failing health.

An early Easter brought no signs of springtime resurrection. The streets of the poor village were muddy from rains and a late snow, but it had been too cold for spring flowers. With barely a month of school left in the term, the parents asked that the children be given a week free to help with spring planting and *Sœur* St. André welcomed the respite.

The two nuns were drinking coffee and planning for a visit on the upcoming Sunday from the Sisters in nearby Keffendorf when they heard a horse gallop up the street and stop in front of their house. So seldom did they have visitors that it took *Sœur* St. André a moment to move toward the door after they had heard the knock. *Sœur* St. André stood in shock when she opened the door.

"Oh, my! Nicolas!" *Sœur* St. André cried aloud. "Is it really you? How are you? *Bienvenue!* Welcome! *Entrez! Comment allez-vous?*" Questions tumbled from her mouth, giving her brother no chance for response.

Taking off his cape and hat and scraping the spring mud from his boots, Nicolas began his response. "I am very well, *Dieu merci!* Our mother sends her best greetings for the Paschal Season and her love." Though he no longer had the boyish appearance that had belied his youth ten years earlier when he had visited her at the

Motherhouse before leaving for Texas, Nicolas still had a youthful smile; and his wild, curly brown hair did not seem to go with his priestly collar.

After introductions, *Sœur* Polycarpe served him a cup of coffee and refilled *Sœur* St. André's cup as well as her own.

"Oh, how I love the aroma of fresh coffee. We don't always have real coffee in Texas and we certainly don't have any of our wonderful French coffee." He took a deep breath. "This smells heavenly. Until one doesn't have them, one doesn't realize how valuable small, simple things are," he finished in a somewhat philosophical tone.

Conversation was lively for the next few hours as Nicolas regaled the two religious with story after story of the faraway Texas wilderness. A diocese the size of half the continent of Europe was nearly unimaginable; and tales of Indians and cowboys, entrepreneurs and immigrants made his experiences as a priest in a mission land seem implausible. Though he had written often to his family, the descriptions in his letters did not bring to life his adventures as a priest in a foreign land as his verbal telling now was able to do. He told his rapt audience of the growing numbers of French and German immigrants who were flooding into Texas because land was cheap and *empresarios* had plenty to sell at give-away prices to men who would promise to work hard and build up the Texas economy.

The first wave of immigrants who had come in the 1840's was now settled into villages that they had carved by hand out of bleak, sometimes desert-like land. Now with growing families, they wanted churches for their wives and schools for their children. His letters had mentioned *l'abbé* Claude Dubuis, the vicar general for the San Antonio area and their bishop, John Odin, who resided in Galveston although he traveled constantly throughout the enormous diocese. In Nicolas' telling these two men were larger-than-life characters who had braved disease, drought, flood, and fierce opposition to the faith to re-establish Catholicism in Texas. The hard work of the Franciscans, according to Nicolas, left behind a number of missions that were operational; but currently, the type of Catholic was shifting from Mexicans and Indians to people from the United States and growing numbers of European immigrants. The few French priests were overwhelmed by the needs that had arisen since the defeat of Mexico by the Texians in 1836. In under a quarter of a century, especially since statehood in 1845, the number of Catholics in Texas had more than doubled; the general population had mushroomed. More priests were needed and, though Bishop Odin had been successful in establishing the semi-cloistered French Ursulines in convents in Galveston and San Antonio, no Sisters were available who could start and operate parish schools in the small villages. So much needed to be done, and Christ never had enough hands to bring His salvation to those who yearned for it.

The nuns, pelting Nicolas with question after question, sat spellbound as he responded so rapidly that they feared he would run out of breath! As he told them of the Comanche Indians, his eyes were as big as saucers. As he spoke of holding his brother Celestin while he died of yellow fever, they were pools of tears. His audience felt every emotion with him. Only because hunger began to overtake them did they stop for supper. While the nuns prepared sliced ham, cheeses, bread, butter, and fried mush, Nicolas went to the rectory to ask the pastor for hospitality. When twilight set in, his sister had insisted that he stay the night, though he traveled extensively after sunset in Texas without giving it a second thought.

Throughout supper and late into the night, the storytelling continued with Sœur St. André sharing her experiences in Heiligenberg, and Nicolas painting vivid pictures of deserts, swamps, pine forests, swollen rivers, wolves, mountain lions, deer, and wild boars.

"You and I were always so competitive when we were children," Sœur St. André confessed to Nicolas. "But, I have to say: your stories are far and away besting mine tonight. My tame-tales of French villages could never keep up with your stories of the wilds of Texas! I surrender," she laughed, holding her hands up in front of her.

"You could share these experiences, too, you know," Nicolas said with only a slight tease in his voice. "Actually, I'm serious," his voice dropped into a somber tone. "We need you in Texas—and as many of your Sisters who would be willing to come. Would you ever consider it?" he asked in a pleading voice. His dark eyes were intense and his jaw set as he rushed on, fearing a negative reply. "I told *l'abbé* Dubuis that I would speak with you and he was very positive toward the idea. I've told him about your congregation and he thinks that you are just the type of Sisters that are most needed for the schools. He also wants some Sisters for hospitals. Do you have nurses?"

"No, we don't have nurses," *Sœur* St. André said, laughing. "I have to admit that the invitation is enticing. I'll have to give this much thought, and, of course, prayer. *Le père* Moye told us: '... **we must leave it up to the Lord, accept guidance from this supreme director whose wisdom is infallible ...**'" His own decision to leave France and go to China is a beacon to us, but so far we have no foreign missions. I doubt if *Mère* Basilisse will be open to the idea. She doesn't think in those terms. *Mère* Constantine, on the other hand ...," her voice trailed off as her next thought brought her back to reality. "And, actually, *l'abbé* Larvette doesn't seem inclined to the foreign missions either. But, I will ask them when I have the opportunity."

"That's all we ask. I'll write to *l'abbé* Dubuis to let him know that I've spoken with you."

It was past midnight when they retired; and though *Sœur* Polycarpe was exhausted, she admitted that she had never had such an entertaining evening. Nicolas came for breakfast the next morning before returning to LaWalck. The brother and sister knew that the vowed life they had undertaken for the sake of Jesus' kingdom would bind them together, regardless of where they served God's people.

The school term came to a successful close and both *Sœur* Polycarpe and *Sœur* St. André were happy to return to St. Jean-de-Bassel for the summer gathering. Attending classes on pedagogy and the catechism filled the days, leaving the evenings free for visit-

---

*   **The Directory, p. 217.**

ing and rest. *Sœur* Polycarpe spent a number of days in the infirmary and *Sœur* St. André was certain that she would be returning to Batzendorf with another companion, or alone.

She was wrong. Both Sisters were reassigned to St. Abrogast's school and *Sœur* St. André barely hid her disappointment as *Mère* Basilisse gave her the assignment. Even *Mère* Basilisse's assurance of her understanding and her prayers were little consolation. *Sœur* St. André knew the year would be hard, if not impossible.

As the winter months of 1861-62 set in, *Sœur* Polycarpe was often feverish and never felt well though she had begun the school term with faithful attention to her students. Having agreed to the same division of classes as the previous year, *Sœur* St. André again took the younger students because there were more of them and they required undivided attention. The fewer older students, requiring less energy, were better suited to *Sœur* Polycarpe who, having had most of them in their primer years, would find them easier to manage. Since teaching the older children often accompanied the duties of directing the school, that assignment also carried more status. This division of classes allowed *Sœur* Polycarpe to save face though the tasks of organizing classes and equipment most often fell to *Sœur* St. André.

During their first year together in Batzendorf, *Sœur* Polycarpe and *Sœur* St. André had established a respectful and professional relationship, but in this, their second year at St. Abrogast's, the strain of the situation required that both Sisters depend on prayer and Providence to maintain their relationship on an even keel.

Unable to go to school at least two days out of each week because of illness, *Sœur* Polycarpe's students and duties regularly fell to *Sœur* St. André. In itself, the task of teaching all the students was not very challenging. *Sœur* Polycarpe simply would not surrender her post, though her health was diminishing by the day. The continued uncertainty, however, was trying and grated on *Sœur* St. André. Though the beads on her rosary had been black in September, now, only two months later, they were worn to a light brown by her prayers for patience.

Grateful that *Sœur* St. Andre had been sent to Batzendorf, the pastor of St. Abrogast Parish was as supportive as possible. *Sœur* Polycarpe was well-loved by the people of the tiny village who kept the two nuns supplied with rich soups, bread, eggs, milk, and butter. Having grown accustomed to dining with the Rohlmans in Heiligenberg, *Sœur* St. Andre's culinary skills had begun to wane and she was very grateful for their generosity.

Sœur St. André, realizing *Sœur* Polycarpe's frailty, took on more and more of the household tasks and a dear friend of *Sœur* Polycarpe, Madame Kübler, occasionally helped them with housework, cooking and laundry. Just maintaining their habits of wool serge, mending them as needed, starching and ironing their *guimpes* and bonnets, and washing their linens required nearly full-time effort.

As fall turned to winter *Sœur* Polycarpe became less and less able to care for herself, and she spent a full day in the classroom only infrequently.

Having planned to visit her family in LaWalck during the two-week holiday for Christmas, *Sœur* St.André made arrangements with Madame Kübler, to look in on *Sœur* Polycarpe, spending the nights if necessary.

Madame Feltin was thrilled to have her daughter home for a few days. Widowhood was lonely for her though Pierre's and Marie-Anne's families took good care of her. The holiday reunion with family and her mother's good spirits buoyed *Sœur* St.André. The time away allowed her to gain perspective on her situation; and when she returned to Batzendorf in time for Epiphany, *Sœur* St. André decided to take her situation in hand.

The two Sisters sat down to a feast to celebrate the advent of the Magi. Madame Kübler had brought them part of a roasted goose, vegetables, a tureen of soup, and fresh bread. Once they had enjoyed their dinner, *Sœur* St. André began the conversation that she had rehearsed a dozen times while she was at her family home in LaWalck.

"*Sœur* Polycarpe, how are you feeling—really. Please don't tell me that you are well. I know that is not the case. Please be honest." Her words were straightforward, but her tone was kindly.

The older nun began as though she were going to give her standard response; but then she leaned heavily on the table with her face in her hands, revealing her constant exhaustion.

"It is no use. I am ill. I know it to be so. It would be an exaggeration to say that you have been caring and tender in the last months," she said with a wry smile, "but you have been concerned in your own way. I know, too, that I am a burden to you, and I am not fulfilling my school duties." She sighed as she covered her eyes, hoping that *Sœur* St. André would not see the tears beginning to well up.

"*Ma sœur*, I admit that I have at times been short-tempered and for that I am sorry. But, I have done my best to keep the school going and to care for you. I simply cannot go on with this uncertainty."

As she lifted her head, *Sœur* Polycarpe's frightened, tear-filled eyes stunned *Sœur* St André. *Sœur* Polycarpe had suddenly realized that her fate at St. Abrogast lay in her companion's hands.

Not wishing to prolong the ill nun's fear, *Sœur* St André hurried on. "It is true: I do not believe that you can continue in the school. Each day is too uncertain. You have become very frail and the winter months will be hard. Here is what I propose. Let's ask Madame Kübler if she will come during the school days and stay here with you, preparing your meals and caring for your needs. You may remain at home and no longer attempt the classroom. Perhaps, if you feel strong on a given day, I can send a child to you for special tutoring. This way, you can remain here in Batzendorf until the summer when we can return to St. Jean together. Will this plan suit you?"

Startled by the proposition, a plan that she herself had never considered, *Sœur* Polycarpe nodded thoughtfully. "I would like that," she replied softly. *Sœur* St. André could feel her companion's relief at not having to return to the classroom and her joy at being able to stay in Batzendorf.

"But, how shall we pay Madame Kübler?" *Sœur* Polycarpe asked anxiously. "We have no money."

"Providence will provide. We'll speak with her together and see what she will require. Then we'll worry about money if we need to."

Both nuns were shocked at the arrangement Madame Kübler suggested when approached with their need. Willing to help with housekeeping and cooking and to tend to *Sœur* Polycarpe during the day, she wanted only her noon meal in return. Admitting that loneliness had begun to creep up on her since her daughters had moved away with their spouses, she would be grateful for *Sœur* Polycarpe's daily companionship.

January and February passed uneventfully. The school year progressed. Unhampered now by the frustration of not knowing whether *Sœur* Polycarpe would be in class, *Sœur* St. André was very able to handle all the students and the administrative duties with the very sturdy foundation in pedagogy and school administration that she had gained in Heiligenberg.

Since the tension that had grown between them was now gone, *Sœur* Polycarpe and *Sœur* St. André became close friends; and Madame Kübler, a very religious woman, was like a third member of their community, often praying the Office and the rosary with them. They spoke easily of *Sœur* Polycarpe's leaving St. Abrogast's and returning for a long rest at the Motherhouse.

The spring term flew by. Bidding a final farewell to Batzendorf was bittersweet for *Soeur* Polycarpe who was actually relieved that she was going home to the Motherhouse to recuperate. The villagers came to bid her *adieu* as the carriage left to take them to the stagecoach way station in Haguenau.

Arriving not too much the worse for wear at St. Jean-de-Bassel two days later, *Sœur* Polycarpe was warmly received by *Mère* Basilisse herself who personally helped her settle into the infirmary so that she could be properly cared for. *Sœur* Polycarpe's smooth adjustment to being a resident of the Motherhouse was a relief to *Sœur* St. André who regularly spent recreation time with her in the evening. *Sœur* Polycarpe took the opportunity of their visits to urge *Sœur* St. André to speak with *Mère* Basilisse about Texas. Though she would be the first to describe *Sœur* St. André as firm, straightforward, and generally lacking a soft or tender manner, *Sœur* Polycarpe also saw in her a spirit that would succeed in the rough wilderness of a place like Texas. Unable to dismiss her brother's repeated invitations to serve the foreign missions, *Sœur* St. André agreed to bring the subject up at her appointment during assignment time.

After the annual retreat, the ritual of posting times for appointments with *Mère* Basilisse's began. *Sœur* St. André spent several days wondering whom they would send with her to Batzendorf as she was fairly certain that she herself would be returning. Finally, her name appeared on the board. While she stood in the hallway awaiting her appointed time, *Sœur* St. André reviewed her thoughts on how to broach the subject of the Texan missions. She was quite surprised when she was called into *Mère* Basilisse's office by *Sœur* Constantine and doubly surprised when *Sœur* Constantine joined them. After initial pleasantries, the two superiors came straight to the point. *Mère* Constantine began.

"*Ma chère sœur*, we want to commend you on your initiative with *Sœur* Polycarpe. She has returned to us satisfied that her years in at St. Abrogast's school were greatly appreciated by the pastor as well as by the villagers. She seems only slightly regretful that she will not return. Your idea of having her friend companion her during school days worked very nicely. However, *ma sœur*, did it not occur to you to write to us and tell us of the arrangement?"

Sœur St. André, not expecting that question, was without response. Sensing her confusion, *Sœur* Constantine continued.

"Perhaps you believed that we would not have been able to offer you any help in the crisis, but we would have welcomed knowing that you were both struggling with a problem that had become insurmountable, and we would have assured you of our support and our prayers."

"But the problem wasn't insurmountable. I truly did not think that our mutually arrived at solution warranted bothering you. *Sœur* Polycarpe never mentioned a need to write to you and I never thought of it! Had we not been able to come to an understanding, I would have written. I was truly at my wit's end. Once *Sœur* Polycarpe and I came to an agreement, all was well."

"For myself, I completely understand your situation. *Mère* Basilisse wasn't even going to bring the matter to your attention as she, too, saw that the solution you and *Sœur* Polycarpe came to was best for the school. Actually, your initiative is appreciated and the success that resulted is admirable. We only suggest that future superiors may not be so accepting."

Sœur Constantine's remarks had caught *Sœur* St. André completely off guard. She felt confused as she realized that once again a well-meaning and creative response to a concern would not always be well received. *Sœur* Constantine's personal security in her authority seemed to welcome initiative and applauded its success. *Mère* Basilisse was somewhat less enthusiastic, but she was aging and her physical frailties probably contributed to her hesitancy. The forewarning about future superiors being noteworthy, *Sœur* St. André decided to develop a communication style that was more forthcoming.

Mère Basilisse spoke for the first time. "It is not really our intention to burden you with guilt about how you handled *Sœur* Polycarpe's needs. You did extremely well with a challenging situation and are to be congratulated. When we received *Sœur* Polycarpe's letter after Easter explaining her decision to return to St. Jean to recuperate and informing us of how you had supported her with a workable solution to her disabilities, we were somewhat impressed. She now seems so happy and settled, and we believe it is in part due to how the last months have gone. But *Sœur* Constantine believed that drawing your attention to the lack of communication was important, mostly for your own future in our congregation."

"*Merci beaucoup, ma mère*," *Sœur* St. André said humbly. She truly valued her Superior's trust in her and would not want to jeopardize it by thoughtlessly failing to keep her informed.

"Now—to the subject of St. Abrogast's in Batzendorf," *Mère* Basilisse continued. "We regret to tell you that we simply do not have another Sister to send with you now. Several of our novices who will conclude their studies in September have potential, but we're not certain that a young Sister will be helpful at this time." She paused to give *Sœur* St. André a chance to respond. *Sœur* St. André, basically grateful that she would not have a young novice pulling on her skirts, said nothing.

Taking *Sœur* St. André's silence for approval, *Mère* Basilisse went on. "Thus, you will once again be alone. Perhaps we can send someone next year. Do you think the pastor will be terribly disappointed?"

"He was hoping that there would be two of us, but he will understand. The school is running very smoothly. However, may I make a suggestion?"

"*Oui, ma sœur*. What is it?" *Mère* Basilisse asked.

"The woman who has assisted us in these past months, Madame Kübler, is widowed and her two daughters live some distance from Batzendorf. Not only was she very helpful with *Sœur* Polycarpe, but she also joined us frequently as we prayed the Office or the rosary. Would you mind if I asked her if she would like to continue helping me in the house, if the pastor approves, of course? She would be a wonderful companion. In addition, her home is in disrepair. Would you consider allowing her, again on the pastor's approval, to join me at the house I live in? She may refuse, but there is talk that one of her daughters might return with her family to Batzendorf. If so, they could repair her home and live there. This arrangement would give Madame Kübler daily chores, a good home, and a quieter environment."

"Yes, go ahead and talk with the pastor about your idea. But if Madame Kübler is in the least hesitant, do not press her."

"*Merci.* I will proceed cautiously. And now I have one more thing."

"What is it?" *Mère* Basilisse realized that their interview had lasted longer than she had intended, but as this was the last one before dinner, she sat back in her chair to listen.

"My brother Nicolas, a missionary priest in Texas in America, came to visit us this spring, right after Easter. He told us of the great needs of the Church in Texas: nursing sisters are needed, more semi-cloistered sisters who can run boarding schools are needed, and Sisters like us who can start up schools in villages are desperately needed. His Vicar is a priest named *l'abbé* Claude Dubuis. I believe he is a native of Lyons. Nicolas told him about us and *l'Abbé* is hoping that we might consider sending some Sisters to America to help him."

Having been caught by surprise with this idea, the Superior sat wide-eyed, stunned at the notion of sending Sisters to another continent.

"Why, *Sœur* St. André, we don't have enough Sisters to staff village schools here in Alsace and Lorraine! Having served alone in Heiligenberg for six years and now facing another mission alone, surely you don't believe we should send Sisters to the other side of the world!" Glancing over at *Sœur* Constantine for confirmation of her stance, she was startled to see that a faraway look had come into her assistant's eyes.

Mère Basilisse hurriedly concluded the interview. "It is nearly time for dinner, *ma sœur.* Thank you once again for your dedication to God's children. *Père* Moye continually reminded us that we should **'keep up the spirit of prayer and instill it in the children. Perform all your duties in union with God.'**[*] Let's remember his words as we begin a new year in the vineyards. We are more

---

[*] **The Directory, p. 169.**

than schoolteachers, *ma sœur*. We don't have to sail away to foreign lands to be missionaries!"

As the days of summer faded, the Sisters of Providence returned to the many villages which depended on them for the education of their children. Life at the Motherhouse continued with a rhythm of its own. The General Council, under the leadership of the beloved *Mère* Basilisse, tended to the needs of the growing numbers of aging and ill Sisters, and provided for the formation of ever-increasing numbers of young women who saw the apostolic religious life as a meaningful way to contribute to the education of the youth and the Church. *Sœur* Constantine, who also served as Mistress of Novices, provided significant support to *Mère* Basilisse who often felt weighed down with the duties of her office. *Père* Larvette continued to visit the Sisters in the villages and found that the pastors who had Sisters of Providence for the schools were mostly pleased. Word about the success of their schools spread from priest to priest bringing more requests from pastors who wrote to St. Jean-de-Bassel asking for Sister-teachers.

The arrival of a letter from *Monseigneur* John Odin, the newly appointed Archbishop of New Orleans, one fall day in 1862 was no surprise to *Mère* Basilisse. His Lordship explained that he was to be in Rome in the late fall and asked permission to call upon the Superiors at St. Jean-de-Bassel to place before them the grave needs of Texas. In her response, written to the Rome address that Archbishop Odin noted, *Mère* Basilisse indicated her reticence to initiate a foreign mission, but welcomed the Archbishop to their Motherhouse, should he choose to visit.

A second letter from Archbishop Odin, this time from Rome, laid out his request for Sisters who could begin parish schools in small Texas hamlets, but begged forgiveness as he was no longer able to make his request in person. The pope had recently appointed Claude-Marie Dubuis of Lyons, France, as the new bishop of Galveston, Texas. Bishop Dubuis' consecration to the episcopate was to be at St.

Irenaeus Seminary in Lyons on November 23, 1862. Odin's regret was apparent as he expressed his hopes that *Mère* Basilisse might be open to allowing even one or two of her Sisters to return with him when he sailed from Le Havre in February.

A long conversation between *Sœur* Constantine and *Mère* Basilisse ensued after the reception of the second letter.

"I believe that it is providential that His Lordship cannot come to ply us for Sister-teachers in person. We simply could not meet his request and the long journey here to Lorraine would have been a waste of his time," *Mère* Basilisse said.

"Perhaps now is not the time, *ma mere*; but, if we are to be true daughters of *Père* Moye, we must be open to sending Sisters to the foreign missions. We now have nearly three hundred Sisters; and though villages are clamoring for them for their schools, we must remember that *Père* Moye himself left the needs of France to spend ten years among those in China who did not even know of Jesus. Could we do less?" *Sœur* Constantine's final question gave *Mère* Basilisse pause.

"I agree that *Père* Moye has given us an undeniable challenge in his own response to God's call to take the gospel to foreign lands ... but, I just don't know. I'm no longer in good health and my days of being Superior General are numbered. *Père* Larvette, too, is hesitant about taking on more than we can manage. Let's wait and agree to look for the Providential signs that *Père* Moye always insisted would accompany God's call to new ventures."

"Very well, *ma mère*, we will wait." *Sœur* Constantine, recognizing that without *Mère* Basilisse's full and enthusiastic support, the Sisters would never feel confident in taking on a venture as bold as going to Texas, a pioneer land in a foreign country. She would be patient in waiting for a sign.

The two years alone in Batzendorf went by quickly for *Sœur* St. André. Meeting with her Superior to receive her assignment had become routine, and sensing an affinity with her, *Sœur* St. André was no longer hesitant about being frank with *Sœur* Constantine, who again was managing assignments in the summer of 1864.

"I am so sorry that *Mère* Basilisse is ill again," *Sœur* St. Andre began. "I fear that she has overtaxed herself. She is very self-giving as our Superior General. I pray that I can be only half as patient as she is. She is always affirming of us. We can only be grateful for all she does for us."

"Yes, but I fear that her days of being Superior General are numbered. She regularly speaks of stepping aside and allowing *Sœur* Adrienne to take more responsibility. Since I have the novices, I am limited in what I can do. *Sœur* Adrienne has more time to give to the detail of administration."

With the news that a change in administration might be in the offing, *Sœur* St. André took the opportunity to ask, "Do you think that we will ever be able to send Sisters to Texas. I still get letters from my brother priest begging me to consider the missions there. And, as time goes by, I feel more and more inclined to entertain the call."

"As *Père* Moye said so often, *'Either the project is God's will or it is not. If it is according to His holy will, He who is all-powerful has a thousand means, a thousand ways, to accomplish it.'* At this time, we must simply wait and see. I myself am no longer as positive about the project as I was two years ago. The terrible war that we hear about in America is frightening. I would never agree to send Sisters to a country that is at war with itself!"

"You are wise to consider that element. Nicolas writes to us that Texas has not been very involved in the war, but the economy there has suffered. I pray that it will be over soon."

"I, too. Now, to your situation for next year. You will return to St. Abrogast's as both teacher and director of the school. And, we have a Sister to send with you—*Sœur* Amarathe Fischer. Do you know her?"

---

* **The Directory,** p. 82.

"*Oui, ma sœur*! We have been in classes together. She seems very capable. I will welcome her. Though Madame Kübler has been a wonderful companion, she now has grandchildren and wishes to live with her daughter. Providence provides!"

"*Très bien*! It is agreed. We continue to be grateful to you for your service to God's people, especially the children. Let us pray for each other, and of course, to *Père* Moye. Providence will continue to provide!"

"*Merci beaucoup, ma sœur.*"

For the first time *Sœur* St. André had hope that the mission to Texas might develop. As the years had passed, she had felt a deepening desire to try the foreign missions. Continuing to reveal how hard life was in Texas, her brother's letters only served to make the minor deprivations in French villages seem insignificant. She constantly asked herself if she would prove strong enough for the trials that awaited her in Texas should she be sent. Her health continued to be good; she knew she had common sense; her background in opening and operating schools was ample.

The Sisters in the Batzendorf area met occasionally to support one another and to mentor those who were new in their positions. Gathering for the celebration of the Feast of the Immaculate Conception had become an annual occurrence. News had come from the Motherhouse that *Mère* Basilisse had turned over her duties to *Mère* Adrienne Frache and everyone had a comment on what the change would mean. Those who knew *Mère* Adrienne predicted a smooth transition; those who had special relationships with *Mère* Basilisse feared the change. Based on her summer conversation with *Sœur* Constantine, *Sœur* St. André was hopeful.

Time seemed to plod on, however, as *Sœur* St. André became more and more drawn to the foreign missions in Texas. Winter eventually became spring; spring melded into summer and her re-assignment in 1865 to Batzendorf, again with *Sœur* Amarathe, drove *Sœur* St. André to examine herself more carefully. Were her interests in serving the Church in Texas grounded in personal ambition and the attraction of acquiring a unique position in the congregation? Or was she motivated by a deepening desire to imitate Jesus who described himself as one who had no place to lay his head? She would like to think the latter, but the simplicity in her self-understanding made her suspicious. She realized that only prayer could bring her to a calm and courageous heart—available for wherever God would send her.

In addition to finding *Sœur* Amaranthe to be an amiable companion, *Sœur* St. Andre had found a good friend in *Sœur* André Keller who was missioned in the very small village of Keffendorf about ten miles from Batzendorf. Finding that they had similar interests, the two Sisters visited each other monthly and exchanged ideas on how to better involve their students in learning, recipes, and hopes and dreams about being good religious. Both parishes had held special devotions on the Sundays during the Lent of 1866, leaving no opportunities for the neighboring Sisters to visit with each other during the season of penance. A few days without school after Easter would be restorative. *Sœur* André had promised that she would find a way to come to Batzendorf.

Having obtained a ride with a Keffendorf farmer, *Sœur* André arrived at *Sœur* St. André's and *Sœur* Amarathe's house by mid-morning the Monday of Easter week. She had barely gotten in the door when she said to *Sœur* St. André, "I have something for you. Last week a letter came for you from the Motherhouse, but it was delivered to me by mistake—I suppose because there is no last name and our names are so similar. You can see how the name of the town is smeared—I suppose they though it was Keffendorf, not Batzendorf. But when I saw it, I knew it was for you." She handed *Sœur* St. André a long envelope. The clear script was unmistakably that of *Sœur* Constantine. What could she be writing? Since the term was nearly over, it was unlikely that the letter was about the school assignment.

"Do you mind if I read it?" *Sœur* St. André asked politely.

"Of course not," both Sisters replied in unison. Receiving a letter from the Motherhouse was an unusual occurrence, and though both on-lookers were curious, they busied themselves with preparations for dinner.

"Oh, my," were the only words that came from *Sœur* St. André as she read the letter carefully. "Oh, my."

Unable to contain her curiosity any longer, *Sœur* André asked, "What is it, ma *sœur*? Is anything wrong?"

"No, no, nothing is wrong. *Sœur* Constantine says that the Council is seriously considering sending two or three Sisters to Texas. She has had a letter recently from His Lordship Bishop Dubuis and he will be coming to St. Jean-de-Bassel while we are all home for the summer. The Council wants to talk with me about the possibility of serving in the missions when I come to the Motherhouse. Nothing is certain, and *Sœur* Constantine warns me not to get my hopes up, but she indicates that *Mère* Adrienne is not completely opposed to the idea of a foreign mission."

"Oh, my," the other Sisters said in unison. Completely surprised by the turn of events, they were speechless.

The contents of the letter set *Sœur* St. André on edge. She continued her duties at St. Abrogast's school, but no longer focused on the needs of her students. She realized that, in a way, her spirit had already gone to America. Though *Sœur* Constantine advised her to accept that all the planning at this point was tentative, her own strategizing felt permanent. Each year, in every mission, she had packed her belongings as though she would not return and had left the schoolroom ready for a newly appointed replacement. But this year was different. As she locked up the school and turned the keys over to the mayor, her tone had a ring of finality to it as she bid him *adieu*. Remaining abandoned to Providence, she understood that she might be somewhere in Alsace or Lorraine in the new school year, but in her heart she sensed that her horizons would be turned westward.

That summer of 1866 was unforgettable. In her meeting with the Council, *Sœur* St. André found *Mère* Adrienne somewhat hesitant about the Texas venture. However, *Sœur* Constantine was very enthusiastic and plied her with questions. What did she imagine her destination in Texas to be? How would she learn English—or could her French and German suffice? Would she be near her brother? Would two Sisters be able to make a difference? Did she feel able to take on the responsibilities for the success of difficult and uncertain duties for the Church in a far-off land?

Her often-tentative responses to these and another dozen questions left her exhausted and basically unclear as to whether or not the Council would push forward with the Texas project.

During the nearly two-hour interview *Sœur* St. André felt an intense scrutiny. As she left the room, she had no idea if the Council would consider her to be a viable candidate for the possible mission in America. All she had been told was that a lengthy letter from Bishop Dubuis had outlined possibilities for the mission and that he himself was coming to St. Jean-de-Bassel in late July to speak with the Council.

When *Sœur* St. André asked the Council whom they were thinking might be her companion, they continued to be vague, but mentioned two or three names. The only Sister that *Sœur* St. André knew personally was *Sœur* Alphonse Boëgler with whom she had served in Epfig over a dozen years earlier. Though they had not remained close, she regarded *Sœur* Alphonse highly, believing her to be a sincere religious. However, she placed the decision about her companion in the hands of Providence. Providence would provide.

A few days before the annual retreat was to begin, *Sœur* St. André was called to the office of *Mère* Adrienne. The tall, gray-haired priest who stood as she entered the office seemed familiar, though *Sœur* St. André knew she had never met him. His kind blue eyes sparkled with a youthful enthusiasm belying his fifty years, and he carried

**Claude-Marie Dubuis,
Second Bishop of Galveston
(Courtesy: Catholic Archives of
Texas, Austin, Texas)**

a worn look about him. His deeply tanned, lined face held an assurance of a wisdom that only the survival of difficult circumstances could bring into a person's life.

"*Monseigneur* Dubuis, may I present *Sœur* St. André," *Mère* Adrienne said simply by way of introduction.

His Lordship extended a hand in a gesture of familiarity that was unheard of in the Church of France. "I am pleased to meet you, *ma sœur*. I also bring you greetings from your dear brother, *Abbé* Nicolas."

The somewhat stilted conversation that followed accomplished little more than to reveal each participant's uncertainty. *Sœur* St. André knew that possibly she was interacting with her future Superior; Bishop Dubuis wondered if this dark-eyed nun with the heavy black eyebrows would be up to the daunting task of carving out a parochial system of education for the Catholic Church of Texas; *Mère* Adrienne's countenance revealed little more than her hesitancy over the entire project under consideration; *Sœur* Constantine's positive demeanor spoke of her own growing commitment to the venture. The short dialogue ended with *Sœur* St. André being dismissed as Bishop Dubuis agreed to speak to the entire Congregation at the four o'clock gathering for spiritual reading, a daily conference which usually focused on some type of spiritual topic.

By four o'clock in the afternoon, over two hundred Sisters of Providence had gathered in Seat of Wisdom salon. Another fifty Sisters lined the wide hallway outside the salon, and most of the remaining one hundred Sisters would have been in attendance if space had allowed.

A short introduction by *Sœur* Constantine presented His Lordship Claude-Marie Dubuis, a native of Lyons, France, and the second Bishop of Galveston, Texas, to the Sisters of Providence of St. Jean-de-Bassel. Always hungry for news and information about the universal Church, the Sisters of Providence who spent their years in small, isolated French villages warmly welcomed their speaker from halfway around the world. No one in the room at the time knew that this encounter would launch a relationship that would change everyone in attendance.

Over his twenty years as a missionary to Texas, Bishop Dubuis, hoping to enlist material and spiritual support for the vast diocese known as Texas, had spoken to legions of groups—seminarians, French parishes, religious brothers and sisters, and other groups of Catholic laity. He began easily with his own story of God's calling him to mission work while he was lying ill in the seminary infirmary at St. Irenaeus Seminary in Lyons, France.

"I have to admit," he noted, "I really didn't think that God would take my promise to work in the foreign missions so seriously. I humbly acknowledge that all I really hoped for was a restoration of my health!" The Bishop's ability to laugh at himself and confess his youthful shallowness disarmed his audience. Each listener was immediately drawn into his confidence.

Tales of being the pastor of an Alsatian parish in the wilds of Texas caught up the Sisters into his narrative. As he told them of eating a monotonous diet of bacon or venison and cornmeal mush, surviving yellow fever, burying his first assistant Father Chazelle, riding endless hours on horseback to his other parish in a German town called Fredericksburg, fighting both flood and famine, Bishop Dubuis loomed larger-than-life to his over two hundred listeners. *Sœur* St. André had taken a chair in a location where she could see the faces of the listening Sisters. She saw that they were spellbound by the Bishop's stories and now and then a gasp of surprise would rise in the room when a particularly grisly episode was related.

A statue of Our Lady of Wisdom holding the Infant Jesus watched over the room full of nuns. The natural-looking folds of her blue gown and the gleaming gold of her halo made the statue seem both life-like and ethereal at the same time. Recent reports of Our Lady's apparition at the small village of Lourdes had roused the French heart and a faith in her abiding presence had also been renewed in the Sisters of Providence. *Sœur* St. André gazed at the statue for a long time as Bishop Dubuis told story after story. The eyes of the Virgin seemed to beckon her directly. She imagined that the Holy Child was being offered to her to hold as Bishop Dubuis finally began his appeal to them to embrace the children of the poor Texas villages in the same way they had so effectively educated the children of France.

Our Lady of Wisdom Statue
St. Jean-de-Bassel
(Photo: Sister Diane Langford, CDP)

"My dear Sisters, our parishes need schools in order for the true faith to be as rooted in Texas as it is France. Germans, Poles, French Alsatians, and Czechs are all seeking solace from poverty and the threat of war in the New World where each hard-working man can find a fortune. The Catholics who are emigrating to Texas and those faith-seekers who are joining the Catholic Church in legion numbers want their parishes to have a place of prominence in their villages and they want their parishes to have schools. I have spoken to your Superior, *Mère* Adrienne and to her assistants. I am hoping that they will allow at least two or three of you to join me in this great endeavor. As I close I place the mission of Jesus in Texas in your prayers and I place an invitation to join in this holy work in your hearts. If any of you have questions, I will try to answer."

Several Sisters had relatives who had immigrated to Texas from the southern region of Alsace, hoping to establish vineyards or farms. Questions about their success brought the Bishop to speak of how difficult life on the frontier really was. Crops were subject to drought, hail, and pestilence and those that did survive those might succumb to the occasional plague of grasshoppers or locusts.

Farmers' wives were laden with the unending tasks of rearing children, preparing meals from nearly inedible provisions, mending the little clothing they had or trying to make new clothes from next to nothing, and attempting to get the dry soil to bring forth a kitchen garden. Their parish community played an integral part in both the support of their faith as well providing them with a modicum of a social life. The women of Castroville, the Bishop was sure, would especially welcome Sisters who could not only teach their children but could offer them spiritual companionship that would strengthen their faith.

The history of Texas was also a subject of interest to the Sisters. They had heard from priests who had gone to Texas as seminarians that Texas used to be an independent country and not part of the United States. Was that true?

Bishop Dubuis gave them a brief sketch of Texas history; and by the time he had finished they were at least conversant on the Battle of the Alamo in 1836, the heroes of the war between the Texians and Mexico—Sam Houston, David Crocket, and James Bowie. He told them that Colonel Bowie, commander at the Alamo had become a Catholic and that he and the other heroes of the Alamo were buried under the altar in the Spanish church, San Fernando, in San Antonio. The years of independence from Mexico under the presidency of Sam Houston had been complicated, the Bishop related, but had yielded an entrepreneurial development of a vast wilderness into cultivated farms and growing villages. Joining the United States in 1845, Texas had taken the final step toward stability. The Bishop now administered a diocese that surpassed in size the nations of France and Spain put together in a state that would always consider itself a land of independence; a state where the visionary Bishop could see vast ranches, mushrooming cities, hundreds of parishes, hospitals, orphanages, schools, academies, and universities in the future that lay before it. If only he could find priests, nuns, and brothers who would help him.

The Sisters loved the Bishop and applauded him at length when he finished by giving them his episcopal blessing. Though he had used every minute of the hour allotted to spiritual reading, the Sisters remarked later that they could have listened to his resonant voice forever.

During the annual retreat, *Sœur* St. André was especially introspective. Her imaginings of *Père* Moye's work in China filled her prayer as she considered the real possibility that she might be sent to America. Would she be able to learn a new language as *Père* Moye had done? Would she be able to tolerate foods that the average Frenchman might consider vile? Would she be able to live in a house that would not be considered fit for animals in France? Would she be able to withstand a climate that sounded like the deserts of Africa? These haunting questions drove her into the arms of Providence for assurance that nothing could happen from which Providence would not protect her. At the end of her retreat, *Sœur* St. André was resolved to accept the call to begin a mission in America.

Thinking that the Council had come to an agreement that the mission to America was acceptable, *Sœur* St. André entered *Mère* Adrienne's office to receive her assignment for the coming year, certain that her life was going to change forever. She was shocked and disappointed that no such plan had been approved. Reasons for the lack of acceptance of Bishop Dubuis' invitation centered on *Mère* Adrienne's own fearfulness that such a mission might disrupt the community or end in the loss of vocations for the Sisters who went to America. Sister St. André couldn't help the tears that came to her eyes, and she knew that *Mère* Adrienne could see the depth of her disappointment. She hardly knew what to say when *Mère* Adrienne told her that she would be returning to Batzendorf with *Sœur* Amarathe and a third Sister, *Sœur* Marie Jerome.

"I see that this development has, to say the least, surprised you, *ma très chère fille*," *Mère* Adrienne said tenderly. "I am sorry. *Sœur* Constantine has continued to support the mission to Texas very strongly. We have arrived at something of a compromise that should help you feel less pained. Bishop Dubuis indicated to us that he would be in Strasbourg in late August. Since Batzendorf is fairly close to Strasbourg, we suggest that you make an appointment to talk in detail with him about this whole venture. If, after that conversation, you truly believe that God is calling us to open a mission in Texas, we will approve. At this point, two other Sisters are willing to accompany you, but we will not make firm plans for their change until you have determined the possibility of a successful experience. *Père* Moye always told us to read the "signs of the times" and, to tell you the truth, I have come to accept that, with more and more Alsatians and Germans going to Texas, perhaps we, too, are being challenged to let go of our comfortable ways and venture forth into the unknown where Providence will await us."

"*Oh, ma mère*, your idea is very encouraging."

"You see, *ma sœur*, this Bishop will become your Superior, your support, your challenger, and your champion. You must know if you can work closely with him and if you can trust him."

"I now understand your wisdom, *ma mère*. I will take a position of caution when I go to see him. Our entire Congregation is being engaged in this venture and I would never want to lead us astray."

"Thank you, my daughter. Here is the seminary in Strasbourg where Bishop Dubuis said he would be and the dates that he thought he would be available. Simply write to him from Batzendorf and ask for an appointment. After you have met with him, inform us of your experience of him. The reason we are sending *Sœur* Marie Jerome to Batzendorf is to insure a smooth transition at St. Abrogast's school in case you are willing to accompany Bishop Dubuis to America. I believe he intends to sail from LeHarve at the end of September."

"*Oui, ma mère.* That is a very good plan. *Sœur* Amarathe is very capable of administering the school. There should be no problem."

CHAPTER VII

EMIGRÉS

Following the close of the retreat on July 26, *Sœur* St. André returned to Batzendorf with immense excitement. Within a few days after arriving at St. Abrogast's parish, she made her way to Keffendorf to talk over her possible future with her friend, *Sœur* André.

"What are you going to say to his Lordship," *Sœur* André asked, her eyes sparkling with enthusiasm for her friend's future.

"I have been thinking about this and I believe that it will be important to tell him of my background in education and the diversities that I have experienced: beginning the school in Heiligenberg, living with the Jewish family there, living alone in Batzendorf. I don't know—I guess whatever else comes to my mind. I think that he will be looking for evidence that I can be flexible and yet stand on my own two feet."

"I concur. Oh, how I wish I were going with you! I spoke to *Mère* Adrienne during my summer interview, you know. I, too, want to be a missionary and this venture would suit me well. Do you think the Bishop would accept me? *Mère* Adrienne sounded as though perhaps I would be given a chance."

"But, *ma sœur*, what about your health? Each winter you seem to have a bad cold and cough. Are you sure?"

"I really want to go. *Mère* Adrienne expressed the same concerns, but—oh, I don't know," she finished weakly. "Maybe I am too frail now." She sounded both resigned and unsure at the same time.

"I've written to His Lordship and expect to hear from him any day. As soon as I hear, I will go to Strasbourg. *Monsieur* Schmitt has agreed to take me. He regularly goes there for business. The journey will take the better part of a day. Then I will stay over two nights with some Sisters His Lordship is acquainted with in Strasbourg. I should be back here in Batzendorf within three days. If my interview with his Lordship goes well, I will simply pack my valise and return to St. Jean-de-Bassel. I saw no reason to unpack my trunk!" Her plans spilled out in waves of excitement. Making this final statement with determination toward her still-unknown future, she smiled broadly in joyful anticipation of the venture.

The two Sisters spent the rest of the day gossiping about their wonderful summer at St. Jean-de-Bassel, especially relishing their memories of the good meals that had come out of the kitchen: the delicious bread, the savory soups, and the pastries. Their mouths watered as they remembered how wonderful the food had been.

"I'm afraid that our noon meal here will not be nearly as delicious. I had only what the villagers have given me to make a soup: some pig's feet from a recent slaughter, a few carrots, and some late potatoes. But we do have good bread and butter!" *Sœur* André concluded proudly.

"Have no concern, *ma sœur*. I will remember your wonderful soup when I am in Texas trying to make do with whatever comes to our table!"

The two friends enjoyed both their meal and one another's company. The day passed all too quickly as both realized that the distance from France to Texas could bring their friendship to an end.

The letter that arrived from Bishop Dubuis the next day was not a surprise and *Sœur* St. André wrote him back immediately assuring him that she would be in Strasbourg on the day given for the appointment.

"Ma chère sœur, come in. *Entrez!"* Bishop Dubuis' hospitality was effusive even though he was not in his own home. "I trust that your arrangements with the Ursulines are satisfactory." This last sentence seemed to be more of a question than a statement of fact.

"Oui, Monseigneur, quite satisfactory." *Sœur* St. André remembered the Bishop as just short of courtly in his demeanor at St. Jean-de-Bassel, and she was pleased that he displayed this same type of behavior toward her when her Superiors were not present.

"Tell me, *ma sœur*, why do you wish to go to Texas?" Bishop Dubuis went right to the subject at hand.

"Monseigneur, I have served in four villages in France, one as a candidate, before entering, and three since my novitiate but, my brother Nicolas's letters have opened my heart to new possibilities. His last letters have been no less than haunting. I simply could not continue to disregard the possibility that God might want me to consider this new work. So many of our Alsatian people have gone to Texas to find their fortune. I believe that they deserve to know their faith no less than those who remain here in France. But, *Monseigneur,* I have one concern."

The Bishop's mind raced as he grew anxious that this teacher might be having second thoughts about coming with him to Texas. However, he calmly asked, "What is it, *ma sœur?*"

"You must know that I have what we call in this area of France an 'Alsatian temperament.' I tend to act quickly, speak brusquely and, sometimes, think only afterwards. It is a great cross for me, but I do work constantly to keep myself in check."

Sœur St. André's candor was both refreshing and appealing to this wilderness Bishop who began at once to see that an "Alsatian temperament" might be an asset in the milieu that awaited her in Texas. His tone was comforting and fatherly. "Oh, *ma sœur,* I'm not certain that we need to worry about that. I am more concerned with your professional background. Do you know how to start schools?"

Relieved that his response was dismissive, *Sœur* St. André, moved quickly to her answer. *"Oui, Monseigneur.* I began the school in Heiligenberg and have had various experiences with different types of villages and different types of living arrangements. I have lived alone; I have lived with a Jewish family; I have lived with a lovely woman in Batzendorf. Providence has provided me with many experiences."

"Ah—Providence. My mother has a deep devotion to Providence which she has instilled in me." The bishop's blue eyes became intense and *Sœur* St. André felt as though they were boring right through her. "Do you truly trust Providence, *ma sœur?*"

Believing that her response to this question could determine her future, *Sœur* St. André said simply. "I pray daily that I can trust Providence more deeply, and I know I could never have survived all that I have experienced in the last nineteen years without depending on Providence. My heart belongs to Providence. I will allow Texas—or any place that I serve—to have a place in my heart. But, it belongs to Providence," she said adamantly. "Our holy founder, *Père* Jean-Martin Moye, said, **'We should rely so much on Providence that we do not know and we do not even want to know what will happen to us in the future, and how our life will end, nor what means God will eventually use to provide our needs.'***"

As the Bishop heard the young Sister speak the words of her founder, he believed that Providence would be the binding force in their relationship. If they could both remain reliant on Providence, Providence would see them through. However, being the practical man that he was, he waited until her answers to all of his questions were complete before concluding the interview with his decision.

"*Ma sœur*, I believe that you will make a good missionary in Texas. Your Alsatian temperament, if reined in," he noted with a smile, "will serve you well. Our life there is, to say the least, challenging. For the men who have come to be priests there, the loneliness of the small villages can be crucifixion. I cannot promise that it will be less for you. Do you accept this?"

"*Oui, Monseigneur*," *Sœur* St. André said simply.

"In that case, I will write to *Mère* Adrienne asking for your services. I believe, too, she has at least one more Sister to send. I will

---

* **The Directory, p. 354.**

leave that appointment to her. It is you that I had to be certain of. I hope that we will work together for a long time."

"And, I had to be certain of you as well, *Monseigneur*. In a way, the rest of my life is in your hands," *Sœur* St. André said with a sparkle in her dark eyes and a smile at play as she spoke the words.

The wise bishop laughed out loud. This woman's humor was another good sign!

His instructions were simple: he planned to leave Lyons for LeHavre around the first of September, and *Sœur* St. André and her companion should be in Lyons by August 25. His party would then travel together to LeHavre where they would sail to New York City in America. Realizing as the—or should she say "her"—Bishop spoke that everything from now on was a strange mixture of beginning and end, *Sœur* St. Andre began to feel queasy, not specifically from fear, but more from an anticipation of the unknown. Each assignment that she had been given previously as a Sister of Providence had been an opportunity to embrace the unknown. Though she had often felt this same distress in her stomach, she had never faltered, for the unknowns always had the same name: Providence.

After returning to Batzendorf, *Sœur* St. André wrote to *Mère* Adrienne at St. Jean-de-Bassel explaining her thoughts about working with Bishop Dubuis and the viability of a mission in Texas. Her letter was filled with enthusiasm, prompting Mère Adrienne to call an immediate meeting of the General Council to discuss the future.

"*Sœur* St. André will be here in a few days, *mes sœures*. How shall we help her prepare for Texas?" *Mère* Adrienne said to her council, hoping that the anxiety in her heart would not be heard in her voice.

"First, we must speak with *Sœur* Alphonse," *Soeur* Constantine replied. "She is expecting this assignment, but the sooner we confirm it, the better."

"You are correct," responded *Mère* Adrienne. "She will return from her visit to her family early next week. You were wise to have her return here instead of going directly back to Mittlebron."

"She has expressed a deep confidence in *Sœur* St. André. I fear that she is not as strong for this venture as *Sœur* St. André is, but Providence will provide. Both Sisters have tremendous faith and courageous hearts. We, too, must trust." *Sœur* Constantine's last remark was uttered in hopes of offering support to her Superior General whom she knew was very anxious about a mission in a foreign land that would take two of her Sisters so far from the Motherhouse.

"Shall we send three Sisters as we had originally planned? *Sœur* André is very willing. In my interview with her this summer, she expressed a deep desire to go to America?" *Sœur* Constantine asked the Council.

"I am not sure," *Sœur* Claire Seyer, Councilor, said. "I had a long talk with her after the retreat. Though she is willing, she herself indicates that her health is not good. She is so pale. I fear that she will not be able to hold up under the rigors of the journey and the deprivations they will find in Texas."

"I concur with *Sœur* Claire," former Superior General Basilisse said immediately. "Each year that I have interviewed *Sœur* André for her assignment, I have noted that her health seems a little more fragile. It would be too much of a risk to send her."

"I agree," *Mère* Adrienne added. "I fear that the Sisters would be devastated if something happened to a Sister on this venture. Let's not send her now. If it is her destiny to go to Texas, she will go in the future. And, it is my consideration that it is much more difficult for three Sisters to come to rely on one another than it is for two. Let's send *Sœur* St. André and *Sœur* Alphonse only. I am presuming as well that we are in agreement that *Sœur* St. André will have ultimate responsibility for eventualities in Texas?"

The other three council members nodded.

Sœur Claire expressed concern over how they were going to keep in touch with *Sœur* St. André. What would be their expectation regarding reports on the mission?

After discussion, they all agreed that, given the circumstances of a foreign mission, *Sœur* St. André should have certain latitude. They further believed that *Sœur* St. André should return to France in the summer of 1870 in order to make a full report. That would give her four years to see what was truly possible in the Texas wilderness.

The conversation then turned to the details of preparing the two Sisters for their departure. *Sœur* Constantine spoke up.

"*Ma mère*, please don't trouble yourself with details. Allow us to review our expectations with *Sœur* St. André to be certain that she and *Sœur* Alphonse have what they need for their journey. The two new missionaries should be here by the middle of next week. That gives us two weeks to get them ready. Don't trouble yourself."

"*Merci beaucoup, ma chère sœur.* I do feel weak and I believe I will need to retire." With a gracious nod to her three assistants, the Superior General concluded, "I gratefully leave everything in your most capable hands." After thanking her council for their on-going support and assistance, *Mère* Adrienne left the council chamber.

Interior, St. Jean-Baptiste Church in St. Jean-de-Bassel, France, 2007.
(Photo: Sister Diane Langford, CDP)

Both future missionaries were at St. Jean-de-Bassel in time for the house's celebration of the patroness of France, Our Lady of the Assumption, on August 15. For centuries, this late summer feast had drawn together the people of France who placed their coming harvests of grain and grapes under her protection. The farming village of St. Jean-de-Bassel used the occasion to pray that their farms would yield all that the village needed for the winter months. The beautiful bell of St. Jean Baptiste parish church rang out in deep, rich tones, calling the residents of the tiny village to the morning Mass.

Since the Sisters at the Convent did not have a chapel, they gathered regularly for daily Mass and on major feasts in the parish church of St. Jean Baptiste just across the courtyard in back of St. Anne Hall. *Sœur* St. André and *Sœur* Alphonse knelt together surrounded by the Sisters who lived in the Motherhouse, the novices who would soon be taking the state examination for teachers, and those who would be going into the novitiate towards the end of September. As *Sœur* St. André looked around the church, soaking in the baroque-styled beauty of the sanctuary, she was struck by how all of those gathered were deeply immersed in the process of waiting: farmers were waiting for their harvest to ripen; novices were waiting for an examination that would be a passport to their future as Sisters of Providence; young women were awaiting the reception of a habit and bonnet that would set them apart forever as Daughters of *Père* Moye; the old and infirm Sisters were awaiting eternity. Her eyes fell on *Sœur* Constantine and *Sœur* Claire who were kneeling in a front pew with *Mère* Adrienne. Were they, too, waiting? Waiting to launch a new project, a new extension of *Père* Moye's dream? Waiting to see what would happen with herself and *Sœur* Alphonse in Texas? Waiting to see how the other Sisters would accept this new venture?

Kneeling in prayer, *Sœur* St. André allowed her thoughts to turn to the meaning of today's feast, a feast that seemed apropos for the official beginning of her focus on a new undertaking. Assured of the fullness of the resurrection for all by Our Lady's assumption into eternal life, each Christian could be confident that worry need not accompany waiting. Each day on this earth was a day of waiting—but not for the insignificant occurrences of new missions or transitory experiences. Each day on this earth was a day to wait in hope for the fruits of the Resurrection of Jesus that are assuredly extended to each person of faith. The Feast of the Assumption was a day to renew one's hope that could grow while waiting.

The days ahead were filled with organizing the items they needed to take to America. The day after the Feast of the Assumption, *Sœur* St. André and *Sœur* Alphonse met with *Sœur* Constantine and *Sœur* Claire to review all of the council decisions in their regard. With only five days remaining before the two Sisters would be leaving for Lyons, both *Sœur* Constantine and *Sœur* Claire spoke with urgency. The missionaries were to defer to Bishop Dubuis in all things, considering him to be their ecclesiastical superior. Bishop Dubuis and the Bishop of Nancy had reached an understanding regarding the ecclesial identity of the Sisters of Providence in America. Though the two religious would remain Sisters of Providence of St. Jean-de-Bassel, for practical purposes they were to rely on Bishop Dubuis, obeying him without question in all matters. Since both *Sœur* St. André and *Sœur* Alphonse were expecting to profess perpetual vows within the next two years, the Bishop of Nancy had given Bishop Dubuis full authority to determine when those vows would be made.

"We will give you your teaching certificates even though they will mean little in America," *Sœur* Constantine said in one of the several planning meetings. "But if you return, you must have them or you will be required to sit for the examination again," she warned.

"We are presuming that you will attract other women desirous of entering the Sisters of Providence who want to give themselves to *Père* Moye's project in Texas. It will be your responsibility to help them to embrace their vocation as Daughters of *le Père* Moye and to know his writings as well as our Congregation's Constitution. We will give you several copies of our Constitution for future members and a copy of *Père* Moye's most well known instructions. In addition, we will send with you a bolt of black serge for capes and one or two bonnets and coifs in addition to your own," *Sœur* Claire added with practicality. "I am afraid, however, that if what you are taking is insufficient, you will be required to adapt what you find in Texas to your needs," she concluded.

Sœur Constantine then opened the letter that she had recently received from Bishop Dubuis. "I want to share with you both what your new Bishop says. He notes that his meeting with you, *Sœur* St. André, went very well. He believes that you are a strong candidate for missionary life. He adds that he trusts us to choose the other missionaries, as we seem to him to be women of good sense with a strong background in working in challenging situations here in France. Thus, he affirms that we are the exact type of Congregation that will be successful in creating a parochial school system in Texas. I might add that the Bishop thinks we are sending three Sisters; but, at this time, we will send only the two of you."

The two missionaries nodded seriously and *Sœur* Constantine went on.

"Bishop Dubuis outlines his travel arrangements. You are to travel to Lyons where you will meet the rest of his party at the Convent of the Sisters of the Incarnate Word and Blessed Sacrament. Everyone will leave together—first for Paris, and then on to LeHavre, where you will board the sailing ship *The Europa* for New York City in America. There you will transfer to another sailing vessel bound for his see city, Galveston, Texas. You will depart for Lyons on August 20 as the Bishop hopes to leave from Lyons for Paris on August 25."

Both Sisters listened intently. As each stage of their journey was reviewed, the excitement in the room grew tangible, and by the end of *Sœur* Constantine's discourse, the two future missionaries, anxious to make their personal preparations, were sitting on the edges of their chairs.

Having received all necessary instructions and agreeing to the expectations of their Superiors, they began to make their final plans. They had decided to take one trunk between them, realizing that transporting baggage could be costly. They also had decided to take one nearly new habit and one old habit each. Traveling in the old habit would save wear and tear on the new one, allowing it to last longer. Whatever else they would need would have to be found in Texas. Recalling their experience with that Christmas pageant in Epfig long years ago assured them both that between them they had enough ingenuity to come up with needed ideas on how to make-do if necessary.

Their departure for Lyons, scheduled for August 20, would give them a day of rest at the Convent of the Sisters of the Incarnate Word and Blessed Sacrament before their August 25 journey to LeHavre. Both new missionaries were ready to leave their convent home when a telegram from Bishop Dubuis arrived indicating that his plans for departure had changed and they were now to be in Lyons by September 20.

"You know, *ma sœur*," *Sœur* St. André said to *Sœur* Alphonse, "as we knelt in the parish church on the Feast of the Assumption, I was thinking about the meaning of waiting. I suspect that this is but the first of many delays that we will experience in the years to come. Perhaps we need to get used to accepting that our fate is not in our own hands, but in the hands of Providence."

"I think you are right, *ma sœur*. There must be some reason for us to spend another month here in the Motherhouse. Perhaps it is so that we can enjoy more of the wonderful meals! No telling what awaits us in Texas, much less on the boat as we cross the ocean!" *Sœur* Alphonse's responded, smiling. "Let's just make the best of having to enjoy *Sœur* Hildegard's delicious *kugelhopf*! It may be the last we'll ever see! I doubt if we can get almonds and raisins in Texas!"

"Yes, and I know that *Sœur* Hildegard will give us some of that special cheese if we ask her! Let's just enjoy ourselves. Providence has provided us with a last month of rest and relaxation." So resolved, they relished those last days with their Sisters.

As they were being jolted and jostled in the stagecoach to Nancy, their first stop before Lyons, *Sœur* St. André and *Sœur* Alphonse reminisced about their last month at the Motherhouse. The time had gone by all too quickly. Goodbyes were always hard, but the finality of this leave-taking was heartwrenching and took its toll on the Sisters at the Motherhouse. Elderly Sisters that *Sœur* St. André and *Sœur* Alphonse had known since they had come to St. Jean-de-Bassel bade them *adieu* with a finality that reflected their advanced age and impending mortality. Novices-to-be whispered about them and novices who were preparing for their state examination seemed distracted by their continued presence.

The two Sisters actually felt relieved when September 17 finally arrived. After the early morning Mass and breakfast, Jean-Pierre, now growing old, pulled the wagon around to the front of the Motherhouse and heaved their waiting trunk into the bed of the wagon. He had taken these two Sisters to the stage station in Sarrebourg each July for over fifteen years and then met them as they had returned in June. He, too, knew that this departure was different and his eyes were wet with tears as he helped them into the wagon. Perhaps he would never see them again. As they waved goodbye to the small group that had gathered in front of the massive entry to their Convent, *Sœur* Alphonse and *Sœur* St. André brushed the tears from their cheeks quickly lest they stain their crisply starched *guimpes*. Their Superiors, *Mère* Adrienne, *Sœur* Basilisse, *Sœur* Constantine and *Sœur* Claire had put on brave faces which they hoped would mask heavy hearts. Though committed to the project as an extension of that earliest venture of Marguerite LeComte who had set out from Metz to Befey with nothing but a knapsack—a project that had been the foundation of the Sisters of Providence of France—these Superiors had given their blessing to an undertaking with unknown consequences. Now they knew how *le Père* Moye must have felt. As they re-entered the main building of the Motherhouse, *Mère* Adrienne said in a voice that trembled slightly in the face of the import of what had just happened, "We will rely on *Père* Moye's insight. If our Sisters whom we have just sent to America **'are worthy daughters of Providence, they will study its designs, adore its dispositions, and far from murmuring at annoyances, they will be content with whatever might happen to them. Let** *us bless Providence.'*"* Having said that, she squared her shoulders and went resolutely back to her office.

The journey by stage to Nancy and then on to Lyons was long and arduous, but otherwise uneventful, and the two Sisters arrived at the Convent of the Sisters of the Incarnate Word and Blessed Sacrament tired but none the worse for wear. Welcomed warmly by Bishop Dubuis, they learned that his plans had been adjusted somewhat because *Mère* Angelique, the Superior of the Incarnate Word Sisters, was not going to give him Sisters for a hospital. The entire incident was a window into his mind, revealing a man who, not to be daunted, could fashion a new plan quickly with seemingly little effort. *Sœur* St. André instantly realized his tenacity and creativity when she met the three young women whom he had "received" into a non-existent religious order which he himself was only then establishing, using the Incarnate Word and Blessed Sacrament Sisters'community as a model. The new order, to be known as the Sisters of Charity of the Incarnate Word, would be nurses who would bring healing and hope to those racked with typhoid, smallpox, yellow fever, and hundreds of other diseases and ailments in the Texas diocese.

In the room they shared in the Convent in Lyons, the two Sisters of Providence recalled their tiny room in Epfig. Though exhausted from travel, they could not sleep in the face of all that loomed in front of them. Sacred silence gave way to their whisperings that night of September 22.

"I hardly know what to think! Imagine, creating a religious order overnight! Can you believe it?" *Sœur* Alphonse said to her companion as they lay awake in the darkness.

"I have given this so much thought since the ceremony yesterday when those three brave young ladies pledged themselves to our Lord and to Bishop Dubuis. He has such a magnetic personality. Who could refuse him! I suspect that he is very much like our own *Père* Moye, creative—even ingenious; tenacious, yet tender; and able to inspire the confidence of anyone! And so devoted to the needs of the

---

*   **The Directory, p. 296 and p. 250.**

poor! He imagines possibilities where others see only problems. So like *Père* Moye, don't you think?" When no answer came, she realized that *Sœur* Alphonse had gone to sleep.

Early the next morning, the two missionaries were awakened by the Convent bell. After the Mass said by Bishop Dubuis and a substantial breakfast, the travelers assembled themselves and their belongings in the front hallway, to await the carriers that the Bishop had hired to take them to the train station. Excited by the impending two-day train ride, first to Paris and then on to the port of LeHavre, a great sense of enthusiasm animated the several communities of Sisters gathered in the entry way. *Sœur* Regis Chavasseiux, a novice of the Sisters of the Incarnate Word and Blessed Sacrament smiled through her tears as she bade goodbye to a Convent she had so recently entered and to which she would never return. The three new Sisters of Charity of the Incarnate Word, clad in the hurriedly prepared habits of their host-Sisters, exhibited a look of fear on their young faces and Bishop Dubuis spent a few moments trying to calm them. Four Ursuline Sisters would meet them at the train station as would a number of seminarians from eastern France.

The Europa
(French postage stamp)

When the entire party gathered in LeHavre for the September 29 sailing of *The Europa*, the number of missionaries totaled thirty-five priests and seminarians and ten women religious, a diverse entourage of travelers whose commitment to Jesus had driven them to undertake an incredible journey. In the six weeks ahead, by sharing meager and monotonous rations, trying to stand upright on a rolling deck, surviving storm and seasickness, praying together and supporting one another with words of hope and encouragement, they would get to know one another in ways that only fellow travelers do.

Each night of the six-week voyage, Bishop Dubuis assembled his troop to pray Vespers and the rosary. Each night forty-five young voices lifted in unison, sending the strains of Gregorian chant into the black night on the deck of *The Europa* as they ended their night prayer by singing the *Salve Regina*. Each morning the missionaries rose before dawn and re-assembled on the pitching deck for Holy Mass. Never a man to waste time, the bishop used the morning and part of the afternoon to instruct them on what lay ahead in Texas and to teach them some basic English. The crossing, focused on progressing in the language and culture of Texas, was not a frivolous experience!

New York City harbor was clogged with masted sailing ships on October 11 as the *The Europa* carefully picked her way to the pier assigned to her. Once the ship's registry was confirmed, Bishop Dubuis and his entourage began to disembark down the swaying gangplank. Deck hands on *The Europa* stopped their work to wave them ashore, wishing them Godspeed. Similarly, the stevedores on the wharf were puzzled by the strange looking group of nuns in habits of various styles, young men in black suits, and a grandfatherly man in a rumpled suit and turned collar who appeared to shepherd the entire assemblage. The stench of floating garbage and open sewers shocked the newly arrived immigrants who had envisioned the proverbial streets paved with gold that lived in the tales of those few who had returned to their homeland. The wooden wharves and piers were rotted, and the group was grateful that Bishop Dubuis quickly brokered a cart to take the Sisters, priests, and seminarians to a nearby parish where they would be housed overnight. The news that the Sisters would stay in the rectory was their first revelation of the religious deprivations of this relatively new country. New York City, the second largest city in the land, had only one Congregation of Sisters in 1866: the Sisters of Charity, founded by Elizabeth

Ann Seton. Because St. Vincent's Hospital, which they operated in Manhattan, was quite a distance away, it would have been an inconvenience to take the women there. The parish near the bowery was the usual first stop for missionaries entering the United States; and the priests assigned there, immigrants themselves from Ireland, were accommodating hosts for the weary travelers who spent their time with him searching for their "land-legs" and trying out their halting English. The troop would not linger in New York, however, as Bishop Dubuis was able to get passage for all the women and most of the men on the *S. S. Tybee* scheduled to sail for Texas the next day.

After the women were settled in two crowded rooms in the rectory, *Sœur* St. André and *Sœur* Alphonse each sat quite still on their beds as there were no chairs.

Sœur Alphonse was the first to speak. "*Ma sœur*, I can't believe we're not moving. I thought we would never be on dry land again!"

"I, too, feared that we might not reach port. But here we are! I think it is best if we try to use as much English as possible. I will begin by always addressing you as 'Sister.' Would you agree?"

"*Oui* ... I mean yes, Sister." The unfamiliar "Sister" sounded like "sees-tear" with the "r" catching on the back of her German throat. "Does my English sound strange?" Her question returned them both to talking to one another in French. They acknowledged that English seemed so hard to speak, but they both agreed to speak it as often as possible. By this time, the ten women travelers had shared nearly everything—beds, basins, pitchers of water, stories of where they had come from, tales of how they had decided to join Bishop Dubuis. Though they were certain that their paths probably wouldn't cross in the future, they felt as though their shared anxieties, griefs, joys, and sorrows had bonded them in a type of friendship that would last into eternity.

Bishop Dubuis spoke with the Sisters, seminarians, and priests only briefly after the six o'clock morning Mass in the parish. After advising them that he would see them on the first of November in

Galveston, he gave them his blessing and assured them of his prayers for their safe voyage. He himself was on his way that very morning to get an early train to Baltimore where he hoped he would be in time for final decision-making at the Council of Bishops which was drawing to a close. His only complaint about their delayed departure had been that he was missing this historic event; but being able to bring Sisters for hospitals, in his estimation, far outweighed what he might have missed in Baltimore. Also, having two Sisters of Providence who could begin a parochial school system for his diocese would give him a certain esteem at this particular Council which would mandate a school in each parish in order to assure the integrity of the Catholic faith in this growing, young country that had expanded from sea to sea in fewer than one hundred years.

Grateful that they did not have to spend too much time in the vile-smelling harbor, the missionaries cheered when the *SS Tybee* set sail into the Atlantic toward the Florida peninsula for the two-week voyage for Galveston. Now worthy sailors, the women and men were lighthearted as they practiced their English, deepened their friendships, and compared ideas of what lay ahead of them. The four Ursulines knew that they were destined for their academies in San Antonio and Galveston; the two Sisters of Providence had visited with Bishop Dubuis and knew that he wanted them to go to the capitol town of Austin to begin a school in *Abbé* Nicolas Feltin's parish; four of the seminarians would be ordained deacons as soon as Bishop Dubuis arrived in Galveston; and the priests would be scattered into parishes throughout the diocese. The lone Sister-novice of the Sisters of the Incarnate Word and Blessed Sacrament would be continuing on to a river-port town, Victoria, where others of her Order were to start a branch of their Brownsville-based Congregation.

On board, Sister St. André watched the diverse religious women, future priests, and missionary priests as they dined together at tables where spoons, forks, and knives slid from one end to other; walked the deck for exercise; prayed the rosary together nightly; attended Mass each morning. She was happy that Sister Alphonse and Sister Regis seemed to be developing a friendship. Worried that Sister Alphonse's grief at leaving her homeland would overshadow her courage for the missions, Sister St. André was relieved to see that her companion was not pining for all that she had willingly left behind. Her own mixed feelings—fearful that she might not be up to the daunting tasks ahead, yet resolutely dependent on Providence who would meet them on the sandy Texas shores—ebbed and flowed with the tides through which the *SS Tybee* navigated. She believed with her whole heart that all would be well, but she had not the slightest notion of how that well-being would be accomplished.

As the steamship threaded its way through the Florida Keys and sailed into the open waters of the Gulf of Mexico, swirling dark clouds gave the passengers pause. The captain announced that his experience had led him to believe that they were sailing into a hurricane and warned them that the end-of-the-season storms could be ferocious. True to the captain's prediction, the storm raged for three days, tossing the craft as though it were a small rowboat. Staying below for protection was miserable as the men and women aboard had no idea how their situation would end.

As they sat together on their bunk, Sister St. André said to Sister Alphonse. "I simply will not believe that we have come all this way to be snuffed out by a storm at sea! This is a worthy ship. Captain Caulkins told me that it had its first sailing only two months ago and is in superior condition. We must have confidence in Providence, *ma sœur*, though I admit that I feel more apprehensive by the hour. I now have a renewed appreciation for St. Peter and the apostles as their fishing boat was whipped by wind and pelted by rain on the dark Sea of Galilee. I would no more get out of this boat and try to walk on the water of this sea—even if I thought I saw Jesus out there on the waves! There is a limit!" This last remark was added with a mixture of humor and vexation.

Sister St. André's tirade against the storm made Sister Alphonse laugh out loud. "Neither I," she said, nearly screaming above the howl of the wind outside. "And, not only is this rocking and pitching about to drive me mad, if I have to eat those dry biscuits and canned beans one more time, I might consider returning to France—except that I would have to get on another ship! No matter how bad Texas is, it can't be worse than sailing across the oceans!"

Her comment put all in perspective and both nuns mustered their faith that Providence would somehow see them through not only this transitory hardship but also whatever challenges they would have to face in the future.

The morning of October 25 dawned bright and clear and everyone was on deck for the final approach to Galveston harbor. The souls of the sea-worn travelers soared with excitement even though their sea legs were wobblier than ever. Breaking into singing the *Te Deum* when the boat pushed into the pier for docking, the crowd of nuns, seminarians, and priests gathered on deck, raised steady voices in the Church's grand hymn of praise and gratitude to a God who brings each person into a safe harbor, no matter how stormy the sea of life.

On the pier Father Chambodut, the diocesan vicar general, other priests and local Catholics were present to welcome the disembarking missionaries who would raise up hospitals in the major cities; schools in villages and towns; parishes in rural and urban areas; and universities, colleges, and academies where both men and women could prepare for their futures.

Piling into a single wagon, with another wagon carrying their trunks and valises, the ten Sisters were driven to the Ursuline Convent. The German-speaking driver, a parishioner from St. Joseph's Catholic Church, turned onto Water Street and over to Strand Street, telling his passengers of the trials that Galveston had experienced during the recent Civil War and the rebuilding that was going to bring his city back to its pre-war opulence. The noise on busy Strand Street, filled with carriages and wagons of every type, startled the horses. As he tried to keep his team under control, their driver shouted his remarks about the wholesale houses and warehouses that lined both sides of this commercial center of the town of over 10,000 people. Sister St. André and Sister Alphonse understood his German, but their French-speaking companions had no idea what he was telling them. The two Sisters of Providence provided translation as their proud driver guided them through the major business district of Galveston pointing out the hotels and banks. Soon they turned northward onto 20th Street past more businesses and after a short distance, the driver stopped in front of a magnificent, new-looking building. Explaining that this was their new customs house, he noted that its size indicated the importance Galveston had to the future economy of the State of Texas. The Sisters of Providence, who had both lived in villages of less than 1,000 inhabitants throughout their lives, were amazed at the number of houses.

As the wagon moved on north, they spoke among themselves, realizing for the first time that this country was not at all what they had expected.

"This city is enormous, perhaps as big as Strasbourg! I had no idea that Texas had cities of this size. Nicolas spoke only of its wilderness character. This is overwhelming!" Sister St. André said to her companion in French, fearing that their German driver would think that they were ill-prepared for the world they had entered.

"*Oui, ma sœur,* "Sister Alphonse responded in a whisper. "But surely we will not be working here. The bishop specifically indicated he needs us to begin schools in small villages. Hopefully, they will be more like where we are accustomed to serving."

Sister St. André could only reply, "I hope so," as she, for the first time, began to feel daunted by the task that lay ahead of her. She had never worked with people from cities. Would they be the same as the villagers she had come to understand over her lifetime in rural France?

The wagon-driver, not understanding a word of French, simply allowed his passengers to visit among themselves as he drove down 20th Street to Broadway, but as he drew up in front of St. Joseph Church, his pride in his parish's newly-built Gothic-style Church prompted him to interrupt their chatter.

"This is our parish church, St. Joseph's. We just finished building it six years ago. Isn't it magnificent?" He spoke lovingly of the small, wooden-frame, white church with its gothic spire and his question revealed a sense of self-achievement as he himself had done some of the carpentry work.

After translating what he had said for her companions, and not wishing to hurt his feelings as she recalled the massive stone Gothic churches in the small villages she had served in France and her own home parish church in Pfaffenhofen, Sister St. André was very complimentary in her response.

"Oh, it is lovely, sir! You can be very sure that this Church will be here for many, many years. A true beacon of the faith for your wonderful city!"

Sister Alphonse smiled to herself as she listened to her friend. Sister St. André had a way with words when necessary! Though the relatively small wooden church was dwarfed by any that she herself had known in France, she was certain that this proud immigrant from her own homeland found his parish church to be a home for his faith which no doubt had brought him through many trials as he came to this new and strange land.

The wagon driver drove down about six blocks and then turned his team northward toward a large, three-story brick building.

Having no idea where they were, Sister St. André asked their friendly driver, "How far is it, sir, to the Ursuline Convent?"

"Why, Sister, it is right here—Saint Ursula's-by-the-Sea!" and he pointed to the tall, brick structure with wide front porches on both the first and second stories.

Sister St. André immediately translated the German to French and all the Sisters began speaking at once, realizing that their journey was at least temporarily at an end.

CHAPTER VIII

GALVESTON

St. Ursula-by-the-Sea Date unknown.
(Courtesy, Ursuline Sisters, St. Louis, MO)

Turning his wagonload of nuns into the grounds of the Ursuline Convent and Academy, the driver shouted *"Wilkommen, Schwestern!* Welcome, Sisters!"

Hearing the clatter of horses hooves and the crunch of wagon wheels on the crushed seashells that formed the drive into the Convent Academy, Ursuline nuns spilled out from the front door and from the back garden, gathering on their front porch to welcome their guests. The three-story building seemed familiar. Even given the limitations of building materials the edifice projected a style in harmony with most French convents, making Sister St. Andrew and Sister Alphonse breathe a sigh of relief that these new surroundings didn't look too foreign.

Bishop Dubuis had never brought so many missionary nuns at one time, and it took more than a few minutes to sort out the new arrivals. Five of the Ursulines, French-speakers from France and Quebec, plunged into trying to identify each emigrant Sister and her place of origin in order to present their guests by name and homeland to their Superior, Mother St. Pierre Harrington who spoke only fragments of French herself. Within minutes, Sister St. Andrew and Sister Alphonse met Sister St. Anne, an Ursuline from Germany and the easy flow of their conversation in German made the Alsatian- and German-born Sisters of Providence feel at home. The hospitable Ursulines took the smaller valises and guided their guests into their first home in Texas: St. Ursula's-by-the Sea. Recognizing exhaustion on the drawn faces of the weary travelers, Mother St. Pierre asked Sister Regine, a French-speaking Ursuline, to help her with some announcements about a light lunch which was prepared in the refectory for those who wished, and the house prayer and meal schedule. Mother St. Pierre, wanting each Sister to feel at home in her new country, asked Sister Regine to assure them that they were to feel completely at home. Following the Superior's welcome, the Sisters were shown to their small bedrooms on the second floor of the convent-academy building. Each room had two or three beds, straight-backed wooden chairs, and small washstands with a large porcelain pitcher and basin already prepared for use. Sisters St. Andrew, Alphonse and St. Regis, the Incarnate Word and Blessed Sacrament novice, were to share a room at the end of the second floor hallway.

"My, it's quiet up here. I thought this was a boarding school. Where do you suppose the girls are?" Mother St. Andrew asked her companions.

"Sister Sigisbert said that they will be in classes and study hall on the first floor until 5:00 so that it should be very quiet up here. Their dormitory is on the third floor. After our experience of the last month, the quiet is deafening!" Sister Alphonse responded. All three chuckled at Sister Alphonse's apt description of their environment.

The wide window was open and a sea breeze stirred the white, lacy curtain. The late October air was warm but crisp since the recent hurricane had blown away the usual humidity that lingered constantly over Galveston City.

"I can hardly keep my eyes open," Sister St. Regis added. "What are we supposed to do now?" As a novice of the Incarnate Word and Blessed Sacrament Sisters, Sister St. Regis Chavassieux, unused to being without supervision, had become dependent on Sister St. Andrew and Sister Alphonse for guidance and support during their ocean voyage. Now that she had arrived in Texas, the loneliness in her voice seemed even more magnified. Until Bishop Dubuis arrived from Washington, DC, her future was completely uncharted. Befriended by Sister Alphonse while they were on the seas, she felt comforted by the continued presence of these two Sisters of Providence whom she had come to rely upon during their month of travels.

"I don't know about the two of you, but I am exhausted," Sister St. Andrew said in a tired voice. "I am going to lie down on this bed that is not moving in any way. They said that we pray the Office at 5:00. I presume that they will ring a bell to call us to prayer. Until then, I am resting!" Her voice revealed her usual sense of self-possession. Seldom had she displayed any apprehension during their journey and once they had walked off the *SS Tybee* onto dry land of the Texas shores, her composure had only grown more secure.

True to Sister St. Andrew's thinking, a bell rang at a quarter to five, rousing the three Sisters from a deep sleep. After washing their faces, brushing the dust from their habits, and resetting their white caps and bonnets, they followed other Sisters toward the convent chapel which was on the first floor. Taking empty pews in the back of the chapel, the missionaries watched as the Ursulines enter their choir stalls and prepare to chant the Office of the Blessed Virgin in Latin. Though the Latin prayers were unfamiliar to Sister St. Andrew and to Sister Alphonse, Sister St. Regis, who had just learned to chant Latin during her novitiate in the Incarnate Word

Convent in Lyons, followed in her own prayer book and seemed to feel at home in the cadenced prayer.

A supper that could have as easily been served in France awaited the Sisters in the refectory, and the travelers, sick of dried meats, hard biscuits, and boiled beans, relished the succulent smoked ham, French-style bread, butter, fresh garden greens, and fresh fruits grown in nearby orchards. After the foods had been passed, the Sisters observed the customary conventual mealtime silence until Mother St. Pierre rose from her seat at the head table and announced *"Deo gratias"** with the ring of a small bell, a signal that the Sisters could enjoy conversation with one another during the meal.

The travelers were scattered throughout the hosting Sisters at the tables in the nuns' refectory, and the girls in their dining room across the hallway were puzzled to hear the excited, high-pitched voices of their teachers who wanted to know all about their guests. The three French Ursulines were especially animated as they probed for news from their homeland. By meal's end, the guests felt completely at home in their host convent and when Mother St. Pierre got up to end the meal with announcements, an audible sigh of disappointment rose from her Sisters and guests.

"My dear Sisters, we are so pleased that you have come to be with us. We hope that the Ursulines just arrived from France will be able to rest before those of you assigned to San Antonio must leave for that school and we are so glad to have the Sister-Hospitaliers, Mother St. Blandine, Sister Mary Joseph, and Sister Marie des Anges, whom Bishop Dubuis has recently received into the religious life. Sister St. Andrew and Sister Alphonse, we are also glad that you will sojourn with us for a short while until Bishop Dubuis is ready to dispatch you to your new mission. And, Sister St. Regis, be assured that you are most welcome to stay with us as long as necessary until your new convent in Victoria is ready.

"I recommend that tomorrow, though we will need to get up and go to school," she nodded at her own Sisters, "you travelers take as long a rest as you care to. Your journey has been arduous and you may need a little time to acclimate yourself to this balmy climate of ours! Though today is rather clear, the humidity will return! When you are ready for breakfast, Sister Cleotilde, who supervises our kitchen, will be happy to serve you. Again, rest as long as you like. We will have our Mass at 6:00. I'm not certain what your schedule is in France, but we receive communion at our Sunday and Thursday Masses. Breakfast follows Mass at 6:45. We begin our classes at 8:00. Our midday meal is at noon and our classes resume at 1:00. The girls will be finished with classes at 4:00 and then will be in recreation and study hall until 5:00. We will have the Office of the Blessed Virgin at 5:00, followed by our supper as we have done tonight. I think that we will have '*Deo gratias**' during supper for a few days until we get to know each other." Her soft blue eyes revealed a kind heart filled with empathy for her foreign guests.

Her last statement, once translated into French by Sister Regine, brought broad smiles to the faces of the travelers who knew that speaking with their Sister-hostesses was their only means of learning about Texas at this point.

"If you need assistance with financial affairs, please don't hesitate to rely on Sister Paul, our treasurer. And, finally, perhaps on Saturday, I could speak with each of you individually to learn how we might best help you with English while you are with us."

Mother St. Pierre's pleasant, light voice assured the Sisters who had braved storms and seas that God's providence was looking after them while they were in Galveston. Seeing in her a model of how a superior ought to be, Sister St. Andrew looked forward to her interview with her on Saturday.

Beginning to feel like herself after a full day of rest, Sister St. Andrew arrived early for her Saturday morning appointment and spent a few minutes looking at the paintings that graced the main hallway of the Ursuline Convent. She was particularly struck by the

---

*   **A Latin phrase meaning "Thanks be to God." In the Convent years ago, it signaled that eating in silence was suspended and those at table could talk with one another.**

painting of their foundress, St. Angela Merici, and when she came to an image of Our Lady of *Bon Secours*, she smiled. The French roots of the Ursulines who had come to Galveston from New Orleans in 1847 were evidenced in the familiar face of the Virgin who had consoled so many people in her own beloved homeland. As she spoke a silent prayer to her heavenly Mother, Sister St. Andrew was interrupted by Sister Regine telling her that Mother St. Pierre was waiting. A short exchange revealed that Sister Regine would be part of the conversation in order to help Mother St. Pierre with the French.

"Sister St. Andrew, we are so pleased to have you and Sister Alphonse. Do you know how long you will be with us?" Mother St. Pierre began.

"I'm not sure, but perhaps as long as a month. Will that be all right?"

"Certainly. You may stay as long as you wish! You are most welcome! Now, how can we help you with English?"

"Is there someone who could help us with vocabulary and grammar? Bishop Dubuis began lessons with us on the ship, but we both—Sister Alphonse and I—need many more lessons. Perhaps we could attend some of the classes for your students? That would give us both exposure to English and ideas of how schools are conducted here in America."

"Wonderful idea!" Mother St. Pierre responded. "Sister Regine, can you and Sister Marie Jeanne work with Sister St. Andrew and Sister Alphonse each day from 3:00 until 5:00? And, then," she turned to Sister St. Andrew, "you are free to attend any classes that you wish. We will give you a schedule."

"Oh, thank you so much. We will work very hard!" Her enthusiasm was genuine and her promise included Sister Alphonse.

"I have another item to discuss with you." At this, Sister St. Andrew appeared perplexed.

"Yes, Mother?"

"Tomorrow, a Mrs. Caroline Rice will arrive to visit you. She is actually from Corpus Christi, but she has relatives here in Galveston with whom she is presently staying. She was here earlier this week inquiring about your arrival date. We sent word to her yesterday that you are here, but suggested that Sunday would be a better day to call."

Stunned at this news, her face a question mark, Sister St. Andrew asked cautiously, "Who is she?"

"I really don't know much about her, but evidently her pastor in Corpus Christi—oh, that is a town in Texas about 200 miles from here. How far is that in leagues, Sister Regine?"

Taking a few moments to mentally calculate the equation, Sister Regine eventually said, "About 80 leagues, Mother."

"Yes," Mother St. Pierre continued. "Her pastor, Father John Gonnard, has written to Bishop Dubuis about Mrs. Rice and her future. I'll let Mrs. Rice tell you her story. After you speak with her, I will be happy to visit with you at greater length about her."

"Thank you," Sister St. Andrew said tentatively. Since Bishop Dubuis had given her no information about Mrs. Rice, she was uncertain as to how she should respond. Having observed Bishop Dubuis carefully during the previous month, somehow she was not surprised. He had been most creative in his response to the Incarnate Word Superior's refusal to send her Sisters to Texas to begin a hospital. Within a few days, he had founded a completely new Congregation with three young women who had intended to come to Texas as nurses with the Sisters from Lyons. Also, he had been so engaging in his lecture to the Sisters of Providence in July that the possibility of beginning a mission in Texas was enthusiastically embraced by her own Sisters who had never even dreamt of foreign missions until this charismatic bishop planted the seed of possibility. Whatever he had arranged with Father Gonnard would no doubt be interesting!

Upon concluding her appointment with Mother St. Pierre, Sister St. Andrew searched for Sister Alphonse. Realizing that opportunities for visiting with her traveling companion were diminishing, Sister Alphonse was in the garden with Sister St. Regis. Sister St.

Regis had no idea when she would be leaving for Victoria, but Sister Alphonse already knew that she would not be in Galveston for much longer.

Sister St. Andrew sat down on a bench and Sister St. Regis asked to be excused.

"Oh, no, Sister. You need not leave. But I need to tell Sister Alphonse of an unusual development." As Sister St. Regis reseated herself on her bench, Sister St. Andrew turned toward Sister Alphonse and in measured tones began.

"It seems that a woman from some town—I don't know where it is—it has a Latin name—Corpus Christi—will be coming here tomorrow to see me. I want you with me so that both of us can hear what she says. I assume she does not know French and we'll need to ask Sister Regine to translate for us. Bishop Dubuis has been in touch with her pastor and they have made some type of arrangement in her regard."

Sister Alphonse was as surprised as Sister St. Andrew had been when first hearing the news. With a stammer, she asked, "Wh-what type of arrangement do you think has been made? Why, we've not been here two days and already unknown events are closing in upon us?" A note of panic had crept into her voice.

"Now, Sister, we have come too far to let something that we do not even know about upset us in any way. We must rely on the words of Father Moye who would remind us: *'Abandon yourselves completely to God; put all your confidence in God and not in others. You will see from experience that those you rely on most will fail you in one way or another.'* I don't believe that Bishop Dubuis will fail us but we must always remember that we are ultimately in the hands of Providence. Bishops will come and go. God endures. And, Father Moye also said, *'... if you entrust yourselves to God, He will never fail you.'"*

---

* **The Directory**, p. 178

"You are right," Sister Alphonse said, taking a deep breath. "You are right. I am not as quick to think that God is with us as you are. But I do trust."

"We all need reminding, Sister. I'll remind you; you'll remind me. We will wait calmly and see who this Mrs. Rice is and what she wants." Sister St. Andrew tried to sound as optimistic as possible, though, if asked, she would have admitted that Bishop Dubuis might be more than she had bargained for.

After Mass and breakfast on Sunday morning, Sister St. Andrew returned to the simple, French-style chapel to spend time in prayer. She expected Mrs. Rice to call in the early afternoon and needed time to recollect herself for this unexpected encounter. She and Sister Alphonse had already decided which questions they would put to the woman, and they wanted to leave her adequate opportunity to ask them questions as well. She had a feeling that the "arrangement" might be longlasting!

Taking the beads of her rosary into her fingers, she began to pray, deciding to meditate on the Joyful Mysteries. The first mystery, the Annunciation, held all she needed to reflect upon: a young woman, thrust into an unplanned-for event of extraordinary proportions— an event that would change the destiny of mankind. Whispering the Hail Marys, she found her present reality paralleling that of Mary. She, too, was only a youth. Though she was a mature thirty-six year-old, she felt very young when she realized that she knew next to nothing about her present situation and less about her future. She could not even imagine the next station on her journey, and she felt as alone in all of this as Mary must have felt in her parent's home in Nazareth. Though Sister Alphonse would certainly do the best she could and was a wonderful teacher, Sister St. Andrew could hear a tremor in her companion's voice at times when things seemed uncertain. Sister Alphonse would need a great deal of support.

The young Virgin of long ago had uttered some of the most profound words known to man: "Be it done unto me according to thy word." With deepened understanding of her reality, Sister St. Andrew prayed to that Virgin who had become a model to all who felt alone. "Dear Mary, let me borrow your very words as I enter into the unknowns ahead of me. I implore your help; intercede for me with your Son Jesus. You walked an unfamiliar road and know its difficulties; help me that I may not stumble."

By the time her prayer was finished, Sister St. Andrew had just enough time for a walk in the garden before dinner. No one else was there, and, grateful for the time alone, Sister St. Andrew admired the lush gardens still filled with tomatoes, peppers, squash, and beans, plants that long since had stopped producing vegetables in France. The temperature that morning was comparable to an August day in France. What must summer be like in this country? Nicolas had always written about the extreme cold in the winter and the extreme heat in the summer. At least she had not arrived during the most severe climes. For that she was grateful!

The ringing of the Angelus bell interrupted her reverie and she paused to say that ancient prayer that was known by every French man and woman: "The angel of the Lord declared unto Mary, and she conceived of the Holy Ghost." Unexpectedly, her eyes filled with tears as she imagined her mother and her sister Marie-Anne in LaWalck stopping their word to pray. Her Sisters at St. Jean-de-Bassel, her friend Sister Andre in Keffendorf were all united in prayer that used the words of the gospel to call the pray-er to a deeper appreciation of God's coming to be with humans as one of them. Wiping her eyes, she hurried into the Convent-Academy realizing that she would be late for dinner.

The Sister-portress found Sister St. Andrew in the garden. A French-speaker, she announced to their houseguest that a woman named Mrs. Rice awaited her in the front parlor.

"*Merci beaucoup, ma sœur,*" Sister St. Andrew responded. "Did you have trouble finding me?"

"Oh, no, *ma sœur, Sœur* Alphonse was waiting in the hallway and she knew where you were. She is with Mrs. Rice now."

"Bon," Sister St. Andrew said as she followed the Ursuline nun into the Convent and down the front hallway to the beautifully appointed parlor.

As Sister St. Andrew entered the room, a tall, thin, light-complexioned woman with dark-blonde hair and blue eyes stood up. Her clothes were fashionable, suggesting that she was a woman of means. Reflecting a wisdom that comes only from loss and suffering, her pale blue eyes were unwavering as she studied Sister St. Andrew's face while Sister Regine made the presentations.

"Ma sœur, je present Madame Rice." Mrs. Rice extended a gloved hand for Sister St. Andrew to take, that unfamiliar gesture used by Bishop Dubuis when she had first met him in early summer. Sister St. Andrew took the offered hand in her own with a warm, reflexive gesture. Mrs. Rice greeted the nun from France in halting but decent French, explaining that she had studied French with Ursuline Sisters from Canada and France in South Carolina, the state of her birth.

After indicating that everyone could be seated and coming straight to the point, Sister St. Andrew, asked Mrs. Rice, using slow and precise French, "Why are you here?"

The story that Mrs. Rice told took Sister St. Andrew and Sister Alphonse through an array of emotions: confusion, shock, disbelief, and finally, resignation.

"I realize that you do not know me," Mrs. Rice began. "I am a widow with a grown son and I live in Corpus Christi. Do you know where Corpus Christi is?" she asked politely. Both Sister St. Andrew and Sister Alphonse nodded tentatively.

"We came here to Texas not quite fifteen years ago after my husband William died in South Carolina. That is a state on the Atlantic Ocean, far away from here." When the look on either Sister St. Andrew's or Sister Alphonse's face revealed confusion or a lack of understanding, Mrs. Rice would turn to Sister Regine for further clarification in French. She went on. "Since I was alone in Charleston after William's death, I decided to join my mother and other family members who had come to Texas to start a plantation in another part of the State. Eventually, I moved to Corpus Christi where I have other relatives and where my spiritual director, Father John Gonnard, is the pastor. Father asked me to come and teach in his school. I've been doing that now for a couple of years." She paused to see if either of the French Sisters had a question. The look on their faces remained unperturbed as they calmly waited for the woman's story to unfold.

"Father Gonnard directed me to read books from his personal library on lives of the saints and on spiritual practices. And," as she began this sentence, Mrs. Rice lowered her voice, speaking simply, "I have provided him with a well-ordered school that now has about thirty-five students—boys and girls. He has said to me that he believes I have a religious vocation, and he wrote to Bishop Dubuis last spring telling him of his thinking on this matter." She stopped again to see if her words had had any type of effect on her hearers. Both Sisters nodded politely, indicating that they were listening.

Sister Regine asked Sister St. Andrew, "*Comprendez-vous*? Do you understand?" After Sister St. Andrew nodded, Mrs. Rice continued.

"At any rate, both Father Gonnard and Bishop Dubuis believe that I should enter your Congregation. I now present myself to you as a subject in your order. Will you accept me?" she concluded with formality.

Recognizing that Mrs. Rice was as straightforward as she herself was, Sister St. Andrew leveled her gaze to meet her eyes and waited nearly a full minute before replying.

Again, in slow French, she began. "*Ma chère aimee*, it is entirely possible that God has given you a religious vocation and it seems plausible that your desire to serve God could be accomplished as a Sister of Providence. The recommendation of your pastor is a first indication and as the Superior of our Sisters here in America I will listen to God's voice as He speaks through the bishops and priests here. However," and she paused here to underscore her intention, "I need to wait to speak with Bishop Dubuis before I answer your question. He is due to arrive this week, thus I cannot have an answer for you until the end of the week. Will that be sufficient?" Not quite a test, this last question was nevertheless key to Sister St. Andrew's future response to Mrs. Rice's request. An overanxious or petulant reply from Mrs. Rice could reveal immaturity, stubbornness, or a sense of proprietorship since she was the American and the two Sisters were recent immigrants.

"I completely understand, *ma sœur*. I am staying with a cousin here in Galveston and am welcome to stay as long as necessary." She gave Sister St. Andrew a calling card with her Galveston address. "Please send for me when you are ready to discuss what is possible."

At this point, Sister Regine broke in. "Would anyone care for a cup of tea? And, I think Sister Cleotilde has baked a lovely cake. I'll bring us a tray." The hospitality of the Ursulines continued to be overwhelming and both Sisters of Providence expressed their gratitude for Sister Regine's kindness. While she was gone, Mrs. Rice asked the two Sisters about their voyage from France and was impressed with their spirit of adventure in choosing to be missionaries to the Texas wilderness. She herself told them more about her life.

"As I said, I was schooled by the Ursulines in Charleston, South Carolina. I know you don't know where that is, but when possible, I'll show you on a map of the United States. My parents were Catholics— of Irish descent—although there are really not many Catholics in South Carolina. I married William Rice, also of Charleston, and we had one son. My husband has now been dead for over fifteen years. Soon after he died, I followed my mother here to Texas where she had settled on a plantation quite a distance from here. My son runs that plantation now, giving me the freedom to reside in Corpus Christi and teach school for Father Gonnard."

"How can Catholics keep the faith here in Texas with so few churches? My brother priest, Father Nicolas Feltin who is in Austin …"

"Oh, I have heard of him! Father Gonnard speaks of him as a very zealous priest. I believe he has been in Austin now for two or three years."

"… yes, two years, I think," Sister St. Andrew continued. "But, about remaining a good Catholic …?"

"Well, it is difficult! We seldom have Holy Mass, except in the towns where a priest resides. Why, on the plantation, sometimes we went months without seeing a priest! So our custom was to gather up everyone on the plantation on Sunday mornings to pray the rosary and say the litanies. My mother would lead the prayers; and when she could no longer, I would take her place."

"I see," Sister St. Andrew said thoughtfully, thinking of the earliest Sisters of Providence who played a similar role providing community prayer in remote French villages which did not have a priest in residence.

"I suppose that one of the reasons I moved to Corpus Christi a few years ago was so that I could go to Sunday Mass regularly. Because Father Gonnard lives in Corpus Christi, I can even go to daily Mass. That is very important to me."

Though Sister St. Andrew was very impressed with Mrs. Rice's strong faith and her devotion to the Mass, she did not know of any widows who had entered her Congregation before and was not sure how to proceed in this case. But Mother Adrienne was a world away; and now, Sister St. Andrew suddenly began to realize that decisions such as this were in her hands alone. She would be glad when Bishop Dubuis returned from his meeting, becoming available to talk this over with her.

After Mrs. Rice departed, Sister St. Andrew and Sister Alphonse took an opportunity to review this new circumstance before Benediction of the Blessed Sacrament at 4:45 p.m.

"Sister St. Andrew, I can't believe that we are faced with this so soon after our arrival! Why, we don't have any way of dealing with a new vocation at this time! What are you going to do? Besides, she is old. She is at least ten years older than we are, don't you think?"

"Perhaps she is in her early forties—that would make her five or six years older than we are," Sister St. Andrew chuckled. "She's not exactly a fossil!"

"But she's been married and even has a son, for heaven's sake! Do we have any similar vocations in France?"

"Actually, I don't think so. But what do you suppose Sister Constantine would do? I have always valued her insight."

"First, she would wait to talk with Bishop Dubuis. There may be more to this than we know at present." Sister Alphonse's response was more prophetic than she realized, especially in regard to her own personal fate.

"Yes. I believe that is what we must do. Let's see: today is October 28. Bishop Dubuis told us he would be back in Galveston by the end of the month. We will simply wait and talk all this over with him. After all, he knows the peculiarities of Texas and he'll know whether or not Mrs. Rice would be a good subject for us. One must admit, the fact that she is able to speak with us in French is very helpful. And, won't we see God's providence in her speaking English?" Sister St. Andrew asked this last question to guide Sister Alphonse to look for God's hand in this unexpected event.

"You are correct. I'll try to be patient—and open to what the Bishop will say."

"Let's go to chapel early to spend some time in prayer about all of this. God provides. Let's give Him a chance."

After Benediction and the Office, the Sisters again gathered in the refectory for Sunday supper. By now, the guests had met all of the hosting Ursulines, and realizing that Mother St. Pierre would announce *"Deo gratias,"* they had taken places with specific Sisters whose company they had grown to enjoy. Once Mother St. Pierre had broken the usual silence at the meal, conversation was lively.

"*Sœur* Regine," Sister St. Andrew began in French, "how did you come to Galveston from Quebec?"

Sister Regine's response gave Sister St. Andrew a short history of how French-speaking Canadians had frequently immigrated into the territory that President Jefferson had purchased from France in 1803. With a number of French-speaking communities settled in what is now the State of Louisiana, immigration from Canada continued. The Canadian Ursulines had been brought to New Orleans by Archbishop Odin who constantly sought more nuns for his diocese. As early as 1727, Ursuline Academy was founded in New Orleans. This academy had been Sister Regine's first destination in the United States, but she had stayed there only a short time and then had gone on to Galveston to augment the faculty for the growing school at St. Ursula's-by-the-Sea. Knowing both French and English had made her an ideal French teacher.

"You are, no doubt, an excellent teacher, Sister Regine," Sister St. Andrew exclaimed after hearing a basic history lesson on the French settlement of New Orleans, the impact of the Louisiana Purchase arrangement, and the development of the Ursuline Academies in New Orleans and Galveston. "Your pupils must listen attentively to your lectures!"

Sister Regine received this compliment with hesitancy. "Oh, I'm not so sure, *ma sœur*. I am afraid that they think of me as a very difficult teacher. But, I have to admit that I enjoy that reputation. It contributes to their studying hard for the subjects I teach. Mother St. Pierre said that you might want to visit our classes. I would welcome you to any of mine. I teach the upper form of French and history in the lower form of the high school."

"I would very much enjoy being your student for the next few days. What are you teaching in history at this time?"

"In our studies on the United States, I am just beginning to lecture on the War of Revolution in 1776. You might find that interesting."

"Yes, I would. I must learn as much as possible about my new country. But your lecture will be in English, yes?"

"Yes, but I have a book I brought with me from Quebec that gives a brief history of the United States written in French. Read that ahead of my class and you will know what to listen for."

"Thank you so very much. I look forward to your class."

Realizing that their conversation had inadvertently excluded others at the table, Sister Regine opened the topic of Galveston and all joined in telling Sister St. Andrew of their town's history and development.

Intrigued by how much had been accomplished in this town since its founding, Sister St. Andrew peppered her table companions with questions about the economy of the town, its growing population, and the place of the Catholic Church in a town that has a majority of Protestants.

"Yes, since we are the only large seaport in Texas, we receive thousands of immigrants, mostly Germans, and a great deal of what Texas exports, rice and cotton for textiles, leaves through Galveston. You might remember passing down a street called 'The Strand.' It is the heart of the business district—quite a metropolitan area for us! I doubt that the town founder, Michel Menard, could have imagined how Galveston would develop. In 1836, when he began to develop the land and sell portions of it to business and ranchers, the little village had under a thousand residents and now—why, the population is just at 12,000!" These remarks came from Sister Mary Paul, the Convent Treasurer, who spent a large portion of her time arranging for business transactions to meet the needs of their growing school for nearly 100 girls. She possessed a great deal of knowledge about the commercial world of Galveston since she spent so much of her time with businessmen and vendors.

Suspecting that in her future she, too, would be engaged in similar transactions, Sister St. Andrew listened carefully to all that was said and found herself feeling regretful that the supper had come to a close when Mother St. Pierre rose to make her customary end-of-the-meal announcements.

"My dear Sisters, I received word today that Bishop Dubuis will arrive in Galveston tomorrow. He has scheduled ordinations of his newest missionaries on the Feast of All Saints. Since we will not be in school that day, we will all plan to attend the ceremonies in the Cathedral. Sister Regine, will you please explain to our Sister-guests how far the Cathedral is from here and when we shall leave in order to arrive for the 10:00 Mass?" She waited while her French-speaker explained that the Cathedral was about a mile away and those who could walk the distance would leave the Convent at 9:00.

"In addition, Sisters, because of our fast before Holy Mass on November 1, we will have a substantial supper on the eve of the Feast. In America, the people follow the English custom of 'All Hallow's Eve,' and we will celebrate with a festive supper and party in the evening." The immigrants, unaware of this custom of 'All Hallow's Eve,' looked puzzled. Sister Regine, seeing the perplexed looks, suggested that she give a short explanation.

Sister Regine explained that 'All Hallow's Eve' had developed as a celebration of English Protestants to deride English Catholics who were honoring the Saints of the Church. But she assured her listeners that in America, "All Hallow's Eve," now known as "Halloween," had taken on a more festive tone with parties for children.

Mother St. Pierre concluded her remarks. "Bishop Dubuis will be with us for our festivities after joining us for supper on Wednesday night. The girls will have their own party in their study room and we will gather in the large community room. Sister Cleotilde may need some help in the kitchen if any of you can volunteer some time. Now, let us pray." Grace after meals and the praying of the Angelus concluded the meal.

As they exited the refectory, Mother St. Pierre caught up with Sister St. Andrew who was continuing to visit with Sister Regine. "Sister Regine, please help me with a conversation with Sister St. Andrew." The two Sisters followed the Superior to her office.

With Sister Regine's assistance, Mother St. Pierre told Sister St. Andrew that Bishop Dubuis would be arriving Wednesday afternoon and that he expressly indicated that he wanted time to visit with her and Sister Alphonse. They were to meet him in the Convent parlor at 3:30 in the afternoon.

Now that she had an appointment with her bishop, Sister St. Andrew didn't know whether to be relieved or anxious. So much needed to be reviewed.

The last Monday and Tuesday of October crawled by as Sister St. Andrew and Sister Alphonse began English lessons with Sister Regine and attended Sister Regine's classes. Finding the Canadian Sister to be an excellent teacher, both Sisters were impressed with how much they learned each day. And, by watching Sister Regine in her classes with the girls, they came to see how teaching was done in the United States. Observing the girls in the classes provided a window on American culture and both missionaries used the opportunity to its fullest advantage.

Both Sister St. Andrew and Sister Alphonse went to the front parlor promptly at 3:30 on Wednesday afternoon. Just as they arrived, the parlor door opened and Sister St. Regis came out. The look of disappointment on her face concerned Sister Alphonse and she made a mental note to find her friend later to learn what was bothering her.

Bishop Dubuis greeted the two Sisters of Providence with enthusiasm and was most solicitous about their present situation. After initial pleasantries and a short account of both the bishop's journey from Maryland, as well as how the two missionaries were getting along at the Ursuline Convent, Sister St. Andrew steered the conversation to her concerns with, "Your Lordship, Mrs. Caroline Rice came to see me on Sunday."

"Oh, yes, Sister, I need to tell you about her, or at least as much as I know." He then informed the two Sisters of his correspondence with Father Gonnard the previous spring, just before sailing for France.

Sister St. Regis Chavassieux, IWBS
(Courtesy: Sisters of the Incarnate Word
and Blessed Sacrament, Victoria, TX)

"So, you see, I never had a chance to meet the woman personally, though Father Gonnard indicated in his letters that she is a very fine teacher and very pious—goes to daily Mass."

"Yes," Sister St. Andrew said, noting her agreement with Father Gonnard's description. "I found her to be very amiable. Do you believe that her age and the fact that she is widowed has any bearing on her being a subject for religious life?"

"Not on the frontier, Sister. How old is she?"

"In her early forties, I think."

"If she is in good health, she could serve the Church for many years. Now, about her marital status. Does she have children?"

"One son, actually a stepson, who runs the family plantation—uh … somewhere …," she stammered, realizing that she had no idea where the plantation was, or actually what a plantation was.

"Oh, yes, I am remembering now what Father Gonnard wrote. Well, what did you think of her?"

"She seems apt. She speaks French, not exactly fluently, but well enough. I see her as being very commanding in the classroom. Of course, she knows much more than Sister and I do about how to manage in Texas!"

"Will you allow me to accept her into the novitiate tomorrow at the Feast Day Mass?"

"My goodness, your Lordship! Our custom is that a woman would be a postulant for at least a year before she would enter the novitiate! I don't think we could ..."

"Now, Sister," Bishop Dubuis interjected placatingly, "I know how things are done in France. But we're in Texas. We move much faster here. The needs are simply too great. Why, I'm going to ordain four men who just got off the boat with you last week to the subdiaconate tomorrow morning, then to the diaconate on Thursday and as priests on Sunday! You see, don't you, that we simply don't have the luxury of time as France has?" His last question was not really open to debate. "What about receiving her into the postulate within the next few days and then into the novitiate at the end of November? Would you be able to accept that?"

Thinking that this was the best compromise her new Superior would offer, Sister St. Andrew nodded in acquiescence.

"There is one other aspect to this. And it will involve Sister Alphonse," the bishop continued.

Sister Alphonse and Sister St. Andrew had thoroughly discussed possible options related to Mrs. Rice and her membership in their Congregation. Sister Alphonse now looked up with apprehension since she had no idea of any other factors.

The bishop addressed her kindly. "My dear Sister, I need your personal cooperation in the second part of the plan in regard to Mrs. Rice. I know that my next remarks will be jarring but I will provide all the support I can to assist you to acquiesce to my request."

The look on Sister Alphonse's face revealed a sense of alarm. What would his Lordship ask? Could she respond with courage? Her eyes went to Sister St. Andrew whose calm demeanor helped her to listen with openness.

"Father Gonnard has a parish school of some forty children in Corpus Christi. Mrs. Rice has been operating this school, successfully as I understand, and Father Gonnard is willing to release her to the religious life if he can have a trained Sister for his school." He paused here to let Sister Alphonse and Sister St. Andrew accept his unspoken request.

Sister St. Andrew's question went to the heart of the bishop's bargain with Father Gonnard. "Are you saying that Sister Alphonse would go to Corpus Christi to take over that school, your Lordship?"

"Yes, that is precisely what I am asking. However, she need not go immediately. That would be most unfair. I propose that she go with you and Mrs. Rice to Austin as soon as Mrs. Rice is received into the novitiate, and then after a few months there, Sister," he turned to her with pleading eyes, "you can go on to Corpus Christi." Not surprised by the anxiety he saw in Sister Alphonse's face, he decided to be gentle rather than demanding.

"Sister," he said, taking her hand in his in a fatherly gesture, "I will not force you to take on this assignment and you need not decide now. I observed you carefully on the boat as we sailed for America. You seem quite able and your interaction with the other missionaries revealed a certain maturity in relationships. I observed that Sister St. Regis truly came to rely on you! And she could not have chosen a better staff to lean on in my estimation." Sister Alphonse colored at the bishop's words of confidence and praise. As her face softened and grew more peaceful, he knew that she was now open to his request. He turned to Sister St. Andrew. "I will leave the final decision in your hands, Mother."

The new title that Bishop Dubuis placed upon Sister St. Andrew startled her. He went on. "You are taken off guard by my calling you 'Mother'?" he asked simply.

"Yes, your Lordship, I am."

"From here forward," he said with both challenge and respect, "that is your position. You are now 'Mother' to all those who will follow you as a Sister of Providence; and, of course, you carry all the rights and privileges of a religious superior. Was that not our agreement with Mother Adrienne?"

"Yes, your Lordship."

"Good. Then I ask you both to pray about all of this, asking our Provident God to bless our endeavors in Texas and to bless Mrs. Rice as she makes this important step in her spiritual journey and in your history here in America. Sister Alphonse, I will pray especially for you, that our dear Lord will bless you with courage and generosity. Father Gonnard is a good priest and, if you go to Corpus Christi in the spring, he will see to your needs. And, Mother, one more thing …"

So much had been said in the previous conversation, that Mother St. Andrew sat quite still waiting for the "one more thing."

"Mother, have you met Sister St. Joseph here? Her last name is 'Holly'."

"Why, yes. She is one of the young ones. Quite friendly."

"You really must visit with her. Your brother, Father Nicolas, is responsible for her being here. It's quite a story! Be sure to speak with her."

"Yes, your Lordship. I will," Mother St. Andrew said with curiosity. Every conversation with this Bishop turned up new information! What will our future here be like, she thought.

Smiling as he looked at the Sisters' faces to see if they had more questions, the Bishop, seeing none, concluded the interview. "Very well, my dear Sisters, I invite you to kneel for my blessing and I thank you for giving yourselves so wholeheartedly to the Church of Texas. *Benedicat Dominus omnipotens Deus, Pater et Fillius et Spiritus Sanctus.*"

Both nuns chorused "Amen," concluding the Bishop's extraordinary visit.

After the Bishop left the parlor, the two Sisters turned to each other, neither quite knowing what to say. Beginning to accept the mantle of her role as "Mother," Sister St. Andrew spoke. "Sister," she said quietly, "his Lordship has given us much to ponder. His plan for accepting Mrs. Rice straightforwardly into the novitiate actually reminds me of our earliest days in the Congregation when we were sent out to teach as postulants without any religious training. And you must pray for the assistance of God as you are invited to take a singular role in our work in Texas. I know that you can be of great use in Corpus Christi, and we came here to serve. Let's take time to pray and reflect before we discuss this situation at length, shall we? Then, it would be kind of you to see how Sister St. Regis is." Her tone was both firm and soothing and provided direction to Sister Alphonse's next hours.

November 1, the Feast of All Saints, was a busy day, with Mass and the subdiaconate ordinations. By the time the Sisters returned to their Convent, they were hungry and welcomed the silent noon meal as a respite from the noisy morning. With no classes in the Academy, the afternoon hours were free for resting and both Sister Alphonse and Sister St. Andrew took advantage of this unstructured time.

With Mother St. Pierre's assistance, Sister St. Andrew sent a message to Mrs. Rice inviting her to come to the Ursuline Convent on Thursday afternoon. Things were moving at a much faster pace than she had anticipated, and Sister St. Andrew decided to write down what she would discuss with Mrs. Rice, lest she overlook an important detail. Since Mrs. Rice's formation could not parallel the formation of postulants and novices in France, Sister St. Andrew knew that she would have to rely on her own creativity to make the reception of this new vocation a success.

Sister St. Andrew had become extremely grateful to Mother St. Pierre who not only agreed to allow Mrs. Rice to move into the Convent for the next month, but who also promised any assistance that might be needed.

Arriving shortly after dinner on Thursday, Mrs. Rice met with Sister St. Andrew whose opening sentence brought them both straight to their mutual concern. "My dear Mrs. Rice, Sister Alphonse and I have spoken with Bishop Dubuis and we now understand the plans that he made with Father Gonnard on your behalf. We have talked all of this over, and we do believe that you may find a place to live a vocation to the religious life with the Sisters of Providence. If you are amenable, the Ursulines have allowed us to invite you to live with us in their Convent until we go to Austin. I will receive you as a postulant in the Sisters of Providence of St. Jean-de-Bassel, and as the month of November progresses we will see how you acclimate to religious life. By the end of the month, we will know whether or not you are ready to be received into the novitiate. If things work out, we will happily receive you and then we'll all leave for Austin together where a school awaits us." Sister St. Andrew paused to give Mrs. Rice an opportunity to answer.

"Oh, thank you so much, *ma mère*! I would feel privileged to live here while we await our departure date for Austin." Continuing the straightforward approach that had framed their conversation on Sunday, Mrs. Rice inquired, "Will you expect me to provide a dowry upon my entrance? I understand that this is customary."

Sister St. Andrew had not thought that through; but on the spot, she replied, "A dowry will be appreciated if you are financially capable, but it is not a requirement."

"I realize that every endeavor carries costs. I will gladly lend some of my financial resources to our Austin project."

"That will be fine. But you do understand that once you enter the novitiate, whatever monies you have must be placed into a fund called 'patrimony,' or turned over to family members, as you wish. If you establish a patrimony, the monies will be earmarked for your use should you leave the Congregation; but should you remain, the monies become part of your estate, only to be disbursed upon your death. This is canon law, Church law."

"Very well. I understand. May I plan to move my things here tomorrow morning?"

"Yes, I believe that will work well. After you get settled here, Sister Alphonse and I will begin to inform you about our—your— Congregation, our history, our founder, and our four fundamental virtues."

"Wonderful! I am very pleased that this is happening. For years I have yearned for a spiritual foundation like this. Father Gonnard is very helpful, but I will welcome the structure of religious life."

"Excellent. Sister Alphonse, do you have anything to add?"

"No, Mother." Her use of the newly bestowed title characterized Sister St. Andrew's position in regards to Mrs. Rice and herself. Sister St. Andrew realized that she must begin to get used to this new role.

After Mrs. Rice had departed, Mother St. Andrew turned to Sister Alphonse. "How is Sister St. Regis doing? Is she still upset that her Convent is not progressing?"

"She is calmer now. She really can't decide whether or not to stay here with the Ursulines until the convent building in Victoria is finished or go on to Victoria and live with a family there."

"For semi-cloistered Sisters that is a challenge. Our life, on the other hand, often finds us living in strange circumstances. I will pray for her."

That Sunday evening, anticipating *Deo gratias*, Mother St. Andrew had maneuvered a seat at the table with the young Sister St. Joseph who quickly initiated a conversation.

"*Ma sœur* St. André, she began in good French, "I have been wanting to meet you!"

"*Oui, ma soeur*, and I you! I understand that we have someone in common—my brother *Père* Nicolas."

"*Oui, ma sœur*. If it were not for Father Nicolas, I would most likely be dead." Sister St. Joseph's words were startling.

"*Ma sœur*, what do you mean?" Nicolas had shared many tales with his sister, but she had never heard of him saving anyone's life!

Sister St. Joseph began her story. "I will begin at the beginning, *ma sœur*. My family came to Texas from Bavaria. My mother and father and I sailed from Brest, and while we were at sea, my sister Katie was born. After we got to Houston, my father found work and he was able to get us a little house. Sometimes we went to Mass at

St. Vincent de Paul Church. Eventually, my little brother was born. Then came the dreaded yellow fever."

A look of horror came over Mother St. Andrew's face as she remembered her brother Celestin's death from the terrible disease in 1853.

"My brother Celestin who came from France in 1852 to be with Nicolas died in that plague," she said quietly.

"So did my mother and father." The two Sisters, now bound together in a common grief, simply looked at one another.

"What about Father Nicolas?" Mother St. Andrew asked quietly, realizing that Sister St. Joseph was still bereaved after these many years.

"He found us: my mother, who was in the last stages of the fever, my sister Katie, and my brother. Our father was already dead. I was only eleven and I was trying to take care of everyone. Mother was so ill; Father had died and Katie and I had dragged his body out to the back shed. I didn't know what to do and was certain we would all eventually perish. Then came a knock at the door. When I went to see who had come, I saw this tall, strong-looking man. He told me he was Father Nicolas and that he would help us. After I told him about Papa, he went immediately to collect the body with a wagon. After he had taken care of Papa, he came back. By then, Mama had died. She was simply too weak to hang on. Father Nicolas took Mother to be buried—he told us that with this disease, burial had to be right away for the sake of the healthy. We understood. Actually, Katie and I understood. Edward was too little. He cried and cried when Father Nicolas took Mama away. He promised to come back for us. And he did.

"He brought Katie and me here to St. Ursula's-by-the-Sea. He told us that he would find a good home for Edward. I hope he did. I never saw him again."

Mother St. Andrew's was astonished at the nun's story. Tears had welled in her eyes and were running down her cheeks by the time Sister St. Joseph finished her tale. The others at the table simply remained quiet in respect for a story that several of them had heard before.

Mother St. Andrew had believed her brother to be a devoted priest, but she had no idea that his commitment to his parishioners was so deep. He was indeed a true missionary! The story only made her more anxious to see him and she was glad that it would be only a few days before she and her two companions would go to Austin.

Breaking the silence which followed the story, Mother St. Andrew said, "*Ma sœur*, you have had a remarkable life. Our Provident God writes straight with crooked lines, doesn't He. The tragedy of your parents' deaths brought you here where you serve your Sisters and your students. I admire you. Others, without the same faith, might have abandoned God, believing that they themselves had been abandoned by Him."

Sister St. Joseph concluded just before the bell announced the end of the meal. "Mother St. Pierre helped Katie and me so much. She replaced the mother and father we lost. From her I learned that God never takes something or someone from us without giving us the grace to sustain our loss—and usually without providing us with more than we lost in the first place."

The ringing bell made a further comment impossible. Mother St. Andrew pondered these last words as the Sisters finished their supper with prayers of gratitude.

The days of the next two weeks flew by. Mother St. Andrew and Sister Alphonse spent hours on their English lessons and taught Mrs. Rice about the Sisters of Providence, Marguerite LeComte, Father Moye, and the world of the St. Jean-de-Bassel Motherhouse. They all found that there were not enough hours in a day to accomplish what they hoped, and each one fell into bed exhausted each night. As the end of November approached, Sister St. Andrew called Sister Alphonse aside.

"Sister, it is decision time. What do you think of Caroline?" During the previous weeks the two Sisters of Providence had grown fond of

Mrs. Rice and used her given name regularly as their lessons on the Congregation's structure and history had progressed.

"Actually, Mother, I believe that she has great potential as a Sister of Providence. She certainly seems abandoned to the will of our heavenly Father and willing to risk as necessary to accomplish His will. She carries the same stalwart personality that Marguerite LeComte seemed to have from the stories that we heard when we were novices. What do you think?"

"I, too, think that she could be a good Sister of Providence. My only concern is that we simply have not had a long enough time to truly examine her. Everything has moved so fast. I am fearful that, even as time goes on, we may not be able to give her as firm a foundation as we should. Her vocation may not last."

"Perhaps not," Sister Alphonse agreed. "But, she is the one God has sent us at this time. We must leave all of this in His hands. Yes?"

Mother St. Andrew laughed out loud. "My dear friend! This time, you outdo me in your abandonment to the designs of Providence. I bow to your insight. We will simply trust. By the way, how are you going to respond to his Lordship? We must have an answer for him by week's end. He's going to want to set a date for Caroline's entrance into the novitiate, and then we'll be leaving for Austin!"

"I have come to the conclusion that taking on this school in Corpus Christi is exactly why I came to Texas. I admit that I am frightened by the idea of going to a completely strange place. I don't have enough English; and I'm not certain that I know how to teach adequately in America. But I will rely on God and say 'yes' to His Lordship."

"Very good, Sister. I had a feeling that you would not fail him."

"I am also thinking of something else, Mother. What would you think if I asked His Lordship if I might change my name in religion?" The look on Mother's face prompted Sister Alphonse to rush on to outline her idea more fully.

"I am quite serious about this. The name I received at St. Jean-de-Bassel is not in my family at all. In over fifteen years I have never been able to truly accustom myself to this identity. I would like to take His Lordship's name—our new Superior's name—and be known as Sister St. Claude. What do you think he will say?"

Wide-eyed at the very idea, Mother St. Andrew replied simply, "I really couldn't say!"

"If you have no objection, I will ask him at our meeting on Friday."

"Very well. I have no objection."

At their second meeting with Bishop Dubuis, Mother St. Andrew and Sister Alphonse acknowledged that Mrs. Caroline Rice would make a good candidate for the Sisters of Providence in America, and they agreed to allow the Bishop to receive her into the novitiate.

The meeting also gave Sister Alphonse an opportunity to commit herself to his needs for a teacher in Corpus Christi; and, having discussed the possibility of her name change with Mother St. Andrew, she brought it up to Bishop Dubuis.

"My Lord, I will do my best for the school in Corpus Christi. And, now, I have a request to make of you."

Surprised, but smiling, the Bishop gave her a nod to continue with her presentation.

"I would like your permission to change my name."

"Change your name? My dear Sister, why do you wish to do this?"

"First of all, I never liked the name I was given when I entered the novitiate. I admit that. This name is not in my family. At this time, I believe that my religious life is, in a way, beginning anew. I simply believe that a new name would denote my new beginning here in America. I have spoken with Mother St. Andrew and she has agreed to allow me to do this, with your permission, of course."

"Very well, Sister. What name do you desire?"

"I would like to be known as Sister St. Claude from now on," Sister Alphonse replied simply.

Shocked, the bishop asked, "Why do you wish that name, my name?"

"Not only have you been especially kind to us and given us every support for this venture, and I do wish to honor you, but this name is also my grandfather's name."

Smiling, the bishop responded, "Your honesty is refreshing. Another might have left her reason as a compliment to me. Your wishing to honor the memory of your grandfather is really much more admirable! I will give you an opportunity to change your name during the religious ceremony that we have just planned. Will that be all right?"

"Yes, your Lordship. Thank you."

"And now that we are asking favors, I have still one more," Bishop Dubuis said. "I know you have not had time to think about this, but I must ask you now, before you go to Austin. Will you both be willing to profess perpetual vows before you leave Galveston? While I was at your motherhouse, I spoke with Mother Adrienne who told me that you were not accustomed to perpetual profession, but that she believed it would soon be an option in the future. Here on the frontier, our lives are so uncertain. Many people do not know nuns and they might have the impression, that without perpetual vows, your loyalty to your state of life is temporary. That could lead men especially to make untoward advances. You will soon see, Sisters, that there are many more men than women out here in the wilds of Texas! And some of them are unsavory characters!" He made this last statement with a broad smile, although both Sisters understood him to be very serious about their possible vulnerability.

"Yes, before we left, we also talked with her about this. Mother Adrienne believed that perpetual vows would be an option for us within a year or two. Realizing that we would be faced with this decision soon, Sister Alphonse and I discussed this on our voyage to America," Mother St. Andrew said. "We agreed that we want to profess our vows for life."

"Good! I am delighted. We'll just add that to the November 27 ceremonies!"

Never a man to spend much time on details, the Bishop took this opportunity to forge a plan with Mother St. Andrew and Sister Alphonse to receive Mrs. Rice into the novitiate of the Sisters of Providence of St. Jean-de-Bassel at a simple ceremony which would precede a solemn high Mass on November 27.

"As I think about this Mass, it will be beautiful! Such a marvelous tribute to the future of religious life in our diocese! Those who attend will never forget it! Thank you both so very much for coming to our diocese. I know that you will face many crosses in the future, but perhaps your memories of our November 27 celebration will carry you through the hard times that are surely ahead of you. May God bless you both! Are there other questions or concerns?" The Bishop, ready to move on to his next appointment, brought the interview to a close before either Sister could phrase a reply.

"Please kneel, now, and receive my blessing."

The next several days were spent preparing various parts of the habit for Caroline Rice and making sure that everything was in order for the reception ceremony on the following Tuesday. Although they both had brought extra pieces of the habit, Mrs. Rice was taller than either of them and a brown dress had to be made in a hurry in order to fit her height. The Ursulines lent their sewing room and sewing equipment to them; and all the parts of their religious habit, including Mother St. Andrew's second cape, were altered to fit their postulant. Caroline herself knew of a hat maker who agreed to fashion the bonnet which was very similar in style to the bonnets used at that time by the women of Texas to keep the sun out of their eyes and off their faces. The extension in the back of the bonnet was added easily by the expert seamstress and by Monday, November 26, all was ready. The two Sisters of Providence and their soon-to-be novice met in the sewing room for last adjustments to Caroline's new garb.

"How does it feel, Caroline? Is the waist too tight or too loose?" asked Sister Alphonse anxiously. "We don't want you to feel strangled by your skirt, but at the same time, we don't want it falling off!" All three laughed together at Sister Alphonse's comment. Over the month of postulancy, they had begun to be friends as Caroline learned about the history of St. Jean-de-Bassel, Marguerite LeComte, and Father Moye.

"I must admit," Mother St. Andrew added, "this has all been like a whirlwind." To Caroline, she said with a serious tone, "Are you sure you wish to do this, my dear? We've had so little time to adequately prepare you. Religious life is hard at best. Are you truly ready?"

"With the help of our dear Lord, I will give myself as generously as I can. That's all I can say. My life has had many ups and downs, as I have shared with you over the last weeks. My husband's untimely death threw me into the station of widowhood when I was merely a girl in many ways. I've actually grown up alongside our son. Thank God he has been a good boy. Coming out here to Texas was a shock after living in urban Charleston. Life on the plantation was often very hard, and not being able to attend Mass regularly was a terrible sacrifice. I believe that my whole life has prepared me for this step and I am grateful that you are allowing me to join your congregation." This was all said quite simply and struck Mother St. Andrew as most sincere.

"Very well, then. We press on. We will leave on Wednesday. Bishop Dubuis has gotten tickets for us on the train to some place called Alleyton. From there we take a stagecoach to Austin."

With the last pins keeping the bonnet in place over the *coif* and the starched *guimpe* resting on her shoulders over her cape, Caroline Rice looked every inch the part of a Sister of Providence of St. Jean-de-Bassel.

"I think that does it, Caroline. You look just fine—as good as any novice!" Mother St. Andrew exclaimed. "Now let's get you out of these clothes. We'll be just in time for dinner. The Angelus should be ringing directly."

Gracious in every way, the Ursulines had agreed to provide special music for the High Mass at the Cathedral and were allowing the girls in the Senior Choir to attend and sing, thinking that some of them might reflect on a religious vocation after being exposed to such an auspicious occasion. The Bishop had also asked the *Mennechor* of St. Joseph's Parish, a group of men who sang the High Masses on Sundays at that church to sing the Mass itself.

And so, the celebration at the Cathedral on November 27 did provide the types of memories that carry one through the hard times in life.

Before Mass began, Mrs. Rice entered the sanctuary where the Bishop sat in his episcopal chair. The newly sewn habit, neatly folded and flanked by two lit candles, was on a nearby table.

A hush fell over the Assembly as Mrs. Rice, dressed in the fashion of a bride of her day, walked alone down the center aisle of the Cathedral Church toward the Bishop. After she had knelt in front of her Bishop and her religious superior who was standing at his side, the Bishop began.

"Caroline Rice, do you come here of your own free will."

"I do," Mrs. Rice answered in a clear voice.

"What is it you ask?" Bishop Dubuis continued.

"I ask to be invested as a novice in the Sisters of Providence of St. Jean-de-Bassel," Mrs. Rice responded.

"As a sign of the gift which you offer our Lord, I cut a lock of your hair." Mother St. Andrew handed him a scissors and he cut off a small piece of Mrs. Rice's hair.

Mother St. Andrew and Sister Alphonse moved to either side of Mrs. Rice to accompany her to the sacristy room where they would clothe her in the habit of a novice. While they were dressing her, the Ursuline Sisters and their student choir sang a lovely Gregorian hymn.

Upon their return into the sanctuary, Mrs. Rice, now wearing the habit of the Sisters of Providence, knelt before the Bishop.

**Sister St. Joseph Rice, Sister
of Providence, 1866-1874
(Courtesy: Sisters of the
Incarnate Word and Blessed
Sacrament, Corpus Christi, TX)**

"Caroline Spann Rice," Bishop Dubuis said in a loud, clear voice, "in religion you will be known as Sister St. Joseph. Just as our dear St. Joseph watched over his little family in Nazareth, we pray that he will watch over you. And, as the Christ-Child Jesus was entrusted to his care, so, too, many, many children will be entrusted to you. Pray to him always for guidance and strength.

He had done this before as he had received the three young nurses into his newly formed Congregation, the Sisters of Charity of the Incarnate Word, but there was a unique pride in his eyes as he welcomed this first vocation into a teaching order for his diocese.

The High Mass at the Cathedral that followed was inspiring. Perpetual vows were made and Sister Alphonse's name was changed, all under the beaming face of a Bishop who had labored so very hard to bring missionaries to his needy diocese. These two women with newly pronounced perpetual vows had now launched the third pillar of his platform to transform his diocese. The new Sister-Hospitaliers would provide the healing ministries under the auspices of the Catholic Church. The growing numbers of missionary priests would offer the Mass and dispense the Sacraments. These Sisters would provide much-needed schools for the children of immigrants who had settled in small remote villages—schools that would meld their homes with their parish.

November 27, 1866, though filled with grand ceremony, in truth mirrored the humble beginnings of Father Moye's project begun nearly one hundred years earlier in rural France. His own reliance on the Providence of God led Father Moye to continually remind his daughters: ***Great things have small beginnings; begin with little.*** *

On her way to Austin the next day, Mother St. Andrew turned those words over and over in her mind: I am beginning with little, just as Father Moye did. All is now in God's Providence.

---

* **The Directory, p. 335.**

CHAPTER IX

AUSTIN

Mother St. Andrew had mixed feelings about the journey to Austin. Though she was eager to get started on the mission of her Congregation in Texas, she felt under prepared for immersion into the life of Texas. St. Ursula's-by-the-Sea had offered a temporary safe harbor. The Ursulines had been more than hospitable, and she felt saddened by the realization that the relationships begun there likely would never be continued.

Continuing to be concerned about Sister St. Claude, Mother noted that each day during their month-long residence with the Ursulines Sister St. Claude had spent some time with her fellow German, dear Sister St. Anne, relishing a chance to visit with someone from her own country. The arrangement made by the Bishop with Father Gonnard entailing Sister St. Claude's imminent move to Corpus Christi was daunting. And, Mother knew that despite her bravado, Sister St. Claude was not looking forward to going by herself to a completely unknown location in this foreign country. Bishop Dubuis had assured her that Sister St. Claude could become accustomed to the wilds of Texas in Austin and would not have to go to Corpus Christi right away. But still, Mother was concerned.

The Mass of Acceptance into the Novitiate for Sister St. Joseph and the Profession of Vows by Mother St. Andrew and Sister St. Claude had been beautiful, but only the beginning of a momentous day. Bags and trunks had been packed and brought to the front entrance of the Ursuline Convent before the Sisters even went to the Cathedral for the liturgical festivities. Upon their return to the

Convent, a breakfast of omelets and sausages continued the celebration, but by mid-morning the wagon to take them to the train station had arrived and was being loaded with trunks and valises.

The departing Sisters had grown fond of the three young women, now Sisters of Charity of the Incarnate Word, who had been their companions on the two-month missionary journey and saying good-bye to them was especially hard. No one could have known at that time how tremendous the impact of that unknown Congregation would have on Texas and the Southwest.

Saying goodbye to the Ursulines was heartbreaking. Those stalwart Sisters, who had survived hurricanes, floods, fire, and war, were incomparable examples of how to manage on the frontier. Mother St. Andrew had watched them carefully and had taken several opportunities to visit privately with Mother St. Pierre Harrington on how to purchase land in Texas, what she thought of the Texas Catholic Church, and her thoughts about Bishop Dubuis. Mother St. Pierre had been straightforward with her and Mother St. Andrew was an apt pupil.

Before joining all those gathered on the lawn for the departure, Mother St. Andrew had taken Mother St. Pierre aside.

"*Ma mère*, I cannot thank you enough for all that you have done for us! Your Sisters have offered us all that we have needed and we have nothing to give you in return. I can only offer you my prayers."

"*Ma chère Mère* St. André! It has been our privilege and pleasure to welcome you and care for you as you begin your great work in Texas! We ask for nothing in return except your prayers. I was not yet stationed here that night that your dear brother brought Sister St. Joseph to us! Father Nicolas fought that outbreak of yellow fever in Houston nearly single-handedly! Sister St. Joseph, my first novice, told me of how so many had died, including another one of your brothers, I understand now?"

"*Oui, ma mère.*"

"Sister St. Joseph—Theresa Holly and her little sister Katie, so young to be alone in the world without parents or family—were well-cared for by your brother. He is described as a man of boundless energy and a 'herculean priest'. He is nearly a legend in the diocese! I never thought I would meet his sister. You seem to be so much like him! In my days of knowing you, dear friend, I believe that you, too, will make an enormous difference in the Catholic Church in Texas. May God bless your works!"

Realizing that they would probably never see one another again, the two Superiors parted with bittersweet emotions. Each had recognized in the other a mirror image of herself: stalwart, to some degree stubborn, and deeply dedicated to the well being of their communities.

The three Sisters of Providence climbed into the wagon and waved through their tears at the Sisters gathered to see them off. The last item loaded into the wagon was handed directly to Mother St. Andrew—a basket full of food for the journey: sausages, French bread, butter, ham, a packet of French coffee, and cheeses of several varieties. It was so heavy that only the caretaker could lift it up and both Mother St. Andrew and Sister St. Joseph had to take it together. It was nearly enough food to last them the entire five days of the journey. And, they would be glad they had it!

The regular life of the Ursuline Convent had been comforting after the tumultuous days of travel; but the Sisters of Providence, not used to a cloister-styled religious life, had said to one another that they were actually looking forward to the adventures that the needs of a parish and school would hold.

Bishop Dubuis had given them money for their tickets on the Galveston-Henderson Railroad to Houston and the Buffalo Bayou, Brazos, and Colorado Railroad from Houston to Alleyton, as well as money for their stagecoach tickets and hotel accommodations along the way. The journey to Alleyton would take the better part of the rest of the day. With luck, assuming that there were no derailments, blocked tracks, or other events that would slow the train down, they hoped that they would arrive at Alleyton in time for the stagecoach north. If they missed the stagecoach in Alleyton, they would have to stay overnight in the hotel there.

Mother St. Pierre had told them of her own trip to San Antonio at the outbreak of the Civil War. Listening to the story, the Sisters, some of whom had heard it dozens of times, hardly knew whether to laugh or to cry as Mother St. Pierre had described the Alleyton Hotel. The hotel owner, not used to dealing with nuns and somewhat fearful of them, had not been especially welcoming. He was not in good humor, as he had to roust men out of their beds in order to accommodate the several nuns and children who were fleeing Galveston, which had been taken over by the Union Army. Sheets on the beds had been filthy and the nuns had spread their shawls on the beds and had not even undressed to sleep. Mother St. Pierre had said that she had refused at first to eat breakfast, dreading a filthy dining room, when one of the children found her and told her that the dining room table wasn't nearly as dirty as the beds! With stories like that and some that Sister St. Joseph Rice had told of her own travels, Mother St. Andrew and Sister St. Claude felt both fear and trepidation as the train left the Houston station for Alleyton at noon.

The three-hour train trip from Houston was uneventful with the train pulling into Alleyton at 3:00 in the afternoon, just in time for their luggage to be transferred and the nuns to board the stagecoach north. With only a couple of hours of daylight left, the stagecoach driver had told them he would be stopping at Frelsburg for the night and that the passengers could find rooms at the hotel there.

The three Sisters settled in as best they could, grateful that the nine-passenger stagecoach held only the three of them and four others: a woman with a baby on her lap, and two men. Both men wore broad-brimmed hats and side arms, the first exposure the two French nuns would have to the usual attire of the West. A third seat between the two main benches was empty and, until other passengers were taken on, Mother St. Andrew used it to hold the basket of food. Food at the way stations was notoriously bad—boiled beans and bread with coffee—and accommodations unpredictable, so the basket would have to last them the entire four-day trip.

Striking up a conversation with the young mother, Sister St. Joseph learned that she was on her way to visit family for Thanksgiving and Christmas near a town called Bastrop. Her German accent led Sister St. Joseph to ask her if she spoke German; and learning that she had been born in Germany, Sister St. Joseph drew Mother St. Andrew and Sister St. Claude into the conversation. Welcoming conversation in her native language, the young mother became very animated. The two men, however, seemed quite satisfied to pull their hats over their eyes and sleep while the four women chatted amiably about who they were and where they had come from. The young German immigrant, a Catholic, acknowledged that she had never met a nun but had heard of them from her parents who had come to Texas from Germany in 1850 when she was only ten years old. She had been fascinated by the Sisters' decision to come to Texas to open schools, and she told them that they would be doing a lot of good since women such as herself with young children needed support from people like them.

The first night of the trip was spent in Frelsburg, a journey of about twenty miles from Alleyton. Bishop Dubuis had told them that if the stage stopped in Frelsburg, they should go directly to the parish church where they would find lodging. The French-speaking pastor, Father Gury, welcomed them graciously, giving them the two guest-rooms in the diocesan seminary. Intrigued with the style of religious life that the Sisters described to him, the priest immediately suggested to them that a school in his parish of Sts. Peter and Paul would be most welcome.

"I assure you, Father, that as soon as we begin to have vocations, we will do our best to open a school in your parish. You know, Sts. Peter and Paul is the name of my own home parish in the small French village of LaWalck-Pffaffenhoffen. I'll not forget its namesake here in Texas!"

Having promised to consider Father Gury's request for a school, Mother St. Andrew looked carefully at Frelsburg while waiting for the stage to be loaded the next morning. Father Gury had told them that his parishioners were from the Rhineland region of Germany and were very proud of their lovely church and the nearby theological seminary the diocese had recently built to train its priests. Though Frelsburg was a predominately Lutheran community, the Catholics were a strong force in their small town that had a growing commerce based on ginning cotton. Perhaps a school here would be a good idea! Frelsburg was exactly the type of town that might provide vocations.

The stage ride the next day, November 28, was equally uneventful. The landscape had begun to change. Rolling, forested hills with occasional small meadows replaced the flat, piney woods nearer to Houston. The air seemed to feel crisper. The three Sisters were actually pleased that they shared the four-foot long bench as they bounced along. Being tucked in together assured them that the cold fall air would keep the coach fresh but would not cause them to feel chilled.

The baby, becoming fussier as the trip became monotonous, was handed around among the women in hopes that the variety would be a distraction. Shortly before noon, the driver stopped the stage at a house with a nearby creek and told all on board to get out to allow the team of horses to rest a bit. The family from the house was scattered around the farm. The farmer was mucking out his barn; the farmer's wife, two small children hanging on her skirts, came out with flour on her hands, genuinely glad for the company. Everyone took advantage of the respite to use their outhouse and take water from their cistern. Grateful for another sunny day, the passengers stretched their legs and the four women passengers collected around the farmer's wife to learn where she was from. The farmer's wife stretched out her arms to take the baby from the tiring mother who was glad for a short rest from the constant duties of motherhood in the confines of the stagecoach.

Since it was time for dinner, the farmer and his wife invited all to their table which was laid with simple foods: roasted sweet potatoes, boiled beans with ham, and bread. Mother St. Andrew had carried in the basket of food from the Ursulines, laying it all out to share.

When the driver said it was time to leave, the farmer's wife packed up all the leftovers into the basket and Mother St. Andrew laughingly said in German: "I think we have more food than we came with! Our Provident God will always take care of us!" Sister St. Joseph asked Sister St. Claude to repeat Mother's comment in French, and then she translated it into English for the farmer and his wife. The couple smiled as they, too, believed that God was taking care of them and their farm.

The rested horses kept up a steady gallop and the stage made good time into the afternoon. By sunset, a small town became visible on the horizon and the driver began to slow his team. LaGrange, Texas, would provide the overnight stop. The passengers were told to find lodging in a two-story hotel on the town square, and Mother St. Andrew, hearing echoes of Mother St. Pierre's tales of her journey to San Antonio, walked toward the hotel in dread with the other two nuns following behind her. Sister St. Joseph spoke with the proprietor, who had a room with two beds and a chair to offer them. After the three travelers agreed that they could accept those limitations, they were shown upstairs.

The room was immaculate! And the bed had clean sheets! When the proprietor's wife came to greet them, her German tongue assured them that her hotel would meet their standards! The weary nuns decided to take a light supper from their basket of food, pray, and then retire early. They had been told to be in front of the hotel at 7:00 in the morning, and the "*haus-frau*" had assured them that breakfast would be ready by 6:30.

After a fairly decent night's rest with two Sisters sleeping in the beds and one in the chair, and a breakfast of eggs, bacon, fried bread, and coffee, the Sisters boarded the stage at exactly 7:00, ready for a full day of travel on their way to a town called Bastrop where they would again spend the night.

Another passenger was taken on in LaGrange, but he seemed amiable as he balanced on the bench between the two seats. He politely asked if he could lean against the Sisters' basket and their positive response set a friendly tone. Excited about being so close to her destination, a farm near Bastrop, the German mother was in high spirits and her baby was in good humor. The two men, who would journey on to Austin, continued to sleep.

Eventually, Sister St. Joseph asked in French, "Did you know that today is Thanksgiving Day?"

"What is that?" Mother St. Andrew responded.

"It is the day that Americans stop to give thanks for all the bounty God has provided for us. In 1863, President Lincoln declared the holiday to be observed on the last Thursday in November."

"What exactly does this holiday commemorate?" Sister St. Claude inquired.

"It commemorates the survival of the first winter by the Puritans who came to this land from England and Holland in 1620. The Indians helped them survive by giving them native foods and teaching them how to hunt and fish in their new land. The story goes that the first Thanksgiving was a harvest banquet to which the settlers invited the Indians. Now we use the holiday as a general day to give thanks to God for all that we have received. Usually families and friends come together for a feast of some sort," Sister St. Joseph said.

"Since we came to this country, my family wants to be good Americans. When I get home this evening, my mother will have her feast. My papa always kills a deer and we have roasted venison!" The German immigrant was proud of her "Americanization."

"In our home in South Carolina," Sister St. Joseph continued in French, we always had the traditional turkey with sweet potatoes. And our cook would make a dressing with cornbread and rice. So delicious!"

The four women enjoyed a conversation on recipes and menus for miles as they translated back and forth so that everyone could be included. And the new passenger, who had been a cook in a hotel, added his culinary knowledge.

Everyone was surprised when they felt the stage begin to slow down and realized that they were in a very deserted place. After stopping his team of horses, the driver walked around the stage very slowly and then called to everyone to get out.

"Well, ladies and gentleman, this is as far as we're going today! I have a wheel that is beginning to come apart. My guess is we're about five miles from Winchester and I think there's a wheelwright there. Anyway, you'll have to walk there, while I walk the team. I think the wheel will stay together if we go slow enough and don't put any more stress on it." The driver's news was unwelcome, and everyone just stood and looked at each other for a few minutes.

Finally, Mother St. Andrew said to the Sisters in French, "*Mes sœurs*, a walk of five miles is really nothing. Let's get started, and on this Day of Thanks, we'll be grateful for good weather!"

The little band began its trek down the barely discernible path toward Winchester, continuing their light conversation along the way. Mother St. Andrew and Sister St. Claude carried their basket of food while Sister St. Joseph helped the German mother with her baby.

Before they reached Winchester, Sister St. Claude noticed a crude farmhouse in the distance and suggested that a stop there would help them all. The smoke coming from the chimney looked inviting as they neared the farmyard and noted several wagons. One of the men called out and a dozen people spilled out of the little house, wiping their faces.

The entourage of travelers was welcomed into the home of Piet and Faustina Schmidt where a true Thanksgiving dinner was in progress. The women scurried around to find more dishes; the men made room for the travelers to sit on the floor near the fire. Laughing and talking in German and English, the farmer and his friends made the modern-day pilgrims welcome. After eating, the Sisters and their companions said they'd better go on to Winchester so they could find a place to spend the night.

"Oh, my, you won't find any hotel in Winchester! It barely has a store! Not even a bank!" *Frau* Schmidt proclaimed. "But, *Frau* and *Herr* Schumann live on the outskirts of town. They will take care of you."

"Thank you very much. You have been so kind to us," Mother St. Andrew said, speaking for everyone. "We just learned about Thanksgiving Day. I can't think of any better way to celebrate! May God bless you!"

"Let us give you some food to take along. Your basket must be nearly empty. We all ate a lot of your sausages!" Frau Schmidt said.

Once the farmer's wife filled the basket, it weighed almost as much as it had when the caretaker at St. Ursula's-by-the-Sea had lifted it up into the wagon. Providence provides generously, Mother St. Andrew thought.

The short walk into Winchester was more enjoyable on a full stomach, and they found *Frau* Schumann's house just as it had been described. The driver, seemingly knowledgeable about where to look for his passengers, reported to them that the wheelwright would work on the repair the next day, but it now would be Sunday before they would arrive in Austin.

As the coach wheeled down Congress Avenue into Austin City on December 2, 1866, Mother St. Andrew saw with gratitude that her new home seemed more like the villages she had left behind in France than Galveston had appeared to be. Small and large homes flanked the main avenue and a number of businesses huddled near the capitol grounds. The stagecoach station was not far from the Catholic Church on Brazos Street and Father Nicolas came to collect his Sisters as soon as he had learned that the stagecoach had arrived.

Father Nicolas settled the three nuns into his own rectory since the convent school building was still under construction. Though he was anxious for news about his homeland, he attempted to control his enthusiasm.

"I will show you everything tomorrow! But, tonight you must rest. Surely you are exhausted!" Father Nicolas was exuberant as he welcomed his Sisters. "I will sleep in the sacristy; there's really plenty of room there. Just like the priests often did in France, right, Sisters?" he said looking at Mother St. Andrew and Sister St. Claude.

"Oh, yes, Nicolas. In fact, there are many stories of our founder Father Moye sleeping in sacristies. Perhaps you are following in his hallowed footsteps?" Mother St. Andrew joked with her brother.

"I don't know about that. He was very holy. You will learn that I am not!"

"The Ursulines think very highly of you," his sister interjected. "Sister St. Joseph of the Ursulines said to give you her regards."

"Who is she?" Nicolas asked with genuine confusion.

"She is the former Theresa Holly. I believe you know her and her sister Katie."

"Oh, my goodness. Those two little girls that I took to St. Ursula's-by-the-Sea those many years ago? I can't believe it. She became an Ursuline nun?"

"Yes, and Mother St. Pierre is very proud of her. She is a fine addition to the community!"

"Well, you never know. I was desperate in those days. People were dying by the dozens in Houston from the yellow fever. It was the same time that Celestin died." At the mention of his young brother's death, his eyes clouded over, but he went on with a choke in a voice. "I buried so many. The parents of those girls did not survive and they had no other relatives—except their little brother. I placed him with a family in Houston but I had no place for the girls. I finally thought of the Ursuline convent and they graciously accepted them. I remember arriving with the two little girls in the middle of the night. The nuns were so generous."

"God has rewarded them with a good vocation," Mother St. Andrew said. "Sister St. Joseph is a very good nun."

The next days were spent learning about Austin and St. Mary's Parish and surveying the building that would house the nuns and the school. Father Nicolas was very busy with his priestly duties: teaching the parish boys, visiting the sick, and going out to the surrounding counties to say Mass when needed. Mother St. Andrew had really never known her brother as an adult and she was edified by his devotion to his priesthood and to the building up of his parish.

Their first Christmas in America was a traditional German festivity with St. Mary's Church decorated with native cedar trees covered with candles. The popular Christmas carol _Stille Nacht_, sung by the men's choir, echoed into the dark, starry night of Mother St. Andrew's first Christmas Midnight Mass in her new homeland. She had had almost a month to reflect on where the Providence of God had led her in the five short months since she had met with Bishop Dubuis in Strasbourg in early August. In her daily meditation since arriving in Austin on the First Sunday of Advent, she found herself reflecting on Father Moye's teaching on the Incarnation: that **_"Jesus Christ is our God, our Savior, our Shepherd, our Physician, our Model, our Victim, our Judge."_** [*] And, her prayer at the Midnight Mass was one of gratitude that she had met this Jesus over and over in her epic travels.

During the days that Father Nicolas and his workmen put the finishing touches on the new school, Mother St. Andrew took over classes for the boys and welcomed the few girls who were now able to attend. Never one to waste time, Mother St. Andrew held classes in the church, dividing the children among the three Sisters. In order to help Sister St. Claude acclimate and not be pressured by her classes, Mother had her teach the children their German and religion. Sister

---

[*]   **The Directory, p. 128.**

St. Joseph taught them English, and she herself taught them ciphering. By the time the school building would be finished in the spring, the children already would be accustomed to a school schedule.

Bishop Dubuis arrived at St. Mary's in Austin toward the end of January, hopeful that Mother St. Andrew and her two Sisters were not too discouraged by the slow construction on the school building and convent. His decision to risk bringing Mother St. Andrew to Texas was validated by her positive spirit, her industrious work at conducting a school without a building, and her indubitable dependence on Providence. During his short visit, Bishop Dubuis spoke at length with Mother St. Andrew about his commitment to sending a Sister to Corpus Christi.

"Mother, you know that I am indebted to you for your courage and industry in getting a school started here without even a building. The people of this parish are impressed by your commitment to their children. Sister St. Joseph seems to fit in with your Order's designs. Is that true?"

"Yes, your Lordship. She is doing fine. But we've been working here only a short two months. Sister St. Joseph has had such little formation. I remain concerned that we have moved her along into religious life too fast." Mother St. Andrew made this last comment with a worried look on her face.

"I am sure that you will do the best you can. I, too, worry about the men I ordain. We have so little time to educate them, form them in the spiritual life, and acclimate them to Texas. We simply must depend on Providence to supply what we lack." After only a moment's pause, the bishop continued. "And now we must talk about sending Sister St. Claude to Corpus Christi."

Mother knew that this topic was coming and she had decided to be frank with her ecclesial superior.

"Your Lordship, I am quite concerned about Sister St. Claude. She is still willing to go, but I fear that any kind of jarring situation may discourage her. She may even lose her vocation. This country is so rugged. We all served in small villages in France which were poor and, in some cases, even crude. But, still people were mostly civilized!"

"I know, Mother. I know only too well what lies before her—and you eventually! Each of your Sisters, and the new vocations that I pray that you will attract, will have to be incredibly strong: strong physically, in the faith, in her vocation, strong in so many ways! For Sister St. Claude, all we can do now is pray that our Lord will take care of her. Perhaps she can return here to Austin during the summer months?"

"I will insist upon that, Your Lordship! It is the custom of our Congregation that we come back to the Motherhouse each summer for rest and retreat. I will not deny our Sisters here in Texas the same privilege!" Her voice was strident as she spoke the last sentence.

"Very well. Do you think Sister St. Claude can be ready to go to Corpus Christi in a couple of months?"

"I will do my best to prepare her, Your Lordship. Will you escort her yourself?"

"If it is possible." The Bishop would make no promises and indeed, when Sister St. Claude was sent to Father Gonnard's school in Corpus Christi on March 7, 1867, the day after Ash Wednesday, she went alone.

Though it was not the custom of the Sisters of Providence to send and receive mail during Lent, Mother St. Andrew had given Sister St. Claude a dispensation from this restriction, and within a few days of her arrival in Corpus Christi, Sister St. Claude wrote to her superior. However, it was nearly Easter before the letter arrived. Mother St. Andrew would remember that Lent as one of the longest in her life as she worried about her Sister whom she had sent into uncharted waters.

Once Sister St. Claude's letter had arrived, Mother read and reread it.

... and, Father Gonnard is very amiable. But he works so hard. He has already begun a school for boys and I am to begin school for girls for which he is very enthusiastic. Father Gonnard is from Loire and his assistant, Father Miconleau, is also from our dear homeland. I so appreciate being able to converse with them in French! The school for boys has over a dozen students and Father Gonnard promises that the school for girls will grow as well.

I live on the second floor and have few comforts and no luxuries! Only the barest essentials! But I am fine and will do my best to begin a school that the Congregation will be proud of. Father tells me that the school term will last until May as the children will be required for farm work during the summer months. Thank God that is only two months away! I miss you and Sister St. Joseph very much. You are so far away!

The last lines brought tears to Mother's eyes each and every time she read them. But, she thought, I may as well get used to this. From now on, each time that I send a Sister away on mission to begin a school, she will be far away from the mother-community. We must all depend on Providence!

Spring months turned into summer and by the end of June Sister St. Claude had returned to Austin. Though she wanted her two Sisters to rest during the months of July and August, Mother St. Andrew believed that they should follow their usual experience at St. Jean-de-Bassel. Having investigated the curriculum for teachers for the State of Texas, Mother had obtained several textbooks that she wished to study so that she could discuss with them the state-required instructional program.

The summer days were filled with study, a review of the writings of Father Moye so that Sister St. Joseph could become familiar with her Congregation's founder, and rest. Mother's main frustration was that there would be no formal retreat for them but she was grateful that her brother Nicolas was a devout priest and provided them with daily Mass and frequent Holy Hours with Exposition of the Blessed Sacrament.

Sister St. Claude entertained them with stories of Corpus Christi; and, Sister St. Joseph, hungry for news of her family and friends there, found that their common knowledge of Corpus Christi now brought her even closer to Sister St. Claude.

Though she was teary-eyed as she said goodbye, Sister St. Claude dutifully returned to Corpus Christi after the three nuns had celebrated the Congregational patronal Feast of St. Anne together on July 26.

The first letter from Sister St. Claude after her return to Corpus Christi worried Mother St. Andrew to distraction.

> *I arrived safely on the second of August only to find that Corpus Christi is under siege from the ravages of the yellow fever. Hundreds are ill and Father Gonnard and I spend day and night nursing our parishioners. This letter will be brief as I must rest for at least an hour before Father and I go out again to tend the sick. Pray for us that we may remain strong.*

Those few lines would be etched onto Mother St. Andrew's heart forever. She suddenly realized that she would always be sending her dear Sisters into harm's way. Disease and deprivation would confront them and she would never be able to adequately prepare them for all the unforeseen pitfalls of working among those on the frontier.

Continuing to worry that Sister St. Claude herself would succumb to the dreaded disease, she asked Sister St. Joseph, also concerned for her family and friends, and her brother Nicolas to join her in a novena to Our Lady of Prompt Succor. The three remained after Mass each day for the prescribed nine days, praying for Sister St. Claude and the people of Corpus Christi.

It was during the novena that Nicolas came to his sister. His eyes were bright with tears as he stammered out the contents of a letter he had just received from their sister Marie-Anne in LaWalck. Pierre had died. Evidently he had been ill only a short while, suffering with pains in his heart.

"Oh, Nicolas. For our dear mother to have to bury a third child. And, poor Eva and little Marie. What will become of them?"

"Here, I'll let you read Marie-Anne's letter," Nicolas said, handing her the small white pages covered in delicate script.

The letter was brief, but Marie-Anne wrote of how devasted their mother was. Over time she had become frail and the death of her eldest son would take its toll, Marie-Anne feared. Eva would keep the store; she was the better grocer anyway.

"I hope that little Marie will be distracting for *Maman*. Let's see—she might be three or four by now?"

"Yes," Nicolas said. "But, it will be hard for *Maman*, won't it? I had to write the letter to her about Celestin's death. I could feel her tears on my heart as I penned the words." Tears streamed down his cheeks as this missionary priest considered the loss of another brother.

"Can your Mass tomorrow be for Pierre?" Mother St. Andrew asked mournfully. "I know that the parishioners will be happy to pray with us for the repose of his soul."

"Of course. Shall we write *Maman* tonight? I believe she needs to hear from us as soon as possible. It could be October before she receives the letter."

"I'll have a page ready for tomorrow morning's mail," Mother St. Andrew assured him.

The two missionaries separated with heavy hearts. Pierre had been only forty-two years old. A sad loss for their family.

Sister St. Claude's next letter, dated September 8, 1867, arriving only at the end of September, truly frightened Mother St. Andrew.

> *Father Gonnard died yesterday. We thought that the devastation of the yellow fever was over and, though he and Father Miconleau were both very ill, Father Padey who came to help us was hopeful that his confreres would recover. Alas! Le bon Dieu must have wanted to reward their labors as both dear priests died last night. Requiescant in pace! I remain in good health, though I am exhausted. We rely totally on Divine Providence!*

Mother's fears did not abate even when she finally received a third letter from Sister St. Claude in November.

> *We are beginning to return to normal here. I was able to open the school for girls; and our new pastor, Father Berthet, has moved the girls' school to a building that had been a seminary. He is now conducting the boys' school in the building I have abandoned. Each of us has an improved situation!*
>
> *Though I have survived this terrible ordeal, I humbly ask if could please come to Austin for the Christmas holiday. I wonder now if I can continue here and I must talk with you.*

The conversation at Christmas revealed that Sister St. Claude was not doing well in Corpus Christi. Though she was not ill, she simply could not rest, as she was now afraid of all that was unpredictable there. The soldiers who dominated the town scared her; the new pastor was more distant than Father Gonnard who had been like a brother to her; parishioners were devastated by the loss of loved ones during the epidemic. Many families, fearing another breakout of yellow fever, had kept their children home from school. Though Sister St. Claude was willing to return to Corpus Christi for the spring term, Mother St. Andrew was certain that the Congregation could not honor this commitment for much longer.

Just before Christmas, Mother St. Andrew received a letter in a familiar handwriting. Hurrying to open the precious possession, she called out to Sister St. Claude and Sister St. Joseph who were in the convent kitchen.

"Sisters, come! We have a letter from home!"

Sister St. Claude, with instant enthusiasm, came running. "A letter from home? From whom?"

"It is from Sister Constantine. She wrote it on October 2, the feast of the Guardian Angels. I will read it aloud.

Mes chères Sœurs,

It is my hope that this letter finds you in good health and that all is going well for you both. I am writing, first of all, to tell you that our dear Mère Adrienne has gone to God. We are saddened by her passing, but we are grateful that she did not suffer. Mère Basilisse bravely took the responsibilities of Superior General, but, her heart being weak, she succumbed on May 1, 1867, only one month after the passing of Mère Adrienne. Our motherhouse was in mourning for months and we are just beginning to recover from the loss of these two stalwart religious who have given us such wise guidance over the last many years.

With deepest humility, I also inform you that last month I was elected Superior of our dear Congregation. I beg your prayers for me as I

begin this calling in the new year. I am sur-
rounded with very qualified assistants and I
will rely on God. As you know, dear Sisters, I am
very hopeful for our mission in Texas as I believe
that our growing numbers of vocations here in
France require us to look outside Europe for
God's needs. I will keep you in my thoughts and
prayers but for various reasons, my letters may
be sparse.

We are well here. The recent deaths of Mère
Adrienne and Mère Basilisse have given us all
pause to reflect on the brevity of this life and the
rewards of eternity.

May God bless your work.
I remain, in Divine Providence,
Mère Constantine, Sup. Genl.

Having read the letter to her Sisters, Mother St. Andrew sat back in the chair, her eyes sparkling.

"I always believed that Sister Constantine would one day be our Superior. She will always support our mission here. In that we can place our trust. Let us each write her a congratulatory note and I will mail them in the morning! Now we must pray the *De profundis* for our dear Mother Adrienne and dear Mother Basilisse. *Requiescant in pace.*"

The realization that her new Superior General was completely in favor of their missionary efforts gave Mother a sense of buoyancy. She had always known that Mother Adrienne was less than posi-tive about the Texas venture, but now that Mother Constantine was in charge it seemed to her that God was smiling down on them. It would be a happy Christmas; Emmanuel—God-with-us—was now much more than a theological idea!

Sending Sister St. Claude back to Corpus Christi after the Feast of the Epiphany was hard, but Mother, now sustained by their letter from Mother Constantine, decided to put the future of that mission in the hands of Providence, finding comfort in Father Moye's own words: ***"Either the project is God's will or it is not. If it is His holy will, He who is all-powerful has a thousand means, a thousand ways, to accomplish it. If it is not according to His good pleasure, I renounce it right now."*** And then she turned her attention to another matter.

Just before the Christmas Season, Mother St. Andrew had answered a knock at the school building door to find Father Nicolas accompanied by two women. Introductions revealed that Mrs. John Wolf and her daughter Phillipina had come to Austin on business, but that Phillipina had wanted to meet the Sisters at St. Mary's Parish. It had taken this young German woman only one encounter with the Sisters of Providence to believe that God was calling her to be one of them.

During the visit, she announced that she was willing to leave the family farm on Walnut Creek, thirty miles south of Austin in Bastrop County, and become a nun if Mother St. Andrew would have her.

The Wolf family was well known both to Father Nicolas and to Bishop Dubuis. Among the earliest settlers in that part of the State, the faithful Catholics often hosted the circuit-riding priests in their home when the clergy came to that area to celebrate Mass. Phillipina Wolf, the twenty-three year-old daughter of the family, had never married and both Bishop Dubuis and Father Nicolas recognized a religious vocation in her and had been encouraging. If Mother St. Andrew agreed to accept her, Father Nicolas said that he would happily go to Walnut Creek to get her after the new year.

Plans were tentatively made to have Phillipina come to Austin after Sister St. Claude departed for Corpus Christi. Mother had thought all of this over carefully. She was sympathetic with

---

*   **The Directory, p. 82**

Sister St. Claude's feelings about being alone in Corpus Christi, but she feared that if Miss Wolf came to Austin while Sister St. Claude was still there, Sister's despondency would thwart Miss Wolf's possible vocation. Best for her to come to Austin after Sister St. Claude had returned to Corpus Christi.

Just after the Feast of the Epiphany, Father Nicolas set off for Bastrop County, promising to return with Miss Wolf by the Feast of the Purification, February 2. Taking this amount of time would allow the devoted priest to stop along the way to celebrate Mass with the many German families who lived in the wilderness of south-central Texas. The month of January would give Mother St. Andrew ample time to prepare for a new candidate. She had always believed that Sister St. Joseph's entry had been too rushed. With a year in Austin behind her, she felt much more settled and would take more time with Miss Wolf.

January 1868 passed quickly. With Nicolas gone, she and Sister St. Joseph taught all the boys as well as the girls; and, though they were pleased to welcome more students after the holidays, the school, at near capacity, was a challenge.

True to his word, Nicolas returned to Austin at the end of the last week of January to announce to his sister that Miss Wolf would be arriving in Austin on the Saturday stage.

Father Nicolas met Phillipina Wolf at the stage station on Saturday, February 1 and, carrying her valise, guided her toward Brazos Street where Mother St. Andrew awaited her newest vocation.

A tall woman with blonde hair, Miss Wolf, spoke some English and fluent German and appeared to be quite capable of just about anything. She was an amiable person; and by the end of the day, Mother St. Andrew and Sister St. Joseph knew all there was to know about the Wolf Family and their emigration from Würges, Germany, to the middle of Texas in 1854. The dozen years of helping her family build a house, scratch for their food, and settle into Texas had made Phillipina into a sturdy woman who had all the makings of a good religious.

Sister Mary Agnes Wolf, CDP Date unknown, but after 1878.
(Courtesy, Texas Catholic Archives, Austin, TX)

In the next few months Mother St. Andrew had her hands full: teaching fulltime in St. Mary's School which already needed another classroom, continuing to mentor Sister St. Joseph in religious life, and spending time forming Phillipina into a Sister of Providence. She wanted her newest subject to understand that she was joining a Congregation whose motherhouse was in France, so Mother took every opportunity to tell Phillipina tales of life in their convent in St. Jean-de-Bassel. Though she was certain that Sister St. Joseph would never feel connected to the French motherhouse, mostly due to her age at the time of entering the Congregation and her American roots, Mother had more hope for Miss Wolf. They could speak German together, and, with the German influence on Alsace and Lorraine, Mother hoped that Miss Wolf might come to feel a kindred spirit with their French-German motherhouse.

Seeing great progress in her postulant, Mother St. Andrew decided to broach the subject of her future in the Congregation on the First Sunday of Lent, March 1.

"Phillipina, I must say that I am very encouraged by your progress in religious life. And, with continued practice and study, I think you'll make a fine teacher."

"Thank you, Mother. I am trying," Phillipina replied.

"Are you happy here, my dear?"

"Yes, Mother. I feel very much a part of this school and its success. I miss my family a bit, but each of my sisters married and left the farm. We were seeing each other less and less because of the distances. I think this is my calling." Her straightforward words evidenced the simplicity expected of a Sister of Providence and Mother St. Andrew was glad to see it. Though the four fundamental virtues of the Congregation—simplicity, abandonment to Providence, poverty and charity—must be developed over the lifetime of a Sister of Providence, the rudiments of the virtues had to come with the candidate at her entrance. The virtues could be developed during the postulancy and novitiate, but the potential already had to be in place. In Miss Wolf Mother saw the seeds of these four virtues and was hopeful about their flowering as she matured in religious life.

Just before Easter, Phillipina Wolf was received into the novitiate of the Sisters of Providence during a simple ceremony at which Father Feltin presided, representing the Bishop. Mother St. Andrew had been able to find brown yard goods and she and Sister St. Joseph made a habit for the young novice. The European-styled headcoverings came from of Mother St. Andrew's trunk and a white bonnet was fashioned by a parishioner who had training as a milliner. The new Sister Mary Agnes looked every bit as nice as any novice at St. Jean-de-Bassel! All that was missing was the large rosary worn from a belt at the waist, but she could do without that.

Thinking that it was time to ask for more items for the habits of future Sisters, Mother decided that her next letter to Mother Constantine would include a list of needed fabrics. Her last letter to France had described their situations: Sister St. Claude's difficulties in Corpus Christi, their successful school in Austin, more about Sister St. Joseph, and now the acceptance of a new novice. Communication with the motherhouse was frustrating at best. In the best circumstances, a letter to France might take as long as four or five weeks. Mother wondered constantly whether or not her letters were being received. News they received through the parishioners about their

German families spoke of little more than impending war, spreading revolutions, and economic unrest. It seemed inevitable that France and Germany would soon come to blows.

Mother St. Andrew brought her fears to Nicolas one day while they were sweeping the classrooms. "I fear, Nicolas, that war will descend upon our dear country. Have you heard any news?"

"*Herr* Gutmann received a letter from his brother in Munich yesterday. There is no doubt in the minds of Germans that war will come. I personally worry about Louis. He is now the age when he could be conscripted into the French army. I have written to him over and over again urging him to come to America. Louis can't get any land around LaWalck; Pierre's wife has the store. Though Eva can make a living in the store and care for *Maman*, she can't support everyone in the family. For Louis, it seems that it is either the army or emigrating. I keep telling him that I have plenty of work for him here!"

"I agree. Coming to America would at least give him a chance. I think you should write to Louis again."

"Yes, you are right. I'll do so tonight."

A letter that came from their family, received just after Easter, confirmed their fears. War, indeed, was impending and Louis had decided to emigrate. Though not certain of Louis' travel plans, the family in LaWalck agreed to give him money for passage and as soon as arrangements could be made, Louis would leave France.

Their second summer in Austin was similar to the first: study, prayer, and rest. Sister St. Claude had come home in a weakened condition; and during Bishop Dubuis' visit to Austin in early June 1868, Mother St. Andrew spoke with him about her Congregation's future.

"Your Lordship, I so appreciate your giving me time to review our status. I know that you are quite busy and that you will be here only a short while."

"Yes, Mother. On this trip I intend to travel to San Antonio, then on to Castroville and Fredericksburg, and back to Corpus Christi. I often say that I spend more time on horseback than I do in a Church! How are you and your Sisters doing?"

"Sister St. Joseph and I are doing very well here. The school continues to grow and Father Nicolas has plans for enlarging the school building. But I remain very concerned about Sister St. Claude. As I've said to you before, she has not been the same since the yellow fever epidemic and the death of Father Gonnard. She needs to be closer to community and I must ask you to allow her to return to Austin. If she does not, I fear for her vocation—and her life."

Mother's voice was firm. She had learned that Bishop Dubuis welcomed a frank assessment and that he would do his best to meet her needs.

"I, too, am worried about Sister," the fatherly bishop responded. "Father Berthet has written to me about her and he also believes that it would be better for her to return to Austin. Are you aware that she is considering joining another Congregation?"

"Sister only mentioned that to me briefly at Christmas, but I think that her return to Austin will settle things for her."

"Very well, then. See how she is after her summer rest. Feel free to make a decision at that time. I'm certain that Father Berthet will adjust as needed." After a short pause, the Bishop continued. "And now I must speak with you about another matter."

Whenever he began in that manner, Mother St. Andrew knew that a big change could be in the offing.

"What is it, your Lordship?" she asked tentatively.

"I have been giving much thought to your future in Austin."

This took Mother St. Andrew off guard completely. Her back stiffened as she prepared to receive his thinking.

"I believe that Sister Mary Agnes," the Bishop continued, "is a very fine vocation. She will endure. I hope that Sister St. Joseph will endure, and Sister St. Claude. But, I had hoped that by now you would have received more young women. Our need is so great and your Congregation is my only hope for providing parochial schools. I therefore propose to you to move your headquarters to Castroville." He rushed through this last sentence and then waited.

"Castroville?" Mother uttered only one word.

"Yes. You know, I myself served there before I was ordained Bishop. The people are Alsatian, as you yourself are. They will welcome you, and I believe they will not only send their children to your school, but they will send their daughters to your convent!"

"Where is Castroville?"

"It is about thirty miles west of San Antonio," the Bishop responded simply. "It is a parish of about 225 families—quite large by Texas standards! I have recently sent the parish a very fine young French priest, Father Pierre Richard, and he plans to lay a cornerstone for a new church—their third!—this summer. I'm going there next month for Confirmation and that ceremony. The diocese owns a large section of land surrounding the first church and I intend to give you that land for a school and a motherhouse."

Hearing those last words gave Mother a new vision of this possibility. To own land! That was exciting! But she did not want to appear too eager.

"But your Lordship, as you know, we have just purchased the land for the new convent building here at St. Mary's. I told you that we would use Sister Mary Agnes' patrimony for that endeavor and that has come about. Will you ask us for this land here in exchange for the Castroville property?" Her talks with Mother St. Pierre at St. Ursula's-by-the-Sea had made Mother St. Andrew very cautious about buying and selling property.

"Oh, no, Mother. Your land here is secure. The Castroville property will be an additional property. If you are amenable to this plan, I will make specific arrangements with Father Richard for you to move to Castroville. Perhaps you could make this move at the end of August?"

Though his plans seemed premature, Mother remembered those three young women from Lyons who were now Sisters of Charity of the Incarnate Word and realized that her Bishop was a man who waited for no one. "Very well, your Lordship. I will think all of this over and give you my answer before you leave tomorrow."

"Thank you, Mother. That is all that I can ask." The Bishop knew that she would not refuse him.

And, the next day, she gave her ecclesiastical superior an answer that would change her life and the life of the Congregation forever.

CHAPTER X

CASTROVILLE

There was so much to be done! Mother St. Andrew felt daunted by the details that needed her attention before she could leave for Castroville. Sister St. Claude's weakened condition had determined the fate of their Congregation's commitment to Corpus Christi, but with the security of the land they owned in Austin, Sister St. Claude and Sister St. Joseph could administer the school at St. Mary's parish for years. Father Nicolas would support them in every way. Mother planned immediately to take Sister Mary Agnes with her to Castroville. That young nun would survive anywhere!

Within the week Mother St. Andrew wrote to Mother Constantine telling her about the planned change from Austin to Castroville. Knowing little about Castroville, she gave few details in her letter about her future home; but she was quick to emphasize that the Congregation would receive a large portion of land which would become the motherhouse property and that the Bishop was certain that the Alsatian settlement would provide a ripe harvest of vocations. Even with nothing more than that to support her decision to change locations, Mother St. Andrew trusted that Mother Constantine would support the Bishop's choice for a motherhouse. The small village of St. Jean-de-Bassel had proven to be an excellent location for the French motherhouse—quiet, almost isolated, with a stagecoach way station only a few miles away. Castroville would have the same qualities, offering a quiet place to prepare novices and to harbor the professed Sisters during their summer rest and study.

July was spent in Austin reviewing with Sister St. Joseph the maintenance on the school and convent building still under construction and helping Sister St. Claude identify how she should best disengage herself from Corpus Christi. It was agreed that she and Sister St. Joseph would return to Corpus Christi at the end of July in order to help Father Berthet find a schoolteacher. This would also give Sister St. Joseph an opportunity to visit her family and friends there.

All four Sisters celebrated the Congregational feast of St. Anne on July 26 with Mass and a special breakfast of German sausages and Alsatian-style pastries. Then everyone walked to the stagecoach station to bid *adieu* to Sister St. Claude and Sister St. Joseph. As the two nuns mounted the stagecoach to San Antonio where they would change to go south to Corpus Christi, they seemed enthusiastic about the rugged six-day trip ahead. They had agreed that they would return to Austin by the end of August.

In the meantime, Sister Mary Agnes spent July and August studying, adding some new pieces to her habit which had been rudimentary when she had received it in the Spring, and making a last visit to her family home on Walnut Creek. In Mother's mind the Wolf family's generosity—both Mary Agnes' inheritance from her father's estate which Mother St. Andrew used to purchase the land where the new school and convent stood, as well as the gift of a daughter for the service of the Church in Texas—needed to be honored. A visit from their daughter was the best possible way. Mother St. Andrew would not cheat an aging mother out of what might well be her last visit with her daughter! And Mother was certain of Sister Mary Agnes' vocation. The young nun would return!

Being alone in Austin for most of the month of August gave Mother St. Andrew time to put her affairs in order. In the fashion of every Sister of Providence, she would leave her school in perfect condition. Sisters St. Claude and St. Joseph would not have to wonder about anything: inventories would be up-to-date; recommendations for future purchases would be filed; recommendations for their ongoing education would be itemized. As she worked on the ledgers of the Congregational accounts and the school accounts, she began to realize that she might not ever return to Austin. She also recognized that though she left assets behind in Austin she had basically nothing with which to begin the Castroville venture. Ah, well! Another opportunity to rely on Providence!

Travel was precarious and she had no idea what she would find in Castroville, but she had a feeling that her own Alsatian people would never let the Sisters go without basic necessities. So much would have to be left in the hands of Providence; but then, God's large hands which had fashioned the world could cradle her small beginnings of a school and convent left behind in Austin and build another for her in Castroville!

By the end of August, the three Sister-travelers had returned. Sister St. Claude and Sister St. Joseph had found a Miss LaFare to take over the school in Corpus Christi and Sister Mary Agnes bravely indicated that she feared her goodbyes to her mother might be her last. *

Mother St. Andrew took time to visit privately with the two she would leave behind.

"How was your departure from Corpus Christi, my dear?" was her opening question to Sister St. Claude. For Mother, this question was broad and she hoped that Sister St. Claude's answer would include her deepest feelings. She was not disappointed.

"Mother, I admit that I was somewhat saddened at leaving Corpus Christi. So many of the people there have been very good to me. And, the parishioners and I became so close to one another during that

---

* **Mrs. Catherine Bermbach Wolf died in 1869. She and her husband John Wolf (d. 1868) are buried near the location of their home on Walnut Creek in Bastrop County outside the town of Rockne, Texas.**

awful epidemic! Why, one of my last experiences was to stand for a young woman at her baptism! I think I made a positive difference there,"—and she added this last with sincere regret—"but I had to leave. If I had stayed … well, I don't know." With this last, her voice trailed off. After a long pause, she added a question. "Do you think I have disappointed our good God? I know that my trust in Providence falters. Perhaps I should have trusted more."

"Sister, none of us can trust enough. We are all weak and we will all disappoint God. I don't know if your decision to return is one that disappoints God or if God is pleased with your wisdom. Each of us is limited: limited in health, in spiritual strength, in intelligence. We can only do what we can do. And, don't forget: it is actually I, as Superior, who made the decision for you to withdraw from Corpus Christi. If God has a problem with what I am doing, He will have to work it out with me in Purgatory!" She said this last with a smile on her face. There was no use preying on Sister St. Claude's fragility and plying her with more guilt than she already carried.

"Thank you, Mother. You always seem to know what to say."

"To tell you the truth," Mother continued, "I only hope that I can follow my own advice. Sometimes my Alsatian heart becomes somewhat stony! And now that I'm moving into an Alsatian village, pray for me, my dear Sister. You above anyone know how we are!" she said, again with humor and an honesty reserved for her lifelong friend.

"Everything will be fine, Mother. You have so very much to offer and being among your own people…. Well, I think Providence is working all of this out!"

"Will you be all right here with Sister St. Joseph?"

"Yes, I think so. She is very nice and we get along. But, Mother, I have not abandoned my thoughts of changing Congregations. I will do my best here, but perhaps I am more suited to a community that is more," she paused as she searched for the word, "'protected,'" she concluded.

"I appreciate your honesty. I invite you to trust the leadings of Providence, as shall I. Please, please, dear Sister, write to me frequently so that I can understand your heart." This last request was made with such fervor that Sister St. Claude vowed that she would write monthly.

"Good. Now—I know that you have much to do to settle in here at Austin. The new school building and convent will be ready within the month and you and Sister St. Joseph will have better accommodations. Now that my brother Louis is here, the construction on the new convent-school is moving very fast. I wish that Sister Mary Agnes and I would be here for the opening of the new building, but, I fear that we will be long gone!"

"Do not worry, Mother. Sister St. Joseph and I will manage. And," she made her last promise looking straight into Mother's brown eyes, "I will depend on the guidance of Providence. I promise."

"That is all that any of us can ask of the other," Mother St. Andrew said with satisfaction. "That's what makes us Sisters of Providence!"

Her conversation with Sister St. Joseph was similarly positive. Sister St. Joseph had devoted herself tirelessly to St. Mary's School and she was very protective of it. Leaving her behind to manage the school with Sister St. Claude was the best decision. She and Father Nicolas worked well together and she continually helped him with parish duties, standing with those who needed a godparent at baptism or couples who needed a witness for the marriage. If Mother St. Andrew had not been so certain of her brother's priestly honor, she might have been concerned about Sister St. Joseph's vocation. But she knew it to be completely secure.

The day of departure arrived. Passage for the two nuns on the September 2 stage to San Antonio had been booked and paid for by Bishop Dubuis who would meet them in San Antonio.

It rained every day of the journey and the barely discernible road, not much more than a path, was nearly impassable. The passengers—the two nuns, three businessmen, and two railroad agents—

crammed into the small seating space inside the coach, strained to keep the canvas covering over the cabin windows to keep the rain from pouring in. Traveling in the darkened, confined, dank space was unpleasant, and the slow-going made for a disgruntled attitude among the men. Uncivil words were exchanged, and one man put his hand on his side arm. The nuns were certain that their presence alone kept tempers under control.

Crossing the Blanco River before their arrival in San Marcos had been treacherous. Both nuns had a deep appreciation of the skill of their driver, a tough old guy who chewed tobacco and swore at the horses, forcing them to do as he wanted.

After an overnight in the muddy village of San Marcos where the streets ran with water, the stage crept along toward the larger town of New Braunfels, founded in 1845. Named for its founder, German Prince Carl of Solms-Braunfels, New Braunfels had been populated with German immigrants recruited by the *Adelsverein* society.

Another overnight, this time in New Braunfels and again in a strange inn, taxed the weary, muddy travelers. At the Comal Hotel, the regular stagecoach stop, the travelers were accommodated for the night in cramped rooms that, because of constant use, looked worn and none too clean. When the rain finally stopped, Mother and Sister Mary Agnes took a short walk through the bustling town. Most of the overheard conversations were in German and she wondered if this town would ever want a Catholic school with her Sisters. Of course, she had no one to send at the moment, but plans should be made! The town looked as though its economy was stable. They walked past a big feed store that looked quite new, a sure sign of a financially stable area. The farms must be large, Mother thought. Another store selling farm implements also looked like its business was doing well.

"Let's stop in this bakery and buy something fresh," Mother St. Andrew said to Sister Mary Agnes, somewhat impulsively. Upon opening the door to Nadler's Bakery, the smell of fresh baked goods brought back memories of LaWalck. "We had such a bakery in LaWalck, my home village."

"It smells like my mother's kitchen," Sister Mary Agnes said. Her tone was reflective, and Mother knew that the young nun realized that she would probably never see her mother again.

They bought a loaf of fresh bread and a German tart for each of them. "Father Nicolas gave me a little money. I think this is exactly the way to spend it," Mother said. She so seldom spent any money on luxuries that Sister Mary Agnes was surprised. She was seeing a side to her superior that was more often hidden. Mother St. Andrew did love her sweets!

After they returned to the inn, the innkeeper gave them cups of steaming coffee which they took up to their room. As they drank the hot beverage and ate their tarts, Mother St. Andrew told her companion Mother St. Pierre's story of an overnight stop on her way to San Antonio at the beginning of the Civil War.

"I wonder who will be at the Ursuline convent in San Antonio," Mother St. Andrew asked as though she were thinking aloud. "Mother St. Pierre spoke of three of their Sisters from Galveston who had founded the new academy: Sisters St. Angela, Augustine, and Marie, along with some others from France and New Orleans. But that was back in 1852. I believe that Sister Augustine was still in San Antonio when Mother St. Pierre took refuge there during their terrible war, but now I just don't remember who she said is still there, except for the two Ursulines who traveled with us from Lyons. I know that we'll have to stay at least one night with them. They were so good to Sister St. Claude, Sister St. Joseph and myself in Galveston. I look forward to meeting these nuns as well. They operate a beautiful school in Galveston, and I am sure this one will be a model academy also. I want you to take time to sit in on some classes if they will permit. That is the best way to learn to teach!" Mother saw in Sister Mary Agnes all the makings of a good school-teacher and director. Capable, resourceful, even assertive in her own quiet way, she would be very effective in helping new schools get started. In her dreaming, Mother St. Andrew imagined being able to send Sister Mary Agnes with new novices entering from Castroville to towns such as New Braunfels to being schools for the German Catholics flooding into Texas.

The next afternoon they arrived in San Antonio. Though the rain had let up, streams were still swollen and crossing the Guadalupe River had been nearly miraculous. The ferry had made two trips: one with the passengers and the other one with the coach. The experienced driver had forced the horses across and was soaking wet upon the conclusion of his task, but he seemed to take no notice. In fact, the two nuns laughingly commented to each other that the river water might have been the first real soaking his clothes had seen in months!

The coach rattled to the station just a block west of the Alamo in San Antonio and upon inquiry, Mother learned that San Fernando Church was a short walk away. They set off west down Alameda Street as directed and within fifteen minutes they arrived at San Fernando Church where the Bishop had said to meet them. San Antonio had not escaped the rain, and the river, usually a sleepy stream, had actually left its banks in places. The bridge over the river was busy with traffic that might have taken other routes in dry weather.

Finding their way to the priests' residence at the rear of the Church, Mother St. Andrew asked immediately for Bishop Dubuis, and within minutes the Bishop came to the parlor where the two Sisters were resting.

"Mother! Welcome to San Antonio. Or, I should say, *Bienvenida a San Antonio!* My Spanish isn't very good," he continued in French, "but even a little bit goes a long way."

He was genuinely glad to see them and wasted no time in showing them around the Church which was being enlarged and updated, and actually was not very large. Mother's own home parish of Sts. Peter and Paul in LaWalck was actually a larger structure!

"I will have Confirmations on September 9, and then at the end of the month we'll lay the new cornerstone right here!" The Bishop's enthusiastic tone revealed his pride in the growth of his diocese. "I have asked a parishioner to take you in his wagon to the Ursuline Convent which is about a mile to the north. You could probably walk, but you are no doubt tired from your journey. *Señor* Perez will be here shortly. I won't be going with you, but Mother St. Angela expects you."

"Thank you, Your Lordship. You always take good care of us."

"Word has come to me from Castroville that the Medina River is everywhere after the rains and the ferry is not able to get across at this time. We'll just wait here for a few days. It is a day's travel and I really don't want to arrive and not be able to cross the river. Mother St. Angela assured me that you are welcome to stay as long as you need to."

"The Ursulines are very kind to us. Your Lordship, I have been thinking," Mother began tentatively. Her talks with Mother St. Pierre in Galveston and the experience of buying the land in Austin had sharpened her business acumen. "Could we possibly meet while we are here before we go to Castroville where I imagine there will be many distractions. We need to know exactly what land in Castroville you want us to have. I would like to have something in writing," she concluded simply.

"I was thinking the very same thing. I will come to the Ursuline Convent tomorrow afternoon and together we will outline the specifics about our arrangement. I think, also, that it is important that you begin to consider which parishes in the diocese you will be able to take on for schools. We will put all of this down in writing."

"Thank you, Your Lordship." Mother knew that the Bishop would not want too much conversation at this point in the negotiations. A man of action, he would prefer to make up the contract as they talked about it tomorrow.

The welcome by the Ursulines was reminiscent of their welcome at St. Ursula-by-the-Sea two years previously. And, true to her expectations, their academy was superb. Both the townspeople and the people from surrounding small villages sent their daughters to Ursuline to be "finished." Both Sisters were welcomed to visit classes as they wished and when Mother St. Andrew tentatively asked if she might speak to the girls about non-cloistered religious life, Mother St. Angela was exuberant.

"Why, of course, *ma mère*! Your work is going to be so important for the diocese. Perhaps some of our own girls might want to join you. In fact, there is one girl, Anna Schultz, who has shown an interest in religious life. But I really don't think we're the right community for her. She's a 'rough and tumble' type. She'll need more action than we will ever be able to offer!" Said with such warm humor, this last comment drew laughter from both Mother St. Angela and Mother St. Andrew.

"Maybe she's just what we need! By her last name I presume she is German?" Mother inquired.

"Yes, her family came from Bavaria, I think. Her mother and father are wonderful people," Mother St. Angela said.

"As you know, there are so many German immigrants in Texas. The small towns, I hope, will want schools. While I was en route from Galveston to Austin in 1866, the pastor at Frelsburg asked me to send Sisters to him. I hope to welcome many young women who will want to be religious. The more vocations we have, the more schools we can provide."

As the two nuns concluded their conversation, a young girl with long blonde hair came toward them as they stood in the hallway.

"What is it, Barbara?" Mother St. Angela asked the young student.

"Mother," she addressed Mother St. Andrew, "I heard that you were here. I want to be a Sister like you!"

"You seem very courageous, my dear, and that is just the quality needed to be a teacher in a village school. But, how old are you?"

"I will be fourteen on my next birthday, Mother."

"And when is your birthday, my child?"

"In November, Mother." This girl, though young, was well-mannered and seemed confident.

"Excellent. When you are fifteen, you may enter, if you still believe that God is calling you."

"Thank you, Mother. I will write to you on my fifteenth birthday!" The girl went off to join her classmates and Mother St. Andrew turned to Mother St. Angela.

"Will I hear from her, Mother? What is your assessment of her?" Mother St. Andrew asked Mother St. Angela.

"Barbara Keller is a very fine, very serious young lady. In fact, her family is one of the original families from Castroville. They came to Texas from the Diocese of Strasbourg as you yourself did, I believe? If she enters your community, she would probably make a good religious!"

"Fine! We will see what happens!"

The next day Bishop Dubuis arrived at the convent in the early part of the afternoon. Never a man to waste time, he began: "Mother, shall we get started? I have some thoughts and I'm sure you do as well."

"Actually, I have given this some thought, Your Lordship." In truth, she had made copious notes about what her little band of religious could do in Texas but she had wisely committed her ideas to memory and was well prepared for this conversation.

"Good. I shall write down our agreed upon plan. Then I will make good copies for each of us to sign and keep. Is that agreeable?"

"Yes, your Lordship." Mother St. Andrew knew that she would never have this golden opportunity again, and she must make the most of it. But, at the same time, she must not appear too eager.

"I, as Bishop," the Bishop began, "agree to give you, Mother St. Andrew ..." At this he stopped, looking pensive. He then continued, "Since you are not incorporated in Texas, I believe it would be best legally to name you personally. Will that be all right?"

After Mother St. Andrew answered in the affirmative, the bishop continued.

"I agree to give you the land in Castroville which lies to the immediate south and west of the parish rectory. Actually, it is the land that the old church, which is now being used as a schoolhouse, stands on—just off the square. This agreement will not describe its exact location, but you shall see when you get there that this is a large portion of land, more than enough for a motherhouse, for a large garden, for a few animals and eventually for a new schoolhouse!"

"That sounds fine, Your Lordship. But, will your successors be similarly committed to this arrangement?" Mother St. Pierre had cautioned Mother St. Andrew to be sure that any agreements she made with Bishop Dubuis would bind future Bishops.

"Very good! I had not thought of that. I will specifically indicate that in our contract." The Bishop sounded pleased that he was dealing with a Superior who was committed to the future of his diocese. "I have given a very clear document to the Sisters of Charity of the Incarnate Word. Do you think that this document should frame your Congregation's mission as well as my commitment to giving you land?"

"I think that is wise. I have come to trust you and to appreciate your style of administering the diocese. I think my Congregation should have a document that protects our future in Texas."

"Good. I have been thinking of which towns and villages might profit from a school operated by your Sisters. To insure that the schools are secure and not mingled with parish properties, I believe that I should indicate that you will own the schoolhouses. What is your opinion?"

"I agree. Which parishes do you propose to give us?"

"I was thinking of those around Castroville: D'Hanis, Fredericksburg and the small missions attached to St. Louis Parish."

"I have made a verbal commitment to the pastor in Frelsburg. I told him that if we get enough vocations, I will begin a school for him. And, when we traveled through New Braunfels, I could see us there as well."

"Very well. I agree to that. South of San Antonio there is a growing community of people from eastern Europe, Polish mostly. What about their parish of Panna-Maria?"

"What does that name mean?" Mother St. Andrew asked with a cautious note in her voice. Though she felt very comfortable with German communities, a Polish community might not be as welcoming of German Sisters.

"It means 'Virgin Mary'."

"In that case, how could I refuse our dear Blessed Mother?"

"Good! I am going to add two more towns, Martines and Bernard. I believe that vocations could come from that area of Texas. Now, for your obligations. I will state that you will abide by Canon Law in your teaching at the schools, that you will not remove anything from the schools without my permission or the permission of my successors, but also that neither I nor my successors will ever be able to take from you the properties of the schools in the towns we agreed upon. Is this sufficient?"

Mother St. Andrew paused. The Bishop had not mentioned the Austin property and she wondered why not. Did his understanding that she owned the land the school and convent were on preclude the need for the mission to be identified in this document? She chose not to ask.

"I believe so, your Lordship," Mother finally said. "I will agree to all we've said."

"In that case, I will draw up the contract and bring it to you in a few days. Perhaps on the 8th? I think we can leave for Castroville the next day."

"Very well, Your Lordship. Sister Mary Agnes and I will be ready."

As it turned out, Bishop Dubuis had over-committed himself and on September 8, after they had signed their contractual arrangement, he gave Mother St. Andrew his blessing. She and Sister Mary Agnes left alone the next morning on the stage for Castroville.

Father Pierre Richard was outside working on the new church when he heard the stage roll into Castroville and stop at the way station across the square. Father Pierre had met every stage for the past two days, hoping that the two Sisters would be on it, and he almost did not stop his work to run across the square to see if this arrival would be they. But he decided to take a chance; and leaving his hammer behind, he dashed across the square, arriving at the station just as a short, black-clad nun climbed off the stage. A second, taller nun followed. Though they had cleaned their habits as best they could at

Father Pierre Richard, Pastor, St. Louis Parish, Castroville 1868-1880. (Courtesy, Catholic Archives of Texas, Austin, TX)

the Ursuline Convent, they still looked muddy and travel-worn.

"*Mes sœurs!* Sisters! I am Father Pierre Richard! *Bienvenue á Castroville!*" Father Richard shouted in his enthusiasm. Without ceremony of further introductions, he embraced them both and kissed each one on both cheeks, as is the custom in France. A young priest, only twenty-seven years old, Father Pierre could hardly contain his excitement at having two nuns come to his parish for his school. Having them take over the education of the children of his parish would leave him free to work on the new church and to devote more time to pastoral duties. "I am so glad to have you here! You're going to love this village. I understand from Bishop Dubuis that you are Alsatian, *ma mère?* The people here are overjoyed to receive

another Alsatian, someone who will truly understand them!"

"*Oui, mon père.* I will do my best." Mother St. Andrew knew that the priest was young, but he seemed like a mere boy. Her conversation with Sister Mary Agnes later that night revealed her thoughts.

"He is so young, our pastor!" Sister Mary Agnes said as they prepared for bed. Father Pierre had given his cottage over to them since there was no proper convent. He himself was sleeping in the sacristy of the church. "But what enthusiasm he has. It would seem that he is able to get the people here to do anything!"

"Yes, he's about your age, don't you think?" Mother St. Andrew asked her young companion tentatively.

"Yes, maybe a year or so older. But he looks younger!"

Mother St. Andrew saw in her new pastor the look that her brother Nicolas had when he visited her in Batzendorf years ago. In Father Pierre's eyes was the same impassioned look of the missionary who truly loves his priesthood and his parish.

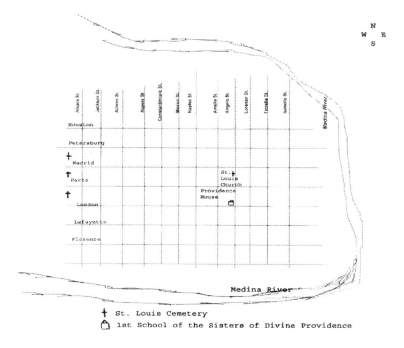

† St. Louis Cemetery
⌂ 1st School of the Sisters of Divine Providence

MAP OF CASTROVILLE, TEXAS

Father Pierre took the full afternoon of their arrival to show them his village—all of which was within a few blocks of his Church. On the same block where the new church was now under construction stood the second church of the village, the one built by Bishop Dubuis. Father Pierre told them the story that he had learned from the Bishop himself about how Dubuis and his assistant Father Domenech had built that church with their own hands, depending completely on Providence for funds and materials.

From the church, they walked across Paris Street to a huge expanse of land. Waving his hand across the acreage, Father Pierre said, "All this is to be yours, Mother. Bishop Dubuis was clear with me on that. We walked the entire property when he was here in July so that I would be certain of the boundaries. Look over there. That's the old church built in 1844. We use it for a schoolhouse now. That's yours, too. Your land continues on the south along London Street back to the west. I'm really not sure how many hectares there are in the property. I know that it goes quite a way up toward the parish cemetery that you can see on the hill. I'll see to it that it is surveyed."

Mother was very impressed with this young priest and his exacting yet pastoral manner. She trusted him immediately, believing that Providence had indeed sent her to the right place.

From her property where eventually a new convent would be built, the priest walked with them eastward down Paris Street past a few homes down to Mann's Store on the corner of Paris and Lorenzo Streets, talking all the while about the layout of his little village.

"We're on Paris Street and the next block over that way," he said as he pointed south, "is London. And that way," pointing the opposite direction, "is Madrid St. The town founder, Henri Castro, loved the major cities of Europe, so he named his streets for them: Paris, London, Madrid, Florence, Naples, Petersburg, Vienna, Berlin, Athens, Constantinople. And now and then he threw in the names of his family members and friends: Amelia St., that's the one the churches face, for his wife; Lorenzo St. and Angelo

St. for his sons; and Isabelle St. for his daughter. Then he named Houston, Washington, and Lafayette Streets for men he admired. You'll find that you've come to a very cosmopolitan little place," he finished with a grin.

At the store Father Pierre introduced the Sisters to Georgius Mann. He told *Monsieur* Mann that the Sisters would be shopping there for what they needed and that he should put their items on the parish bill. A bakery facing the square on Lorenzo Street and a meat market were the next stops with similar instructions to each shopkeeper. In each case Father Pierre seemed to be well liked even though he had been in the parish less than a year. Mother St. Andrew made a mental note of this.

After their initial introduction to the parish environs in the village, Father Pierre invited the Sisters to join him for vespers and supper.

"I hope you will be comfortable in my little rectory, *mes sœurs*. I regret that we do not have better accommodations for you," Father Pierre said apologetically. "How soon do you think you'll be able to get the school started? The children are usually free to begin classes around the first of October."

"Then we will open the school on the first Monday of October," Mother St. Andrew said with conviction. Looking at Sister Mary Agnes for confirmation, she added, "We can be ready. How many pupils will we have?"

"Maybe thirty or so. I have to admit that the people here are not very good at keeping their children in school. But maybe you will be able to inspire more cooperation!" he said with hope in his voice.

"Very well. Not to worry. It is often like this in France as well. We will begin with the children God sends us."

"I am sure that you are both tired," Father Pierre said courteously. "I am going on over to the sacristy where I have set up a cot. I want to do some reading before I retire. Please make yourselves at home here! *Duermen con los angeles!*"

"What does that mean?" Mother St. Andrew laughed. "Do you speak Spanish?"

"Only a little, but I do need it with some parishioners. It means 'Sleep with the angels.'"

"Thank you for your good wishes. Good night." Both nuns chorused.

First St. Louis Church, Castroville.
Constructed in 1847. First school.
(Courtesy, Castroville Chamber of Commerce.)

The next days were spent preparing for "thirty or so" pupils of all ages and abilities, just as it was in France. And true to their word, the nuns opened the school on October 5. Thirty-six students were enrolled by the end of the first school day.

By November, the St. Louis School was filled to capacity with the second and third generations of the founding families of Castroville who had emigrated from the Diocese of Strasbourg in Alsace. Sitting up straight by order of their parents, little Rihns, Christelles, Kempfs, Habys, Manns, and Zimmermanns, hoped that they would make a favorable impression on these women who wore strange coverings on their heads underneath their prairie-bonnets with the long sides.

On November 26, her third Thanksgiving Day in her adopted country, Mother St. Andrew sought out her pastor to discuss a concern.

"Father Pierre, I know that you are working hard for the new church, and it is true that the parish desperately needs it! But, Father, is it possible for you to entertain the idea of building a new school and convent for Sister Mary Agnes and myself? As of yesterday, we now have almost fifty students. We simply cannot take any more in the building we have. Besides, you would have your rectory back!" She said this last with a smile of hopefulness. Having the two nuns living in his rectory had been but a minor inconvenience for the young pastor.

"I've been thinking about the same thing, Mother. I know that you cannot take more students without a better building. Yes. We can discontinue work on the church and have the same workers get started on a new school building for you. Do you think a convent on the second floor of that building would be feasible?"

"That would be ideal, Father. But before you get started, I would like to review the plans."

"Of course, *ma mère*! And please tell me how you want the school designed. We will build exactly as you wish!"

"And, Father, there is one other thing I wish to mention."

"What is it, Mother?"

"Next month Sister Mary Agnes and I will welcome a new candidate for our Congregation, a Miss Anna Schultz of San Antonio. Would there be a third cot for her?" Father Richard had been so amenable to their use of his house that Mother was hesitant to ask for more. But he did not disappoint her.

Always ready to help "his" Sisters, Father Pierre replied, "Of course, Mother. I will talk with a few parishioners. Perhaps someone has an old bed not being used."

During the month before Christmas both Mother St. Andrew and Father Pierre received letters from Bishop Dubuis with essentially the same message. Though Mother was surprised to receive hers, she nevertheless saw the wisdom in Bishop Dubuis' decision and read the letter aloud to Sister Mary Agnes with a positive tone.

December 6, 1868—First Sunday of Advent and
Feast of St. Nicolas

My Dear Mother André,

As perhaps you may have heard, I will be leaving the first of the year for Rome for the opening of the Vatican Council which His Holiness Pius IX has called into session. This is a very important moment for the Church and I dare not miss it. My being at a distance from you for an undetermined period of time might leave you without proper assistance in making decisions that will affect the future of your Congregation. I am therefore appointing Father Pierre Richard as your ecclesiastical superior.

As of January 1, 1869, Father Richard will have all of the rights, privileges, and responsibilities of this position. I believe him to be an honorable and trustworthy priest. He speaks highly of you and acknowledges your positive future in our diocese. Please accept the advice of Father Richard as you would my own.

Sincerely in Christ,
I remain,
Claude-Marie Dubuis
Bishop of Galveston

"What does this mean, Mother?" Sister Mary Agnes asked.

"Since we are a diocesan congregation in France, the Bishop of Nancy, our Diocese, appoints a priest who serves as our Superior. We defer to him in all things and he assists Reverend Mother Constantine with decisions. Here, we would not have recourse to *l'abbé* Michel, and at the time we came to Texas, he agreed to extend the right of ecclesiastical superior to Bishop Dubuis. Now Bishop Dubuis has named Father Richard as our ecclesiastical superior in this diocese."

"But, Mother, he is so young." Sister Mary Agnes' comment carried not so much a criticism of the bishop's decision as simply surprise.

"Yes, I admit that, but I like what I see in him so far. I believe that Providence will guide us and all will be well. We will trust."

In truth, Mother St. Andrew had begun to grow fond of the boyish priest. Though young, he had a wisdom that the parishioners turned to when they needed consolation or encouragement. She believed she would have no difficulty relying on him as she moved into the future.

Within an hour, Father Pierre stood at the rectory door asking to be admitted.

"Mother, did you receive a letter from his Lordship?"

"Yes, I did."

"What do you think," he asked nervously. Having no experience with nuns, Father Richard was not as ready to accept this seemingly awesome responsibility, as the Bishop had been to bestow it.

"I believe that Providence will take care of us. In France, the priests who were named our ecclesiastical superiors at St. Jean-de-Bassel always seemed to offer us just what we needed at a given time in our Congregational history. God always provided in France. I expect no less from God in Texas," she said with a twinkle in her eye.

"Very well," Father Pierre said. "I yield to your greater wisdom. I will do my best."

"I know you will, Father. I know you will." Her smile was warm and her tone was motherly as she pledged herself to honor this young priest with her confidence. "And, Father, may I trouble you for another bed? We will be receiving another postulant after Christmas. This new postulant, Miss Isabelle Zimmerman, will need to finish her schooling before entering the novitiate. I hope your thinking is like mine, Father. If we can, I want our new vocations to be as well prepared as possible before they enter the novitiate. Once they have donned the habit, I will be sending them out to begin schools. Bishop Dubuis did not give me specific time frames for beginning schools, but I know that he will not be too patient."

"I concur, Mother. The more training they have here, the more likely the vocation will endure. And, by the way, Isabelle will be a good, strong candidate."

"Thank you, Father." Somewhat hesitantly she added, "Father, we really do need that new school and convent!"

"I know, Mother. I know. It will be ready in the spring; I promise."

Since they were less entangled in their own farm duties during the winter months, the men of the parish built the convent-school building in near record time. The two-story wood and stone structure, built in the Alsatian-style with cypress beams and pilings hewn from trees along the Medina River, occupied the southeast corner of the property at Amelia and London Streets, facing London. Two large schoolrooms on the first floor and then a two-room residence for the Sisters, accessible by outside stairs near the back doors of the schoolrooms, made for a very compact appearance.

First St. Louis School, Constructed in 1868-1869.
(Courtesy, Castroville Chamber of Commerce.)

The parish celebrated the completion of the convent school with a Mass of blessing and dedication on Sunday, March 21, the Sunday before Easter 1869. Though there would be only two months in the new school before the end of the term, Mother St. Andrew believed that being in the new building before the end of the first year would give the school stature in the eyes of the parishioners. The day after the dedication, with the help of their students, Mother St. Andrew, Sister Mary Agnes, and Postulants Anna Schultz and Isabelle Zimmermann moved all of the furniture and school equipment out of the little church and established St. Louis School and Providence Convent in its brand new building. Since the Sisters had no furnishings for their new house and remembering their own meager possessions as they started their homes in this country, the parents of the children brought chairs, a couple of tables, dishes, and pots with them to the Mass of Dedication and Blessing. Father Pierre gave the beds. By the Monday after Easter, the two nuns and their two postulants were settled into their new home and the school-rooms downstairs already smelled of chalk dust.

Mother St. Andrew heard regularly from Sister St. Claude during the 1868-1869 school year, but the tone of her letters suggested that the rigors of her experiences in Corpus Christi had taken their toll. Though she remained faithful to her teaching assignment in Austin, she continued to suggest that she felt more drawn to a less stressful religious life. Her health also remained a concern. Sister St. Claude spent much of the spring of 1869 with one type of ailment or another. She sounded more and more tired in each monthly letter.

Anxious to establish the practice of the summer homecoming for her Sisters, Mother wrote to the two Sisters in Austin suggesting that they begin to make plans to come to Castroville for June and July and was keenly disappointed when Sister St. Joseph wrote back declining the invitation. Her excuse was flimsy, or so thought Mother St. Andrew. But Mother was not entirely surprised. Though a fine teacher and an admirable religious, Sister St. Joseph simply did not have a firm foundation as a Sister of Providence. With such a hurried and distracted period of formation, she had never internalized the true spirit of the Congregation.

But Sister St. Claude's declination was another story. Mother felt hurt that her lifelong companion in religious life was choosing not to come to the motherhouse. She wrote them both of her feelings, hoping that at least Sister St. Claude would change her mind. In the letter that arrived in Castroville at the end of May, came words that dashed all hope.

> *... I am sorry, dear Mother, but I simply feel so very tired. I do not feel able to make the stage-coach trip to Castroville and I ask your permission to remain in Austin. I will rest; I will pray; I will study. But, I need to remain here. Please, try to understand.*

Mother's heart felt heavy as she penned her response.

> *... Of course, I want the best for you, my dear Sister. Perhaps I was thinking only of my own loneliness which would be assuaged by your company. I will pray for your health. Please take care and get good rest in the months ahead.*

As she walked the three blocks to the post office to post the letter herself, Mother began to brace herself for a loss and renewed her commitment to imbue the spirit of Father Moye into his newest daughters in Texas.

Although the two Sisters from Austin did not come home for summer rest, the two Sisters and postulants in Castroville spent their days studying so that they might keep pace with educational changes. Mother asked the Ursuline Sisters if she and her little community could join them for their summer retreat. A week at the Ursuline Convent would give them all a respite from their meager lives on the frontier.

Coincidentally, the retreat at the Ursuline Convent would end in time for the two Providence Sisters and their postulants to return to Castroville for the celebration of the Feast of St. Anne. Mother St. Andrew had made arrangements with Father Pierre to receive Anna Schulz into the novitiate at the morning Mass on that day, and Father Pierre was excited but nervous as he took the honored role of ecclesiastical superior as Anna was received into the Congregation.

Coached by Mother St. Andrew on how to conduct the ceremony, Father Pierre gave Anna the name Sister Theresa as he invested her with a makeshift habit of a simple brown dress of rough wool and the traditional white bonnet which fitted over the *bandeau* and *coif.*

Pieces of the French habit were becoming scarce and worn and Mother had decided that the three of them must be serious about spending the summer months sewing or they would spend the winter months without proper religious clothing! Well-trained by the Ursulines in San Antonio, the new Sister Theresa was a good seamstress, and threw herself into the project of making new parts for their habits. And, Isabelle Zimmermann, the daughter of a farmer, was wonderful at the garden. By the end of August, each Sister had several new *coifs* and *bandeaux*, and each one had a new cape and *guimpe;* and the community was beginning to enjoy beans and squash.

Sister Theresa was ready to teach in a classroom at the opening of the new school term, but Isabelle would continue her studies as a postulant. Another year in school, Mother thought, would only serve to better prepare her for her future. Each Sunday afternoon Mother devoted not less than three hours to instructing her postulant, novice, and Sister on the four fundamental virtues and the writings of the Founder.

The second school year began uneventfully on the first Monday in October 1869, with all the students returning. Work on the church resumed at a fast pace after the harvest was complete, and Father Pierre was very pleased with the progress made. He was certain that another year of work would bring the church to a point where services could be held.

Two months later toward the end of November 1869 a letter from San Antonio arrived for Mother St. Andrew. The now fifteen-year-old Barbara Keller, true to her word, was asking for admission to enter the Sisters of Providence. How could Mother say "no" to such a persevering young girl? And then, the day after Thanksgiving, a wagonload of people drew up to the front of the school building and three girls and their parents got down. Mary Merian, daughter of Mr. and Mrs. John Merian, and Amelia and Caroline Bader, the nearly fifteen year-old daughters of Mr. and Mrs. Sebastian Bader of Bader Settlement, had come to request entrance.

Though the growing numbers of vocations indicated a promising future for the young Congregation, Mother St. Andrew feared that Father Pierre would soon get tired of her requests for more beds!

At the end of the school year in May of 1870, with Texas having been re-admitted to the Union after the hiatus of the Civil War, various laws related to education were put into effect which, if carried out, would bring income to the Sisters of Providence for the education of the children of Medina County. However, the fall term of 1870 would be underway before actual monies would come into the coffers of the Sisters. In the meantime, Father Pierre and the parishioners of St. Louis were very generous and attentive to "their" Sisters, which now included daughters of the town. Gifts to the Sisters regularly included recently butchered meat and vegetables from kitchen gardens. With six pairs of young hands tilling, hoeing, weeding, tending the cows and milking, the Sisters of Providence had all the vegetables and dairy products they could use and always had some to share with Father Pierre.

Each of the new vocations seemed to be doing well and, with so much help at the school, Mother St. Andrew was able to devote her time to their instruction. Only Caroline Bader chose not to continue and Mother was certain that the young girl would be much happier as a wife and mother than as a nun.

As the work on St. Louis Parish's new church was nearing completion with only the church spire to be placed, Father Pierre decided to use the parish celebration of the feast of St. Louis, August 25, as the occasion of the for the first services. A special procession opened the celebration. Various participants—girls carrying flowers walking in front of the statue of the Mother of God, boys holding banners, a cross-bearer in the lead—circled the new church in an act of thanksgiving for its beauty. The Mass was beautiful with the men's choir singing favorite hymns in Latin and French.

Father Pierre with Mother St. Andrew standing at his side bestowed new religious names on four postulants accepted now as novices: Isabelle Zimmermann—to be known as Sister Mary Louis; Barbara Keller—to be known as Sister Mary Paul; and Mary Merian—to be known as Sister Joseph. He had been well instructed by Mother St. Andrew and his voice was strong and sure as he made these first three pronouncements. But, tears filled his eyes, and he audibly choked when he read the last name, for Mother St. Andrew had given Amalia Bader his name. She was to be known as Sister Mary Pierre. He was touched by the honor of having a young nun who would serve God's missionary church carry his name. The four new novices made their pledge to be faithful to the Constitution of their new Congregation and the number of Sisters of Providence increased to nine.

CHAPTER XI

EXPANSIONS

The little band of young religious had been told to assemble in the schoolroom as soon as possible after breakfast and chores on August 26, 1870. The feast of St. Louis was over; the novices had been named and vested; and Mother St. Andrew, in consultation with her assistant, Sister Mary Agnes, had made decisions about where individuals would be stationed in the coming school year. Though the procedures at St. Jean-de-Bassel always cloaked assignments in an aura of secrecy with individual Sisters receiving their "Obediences"* from the Superior General in private, this little group was small and general conversation had informed everyone of plans to open schools in D'Hanis and Haby's Settlement and to send Sisters to Fredericksburg for the parish school there. Mother had decided to call everyone together for spiritual reading and afterwards to make the Sisters' assignments to all at the same time. In years to come, she imagined, it would be more proper to follow the traditional procedures used at St. Jean-de-Bassel, but for now this would do.

The young girls, now habited in their brown dresses, capes and specially made bonnets with the long sides, took their places at the tables and benches in the schoolroom. Each day of the summer and every Saturday and Sunday in the school term, Mother St. Andrew had gathered her young Sisters and novices for lessons in peda-

---

* **Familiarly, the assignment of a religious is called an "Obedience" because under the Vow of Obedience, she is required to take the assignment given.**

gogy and spiritual talks on various topics related to religious life as Sisters of Divine Providence.

"My dear Sisters," Mother St. Andrew began, speaking in German and English, "each of you has, in some way, begun a new year. Those of you who are new novices know that some of you will be leaving here soon and traveling to a village that needs a good school for its children. You will make another new beginning in your life, just as leaving your home and coming here to Providence House made a new beginning for you. Those who will remain here in Castroville will be given more responsibilities as you learn to teach in the very school where you were a student. Since today will be one of my last opportunities to address all of you before you leave for your various missions, I want to focus my remarks on some advice that we have from our dear founder, Father Moye. He himself was a brilliant educator who continually sought out places of hardship, such as China, in order to bring the gospel into the lives of those who were most needy. You must never forget that your assignment is merely cloaked in teaching the secular subjects of reading, writing, ciphering, geography. The heart of your assignment is to help your students, and as possible help their parents, to know more about Jesus, our Lord and Savior, and the mysteries of our Faith.

"I see that each of you has brought a pencil and paper. Good. Perhaps you will want to write down these statements from Father Moye's advice to us, his daughters."

As she spoke the words of Father Moye, her tone became quiet, reverent.

"Are you ready to take down his words? *'The first spiritual work is to teach the ignorant. This will be your main duty. Teach not only the children but also all those whom you know are not sufficiently instructed.'*[v] Now you have heard this many times before during spiritual reading. Today, I want only to remind you that we must never see the word 'ignorant' as a negative judg-

---

∇   **The Directory, p. 95**.

ment of another. Each of us is ignorant at one time or another. All of you came to Providence House 'ignorant' of religious life and how to live it. Though your pupils may come from homes where little reading is done, their mothers and fathers must be people of extraordinary wisdom and knowledge to come to a foreign land and create a home and a livelihood in a sparsely populated wilderness. Never forget that the immigrants whom you will serve at Haby's Settlement, D'Hanis, and Fredericksburg come from roots that go deeply into a very learned culture. Above all, be respectful of that!

"As you travel to these villages to begin schools for them or to continue schools which they cannot sustain, remember that where one of you is, all of us are! Whatever you do will reflect on the entire Congregation, not only those of us here in Texas but also on those in Germany.

"Father Moye was clear," and again her tone changed. *'It is charity alone that should activate you in everything and everywhere.'*[*] If you act with charity towards your pupils and their parents, toward the pastor, towards the villagers—and especially toward each other—then the Sisters of Divine Providence will be appreciated and loved. Those who follow you will be received warmly. Pray daily that Jesus and His holy Mother will be your models. Never raise your voice; never spend time alone with the pastor or any man in the village, for that will raise questions; never single out any family or child for special favors; never roam around the village idly as though you have nothing to do. There is always a temptation to give ourselves to the more attractive, the better educated, the wealthier in a town; but remember what Father Moye said:

> *... take greater pains with those who have nothing attractive, who are stubborn, who have uncouth manners and appearance, who are poor, badly dressed, dirty, because they are the ones with whom the best results can be achieved,*

---

[*]   **The Directory, p. 95.**

*I mean supernatural and solid results. For God
often chooses the weak, the refuse of the world, to
make them vessels of election.* ∇

Do you understand, my dear daughters?" She looked the small
group of six young nuns over carefully, as their bright eyes, riveted on
her face, revealed their seriousness. Their heads nodded in assent.

Mother then went on. "When you have extra time, go to church for
prayer or spend time in your own quarters cleaning your habit and
mending. Our habits are somewhat 'piecemeal.' Why, Sisters Louis
and Sister Mary Joseph are still wearing skirts cut from an old skirt
of mine! No matter what you are wearing, you can always be clean
and neat! The Germans will expect that!"

As she finished this last sentence, Mother St. Andrew, noticing
that her young daughters were listening with rapt attention and
serious faces, laughed aloud.

"You know how the Germans are," she went on, with a smile. "Why,
all of us from Alsace are influenced by their meticulous ways. Some
say that the women of Alsace would rather clean than eat! Now, we
French, on the other hand," she smiled again, waving her hand, as
she found herself drifting away from her topic, "well, I won't go into
to how we French are!" All of these young nuns had heard some type
of reflection on this topic many times and they smiled as they heard
Mother laugh at herself.

"Sister Mary Agnes, you and Sister Mary Paul will be going to
D'Hanis—not so far down the road. I am hoping that you will be
able to come back to Providence House monthly as you, Sister Mary
Agnes, will remain my assistant for Community business. I have
been to see the D'Hanis school and the arrangements for your housing. You will have an opportunity to practice poverty," Mother St.
Andrew said this simply, almost as though their coming experience
was to be seen as a privilege.

∇ **The Directory, p. 143.**

"Sister Theresa and Sister Louis, Fredericksburg, as you know is the furthest mission, and I have not yet been there. We will go together, leaving in about a week or so. As I understand from Father Tarrillion, their school has been in session for many years and the building should be very serviceable. Father promised me that he would provide more than adequate accommodations for you. We must trust that Providence will provide. We will take the stagecoach to San Antonio and then take another coach to Fredericksburg. But, once you are there, I doubt that you will be able to return to the Motherhouse before the school year is over." As she mentioned this, she looked directly into the eyes of the two Sisters. Their clear, young eyes met hers evenly, assuring her of their readiness for a period of separation.

Sister Theresa, the senior of the two, had shown herself to be especially suited to religious life. Her parents were quite supportive of her vocation, and her education from the San Antonio Ursulines gave her a firm platform from which to run a school. And Sister Louis seemed equally up to the challenge before them. Mother wouldn't need to worry about Fredericksburg!

"Now about Haby's Settlement. It, too, is a short distance from here and, I must say, is in the direst of circumstances. The people have barely been able to provide a schoolhouse. Sister Joseph, you will stay in their school building. But, due to the extreme destitution of the situation, I will insist that you come back here to the Motherhouse each Friday afternoon after school and then return to the school only on Sundays. We will provide your food from here. The people there have told me they simply cannot afford more than a roof over your head. And, I might add, that roof probably leaks!"

With that remark, Mother smiled at Sister Joseph. "Now, Sister, don't worry. Our Blessed Savior had nowhere to lay his head. I think they are going to give you a bed!" Everyone laughed aloud and those sitting near Sister Joseph reached out to pat her arm in support. Seeing the community's consoling attitude, Mother St. Andrew expressed aloud their feelings. "Sister, remember: where one of us goes, all of us go. We will be with you and you will feel our prayers. You are not to worry. Though the housing is spartan, the people seem warm and friendly. Providence will take care of you. Oh, one more thing. D'Hanis and Haby's Settlement will not have daily Mass, but at least at St. Dominic's in D'Hanis, the Blessed Sacrament is reserved in the Church. I ask you two who are going to St. Dominic's to take at least an hour of prayer in front of the tabernacle each day. Sister Theresa, after you have been in Fredericksburg for a month or so, you may speak with Father about helping care for the sanctuary of the Church. But, under no circumstances, are you to spend time alone in the Church with Father Tarrillion, The people will talk and your mission there will be compromised. Always take Sister Louis to church to work with you. Never forget: where one of us goes, we all go. We must never give the slightest opportunity for gossip." This last sentence she directed to all of her young nuns.

By the time Mother finished, it was nearly eleven o'clock and she recognized that many of the Sisters had duties to perform before dinner could be served at twelve-thirty. She dismissed them with the singing of the *Salve Regina.*

As the Sisters left the schoolroom, Mother said to Sister Mary Agnes, "Sister, are you free until dinner? I need to review some things with you."

They resettled themselves at a table in the schoolroom and Mother St. Andrew began. "Sister, I received another letter today from Father Nicolas. It seems that he is almost certain that St. Mary's Parish in Austin will be transferred to the Holy Cross Fathers.* However, he is not sure about the school. As long as both Sister St. Claude and Sister St. Joseph are there, I feel that it is secure. But, Sister St. Claude continues to think about leaving us. At least she writes that she might join the Sisters in Victoria."

"Oh, Mother. I wonder if we can sustain Austin without Sister St. Claude. And if Father Nicolas is changed, as he surely will be if the

---

* **The reader may want to read the Endnotes to Chapter XII if she/he has not already done so.**

Holy Cross Fathers take the parish, I'm not certain that Sister St. Joseph can manage the entire school by herself. Are you thinking of sending someone to Austin at this time? Who would it be?"

"I really don't have anyone to send. We've already committed ourselves to D'Hanis and Fredericksburg and Haby's Settlement. And I must be faithful to my contract with Bishop Dubuis. New vocations will require that I open a school in Frelsburg and in New Braunfels, as well as those Polish settlements south of San Antonio." Her tone suggested that she felt overextended.

"I suppose we will just have to wait and see how things go in Austin. Surely, those types of arrangements take time." Sister Mary Agnes' tone was positive, though her words betrayed her uncertainty about the situation. "Perhaps you should talk all this over with Father Pierre?"

"Yes, I intend to. He always offers sound advice. Perhaps he knows the Bishop's thinking as well."

"While you're speaking with Father Pierre, Mother, do you think you could bring up the idea of a new building for us? You might be able to manage with this school building, but I predict that in one more year we won't have room for the vocations that God will send us."

"That is true. When Father Tarrillion wrote asking for our Sisters in Fredericksburg, he was very enthusiastic about possible vocations among his young girls. He even mentioned two by name. I believe you saw that letter?"

"Yes, and that is what is prompting me to urge you to talk to Father Pierre about a new building. If, by next summer we have received even two or three new postulants, we won't be able to manage in this space. I suppose we could set up some beds down here in the schoolrooms, just for June and July, that is."

"That is a very good idea, Sister. I will talk with Father Pierre as soon as he returns from San Antonio. I'm glad he is taking a few days off to visit his priest friends there. By the time St. Louis Day is over, he is exhausted. I fear that he will not keep his health and

I have grown very dependent on him in the last year. And if he does allow us to build, what do you think of taking boarders? I think it would help our income considerably."

"I agree. If we took in boarders, it would also allow farmers in the outlying areas to send their daughters to us for an education that is more like the one provided by the Ursulines. We've all learned so much from you, Mother: sewing, embroidery, music. I think we could offer a good school for girls!"

"Of course, that is in the future. And I do believe in looking ahead!"

The ringing of the bell at St. Louis Church interrupted their conversation.

"Oh my, it will be time for dinner soon. Is that the *Angelus* already?" With that question, Mother St. Andrew began the ancient prayer that marked the coming of the dawn, the noon hour, and the close of day in every Catholic community and family. "The angel of the Lord declared unto Mary," she prayed in German. Sister Mary Agnes bowed her head and answered, declaring the essence of the mystery of the Incarnation of Jesus: "And she conceived of the Holy Ghost." They finished the prayer together, and then each went off to finish her morning tasks before dinner would be served.

Father Tarrillion had agreed to receive the Sisters in Fredericksburg after the first of September, and he consented to beginning school on the first Monday in October 1870. Sisters Mary Theresa and Louis, accompanied by Mother St. Andrew, took the stage to San Antonio and then on north from San Antonio to Fredericksburg. Once again Mother had called upon the hospitality of the Ursulines so that she and her two young companions could be on the early stage northwest out of San Antonio. The two-day trip required several stops along the way before the overnight stop in Boerne, Texas, where the three nuns spent the night in the inn used by stagecoach passengers. Accommodations were clean but limited. Since the stagecoach had been full, the three nuns shared a room and were crowded into one bed for the night. No one slept much and all three spent the next morning napping on and off in the cramped quarters of the carriage.

Never having been into the country northwest of San Antonio, Mother St. Andrew and her two young companions had been amazed at the change of landscape as the stagecoach headed out of Boerne on the road to Fredericksburg. The more mountainous terrain reminded Mother St. Andrew of her years in and near the Vosges Mountains. Though these hills were not as ominous as the Vosges, it was still slow going for the horses as they pulled the stage higher and higher into the cedar-covered hills. At times the brush was so dense that a road was hardly discernible, but the experienced driver seemed to know his way. It was nearly dusk by the time the stage turned onto the *Hauptstrausse* of the thirty-five year old village of Fredericksburg, and Mother breathed a sigh of relief at a relatively uneventful journey. She was not yet at ease as she traveled in Texas, and her two young and inexperienced nuns looked to her for direction. She was glad this journey was over.

The driver guided his team down the busy street teeming with horses and wagons. Saturday was the day the area farmers came into town to buy supplies and to sell the produce from their wives' gardens. Some of the families would stay overnight at a local inn, with relatives, or in their town houses so that they would not have to drive the long distance back into town the next morning for Mass. The bakery was just closing, and the owner of the general store was pulling down the shades on the windows of his store.

When the driver stopped at the stagecoach station on the west end of the main street, all the passengers disembarked. Mother St. Andrew and her two companions picked up their valises and began walking south toward the church steeple that rose behind the one-story buildings along the *Hauptstrasse*.

Father Tarrillion, the pastor of St. Mary's Parish, had heard the stage come in and met them before they reached San Antonio Street. He was so excited to receive "his" nuns that he insisted on showing them the schoolhouse even though it was almost dark and they could barely see the outline of the building. Father explained that he thought that a second floor could easily be put on the school-house for a permanent residence for Sisters Theresa and Louis. In the meantime, *Frau* Lange, a faithful parishioner who lived across the street from St. Mary's Church, had offered to keep the nuns at her house as long as necessary. Mother agreed to his plan.

Frau Lange, whose grown children now lived on their own farms outside the village, was so excited to receive the nuns that she laughed and talked at the same time, welcoming them to her home, rushing to set her table with her finest Bavarian dinnerware and silver. Though she did not have a full set for three place settings, what she did have was delicately beautiful and obviously carefully tended for years. When Father Tarrillion had asked her to care for the nuns overnight, she had been delighted, and true to her German nature, had produced a meal of grand proportions: a roasted chicken, sausage, kraut, beets, and a delicious pastry made with cinnamon and apples. Sister Theresa and Sister Louis began to relax as they realized that if Frau Lange were an example of the villagers, they would be made to feel right at home among them.

Mother spent the next day speaking with Father Tarrillion about his expectations of his new teachers. She learned that he believed that at least fifty pupils would be in their places on the first Monday of October. Some of the families lived in town, but those with outlying farms boarded their children in town with friends and relatives during the week so that they could attend school. In some ways, Fredericksburg reminded Mother of Batzendorf. Close to the border between France and Germany, Batzendorf had a more German-than-French flavor to it. Her years there had taught her that the education of their children was indeed prized by parents who themselves had been denied the privilege of learning.

By the time Mother left Fredericksburg at the beginning of the following week, she was convinced that this mission would last. The people were open and friendly, their choir at Sunday Mass had revealed a true love of music, and the men's voices were strong and true. She was sure that Father Tarrillion would do everything he could to make his school a success. As she rode the stagecoach back to Boerne Mother made a mental note to begin music lessons with the Sisters in the coming summer. She would begin immediately looking for someone in Castroville to teach the Sisters piano and violin. Somehow she would obtain the instruments needed. The Sisters voices for their sung hymns and prayers were pleasant, but she wanted them to be trained to teach singing. She also decided to write to Mother Constantine to see if some Sisters with musical abilities might want to come to Texas. She wrote regularly to Mother Constantine but had been hesitant in asking for anything. Mother Constantine had so many plans and needs at the Motherhouse at St. Jean-de-Bassel that Mother St. Andrew tried not to impose her own needs on the Motherhouse. The transition from being a French community to being a German community had begun and resources would be dear in the years to come. Mother Constantine's last letter, earlier in the year, had revealed grave concerns.

The school year in Castroville progressed. Sister Mary Pierre took on more and more responsibilities in the school, and new postulants from Fredericksburg were expected at the beginning of Lent in 1871. The letters that Mother received from Sister Theresa indicated that St. Mary's in Fredericksburg was doing well. The Sisters had remained with *Frau* Lange for only two weeks since the men of the parish had arranged part of the second floor of the schoolhouse to provide the Sisters with a bedroom and a living area that included a kitchen. The cistern that served the school was easily reached. All in all, the accommodations were nearly exemplary. In October and November, Sister Theresa had met regularly with four girls, two of whom were sisters, who had expressed interest in entering the convent almost since the Sisters of Divine Providence had arrived. Letters to Mother St. Andrew spoke of the girls as "well-mannered, intelligent, and usually balanced," words that seemed to recommend them for the religious life. Mother agreed to receive them in March and then to prepare them to be received as novices in August 1871.

As she began to perceive serious vocations in the four young girls that Sister Theresa described in her letters from Fredericksburg, Mother decided to take Sister Mary Agnes' advice and speak to Father Pierre about a new convent building. Since the students were on holiday on Thanksgiving Day, she took that opportunity to call at the rectory.

"Why, hello, Mother, how are you today? Have you had your turkey? That is becoming the main fare for a Thanksgiving meal. Surely someone provided you with a bird!" Father Pierre was always enthusiastic and Mother enjoyed her conversations with him.

"*Oui, mon père*," Mother said, addressing him in comfortable French. "The people of Haby's Settlement gave us a turkey. They offer us nothing for the education of their children, but then they seem to have nothing. We did enjoy their gift to Sister Joseph. But I think Sister is enjoying being home with us for a few days more than we enjoyed the turkey. That is a hard mission; she has so little there. We try to send provisions with her that she can share with her few neighbors."

"Good. I know how hard it is for her. But what an opportunity to trust in Providence!"

"*Oui, mon père*. I hope she will persevere. But, *mon père*, I came to speak with you about quite another matter."

"What is it, *ma mère*?"

"*Mon chèr père*, as you know we hope to receive more vocations in the year to come. Sister Theresa has already begun to tell me of four girls in Fredericksburg who want to come in the spring, and I think there is at least one more from Castroville. The schoolrooms are adequate for the children now. It seems that we will have between fifty and sixty pupils a year, but I anticipate that the school will grow. I cannot imagine the second floor meeting our future needs as a Community. *Mon père*, to put it simply, we need another building, a proper motherhouse."

"*Mais, ma mère,* we are still trying to finish the church. I don't know if we have the ability ...," he drifted off. Seeing the disappointment in her face, he immediately said, "Now, don't worry. I will do the best I can. Let me talk to *Monsieur* Zimmermann and *Monsieur* Tondre. They always know how the wind blows here in the parish. If they think we can do it, we'll begin immediately. Is that sufficient?"

"*Mais, oui, mon père.* I trust you implicitly. Let me tell you what I am hoping for."

At that Mother St. Andrew began to outline her dream for a long, two story building that would face Paris Street, just to the south of the new Church. The rear of the building would have a first and second floor porch overlooking the gardens already been planted. In the two years that she had been in Castroville, Mother had begun a small apple orchard and the postulants tended a good-sized kitchen garden that had produced both squash and beans the past summer. She told Father Pierre that the building could be made of local stone and cypress beams, just like the church had been. A separate small kitchen building would be appreciated, she had said, and would make the large building safer for her nuns and for pupils that she hoped would come to board. By the time Mother finished telling Father Pierre of her vision of the new structure, he, too, could see the edifice.

"Very good, *ma mère!* I can see it now. I will speak to my parishioners tomorrow."

"*Mon père,* there is one other thing, an item of great importance." As always, Father Pierre was very attentive.

"Have you heard the Bishop mention anything about the future of St. Mary's Parish in Austin? Father Nicolas seems to think that the Holy Cross Fathers will get that parish as part of arrangements for their college that they want to build near Austin. At least this is what Nicolas thinks."

"Actually, I have heard nothing more than that, *ma mère.* You seem to know as much as I do."

"I remain quite concerned for our school. Sister St. Claude, whom you have not met, continues to seem—how shall I say—fragile perhaps, in her vocation. She has been a Sister of Divine Providence for twenty years, but she now seems to require a less solitary religious life than ours. She has written to me suggesting that she might be interested in joining the Sisters of the Incarnate Word and Blessed Sacrament in Victoria. Do you know them, *mon père?*" Though her words were questioning, her tone was somewhat caustic, revealing her sense of being betrayed by her dear companion.

"Why, yes. They are a wonderful group, so I hear. Semi-cloistered, I believe. They have had an academy in Brownsville for some years, but Nazareth Academy in Victoria was begun only a few years ago." His quiet, positive response was calming for Mother, and her next comment was more conciliatory.

"Yes, that is what I understand. One of their novices from Lyons was on the boat with us coming over. She and Sister St. Claude became friends. I suspect that this relationship draws Sister St. Claude to them—at least in part."

"What will happen to your school if Sister St. Claude changes congregations?"

"Sister St. Joseph is very capable and could run the school alone for a while, at least as long as Father Nicolas will teach the boys. However, if the Holy Cross Fathers take the parish, Father, do you think they will take the school as well?" This seemed to be the first time Mother had imagined that course of events.

"Oh, I don't think so, *ma mère.* The school is yours. Didn't you tell me that you own the property? It's on that list of properties that we drew up, isn't it?"

"Yes, Father. But, the question is, is it secure?"

"I rather think so. I will ask the Bishop the next time I see him."

"Thank you, Father. And please pray for Sister St. Claude. She needs our prayers at this time more than ever."

"I will, *ma mère.* Don't worry about St. Mary's. Providence will provide."

By the middle of December 1870, Father Pierre had begun to draw the plans for the new convent and the men of the parish had promised their time and talent as well as the donation of materials. Donations came from other sources, including Bishop Dubuis, who heartily approved of the new structure.

In a conversation just before Christmas, Father Pierre assured Mother St. Andrew that construction could begin in the new year. Although they did not have the total monies needed for the project, both the Superior and her young pastor agreed to rely on Providence for what was lacking.

Though Sister Theresa and Sister Louis were unable to come to Castroville for Christmas, Sisters Mary Agnes and Mary Paul arrived on Christmas Eve with plans to remain in Castroville during the holiday vacation period. Since the days off school were an opportunity for everyone to rest, Mother saw no reason to deny Sister Mary Pierre the privilege of visiting her home and was not surprised when she brought interesting news back to the convent.

"Mother, I had a long talk with my aunt Emma while I was home. You remember her—my father's youngest half-sister? She's three years younger than I am. Have you been watching her lately?"

"Yes, as a matter of fact. But what are you suggesting? Did she say something to you about joining us?" Mother had seen in young Emma Bader a leaning toward religious life; she loved to help in the classroom, teaching the younger students and cleaning up after school. She also seemed to enjoy her time with Sister Pierre after school and frequently came up to the convent quarters for a glass of milk after her chores in the schoolroom were finished.

"I think she wants to join us, but is too afraid to ask," Sister Mary Pierre said. "Do you think you could ask her to join us? I know that is not exactly the procedure, but Emma would be a good teacher and a good nun. She is young, only thirteen; but she is very mature."

"I won't hold her youth against her if she is truly determined to be a religious. As soon as school begins I will talk with her."

"Thank you, Mother. I don't think she will disappoint you."

As soon as school reconvened in the new year, Mother St. Andrew took Emma Bader aside.

"My child, I understand that you are interested in being a Sister. Do you understand what that means?"

"Yes, Mother. I would be like Sister Mary Pierre and would pray and teach school."

"Do you want to do this?"

"Yes, Mother. Very much."

"Very well, Emma. As soon as we speak with your mother and father, you may begin living upstairs with us."

The young girl beamed as she began to comprehend that her dream of being a Sister of Divine Providence was going to come true.

When Joseph Bader, a huge man who had to have a specially-built buckboard wagon, and his second wife Theresia came into Castroville from Bader Settlement that afternoon, Mother St. Andrew told them of their daughter's desire and of her acceptance. Though *Monsieur* Bader was surprised, *Madame* Bader, with wet eyes, merely nodded her head as she had known her daughter's heart.

"When may she enter, Mother?" Madame Bader asked.

"When you give your permission," Mother answered simply.

"What does she need, Mother? Do we need to give money? I cannot afford that," *Monsieur* Bader asked, unsure of what commitment would be asked of him.

"Even if you cannot provide a dowry, we will take her. I think she will prove to be a good vocation. God would not ask you for your daughter as well as for money you do not have." Mother smiled as she spoke, hoping to lessen *Monsieur* Bader's self-consciousness about his poverty. "But is it possible for you to buy her a uniform? All she needs is a black skirt and two black blouses. She will wear that until she enters the novitiate on the Feast of St. Louis."

"Oh, we will be happy to get that for her. I saw some black goods in Mann's Store just the other day. I'll be happy to buy the materials. Do you wish to make the skirt and blouses, or shall I?"

"I really don't have time. Is it possible for you to do so?"

"Yes, of course. I'll bring the uniform by the end of next week."

Mother turned to young Emma. "If you are ready, you may stay with us now, Emma, and prepare for your entrance into the novitiate. Are you willing to work hard at learning what it means to be a good religious? And will you try to live our virtues of simplicity, poverty, abandonment to Providence, and charity?"

"Yes, Mother. I will try with all my heart."

"Then go on upstairs now. You may stay with us. Sister Mary Pierre needs help with supper. I want to talk with your mother and father just a bit more."

Mother recognized how hard it was for parents to give her such a young daughter. She recalled her own father's somber face when she told him of her desire to become a religious teacher those long years ago when she was fifteen! It would help the Baders if she would spend a little more time getting to know them and letting them get to know her. When she told them goodbye they were getting used to the idea that their daughter would not be coming home to stay ever again.

After the early morning Mass on the Feast of the Purification,* Mother approached Father Pierre, asking if he had time to visit with her that morning. He agreed to see her at ten o'clock. These days she was needed less and less in the school. Sister Mary Pierre was comfortably in charge and doing a very good job while young Emma was a good right hand.

Promptly at ten o'clock Mother arrived at the rectory.

"*Bonjour, mon père.* How are you? Tomorrow is the Feast of St. Blaise. Will you be able to bless the throats of the children?"

"*D'accord, mais oui, ma mère.* What time will be convenient?"

---

*   **February 2**

After the two agreed on the blessing of throats at eleven o'clock the next morning, Mother St. Andrew continued with her agenda.

"*Mon père*, I need to go to Austin. I continue to receive letters from Sister St. Claude indicating that she is writing to the Sisters of the Incarnate Word and Blessed Sacrament in Victoria. She wants to join them, *mon père*. And perhaps she should."

"Why do you say that now, Mother? You were holding on to her so tenaciously before Christmas. Have you changed your mind?"

"Actually, I have." Her voice was peaceful. "I cannot ask Sister to be someone she cannot be. As stubborn as I am—and as hard as I've tried to get her to reconsider—I now believe that it is in her best interest to transfer to the Incarnate Word and Blessed Sacrament Sisters. She is so distraught now and, in her distraction, she is no longer a strong teacher in her present circumstances. My brother has talked with her; Sister St. Joseph has been supportive. But, if she is to remain in religious life—which I truly hope she will—she needs a different type of life. She needs something more like a cloister, something more stable, more secure."

"I see your wisdom. And I must say, I admire your courage, *ma mère*. It is very difficult to accept a young vocation like Emma Bader, realizing that you must provide so much for her. But, it must be heartbreaking to let go of Sister St. Claude. She, after all, will take part of your heart with her."

The young priest was very wise and he had grown to know Mother St. Andrew well. This loss would be heartwrenching.

"The Lord gives and the Lord takes away," Mother St. Andrew began, prayerfully submitting to the designs of Providence, and Father Pierre joined her for the rest of the adage: "Blessed be the name of the Lord. Amen."

"Very well, *ma mère*. When do you plan to go to Austin?"

"I would like to leave on Monday, February 6. I understand that Bishop Dubuis may be there this month to continue arrangements regarding the future of the Holy Cross Fathers in the diocese, at least that's what Father Nicolas tells me. The coach will take three days. I will be so glad when the railroad from San Antonio to Austin is finished. These stagecoach trips are killing me!" Mother laughed at herself and Father Pierre sympathetically joined in.

"When do you plan to return?"

"I want to be back by the first of March. Those girls from Fredericksburg will be joining us around that time. I want to be here to welcome them."

"That sounds fine. I'll pray for you, *ma mère*. I understand what all this means to you. Providence will provide." Father Pierre's wisdom and support belied his youth, and as she left the rectory to return to Providence House, Mother St. Andrew once again offered a prayer to God in thanksgiving for his guidance. She realized that this relationship was unique in its mutuality and maturity; she also knew that given other circumstances the relationship could be different.

Austin held mixed emotions for Mother St. Andrew. She had not always agreed with her brother Nicolas, but he had been very supportive when she had first arrived in 1866. He also had helped her immensely to get the school started and to buy the property. But now he seemed vague about his plans. She feared that his Alsatian ways would frustrate the bishop. He had written her that the bishop was offering him the German parish in Bastrop after the transfer of St. Mary's to the Holy Cross Fathers, but Nicolas had not accepted. Once he even wrote of remaining in Austin and joining the Holy Cross Fathers. She simply could not imagine that. He would never be able to serve obediently!

Now that it was inevitable that Sister St. Claude would transfer to the Sisters in Victoria, Sister St. Joseph's future was in jeopardy. Sister St. Joseph had never been anywhere other than Austin since joining the Sisters of Divine Providence. Mother was certain of her loyalty to St. Mary's School, but she was not convinced that she would remain loyal to the Congregation. So much remained to be seen.

Mother was gratified to see how well the school was doing. Both Sisters were excellent teachers, holding themselves to high standards. The people of the parish had become very fond of them both, and many of the people who came to greet Mother St. Andrew after the Sunday Mass indicated that they would not want to lose the Sisters of Divine Providence. It was apparent that the future of their parish worried the parishioners who had only recently learned of the coming of the Holy Cross Fathers.

Mother stayed two weeks in Austin, renewing friendships and trying to assist Sister St. Claude with her decision to leave the Congregation. In her conversations with Sister St. Joseph, it became clear to Mother that if the Sisters of Divine Providence lost the school, she might join the Holy Cross Sisters. It was apparent that Sister St. Joseph and Father Nicolas had spoken together about their futures, and she was disappointed in Nicolas for obviously influencing Sister St. Joseph.

While in Austin, Mother St. Andrew took the opportunity to visit with her brother Louis who had come from France in the summer of 1869, just escaping the war with Prussia that erupted at the end of that year. Louis had done a great deal of carpentry work for Nicolas and was presently busy with the construction of Nicolas' new church. He and his beautiful blonde bride, Theresa Fruth, the daughter of Bavarian immigrants had been married only three months; and Mother St. Andrew was happy to see her now grown-up brother and meet her new sister-in-law. Theresa and Louis seemed like a happy couple and both were very involved in Nicolas' parish.

On her journey back to Castroville Mother had much to think and pray about. She had promised Sister St. Claude that she would come back in the summer, but she knew that the visit would be for one final goodbye. Sister St. Joseph was dedicated to St. Mary's and would run the school as long as Father Nicolas remained the pastor. With the advent of the Holy Cross Fathers, whenever that would be, her future was uncertain. However, Mother had little hope that she would remain in their community. And Nicolas: it was impossible to know what he would do. He had told her that he was waiting to see how the Diocese of Galveston would be divided before he accepted a new assignment. The division was inevitable and the bishop was talking about it with his priests, though no firm plans had come from Rome. Bishop Dubuis had told Nicolas that he himself wanted to serve the western diocese which included San Antonio, Castroville, Fredericksburg, and St. Hedwig, the area he knew so well. Of course, Rome would decide.

March was a busy month. On Sunday, March 5, 1871, Mother St. Andrew and Sister Mary Pierre and little Emma Bader welcomed new postulants: the Misses Koehler, Miss Fritz and Miss Becker, all from Fredericksburg. Adding four pairs of hands lightened the work at the school and convent considerably for Sister Mary Pierre and Emma, but Mother St. Andrew found herself burning the candle at both ends in order to keep up with her duties as both Superior and Mistress of Novices and Postulants.

Positive letters from Sister Theresa indicated that the Fredericksburg school would complete a successful year in May, ending with an enrollment of more than fifty students. Sister Mary Agnes had been coming back to Castroville one weekend each month to assist with congregational decisions and was able to stay a day longer at Easter since St. Dominic's would not have school on Easter Monday. Two letters needed the attention of Mother St. Andrew and her assistant.

Mother Constantine's Easter letter had arrived before the Feast of the Pasch. Several paragraphs were of importance to the Sisters in Texas:

> *It is with great pleasure that I tell you that we are in the process of building a grand chapel for the Motherhouse. It will fill the space that our predecessors left for it between the front entry and Ste. Anne Hall. Plans are com-*

ing along nicely and we hope that we can begin construction soon. Of great concern to us is the State Certification for those of you who teach in our schools. Regulations are now changed and most of you will need to prepare to sit for the State Examination once again. When you are home this summer, we will identify who needs to take examinations and where the examinations will be given. If necessary, we will ask some of you who have more experience to tutor those with less. In addition, I want you all to know that our official name is now "Sisters of <u>Divine</u> Providence." Many of you who have served in villages with German influence have used "Divine Providence" in the past, since the Germans do not recognize "Providence" as a reference to Almighty God. With "Divine" affixed, there will be no doubt. With all the coming changes, I fear that we will need to expect a very busy summer.

An added page was included with the letter mailed to Texas.

My dear Sisters,

I know that distance keeps us from frequent communication. I want you to know, Mother St. Andrew, that I am grateful for your work and I find your descriptions of Texas to be very enlightening.

I do not write with regularity due to changes in our world since the war. Perhaps one day I can share personally with you what has truly transpired. I wish that I could tell you that I will come to visit you, but, as you remember, my old legs are sore and won't allow me to travel. My prayers, however, cross the ocean each day. I hope one day to meet your new Sisters. How wonderful for you to be training so many Sisters so soon! I pray that they persevere.

I regret that I cannot send you money. The construction of the chapel and projects on the farm take our resources and we don't know how long we will be able to keep our Sisters in the classrooms without further education. Everything costs money. Also, we lost a lot when Lorraine changed from the French franc to the deutschmark. I know you understand.

I know that we agreed in 1866 that you would plan to come to the Motherhouse in 1870. Now I suggest that we put that visit on hold. Those with French surnames are experiencing jarring treatment. Please do not refer to this in any future correspondence. Please give my regards to your dear Bishop. What an admirable disciple of our Lord Jesus Christ! You, too, my dear Mother, are an exemplary missionary. Remain faithful to your vows and live our virtues. Divine Providence will reward you.

In our Providing God, I remain,
Mère Constantine Eck
Superior General

The second letter, though expected, was crushing in its finality.

My Dear Mother

In some ways I write this letter with a heavy heart. In other ways, my decision has lifted a burden from me that had become too heavy to carry. I assure you that I have prayed about this decision for months and, true to my word, I have written you each month. I suspect that you know my heart and you will not find what my hand pens to be a surprise.

It is my wish to transfer to the Sisters of the Incarnate Word and Blessed Sacrament convent in Victoria. I am assured that Mother St. Clair will welcome me. I will not go into detail about my reasons, as I believe you already know them. Suffice it to say, that my heart longs for a more peace-filled environment where more Sisters are present to support me in the religious life. I simply do not have the constitution for the rigors of this frontier life. I know that you need for us to manage schools in towns and villages at a great distance from the Motherhouse in Castroville and from one another. I cannot do that any longer. I beg your understanding and your forgiveness for I fear that I have greatly disappointed you.

Please pray for me. I will make arrangements to travel to Victoria at the end of the summer. Hopefully, I will be able to teach in their new school and make myself useful in the house. Perhaps I can teach German and I do sew pretty well.

I will always be your daughter—no matter where I go. I pray that you will forever remain my Mother.

In God's Providence, I remain,
Sister St. Claude

Sister Mary Agnes read both letters thoughtfully when she and Mother St. Andrew met after dinner on Easter Sunday. Knowing how deeply Sister St. Claude's decision cut Mother's heart, Sister Mary Agnes' eyes filled with tears as she saw the tears spill out of Mother's sad eyes. She had never seen Mother so distraught. The letter from Germany had only added to the sadness of Sister St. Claude's letter. It was obvious to Sister Mary Agnes that Mother felt very alone.

"Is there anything I can do for you, Mother?" the young nun asked helplessly.

"No, my dear. I simply never thought I would have to say good-bye to Sister St. Claude like this. I know it is right for her to make this transfer to the Victoria Sisters, but ..." Her voice trailed off, despondently.

"I know, Mother. It is hard to say farewell to someone we have grown to love. But, like you, I believe it is best for Sister St. Claude to make this change."

"That is the one hopeful note in this. I do want Sister to be happy."

"She will be, Mother. She will be." Sister Mary Agnes so wanted Mother to believe that Sister St. Claude's future was positive. "Don't you think, Mother, that it is significant that Sister St. Claude is not returning to Germany? She has the heart of a missionary. She simply cannot sustain our difficult and sometimes lonely life. But she will do much good in Victoria. That area, just like the ones we will serve, is desperate for solid schools for their children."

"You are quite right, Sister. And the change to the other Congregation may allow Sister St. Claude to serve the Church of Texas faithfully for many years. After all, that is what we came to do."

"I'm certain of it, Mother. As you always tell us, 'Providence will provide.' In this case, Providence will provide you with the strength to endure this loss."

"Thank you, my dear Sister. Your words are very encouraging. Now, while you are here, we must make firm plans for the summer. I want to go over with you which classes we will offer for the young Sisters. I brought back new textbooks from Austin and am hoping to teach from them this summer. Also, I really want to include music lessons. I am hoping to engage Miss Schott. She could teach our Sisters both piano and violin. What do you think?"

"Oh, Miss Schott would be perfect. She is quite accomplished and, if she is willing, music lessons would help each of us. What about singing lessons?"

"I've thought of that as well. One of our girls from Fredericksburg, Francisca Koehler, could give us lessons in singing. What do you think?"

"She has a beautiful voice, Mother. I, too, believe that she could teach us how to teach singing. And I, for one, would appreciate the help!"

"Good. We've got the summer schedule underway then. I'll work out a detailed plan after I speak with Miss Schott."

"Excellent, Mother. The building is coming along nicely, too. We won't be able to move in this summer, but I think by next summer it will be finished. Don't you?"

"Yes. Your idea about changing the schoolroom downstairs into a dormitory for the summer is a good one. I had to ask Father Pierre for additional beds for the girls from Fredericksburg; and when we're all here for June and July, I'll have to ask him for more. He'll have a good laugh. All we ever seem to talk about is beds!"

"That is a good problem to have, Mother! Father Pierre won't mind. He seems very excited that we are growing."

Father Pierre was delighted to receive seven new novices at the annual St. Louis Day Mass. After vesting the young novices with bonnets, *coifs, guimpes*, and capes, he conferred on them the names by which they would be known in religion: Sisters Angela and Virginia Koehler, Sister Odilia Fritz, Sister Regina Becker, Sister Mary Clare Schorp, Sister Mary Rose Bader, and Sister Mary Philomena Bretner.

With the new novices, Mother St. Andrew was able to open four more schools in the fall of 1871. Sister Mary Pierre Bader, now prepared for teaching by Mother St. Andrew at St. Louis School in Castroville, was sent to New Braunfels where Father Peter Behr, the new pastor, had stabilized the parish financially and was ready now to open a school. Frelsburg's pastor, Father Peter Gury, who had invited Mother to send Sisters to him as she passed through his parish on her way to Austin in 1866, welcomed Sister Mary Agnes Wolf and Sister Mary Rose Bader. Though she was very young and barely out of school herself, Sister Mary Rose was a capable companion and teacher, fully prepared to assist the veteran Sister Mary Agnes in beginning a school.

Sister Theresa and Sister Louis returned to Fredericksburg and Sister Mary Paul continued at St. Dominic's Parish in D'Hanis.

Only after the young nuns were settled in their missions for the 1871-1872 school year, did Mother St. Andrew make the heartbreaking journey to Austin where she counseled Sister St. Claude one last time.

After the two old friends were alone, Mother St. Andrew asked her lifelong companion in religious life: "Are you certain, *ma chère amie*, that you wish to make this change? I ask you not out of an attempt to change your mind, for I feel that the Sisters in Victoria will give you life. I ask only because it is a formality before we sign the papers that dissolve your relationship with the Sisters of Divine Providence."

Sister Alphonse Boëgler (Sister St. Claude)
(Courtesy: Sisters of the Incarnate Word and Blessed Sacrament, Victoria, TX)

"Mother, I have no quarrel with our dear Congregation. If we were able to live as we did in France—I mean Germany—with Sisters being close enough in the small villages to visit and to help each other, I would happily remain with you. I have admired you for twenty years now. Had you remembered that it was twenty years ago this month that we began our year together in Epfig?"

"Yes, that coincidence has not gotten past me." Mother's voice cracked as she recalled that year: her own naiveté, Sister St. Claude's help with her classroom, their challenges with the now-infamous Christmas pageant. So many memories. So long ago.

"Though it saddens me greatly to bid you *adieu*, I must, Mother. I must." Sister St. Claude's last words were a mere whisper. "Please forgive me."

"Oh, my dear daughter. There is nothing to forgive. Yes, at first I was tenacious and could hardly imagine letting you go to another community. But seeing how even the planning for your transfer has brought color back to your cheeks and a sparkle back to your eyes, I have no further worries about you. I am sad only because you alone of all the Sisters here in Texas know my true heart. It is my own selfishness that wants to hold you fast."

"Thank you, Mother, for everything. Especially for being so understanding. You know that I will never forget you. I can only hope that Mother St. Clair will be half as kind as you are."

"I, too, hope that you will find a warm welcome in your new home, Sister. You will always be in my thoughts and prayers. Perhaps one day you will write to me and tell me of your new life? And I know that Mother Constantine will be happy to hear from you from time to time."

"Yes, I will write to you both as I am allowed."

"Then I believe this settles things. Nothing is left now except to sign the papers." At that Mother St. Andrew picked up the pen, dipped it into the well of ink, and affixed her name to the Latin text that released Sister St. Claude from her vows and her affiliation with the Sisters of Divine Providence. She then handed the pen to her missionary-companion and pointed to the space where her signature should be placed.

With the writing of her religious name, taken at St. Mary's Cathedral in Galveston only five years earlier, Sister St. Claude Boëgler concluded her twenty-one years as a Sister of Divine Providence of St. Jean-de-Bassel.

As the stagecoach pulled away from the station in Austin, Mother sighed, thinking that she could never have imagined the turn of events of the past five years: beginning a school in Austin that she might very well lose in a thorny battle between her brother and the Superior of the Holy Cross Fathers; losing her old friend to another religious community; receiving, educating, and sustaining fourteen new members of the Sisters of Divine Providence of St. Jean-de-Bassel in Texas; starting seven missions in six years; and attempting to fend off anxious pastors in Panna Maria and St. Hedwig who were clamoring for schools for whom she had no nuns. Without her faith in Providence, she realized she would be adrift in a sea of uncertainty. However, with Providence, it seemed that anything was possible. Alone with her thoughts on this crowded stagecoach, she let her fingers fall to the rosary hanging from her belt. The fingers found the crucifix and caressed the Body of Jesus, affixed there to remind her of her salvation. With gratitude she began to pray for the strength she would need to meet the future with faith.

The school year of 1871-1872 passed without incident. Letters from Sister Theresa in Fredericksburg, Sister Mary Agnes in Frelsburg, Sister Mary Paul in D'Hanis, and Sister Mary Pierre in New Braunfels described their lives as Sisters of Divine Providence and related the successes of their schools. Sister Mary Agnes was particularly taken with Frelsburg, a town not too far distant from the Bastrop area where she had grown up. The diocese had seen a great future for the small village which was developing into a ginning town where Bishop Dubuis had tried once to begin a seminary. The huge seminary building had stood empty for several years, however, until Father Gury converted the building into a school for the children of the whole village.

The summer of 1872 brought everyone but Sister St. Joseph Rice home for study, retreat, and rest. More music lessons now improved the curriculum which included studies in geography, history, and reading. Parishioners with violins loaned them to the Sisters so that at any given time a half-dozen young nuns could be heard practicing their scales in the fledgling orchard between the new building and the schoolhouse.

In early June, shortly after she had returned to Castroville from Frelsburg, Mother St. Andrew called Sister Mary Agnes aside and said, "Sister, I have just received a letter from my brother, Father Nicolas. I am not sure what he is telling me. Would you read it and give me your opinion. I have also spoken to his Lordship about all this."

"Of course, Mother." She took the letter and said, "It's in French. It may take me a minute. I don't read French as well as I do German."

"Take your time, Sister."

Sister Mary Agnes read the letter over several times, being sure to ask Mother about words that were not clear.

"What do you think, Sister?" Mother St. Andrew asked at last.

"It seems to me that the future of our Austin property is in jeopardy. Father Nicolas indicates that the title was never clearly in your name, but rather is listed with the rest of the parish property. He says that the property that is in his name does have a clear title. He thinks that you should write to Father Sorin explaining your position as rightful owner. Is that what you understand?"

"Yes, it is. I had hoped I wouldn't have to make the trip to Austin about all of this, but I am afraid that I should. I believe I should go at the beginning of next month, before our retreat. I want you to accompany me. You are much more proficient in English than I am and if we have to do business at the capitol, I would want you there."

"I would happily assist you, Mother. I am ready to go whenever you wish.

"Very well. Let's plan to leave on July 5; that's a Friday. Then we can remain through the next week in case we have to do business. We can return by July 15 or 16. Our retreat is scheduled to begin the evening of July 18 and I wish to be back in time to begin with the Sisters. Do you think that Sister Theresa can take charge while we are both away?"

"Yes, she will manage quite well. The curriculum for study is set and the Sisters will all be in classes. There should be no problem with both of us being absent." Then Sister Mary Agnes added thoughtfully, "Mother, what did his Lordship say about all this?"

"Actually, he was somewhat evasive. He said that 'he thought' that the land was secure, but because we do not hold the title—the diocese has that—and since it is all with what is considered 'parish property,' he simply could not promise that we would be reimbursed for our expense. I am quite disheartened at that. But, you know, his Lordship did not put the Austin school in our contract. I should have asked him about it then. From now on I will be more careful."

"My father is no doubt turning in his grave over all of this! He would have wanted that property to stay with us or, at least, he would want us to be paid for it!" Sister Mary Agnes' tone was angry as she thought of her father's estate going to strangers.

Sister Mary Agnes and Mother St. Andrew talked for a long time about the future of St. Mary's. Once again, they had no one to send to assist in the school; and, without a diocesan priest as pastor, they were doubtful that the Bishop would be able to offer the same support that he did for other parish schools. Also, they were very certain that working with priests from an Order would be different from working with diocesan priests. Both of them suspected that the people of St. Mary's Parish would be distressed about losing the Sisters of Divine Providence, and the unknown future of their parish was also disconcerting for them. In the end, they agreed that a letter to Father Sorin might be necessary. Both believed that if they wrote it, it needed to be strong, but diplomatic, leaving no room for misunderstanding on the part of Superior of the Holy Cross Fathers.

They began to draft the letter together over the next few days but Mother wanted to wait until they had returned from Austin before actually writing the final missive.

"I really don't have a good feeling about all this," she said to Sister Mary Agnes. "Please pray with me that we act only on behalf of Divine Providence."

"Very well, Mother. But we have put our resources into that property which is quite valuable. You are always speaking of how Father Moye would stand for justice. Can we do less?" Sister Mary Agnes added.

Mother was so grateful to be able to lean on Sister Mary Agnes. She had turned out to be a very thoughtful and intelligent religious. She also had a good head for business. With Sister St. Claude gone, Mother needed to begin to trust her young assistant.

Once they were in Austin, it became clear to Mother St. Andrew that even though the negotiations related to the transfer of St. Mary's Parish to the Holy Cross Fathers were moving slowly, the situation was causing great consternation in the parish. One of Father Nicolas' parishioners had changed her will in order to give her entire farm to the Holy Cross Fathers for a college, and though Bishop Dubuis had found this satisfactory, Nicolas' feelings about it changed by the day. At times he was supportive of the whole idea of the Holy Cross Fathers taking his parish, but there were days when he was broken by the idea of leaving his beloved Austin. Having declined the Bishop's offer of the Bastrop parish, Nicolas had decided to remain in Austin until the Holy Cross Fathers had priests to send to the parish. Some days he even talked of joining the Holy Cross Order, and Sister St. Joseph mentioned that she might stay in Austin even if the Holy Cross Sisters took over the school. Early in the visit, Mother learned that Sister St. Joseph was also thinking of joining the Holy Cross Sisters.

Mother St. Andrew knew that she would have to give up the school— that was inevitable. But, she believed that she had a right to be paid for the land on which the school stood!

The day after arriving in Austin, Mother St. Andrew and Father Nicolas sat down to talk over the future of her school.

"So, Nicolas, you are certain that the Holy Cross Fathers will take St. Mary's School as well as the parish?"

"Yes. However, they are very slow in sending a priest. And I refuse to leave until someone is here. Father Sorin seems to keep putting this final commitment off, and I don't know why. Mrs. Doyle, the woman with the farm, is ready to give the acreage to him if he'll start building the college right away. I don't know why he is delaying so." As he spoke, Nicolas' voice became strident; he sounded angry and confused.

"I just want to know: will we get our money?" Her tone was serious and her lips were tight as she spoke.

Nicolas was somewhat noncommittal. "When the time is right, I plan to write to Father Sorin to explain what he owes me for the lots I bought for parish expansion. As I said in my letter, I think you should write to him as well. Explain that the right thing to do is to pay you for your property."

"What type of man is Father Sorin?"

"He's very French! Stubborn and self-assured. His Lordship says that Father Sorin has done phenomenal work with his priests, Brothers, and Sisters here in America. Why, his college in Indiana, Notre Dame du Lac, is growing by leaps and bounds. He is certainly a man with a vision. I just wonder if he has the resources to accomplish all that he promises."

"Will he listen to me?"

"I really couldn't say. Perhaps. Perhaps not."

"I will talk this over with Sister Mary Agnes. If she concurs, we will write the letter when we return to Castroville. What language should we pen it in?"

"He prefers French," was Father Nicolas' simple answer.

"Then, French it will be."

After they returned to Providence House in Castroville, Mother St. Andrew began working on her letter to Father Sorin.

"I will let you read the letter when I'm finished with it, Sister," she had said to Sister Mary Agnes. "Your help is much appreciated."

A few days after the summer retreat had begun, Mother called Sister Mary Agnes to her small office-space that she had established in the corner of one of the schoolrooms.

"Sister, I am sending the letter to Father Sorin tomorrow, but I want you to look it over once more. I made no changes in our message."

Sister Mary Agnes read Mother's fine French script.

Castroville, July 21, 1872

Very Rev. Father Sorin

Very worthy Father.

In the name of the Holy Trinity and under the protection of the Blessed Virgin, our good Mother, I write you these lines.

It is now six years that I have been in Texas. With the approbation of my venerable Superiors and the desire of Monseigneur Dubuis, Bishop of Galveston, I founded the House of Providence in this diocese. At Austin, the capitol of Texas, I began my mission. The house at Austin was not founded without great sacrifices. After two years of assiduous work, his Lordship deemed it fit to send me to Castroville to spread the good work; afterwards, the House at Castroville became the Mother House, and Austin remained a branch of it, since the Sisters of Divine Providence have continued the work begun up until the present time.

One of our good Sisters, Sister Mary Agnes, gave her patrimony for the purchase of the lot on which the convent [in Austin] is built. All the residue from the tuition which remained after expenses was probably employed in covering part of the debt on the convent which rightfully belongs to us. The Sisters of Austin have never said or written to their Superiors that they were going to leave the Congregation and the Congregation of Divine Providence has never excluded them.

As Superior and foundress of the Sisters of Providence, I have at heart the honor of the Congregation. Eight days ago I was in Austin and I saw with great pleasure that the Catholic population does not want to see our Sisters removed, and they look upon these actions as a real scandal.

The good ladies of Austin say, "we do not wish to have any other Sisters; we do not wish to see other veils; that is an injustice; oh! that is dreadful."

Now, I ask, my dear and worthy Father, why you, who also have charge of a congregation, why you, who should know what it is to have the care of a congregation, why do you cause me this sorrow in wishing to take the fruits produced by the sweat of others; and what recompense do you expect from these actions!

Divine Providence still lives and certainly it will not abandon Its children. I have always understood that the laws of the Church forbid beginning a similar work in the same diocese without the permission of those who began the original work. To begin a College at Austin for boys would be a very praiseworthy and useful thing; but to drive away the daughters of Providence to make room for the Sisters of the Cross, that is an injustice and Providence will be avenged. Very worthy Father, I have nothing in writing to call upon. I have no papers or documents [proving my ownership of the land in question], but I am the instrument of Providence; therefore, respect the rights of the instrument.

Your very humble and very respectful servant,
Sister M. André
*Superior of the Sisters of Divine Providence**

---

* This letter is a very close rendition of the copy of the original which is in the Archives of the Sisters of Divine Providence, San Antonio, TX. The additions (in brackets) do not change the sense of the letter. The reader will want to remember that translating from 19th century French to 21st century English is a challenge. The author presumes that the translation was done by Sister James Aloysius Landry, CDP, or Sister Ann Linda Bell, CDP, who did translation work for Sister Generosa Callahan's book, *The History of the Sisters of Divine Providence of San Antonio, TX.* At this point, the reader may want to read the Endnotes for Chapter XII if he/she has not already done so.

"That's good, Mother. I will pray that the letter is received with the same sense of rightness with which it has been sent."

Like every religious superior before and after her, Mother St. Andrew had begun to lead two lives. One life was available to her alone—a life lived in the recesses of her heart where the pains and sufferings of loss and disappointment, fears and inadequacies were kept hidden from the many publics she had to meet. The other, her public life, the one her Sisters, students, friends and neighbors saw, portrayed joy and enthusiasm, and most importantly, hope in a future where Divine Providence would provide.

Those present at the reception of the new novices vested on the Feast of St. Anne[V], Sister Josephine Krust of Castroville, Sister Christine Zuercher of D'Hanis, and Sister Mary John Campbell of San Antonio, saw only her hope in the future, never seeing the fear in Mother's heart at the uncertainties facing the little Congregation. Her smiling eyes revealed only her enthusiasm for the great progress being made on the new motherhouse building and the addition of new members which would allow for the opening of schools in Danville, south of New Braunfels, Panna Maria and St. Hedwig. Thanks to two Castroville builders, Josephus Schorp and Andreas Stein, who had set aside other projects to concentrate on the two-story stone convent, the building was expected to be finished by the next summer.

As she returned to Providence House after the Mass of Reception and Investiture, Mother strolled through the small but beautiful orchard and gardens on the south of the new building. The arbor reminded her of the inner courtyard at St. Jean-de-Bassel. Mother St. Andrew had planned for wide porches on both the first and second floors of her new convent. In her mind's eye she could see future Sisters of Divine Providence choosing to sit in the arbor-like area, asking Providence to provide grace for the year ahead on the mission, while the aged and infirm Sisters would be sitting on the porches resting from their years of labor in the vineyard of the Lord.

Once again, her hope in the unknown future outweighed the fears that clutched at her heart.

CHAPTER XII

UPS AND DOWNS

Tempted though she was to spend the rest of the morning on a bench in her growing apple orchard, Mother St. Andrew walked resolutely to the back steps of the schoolhouse and, entering the door to the west classroom of St. Louis School, went directly to the desk that she laughingly called her "office" during the summer months while all the Sisters were at home.

The room smelled of chalk dust and floor oil. That summer's lessons were focusing on United States history and geography while the spiritual reading sessions held each day followed her precious copy of Father Moye's letters from China written to the Sisters in France in the late 1700's. Each letter was filled with both instruction in the four fundamental virtues and inspiring lessons for the life of a missionary. Her young Sisters would need both. Just as she and every other Sister of Divine Providence had memorized passages from these letters and Father Moye's various other admonitions, so, too, she required these newest of his daughters to do the same.

The chalkboard was filled on one side with important dates in United States history; on the other side were short instructions from their holy founder. In Mother's mind, the Sisters must always remember that their earthly success might lie in their knowledge of what and how to teach, but their eternal success was dependent on their faith and the way they lived their lives as Sisters of Divine Providence.

She turned her attention to letters received in the last two months: one from Nicolas, received just the previous week, again noting the uncertainties in Austin; another from Father Zwiardowski at Panna Maria; a third from the pastor at Bernardo Prairie; and another from the pastor at Martines.

Father Zwiardowski's letter was the last in a series he had written over the past two years always begging for Sisters so that he might have a good parish school. After sending so many letters of regret, Mother had been relieved to be able to answer that letter with news that she would send Sister Louis and Sister Joseph to the Polish settlements to begin schools.

These assignments allowed her to write to Bishop Dubuis noting that the only schools now lacking under her contract with him were Martines and Bernardo. She had assured him that several of the newest vocations were progressing well in their lessons and perhaps the pastors of Bernardo Prairie and Martines would receive letters soon indicating that she had Sisters ready for their parishes. Reminding His Lordship that St. Mary's School in Austin actually opened in March, she suggested that this frontier world would welcome the beginning of a school regardless of the month of the year. When she had novices ready, Mother promised the bishop that she would send them out. That is exactly how Father Moye would respond, she thought.

His Lordship had set no time frame for establishing the agreed-upon schools, but Mother knew that he was anxious to have these commitments honored before the Diocese of Galveston was divided. Though he himself was very positive toward the Sisters of Divine Providence and Mother St. Andrew's work, future bishops might not be of like mind.

Father Behr in New Braunfels had been so delighted with Sister Mary Pierre that he wanted two Sisters for a school in his mission parish of Solms, eight miles south of New Braunfels. This type of arrangement mirrored those in Germany: Sisters staffing schools in small villages that were close enough to each other to provide the Sisters with community support. Mother agreed to send him Sisters Christina and Mary Paul. In addition, Father Gury, the pastor in

Frelsburg, was so pleased with the work of his two Sisters that he wanted to open a school in Mentz, his mission parish near Frelsburg. Perhaps with support from Sister Mary Agnes, Sister Josephine could manage to open a small school there.

Assigning Sister Louis to Panna Maria and Sister Joseph to St. Hedwig would mean that Sister Theresa would have to take a novice teacher with her for Fredericksburg and that Haby Settlement would also get a different Sister. As long all of the Sisters remained healthy, Mother felt sure that she could cover all of the schools with the Sisters she had, even though they would need additional teachers' training in the summer.

When she had accepted the two Koehler sisters from Fredericksburg, Mother had not realized that placing them would be challenging. She did not want to put them on mission together; she did not want to send either one of them to their hometown of Fredericksburg. So, Sister Virginia was sent with Sister Odile to St. Dominic's in D'Hanis and Sister Angela was sent to Haby's Settlement. Those assignments placed three novice-teachers in established schools. With a prayer to Providence, Mother hoped for the best.

That left Sister Mary Paul, now a veteran teacher, and Sister Christina, a new novice from Castroville, to open Solms. Sister Mary Paul had done very well in D'Hanis under the tutelage of Sister Mary Agnes. She would be able to begin a school.

Deciding to write letters before noon to Father Behr about Solms and Father Zwiardowski about Panna Maria, Mother set about her task. Both priests would be pleased. Since Father Behr was already accustomed to the needs of a school, Mother felt certain that Sister Mary Paul and Sister Christina could open the Solms school without her assistance, but she did not have the same confidence in Sisters Louis and Joseph. She wrote to Father Zwiardowski that she would accompany the two Sisters to Panna Maria to help them get the school in operation. She requested housing for the three of them and, since she had not yet seen his schoolhouse, she also inquired about it in detail. Where was the cistern or well? How large was the schoolroom in each school? Who tended the buildings? Who provided firewood? Only forty miles south of San Antonio, Panna Maria and St. Hedwig were fairly close to Castroville. But Mother didn't want either of her two young Sisters to encounter any surprises. Letters she had received previously from the Polish priest who served as Superior for the priests of his Order in the area indicated his readiness to provide all the Sisters would need. This would be Mother's first experience of working with a priest from a religious order, and so far Father Zwiardowski seemed amiable.

The situation in Austin remained a conundrum. I'll wait before writing again to Nicolas in Austin, she thought. His speculative posture had begun to be unnerving. Would he remain a diocesan priest? Would he join the Holy Cross Fathers? Would he take another assignment from Bishop Dubuis? Would he wait until new bishops have been appointed for the new dioceses to be formed? Anything she might say would probably rile him up, she thought. If only he weren't so stubborn. But, then, perhaps she shouldn't question her brother about stubbornness! The characteristic certainly ran in the family!

While at her desk, she finished her letters, made notes about her next tasks, and re-read Father Moye's last letter, written at sea in 1784, while he was en route from China to France. She decided to use two pieces of the letter for tomorrow's spiritual reading: ***"Someone wrote to me from Europe,"*** Father Moye wrote, ***"that there are among you, Sisters who are too familiar with priests and that this caused scandal. This news grieves me. ... I told you in my former instructions that the respect you owe to priests ought to incline you to act toward them with extreme reserve, to see them and to speak with them only in cases of necessity and with so much precaution that wicked tongues cannot find anything to say against you."****

---

* **The Directory, p. 253.**

Their holy founder had been so adamant about this point; and, now that her Sisters were dealing with more and more priests whom she really did not know, Mother believed the instruction apropos.

The second point of instruction was from the Moye's same letter: **"As long as you are despised, poor, humiliated I trust everything will be well. The cross, if you carry it, will carry you, keep you, sanctify you. But I fear prosperity for you. When you have your comforts, when you exalt yourselves, then you will fall."**[V]

Anticipating the gratitude of the people of Frelsburg, D'Hanis, Solms, New Braunfels, Fredericksburg, Panna Maria, and St. Hedwig, Mother could imagine that they would donate their best foods, bedding, and furniture to their Sister-teachers. As a consequence, the Sisters would be living in greater comfort than were the people whom they were serving. This admonition from Father Moye bore memorizing. Tomorrow she would have to be quite serious with her young charges. Soon each one would be on her own; whatever they received from her would have to be enough to see them through the school year until they gathered again the next summer. So much to impart. So little time.

Realizing her own limitations and how much yet remained for her to teach her novices, Mother felt frustrated. The ringing of the Angelus bell, signaling the noon dinner break, led her to pray: "The angel of the Lord declared unto Mary ... And she conceived of the Holy Spirit." The timeless words of St. Luke's gospel led her to pray aloud: "Dear God, if You dared to immerse Your precious Son into our weak human condition, perhaps You trust each of us to do the best we can with our frailties. Give me the strength to trust in You as You seem to trust me."

Over the next weeks Mother laid plans to send the Sisters to their various destinations at the end of August for the 1872-1873 school year. With all the schools well-established, except for Solms, Mentz, and the Polish settlements, the month of September would

---

V   **The Directory, p. 255.**

give everyone ample time to prepare for starting classes in October. Sister Mary Pierre had agreed to help Sisters Mary Paul and Christina set up their school in Solms; Sister Mary Agnes would assist Sister Josephine in Mentz; she herself would help the two Sisters who would begin the Polish schools in Panna Maria and St. Hedwig. Hoping that Father Zwiardowski would assist in bridging the language barrier, Mother decided to spend some extra time with Sisters Louis and Joseph in English lessons. Their German would be of little use.

After she had Panna Maria and St. Hedwig schools underway, she believed that she could take Sister Mary John and Sister Regina to Bernardo Prairie. That village was small and a letter from the pastor had assured Mother that his parishioners would welcome the Sisters no matter when they came.

Mother had no real alternative to her plan for staffing all the schools now under her supervision. The most serious consequence of her decisions, however, was the loss of Sister Mary Agnes as a consultor on Congregational matters. Now that she was in Frelsburg, Sister Mary Agnes was too far away to be of real assistance on day-to-day concerns. Mother found herself turning to Father Pierre weekly as she discerned how to respond to letters from pastors who wanted Sisters and interviewed girls who believed they wanted to be Sister. There were many times that Mother's prayers were filled with gratitude that Father Pierre was so gracious and, despite his age, quite mature.

By the end of 1872, the new motherhouse building in Castroville was taking shape. The walls of the two-and-a-half story structure were up and the rooms were being framed. Now that winter had set in and the farmers had more time, many parishioners gave their time to the construction. Mother was pleased with the quality of the workmanship and often said to Father Pierre that this new building would serve her Congregation for the next hundred years.

The young priest had such a positive manner of working with his flock that people wanted to help with projects, and refinements on the new church continued alongside the work on the motherhouse. Mother St. Andrew, too, had become a daughter to the parish. The first generation Alsatians in Castroville, now themselves grandfathers and grandmothers, took her under their wings as they would their own children. Regularly wagons would arrive at Providence House with usable furniture for the new motherhouse. The old church became a storage place which soon would be filled to capacity with cast off items brought by parishioners.

A devastating epidemic of typhoid fever struck Austin in January of 1873. Concerned that her Sisters in Austin and New Braunfels might be in jeopardy, Mother decided to visit those missions in the spring of 1873. She found Nicolas and Sister St. Joseph bereft at the death of their friend and benefactor, Mrs. Mary Doyle. The Holy Cross Fathers had not yet sent a priest for St. Mary's Parish and Nicolas was hopeful that Mrs. Doyle's death would certainly speed up Father Sorin's plans since the Holy Cross Fathers inherited the lion's share of her estate. Mother found that her brother remained uncertain as to his own plans since he spoke less frequently about joining the Holy Cross Congregation. Conversations with Sister St. Joseph led Mother to resign herself to Sister's leaving the Congregation. Sister St. Joseph's plans, however, remained vague. Nicolas and Sister St. Joseph continued to work together to keep St. Mary's School operational. She taught the girls; he taught the boys.

Nicolas had learned that three dioceses in Texas were being designed: Galveston, San Antonio, and either Brownsville or Dallas. In addition, he told his sister that he had heard that Bishop Dubuis had become exasperated at Father Sorin who had never sent priests to take the missions in San Antonio and still seemed to have no plans for sending a priest to Austin.

During her visit to New Braunfels, Mother St. Andrew found Sister Mary Pierre exhausted from keeping up the school while nursing parishioners who had fallen to typhoid. The young nun's color was jaundiced and she had a racking cough. Mother St. Andrew wanted to take her home to Castroville; but fearing that Sister Pierre wasn't strong enough for the trip, Mother asked Sister Christina to leave Solms and come to New Braunfels so that Sister Mary Pierre might find time to rest. Mother left New Braunfels with a heavy heart, suspecting that Sister Pierre might succumb to pneumonia or a relapse from the typhoid fever before the end of the school year.

The remainder of the spring of 1873 passed without incident. Just before Lent, Mother received a letter from Father Zwiardowski introducing her to two of his parishioners, Cecilia Felix and Albina Musiol. He was enthusiastic about both girls, assuring Mother that he saw two very good vocations in them. His letter requested her to accept them immediately. The proud pastor agreed to bring the two Polish girls to Castroville as soon as he received her positive response to his letter.

Mother wrote back immediately that she would be happy to have the two girls. Convinced that the only way her little community could grow would be to take young girls with willing hearts, she never turned down the opportunity. These girls, however, would be the first entrants who did not speak German. This would force her and her other Sisters to embrace English more enthusiastically. Up to then, they all had had the luxury of speaking with one another in a familiar German tongue and, since none of them knew Polish, they now would have to find a common language in English.

Cecilia and Albina arrived in Castroville on *Laetare* Sunday, three weeks before Easter. Anna Ebers and Catherine Muller of Castroville entered as well. True to Mother's supposition, neither of the Polish girls knew German; and their English was sketchy at best. The two girls from Castroville knew German-Alsatian and English. Mother would be spending many hours with them before communication would come easily. But four new vocations would assure the continuation of present schools and perhaps the opening of new ones. All four girls were apt pupils. The other children in St. Louis School, welcoming the new Polish students, were happy to help them learn Alsatian and English.

After early Mass on the Monday of Holy Week in 1873, Mother St. Andrew asked Father Pierre if he had time to confer with her. He agreed to a mid-morning meeting, and she took the time before the conference to make her list of concerns she needed to explore with their Ecclesiastical Superior.

Mother wanted to talk about the upcoming summer retreat, a date to move into the new motherhouse building, the Austin property, plans for dividing the diocese and the effect that division might have on her schools.

After introductory pleasantries during which Father Pierre shared a letter he had received from his mother in France, Mother St. Andrew then proceeded to her agenda.

"*Mon père*," she began as she steered the friendly conversation to her business items, "may we turn to my concerns?"

"Of course, *ma mère*. What is it you wish to discuss?"

"My first concern, *mon père*, is the summer retreat for our Sisters. As usual I will present spiritual reading on our virtues and our Congregational history and mission each day while the Sisters are home. We now have eighteen members, *mon père*. I believe that we should have a preached retreat of five days this summer here at our own new motherhouse. As you know, in past summers we have taken advantage of the hospitality of the Ursuline Sisters in San Antonio. I think it is time for us to stay at home and have a priest preach to us alone. What do you think?"

"Whatever you think is appropriate, *ma mère*. Whom do you wish to ask?"

"If we were in Germany, *mon père*, we would occasionally have our own Ecclesiastical Superior," Mother said with a slight smile.

"Oh, *non, ma mère*," Father Pierre said emphatically with a shake of his head. "I am completely unable to oblige you in this regard. I simply cannot ..."

Before he could continue with his refusal, Mother broke in gently. *"Mon père*, there is no reason you cannot do this. I am giving you ample time to prepare. We would hope for two short talks each day in addition to a short sermon at daily Mass. Please say that you will. I see tremendous potential in you." Her tone was motherly and patient.

"I ... I ...," the priest stammered.

"Non, mon père. At least pray about this during our great holy-days at this week's end. Then we'll talk again next week. *Bien?"*

"All right," Father Pierre said meekly. "I will pray. What else, *ma mère?"*

"Merci beaucoup, mon père. I will pray with you. Now—my other items. When do you believe the motherhouse will be finished? I have no idea where I will put all of our Sisters as they return from their missions in June if it is not ready by then." Mother did not want to pressure her Superior regarding a matter that was largely out of his control, but she was beginning to feel desperate about living arrangements for the summer.

"Oh, *ma mère*! I am happy to report that *Monsieur* Schorpe told me yesterday that he thinks all of the work will be finished by the end of next month. You may begin to move in on June 1. Will that be all right?"

"Wonderful, *mon père*. The postulants who are here—and perhaps a few students from school—will begin cleaning and then we'll move the stored furniture. I want to have the building ready by the time the Sisters come home. June would be fine!"

"Trés bien. What is next?"

"I am hoping that Sisters Mary Agnes and Mary Theresa will wish to profess their vows this summer. Sister Mary Agnes, as you recall, entered in Austin in January 1868; Sister Mary Theresa entered from San Antonio in December 1868 just after we arrived here. May I invite them to these vows, *mon père?"*

"Of course, *ma mère*. I observe strong vocations in each of them. I am certain that they will be faithful to their holy vows for life.

And I myself will feel privileged to receive them. And your other concerns?"

"Do you have any news about the Holy Cross Fathers in Austin? I fear that the Alsatian in me is vexed over the considerable delay. Nicolas has asked them for the money that justice requires them to pay me for the property there. Do you know anything?"

"No, *ma mère*. I am afraid not. When I saw Bishop Dubuis at the priests' retreat at the beginning of Lent, he was very vague about the future of St. Mary's Parish. The Holy Cross Fathers are supposed to send a priest, but, to this date, no one has arrived. I think that His Lordship is becoming—what was your word—'vexed' as well. And, if I were Father Sorin, I would not want to 'vex' our bishop!" Father Pierre said this last with humor. "The priests' experience is that Bishop Dubuis is seldom irritated since the frontier requires tremendous flexibility. But when he is, we know to run the other way!" he finished with a broad smile. "And you wish to know about plans for dividing the diocese, I suppose," Father Pierre anticipated.

"Why, yes. What plans do you know and how will they affect our schools?"

"The four vicariates—Galveston, San Antonio, Laredo, and Brownsville—seem to be working well. His Lordship has asked Rome to divide the diocese into three dioceses: Galveston for the eastern and central parts of the state, San Antonio for the north and west, and Brownsville for the south and west. However, no decision has come from the Vatican. That is all I know. Now, about your schools. Actually, I believe that your relationships with pastors are more predictive of your future than anything else. My advice: work with your pastors, *ma mère*."

"*Merci beaucoup, mon père*. I will take your advice." Mother continued to find her relationship with this young prelate quite satisfactory. Father Pierre was a man of prayer, compassion, and wisdom whom his parishioners loved. She was certain that he would offer a fine retreat to her Sisters. Would that all of her Sisters had such a priest as their spiritual guide in the parishes where they served!

"And, there is one final thing, *mon père*." A note of sadness entered Mother's voice. "I continue to receive letters from Sister Christina in New Braunfels that Sister Mary Pierre remains weak. She is able to be in the classroom only irregularly. I am very worried about her."

"I, too, am concerned. Sebastian Bader told me that the letter they received from Sister Pierre before Lent sounded vague, as though she were guarding them from the truth. Her mother and father are very worried. Do you think you should make a visit to New Braunfels? You could leave next Monday if you wish." Father Pierre's suggestion followed Mother's own instinct.

"*Oui*. You are quite right. I could go next week and see for myself."

The visit to New Braunfels during Easter Week served only to underscore Mother St. Andrew's misgivings. Sister Mary Pierre was weak, remaining in bed much of the time. She complained only of being tired and was certain that when school closed during the spring planting week at the beginning of May she would be able to rest sufficiently and "would be as good as new." Though she tried to be positive, Mother had her doubts and left New Braunfels with a troubled heart, fearing the worst for her young daughter.

Mother's first act upon returning to Castroville was to write Mother Constantine in St. Jean-de-Bassel. Though eventually she might have to pen the news of the death of Sister Pierre, Mother preferred to soften the blow with less dire information first. She took the opportunity of the letter to share that Father Pierre would be giving their retreat in July and that the new motherhouse would be completed and ready for use in June. Since there was no firm news regarding the Austin property, Mother chose to omit her confusion about its future. No need to worry Mother Constantine about something neither of them could do anything about! A list of the four newly received postulants and plans for the professions of vows by Sister Mary Agnes and Sister Mary Theresa completed the letter.

With pride in her accomplishments during the eight years she had been in Texas, Mother assured her Superior that all was well and promised prayers for the entire Congregation during the Easter Season.

On the day she wrote to Mother Constantine, Sebastian Bader and his wife Josephine came to see her to inquire about their daughter, Sister Mary Pierre. After they left Providence House to return to Bader Settlement, Mother told her young postulants that she was going over to St. Louis Church and that she wasn't certain of the time of her return. They were instructed to continue with supper without her if she hadn't come back by the time the Angelus rang.

During prayer Mother recalled her conversation with the Baders. She had felt so grieved as she told them of their daughter's weakened condition. Their faith, however, had edified her. Not unlike their relatives left behind in Alsace, these first generation Texans were of hardy stock and had come to expect tragedy and loss as part of the price of their new life in America.

Holding Josephine Bader's hands while she spoke of the frailties of her dear daughter, tears had welled up in Mother's eyes as she had tried to console a mother whose daughter most surely would not return home again.

"So, Mother," Josephine had asked in a low whisper, "you don't think we should try to bring Amalia home?"

"I fear that she is not strong enough to travel. But I urge you to make the journey to see her if you can."

"What do you think, Sebastian? Could we go?"

"I don't know, Josephine. If I can get the corn in the ground in the week ahead, perhaps then ..." Sister Mary Pierre's father's voice seemed empty as he realized that taking a full week for the two-day trip to New Braunfels could jeopardize his family's livelihood. Life was hard. He bent his head as though he had been defeated by an unseen enemy.

"I know this is hard for you as well, Mother, but please pray for us. We gave our daughter to you freely. We will try to leave her in the hands of Providence." Josephine's words recalled words that Mother St. Andrew had heard her own mother utter so many times before.

"I ask you, my God," Mother prayed in the darkened church, "give me the strength that my own mother had, the faith that my mother had, the understanding heart that she had in this life. I know that I am hard on these young women who come to me as girls. I want so much for them to serve you with generous and honorable hearts. Perhaps I ask too much of them. Soften my heart to be that of a mother for them. Give me courage tempered with compassion; fortitude tempered with understanding. Bless the Baders in this time of their sorrow. Give us all the grace we need to accept Your holy will."

It was quite late when Mother returned to Providence House. The sleeping postulants never heard her creep up the stairs in the moonlight only hours before they would rise for a new day.

Sister Christina wrote weekly about the situation in New Braunfels. Her news of Sister Mary Pierre changed with each letter: one week she was stronger; the next, her cough was worse; the next, she had been in the classroom for two days; the next, she was feverish. The letter on the first of June asked Mother St. Andrew if they might both remain in New Braunfels for June and, if possible, they would travel to Castroville for the summer retreat. Mother wrote immediately that she honored their request. Perhaps a full month of rest would restore Sister Mary Pierre enough that she might travel. Then, when she was safely home in Castroville, Mother, promised, she would build up the young nun with teas and soups. After the retreat, she would allow the weakened nun to be at home with her mother for the month of August. Mother had already decided that Sister Mary Pierre would stay in Castroville for the next year.

The Sisters began coming home from their missions during the first week of June. Though the railroad was making progress in establishing the line between Columbus and San Antonio, all of the Sisters still made the journey home by way of stagecoach. The people of Castroville welcomed their daughters and adopted daughters home; and farmers, bringing extra milk, cream, and fresh vegetables for the houseful of nuns, came daily to the new convent. The Zimmermans, Sister Louis' family, butchered a hog, supplying the Sisters with meat for the entire summer. In addition to their studies, the Sisters spent every day in June waxing the floors of the first-floor classrooms and parlors and preparing the second-floor dormitories and bedrooms.

First Motherhouse of the Sisters of Divine Providence in Texas, Castroville, Texas (Photo in Congregational Archives, San Antonio, TX)

The new building had been planned in order to provide ample room for a growing Congregation that would need large rooms for classes, study, recreation, and prayer. The main door on Paris Street, opposite the new church, opened on an entryway with a staircase to the second-floor bedrooms and an unfinished third floor. To the west of the entry a large room served as a parlor for receiving guests. Other first floor rooms were large, including airy classrooms which opened onto the orchard and gardens in the back of the building. On the west end were a smaller reading room and office that also opened onto Paris Street. Eventually, a veranda would be added to the south side of the building.

To the east of the entry was a large dining room; in a smaller, separate building was the kitchen. A cistern just outside the kitchen building held water for the convent's use.

The second floor had a few private bedrooms on the east end with dormitory space on the west end. If the growing Congregation needed more sleeping quarters in the future, there was ample space on the unfinished third floor for more dormitories. The building had been well planned and equally well constructed.

Classes in that summer of 1873 covered music pedagogy and English. Now that the schools were no longer located in purely German communities, Mother felt compelled to improve the young Sisters' English. It was safe to presume that the future of Texas would mean less German-speaking and more English-speaking in all locales.

Mother St. Andrew also spent time with each Sister individually, allowing the Sister to evaluate her past year and to reflect on best practices to be adopted both spiritually and professionally in the academic year ahead.

After interviewing each Sister, Mother decided to make some changes in assignments for the fall of 1873. Sister Louis, though well liked by the people of Panna Maria, struggled in both Polish and English, making progress in the quality of the parish school tentative. With the investiture of Cecilia Felix and Albina Musiol coming up in August, she would have two native Polish-speakers to send back to Panna Maria and she could move Sister Louis to New Braunfels with Sister Christina.

In one of her frequent conversations with Sister Mary Agnes, Mother pondered her situation: "I am still unsure how to proceed with Panna Maria. Father is very satisfied with Sister Louis and I am somewhat uneasy about sending Cecilia and Albina back to their home village. Their vocations are untested and both seem somewhat immature. What do you think?"

"I see your point, Mother. However, I'm not certain that you have many options. We have so many more German-speaking parishes; only Panna Maria and St. Hedwig are Polish-speaking. You've had good relations with Father Zwiardowski. Don't you think, since he is a religious priest, that he will take Cecilia and Albina under his supervision? That should help them in their vocations." Sister Mary Agnes brought a good insight to the situation. Mother agreed that Father Zwiardowski's being an order-priest did make a positive difference. "What about sending Sister Louis with the two new teachers to help them get started? She could then go to New Braunfels from Panna Maria."

"I like that idea. We'll trust in Providence. That's all we can do. So, Cecilia and Albina will be sent to Panna Maria; Sister Louis will accompany them and later will go on to New Braunfels to be with Sister Christina. I think Sister Mary Paul can handle Solms by herself. Don't you?"

"I do," Sister Mary Agnes replied. "Now that the train runs all the way from Columbus to Austin, if necessary, I can go to New Braunfels if any of them needs support. Sister Mary Rose is doing very well with me and I feel that I can leave the school in her hands if I need to be absent. Will you send Sister Joseph back to St. Hedwig, Mother?"

"Yes. According to Father Zwiardowski, her Polish is better than Sister Louis'. While we're talking, let's look at all the other assignments."

"Very well," Sister Mary Agnes said amiably. "What are you thinking, Mother?"

"I want to keep Sister Angela in Haby's Settlement. That is a hard mission, but she seems to manage. And it is good for her to come here to the Motherhouse each weekend." Sister Mary Agnes nodded in agreement. Mother went on. "I'm not certain how long we can remain at St. Dominic's in D'Hanis."

"Oh, Mother! I so love that place. Are you certain that we can't keep the school going?" Sister Mary Agnes' words carried a deep regret at the thought of closing the mission she had begun.

"I know you do, my dear. You gave the school a fine beginning, but it isn't growing. Perhaps the parish just doesn't have enough students; or maybe the parents don't value their children's education as we thought they would. I'll send Sister Odile and Sister Virginia with hopes that the two together can strengthen the school. Anna Ebers will be able to take over the classroom here at St. Louis. That leaves Catherine Muller to send with Sister Theresa to Fredericksburg. That will give both of those girls more supervised teaching time after their investiture in August. What do you think?"

"A very good plan, Mother. I regret that I don't really know these newest entrants. Sister Theresa will be a wonderful model for Catherine and you can continue to work here with Anna."

"I suggest that we leave everyone else where she is, except Sister Pierre who will come home for rest until she is completely well." Sister Mary Agnes' face clouded as she realized that Mother was truly worried about Sister Mary Pierre. Then Mother continued. "There is one other thing. This summer I would like to begin visiting with each Sister individually to give her the assignment for the coming year. You've heard me say that Obediences are done with private appointments in Germany. With seventeen Sisters, I would like to begin the more structured practice."

"I concur. While we were small, our procedure of presenting the plan for Obediences to all of us at the same time seemed to work well. Now the Sisters may have specific thoughts best voiced to you alone," Sister Mary Agnes said thoughtfully, indicating complete agreement.

"Very well," Mother St. Andrew concluded. "I believe that is all. Let's see. The retreat will begin on July 20 and we will conclude with Mass on the Feast of St. Anne. That leaves a month to prepare for your and Sister Theresa's profession of vows and the four investitures on St. Louis Day. I have been thinking that Father Pierre should invite Father Zwiardowski to join him in celebrating the Mass of Thanksgiving."

"A fine idea, Mother. Father Pierre may have other area priests he may wish to invite."

Sister Mary Agnes had noticed that Mother appeared tired. Dealing with various priests, preparing new candidates for religious life, supervising St. Louis School, tending to the curriculum for summer studies, getting the new motherhouse cleaned and furnished seemed to be wearing their Superior down. And the worry about Sister Mary Pierre and the future of St. Mary's in Austin only added to Mother's burden.

The summer schedule provided the nuns with a full day: secular studies and music lessons in the morning, various chores after dinner, study and music practice in the afternoon, and then spiritual reading after supper.

Just before noon on July 9, Father Pierre came to the new motherhouse looking for Mother St. Andrew. The Sister who answered the door showed their Ecclesiastical Superior to Mother's office in the corner of a unused classroom.

"*Mon père*, good morning. How may I help you?" Mother gave her Superior an inviting welcome, gesturing to a chair near her desk. As the priest sat down, Mother noticed the yellow paper he was holding. Their eyes met and though neither spoke, both knew that this call would never be forgotten.

"*Ma mère*, I just received this telegram. Father Behr did not want you to receive this message alone."

Mother braced herself, realizing that the news would be piercing.

"The telegram reads:

CONVEY TO MOTHER ST. ANDREW MY DEEPEST SYMPATHIES. SISTER PIERRE DIED PEACEFULLY 1:00 PM JULY 8. SISTER CHRISTINA AND I WITH HER. GAVE HER LAST RITES AND VIATICUM. FUNERAL JULY 10. BURIAL IN OUR CEMETERY. FATHER BEHR."

Mother St. Andrew and Father Pierre sat in silence. The tears on Mother's cheeks revealed her pain; the young priest was silent in his own grief. His namesake in religion had gone to God.

Mother was the first to speak. "Come, Father, we must go out to Bader Settlement to speak to the Baders. Can we go at once?"

"Of course, *ma mère*. My horse and buggy are ready. I will be on Paris Street in fifteen minutes."

In the next few minutes, Mother went through the new convent building, ringing the bell that ordinarily summoned the Sisters to prayers and meals. It took the Sisters only a few minutes to gather in the dining room. With a catch in her voice, Mother told the Sisters of Sister Mary Pierre's death and funeral arrangements.

"I'm going now with Father Pierre to the Bader farm. Pray for all of us, dear Sisters."

When Sebastian Bader saw Father Pierre's buggy drive into his yard, he instinctively suspected the worst and went immediately to Josephine's side. He braced his wife as they readied themselves for the news.

Mother herself spoke. "Our daughter has been called home. She is now with God," she said simply. Having surrendered their daughter to God, both mothers then fell into one another's arms in tears.

Finally breaking through her grief and wiping her eyes, the brave Josephine Bader said, "Come in for a cup of coffee. Thank you for coming to tell us in person." Having expected this news for over two months, the Baders resolutely regained their composure. Death was not an enemy for people of such deep faith.

Father Pierre eventually turned the conversation to the rituals of the Church. "Shall I read the Mass on Friday for Sister Mary Pierre?" he asked.

"Thank you, Father. Yes. The Bader Family will be there," Sebastian said. And Josephine nodded. Mother St. Andrew volunteered the Sisters of Divine Providence, Sister Pierre's religious family, to sing the Requiem.

Mother St. Andrew and Father Pierre returned to Castroville in silence. There was nothing more to say.

Sister Mary Pierre's tragic death cast a pall over the rest of the summer activities, and in his retreat talks Father Pierre used the timeless lessons that the death of a loved one offers.

Realizing that the young community was shaken by the death of their companion in religion, Mother spoke to them on the congregational Feast of St. Anne after Father Pierre's last retreat talk.

"My dear Sisters: we can truly never anticipate the depth of the designs of Providence. I would never have suspected that in barely five years here in Texas I would have the experience of admitting you to the Congregation. With your generous spirits we have been able to open so many schools for God's children. I also would not have imagined bidding goodbye to my companion in religion, Sister St. Claude. I would not have thought that one of our young nuns would be taken to her eternal home. But this is God's work, not mine, not yours. We all work in God's plan.

"It is time now to look forward. I cannot cling to what has already been accomplished. We cannot cling to our past friendships. God is calling each of us into the future where He Himself awaits us. In the next month, I will meet with each of you individually, as is the usual custom of our Congregation in Germany, so that I can inform you of your mission assignment for next year. Then, on the Feast of St. Louis, Father Pierre will receive the profession of vows of Sister Mary Agnes and Sister Theresa. Anna, Catherine, Albina, and Cecilia will be invested in our hold habit and receive new names. For you a new life in Providence will begin. Let us now thank God for all the blessings we have received and pray for the grace to do God's will in the year to come." Mother's positive words broke through the pall that had settled over the little community in the days following Sister Mary Pierre's Requiem Mass. "And," she concluded, "at dinner today in celebration of the Congregational feast, we will have *Deo gratias*."

The Mass on St. Louis Day, August 25, brought the summer to a festive end. Father Felix Zwiardowski from Panna Maria, Father John Neraz from San Fernando Church in San Antonio, and four other priests from the area joined Father Pierre in celebrating the high Mass.

A grand procession with boys from St. Louis School, men from the St. Louis Society carrying banners, Children of Mary in their white dresses with blue sashes, Sister Mary Agnes and Sister Theresa, and Albina Musiol, Cecilia Felix, Anna Ebers, and Catherine Muller began at the schoolhouse and walked down Amelia Street to St. Louis Church. The three bells, "baptized" St. Louis, Ste. Marie, and St. Joseph in an elaborate ceremony which Mother St. Andrew herself had suggested and designed when they were installed in 1871, pealed a joyous chorus that could be heard for miles. After all had entered the church, Sister Mary Agnes and Sister Theresa approached the altar, prostrating themselves on the sanctuary steps in humble prayer. At Father Pierre's invitation, they rose and each in turn placed her hands in Mother St. Andrew's hands, professing the vows of chastity, poverty, and obedience.

Next the four young girls, two from Panna Maria and two from Castroville, were called into the sanctuary by Father Pierre. Assisted by Father Zwiardowski, Father Pierre handed each girl her habit. Sister Mary Agnes and Sister Theresa accompanied the girls into the sacristy where the two newly professed Sisters helped the Congregation's newest members to dress in the simple brown dress and black cape. A coif was drawn tightly over each one's head, a bandeau was tied over the forehead, and then the traditional bonnet was pulled over the head coverings, completing the dressing. While the young girls were being vested, the men's choir of St. Louis Parish sang several hymns in Latin. Now dressed, the four young novices were led back into the sanctuary and each knelt in front of Father Pierre who gave them their new names: "Albina Musiol, you will, from now on, be known as Sister Mary Stanislas Kostka; Cecilia Felix, you will, from now on, be known as Sister Mary Casimir; Anna Ebers, you will, from now on, be known as Sister Mary Celestine; Catherine Muller, you will, from now on, be known as Sister Mary Felicitas."

After Communion during the high Mass which followed, the rest of the Sisters kneeling in the front pews proceeded forward to renew their promises to live the virtues of chastity, poverty, and obedience, simplicity, poverty, abandonment to Divine Providence, and charity in the year ahead.

Festivities for the parish continued after the Mass in Koenig Park while the Sisters went to their new convent for a feast day dinner of roasted pork, sweet potatoes, and new sweet corn.

During the next two weeks each Sister readied herself for her new mission, and by the first of September quiet had descended on Providence House. Classrooms were empty, bedrooms and dormitories were cleaned, beds and cots were stripped of linens.

On the Feast of the Birth of Mary, September 8, Mother St. Andrew, grateful for a quiet morning, took the opportunity to work uninterruptedly in her office. As she looked over the materials on her desk, a conversation she had had with Father Zwiardowski on August 25 came back to her. He had been joyously enthusiastic as the two daughters of his parish had donned their habits and received new names. One remark stayed in Mother's mind: "I congratulate you, Mother," Father had said. "You have given Cecilia and Albina a very good start in religious life. I see them as the beginning of great things in Panna Maria."

What could he have meant by that? The throngs at the St. Louis Day Mass had pre-empted the possibility of a real exchange, and she had let the comment go. Had she been wrong in sending the two new novices to their hometown? But she had so few options, and she needed Sister Louis for New Braunfels now that Sister Mary Pierre was gone. Having lost Sister St. Claude to the Incarnate Word Sisters and the probable loss of Sister St. Joseph, Mother was concerned about the stability of the youngest members of her community.

In the next few days a letter from Father Zwiardowski answered her questions.

> **Mother, I am so pleased with Sisters Stanislas**
> **and Casimir, but I feel that moving Sister Louis**
> **right now would not be good for Panna Maria. I**
> **am asking you to leave her here so that she might**
> **guide the two young Sisters as they take on our**
> **school.**

Mother's reply went in the next day's mail: Sister Louis was needed in New Braunfels; Sister Joseph in St. Hedwig was very competent and would help his two new Sisters.

At the end of September 1873, came Father Zwiardowski's jarring response.

> **Sister Louis will remain here. We require her**
> **services.**

As she read the short note over and over, Father Pierre's advice filled her mind: My advice: work with your pastors, *ma mère*." Did "work with your pastors" mean that she should defer to their wishes as to who would be sent to their parishes? She felt her Alsatian temperament begin to flare. No! She was the Superior; she would decide where Sisters would be missioned! But Father Zwiardowski had sounded final in his response. Would it be better to let him decide who would serve in Panna Maria; or, should she take a stand on her authority with the Sisters? Bishop Dubuis was out of the country and had turned over most of the affairs of the diocese to Father Chambodut, the Vicar General.

She consulted Father Pierre.

"I'm not sure what to say, *ma mère*," Father Pierre responded to her dilemma. "I know I said that you should work with your pastors, but I never dreamed that one of us would begin to assume the authority to make decisions about the placement of your Sisters! Shall I write to Father Chambodut?"

"*Non, mon père.* I don't want to take this further than we absolutely must. I believe that I will treat Father Zwiardowski's letter as a 'request' and reply in the affirmative. After I write my letter, will you read it for approval?"

"Of course, *ma mère.* I suggest that you be polite, but firm. You are in the right here." Father Pierre was very encouraging.

Upon Father Pierre's approval, Mother sent the following to Father Zwiardowski:

> *I am very pleased that you find Sisters Stanislas and Casimir well-prepared. The girls from your parish came to me with a deep faith. Congratulations on your cultivation of such admirable vocations. Now, to the matter at hand. Though we need Sister Louis for New Braunfels since the tragic death of Sister Mary Pierre, I will acquiesce to your request to allow her to remain in Panna Maria. This concession is for this academic year only. I will require her to take another mission in the fall of 1874.*

With everyone settled at the missions, Mother was able to concentrate on developing a curriculum for summer school that would allow her Sisters to be paid by the State of Texas in some of the schools they conducted. The money would help to pay off some of the debt for the new Motherhouse; however, because of so many volunteer workers and donated materials, little was still outstanding. But she did want to pay Bishop Dubuis the money he had lent her. Although no one had any idea who would take His Lordship's place, rumors abounded that he would not be serving as bishop much longer.

Just after Christmas, Father Zwiardowski surprised her with another letter. Again noting his pleasure at the service of his four Sisters of Divine Providence, he asked her to accept three more

Polish girls into the novitiate. If she would allow them to come, he would bring them himself in February.

Believing that their relationship was no longer strained, Mother wrote that she would accept the new candidates and be happy to welcome them in February or March. Return mail brought a letter from Father Zwiardowski saying that he would bring three girls for candidacy in the Sisters of Divine Providence on the Second Sunday of Lent, March 1, 1874. As she read the letter carefully a second time, Mother sensed that Father sounded positive and would be supportive of her position as superior.

True to his word, Father Zwiardowski brought the four girls to Castroville, arriving late in the afternoon of Sunday, March 1. He told Mother how delighted he was with his teachers, Sister Louis, Sister Joseph, Sister Casimir, and Sister Stanislas. Staying at the Motherhouse only long enough to help the girls bring in their things, the Polish priest said that he wanted to be on his way as he wanted to visit Father Barzynski, another Polish Resurrectionist priest who served St. Dominic's Parish in D'Hanis.

Just before Easter 1874, two letters were delivered, both from Austin. The first one Mother chose to open was from her brother, Father Nicolas. Bishop Dubuis, no doubt anxious to finalize his negotiations with Father Sorin, had finally prevailed upon the Holy Cross Congregation to send a priest to St. Mary's Parish. Nicolas indicated that he, as pastor, would transfer the Austin parish to Father Sorin on the Sunday after Easter, April 12, 1874. Nicolas' relief that the transition was imminent spilled from the page. He had grown tired of being 'in limbo' and finally told His Lordship so. Prompted by Nicolas' discontent, tired of Sorin's maddening delay, disappointed that the Holy Cross Fathers would not be taking vital parishes in San Antonio, Bishop Dubuis had written Sorin demanding that he pay for the schoolhouse property in Austin and send a priest for St. Mary's Parish. Nicolas said that he would be staying in Austin only long enough to acquaint the new pastor with the parish, and then he would be taking several months to rest before moving to his next assignment. Perhaps he would visit Germany, but with the political situation in Alsace-Lorraine as it was he was not particularly drawn to that. Perhaps he would take a few months of rest at St. Mary-of-the-Barrens Seminary in southeast Missouri. Perhaps he would help in parishes in the newly established Diocese of San Antonio. With Dubuis soon off to France, the appointment of a new bishop would be within a few months at most. So Nicolas did not feel compelled to immediately take up the pastorate of his new parish—St. Joseph's German Parish in San Antonio. His letter indicated that he would simply take his time.

Just two years ago, the money for the school property in Austin had meant everything to her. Nicolas had barely mentioned it, and Mother was certain now she would never see a penny! Father Moye's words came to her mind as though he were speaking directly to her: **Be assured that the more you abandon yourselves without anxiety to God, the more He will take care of you.** * Perhaps abandonment to God had crept up on her. Even in the face of tremendous financial loss, the peace she felt was her consolation.

Mother fully expected the next letter she opened that day. In a short note, Sister St. Joseph said that she would remain at St. Mary's School in Austin through May, assuming that Sisters of the Holy Cross would be coming with the new pastor. Should no Sisters arrive, she would finish the year and close the school. Having no specific plans for herself, but not feeling drawn to continue life as a Sister of Divine Providence, she informed Mother that she would be returning to Corpus Christi where she "may be of some help in the parish school."

Laying the letter in her lap, Mother leaned back in her chair and looked out the window. Paris Street was not particularly busy this morning. Today was like most days in Castroville. All appeared to be business as usual around the town square. Sister St. Joseph, she thought, a woman with incredible talent as an educator. Selfless in

* **The Directory, p. 225.**

her work for St. Mary's School. True pioneer stock. An exemplary Catholic. But never really a true Sister of Divine Providence. God had placed her in the initial years of the Congregation's mission to Texas, however. Providence knew that an English-speaking pioneer Catholic Texas woman was exactly what was needed to inaugurate the Sisters of Divine Providence in Texas. Providence had known exactly what was needed. Providence had known.

Though Mother St. Andrew had hoped against hope that Sister St. Joseph would honor her commitment as a Sister of Divine Providence and come to Castroville where she could be such an asset in preparing the young novices for teaching, Mother had admitted to herself a year ago that that was quite unlikely. And now, just as she had been required to surrender Sister St. Claude, just as she had returned Sister Mary Pierre to God, Mother now let go of Sister St. Joseph. With a sigh, presuming that no one could hear the prayer of her heart, Mother prayed aloud: "*Mon Bon Dieu*, I confess that in the beginning I relied on Sister St. Joseph—a human means for accomplishing your work in Texas. Thank you for lending her to the project. Assuage my fears and anxieties about our future and fill me with confidence in You alone. Help me to be more like Father Moye. He cautioned us not to worry about the means that You will use to provide for our needs. I cast all of my cares this day into Your arms, O Providence."

Her prayer ended in a silent request that God would shower His blessings upon Sister St. Joseph. The uncertainties that lay ahead of her in Corpus Christi might prove daunting.

Mother St. Andrew could hardly believe that May was nearly over. She had decided to write a short note to each community of Sisters telling them that she would be happy for them to come home to Castroville by the middle of June so that classes could begin.

On June 1 a letter came from Father Zwiardowski that shocked the Superior.

My dear Mother,

I wish to inform you that the Sisters at Panna Maria and St. Hedwig will remain here through-out the summer. They have had an exhausting year and I do not believe that study is warranted at this time. The families of Sisters Casimir and Stanislas wish to keep their daughters at home. I myself will spend time with Sisters Louis and Joseph helping them with their Polish. Thank you for your consideration.

I remain,
Father Felix Zwiardowski

Mother was furious! How dare he demand that her Sisters remain in his village! How dare he! Leaving her office and slamming the door behind her, she walked as fast as she could to the rectory. Father Pierre would simply have to do something about all of this.

But Father Pierre was out on a sick call. The note he had pinned to the front door of the rectory gave no indication of when he might return. Mother decided to take a walk as was her habit each day. She had to walk off this anger before she faced the new Polish candidates at supper. If they uttered one word in Polish, she feared she might explode. That Polish priest had no right! Simply no right!

Usually Mother walked all the way down Amelia Street to the Medina River and then along Washington Street and back along the bending river to Paris Street, and west on Paris Street back to the Convent. Given her fury this time, she did not turn westward onto Paris Street but continued along the river road southward past the Landmark Inn. Then she decided to walk westward toward the cemetery. Reaching the cemetery which lay at the foot of Cross Hill and having circled the small town, she turned back eastward along Lisbon Street to Amelia Street. Walking the final blocks over to

London Street, Mother realized that finally she had calmed down. But not trusting herself with the Polish girls, she excused herself from supper and instead took a plate to her office to dine alone.

The next day a letter came from Sister Louis explaining that on orders from Father Zwiardowski, she and the others would be staying in Panna Maria for the summer. She begged Mother to understand, indicating that she believed that she really had no choice since a priest had given her direct instructions.

The next day Sister Louis' mother and father came to the Motherhouse. Irate that their daughter was not coming home for the summer months, they took their feelings out on Mother St. Andrew. Their emotions only served to stir her own again so that by the time Mother finally saw Father Pierre, she could barely speak.

"Please be calm, *ma mère*," the sympathetic priest said gently. "I hardly know what to say. I never thought that Father Zwiardowski would take this attitude toward our Sisters. Why, he treats them as though they are his own!" Father Pierre's voice, though more modulated than Mother's was, bespoke his deep concern. "If only we had a bishop," he lamented. "I don't know how to remedy this. I actually don't believe that Father Neraz will do anything. He is doing his best to administer our new diocese; this will not draw his attention, I fear."

"I believe you are correct, *mon pere*. So, what shall I do?"

"You need not respond at length to Father Zwiardowski's letter. Something simple and curt is required: 'Thank you, Father, for letting me know your plans. Should you change your mind, my Sisters are welcome here at Providence House at any time.' Can you write that, *ma mère*?" Father Pierre looked at her with pleading eyes. She was intensely angry—and legitimately so, in his opinion.

"Now," he continued. "when you answer Sister Louis, let her know of her parents disappointment, and your own. But I wouldn't apply too much pressure. After all, she is caught between you and her pastor. And I confess, her pastor will prevail, though not admirably. I don't think filling your letter to Sister Louis with your feelings about her pastor will be helpful. Simply write affirming her efforts in religious life and reminding her that her Obedience to God is through you as long as she is a Sister of Divine Providence. Can you do this?" His steady gaze lent her courage to do one of the hardest things she had ever had to do as Superior. He realized that this entire affair could end disastrously. In fact, though he did not say so, he had heard from other priests that Father Zwiardowski was renowned for his stubbornness—and for his cunning. But in loyalty to his brother-priest, he did not share these insights with Mother St. Andrew.

The summer of 1874 could only be characterized as lonely. Though Sister St. Joseph had never come home in the summer, the realization that she was gone for good left an emptiness in Mother St. Andrew's heart which was only exacerbated by the absence of Sisters Louis, Joseph, Casimir, and Stanislas.

In consultation with Sister Mary Agnes, Mother St. Andrew decided that she would not invest the three new Polish girls with the habit on St. Louis Day. In all honesty, they were not ready. Their English was insufficient; their German, non-existent. She had no place to send them other than Panna Maria or St. Hedwig.

Believing that sending them back to Father Zwiardowski was a good as dismissing them from the Congregation, Mother and Sister Mary Agnes told all three girls that they would remain at the convent school for one more year. The three girls surprised their Superiors. They were pleased to remain in Castroville. They had made friends at St. Louis School and they liked the convent life. But when the girls wrote their families explaining their future, the letters Mother received from their parents revealed a much different attitude. Supported by Father Zwiardowski, the Polish parents were infuriated. All three sets of parents threatened to come to Castroville for their daughters. To his credit, Father Zwiardowski calmed them, suggesting that the lengthened candidacy would, in the end, make their daughters stronger religious.

Mother felt strangely grateful to her Polish adversary. At least, she thought, his own understanding of religious life gave him a foundation for some sensibility! Given time and patience, perhaps the Panna Maria situation would work out.

Bishop Anthony Dominic Pellicer, First Bishop of San Antonio, TX
(Courtesy: Catholic Archives of Texas, Austin, TX)

Bishop Anthony Pellicer was consecrated the first bishop of San Antonio at the cathedral in Mobile, Alabama, on October 8, 1874. When the new bishop began his short tenure in early 1875, one of the first problems to greet him on his arrival in San Antonio was the conflict between Father Zwiardowski and Mother St. Andrew.

In early February 1875 Father Pierre came to Mother's office.

"I have a letter from His Lordship, *ma mère*." His tone was flat and, fearing the worst, Mother led him to her office in silence.

"What does he say," she said curtly.

"He has given Father Zwiardowski permission to organize a new order of nuns* who will serve the Polish people of the diocese. In addition, His Lordship has appointed Father Zwiardowski as 'superior of all the Missions and of the teaching Sisters, and the clergy, whether secular or religious, and the Vicar-General for the Polish mission.'" He handed the letter to Mother St. Andrew so that she might read it for herself.

---

* **The Blue Sisters, as they were known, was a short-lived Congregation. Having no mature members and only the rule provided by their founding-priest, Father Felix Zwiardowski, the fledgling community was disbanded in 1879. Sister Joseph Merian was one of the thirty that Father Zwiardowski sent to the Sisters of the Incarnate Word and Blessed Sacrament in Victoria; Sister Louis Zimmerman returned to her parents' home in Castroville.**

"So," she said simply. "So. We have lost."

"I am afraid so," Father Pierre said with a sigh.

The next week Sister Louis Zimmerman's mother appeared at the Convent demanding to see Mother St. Andrew. From the distraught mother, the Superior learned that on February 14, 1875, *Quinquagessima* Sunday, Father Zwiardowski, over the objection of the Polish Superior of the Sisters of the Immaculate Conception, had invested all of the Sisters in Panna Maria and St. Hedwig with the blue habit of that Congregation.

On the First Sunday of Lent, February 21, 1875, the father of Balbina Sowa came in his wagon to fetch his daughter and four other Polish girls from the Castroville convent. Zygmunt Moczygemba came for his daughter Anna and their neighbor Louise Neimetz. All these young women had been with the Sisters of Divine Providence for just under a year.

Mother's heart was crushed by the loss of eleven vocations to the scheming of the person she would forever refer to with bitterness as "that Polish priest."

CHAPTER XIII

GRAY DAYS

The Lent of 1875 seemed interminable. The gray weather and unusually severe spring storms only served to further dampen spirits at Providence House. Mother's usual optimism waned more and more as the weeks dragged on. She felt the loss of her young charges keenly, and angry feelings against Father Zwiardowski gnawed at her. Even the hours she spent talking with Father Pierre brought her no hope. Prayer seemed empty and the long hours that she spent in their makeshift second-floor chapel served only to leave her feeling more bereft. How had it come to this? How had she lost those fresh young vocations? Was it her Alsatian stubbornness that held her back from negotiating with the Polish priest who was just as stubborn in his own way? Was it her lack of finesse that kept Bishop Pellicer from accepting her side of the story and supporting her authority over her nuns? She supposed that she might never find an answer to these questions. She imagined that the experiences of the last two years would haunt her to her grave.

During Holy Week, upon the advice of Father Pierre who was truly worried about her mental well being, Mother St. Andrew agreed to visit Nicolas after Easter. He had recently taken up his pastorate of the German parish in San Antonio and had invited her to talk with him about the possibility of a school. A recent letter indicated that he had very good news for her. She definitely needed good news.

Easter Monday was a crisp spring day and Herbert Tschirhart agreed to give Mother a ride to San Antonio. Bidding the Sisters in residence at the Motherhouse farewell, she told them that she would return by the end of the week. Truth be told, they were all glad to see her go. The weeks of watching her grieve the loss of the Sisters and candidates who joined the Blue Sisters had burdened them all.

Nicolas' greeting was warm and his words were supportive. He and other priests had been suspicious of Father Zwiardowski's intentions for some time and Nicolas told his sister that it was only a matter of time before the small community of Polish Sisters that Zwiardowski had founded in Panna Maria would disband.

Nicolas' enthusiasm for his new parish and his plans for all that could be accomplished in the San Antonio German community brought a spark of life back to Mother's heart. Nicolas seemed like his old self—the priest he had been when she had first arrived in Austin nearly ten years ago.

After relating how he saw the future of St. Joseph's Parish, Nicolas finally came to the real issue that he wanted to discuss with his sister. Bishop Pellicer believed that much could be done at St. Joseph's even though presently the parish was covered in debt. Nicolas knew that it would take him weeks—perhaps months—to earn the trust of his skeptical German parishioners and begin to build up the parish's treasury, and time was of the essence. Nicolas saw a school in the parish as just the spark that might ignite the debt-ridden parish. Bishop Pellicer agreed and pledged the diocese to purchase a large piece of property on Bonham Street, just next door to the Church, which, if they wanted it, the Sisters of Divine Providence could buy from the diocese for a school. The Bishop assured Nicolas that "the price would be right."

"Perhaps this is His Lordship's way of making amends for all you've lost to Zwiardowski. I think that His Lordship was simply caught. Every bishop has to support his priests. Sometimes that support is misplaced and wrong is done," Nicolas said wisely.

"When did you acquire such wisdom?" his sister asked with a smile. The idea of owning property and building a school in San Antonio was very tempting. Even Bishop Dubuis had not suggested anything this expansive. And Mother had not imagined her Sisters with schools in the larger towns. Those endeavors seemed best left to the Ursulines who had a long history of urban academies. "How much do you think His Lordship wants for the property?" she finally asked.

"He said 'the price would be right,'" Nicolas responded. "Do you want to walk over and see the land? It has three buildings—well, of a sort. One building is nothing more than a stable. And, since the property is right on Bonham Street, then we'll go on over to the Menger Hotel. *Frau* Menger has offered you hospitality while you stay in San Antonio. She and her husband who is now deceased are founder-parishioners of St. Joseph's. Father Pfefferkorn, the former pastor, came to rely heavily on them and I know that I will as well. While you're here this week, I'd like to show you this part of San Antonio. The Germans are really making their mark on this end of town!" With that he picked up her small valise and led her out of the church.

"Where do you sleep, Nicolas?" Mother asked as they walked down Alameda* Street and around the block toward Bonham Street.

"Oh, I have a small room above the sacristy. I suppose I am destined to follow in the footsteps of the many French priests who lived in their churches. This parish has no money and I don't imagine building a rectory is even on the list. Why, did you know that this parish doesn't even have a cemetery? Parishioners who die are buried in the City Cemetery. That is simply unacceptable. My first goal is to buy some land east of here for the parish. Here we are," Nicolas said, pointing to a block of land which was behind the parish property as they rounded the next corner on to Bonham Street. Two dilapidated buildings and a stable which had been long abandoned took up most of the land. This is all for sale and the Bishop has placed a bid on it. The owner is a Catholic and he has given His Lordship a very good price."

---

* **Known today as Commerce Street, in 1878, the street in front of St. Joseph's Church was Alameda Street.**

"Well," Mother began thoughtfully. "One building could be a school; the other could be a residence for the Sisters. I suppose that stable could be made over into a kitchen or something." Mother's missionary eyes saw the potential in the property. "Would this school be associated with your parish?"

"Yes, but you would own the land and the buildings. Isn't that the arrangement you ordinarily have?"

"Yes. This time I will exact a proper deed. I am not going to risk repeating what happened to my property in Austin," she said, emphasizing this last sentence with a determined look in her eyes.

"I don't blame you," Nicolas said. He continued sheepishly, "Perhaps the fact that you lost the Austin property was my fault. I should have been more careful with the deed."

"I won't dispute you on that, Nicolas. But neither will I rebuke you for it. What is past is past. I want to look forward from now on. I can't go back and retrieve what is gone—either lost land or lost Sisters." Her words were resolute and Nicolas recognized the hopeful heart of the missionary that his sister had begun to be known for.

"I want to say that I'm sorry for what happened in Austin. Sorin was not fair to you, nor to me for that matter. I, too, experienced a great loss. I had built that parish from next to nothing only to have His Lordship give it away. It has taken me many months to begin to surrender that outcome to God's holy will. I wish I had our mother's great confidence in God's Providence. Too often mine wavers."

"Ever since *Maman* died, I have prayed to her that she might ask our dear Lord to give me a hopeful, trusting heart also. But too often I lack confidence. And then, something completely outside of my control happens to restore my hope. Like this property and the possibility of a school here in San Antonio. If the diocese had not given St. Mary's Parish in Austin to the Holy Cross Fathers, we would not have lost that school. As I see now, I think providing seasoned Sisters for that school would always challenge us. Sister St. Joseph might not have persevered even if we had kept the school. And you might not have been moved to San Antonio. I can certainly see the hand of Providence in all of this. But the better part is to trust Providence before one sees His works. Yes?"

"Yes, Mother," Nicolas agreed, addressing his sister with her religious title. "You are exactly correct. If you begin a school here, I believe it will be of great service to families who don't really have the means to send their daughters to the Ursulines and their sons to the Marianists. The school will be welcomed."

"So you see it serving families who cannot afford the private academies, Nicolas? I would not really want to begin a school that would serve only those with means. Our holy Father Moye was always insistent that we serve the poor."

"A number of my parishioners have new wealth, but most struggle. Hence, the debt on the parish. Your school will serve a great purpose for those in need. Mark my words."

"Very well, then. I will talk this over with Father Pierre and then I will let you know soon."

"I believe that you and Father Pierre can communicate directly with His Lordship. I truly don't want to get in the middle of these negotiations. I learned my lesson in Austin! And, too, His Lordship may be feeling badly about what happened to your young Sisters in Panna Maria. Give him a chance to redeem himself."

"That is good advice, Nicolas. I will offer a generous spirit to these arrangements."

The Lent of 1875 had been a true death to self for Mother St. Andrew in many ways. Perhaps the days ahead when the entire Church would relish the presence of the Risen Lord would be a resurrection for her as well.

Mother spent the rest of the week in San Antonio getting accustomed to the city and looking carefully at its commercial establishments. When she returned to Castroville at the end of the week, she was ready to ask Father Pierre to support the purchase of the Bonham Street property for St. Joseph's School.

The summers had settled into a routine of classes in music, pedagogy, geography, ciphering, and English. Most of the Sisters who were native German-speakers were not proficient in English and new candidates came with both Alsatian and English or German and English.

Since she was closer to Castroville when missioned in Fredericksburg, Sister Theresa Schultz had become Mother St. Andrew's councilor for matters during the school term. However, upon her return to Castroville in the summer months, Sister Mary Agnes Wolf joined them in conferring about decisions to be made.

All three sat down in early June to review the missions and to try to plan for personnel placement for the next school year.

Sister Mary Agnes, always the practical one, began. "Mother, we continue to be stretched to the limit. Without the vocations taken by Father Zwiardowski, I'm not certain that we can staff every place in the coming year. What are you thinking of doing?"

"I have prayed long hours over this, Sisters. If we cannot place our trust in Providence, how might we expect our younger members to become abandoned? No matter what we are faced with, we must not appear to be jarred. The younger Sisters will feel our panic and they might lose heart as well. After losing so many Sisters to the Panna Maria community, we must present a positive and steady posture. In addition, the people of Castroville will not send us any more of their daughters if we appear to be shaken."

"I agree with Mother," Sister Theresa said. "The people of Fredericksburg, since they know Sister Louis, were somewhat disturbed by rumors of what has happened in Panna Maria. I have tried to maintain an outward appearance of certainty, but we must not be disheartened. I think that we should talk all this over with the younger Sisters as soon as we have assignments prepared for next year." Nods from both Mother St. Andrew and Sister Mary Agnes indicated their acceptance of Sister Theresa's position. She then went on. "Are we really going to open a school in San Antonio, Mother? Won't that stretch us even more?" Sister Theresa was the first to question Mother's plan for St. Joseph School, but Sister Mary Agnes had reservations about the new school in downtown San Antonio as well. Her concerns, which she voiced, included the urban setting. "Isn't this out of character for our Congregation?" she asked.

The conversation about assignments and St. Joseph's School continued for quite some time; and by the time the dinner bell rang, the three Sisters had not come to complete agreement.

Mother St. Andrew finally said, "Sisters, after we have dinner, let's go to chapel to place all of this before Our Lord before we meet again. I will pray to be open to your concerns and I will pray that I will be more reliant on God's work and less concerned about what our poor efforts might accomplish."

"I will pray in the same vein, Mother," Sister Mary Agnes assured her. Sister Theresa pledged the same fervor and they all agreed to meet again at three o'clock in the chapel to say the rosary with arms extended.

Later, after praying the rosary, the three walked together to Mother St. Andrew's office.

"Now we must come to some agreement, Sisters. What are you thinking now?" Mother St. Andrew began.

"I have less trepidation, Mother," Sister Theresa said in a surprisingly calm voice. "Father Moye would expect us to take the little we have and, after we have asked God's blessing upon it, to simply give it away. Isn't that correct?"

"Yes," Mother nodded with a slight smile on her face. "I believe our holy founder would say those very words to us were he here. Sister Mary Agnes, what are you thinking?"

"I am now at peace about St. Joseph's School as well. We actually need to be in centers with larger populations. It doesn't make any sense not to begin a school in San Antonio. It is so close to Castroville. And the railroad to San Antonio should be finished in a year or two. If we have a house there, our travel to and from this area might be easier. I am now in favor of St. Joseph's School. Whom do you wish to send there?"

"Based on what Father Nicolas says, I believe that we should expect a large enrollment. I think we should place four Sisters there. It might mean that we'll have to close D'Hanis, however, since I was thinking of including Sisters Virginia and Odile in the San Antonio community. If we do that, we can send Sister Clare and Sister Ursula as well. Sister Felicitas can go with you to Fredericksburg, Sister Theresa. I myself will take the school here. Our newest entrants can help me." She said this last with a sigh, realizing how the addition of those duties would surely overextend her. "I wish we had not opened Ellinger last year," she mused. "But I simply don't have the heart to tell Father Gury that we will close it after only one year because we don't have religious. I may have done poor planning with that decision, but I don't want to have to admit it publicly," she finished with a laugh at herself.

The other two Sisters smiled at their Superior who so humbly accepted responsibility for plans that might seem to be going awry.

"So," said Sister Mary Agnes, "our assignments for 1875-1876 will be: Sister Angela at Haby's Settlement; Sister Christine in New Braunfels; Sister Mary Paul in Solms; Sister Celestine in Ellinger; Sisters Mary Clare, Odile, Virginia, and Ursula for St. Joseph's School in San Antonio; Sister Mary Rose in Mentz; Sister Theresa and Sister Felicitas in Fredericksburg; myself in Frelsburg; and you, Mother, here at Castroville?"

"Yes. Let's hold off on a decision about D'Hanis. Perhaps one of the new novices may be able to take on that school. Do we all agree?" Mother asked.

Both councilors nodded.

"I shall write to Father Nicolas and ask him to try to get that shed ready for our Sisters. He has three months; surely he can get it habitable by then. And he did promise me that the stable would make an adequate kitchen. I'll hold him to that." Mother laughed and went on. "I think he knows better than to get on my bad side!" Both nuns laughed with their Superior. They also knew better than to "get on her bad side" and they felt for her brother-priest should he fail.

"How do you think our present candidates are doing?" Sister Mary Agnes asked, moving ahead on their agenda.

"They are working very hard in school and their English improves by the day. But after our experience in Panna Maria, I am certain that we send them out too soon. They are quite immature in religious life and their having to contend with the pressures from schools and pastors ...," her voice trailed off. "I now see that we must give them more resources. Perhaps soon we may be able to keep them here at Providence House one more year. At least, that is my hope."

"I acknowledge your wisdom, Mother," Sister Theresa said. "I have had a wonderful relationship with Father Tarrillion, but our losses to the Polish priest have given me cause for concern. More time here at the Motherhouse may be the answer."

The three women finished their conversation and reviewed the house accounts before going to evening prayer. Mother had always operated the Congregation very frugally and somehow managed to save money each year, even though the parishes sent her very little for the services of the school Sisters. Father Pierre had assisted her to create a workable arrangement with Bishop Pellicer, thus making the purchase of the San Antonio property possible.

Before the summer retreat began, Mother took her two assistants to San Antonio to look over the renovations on the Bonham Street property. All three were very pleased with the work that Father Nicolas had accomplished. In addition to building up the treasury of his parish, the seasoned missionary was a master at drawing parishioners into building projects and had been able to put the smaller building into a passable condition for the convent and the larger one into shape for the school rooms. Talk in the parish about the opening of their school was lively and a good enrollment seemed likely.

"How many Sisters will you send us, Mother," Father Nicolas asked timidly. "I think we'll need six to manage the situation."

"Six!" Mother's face showed more shock than surprise. "I will try to send you four, Nicolas. And you will be grateful for that many!" The other two Sisters had never had the opportunity to observe the relationship between these two Alsatian siblings. Sometimes it was difficult to determine whether they were teasing one another or actually arguing. But in this exchange, Nicolas seemed to recognize that he had no power of negotiation and merely responded, "Very well. We will welcome four." Then he pushed his sister further. "Could one of the Sisters be a musician? I desperately need someone to help our parish choir. It is quite pitiable and I have no idea how to improve the situation."

"I will try," was Mother's reply and Nicolas seemed to know that he had heard her final word on the subject.

Further conversation at the site included each person's vision of the new school; but once they had returned to Castroville, the three Congregational leaders were frank with each other.

"Mother," Sister Theresa began, "I know you want to open this school in October. But, will the buildings really be adequate?"

"Actually, I don't think they will be adequate. But many, many of our Sisters in France and Germany teach each and every year in cold, drafty, dilapidated buildings and then live in worse. We will manage here as well as they do. We are sending some of our stronger Sisters to Bonham Street. Starting the school and living in that excuse for a house will take more than courage and abandonment to Divine Providence! Each Sister must be healthy as well!"

"When I went to Frelsburg," Sister Mary Agnes added, "Father Gury was so excited about having Sisters that he was able to get the townspeople to supply almost anything we needed. I think Father Nicolas will have the same effect."

"Oh, yes," Mother agreed. "Nicolas has an uncanny ability to draw the parishioners into a project. He's new at St. Joseph's, however, and assistance may be slower in coming than it was for us in Austin. But Providence will provide."

Sister Clare led the small band of Sisters of Divine Providence to San Antonio in September 1875 when the Sisters of Divine Providence opened St. Joseph's Academy on Bonham Street. Sister

Virginia accepted the added responsibility of assisting Father Nicolas with his parish choir and all four Sisters contributed their considerable musical talents to the parish Masses.

But the situation at St. Joseph's proved physically hard. The 150 pupils occupied every square inch of the inadequate schoolhouse while conditions in the so-called convent were deplorable. The makeshift kitchen lent itself to only "picnic-style" dining and many days the Sisters took their meals under the cottonwood trees. Sister Ursula, whose sister, Sister Josephine, had been absorbed into the Polish "Blue Sisters" in Panna Maria found her own vocation waning and left the Congregation from St. Joseph's during the first school year. Mother had to send one of her young, untried novices, Sister Clothilde to take Sister Ursula's place.

When the school year of 1875-1876 ended, Mother sighed in relief. She had spent anxious months, fearing that illness or some other disaster would jeopardize all of their missions.

After an uneventful but productive summer, most of the Sisters were re-assigned to the same schools they had served during the previous year. The final preparations before they were sent off included a general meeting with Mother St. Andrew the day after St. Louis Day. The sixteen religious gathered as instructed in the large community room on the first floor. By now the Motherhouse had a lived-in look. Crucifixes graced the walls of each room; desks and chairs held inkwells, pens, and notepaper. Mother's office was in an unused classroom behind the community room; and after she believed the Sisters to be settled at their desks, she entered, taking her place at the small desk in the front of the room.

"My dear Sisters," she began, "on Monday, most of you will be taking up your assignments for the coming school year. We are happy to send Sisters Theresa, Scholastica, and Celestine to open a new school in Galveston, but I am the first to admit that I am uneasy about extending ourselves that far. At least the railroad from Alleyton to San Antonio is almost finished! I want to announce that Sister Mary Agnes will oversee all of our missions to the east: Mentz, Ellinger,

Galveston, and Frelsburg. From Frelsburg, she will be able to take
the train to Galveston should you need her. But Sister Theresa will
represent us well as the first principal of the new school. Galveston
welcomed us poor missionaries so generously ten years ago. I simply
could not refuse to staff Father Grenyenbeuhl's school in St. Joseph's
German parish in Galveston in this, the tenth anniversary year of
our coming to Texas. I know Providence will provide."

She walked over to the crucifix hanging on the wall, and, quoting
the Founder, said, "***Let the crucifix be your book of meditation.
May Jesus crucified be in your heart and all His sufferings be
in your mind so that you can never forget them.***"* Sisters, you
have heard me quote our Holy Founder on this point many, many
times. But the words always bear repeating. We never take on new
missions—or any responsibility—because we believe we have the
resources to be successful. No! We accept new schools because we
believe that Providence will provide us with our needs as long as we
are open to His designs. Ten years ago we came to Texas with nothing but our hope in Providence. Despite the trials and losses of the
last few years, Providence has not abandoned us.

"I know how busy you are during the year with lessons, housework, laundry, care of your classrooms, and visits to the sick of your
parishes. Our duties are very important, but I urge you to be faithful to our deepest calling. Our fidelity to the cross of Jesus will see
us through any adversity. Be faithful to prayer; be faithful to our
Fridays in silence. Thinking that the conversations that engage us
are so important, we often find ourselves breaking Friday silence.
Yesterday, St. Louis Day, is a good example. With all that was happening, I dare say none of us spent any time in silence yesterday!
Our Founder, however, characterized anything that would take us
away from interiorly being with our Suffering Lord a mere distraction. As our Founder has directed us, I urge you to resolve to '***recollect yourselves, purify yourselves, and renew yourselves at the***

---

*   **The Directory**, p. 210.

foot of the cross in meditation on the death and passion of Our Lord Jesus Christ as much as your occupation will allow.'[V]

"With your example, your pupils will do the same. A good teacher leads by example. I recommend that you give your pupils quiet time on Friday afternoons. Perhaps you might read aloud to them from the Bible, if you have one; or you might tell them stories from the life of Jesus; or you might simply lead them in being silent, telling them to mediate on the sacrifice Jesus has made for their sins. Let this time of silence occupy the last hour or so of your Friday afternoon. All of your children will return to their homes to take up many chores. A time of quiet will serve them well.

"I am the first to confess that yesterday, St. Louis Day, we did not heed this advice of our Founder. It was a very busy day. For the next hour, we will take upon ourselves the silence recommended by Father Moye. We will go to our little chapel and be still, begging God for the graces we will need as we re-enter the vineyards of the Lord."

At this she led her little community in silence to the nearby chapel-room where they spent the rest of their afternoon in silence.

Staffing all the schools in operation during 1876-77 again depended on sending newly invested novices to teach in Fredericksburg and D'Hanis; and, once again, Mother, assisted by the candidates, would manage St. Louis School in Castroville.

With the grace of Providence, the 1876-77 school year was uneventful. Father Grenyenbuehl warmly welcomed the three Sisters to his parish in Galveston, even though the school building was still under construction upon their arrival. The three Sisters lived in a rented cottage and taught classes on the first floor of an old hall until the permanent structure could be completed. Sister Scholastica, having only one year of teaching experience, and that in a small country school, was unaccustomed to the rowdier city children. Also, she had

---

V   **The Directory, p. 300.**

the boys in grades four through eight! Her cedar switch and tap bell had no effect, causing Sister Theresa to make numerous trips to the bedlam-like classroom to restore control. Each day was better, however, and by Christmas, Sister Scholastica ruled her kingdom! The three Sisters gave the school a solid beginning.

In June 1877, after everyone was back at the Castroville Motherhouse and settled into classes, Mother St. Andrew began meetings with her school principals. Most schools were growing: St. Joseph's Academy needed more teachers; Father Grenyenbuehl wanted the Galveston Sisters to open a girls' school at the Cathedral parish; Fredericksburg wanted a music teacher; and parishes just opening in Schulenburg and High Hill were writing for Sisters.

Once she had a firm picture of needs for the coming school year, Mother met with her Sister-consultors. Their frustration at not having enough Sisters for growing needs was apparent. Finally, Sister Mary Agnes offered a suggestion.

"Mother, have you ever thought of returning to Europe to seek more Sisters to join us here in Texas? The letters we receive from Mother Constantine seem so supportive, and she continues to indicate that they are receiving many vocations there. Perhaps they could help us." Her voice held her trepidation at bringing this up. Though she told numerous stories of the Motherhouse as she had known it and relished her letters from Mother Constantine, Mother St. Andrew had always taken a self-reliant position in terms of the now-German Motherhouse. Her constant concern had been to stand on her own and not be a burden to Mother Constantine who so generously supported the mission in Texas as best she could, given the circumstances in Europe over the past six years.

After a very long pause, during which Sister Mary Agnes and Sister Theresa sat perfectly still, Mother said, "I'll think about it. Now, let's get back to our plans for the next school year." With that, both of the consultors knew that the topic was closed, and both knew better than to press the subject further.

"I continue to get letters from the pastor in Schulenburg who wants Sisters for two schools and there's going to be an Austrian parish in a place called High Hill. I'd love to begin a school there! Also, Father Gury writes on behalf of Father Orth in Columbus." As she spoke, Mother shuffled through a half-dozen letters. Laying the correspondence down, she sighed. "This year, however, I do not believe we should stretch ourselves further. We now conduct twelve schools with twenty-three Sisters. I regret that we cannot do more."

"Mother, you are quite right," Sister Theresa affirmed. "We can do only what we can do. I think that our virtue of simplicity calls us to acknowledge our limitations."

"Very insightful, Sister. Our Holy Founder always placed simplicity and charity as the bookends of our four fundamental virtues. In this case, perhaps we might, in charity, realize that we cannot burden our Sisters with more than they can take on. For each mission school that we open, the numbers of Sisters in our present schools are diminished. Each mission is hard in its own way; but, so far, except for Haby's Settlement, Solms, and D'Hanis, we have been able to keep at least two Sisters in each of our schools. Our Sisters all struggle to operate good schools for their parishes. I must accept that, in charity, we cannot ask more of their generous hearts."

"Mother," Sister Mary Agnes began, changing the subject, "all the Sisters are expecting to visit their families at the end of July. Rather than visit my sister at that time, I could remain here. Perhaps I can be of use with the new candidates before they are invested on St. Louis Day. I will stop in Bastrop on my way back to Frelsburg in September. Would that be all right?"

"I would be very grateful, Sister," Mother replied. "I would welcome both your company and your assistance." Over the years, Sister Mary Agnes and Sister Theresa had matured into dedicated religious and confident educators, and Mother had grown fond of them both.

As the meeting concluded, Mother made a mental note to speak with Father Pierre about going to Germany to seek help from Mother

Constantine. Their Superior General had never given the impression that Mother St. Andrew would not be welcomed home. In the days of June and July, Mother found herself longing for the quiet and peace of the cradle of her vocation. If she went to Europe, she would take one of her two consultors with her, giving the Texas vocation an opportunity to experience the Congregation's roots.

All of the Sisters had returned from their home-visits to the Castroville Motherhouse by the Feast of St. Louis and each Sister appeared rested and eager to begin the new school term. All, that is, except for Sisters Virginia and Angela. Something had evidently occurred during their home-visit to Fredericksburg and the two young siblings were not speaking to each other when their father dropped them off at the Castroville convent on his way to San Antonio. Slammed doors and angry looks announced their arrival.

Sister Mary Agnes greeted them warmly, but her overtures were returned with silence. Concerned that their sisterly quarrel would spill out onto the rest of the Sisters arriving from their vacations, Sister Mary Agnes spoke to each of the Koehler sisters individually, learning nothing. Each sister blamed the other for "the worst two weeks of my life."

As each group of Sisters left for their schools during the week following St. Louis Day, the Motherhouse returned to a place of peace. Mother St. Andrew took the lull in activity as an opportunity to speak frankly with Sister Angela who would be living at the Motherhouse until further into September when she would return to Haby's Settlement.

"Sister Angela, please be frank. What is your difficulty with your sister?" Mother's question was straightforward and her black eyes commanded an answer.

"I ... I ...," Sister Angela began with hesitation, but the more Mother's eyes bore into her own, the more the young religious knew that she had to say something. "I," she began again, "I wish I didn't have to tell you this, Mother, but I think that Sister Virginia is in love with your brother." Sister Angela spoke simply and Mother, realizing the temptations of life, chose to believe her.

Within the next two weeks, Mother consulted both Sister Mary Agnes and Father Pierre to design a plan to deal with this disconcerting news. Father Pierre's advice went straight to the heart of the matter. "Mother, you must change Sister Virginia. Whether the accusation is true or not, I believe you should act in a manner that will protect the reputation of your brother, should Sister Virginia's behavior become improper. You must protect your Institute from scandal. Yes, remove Sister Virginia from St. Joseph's. Basically, she is a good young religious. Another school will give her a fresh start and will eliminate her present distraction."

Taking that advice, Mother went herself to St. Joseph's Academy in San Antonio, in early September to tell Sister Virginia that she was being changed to Frelsburg. Sister Mary Agnes would be just the right influence on this young vocation.

Little did Mother know that her greatest challenge to her decision to move Sister Virginia would be her own brother! First, he was furious that his own character was being called into question.

"Nicolas, I am not questioning your character! I merely want to stop a problem before it begins. It won't be long before all of the Sisters in the community know of Sister Virginia's alleged feelings about you. I am not even sure that Sister Angela is telling the truth. But after all that happened with my Sisters in Panna Maria, we can ill afford further controversy! Be patient with me and help me." Her last words were pleading.

"I will not!" Nicolas retorted. "No change here is necessary. Our school is just now getting started. Sister Virginia is doing a fine job; besides, I need her to direct our parish choir. She cannot be moved!"

"I am the Superior, Nicolas, and if I think it best to move her, I will move her," Mother said in an even, low tone. The two Alsatians were at an impasse. Nicolas walked off in anger and Mother tried to regain her composure before telling the St. Joseph's Academy community of the change planned. As she prayed for calm, she was struck by the irony of the situation: a ridiculous quarrel between two immature sisters had inadvertently weakened her own relationship with her brother, which had been mended only recently after the problems over the Austin property. How fragile our relationships are, she mused to herself.

Mother met with Sister Virginia the next morning, hoping that her overnight rest would give her wisdom for the encounter.

"Sister Virginia, I have thought this over carefully. I no longer believe that you can give your best service here at St. Joseph's. Therefore, I am going to send you to Frelsburg. Sister Mary Agnes has much more than she can manage there; and since you have so many talents, you will be a great help to her."

Sister Virginia sat open-mouthed. She had no idea that this was coming and her first words indicated her shock. "But, Mother, why are you changing me? I am doing well here, am I not? Sister Clare has always praised my classroom work and Father Nicolas appreciates my work with his choir. What has happened to bring about your decision?"

"Sister, I would rather not discuss that with you at this time. I know that change is hard. But our life is one leave-taking after another. Our dear founder frequently told our earliest Sisters: *'Go everywhere they send you without murmuring.'** And our first Superior, Sister Marie Morel, gave us the best example. Father Moye wrote that she was ready to leave wherever she was in order to go where God might call her. Sister, this is our life as Sisters of Divine Providence. This is your opportunity to join your sufferings at being moved with those of our Savior, asking Him for the grace to withstand the pain of abandonment as He Himself did."

"Yes, Mother," Sister Virginia said, but her words did not reassure her Superior who detected a look of rebellion in her subject's eyes.

"I will purchase your train ticket while I am here. Perhaps you might leave by the end of next week? That should give us time to bring someone here whom you might instruct on your present

---

*   **The Directory, p.209.**

duties. I would not want anyone to feel a disruption because of your transfer."

In the next week, unknown to Mother St. Andrew, both of the daughters of *Herr* Koehler of Fredericksburg wrote their father. Sister Angela's short letter indicated in veiled terms her "worry" about her sister in San Antonio and the relationship she "seemed to have" with the pastor. Sister Virginia's short letter complained of the change that was in the offing and revealed her ire at her Superior's decision.

Herr Koehler headed for San Antonio immediately. No priest was going to tempt his daughter! No daughter of his was going to be involved with a priest!

Koehler arrived in San Antonio within a few days and went directly to St. Joseph's Church looking for the pastor. Father Feltin was east of town looking over property that the parish had just purchased for a cemetery. Plans were in the offing to clear the ground of the cactus and scrub brush in order to make the ground suitable for burying the dead.

Koehler remained in the church, not even going to St. Joseph's Academy to see his daughter. He wanted no explanations that might lessen or distract his fury. When Feltin returned, he was delighted to meet *Herr* Koehler; and though he was put off by Koehler's angry demeanor, Feltin's own innocence of any wrongdoing prevailed and he persuaded Koehler to have supper with him.

When Koehler left Feltin's table to find a room for the night, he was somewhat mollified and indicated that he would let Mother St. Andrew handle her problems with his daughters. Feltin was pleased with how the event had ended.

But that night, Koehler fell desperately ill. His stomach pains were so severe that the hotel owner called a doctor.

Standing over the bed of his sweating, writhing patient, the doctor confessed, "Sir, I have no idea what is wrong with you. Have you eaten any bad food? Have you drunk any bad whiskey?"

Koehler replied to the doctor's innocent questions with outrage. "Do I appear drunk, sir? I have had nothing except dinner at the table of a priest! I am going to die! Help me!" Koehler bellowed.

The doctor, recognizing that any number of things could be wrong, stroked his beard and finally said, "Perhaps you had spoiled food. I can do nothing but give you Syrup of Ipecac. That might relieve your pain and expel the toxins." His last word led Koehler to believe that he had been poisoned—and Koehler decided then and there that the priest had poisoned him on purpose.

Only after several days was Koehler able to leave his bed; and when he did, he went straight to the sheriff of San Antonio, demanding the arrest of one Nicolas Feltin, priest, on the charge of attempted murder! Verification of Koehler's near-fatal attack by the doctor and hotelkeeper, Koehler's witnesses, required the sheriff to arrest the dumbfounded priest.

That day's *San Antonio Daily Express* carried the bold headline: *Local Priest Arrested for Murder!* Though the entire matter was cleared up before Judge George Noonan within ten days, everyone involved was angry with everyone else. Mother St. Andrew was once again angry at Nicolas who had been in the middle of another problem; Koehler was angry with the priest, the Mother Superior, his daughters, and the San Antonio judge who threw out his case; Sisters Virginia and Angela—who both left the Sisters of Divine Providence—were angry with each other, Father Nicolas, their father, and Mother St. Andrew; and Father Nicolas whose character had been besmirched and his arrest cause for scandal for the entire San Antonio Catholic Church was furious with everyone.

Bishop Pellicer had once again been drawn into a thorny mess in which the Sisters of Divine Providence were involved. This time, however, he made a personal call on Mother St. Andrew at Castroville. In a meeting with Mother St. Andrew and Father Pierre, the Bishop learned that Mother was acting within her rights to move Sister Virginia. His Lordship came to appreciate this Superior whose integrity had led her to a difficult action in order to maintain the reputation of her Sister and one of his priests. In the end, the Bishop of San Antonio expressed his deep regard for Mother St. Andrew and his regret that all concerned had been slandered by what he termed "that local rag of a newspaper."

Three Sisters left the community over the San Antonio fracas: Sisters Angela, Virginia, and Odilia all returned home to Fredericksburg.

By fall of 1877, having lost three more Sisters, Mother St. Andrew decided to talk with Father Pierre about her dwindling numbers.

"Father, no matter what I do, it seems that we take one step forward and two steps back. We are now losing Sisters faster than we are gaining new vocations. Tell me what to do." Her defeated tone revealed her desperation and Father Pierre was gentle in his response.

"Mother, you have done all you can alone. You simply cannot continue to rely only on your resources in Texas. You need help. Perhaps someone who can focus only on training your novices? Perhaps more Sisters who are mature vocations? Perhaps ..." He stopped as he saw panic in Mother's face. He thought to himself: am I being premature with my advice? Will she feel too defeated if she has to ask for help from Germany?

But, Mother recovered almost instantly from her sense of panic. Her voice was steady when she answered her friend of nearly ten years. "You are right, *mon père*. With your permission, I will return to St. Jean-de-Bassel after the New Year."

"Excellent, *ma mère*! Shall I use our diocesan offices to obtain your tickets? I believe we can save some money making the arrangements through the chancery." Enthusiasm returned to this kind priest who himself had weathered so many storms with this young Congregation.

"Thank you, *mon père*. I would greatly appreciate the assistance. I, however, can afford the passage money; just tell me what I will owe." Ever the self-reliant, Mother might have to go to St. Jean-de-

Bassel with her hand outstretched, but she could at least pay her own way!

That very night she wrote to Mother Constantine.

Castroville, Texas
Feast of the Guardian Angels
October 2, 1877

Ma Chère Mère!

I hope that this letter finds you and the other members of your Council well. I, too, am well but experiences of the last months have left me tired and frustrated. I take pen in hand to ask for your assistance. You have always been more than a Mother to me, supporting me, helping me to curb my Alsatian temperament, advising me to place the well-being of the community before all.

That is my reason for writing. My community is struggling. I would rather tell you of these challenges in person, and thus, ask for an invitation to come home to St. Jean-de-Bassel. It has now been nearly a dozen years since I left our beloved motherhouse and I have grown weary of continuing a patchwork plan for providing proper formation to our Sisters here in Texas. I ask for more Sisters from Germany to join us here in Texas. More and more pastors ask for Sisters for schools. The Sisters we have are fragile vocations who need a deeper foundation in the religious life. Though I will not ask you for monetary assistance, I would be grateful for a Sister who has strength in money management.

I pray that you will receive my request with a generous heart. Be assured of my prayers for you and for our entire Congregation.

> *Your loving and obedient daughter,*
> *Sœur St. André*
> *Superior in Texas*

The weeks between the mailing of the letter to Mother Constantine and the day the response came seemed as long as a year. Only just after Christmas did Mother receive a reply.

> *St. Jean-de-Bassel, Lorraine, Germany*
> *Feast of St. Albert*
> *November 15, 1877*

Ma Chère Fille!

It was with great pleasure that I received your recent letter and I beg you to come home. Your work in Texas will endure without your presence for a few months. We continue to receive more and more vocations yet we remain unsure what God is truly asking of us as Père Moye's Daughters. Our life as Germans remains complex, but I feel that we are now more secure. You should have no difficulties in coming at this time. I have heard your request and we will review possibilities. When may we expect you? Come as soon as you can arrange your travel.

> *Your Mother,*
> *Mère Constantine*
> *Superior General*

Mother St. Andrew sat in her office for a long time pondering Mother Constantine's letter. She said so much and yet she said so little. Other recent letters had been equally as cryptic. Vocations were plentiful, yet Mother always seemed vague about what the Sisters were doing. Her descriptions in previous letters of the building of the new chapel and other improvements to the Motherhouse grounds were Mother Constantine's only thinly discussed topics. The Superior's letters had been newsy but the politics of their situation as a German Motherhouse were always veiled, and she never discussed the impact of German politics on their schools. News that others in Castroville received from family members in Alsace painted a grimmer picture: German bureaucrats required strict standards to be met by schoolteachers and town leaders, prompting the closing of many Catholic schools whose teachers could not meet state requirements. And the Church, too, fell under persecution as the German government openly favored the Lutheran Church over the Catholic Church. Neither letters Mother St. Andrew received from Mother Constantine nor letters she wrote to Europe referred directly to any of these circumstances. Since the people of Castroville shared their letters with Mother St. Andrew regularly, however, she felt that she had a clear understanding of the bleak situation of life in Lorraine and Alsace since 1870.

Sister Mary Agnes and Sister Theresa were thrilled to receive Mother's notice that she was planning to sail in the early spring of 1878. Mother had decided to take one of her two oldest Texas vocations with her and felt that priority should be given to Sister Mary Agnes since she had been with Mother since Austin days. But Sister Mary Agnes declined. Having been born in Germany, Sister Mary Agnes felt that she might not be able to present adequate papers for traveling; and, because she had given up one of her Sister-teachers for St. Joseph's Academy when the two Sisters there left in October, she did not feel that she could leave the Frelsburg area. On the other hand, Sister Theresa was very happy to accept when Mother wrote to her after receiving Sister Mary Agnes' declination. Though Sister

Theresa had been born in Germany also, her father had made certain that he and his family all had proper papers from the earliest years of their emigration to San Antonio.

Mother asked Father Pierre to obtain passage for herself and Sister Theresa on a sailing from Galveston in late February or early March. Sister Theresa had assured her that Sister Scholastica could take the principalship for the last few months of the school term. Sister Mary Agnes agreed to take responsibility in Castroville for the summer classes, the annual retreat, and assignments for the 1878-79 school year. The more she thought about this turn of events, the more Mother was convinced that the hand of Providence was guiding everything. Sister Theresa would be able to experience the Motherhouse; Sister Mary Agnes would gain experience in Congregational leadership; she herself would be able to rest and see her family.

Now that Mother was back on speaking terms with Nicolas, he ladened her with letters for everyone he knew in Strasbourg and LaWalck and asked her to find him some specific appointments for his sanctuary. He wanted a "decent" monstrance, candlesticks, and a new *prie-dieu*. When Mother agreed to find these items, he gave her enough money for them and for other items that she might find for her own chapel in Castroville. Nicolas knew that he had been a thorn in her side and hoped that his generosity might make up for his stubborn behavior in the previous fall.

Crossing the Atlantic was uneventful and after long train rides from LeHavre to Paris and then on to Germany, travel-worn Mother St. Andrew and Sister Theresa arrived at the Sarrebourg station. Their train was met by a young man who seemed quite familiar, but Mother knew that she had not met him.

"Hello, *Schwestern*," the young man said in German. "My name is Jean-Louis. Let me take your valises and help you into the wagon. The Sisters expect us by supper."

"Why thank you, young man. You look quite familiar, but I know that we have never met." Once the young man heard Mother's accent, he slipped easily back into French.

"No, *ma mère*, we have not met. My father is Jean-Pierre. He remembers you very well."

"Oh, my goodness. How is your father? He met us here so many times when I taught in Alsace! Do you work at St. Jean?"

"My father is well, but he does not take on as many duties. I have been working with him for the last six years. I am the one who now meets the trains and stagecoaches. Father takes less strenuous duties on the farm."

Over the next miles young Jean-Louis and Mother St. Andrew chatted, going back and forth in French and German. By the time they reached St. Jean-de-Bassel, Sister Theresa, whose German was tested by the conversation, had begun to feel like she, too, was coming home.

As the wagon pulled around the buildings to the back stables, Sister Theresa let out a cry of excitement. "Mother, I had no idea that your Motherhouse was so grand. Our house in Castroville is very small in comparison! Will I ever find my way in all these buildings?"

As tired as she was, Mother laughed out loud. "That is exactly what I thought that summer day in 1845 when Jean-Louis' father drove me up this same path. Yes, just as I learned my way around so will you," Mother said encouragingly. She was visibly pleased that Sister Theresa did not seem too daunted by the enormity and complexity of the buildings. Sister Theresa's principalship in the large city of Galveston had given her a bit of sophistication that Mother was glad to see. As the wagon had come down the front drive, Mother's own attention was drawn to the new chapel to the right of the front entrance. She could hardly wait to see the interior!

Scores of Sisters poured out of the buildings to meet the missionaries from Texas. In the lead, but limping significantly, was Mother Constantine herself, the first to greet Mother St. Andrew. Taking her spiritual daughter into a warm embrace and placing a kiss on each cheek, Mother Constantine's own tears of joy mingled with those of the Sister she had not seen in almost twelve years.

Mother St. Andrew's first remarks were an apology. "*Ma mère*, I beg your pardon for our attire. None of us in Texas has had full habits like yours for many years. It is impossible to get proper fabrics in the wilds of Texas. Please excuse us for appearing so poorly dressed!"

"We joyfully accept you as you are, *ma fille*! *Père* Moye always thought we should be dressed as the people we serve. I think he would approve of your simple dress. Here at St. Jean we are changing this habit for something more fitting our vocation soon. By the time you leave here, you and I will both be dressed in new garb!"

Enthusiastic introductions enfolded Mother St. Andrew and Sister Theresa into their Motherhouse community. Realizing how exhausted the travelers must be, Mother Constantine insisted on a light supper and then an early retirement, assuring Mother St. Andrew that they could spend the next day catching up on all that had happened during the previous dozen years.

But before being shown to her bedroom in the section of *Maison Ste. Famille* where the General Council slept, Mother St. Andrew asked, "May I please visit the new chapel before I retire?"

"Of course, *ma sœur*, of course," Mother Constantine replied. "*Ma sœur* Richard, my old legs will not carry me downstairs one more time this evening. Please take *Sœur* St. André to our new chapel. Spend as much time with her as she wishes and then take her to her bedroom."

Mother St. Andrew walked into the new chapel, now in complete darkness except for the glowing sanctuary candle near the tabernacle.

"Do you wish me to light candles for you, *ma sœur*, so that you might see?" *Sœur* Richard asked timidly. She did not know Mother St. Andrew and was not sure what to expect from this foreigner.

Ste. Anne Chapel, Motherhouse, Congregation of Divine Providence of St. Jean-de-Bassel, France.
(Courtesy, Congregation of Divine Providence, St. Jean-de-Bassel, France)

"Non, ma sœur. I wish only to pray for a moment. When I left eleven years ago, we were gathering for Mass and prayers in St. Jean Baptiste Church. I only want to spend a moment with Our Lord, thanking Him for a safe homecoming. I will look more carefully at this beautiful place in the morning light. Will morning prayer be at 5:30 as usual?"

The other nun was surprised. Rumors abounded in the Motherhouse and those who did not know Mother St. Andrew personally had wondered about the religious decorum of a Sister who had lived in the wilds of Texas for over a decade. *Sœur* Richard made a mental note to assure her Sisters that Mother was a woman of prayer, holding to the traditions of the community handed down from the Founder: ***"When they arrive in a place, the Sisters will go first to the church to adore the Blessed Sacrament and ask Our Lord to bless them. There they will offer anew to God what they are going to do ..."****

Mother slept that night with the sleep of those who rest in their mother's arms and woke to the bell for rising, refreshed and ready for the beginning of a wonderful visit with her Superior and Sisters. After dressing, she entered the hallway, following the other Sisters in silence down the wide staircase to the first floor. Noticing Sister Theresa ahead of her, she was delighted to see that the Texan had

---

* **The Directory, p. 299.**

already been embraced by her French and German Sisters. The comforting Latin prayers provided a common language for worship, transcending other languages which often brought discord and misunderstanding. Though the chapel space was new for her, Mother felt completely at home as she watched the candlelight play on the walls. Her spirit, hungry for the beauty of French art and architecture, drank in the blue- and red-tinted sunlight streaming through the glorious stained glass windows above the altar.

That day and the others that followed were filled with hours of conversation with Mother Constantine. The two Alsatians visited as equals, each one taking her turn with the other to share the successes and failures of the previous years. Mother Constantine shared her experiences and exasperations of shepherding their Congregation through the tumultuous years of the Franco-Prussian War with its disastrous aftermath. She confessed her fear that the government might still disband her community as it had done to others.

"I hope that our new habit will afford our dear Sisters both stature and protection in small villages with German sympathizers. Bismarck has actually commanded that all of us who continue to wear the headpiece of peasant women take on a veil that is more in keeping with cloistered nuns. We have worn the dress of peasant women for so long—and that was *Père* Moye's wish—but now I believe that we must take steps to safeguard our Sisters in troubled times," Mother Constantine was frank with Mother St. Andrew about her trials during the eight years under the Reich. Mother St. Andrew learned why her Superior's letters had been so vague, so cryptic at times. The German government early on began to pressure the teaching orders in Lorraine and Alsace to disband, thus turning over hundreds of Catholic schools to lay teachers.

"If *Père* Moye had not left us such copious writings, we would have no way to defend our existence! *Abbe* Michel has spent days in Strasbourg arguing on behalf of our teachers; but, thanks be to God, our Founder's plan was to establish a group of women who would do all of the works of mercy in tiny hamlets such as tending the sick, sitting with the dying, and helping the old people. *Abbé* Michel has been the essence of patience in working with the German officials. His persistent work has led to our security—at least for now. So much has happened since 1871. You can see, now, can't you, *ma chère*, why I have written such sketchy letters. If any one of them had fallen into the wrong hands and I had been too specific, I might have jeopardized our very existence." Mother Constantine seemed relieved to be able to speak frankly to this fellow Alsatian whose missionary work she admired so very much.

"I had no idea, *ma mère*," Mother St. Andrew said softly, reaching out her hand to touch her Superior's arm in support. "What an ordeal!"

"Yes, and I fear it is not over. I am hoping that your work in Texas can be sustained. In case we are unable to endure here, at least the Sisters from Portieux, Gap, and now Texas, will last!" Her last words were filled with hope and her eyes met Mother St. Andrew's evenly as though with a look she might insure the future of the Texas foundation.

"I have done my best to establish us in Texas, *ma mère,* and to continue our Founder's project there. Our twelve schools are doing well. Losing our property in Austin was a great distress, but I have presumed that Providence did not want us there. Castroville is an ideal setting for the Motherhouse—so much better than Austin. The Castroville people are true Alsatians, with every Alsatian strength and limitation! They are very generous to us and have helped us build a magnificent Motherhouse. I so wish that you could come to see it! Is that out of the question?"

"I'm afraid so, *ma chère*. My legs are no good. I don't even travel outside of the Motherhouse here any more. However, I have been thinking of whom to send with you to Texas. Once the Council comes to a final decision, we will let you know. But each one whom we will send will be my personal ambassador. We are discussing the possibility of sending our own Mistress of Novices, *Sœur* Marie-Ange. What is your thinking about that? Do you need her?"

"Oh*, ma mère,* that would be wonderful. At present I fulfill those duties, but I am so distracted and pressured by other administrative work that I fear our youngest members often are denied my full attention. Is *Sœur* Marie-Ange willing to come? You know, she and I were novitiate companions!"

"*Sœur* Richard is speaking to her this week. We believe that she will be open, perhaps even eager. She has served as Mistress of Novices here for some time and she herself needs a change. Perhaps the challenge of Texas would be good for her," Mother Constantine said with a twinkle in her eye.

"If she can withstand sweltering heat, is willing to learn English, and is fond of Alsatian sausage, she'll be fine!"

"I myself was surprised at her willingness when we first brought up the possibility of Texas. She may not be young, but she has a hardy constitution, and she is an Alsatian to her very core!"

"Castroville will love her!" Mother St. Andrew assured her Superior. "And so will I! *Merci beaucoup!*"

"The Council and I have had a number of discussions since I received your letter. We do not have all of our thoughts finalized, but we would very much like to have you speak to all of us about the needs in Texas. Would tomorrow be all right?"

Mother St. Andrew spent all the next day speaking with Mother Constantine and her Council about the progress and the problems of the Texas foundation. The Councilors, eager to learn, asked numerous questions. Though Mother St. Andrew had written regularly over the past years, only the spoken word could adequately paint a picture about how things were in Texas.

The days of spring sped by; and after Easter, seeing that Sister Theresa was quite settled in among her German Sisters, Mother St. Andrew decided to visit her own family in LaWalck. In several recent letters Marie-Anne had begged her to come. Though she knew that her first home visit since their mother's death would re-open the wound in her heart, Mother St. Andrew made plans to go to LaWalck. She had nieces and nephews whom she had never met; her mother's grave beckoned her, as did the grave of her brother Pierre.

Her sister's husband Isidore met her stagecoach in Haguenau and by the time they reached LaWalck, Mother St. Andrew was caught up on all the family. Marie-Anne and Christine were the only two Feltins left in LaWalck. Celestin had joined baby Rosalie in heaven in 1853; Francois had gone to Paris; Pierre had died in 1867; Nicolas, Louis, and herself were in Texas.

The spark of friendship that had existed between the two sisters since they were little girls huddled together in that cold kitchen in Geispolsheim watching their mother and father suffer after the death of baby Rosalie rekindled. Opening their age-old friendship to Christine, Mother St. Andrew and Marie-Anne and their young sister spent hours each day filling in one another on all the details of their very different lives. Thrilled to welcome a returning daughter, the people of LaWalck extended numerous invitations to *Mère* St. André. There were numerous afternoon teas; the parish of Sts. Peter and Paul held a special celebration; the Office of the Mayor—a position her brother Pierre had once held—sponsored a *féte* for the entire village.

Her two weeks at home were gone before she could realize it, and in their last embrace, Mother St. Andrew whispered to Marie-Anne, "I won't be gone so long again, *ma chérie!*"

As the Sisters began to arrive for the summer homecoming, specific plans began to take shape regarding who would be sent to Texas. Sister Marie-Ange Huver was to relieve Mother St. Andrew of the training of novices; Sister Mary Angelique Decker, the general treasurer at St. Jean-de-Bassel was to take over the administration of the Motherhouse in Castroville; Sisters Marie Pierre Hetzel, Sigisbert Megel, André Reisdorf, Arsene Schaff, and Donate Claude, all experienced teachers, were to provide pedagogy classes for the young Texas Sisters and monitor their classrooms. Each of them had taught under French certification and was unenthusiastic about having to sit for examinations for German certificates. To them, Texas was an escape!

By the summer retreat all plans were in place and travel arrangements were made. Mother so relished being able to make her retreat at St. Jean-de-Bassel. On the last day, as she sat on the same bench near the orchard that she had occupied a dozen years earlier, she allowed her mind to drift over her life. Only the Providence of God could have designed all that had happened: her good fortune to be called into the Sisters of Divine Providence; the cradle of faith that her parents had provided for her; the Sisters with whom she had served in Epfig, Heiligenberg, and Batzendorf, some of whom had gone to God in the past years; her dear, dear friend, *Sœur* André Keller who had hung on every word of her tales of Texas, longing to be able to join in the missionary work; her gratitude to Mother Constantine who so wanted Texas to succeed; her own dear Marie-Anne, the sister of her heart who now tended alone the hearth of the Feltin family in LaWalck. The grace of gratitude flooded over her as tears spilled over onto her cheeks now browned forever from the Texas sun.

The new habit was still uncomfortable, especially the new, larger *guimpe*. But she supposed she would get used to it. At least she now looked like all of her Sisters. The change of habit that had occurred on the Feast of the Sacred Heart required everyone to adjust, and Mother St. Andrew was glad that she and Sister Theresa had been at St. Jean-de-Bassel for the event. They both agreed that the Sisters back home would find the stories of the change very entertaining, though they might not appreciate the formality of the new garb! The Sisters in Castroville would rely heavily on Sister Theresa's ability as a seamstress since she had spent long hours in the Motherhouse sewing room learning how to make the various parts of the new habit.

Just before the retreat had begun, Mother Constantine had had one last long conference with her Texas counterpart. It seemed that one of the household Sisters, Sister Gabriel, had come to Mother

Constantine asking to be sent to Texas. Mother Constantine had been reticent, not wanting to burden Mother St. Andrew with someone who does not teach. But Mother St. Andrew had been thrilled.

"*Ma mère*, I would love to take *Sœur* Gabriel! The new Motherhouse definitely needs the touch of a true housekeeper. The candidates keep things orderly under my direction, but you know that I am not a true homemaker. She will be able to provide so much more for us. I simply keep the dust scooped up," she laughed. "We truly need *Sœur* Gabriel if she is willing to come."

"She really wants to. If you wish, we will send her."

Sœur Gabriel Stephen became the eighth Sister of Divine Providence of St. Jean-de-Bassel to come to Texas in August of 1878.

On the morning of August 10 all were in readiness for their leave-taking. They would travel by stage and train to LeHavre where, on August 13, they would sail for New York. The newly designated missionaries were gathered in the quadrangle where Jean-Louis and his assistant had two wagons hitched and ready to go.

"Where is *Mère* St. André?" *Sœur* Richard asked Mother Constantine.

"I suspect that she is in the chapel. Would you please fetch her, *ma sœur*?"

True to Mother Constantine's suspicions, Mother St. Andrew was in the chapel and had been there since breakfast. Not wishing to startle her, *Sœur* Richard tapped her gently on the shoulder. "It is time, *ma mère*."

Bending her head—though not far because of her stiff new *guimpe*—Mother rose, stepped out of the pew where she had been kneeling, and genuflected slowly and reverently. As Mother turned toward *Sœur* Richard, the General Councilor who had met this legendary missionary less than six months previously, was startled to see that Mother had been crying. *Sœur* Richard handed Mother a fresh handkerchief and, after wiping her eyes, Mother spoke simply and sincerely: "I was taking this beautiful chapel into my heart, *ma sœur*.

Ste. Anne Chapel Interior, St. Jean-de-Bassel Motherhouse.
(Courtesy: Congregation of Divine Providence of St. Jean-de-Bassel.)

When days in my future are hard, I will go there to pray. Sometimes I will pray for guidance; often I will pray for mercy and forgiveness. This chapel will be in my heart until I can return."

Every cheek was damp with tears as the crowds of Sisters at St. Jean-de-Bassel bade *adieu* to the two Texas missionaries and the eight Sisters joining them. After settling on the wagon seat, Mother St. Andrew looked with love at her Superior who had placed so much confidence in her. "Praised be Jesus Christ," she said, binding them both in the century-old traditional prayer of their foundation.

"Now and forever. Amen," Mother Constantine returned with a wave and a smile.

Mother St. Andrew, circa 1880.
(Congregation of Divine Providence Archives, San Antonio, TX)

CHAPTER XIV

RETURN TO HOPE

The din coming from the crowd was overwhelming! As the carriages and wagons crossed the Medina River, the people gathered along the way began to beat on whatever they held, heralding the arrival of Mother St. Andrew, Sister Theresa, and the Sisters from Germany. Having rested at St. Joseph's in Galveston for only two days before boarding the train from Galveston to San Antonio, the travelers were road weary. Father Nicolas had met the train in San Antonio where he had received candlesticks, vestments, and a *prie-dieu* for St. Joseph Church from Mother St. Andrew before she and her companions had boarded wagons and carriages for Castroville.

The German Sisters, having no idea what to expect from the wilds of Texas, were agog at the array of Castrovillians lining the road from the river to Providence Motherhouse. Children ran up and down waving and hollering. With eyes hidden by broad sunbonnets quite similar to the Alsatian bonnet that had been the habit of the Sisters of Providence for over one hundred years, women with babies on their hips, waved and shouted words of welcome. Men banging on anvils only added to the chaos. Mother St. Andrew had come back and those who loved her gave her a true Texas welcome.

The wagons and carriages filled with nuns, valises, and trunks of fabric for new habits now clattered down Paris Street where still more townspeople lined the dusty path. The excitement was tangible as the travelers approached the town square. Nearing Amelia Street, the nuns in the wagons craned their necks so that they could take in the tall steeple of St. Louis Church. The rising pitch of their voices suggested that they were not expecting to see a massive stone church in the middle of Texas. Finally reaching the front door of Providence Motherhouse, Mother St. Andrew, alighting from the first carriage, was taken up in a bevy of hugs by the Texas nuns who gathered in the yard. The Texas nuns then became quickly silent as they realized that Mother St. Andrew, Sister Theresa, and their companions were dressed completely differently. The simple bonnet was gone, replaced by a more formal-appearing veil covering a stiffly starched linen headpiece. The brown dress, worn by the Sisters since the time of Father Moye, had given way to some type of black skirt and waist.* At least the familiar cape seemed to be the same, but the *guimpe* was larger.

As the newly arrived German Sisters were helped out of their carriages by the men who had come to San Antonio to bring their Sisters to Castroville, Mother introduced each one to the waiting Sisters.

In muted voices of amazement, the Europeans, repeated over and over: "*O mon Dieu donc, ce ne sont que des enfants! Oh, my God, these are only children!*" Sister Mary Ange, sent to be the new Mistress of Novices, felt the weight of her new position as she whispered to Mother St. Andrew, "Why these are just little Sisters! *O les petites sœurs!*"

In keeping with the directives of Father Moye, the new Sisters, the Texans, and the people of Castroville filed into St. Louis Church where Father Pierre intoned the *Te Deum*, the grand hymn of thanksgiving to God for blessings received. All voices joined in the familiar Latin words, which washed over those assembled, joining them together as God's grateful children.

After the singing of the *Te Deum*, Father Pierre spoke from the pulpit.

"My dear Sisters from St. Jean-de-Bassel, we welcome you to our humble village. Your arrival reminds me of the wonderful September day in 1868 when I met the stagecoach which carried your esteemed

---

*   **Blouse**

Superior, Mother St. Andrew, to our little town. Since that day, we have all been touched by the presence of the Sisters of Divine Providence in our midst. When I look out at the young people who have been educated by these wonderful Sisters in our parish school, I see the faces of women and men whose faith is stronger because our Sisters share their faith with us. I myself cannot imagine our parish without our Sisters. It is now a true blessing to receive more Sisters and to anticipate your influence on our still-wild Texas. Don't be daunted, dear Sisters, as you experience our rustic world. We may not be as refined as those in our native homeland, but we assure you that our faith is every bit as deep as the faith of our mothers, fathers, brothers, sisters, and friends that we left behind in France and Germany.

"Sisters, we need you here. We need your wisdom, your courage, your trust in Divine Providence. Thank you for coming, and may God bless us all as we grow to know one another and love one another. Please join me now in singing the *Salve Regina.*"

As voices began the chant *"Salve Regina, mater misericordiae; vita dulcedo, et spes nostra, salve ..."* the Sisters who had willingly traveled untold miles from their dear motherhouse in St. Jean-de-Bassel, who knew that they would never return to their homes and families, who had nothing now but their trust in Providence, felt tears of joy and relief stream down their cheeks. This ancient song, these comforting words, "Hail Queen, mother of mercy, our life, our sweetness, our hope ..." sung at St. Jean-de-Bassel at every gathering, for one mystical moment both bound them to their Sisters across the ocean and made them feel at home in a foreign land.

The next days were a flurry of activity. The Sisters from Germany, finding the schedule at Providence Motherhouse to be identical to that of St. Jean-de-Bassel, easily settled into the routine of the house. But getting used to the diet of Texas was another matter. The day that ears of sweet corn appeared on the table caused raised eyebrows among the new arrivals. People in France and Germany do not eat corn-on-the-cob! That is animal fodder! Catching one another's eyes at the silent table, the German Sisters could read one another's thoughts: do these people eat like animals here? Once the meal was over and the Sisters had left the silent refectory, questions from the newcomers about food in Texas brought peals of laughter from the Texas Sisters. The second and third generation Texans took the opportunity to tell more stories of their own French and German grandfathers and grandmothers who had eaten everything from rattlesnake to boiled cactus in order to survive in the "old days" of Texas.

The first order of business was determining how new habits would be prepared. Sister Mary Agnes and Sister Theresa wisely advised Mother to simply let the Sisters go on mission in their old habits. New habits could be prepared during the school year, scheduling the change to take place at the beginning of the next summer. Once the announcement about habits was made, everyone seemed more relaxed. Ever since seeing the new habit on their European counterparts, the Texas Sisters had seemed hesitant to make a change just before going back to their schools.

The European Sisters' arrival in Castroville just before St. Louis Day left little time for socializing and getting acquainted before the Texans had to leave for their mission schools. But the annual celebration did give the people of St. Louis an opportunity to enfold their new Sisters into the parish community.

Monday, August 26, Mother gathered everyone in the largest classroom on the first floor of the motherhouse. In years past, this last general conference before everyone left for her mission gave Mother a final opportunity to review Father Moye's words that would sustain the Sisters in the months ahead. However, on the boat coming over, Mother had asked Sister Mary Ange to speak on the Constitution.

When Sister Mary Ange had finished, Mother said, "Now, Sisters, I want us to conclude with Father Moye's instruction to us: *'It is by the cross that Jesus Christ engendered us; it is by the cross that we engender souls for Jesus Christ; it is by the cross also that I engender you ...'** And in another place Moye says, **'Pray that the power of the cross may attract the whole universe to Jesus Christ.'**ᵛ

"Most of you here know our Superior General, Mother Constantine, only through her letters to us. I spoke with her daily while I was in Germany. If she could, she would come to visit us. But her own cross, her poor health and her crippled legs, prohibits travel of any kind. In my last visit with her, she asked me to embrace each one of her Texas daughters and assure you of her love and prayers. In her name, I now invest each one of you with the new cross of our Congregation."

At these words, Sister Angelique Decker, the new general assistant, walked to the front of the room with a tray of crosses on black ribbons.

Mother continued. "As I call your name, please come forward." Beginning with Sister Mary Agnes, the oldest member of the Texas Congregation, down to the last one professed, all seventeen nuns came to the front of the room. Their poor patched and mended brown dresses, which had endured the dust of drought, the damp of unexpected downpours, hundreds of brushings to clean away dirt from dozens of journeys by stagecoach and railroad, and uncountable washings made appropriate backdrops for the new crosses. With shining dark eyes that spoke of her pride in her Texas vocations, Mother St. Andrew placed the new black cross around the neck of each Sister. For Sisters Mary Agnes and Mary Theresa, both perpetually professed, the cross bore the Eye of Providence in silver on one side and a silver Corpus on the other side. The crosses received by the others bore only the Eye of Providence. At each investing, Mother spoke Father Moye's own words with reverence: **"Always love poverty and simplicity."***

---

*   The Directory, p. 198.

ᵛ   The Directory, p. 210.

*   The Directory, p. 179.

After the Sisters left for their missions, Providence Motherhouse returned to its regular peaceful routine. Mother St. Andrew, Sister Angelique, and Sister Mary Ange took an afternoon to sit together to more fully orient the two new arrivals with Congregational operations in Texas and to plan for the year ahead.

"I am so very happy that you both of you are here. We have greatly needed your expertise and maturity. Sisters Mary Agnes and Theresa have been valiant in their assistance, but they, too, are young vocations. Without you, I fear that we would have eventually had to disband," Mother St. Andrew confessed humbly.

"Mother, we see so much to be done, to be sure. But you have begun a heroic endeavor. There is much to work with," Sister Mary Ange said. "I am impressed with the type of young girl you are attracting. Regina Friesenhahn, for example, has been so generous in helping us to find our way! She will make a fine novice," Sister Mary Ange quickly asserted.

"Regina is typical of second generation German-Texans. Her parents modeled generosity to their children, inviting our Sisters to live with them when we first began the school in Solms. I am certain that Regina's home was the cradle of her vocation!" Mother said.

Hoping that Mother would realize that she was growing to like the girls in her charge, Sister Mary Ange said with enthusiasm for her new ministry, "I assure you that I will do my best with these lovely girls. Don't you think that I should begin by translating the Constitution into English? Perhaps that would serve us well, giving us a common document for study next summer. I am not yet proficient in English, but I did begin a study of English while at the Motherhouse. And several of the candidates and novices can help. I'm certain that I can complete the translation by next summer if I begin now."

"Sister, that would be excellent!" Mother's gratitude was heartfelt. "May I tell you both a little bit about our schools?" With that Mother St. Andrew launched into a thorough description of each school, beginning with the oldest, St. Louis in Castroville. By the time Mother had finished describing all thirteen schools, Sister Angelique, impressed with the scope of activity of the Texas branch, volunteered: "Mother, you seem to have relied on reports from your principals for several years. Do you think that this year is the time for you to visit each house? With me here at the Motherhouse, and Sister Mary Ange with the candidates and novices, I should think that you would have more freedom to travel. Is that your desire?"

"Oh, yes, Sister! I haven't been to Fredericksburg in years, and now that Sister Theresa who founded the school is no longer there, I feel a great need to visit, especially after our difficulties with the Koehler family. And I haven't been to New Braunfels or Solms recently either. I've depended on Sister Mary Agnes to supervise that entire area. But now I must see for myself."

"Where shall we send the Sisters who came with us from Germany?" Sister Angelique asked.

"I was wondering the same thing. St. Joseph's in San Antonio is growing and could use another teacher. Bernardo Prairie—we opened that school only last year—really needs a seasoned principal and superior. St. Joseph's in Galveston is desperate for another teacher. You know the others from Europe better than I. What do you think?"

After deliberation, the three decided to send Sister Marie Pierre to be the superior in Bernardo; Sister Mary Andrew to St. Joseph's in downtown San Antonio; and Sister Arsene to St. Joseph's in Galveston. They agreed to have Sister Sigisbert and Sister Donate remain at St. Louis School as master-teachers supervising the candidates.

Realizing that the conversation was drawing to a close, Sister Mary Ange asked, "Mother, will we receive any new candidates in the months ahead?"

"Why, yes, Sister. I recently received a letter of application from a young lady from nearby—Mary Neeb. If you are prepared, I believe we could receive her before Christmas." Not wishing to rush Sister

Mary Ange into her work as Mistress of Novices, Mother's last statement sounded tentative.

"Of course, Mother. I will be ready to receive someone by the first
of December. Will you want me to write to Mary and give her details
about entering?"

"I would greatly appreciate your taking on that task. The girls
who are here have been meeting with me weekly and then working
on their lessons independently for the rest of the week. Please take
over as soon as you feel settled. And, of course, you may establish
any schedule you wish."

"When everyone begins school, I will be ready. What is the date
St. Louis School opens for the new term?"

"The parishioners need their children at home to help with the
fall harvest. Let me see," Mother paused as she consulted a calendar. "I suggest that we begin school as usual on the first Monday in
October, October 7."

"Very well. I will begin daily classes with the candidates in a
few days, concentrating on the four fundamental virtues. That will
help them to know me before school begins. When school begins, the
candidates will assist in the classroom under Sisters Donate and
Sigisbert."

"Wonderful! I am feeling relieved already!" Mother said with genuine gratitude.

"I will work with Sisters Donate and Sigisbert to be certain that
the girls become strong teachers as well as strong religious. As they
enter the novitiate, we will begin a more formal teaching schedule
for those who don't go immediately to the missions."

Thrilled with the idea of a firm regimen for the novitiate, Mother
St. Andrew let out an audible sigh. "Thank you so much, Sister Mary
Ange. Providence certainly knew what we needed when He called
you to Texas!"

"What do you wish from me, Mother?" Sister Angelique chimed in
with enthusiasm. "Shall I begin to work with the accounts now?"

Mother laughed out loud. "Of course!" She turned to a ledger that she had brought into the room earlier. "Here is the ledger. It is all yours! I am happy to pass this chore on to you! Tomorrow I will walk with you to Mr. Mann's store, to the bakery, and the butcher. Once you have met the town's merchants, you can then order all of our provisions. Not that we have much money, but Father Pierre and I have tried to make it stretch. So many of the townspeople bring us provisions of one kind or another and all of the merchants are very good to us, extending us credit as needed. We try to pay our bills as soon as possible, but we are truly dependent on Providence as we have been since the days of Father Moye. Father Pierre will welcome your attention to our accounts as much as I do." She smiled broadly before stating with pride, "We may be beholden to almost everyone in Castroville, but at least we are not in debt!"

The rest of the afternoon was spent on the back veranda where the Sisters could enjoy the Texas-blue sky. Mother St. Andrew, Sister Angelique, and Sister Mary Ange enjoyed one another's company. They planned together for making the new habits and exchanged ideas on curriculum revisions for the novice teachers' further education. For Mother St. Andrew the opportunity to work with her educational and spiritual peers was priceless and exhilarating. As the afternoon meeting came to a close, Mother realized that a nearly indescribable deprivation had crept into her life over the last twelve years. The wisdom and companionship of her religious peers now filled an unexpressed void.

After schools opened in October, Mother St. Andrew, true to her commitment to visit their missions, made a visitation to Fredericksburg. Since Sister Theresa had become the principal and superior at St. Joseph's in Galveston in 1876, Sister Felicitas had been alone in Fredericksburg. Mother hoped that when new novices were received in the next months, one could be sent to help at St. Mary's. After seeing for herself how things were going in the German town seventy miles from Castroville, Mother would be able to make a better decision on whom to send. Possible problems associated with the Koehler sisters still worrisome. Though Sister Felicitas had taken a very mature position about that debacle, Mother hoped that she might be able to bolster Sister Felicitas' resolve. People in a small town could be cruel, and the entire Koehler family had extremely strong feelings about the Sisters of Divine Providence. Mother wanted to talk personally with the pastor in order to assure him of the Congregation's stability and learn his impression of all that had happened.

The visit to the hill country town went better than Mother expected. Father Tarrillion was quite hospitable to her and seemed to understand how the situation between *Herr* Koehler and Mother's brother had gotten out of hand.

"Actually, Mother," Father Tarrillion had said, "I understand what happened and am very sorry for how much grief this must have caused you. Bishop Pellicer was very frank with me about the situation since *Herr* Koehler is my parishioner. To tell you the truth, knowing *Herr* Koehler as I do, I wasn't too surprised. Father Nicolas is a very fine priest and I regret that he was humiliated as he was. There is no excuse for all that. All we can be sure of is that as quickly as the problem blew up, it will dissipate. Memories are not long. And Angela and Virginia seem to be all right. Their mother is a very good woman and she knows her daughters! Time will heal all of this."

Later, in her classroom, happy to show off her pupils to the Reverend Mother, Sister Felicitas glowed from Mother's praise for her teaching abilities. She was extremely proud of how well the children recited poetry in both English and German and how well they sang their German hymns. During Mother's visit, the older students enacted a play on the life of Our Lady, and Mother, remembering her days in the classroom in Epfig, complimented them liberally on their expression and creativity. Sister Felicitas beamed.

That same night Mother herself cooked the supper, talking to Sister Felicitas as she fried bacon and boiled cabbage and potatoes.

"I miss the classroom, Sister, but realize that I no longer have the patience to teach full time. I admire how you have worked with the children, especially in the areas of poetry and music. Did I ever tell you the story of my first year of teaching in Epfig when Sister St. Claude and I had to prepare and orchestrate the annual Christmas pageant?" With that Mother St. Andrew launched into one of her favorite stories about herself.

Changing the subject, Mother concluded: "You seem very well accepted by the people here, Sister. That is important. But even more important is that you maintain a professional distance. The longer you are here, the more familiar you will become to them. They may take you into their confidence, and unwittingly you might find yourself spreading or listening to gossip."

"I know what you mean, Mother. When Angela, Virginia, and Odilia returned home, so many people wanted to know what had happened. I must admit that I was tempted to join in their speculations. I was actually glad that I really had no factual information. But Father Moye's admonitions came to mind and I resisted temptation. Now I think that the storm basically has passed. Thank God that is all behind us. Now when I see Angela and Virginia, they are quite friendly. I'm a little concerned about Odilia, though. She remains distant. I heard that the village to our east, Stonewall, might want a teacher. Odilia would be good for them. She also lives in that direction. I hope she applies."

Sister Felicitas was refreshed by Mother's visit. Mother, too, found her time with Sister Felicitas very invigorating. This was actually her first true visitation that was not a response to an emergency. Returning to Castroville, Mother used her time on the stagecoach to San Antonio to plan her visitation itinerary for the next few months. She wanted to go to both New Braunfels and Solms soon, and she scheduled her visit to the Frelsburg area for spring. She had never been to Mentz and had visited Ellinger only once. Her mind was at ease: the administration of the Motherhouse was in the capable hands of Sister Angelique; Sister Mary Ange would take care of the novices and candidates.

Upon her return, Mother continued to be encouraged by what she found. Sister Angelique had made workable schedules for cleaning the Motherhouse and the school building. One day each week all the floors in the Motherhouse were scrubbed; a second day was devoted to the laundry. Sister Mary Ange held spiritual reading for the novices and candidates every day, covering the writings of Father Moye and the Constitution.

St. Louis School was doing well. The nearly fifty students seemed to enjoy their lessons. They had several teachers so the students never found the day boring. Since the novice-teachers were being strictly supervised, their lessons were well prepared and stimulating. Even Sister Angelique was called into the classroom to offer critiques of the lessons on ciphering.

Never complaining about the rustic situation in which she found herself, Sister Gabriel had taken over the kitchen with a chef's expertise. Her meals were both ample and tasty. Mother St. Andrew complimented her regularly on being able to do so much with so little!

Her second visitation, to D'Hanis, proved to be an eye-opener for the Congregation's Superior. Though the Sisters at St. Dominic's School had always been frank with Mother in her summer conversations with them, until she visited them on site, she had not truly appreciated the poverty of their spiritual life. The living conditions were primitive, but those types of deprivations never worried Mother St. Andrew. Father Moye had regularly pleaded with his daughters to welcome hardships. However, the fact that no priest was in residence in D'Hanis meant that the two Sisters did not have access to the sacraments of the Church. Unless a priest would be assigned to live in D'Hanis Mother thought that the school would need to be released to the pastor and his people. Keeping one's vocation in a small frontier village was hard enough without tempting fate by denying her Sisters the graces of the sacraments!

Just after returning from D'Hanis, Mother found an opportunity to meet with Sister Mary Ange and Father Pierre. Mother wanted to discuss with both of them plans for the reception of novices after Christmas. Time was flying by so rapidly that she feared it would soon be Christmas and Father Pierre would be preoccupied with his pastoral duties. Lately, she had begun to notice how tired he appeared at daily Mass.

I wonder if he is feeling well, she thought; he works so hard. I know he doesn't really take care of himself.

Since Pierre Richard was somewhat younger than Mother, she felt motherly toward him. He really ought to take a vacation—spend some time with his family in France, she thought with maternal concern. Pledging to herself to approach her ecclesial superior on the subject of his health, Mother turned her attention to other matters on her desk.

A letter from her brother Nicolas had come while she was away. He was deeply grateful for the items that she had purchased for St. Joseph's Parish while she was in France and Germany. He loved the *prie-dieu*! "My first prayers on the beautiful kneeler were for you and your beloved Congregation, my dear sister. I commended you and all that you do to Divine Providence whom you love and adore." I must answer this letter right away, she noted. Nicolas might be thinking that she was still peeved at him for the humiliation of the Congregation over Sister Virginia's father's accusations against him. She would have to assure her brother that she was no longer concerned about that and to tell him of her visit with Father Tarrillion.

The next letter she picked up was from her brother Louis. Now the father of three children with one on the way, he complained that since Nicolas had left Austin his opportunities for steady work were diminished. Would she know of work that he could do in San Antonio or Castroville?

Mother thought of the Motherhouse. Part of the second floor and the entire third floor were a mere shell. If she were to continue to welcome new candidates, novices, and professed Sisters from

Germany and other parts of Europe, as well as from the villages of Texas, dormitory space would be needed. Perhaps Louis might be put to work here. She also had designs on extending cultivated land into the west pasture. Maybe he and his eldest son John Isidore could help with that, too. She would talk with Father Pierre and her Sister-consultors about these possibilities. But she simply could not be responsible for Louis and his family. He would have to understand that from the beginning. She would have to talk this over with Sister Angelique, as she would have to supervise the construction.

With the approval of Father Pierre, Sister Mary Ange, and Sister Angelique, Mother St. Andrew wrote to Louis explaining the work to be done and offering him enough money to move his family and rent a house. The rest of the arrangement would need to be worked out after he and his family arrived. If Louis accepted the job, he was welcome to move his family to Castroville.

Louis' response came by return mail suggesting his desperation; yes, he and Theresa would move to Castroville after the first of the year. The baby was due any time, so they would wait until Theresa was strong enough to travel.

Every chair in the refectory at Providence Motherhouse was occupied for Thanksgiving Day dinner on November 28, 1878. The two Sisters from D'Hanis, the four Sisters from Germany, five novices, and the new candidates preparing for the novitiate bowed their heads in gratitude as Father Pierre blessed Sister Gabriel's first effort at cooking an American Thanksgiving dinner. Candidate Regina Friesenhahn, having grown up in Solms, was more than helpful to the German Sister-cook who had many questions about preparing the turkey that Haby's Settlement had provided.

The next day, Friday, was a quiet day of solitude and prayer in keeping with the directives of Father Moye. Mother spent the rainy day in the first floor chapel room, polishing candlesticks and oiling the woodwork. She loved working in the Lord's own house, making the simple prayer room as beautiful as possible. Assuring Mother that Jesus had slept in worse surroundings, Father Pierre allowed the Sisters to keep the Blessed Sacrament in their unsophisticated place of adoration.

Just as the community finished their evening meal, a rider from St. Joseph Parish in San Antonio arrived. His news was ominous: Father Nicolas had become very ill. Though he had preached as usual the previous Sunday, he had become overcome by a racking cough and had taken to his bed with a fever. The Bishop thought that Mother should know about this and perhaps come to San Antonio.

"Tell his Lordship that I will come tomorrow afternoon," was Mother's simple reply.

"I think you should come now, Mother," the messenger said with a plea in his voice. "Father Nicolas is not very good."

She was worried. Bishop Pellicer would not have sent for her if the situation were not serious. It might have taken her a day or so to arrange for transportation to San Antonio except that as soon as they heard of the seriousness of Father Nicolas' condition, the people of Castroville rallied their resources, offering to drive Mother the thirty miles to San Antonio in wagons and carriages.

A group of men arranged for the fording of the rain-swollen Medina River and Father Pierre offered to accompany Mother on this solemn journey.

Her prayer along the way commended her brother to God's Providence.

Sometime after midnight the rain-soaked travelers finally arrived in downtown San Antonio. The candles in St. Joseph Church were all lighted, causing strange shadows to dance on the church walls. With assistance, Mother climbed the steep stairs leading to Father Nicolas' small room above the sacristy. My, this place is cold, she thought. No wonder Nicolas is ill!

The tiny bedchamber was crowded with the Bishop and Father Nicolas' fellow priests who had been called to his bedside. The group parted, allowing Mother St. Andrew to approach the cot upon which her brother lay. His face was bathed in sweat and his breathing was

Rev. Nicolas Feltin, c. 1875.
(Courtesy: Catholic Archives of Texas, Austin, TX)

shallow. Pushing his damp hair back from his forehead, Mother felt his hot forehead. A racking spasm took his breath, and Nicolas moaned in pain. It was clear that he was dying.

Mother looked at Bishop Pellicer who simply shook his head. His Lordship's moist eyes met Mother's, announcing the inevitable. The end was near.

Everyone knelt, surrounding the brother and sister who had come to Texas in response to God's call to serve those who had no one to support their faith. Bishop Pellicer began the prayers of Extreme Unction* and anointed his priest with the *Oleum Infirmorum.*[∇] Since Nicolas was already unconscious, the Bishop had been unable to offer this man of God the Viaticum[∞] which the dying priest had carried to countless dying people during his ministerial service. Lifting the Host in blessing, the Shepherd of the Diocese of San Antonio sent this son of the Church on to God with a final Eucharistic blessing.

The priests huddled in Father Nicolas' bedroom heard his sister's whispered words: "I'm so sorry, Nicolas—for everything that kept us from loving one another as we should have. You know my failings better than anyone else. Pray for me as you enter the Kingdom of God." Then silence settled over the room as they listened to the death rattle that emanated from the heaving chest of the suffering priest. At daybreak, the faithful missionary entered into his own

---

*   **Now called the Sacrament of the Anointing of the Sick**

∇   **Olive oil blessed by the Bishop used for anointing the sick and dying.**

∞   **Viaticum is the Body of Christ (communion) given to the dying. "Viaticum" means "with you on the way."**

resurrection, finally coming out of the tomb and joining the Lord whom he had served faithfully for twenty-five years without regard to his own health.

"I myself will prepare his body for burial," Mother St. Andrew said to Bishop Pellicer. "Could Father Pierre assist me?"

"Of course, Mother. May I suggest that you ask *Frau* Menger for information on which ladies of the parish might help you. She is very fond of your brother. He served this parish well and the people will help you."

"Thank you, Your Lordship. I will."

"Mother, you are no doubt exhausted. Let's just tend to the immediate concerns and then I want you to go to the convent for a rest. After we have rested, we'll dress your brother as is fitting a priest for his burial. I'll find a coffin maker." Father Pierre was solicitous and Mother appreciated his care. Though she often spent the night in prayer at Providence Motherhouse, this night had been emotionally exhausting. She was beginning to feel its effects.

"Thank you, Father. That is a good plan."

The two then set about washing the dead priest's body. Mother had to search through every box and drawer to find a clean nightshirt that could be used. Never one to spend money on himself, Nicolas'clothes were shabby. Once they had Nicolas' body prepared, Mother commented, "It's a good thing that he will be buried in clerical vestments. He doesn't have a decent suit of clothes to his name. Every pair of pants is so patched and worn that they might as well be taken out and burned. His cassock is a disgrace! It is so threadbare that we can't even offer it to another priest without appearing insulting!" She turned to her brother. "Oh, Nicolas. I wish we had had time to set things right. I have been so foolish." Tears spilled onto her new *guimpe*, leaving blotches of wet stains on the starched linen. Then she remembered: she had never answered his last letter. Tears of sorrow for her sins of omission accompanied the tears of grief running down her cheeks.

Father Pierre, his heart aching for Mother St. Andrew, said, "Don't be so hard on yourself, Mother. It is usually our own family members that we fail first as we try to live the life to which God has called us. Nicolas now understands your heart. He wouldn't want you to berate yourself on his account. Allow our good God to stitch up the tear in your heart that Nicolas' death has wrought. Only God can mend our broken hearts in a case like this." Once again her young superior's words brought comfort and hope to the grieving nun.

Coming to the church on Saturday, November 30, as soon as they had heard that their beloved pastor had gone home to God, the women of St. Joseph's parish polished the dark pews and the altars, draping them with fresh altar linens, readying everything for the funeral Mass. The new golden French candlesticks gleamed. The church and its sanctuary had never looked better.

Dressed in an alb and white chasuble, Father Nicolas Feltin lay in state in his parish church after the Sunday Masses on December 1. People of the parish, feeling honored to serve their pastor once more, took turns staying in the church with the body overnight.

At the funeral the next day, crowds of parishioners and people from various sectors of San Antonio filled the stone church, spilling out onto the sidewalk and into Alameda Street. The Sisters of Divine Providence from St. Joseph's Academy and Castroville knelt in the front pews on the west side of the church with Mother St. Andrew, while the men of the Society of St. Joseph filled the first rows on the east side of the church.

Draped in black and surrounded by tall candlesticks, the closed coffin rested on the bier in the center aisle.

"*Dies irae, dies ila*," intoned the full-voiced *mennenchor* before the gospel.

Bishop Pellicer's sermon eulogized a sainted priest whose twenty-five years of service to Catholics and non-Catholics alike had edified all who knew him.

Upon her return to Castroville, Mother was introduced to Mary Neeb who had entered on Sunday and was just getting acquainted with the schedule at the Motherhouse. Recognizing that Mother was extremely tired from the ordeal of burying her brother, Sisters Angelique and Mary Ange took the lion's share of administrative work, urging Mother to rest.

Though Nicolas had begun the Season of Advent in the heavenly courts, of that she was certain, Mother herself was bereft of the hope to which the Church called those still awaiting the coming of their Lord. Noting her pained expression at the communion railing, Father Pierre decided to visit the Superior.

"Mother, I am worried about you. Please tell me what is wrong," Father Pierre began in a kind voice after he was seated in Mother's office.

"Why, nothing is wrong, *mon père*. What do you mean?"

"You know perfectly well what I mean. Things here at the Motherhouse could not be better; the Sisters on the missions are doing well. Yet, you look—what shall I say?—pained." Father Pierre had decided to be very frank.

Seeing no reason to mislead her superior, Mother said simply, "*Oui, mon père*. My heart is breaking. How can I inspire these young vocations if I myself have no hope? My prayer is empty; God is far away."

"Very well, *ma mère*. Your words themselves will be your confession, giving your soul room to receive God's loving forgiveness. I have never known anyone as hard on himself as you are. Can't you allow our good God to be compassionate towards you?" Though he had promised that he would not scold, Father Pierre's tone held exasperation.

"If only I had been kinder to Nicolas; if only I had assured him that I held nothing against him; if only I had written to him after I had returned from Fredericksburg. At least he would have died in peace."

"Oh, *ma mère.* You were never in charge of Nicolas' peace!" Father Pierre said with a smile. "Only God is able to give us peace. How do you know that Nicolas did not have peace? How do you know the impenetrable mind of God?"

Mother felt duly chastised. "Of course, you are correct, *mon père,*" she said in a whisper. "What do you recommend?"

"I recommend that in the next week before Christmas you read carefully the Book of Job. Concentrate on who is God and who is not."

Refreshed by Father Pierre's visit and advice, Mother herself led the self-accusations at the Chapter of Faults* after the next day's noon meal, confessing to failure in simplicity, failing to trust in the forgiving goodness of God, and failing to offer a model of hope to her Sisters. The newly arrived candidates had their first experience of their Mother General's participation in the Chapter of Faults. It would not be their last.

The ritual seemed to break through the pall of sadness that had fallen over the convent after the death of Father Nicolas. By the time Christmas Eve arrived, the Sisters were once again filled with the spirit of joy which celebrating the coming of the Christ-Child brings to all Christians.

The year 1879 came and went without incident. Regina Friesenhahn and her companions were received as novices in February. Bishop Dubuis wrote asking for a branch novitiate house for his Diocese of Galveston. And, after moving his wife and four children to Castroville, Louis Feltin began to finish out the second and third floors of Providence Motherhouse.

The coffers of the Congregation increased since the School Law of 1876 provided remuneration from state funds for the Sisters who taught in Texas villages which had only one school, the Catholic school. Though the same law forbade the expressed teaching of reli-

---

*   **The Chapter of Faults was a weekly ritual in most convents and monasteries at this time in history. Following the noon meal, all present in the refectory said aloud their faults and failings in an expression of humility and contrition.**

gion during the school day itself, each locale managed to provide religious instruction either before the school day began or after it had ended. Beginning in 1879, Mother St. Andrew received letters from the pastors of Schulenburg, High Hill, Palestine, Marienfield, St. John's and St. Joseph's near Schulenburg, Dubina, Fayetteville, and Columbus requesting Sisters to establish parish schools in these towns.

Though available personnel might have afforded the opening of at least one new school in 1879, Mother and her council wisely decided to forego extending their resources and declined the invitations. Realizing that native vocations would never keep up with requests, the Congregational leadership used an unplanned development to acquire help once again from their European Motherhouse at St. Jean-de-Bassel.

As 1879 wore on, Mother began to be genuinely concerned about Father Pierre's health. Always tired, the overworked pastor looked more and more wan as fall turned to winter. Mother invited him to join the Sisters for their celebration of the Feast of St. Nicolas on December 6. When he begged off claiming that he was "too tired," Mother was alarmed. She immediately went to the rectory.

Father Pierre opened the door and invited her into his parlor. "What can I do for you, *ma mère?*" he asked in a voice that was barely above a whisper.

"*Mon père,*" she began in her most maternal tone, "the time has come for you to take advice from me, for once."

Father Pierre's raised eyebrows revealed his surprise. "What do you mean, *ma mère?*"

"It is time, *mon père,* for you to return to your home in Loire where your dear mother and father can put you on a regimen of rest; ply you with good cheese, bread, butter, and wine; and hopefully restore you to health!"

"But ..." he began.

"This time there will be no refusal, *mon père*. You are sick. I will not want to write your dear mother that we have buried her son!" Now her tone was stern.

"You are correct, *ma mère*. But I fear that I am now too tired to make that long journey. Just thinking of being on a ship at sea for three weeks exhausts me."

Mother thought he might cry as he realized that he had allowed himself to become so run down that he now might not even make it to his homeland.

"I have been giving the situation some thought as well. I myself will go with you. Taking you home to your mother will give me a chance to return to St. Jean-de-Bassel. We need more candidates, novices, and, hopefully, professed Sisters. Mother Constantine wrote saying that I may ask for more help. And so I will. Now, *mon père*, take your own advice. Don't try to rely only on yourself!"

"You have cleverly turned my own words against me, *ma mère*," Father Pierre said with no offense. "When shall we go?"

"I think in the spring, *mon père*. Perhaps in April?"

"Very well. April, it is, then."

"And, in the meantime, you are to rest more, eat better, and take better care of yourself. From now on, you will take all of your meals at the Motherhouse. If you cannot be at the meal, Sister Gabriel will take food to you. Do you understand?"

"Yes, *ma mère*," Father Pierre's voice was that of a small boy addressing his mother. "I will do as you say. And, *ma mère*, may I ask a favor?"

"Anything, *mon père*," Mother replied quickly. Her superior had been so compliant with her directives for his health that she knew she could deny him nothing.

"I have wanted to re-build the pulpit to our church, *ma mère*. I would like to have it begun by the time I leave in the spring. Do you think your brother Louis could carve the pulpit for the parish? We can't pay him much, but at this time we have no debt. Perhaps even the little we can pay will help him with his family."

"I'm certain that he can do as you wish. Please feel free to ask him as you know your requirements."

"Thank you, *ma mère*. I will mind your instructions for my health," he finished sheepishly.

Barely two weeks before Father Pierre was to take the train to Galveston and sail for France, he raced over to the Motherhouse looking for Mother St. Andrew. The candidate who answered the door asked him to come in, saying that she thought Mother was in their small chapel. If Father would go on to Mother's office, Mother would be there shortly.

As Mother entered her office, the look on the young priest's face startled her. "*Mon père*, what is it? You look shocked."

"I have just received word, *ma mère*, that His Lordship is quite ill. They fear that he will not recover. I believe that we should go at once to see him."

"Oh, *mon père*! This cannot be. I know that His Lordship has health problems, but surely they are not fatal."

"It is best that we go. We would never forgive ourselves if something happened to him and we had not taken time to visit him."

"But, *mon père*, your own health! The trip to San Antonio is too arduous for you!"

"*Ma mère*, he is our bishop. We must pay our respects!" Given the tone in his voice, Mother St. Andrew knew not to argue with her superior.

"You are quite right. When shall we go?"

"We ourselves are leaving in less than a month. I believe we should go tomorrow. I have a number of things to do here in the parish before sailing and would rather see His Lordship sooner than later. And, Mother, though His Lordship will probably see me, the message I received said he is not receiving other visitors. He may not receive you, but you should try anyway, don't you think?"

"Absolutely. I will be ready in the morning. But let's plan to stay at least two nights. I would like to visit the community at St. Joseph's while we are in San Antonio. I want to see how things are going with Father Pefferkorn.

After arriving in San Antonio the next day in early afternoon, Father Pierre and Mother St. Andrew went directly to Bishop Pellicer's residence at the Cathedral. The porter admitted Father Pierre, but said to Mother St. Andrew, "I'm sorry, Mother, the doctor insists that visitors be limited to priests only. His Lordship is very ill."

Mother was disappointed, but replied, "Very well. *Mon père*, you go ahead and see His Lordship. Please tell him that he is in my prayers. I will remain here in the parlor praying the rosary for His Lordship. Take your time."

Father Pierre followed the porter to the Bishop's bedchamber; Mother St. Andrew knelt on the parlor floor and began her rosary.

Within minutes, the porter returned. "Mother, His Lordship wants to see you."

As she entered the darkened bedchamber and approached His Lordship who was propped up on a long chaise, she immediately fell to her left knee and took the hand His Lordship weakly offered, kissing his episcopal ring.

"Mother, I had no idea you would come."

"Your Lordship, I bring you the prayers of all my Sisters who are deeply saddened to learn of your sufferings. Is there anything at all we can do for you?"

After dismissing her solicitous attitude, Bishop Pellicer, realizing how few days he had left on this earth, asked Mother St. Andrew's forgiveness for misunderstanding her trial with Father Zwiardowski. "I fear," he said, "that my lack of understanding caused your loss of nearly a dozen vocations."

"Your Lordship, you have no need to apologize. God writes straight with crooked lines, yes? We must believe that what happened years ago was the design of His Holy Providence."

"You are too kind, Mother. I offer to you and to all of your Sisters one of my last episcopal blessings for I fear that my days here are numbered."

Mother knelt as Bishop Pellicer concluded their visit. "With all my heart I give my blessing to the Sisters of Divine Providence. *Ostende nobis, Domine, misericordiam tuam.* Show us Thy mercy, Lord," His Lordship began.

"*Et salutare tuum da nobis.* And grant us Thy salvation," Mother St. Andrew and Father Pierre replied in unison.

"*Domine, exaudi orationem meam.* O Lord, hear my prayer," the bishop continued.

Et clumor meus ad te veniat. And let my cry come to Thee," Father Pierre and Mother St. Andrew responded.

"*Benedicat vos omnipotens Deus, Pater, et Filius, et Spiritus Sanctus,*" Bishop Pellicer said, as he weakly traced the cross in front of Mother St. Andrew and Father Pierre in a gesture of blessing.

"Amen," concluded the Bishop's two guests.

Having received His Lordship's blessing, Mother St. Andrew left the room, giving Father Pierre privacy with his bishop.

"Are you still returning to France, my son?" the Bishop asked kindly.

"Yes, Your Lordship. I am worn out. Perhaps a time of rest in my home will bring me strength."

"Are you traveling alone?"

"No, Your Lordship. Mother St. Andrew and Sister Angelique will travel with me. I don't feel strong enough to go alone."

"Very wise of you, Father. I had forgotten that Mother asked my permission to make this journey. She is returning to her Motherhouse for more Sisters; is that correct?"

"Yes, Your Lordship." Father Pierre paused and then said, "You are obviously quite tired, Your Lordship. I will take my leave now. I wish you Godspeed."

"Thank you, my son. And thank you for your service to this diocese. You have been an extraordinary priest." Just before leaving his bishop, Father Pierre took the sick man's frail hand in his own, raised it to his lips and reverently kissed the episcopal ring.

Father Pierre knew that this exchange with his bishop would be his last.

Bishop Anthony Pellicer died on April 14, 1880; Mother St. Andrew and Father Pierre sailed for France two weeks later.

Once again in August of 1880, the Sisters at Providence Motherhouse and the people of Castroville turned out to welcome Mother St. Andrew and Sister Angelique home. With them were four professed Sisters newly recruited for the Texas foundation: Sister Mary Luca Denniger, Sister Mary Bertilda Thiel, Sister Mary Rosine Vonderscher, and Sister Mary Florence Walter. Sister Mary Ange, Mistress of Novices, received four novices: Sister Mary Muechler, Sister Mary Anna Ehrismann, Sister Augusta Rudloff, and Sister Mary Floride Seyler.

The next day, Mother consulted with Sister Angelique, Sister Mary Ange, Sister Mary Agnes, and Sister Theresa Schultz to learn how things were going in the parish and the diocese.

"Mother, how did you leave Father Pierre?" was Sister Mary Agnes' first question.

"He is really not well. His mother was thrilled to have him home and I found his family to be a beautiful example of the generosity of French villagers who have given so many sons and daughters to missionary endeavors. I like his mother very much. In truth," she said with regret in her voice, "Father Pierre may never be strong enough to return to us."

The other Sisters looked around at one another suspecting that this news might affect their lives as Sisters of Divine Providence.

"Do we have a bishop?" was Mother St. Andrew's first question.

"No, Mother," Sister Angelique replied. "In fact, no one seems to have any idea when a bishop will be appointed. In the meantime, Father Neraz is administering the diocese. Perhaps he himself will be named the bishop."

"He would make a fine bishop," Mother said. "He certainly knows the diocese. Is there any other news that could affect us?"

"Actually," Sister Theresa replied, "there is quite a bit of talk that Bishop Dubuis is planning to retire to France. He, too, has begun to suffer ill health. That could make a significant difference to us."

"If Bishop Dubuis returns to France, do you think it will be soon?"

"No, Mother. No one has mentioned any time frame for this possibility." Sister Theresa seemed confident that Bishop Dubuis would be with them at least throughout the rest of that year. In recent years, however, the pioneer missionary had experienced several mishaps which, though not life-threatening, when taken together had worn him down. While crossing the Atlantic in 1874, a shipboard accident left him with a severely broken arm. Nothing short of a miraculous healing at Lourdes restored the use of his arm to him. A carriage accident in 1877 left him shaken up. However, his mother's death in the summer of 1876 may have been the most jarring episode. In 1880 Bishop Dubuis was no longer a young man, and Mother St. Andrew was not looking forward to the effects of his retirement on her Congregation in Texas.

"I believe that we should proceed more definitely with our plans to open a branch novitiate in Frelsburg," Mother said thoughtfully. "Bishop Dubuis has given us permission to open a novitiate there. The next Bishop of Galveston may not see the same need."

"But, Mother," Sister Mary Agnes interjected, "who could you send to be Mistress of Novices? I have my hands full with the school. Surely, you don't expect ..." Her voice trailed off.

"Oh, no, Sister Agnes, of course not. You are correct; another person would need to be in charge of novices and candidates." Mother was quick to clarify her intentions. "But, like you, I don't know whom to send. Sister Mary Ange, you are needed here. And with Sister Angelique opening the school at Schulenburg, that leaves us somewhat short-handed here at the Motherhouse. Maybe we won't be able to open the novitiate until next year." Mother's words were realistic, but her tone of voice betrayed deep disappointment.

Heads nodded in clear agreement with Mother. A novitiate at Frelsburg was out of the question until next year.

"I have one other concern, Mother," Sister Mary Ange added. Receiving Mother's nod to continue, she said, "It has come to my attention that Sisters Mary Agnes and Theresa, though having made their vows years ago, have never made their solemn perpetual profession." With a look at the two young Sisters, Sister Mary Ange said, "If they are willing, I believe that we should plan for this ceremony next summer when we are all gathered here at Providence House. This momentous step by these two young nuns will serve to encourage our young Sisters in their vocations."

Sisters Mary Agnes and Theresa sat quite still, their pink faces and wide-eyes indicating their complete surprise. They knew that this final step in religious commitment was now allowed in Germany, but no one had ever mentioned perpetual profession here in Texas.

Mother gave the two Sisters a long, tender look. Each one had been so devoted to the Congregation and its works. Her eyes held the deep appreciation she felt for both young nuns. "What do you wish, my daughters?"

After but a moment's hesitation, both Sisters smiled and said in unison, "Oh, yes!"

"Good," Mother St. Andrew said, finalizing the decision. "Sister Mary Ange, will you please make all the arrangements for the celebration next summer. Perhaps whoever is named our bishop should receive their perpetual vows."

"Very well, Mother," Sister Mary Ange answered simply.

The next days were spent helping the newly arrived German Sisters and novices to settle into Providence Motherhouse. Remembering the difficulty that she herself had at first with eating corn-on-the-cob, Sister Gabriel decided not to serve that delicacy until the immigrants were more acclimatized. Sensitive to the challenges they would find with Texas food, Sister Gabriel cooked meals that were more like the ones they would have had in the German motherhouse. And she had learned to make a delicious *kugelhopf* even though she did not usually have all of the necessary ingredients. Pecans made a good substitute for almonds, and apples would replace the raisins. She was proud of her concoction and the Sisters from both sides of the Atlantic seemed to love it.

Mother and her advisors agreed to open a school for the Austrian parish in High Hill, St. John's School for the Schulenburg parish, and another school in nearby St. Joseph parish. The geographical proximity of these three parishes, reminiscent of villages in France and Germany, led Mother St. Andrew and her advisors to believe that new vocations would come from the area and the Sisters in the villages could support and help one another as they do in Germany. Long distances between the villages in Texas militated against both the growth of the Congregation and stability in vocations, Mother and her advisors had concluded. Even by twos, Sisters felt very isolated in small villages when the nearest Sister-neighbor might be as much as thirty or forty miles away and sometimes farther.

After the Sisters had been sent off to their missions, but before Sister Angelique left for Schulenburg, Mother met with her advisors again.

"Now that we have more vocations," she began, "our situation should begin to stabilize. But I remain concerned. If we are going to continue to take village schools throughout central Texas—and I have a letter from the pastor in some place called Palestine," she said. Then looking at her advisors, "Does anyone know where that is?" Mother asked. "I also have a letter from the pastor in Fayetteville, a town about thirty miles from Frelsburg; another request from the pastor of Marienfield; and a third from the pastor in Columbus; and a growing Czech community in some place called Dubina is asking for a teacher." Before she could finish her thought, she sounded exhausted.

She began again. "I think we have a fundamental problem: since Sisters are in small towns and quite far from one another, I wonder if we shouldn't plan to send more than two Sisters to the schools so that girls in the villages can see how we live and the Sisters themselves will have a greater sense of community. What do you think?"

An exchange in the conversation led those gathered to see the wisdom of the ideas, yet they felt frustrated since they were not yet receiving vocations at a rate that could support sending larger numbers of Sisters to the villages.

"Mother, I think you will have to return to Europe. But I would write to Mother Constantine and ask her what she thinks. Also, this time, perhaps you and your companion would imagine recruiting in the villages of Lorraine and Alsace yourselves. I know you could bring many young girls back with you. We are stable enough here at the Motherhouse to take in—oh, maybe as many as fifty." This suggestion came from Sister Mary Ange. Since fifty new candidates would mean an enormous amount of work for her, Mother smiled ruefully.

"Do you know what you are subjecting yourself to, Sister? You are truly making a suggestion that will require a great deal of generosity from you!" Mother smiled at Sister Mary Ange. They had an easy relationship and Sister Mary Ange was used to Mother teasing her a bit.

"I know," she confessed. "I'll probably be the first to complain when you bring me fifty 'green' girls to transform into nuns! But, I am not backing away from my idea!"

"Do the rest of you agree?" Mother asked.

"I see this as a real way to gain large numbers. All of us have relatives in villages throughout Lorraine and Alsace. Our own families can help recruit. If Mother Constantine agrees, we can each write to our sisters and brothers to help us find girls with missionary hearts," Sister Angelique added.

Not wishing to leave her native Sisters out of the conversation, Mother turned to Sister Mary Agnes and Sister Theresa. "What do you think?"

"I think that this is a grand idea. If we succeed, we would have Sisters who could be placed in Frelsburg where we might actually get the new novitiate started there," Sister Agnes said with enthusi-asm. Sister Theresa agreed.

"I will write to Mother Constantine soon. If she agrees, I will make plans to go to Germany in the spring. Perhaps you might be the one to accompany me, Sister Mary Ange?" Mother asked. "You know best the type of girl who would have the characteristics we need."

The plan, dependent upon Mother Constantine's approval, began to develop.

In November, Mother received a letter from her friend and men-tor, Mother Constantine.

After a page of news about circumstances in Germany and at the Motherhouse, Mother Constantine wrote,

> *I am afraid that it is too soon for you to return for more volunteers for Texas. Though I continue to support the missions there, I do not think that your coming in the spring will be beneficial.*
>
> *I ask that you wait a year and then come. By that time, we cannot only support your recruit-ing throughout Lorraine and Alsace, but we can have more professed Sisters ready for you. Can you be patient? That virtue is not strong in our Alsatian temperament, but I will pray you can accept.*
>
> *My old legs hurt all the time now. I walk with difficulty and never leave the Motherhouse. But my heart travels far and wide. I visit you and all of our Sisters in Texas regularly in my prayers.*
>
> *Please accept my blessing upon your most cou-rageous work.*
>
> > *In Divine Providence,*
> > *Mère Constantine*

Mother and her advisors met during Christmas vacation. By that time, Mother had calmed down. Her first reaction to Mother Constantine's refusal, anger at being denied and rejected, finally dissipated when she came to understand the wisdom in the Superior General's time frame. Her last trip to Germany had brought only four professed Sisters. If the plan to send more Sisters to the villages to open additional schools was to work, receiving seasoned vocations was imperative. Mother St. Andrew shared Mother Constantine's letter with her advisors. She noted their faces: surprise tinged with anger. Once their feelings were under control, she explained to them how she herself had come to see the wisdom in Mother Constantine's plan.

Sister Angelique, who knew Mother Constantine quite well, acknowledged that her insights were well founded. One by one, each Sister came to accept their Superior General's thinking and all agreed to pray for one another's patience.

"I admire your humility, Mother," Sister Mary Ange noted. She had been the only one who had known Mother's original depth of emotion when she had received Mother Constantine's letter. Mother had been quite furious; but as time passed, she let go of her own desires, giving way to her Superior General's. "We all agree to support your idea. In God's Providence, I believe that we will return next year from St. Jean-de-Bassel with exactly the Sisters we need to advance the Texas mission. I am reminded of Father Moye's predicament when his own bishop lost faith in him and would not approve the opening of more schools by our earliest Sisters. You remember how he placed his disappointments within the passion of Jesus. Is that how you managed through this, Mother?"

"I must admit that I wish I could say 'yes.' I suspect that grace has overtaken me without much of my own cooperation. Thanks be to Divine Providence!" With this last declaration, Mother laughed out loud. "However, Sister, I shall try to remember Father Moye's more prayerful solution for next time!"

Mother's humor ended the meeting on a positive note. In reality, she was glad that she had more time in Texas and would not be traveling to Europe again so soon since remaining in Texas gave her time to travel to Galveston.

Early in 1881, while visiting St. Joseph's School in Galveston, Mother had a meeting with Bishop Dubuis. Their conversation led to a formal contract for establishing a novitiate branch in Frelsburg.

Bishop Dubuis' parting remarks once again revealed his confidence in Mother St. Andrew. "Mother, it is a pleasure to establish a novitiate of the Sisters of Divine Providence in the Diocese of Galveston. The Church continues to need what your community alone seems to be able to offer. Sisters who are willing to go to the smallest hamlets, live with the people, and educate children who have no other possibility for an education. Your successes in Castroville, Fredericksburg, and Frelsburg can be duplicated in the villages of eastern European immigrants that are springing up throughout central Texas. I wish you well!"

"I, too, am very happy to plan for this new novitiate. I will be returning to Germany for more vocations soon. Perhaps some of them can be trained here. Will you be coming to visit us in Castroville soon, Your Lordship?"

"I plan to be present when your new bishop is consecrated at San Fernando Cathedral. I think Rome will name a prelate any day now. I will also plan to come to Castroville. That may be my last visit to my old friends there." Bishop Dubuis' remark was cryptic, but his desire to retire in France was known by many.

"We will welcome you whenever you can come, Your Lordship. I want to show you our new motherhouse. Our house is your house. *Mi casa es su casa!*"

"Mother, you have picked up a little Spanish! Very good!"

"Don't test me, Your Lordship. I don't have much!"

With that the two old friends parted to meet again in Castroville later in the spring.

Just at the beginning of March 1881, Mother St. Andrew found a letter in a vaguely familiar hand in her stack of mail. As she glanced at the postmark, her heart stopped. "Loire." This could contain only one message. A quick reading of the contents confirmed her worst suspicions: Father Pierre Richard had been called home to God. The brief note from his mother brought only news of her son's death, giving no details of his last days. The bereft mother expressed her deep gratitude for Mother's enduring kindnesses to her son.

> *If you had not insisted, our dear son would never have come home to us. Though we had him with us for such a short time, his last months were restful and happy. I will forever be grateful for your solicitude.*

On March 8, Mother wrote to Madame Richard:

> *My sorrow has been too great to find words of consolation. But then, what are we to do? We must be resigned. We prayed the Good God and the Blessed Virgin for his cure, but God decided otherwise. We are not better than the Blessed Virgin who also had her heart pierced with sorrow.*
>
> *Here in Castroville people are always speaking of his virtues. He lives in his work; he lives in the heart of each and every one. Since he has gone, we seek consolation, repeating to ourselves how devoted he was, how he made himself all to all in order to win all souls for heaven*
>
> *... There are still several pictures here; if you want some, I will send you some. Here if people have only a little souvenir, something that he used, they are happy ... As for myself, I am still disconsolate; I cannot forget him so soon. Please*

have the goodness to tell me how he died; this is a great deal to ask of you, but I hope that that will give me a little consolation. Adieu then, good Mother; let us place our grief in the Hearts of Jesus and Mary.

Your very devoted,
*Sister St. Andre**

In the late spring of 1881, an event took place that caused Mother to reflect on Providence's action on her behalf. Father John C. Neraz, the diocesan administrator, had been named the second bishop of the Diocese of San Antonio; his ordination was planned for May 8, 1881. Rumor had it that Bishop Claude Dubuis of Galveston and Bishop Dominic Manucy of Brownsville would join Bishop Edward Fitzgerald of Little Rock to consecrate the first bishop to be ordained in San Fernando Cathedral.

First Motherhouse of the Sisters of Divine Providence, Castroville, Texas
(**Congregational Archives, San Antonio, TX**)

Realizing that he would never travel to this area of Texas again, Bishop Dubuis took the opportunity to make an extended visit to his beloved Castroville. The new pastor, Father Henry Japes, gave the Bishop hospitality in the rectory, but the gregarious missionary spent all of his time in the homes of his former parishioners and in the convent with the Sisters. One of his first visits was to the little Alsatian nun whom he had brought to Texas in 1866.

---

*   **Excerpted from the actual correspondence.**

"Your Lordship," Mother said in a tender voice, as she herself opened the door of Providence House to her friend and first superior in Texas. "Please come in. You are most welcome to our humble motherhouse."

"Oh, Mother, this," the Bishop said, looking around admiringly and waving his hand over the entryway, "is not humble. This is a grand house. You have done well!"

"Come to our parlor and sit down. One of our novices will be bringing us some coffee. How are you?"

"I am pretty well. Oh, actually, I'm getting old, Mother." His whispered comment sounded conspiratorial, prompting Mother's laugh.

"I am, too, Your Lordship. Fifteen years takes its toll, doesn't it?"

"Yes, it does," Bishop Dubuis said as he settled into a comfortable rocking chair in the front parlor. "It is fifteen years since we first met, isn't it? Time has gone by so fast." A pause revealed the bishop's reflective mood. "Coming back to Castroville has brought many memories to mind. I still meet people here whom I baptized or married!"

"I am so grateful to you for bringing us here, Your Lordship. I know that this was the will of Providence. At the time, I admit, I was not certain. But, as time has passed, this village has become our home."

"Father Japes tells me that the railroad will not be going through the town. The people rejected their opportunity to be on the line?" Bishop Dubuis asked with some disbelief.

"Yes. The word around the town square is that the people of Castroville were fearful that if the railroad passed through our town, it would bring riff-raff that would eventually spoil our quiet atmosphere. I personally am sorry. Having to take our Sisters to the train so that they can get to and from their missions is becoming a nuisance. I had hoped that Castroville would be a stop."

"I see what you mean, Mother. As a result of their decision, I think the citizens of Castroville have fated their village to the quiet they think they want. I hope they will be satisfied. Time will tell." This missionary continued to keep up with trends in Texas, and his words indicated that he thought the Castrovillians may have acted in haste. "Tell me about your community, Mother."

As Mother St. Andrew told Bishop Dubuis about her two trips to Germany and the new members for Texas that she brought back, he smiled.

"You have been able then to open more schools?" he asked.

"Yes," Mother replied. "We now have fourteen schools, including Haby's Settlement. D'Hanis is presently closed, but I think that we may be able to re-open if the new bishop will send them a resident priest. And four of those schools are in your diocese." Mother's smile betrayed her feelings of pride at being able to speak of her Congregation's accomplishments. "I continue to receive letters from pastors; several are from your diocese. I am hoping to make another trip to Germany next year in order to find more vocations."

"Wonderful! I wish you the best." He paused then as though weighing his next words. "I'm not certain that I should confide this to you, but I think I will. We go back a long way, Mother. I'm going to write His Holiness soon tendering my resignation. I really cannot do justice to the needs of the Diocese of Galveston. Also, attempts to appoint a coadjutor bishop have failed. If I don't resign, the Vatican will never take me seriously."

"Oh, Your Lordship. I had no idea!" Hardly knowing what to say, all Mother could think of was the eventuality of losing another strong proponent of her Congregation in Texas.

"Yes, it is for the best. I will return to my home diocese in France and be of service as the bishop there wishes."

"You leave behind a very strong legacy in the Church in Texas, Your Lordship. It has been a privilege to serve under you," Mother said humbly.

"Please don't say anything to anyone, Mother," Bishop Dubuis added. "Your words are kind. I do think that I, along with all of you incredible missionaries who have joined in spreading the gospel in Texas, have made an enormous difference. Imagine: you have begun fourteen schools in fifteen years—not counting the schools you no longer serve. That is laudable! I guess I knew what I was doing when I asked you to come with me that day in Strasbourg in 1866. We took a chance on each other and left the rest to Providence!"

"Yes, Your Lordship, we did," Mother agreed, smiling. "Do you have any regrets?"

"Not really. Except that I wish we could have done more. I wish your Congregation had a novitiate in my diocese. Perhaps with new European vocations, you could train some of them in Frelsburg?" The bishop was very eager to have an active Motherhouse of the Sisters of Divine Providence in his diocese.

"Perhaps so," Mother said tentatively. "However, I have only one Mistress of Novices. I am still hopeful for Frelsburg and I am glad that we established the second Motherhouse there."

The Bishop continued. "We should have worked harder to make that happen. But we can't do everything, can we?"

The rest of their conversation recalled the Texas of days gone by, their mutual struggles to build up the faith through the sacraments and through education. The afternoon visit ended with the two legendary missionaries bidding one another adieu for the last time.

"I will be at the consecration next Sunday, Your Lordship, but I realize that many people will want to talk with you," Mother said as they stood together on Paris Street. "I will tell you good-bye now. Go with God," she concluded simply. "May I have one last blessing?"

"Of course, Mother." Mother St. Andrew knelt in the street, acknowledging with her simple action the homage she believed she owed the prelate who had brought her half-way around the world to serve their Lord.

"*Adieu*, Your Lordship," she said upon rising.

"*Adieu*, Mother."

The two missionaries parted company. Bishop Dubuis submitted his letter of resignation in early summer 1881 and returned to France within the year.

CHAPTER XV

UNRAVELINGS

Just at the end of the 1881 annual retreat, Mother St. Andrew found a letter from Germany in the familiar hand of Mother Constantine on her desk.

> *My dear Sister,*
>
> *I am taking a moment after our council meeting to write. We all want to let you know that we would welcome you next year. We know that the winters here are hard for you now so perhaps you would like to come in the spring and remain through the summer.*
>
> *We continue to receive many vocations and we also think that some of the German and Polish villages would be a ripe harvest for you. We will happily assist you to travel through Alsace and other territories if you wish to personally recruit.*
>
> *Sister Marie offers her prayers and love—as do we all.*
>
> *In Divine Providence,*
> *Mère Constantine*

Mother called a meeting of her advisors.

Once they had assembled, she began with excitement. "Mother Constantine invites me to come to St. Jean in the spring and to recruit in Alsace—and perhaps, if I wish, all the way to Poland." The tremor of her voice revealed her hope.

The advisors began talking all at the same time. Finally, the voice of Sister Angelique rose above the others. "Mother, I think I can speak for us all. We believe that this is Divine Providence taking care of us. I recommend that we return to our earlier idea: write to our relatives—and invite the other Sisters to write as well—so that you might find fertile fields when you go to Europe in the spring."

Everyone nodded enthusiastically.

"I'll take charge of asking the other Sisters to write. We'll get these letters off to our families before we go on mission!" said Sister Mary Ange.

"While we are assembled, I want to talk with you about two other things," Mother said. "During retreat, Sister Agnes asked me to relieve her of her services at St. Joseph's Academy," Mother continued, nodding toward the faithful Sister who had journeyed from Austin with her nearly thirteen years earlier, "Though she has served well there, she believes that someone with a broader background should be placed there as Superior and Principal. Is there anyone you would suggest?" This last question was addressed to all those gathered.

"What about Sister Florence?" Sister Mary Ange asked. "She is young, but she seems mature and appears very secure. We especially need someone there who can deal with parents of city children."

Others nodded in agreement.

"Without objection, then, I will approach Sister Florence," Mother said. "Now that Sister Angelique is in High Hill, I suggest that Sister Mary Agnes split her time. She can help with operations of the Motherhouse here so that Sister Mary Ange will not have to provide guidance for our youngest members and oversee the running of the house. Since she knows the area so well, she can also supervise the opening of our novitiate at Frelsburg. Though we have no subjects there at this time, I remain hopeful that our growing presence in the area will draw vocations. Bishop Dubuis was wise to establish Frelsburg as an extension of this convent."

Again everyone nodded in agreement.

Summer classes for the Sister-teachers continued each June and July. Several European Sisters who had special training in pedagogy gladly shared their knowledge of teaching techniques with the others. The members of the Congregation had grown especially adept at teaching the primary grades and pastors learned from one another that the Sisters of Divine Providence could provide their parishes with orderly and successful schools.

After the annual retreat, the final days of summer were filled with Mother St. Andrew's appointments with the Sisters to give them their assignments for the new school year. A hush settled over the house as Sisters lined the hallway outside Mother's office, standing in silence awaiting their time with their Superior. Mission changes were seldom, but occasionally, as with the case of Sister Mary Florence, something came up that required moving a Sister to another school.

The council of advisors had looked carefully at the assignments in early June and one change always unsettled several other Sisters. Those who had been in a school for a long time usually appeared particularly tense during these days after the retreat as they suspected that necessary changes could affect them.

Once the appointments were finished, the atmosphere in the house reverted to its usual hustle and bustle as preparations were made for receptions into the novitiate and for profession of vows.

Vacations were over by the beginning of September. The tasks of packing, making train reservations, and planning for transportation to nearby La Coste to catch the train occupied those who would be returning to their former mission and those nervously anticipating a new school.

Remembering the waving handkerchiefs of the Superior General and other Sisters gathered to send them off to mission from St.

Jean-de-Bassel, Mother St. Andrew personally dispatched each wagonload of Sisters pulling away from the Paris Street door on its way to train stations in San Antonio or La Coste.

The last group left in late fall for Ellinger. With the weather beginning to cool, Mother pulled her shawl tightly around her shoulders as she stood on the street waiting while the departing Sisters loaded their valises into the back of the wagon. The horses seemed skittish in the fall air but Sister Victoria held the reins tightly. After all were in place, Mother took one last opportunity to tell the young missionaries to be good religious, welcome the crosses that would come, and depend always on Providence.

As she glanced at Sister Rosine who had come from Germany with her in 1880, she laughed out loud.

"Now, Sister Rosine,* my remarks about depending on Providence do not extend to a lack of good sense! Where is your shawl, my dear? What are you thinking? I've been on that hill in Ellinger, and there is not a single tree to protect you from the chilling wind." Then, she took off her own shawl, handed it to Sister Rosine, and concluded, "There, wrap that around your shoulders!" She then said to everyone, "Sisters, Providence expects us to use good sense at all times. Remember that!"

"Yes, Mother," they replied in chorus, laughing. And with that, Sister Victoria brought the reins down on the rumps of her team of horses and the wagonload of Sisters headed east on Paris Street toward the river ferry.

As the fall months slid into winter, Mother St. Andrew found herself relying heavily on Sister Mary Agnes and realized once again how wise the Providence of God truly is. Sister Agnes proved to be a capable supervisor for Mother's brother Louis, now working on various projects in the motherhouse since moving to Castroville. Mother had found that supervising her own brother frequently led to sibling

---

* **This episode was recalled in the memoirs of Sister Rosine Vonderscher, Archives of the Congregation of Divine Providence in San Antonio, Texas**

conflict, and Sister Mary Agnes was much more successful at cajoling Louis into working at a faster pace. Mother was just as happy to be relieved of that duty. Likely, Louis could finish the dormitory on the third floor by the end of next summer in time to accommodate new candidates. Then he could begin on the west end addition to the building that would include a proper chapel.

"Before Thanksgiving," she said to herself as she worked on correspondence at her small desk, "I must write to Bishop Neraz to ask him if he is available for Midnight Mass. He probably will want to celebrate at the Cathedral, but the invitation should be offered." Writing herself a note to that effect, Mother returned to reading letters from priests. The priest at Schulenburg wanted a Sister for nearby St. John's School; priests in Palestine, Fayetteville, and Dubina also were asking for Sisters.

It's a good thing I'll be going to Europe in the spring, she thought. Without more vocations, we'll never be able to keep up with requests.

Midnight Mass in their humble first-floor chapel was simple yet lovely. Ever since her 1878 trip to the St. Jean motherhouse, Mother St. Andrew had longed for a "proper" chapel. After gazing around the humble makeshift chapel, she thought that perhaps this was fitting a place to celebrate the birth of the poor Savior anyway. Louis had to take on extra jobs outside the convent to feed his family causing various projects to move more slowly. But Mother was trying to be patient.

Sisters in San Antonio who had come home for Christmas, together with Louis and Theresa and their little ones, filled the small chapel room. The Oblate Father from San Antonio who sang the high Mass had a rich, baritone voice which was nicely balanced by Sister Mary Ange's well-prepared choir of Novices and Postulants. Though the little temporary chapel had no heat, the number gathered made a cozy group and the rather mild December night helped. The glow of candlelight cast dancing shadows on the cream-colored walls creating a magical atmosphere.

Little Mary Teresa Feltin carried the statue of the Infant Jesus down the main aisle, placing it into the crèche beneath the evergreen tree near the tiny sanctuary. And her mother's swelling torso reminded them all that each birth is God's way of re-blessing the human race, just as He did at the Incarnation. Theresa had told Mother that the baby was due in March, and, though the expectant mother looked rather wan, her blue eyes sparkled in anticipation of their new child.

After Mass everyone gathered in the refectory for traditional Christmas goodies. Sister Gabriel's special *kugelhopf*, risen to perfection and filled with pecans and raisins, graced the center of the table. Other traditional Alsatian dishes surrounded the cake: local sausages wrapped in risen dough; *parisa*, a meat dish of raw ground meat, onions, and cheese flavored with coarse ground pepper and lemon juice; and a huge bowl of *rumtopf*, filled with local pears, apples, figs, and Fredericksburg peaches floating in a rich liqueur.

After all had eaten the delicacies and the adults were sipping their wine or *rumtopf*, Sister Mary Florence took her violin out of its case and began to play softly, moving easily from one Christmas carol to another as the Sisters and guests lifted their voices in song.

In late January 1882, Mother wrote to Bishop Neraz asking his permission to go once again to Europe for more candidates and Sisters. Recognizing this Congregation's importance to the future of Catholic education in his diocese, he responded immediately with an affirmative answer, suggesting that Mother use the resources of the chancery to book a discounted ticket. Plans were made for an April 1882 sailing with the hope of avoiding the beginning of the hurricane season in Galveston.

Mother was welcomed with exuberance at St. Jean-de-Bassel and spent her first days there telling Mother Constantine about circumstances in Texas. Recounting how the geography of Texas differed from that of Lorraine and Alsace, Mother St. Andrew reported that they had added only a few schools since her visit in 1880.

Bishop John C. Neraz, Second Bishop of San Antonio, TX
(Courtesy: Catholic Archives of Texas, Austin, TX)

"Mother, the situation in Texas is so very different. Why, when I was in Batzendorf, for instance, the nearest village was only three or four kilometers away. We Sisters could easily visit from village to village, meeting together, praying together, and supporting each other. In Texas, the villages are simply too far apart to provide community for those Sisters who are alone. To lessen the loneliness and temptations that creep in, we've decided to place Sisters in groups of two or three, and, in some cases, even four."

Mother Constantine was impressed. "Very good thinking, *ma fille*. I wish I could send more with you this time, but I'm afraid I have only seven professed Sisters and two novices. However, I understand that you are willing to recruit in the villages yourself?"

"Yes, in fact, as I wrote to you, our Sisters have written to their home villages urging their sisters and nieces to consider religious life in Texas. Based on their replies, I think we'll be able to find ten or so to come back to Texas with me."

"I have another idea. Have you heard of Our Lady of Knock?"

"No, I have not. Who is she?"

"About three years ago Our Lady appeared in Knock, Ireland. We've heard nothing but good about this circumstance, though the Church is not saying anything about the veracity of the apparition. I've been thinking that you should go to Knock and pray to Our Lady for the Texas missions. If my old legs were any good, I would go with you. But, alas, I cannot. Would you consider the pilgrimage? Sister Marie is willing to accompany you."

"Of course, at your request, Mother. I wonder if there might not be Irish girls interested in religious life? We're finding that we need more English-speaking Sisters. Perhaps this is an answer."

"Very well. Ask Sister Marie to arrange your transportation. Our suggestion is that you go to the villages to which you have written; and if there are possible candidates, have them come to St. Jean to meet you here in August before you go. Then, that plan allows you to make the pilgrimage to Ireland at the end of July or so. Does that sound plausible?"

Mother St. Andrew felt that Mother Constantine's ideas were both helpful and creative, her attitude remaining supportive. The two strong-spirited missionary women spent hours during Mother St. Andrew's short visit planning how to best strengthen the Texas foundation. By the time she recruited in ten Alsatian villages, traveled east of the Rhine into Bavaria, visited her own family in LaWalck, and met several times with the General Council, her time in Europe flew by.

In mid-July Mother St. Andrew took the train from Sarrebourg to the west of France and then embarked from LeHavre to Ireland. Her plan was to visit the shrine of Our Lady of Knock to place her needs before the Blessed Mother.

While at Knock, hearing of a newly begun community, Mother sought out its foundress, Mother Francis Clare Cusack, a convert to Catholicism whose reputation as a philosopher, theologian, and writer was becoming well known. What she found was a small frame house where nearly twenty girls were in training for religious life. Mother Francis welcomed Mother St. Andrew and Sister Marie, inviting them to stay with her community while they were in Knock. The two foundresses discovered a kindred soul in each other.

Over a cup of strong tea and a piece of Irish soda bread, Mother St. Andrew plied Mother Francis with questions: What precipitated your leaving the Sisters of St. Clare? How have you designed this new foundation? Are you well accepted? How have you attracted so many vocations?

Mother Francis Clare finally held up her hand. "Stop, Mother! Your questions are good ones, but I am afraid I have very few answers. I simply found the lifestyle of the Sisters of St. Clare to be too confining. I think the Church needs more flexibility in religious life, and I wanted to found a community that can do more than teach school. So I went to Rome and asked His Holiness if I could begin something new. Now young ladies are flocking in. I have no place for more novices!"

"How do you account for the vocations?" Mother St. Andrew inquired

"Ireland is in terrible turmoil. No one can really make a living. The English are despots. More and more young people—both girls and boys—are seeking solace in service to the Church. And many are going to America. I have a list of girls who wanted to join us in September, but we simply have no room. You can see how tiny our house is! Perhaps you would like to contact them? Some of them might want to go to America!"

"Oh, I couldn't take your prospects," Mother St. Andrew protested.

"Never fear, my dear. Literally hundreds of girls are looking for a path to take from the drudgery of their poor family farms. Now, don't misunderstand me. They are good girls with high moral character, very devoted to seeking a life of service. They would serve you well!"

"Then I'll take your list. May I write to them from here, asking to interview them here at your house?"

"Of course. Write today!"

Mother St. Andrew heard from all five girls on Mother Francis Clare's list. All wanted to meet her. All lived in the same town but could not make expedient travel arrangements, giving Mother no choice but to write to them: If you wish to join me and go to Texas, meet me at the wharf in LeHavre on July 23. I will await you there. We will sail for Texas on July 25.

After writing the letter, Mother had a final cup of tea with Mother Francis Clare. "I have to admit I am not sure who is taking the greater chance! I am going to accept these girls sight-unseen. If they choose to come, they have no idea what they are risking. If they meet me in LeHavre, they truly have the potential to be good Sisters of Divine Providence. No one else would take this type of risk!"

Upon her return to St. Jean-de-Bassel, Mother collected her professed Sisters, her novices, and thirteen girls from the territories on either side of the Rhine River. Together they took the train from Sarrebourg to Paris and then on to LeHavre.

Arriving on the wharf in LeHavre, Mother was barraged with information about five young Irish girls who were looking for her. Various sailors had sent them to a local boarding house where the landlady was looking after them.

To one sailor, Mother said, "You mean these five girls are here alone?"

"Oh, no, Mother," he replied. "They are with a priest—an uncle, I believe."

That gives me comfort, Mother thought to herself. I want girls who will take risks, but I don't think I can manage foolhardy ones!

Within a few hours, Mother had all of her subjects rounded up and boarding the *St. Laurent*. As they stood on the deck watching the sailors cast off, young Joanna Sheehan spoke sheepishly to her new Superior. "Mother," she began.

"Yes, Joanna, is it?" Mother answered.

"Yes, Mother. I want to apologize. It was my fault that we were unable to meet you in Knock. You see, my dressmaker took too long to finish my travel dress. This delayed us. I'm so sorry." Then, turning around, she continued. "Do you like the dress?"

Mother chuckled. "Why, yes, Joanna. It is lovely. But I am afraid that your future will hold very few new dresses. Are you ready for that?"

"Oh, yes, Mother. But it's all right to enjoy this one while I can; isn't it, Mother."

"Of course, my child." Mother then began to realize how very young all of these new candidates were. Most were fifteen years old or younger. They had forsaken pretty dresses, the possibility of dances and parties, boyfriends, and every other material possession for the sake of a religious vocation. "Father Moye, I implore you to help them. I pray that Providence will be enough for them; it is all they will have."

The *St. Laurent* cast off on schedule, sailing into the channel between England and France and arriving in New York as scheduled on August 4. The travelers changed then to the *Rio Grande* and steamed onward to Galveston. After a short rest at St. Joseph's in Galveston, they took the train to Castroville.

Once at their new Motherhouse, the candidates set about recuperating from seasickness and learning the way of life at Providence House. As the young girls began to feel at home in the little Alsatian village, the professed Sisters soon left for missions in other tiny Texas towns.

The new candidates were busy caring for the convent's cows, pigs, horses, and chickens and several of the young girls worked hard to transform the property in back of the Motherhouse into a garden. The thin soil gave little hope to the girls who had come from beautiful farms in Bavaria and Alsace. With the help of Sister Victoria, they brought in wagonloads of rich dirt from the bottomlands along the Medina River. They even went up to Cross Mountain above St. Louis Cemetery to find white stones with which they edged their furrows. Their garden was beautiful!

The business of the Congregation occupied Mother St. Andrew's time upon her return to Castroville. She had few responsibilities in the running of the Motherhouse with Sister Mary Agnes in charge and therefore was able to visit the new missions in Schulenburg and High Hill before Christmas.

At their Christmas holiday meeting in 1882, Mother placed two important items before her council of advisors.

"Sisters, as I told you in August, Mother Constantine was thrilled with our recruiting efforts this past summer and urged me to return to Germany and Poland next summer to seek more candidates. She could not assure more professed Sisters, but supports our recruiting in the villages. I have had another letter from her to that effect. What is your thinking?"

"I think you should go, Mother. I also think you should contact Mother Francis Clare in Ireland to ask her for more possibilities. Perhaps she still has more vocations than she can handle," Sister Theresa said. Mother's tale of her visit to Knock, Ireland, had intrigued them all; and the hard-working Irish girls who had come in August had brought new life to the Motherhouse.

"Is there any objection?" Mother asked.

The advisors shook their heads, indicating their support for the European trip.

"Do any of you wish to accompany me?"

"From what I observe, Mother, you should take Sister Clemens back to St. Jean," Sister Mary Ange replied. "She is simply unsuited to our life here."

"She will be the only Sister ever to return, but I agree that we must take her home," added Sister Florence, who had joined the advisors since her appointment to St. Joseph's in San Antonio.

Others nodded in agreement.

"Very well. I'll contact her soon to tell her that she may return with me if she still wishes. And there is one other thing. Sisters, before he returned to Europe, I received a note from Bishop Dubuis thanking us for our hospitality when he visited with us. He also made a suggestion to me. Each time I sail away, I am concerned because all of our properties are in my name as per the contract that I made with Bishop Dubuis in 1868. Until now I really never gave his suggestion much thought; however, if something should happen to me, I fear you would have difficulties with deeds and other legal matters. His Lordship's advised me to incorporate with the State of Texas, and I think his suggestion bears review.

"This action would assure that our lands and properties would be held securely in the name of the Congregation, and we would have the right to buy and sell our properties without the confusion that happened in Austin. Could you give me your immediate thoughts? We'll not make a decision today, but before you return to your missions this weekend, I do want a decision on this." Mother's face had taken on a serious look.

Silence fell over the group, as the Sisters did not quite know how to respond. Finally, Sister Mary Agnes spoke,

"I think this is a wise move. My brothers continually speak of the complications of buying and selling properties, and I shall always feel a personal loss in terms of our Austin property. With Bishop Neraz retaining the position of our Ecclesiastical Superior, he will not necessarily be easily available to us as was Father Pierre. God rest his soul. Incorporation might secure us."

"Is this type of thinking against Providence? Father Moye was so quick to admonish the early Sisters who wanted to acquire property and save for the future," Sister Mary Ange questioned. She carried a copy of the Founder's writings to each meeting and believed that she could present Father Moye's values to the young members only if those values were lived concretely by everyone. Now, turning to the quotation that she referenced, she read,

> **As soon as we rely on some human means, we begin little by little to lose confidence in God. Without our noticing it, our confidence becomes only verbal and speculative; in practice in reality, we rely on those funds, we congratulate ourselves for them; like the rich man in the Gospel we say, "I will not lack anything; I have goods for the remainder of my life." And that is how, in**

> *proportion as we turn to creatures, we lose sight*
> *of the Creator, and He loses sight of us.* [*]

The Founder's words silenced the Sisters, driving them to reconsider their thinking on incorporation. Finally Sister Angelique spoke.

"I suppose that I am the senior member here," she said with a wry smile.

"I'll take that posture to support my response. While I was *econome* at St. Jean-de-Bassel, I brought to both Mother Constantine and Mother Adrienne any number of documents that required study and signature. Especially when the Prussians took over Lorraine and Alsace in 1870, we had to defend our identity in order to sustain our existence. If Father Moye's descriptions for our Congregation's mission had not been so clear, if he had not included care of the sick with our mission for teaching, the Prussian government would have disbanded us as it disbanded so many other communities. For me, the incorporation is an opportunity to record with the State of Texas exactly who we are and why we are in existence. This documentation may mean little to us now, but to our future Sisters, it may mean everything."

"I think that our *two* senior members," Mother began, indicating with a nod that she was speaking of both Sister Mary Ange and Sister Angelique, "have given us much food for thought. When we turn to Providence in prayer, we so often find that two positions that seem on the surface to be mutually exclusive are, in fact, two sides of a thin coin. I suggest that we take this question to prayer in the next few days. I would ask us all to re-assemble at the end of the week for a final decision. If we decide to incorporate, I would like to get the transaction completed before I leave for Europe in the spring."

Mother's words calmed the group, allowing them to part without friction.

Re-gathering at the end of the week, Sister Mary Ange opened the conversation. "Sisters, I have completely re-read the <u>The Directory</u>

---

[*]   **<u>The Directory</u>, p. 353.**

in hopes that Father Moye's words might shed light on our concern. I was struck by two passages: *'Let us leave the future to Providence and take advantage of the present. Let us do everything that depends on us and God will take care of what concerns us.'** In another place he says: *'People in their very scheming are only the executors of God's designs for those who abandon themselves sincerely to Providence and who follow its dispositions.'ᵛ* You can see from these two segments of <u>The Directory</u> that Father Moye himself suggests that we have to do those things that seem right and sensible. Only then will God take care of us. Perhaps with the incorporation we will become 'the executors of God's design'! I withdraw my former objections."

The other nuns sat in stunned silence, completely surprised. Several had taken time to review the <u>The Directory</u> looking for support for the position that they should incorporate the Congregation, but they had not discovered these points.

Sister Angelique finally spoke. "I yield to Sister Mary Ange's extensive understanding of our Founder's writings. I suggest that we follow her example and read our Founder more diligently as future decisions will need his wisdom."

"Without objection, then, I will move forward on the transaction. I will talk with August Kempff at the county offices to determine how we do this and will take the Articles to His Lordship once they are finished. You will all have to re-assemble here when the document is ready for signature. Agreed?"

"Yes, Mother," they chorused.

Kempff, the County Clerk, had designed the Articles to Mother's satisfaction by early February 1883. Mother then made an appointment with Bishop Neraz to obtain his approval. The meeting also would give her an opportunity to ask his permission for her next visit to St. Jean-de-Bassel.

---

*   <u>The Directory</u>, p. 213
ᵛ   <u>The Directory</u>, p. 349.

The meeting with His Lordship took place at his office at the Cathedral.

"Thank you for seeing me, Your Lordship," Mother began after she had been seated opposite his desk.

"Very good, Mother. How are things with the Congregation?" Neraz seemed genuinely interested. He was known to be very solicitous about the Sisters at the Orphanage and Infirmary in San Antonio; but this Congregation, which dealt with priests throughout his diocese, was also of concern to His Lordship.

Mother reported on each school, noting that the building plan at St. Joseph's Academy was coming along. She also informed Bishop Neraz that because Sister Clemens at New Braunfels did not seem well, her return to St. Jean-de-Bassel was recommended. "I myself wish to return to St. Jean-de-Bassel in the summer. We were so fortunate to recruit thirteen girls from Alsace and Bavaria, and five from Ireland. I want to see if more would like to come! May I have your permission, Your Lordship?"

The Bishop sat in silence for a long moment. "Mother, I am afraid that more vocations from Europe only will serve to stifle vocations from Texas. I forbid you to return to St. Jean."

Mother could hardly believe her ears! Not return to St. Jean! What did the Bishop mean? She attempted to refute his thinking; but he would not relent, and she proceeded to ask his approval for the Articles of Incorporation.

After giving his consent for the business transaction, the Bishop then perfunctorily dismissed the Superior of the Sisters of Divine Providence.

Since she was staying at St. Joseph's Academy overnight, Mother took Sister Mary Florence, one of her advisors, into her confidence, telling her of the Bishop's refusal to allow her to travel to Germany. Sister Florence, too, was surprised. Their conversation took them no closer to understanding the Bishop's position, but Sister Florence finally had an idea.

"Mother, I think you should send Sister Angelique and Sister Mary Ange to His Lordship to ask him to change his decision about your voyage to Europe. Perhaps if they emphasized the need for more English-speaking vocations and the possibility of Polish-speaking vocations, he will relent. It's worth a try, isn't it?"

"Yes. I believe you're right. I will write to Sister Angelique in Schulenburg. She could come and return on the train in one day, and I know Sister Mary Ange will agree. Perhaps everything will work out."

"We shall depend on Providence," the young Superior at St. Joseph's said. "That's all we have, Mother."

As it happened, Sister Angelique and Sister Mary Ange did persuade the Bishop to allow Mother St. Andrew one more trip to Europe. Their selling point was that Mother hoped to find vocations in eastern Germany and eastern Europe, girls who speak Polish and the Slavic languages. Teachers with these languages would facilitate the opening of more schools in the area around Columbus and Schulenburg where many settlers were from eastern European countries.

By early 1883, the young nun at New Braunfels, Sister Clemens, had become very melancholy; and Sister Barbara, the Superior, wrote a second time of her concerns to Mother St. Andrew. Worried that Sister Clemens' frailty might lead to some type of disaster, Mother immediately changed the new missionary to Solms, about eight miles away, thinking that a smaller, less populated area would be less stressful.

But even the small school in Solms proved too much for Sister Clemens, and the distraught nun asked the Superior there to take her back to New Braunfels.

"Now, Sister," the Superior said in a kind tone, "I know that you are not feeling well. Let's plan to go to New Braunfels on Friday after school is out. You can remain there, and I will write to Mother St. Andrew asking that you be received back at Castroville."

"I just want to go home," Sister Clemens cried. "I just want to go home. I hate it here!"

"Very well. All in due time. After you get back to Castroville, Mother can arrange for you to return to St. Jean-de-Bassel. But all this takes time, Sister."

The Superior believed that Sister Clemens had gone to her bed to lie down, and she missed her only as evening came on. She called together several men, the fathers of her pupils at Solms, and at daybreak they began a search for the missing nun. When they checked in New Braunfels and learned that Sister Clemens never arrived there, they began to give up hope. The wilderness simply held too many perils.

The troubled nun was never found.

Mother received a telegram from Sister Barbara telling her of the calamity. Asking for their prayers, she immediately announced the tragedy to the Sisters, Novices, Postulants, and Candidates at the Motherhouse.

The grief of their tragic loss was felt keenly when Sister Barbara's letter to Mother St. Andrew came just after Easter.

Dear Mother,

It is with a heavy heart that I write these lines. A young boy found Sister Clemens' habit this morning while he was hunting. The habit was completely intact. Only Sister's skeleton remained. Presumably she became lost and was overcome by the cold night. Perhaps her corpse was eaten by animals. We will bury her remains here, next to Sister Pierre, if that is your wish. I am so sorry.

In Divine Providence,
Sister Barbara

As she read the letter, thinking of the sad death of Sister Pierre twelve years earlier, Mother said to herself, "I wish I had never heard of New Braunfels. For us it has meant nothing but tragedy." Then she sat down to write to St. Jean-de-Bassel and to Sister Clemens' family. Her letter to Mother Constantine would be explicit. Her letter to the Guebels family, on the other hand, needed gentleness. Perhaps, she thought, the grisly details of their daughter's death might not be necessary.

The Articles of Incorporation were signed on May 19, 1883, in August Kempff's office by Sister Mary Theresa Schultz, Sister M. Agnes Wolf, Sister M. Arsene Schaff, Sister M. Florence Walter, Sister M. Paul Bader, and Mother St. Andrew. The newly incorporated entity was valued at $20,000 in land, buildings, and furnishings.

Shortly after the signing, Mother St. Andrew returned to Europe to recruit throughout Germany, Poland, and Ireland where she found a total of fifty-two eager, new missionaries. Mother returned to Texas in August with thirty Alsatian and German girls, four Polish girls, and eighteen Irish girls. All the European girls met at St. Jean-de-Bassel and the Irish girls were instructed to meet Mother St. Andrew in LeHavre where they sailed on August 25, 1883, on the *St. Germain.*

At nightfall, Mother called all her new missionaries around her. After leading them in the singing of the *Salve Regina*, she gave them her blessing for the night. Tired from a hard day's journey, they were soon settled in the bunks assigned to them.

Shortly after midnight, a terrible crashing noise awakened the six hundred passengers. Pandemonium set in as everyone realized that something was terribly wrong.

"Quick, girls, get up immediately," Mother shouted above the rising din. "Dress and come directly to me. We must be ready to abandon the ship if directed. I fear the worst!"

The sisters-to-be obeyed instantly, huddling around Mother awaiting further instructions. Within minutes a sailor came below and shouted, "All women and children to the lifeboats! We are sinking. Move as fast as you can!"

Mother led her new daughters topside and watched as they piled into a lifeboat. After counting heads to be sure all were there, she herself stepped into the boat just as the sailor in charge gave the signal to swing the craft overboard. The lifeboat slammed into the inky water, splashing all on board with a cold spray.

"Are you all right, girls?" Mother screamed over the crash of waves and yelling from the other boats. "Is everyone all right?"

They answered back in one voice, "Yes, Mother!"

"Then we will begin the rosary: In the name of the Father ..." The repetition of the soothing prayer consoled and calmed all in her charge even in the pitch-black darkness. In the early morning dawn, when they were taken aboard the Recovery, the ship that had been towing the boat with which the *St. Germain* had collided, those in this lifeboat were models of self-composure.

Only after they had boarded the *Recovery* were the girls able to take a good look at each other. Now safe from peril, all had to eventually sit down on their bunks as they burst into laughter.

"Look at you!" They said to one another.

"You have on my shoes!"

"You have on my dress!"

Another said, "At least you have a dress and shoes! Look at me! I'll have to wear this shabby old thing!" The young girl complaining was wearing the battered coat of a sailor and was in her stockings.

The banter continued. "That left shoe is mine! Is the right one yours? Perhaps I am wearing yours!"

Mother, too, was doubled over in laughter. "Well, never mind now, girls! You won't really need these clothes for long. I'm certain that they'll be bringing our luggage soon. You can travel to New York and then on to Galveston in your other clothes!" The laughter over the great mix-up in clothes released the tension that had built in the terrified girls and their Superior during their near-death experience.

The *St. Germain* was towed by the *Recovery* into Plymouth harbor where the missionaries were housed in army barracks until another ship could be fitted for sailing. The voyage resumed when the *Amerique* sailed on September 1 and all hoped for an uneventful journey.

Just halfway across the Atlantic, disaster struck again as the *Amerique* sailed into a terrific storm. Tossed about like a matchbox by angry winds, all on board were certain that they would meet their God this time.

After the fifty-two candidates had said the rosary for the sixth time, one of the youngest girls whispered to Mother St. Andrew, "Mother, I think we have made a terrible mistake. Perhaps we should not have come after all. Please pray for us, Mother."

"Now, now, daughters. These misadventures are all the strengthening works of God. You must never make a decision in the midst of trauma. After we have arrived safely in Castroville and you have had a chance to settle into your new home, then we'll see what God is really asking. If this is a mistake, you may then return to your homes. Will that be all right?"

"Yes, Mother," the young girls said. Mother could tell from the tremor in the young voices that everything was not "all right." But nothing could be done about it now.

A mishap in their New York hotel, putting the lives of a number of the young girls in danger, alarmed even Mother. A gas jet in a hotel room had inadvertently been left on after the flame had gone out. It was a near miracle that her girls had not perished. Recalling her own words the night of the perilous storm at sea, Mother asked God in prayer, "Are you strengthening me, O Lord? And for what?"

The words of Father Moye came to her: ***"At certain times it seems everything is lacking, but those are moments of trial designed by divine Providence to awaken our faith and confidence."****

"All right," she continued in prayer, "after all of the trials in the past two weeks, I place myself confidently in Your loving hands. You

---

* **The Directory, p. 238.**

never promised that it would be easy! I entrust myself to Your providential designs. But, please, Lord, no more problems at sea!"

As they finally docked at Galveston after the steamer *Guadalupe* had run aground on a sandbar and they had rocked uncertainly on the Bolivar peninsula, Mother recalled her prayer in New York and added: "All right, Lord, I now know better than to ask for an altering of conditions for my own consolation. Thy will be done!"

A puzzling letter came to Mother's desk in October 1883. Sister Marie, worried that the mishaps at sea and in New York may have resulted in permanent disaster, wrote from St. Jean-de-Bassel on September 26, 1883, asking Mother to write the German motherhouse as soon as possible because "All the sisters are ... deeply interested ... and eager to have news of you."

The second to the last paragraph confused Mother St. Andrew. Sister Marie wrote:

> *On the day of the close of the first retreat we had a visit from your bishop, Msgr. Neraz, who came with M. Tarillion and the curé of Insming. His Excellency paid a visit to our dear Mother, with reverend Father Superior. I was also present. He asked us if the Congregation, or rather the House at Castroville depended on ours here. We said that that was impossible, considering the distance one from the other. He also said that he thinks that you ought to hold an election in your convent. He manifested much interest and solicitude for your Congregation, and showed much satisfaction when we told him that you had taken along so many postulants. He said*

*that the Congregation renders very much service
to the cause of religion: that gave us pleasure.* *

Not sure of the import of the letter, Mother took it immediately to Sister Mary Ange and asked her to read it carefully.

"What do you make of it, Sister?" Mother asked with caution in her voice.

"Actually, I couldn't say, Mother. There are several puzzling factors. First, the letter is from your friend, Sister Marie. Though she is on the Council, I would have thought that if the meaning of the Bishop's visit to St. Jean-de-Bassel has lasting consecquences, Mother Constantine would have written herself and would have been more explicit. Also, did you know that Bishop Neraz was going to Germany?"

"No, I did not. I learned that he had gone to Rome only after I returned from Europe."

"What do you think about an election?" Mother continued her questions.

"Perhaps it is a good idea. With the recent new *Constitution*, it might be prudent to allow our professed Sisters to choose their Superior as we do in Chapter at St. Jean. I suppose we could hold an election next August after our retreat. We probably have only 15 Sisters who are eligible to be capitulars."

"How do you read the part about our dependence on St. Jean-de-Bassel?"

"To tell you the truth, Mother, I think that it accurately captures our reality. We are at a distance and you manage our day-to-day situations. I have had the impression that this arrangement works well for both you and Mother Constantine. Am I not correct?"

"Yes. Mother Constantine seems to have full confidence in me. If she did not, she could have removed me and asked any of you to take

---

* **Actual excerpt from the letter which is held at St. Jean-de-Bassel, copy in the Archives of the Sisters of Divine Providence of San Antonio, TX.**

the reins! Should I talk this over with His Lordship?" was Mother's final question.

"Mother, I don't think I would. If he has some concern, he should bring that to you," Sister Mary Ange replied.

When she met with her advisors at Christmas, Mother showed them the letter as well. Conversation was both lively and questioning. Although the group could not agree on its meaning, all affirmed that an election could be a good thing. The advisors appointed Sister Mary Agnes to call and monitor the election in August.

Though she took Sister Mary Ange's advice, in just three years Mother would look back at this letter with a very different attitude.

In the fall of 1883, the Sisters of Divine Providence opened an academy in Palestine, Texas; and in the early months of 1884, plans were made to open schools at the invitation of the pastors of Fayetteville, Dubina, and Marienfield. In addition, Sister Florence was able to expand the buildings at St. Joseph's Academy in San Antonio to accommodate an increasing enrollment.

Sister Sacred Heart came to her Novice Mistress after morning prayers early one spring morning in 1884. "Sister, I don't feel well. I would like to be excused from my duties today. May I please go to bed?" Feeling the young novice's warm, flushed face, Sister Mary Ange immediately granted the request and rushed to ask Mother St. Andrew to send for the town doctor. The doctor's face was grave when he came out of the second floor dormitory where Mother St. Andrew and Sister Mary Ange stood outside waiting in the hallway.

"Mother, I am afraid your Sister has typhoid fever. Since we've had the drought I have been concerned about the town's water. Are you still using water from that old cistern to the east of your kitchen?"

"Why, yes, Doctor."

"I'm going to talk to Sister Gabriel. She should start boiling all the water from there that you use. That's all I know to do. Keep an eye on Sister. I don't like how she sounds."

During Holy Week, Sister Sacred Heart's conditioned worsened and the doctor was called in again. This time, as he left the room, he said, "Mother, Sister should be moved to a private room, and someone should stay with her at all times. Her situation is quite grave. She may not live until Easter. And please take precautions. I recommend all Sisters wash their hands frequently. Also, avoid direct contact with Sister."

The Sisters set up a schedule for sitting with Sister Sacred Heart, but all precautions were to no avail. On Good Friday afternoon, April 11, 1884, her Savior said to the novice the same words He had spoken from the cross to the Good Thief: "This day you shall be with me in paradise."

Now truly frightened by the threatening disease of typhoid, Mother suggested that a novena to the Sacred Heart be started. Her announcement in the refectory on Holy Saturday struck at the hearts of all who listened.

"My dear daughters, Monday we shall bury our dear Sister Sacred Heart. We shall miss her lilting Irish laughter. But our vigilance must now be doubled. We will continue to boil all water that we drink; those among us who have been diagnosed with tuberculosis will, beginning tonight, sleep apart at the west end of the first floor. We'll prepare that room that we seldom use for their beds as soon as we've finished our noon prayers. Finally, we will begin today with a novena to the Sacred Heart asking for Our Divine Lord's mercy at this time of peril."

All in the refectory nodded, assenting to Mother St. Andrew's plans.

"Now, let us continue on this Good Friday with our Chapter of Faults, recognizing that it was our sins which nailed our Blessed Lord to the cross."

Beginning with their Superior, each Sister confessed to her community recent strayings from the Holy Rule, words and acts of unkindness, careless behavior that may have wasted resources, and myriads of other small or large faults that piqued their consciences. When all had confessed, the Sisters left the refectory in silence and remained in silence the rest of the day, as was the custom on Good Friday.

That night, as she was on her way to bed, Sister Mary Ange stopped in their small chapel on the first floor. The usual glow from the sanctuary lamp was gone since, like all repositories on Good Friday and Holy Saturday, the Blessed Sacrament was not present. Once her eyes were accustomed to the darkness, Sister Mary Ange was startled to see a habited figure prostrate on the chapel floor near the altar. Mother St. Andrew. Frequently various novices mentioned seeing Mother late at night in the chapel, but Sister Mary Ange had never personally witnessed her Superior's devotion.

Actually, thought Sister Mary Ange, I am not surprised. Mother has never asked of us what she herself is unwilling to do. For every hour of prayer she requires of us, she gives two hours. I wouldn't be surprised if she is here all night praying to Our Lord on this night of His burial. With that, Sister Mary Ange slipped out of the chapel, quietly closing the door so as not to disturb her Superior.

The summer of 1884 was a busy one. Health concerns occupied everyone as more Sisters came down with typhoid fever and tuberculosis. Mother and her advisors decided to lighten the load of studies to allow Sisters to have more rest. Everyone was encouraged to eat more vegetables from the bounteous convent garden. Even though Sister Gabriel was scrupulous about boiling water from the cistern, Mother asked each Sister to take a holy hour to pray for rain which could give them untainted water.

Mid-summer, Mother was approached by Sister Barbara who asked to see her.

"Come in," Mother said from her desk as Sister Barbara appeared in the doorway of the Superior's office at the appointed time. After

Sister Barbara was seated, Mother asked, "What can I do for you, my daughter?"

"I have been hesitant about coming to you, Mother. I don't want to tell tales and I certainly don't want to misinterpret innocent behaviors. But I feel that I must mention something to you before the summer is over and we return to our missions. Let me ask first: will Sister Christine be returning to New Braunfels?"

"Why, yes. We did not see any reason to move her this year. Is there a concern?"

"Possibly not. Sister is an excellent teacher; and having been in New Braunfels so many years, she is well-known and is well-liked by our children and their parents. But …," her voice trailed off.

"But what, Sister," Mother St. Andrew pressed.

"Perhaps I should start from another perspective. Father Kirch was very helpful during our crisis last year with the death of Sister Clemens. He could not have been more solicitous, Mother. He often came to the convent asking if we were all right, especially during the weeks that Sister Clemens was missing. And when the boy found her skeleton, Father was wonderful. The funeral Mass and his sermon were so consoling to us. But, as this past school year progressed, the good Father continued to visit us regularly and he appears to have a special regard for Sister Christine." This last information caught Mother by surprise.

"Could that be so? I've never had any concerns about Sister Christine before. She's been in New Braunfels for more than ten years now. Are you certain?"

"Perhaps I am being overly cautious," Sister Barbara admitted.

"Let's not make too much of this, Sister. In my closing remarks to the Sisters before you leave for your missions, I will emphasize the decorum that our Holy Rule requires, particularly with priests. I appreciate your candor, but I think perhaps we should wait and see. Do you agree?"

"Yes, Mother. That is the best approach."

"Thank you, Sister, for your solicitude. I will ask you to keep an open heart toward Sister Christine, but you might keep an open eye as well. We're all only human, you know," Mother concluded thoughtfully.

"Thank you for your time, Mother. I will heed your advice."

Following the directives of the consultors, Sister Mary Agnes organized an election for the position of Superior of the Texas Sisters. When the retreat opened, she announced the impending election, scheduled for August 24, 1884, the day before St. Louis Day, indicating also that the suggestion had come from the motherhouse at St. Jean-de-Bassel. Twenty-two professed Sisters had the right to cast a ballot, she informed them. She asked for prayers during the retreat for the success of the election.

On Sunday morning August 24, 1884, the singing of the *Veni Creator Spiritus* concluded the Mass as the entire community called upon the Holy Ghost for guidance and protection. After the hymn, the youngest members of the Sisters of Divine Providence exited. The twenty-two electors remained in the chapel, each receiving a slip of paper.

"Please write the name of the Sister whom you believe should serve us as our Superior," Sister Mary Agnes instructed. "When you have finished, bring your ballot and place it in the bowl on the altar. Sisters Mary Ange and Angelique, our senior members, will count the ballots."

A hush fell over the chapel as the Sisters knew that they were participating in a history-making event.

When the ballots were counted, Sister Mary Agnes stepped forward.

"Sisters, we have elected Mother St. Andrew," she announced simply, and the electors applauded their work.

True to her word, Mother St. Andrew's final conference with the Sisters before they left for their missions cautioned them to heed the Founder's admonition to avoid casual relationships with their pastors.

"Sisters, we are all only human. And priests are only human. In obedience to our Holy Rule, you must honor your vows and you must live impeccably. Only a small crack allows Satan to get into your very soul and distract you away from our good God's plan. Do not give Satan even a crack. Stay alert. Help one another. Pray daily for perseverance in your vocation. And also pray for all priests.

"I ask that you curtail visiting with your pastors in your school-rooms when the children are not present. I exhort you to remember that in the past I have asked that you not fraternize with your pastor while taking care of the church sanctuary or on other similar occasions. Simply be careful. Pray for the virtues of our state of life."

The sternness in their Superior's voice and the set of her jaw conveyed to the Sisters that this topic was serious. They knew not to take these remarks lightly.

Only the deaths of Sister Theresa Schultz and Novice-Sister Felicite Bastian marred the last few months of 1884. The day after Sister Theresa died, Mother sat in conversation with her confidants Sister Mary Agnes and Sister Mary Ange. All were broken with grief.

"God has taken our Sister at such a young age," Mother began. "Sister Theresa is three years younger than I was when I came to this land. She was just finishing her studies at Ursuline Academy when I stayed there en route from Austin to Castroville in 1868. The Ursulines saw a vocation in her, but knew that she was too—let's see, what did they say?—rough and tumble, for them. She came to us at Christmas." Mother got a faraway look in her eyes as she seemed to be transported into a less-complicated time gone by.

Breaking the reverie, Sister Agnes said, "Sister Theresa was always so generous. We knew we could count on her, no matter what needed to be done. She was deeply revered in Galveston during the years she served there. I so wish that she hadn't suffered such agony. Her last hours were an edification to us all."

Sharing memories of Sister Theresa's sixteen years in the community continued for a while, comforting the mourners.

Finally, Mother brought the conversation to a close. "Each death takes a bit of my heart with it. I thought I should not survive the death of Sister Pierre, and then Father Pierre left us never to return. The tragedy of Sister Clemens demise was crushing. Now Sister Theresa. The death of each Sister is like the death of a daughter. I now know the burden of grief that my own mother experienced when my little sister Rosalie died."

After a short pause, she said, "The Lord giveth and the Lord taketh away."

The others responded: "Blessed be the name of the Lord."

During the summer of 1885, Mother St. Andrew made it a point to visit with Sister Barbara about the concerns the New Braunfels superior had brought forward the previous summer. Learning that Father Kirch continued visiting the convent regularly, Mother decided to speak directly to Sister Christine before summer's end. Sister Christine's defensive response gave Mother pause, and she reminded her subject that decorum was essential to their way of life, especially in small towns. Sister Christine gave a half-hearted promise to be less available to Father Kirch's attentions.

During that same time period, between May and November of 1885, five more deaths would unravel the heartstrings of Mother St. Andrew and her Sisters.

Sister Gabriel Stephan, barely thirty-six years old, succumbed to disease, followed by three young Irish novices in July, August, and October. Sister Vincentia Wipff of D'Hanis died on All Hallow's Eve.

"The Lord giveth and the Lord taketh away," was whispered over and over again by those left behind. "Blessed be the name of the Lord."

A letter from Sister Barbara to Mother St. Andrew in the winter of 1886 led Mother to seek out Sister Mary Ange for advice.

"Oh, Sister," Mother began after Sister Mary Ange had had a moment to read Sister Barbara's letter indicating that Father Kirch and Sister Christine were not 'using good judgment,' "I believe that my heart is breaking! If these frequent visits do not stop, I fear that once again we have nothing good to expect from New Braunfels."

"Since Sister Christine is still in annual profession, I suggest that I write to her and indicate our displeasure at her relationship with Father Kirch."

"I would sincerely appreciate that, Sister. I don't believe she will be open to anything I have to say," Mother responded dejectedly.

Almost immediately, Sister Mary Ange wrote to Sister Christine.

Another letter to Mother St. Andrew from Sister Barbara brought the Superior General and the Mistress of Novices together again, this time with grave misgivings.

"I simply cannot believe that Sister Christine shared my letter to her with Father Kirch," Sister Mary Ange said angrily. "That letter was intended for her alone! The very idea that the pastor would take the letter to His Lordship! I can hardly speak I am so disturbed."

"I, too, have no idea where this is going," Mother St. Andrew said, trying to remain calm, though her own temper was just barely under control. "I wonder if we should speak with Father Brücklin about this. Since he has come to St. Louis Church, he has been very helpful to us. Perhaps he would know what we should do."

After Sister Mary Ange agreed to consult with Father Brücklin, the two nuns went together to their pastor-chaplain. The priest, who had been at St. Louis for only a short time had little to say.

On the way back to Providence House from the rectory, Mother St. Andrew said to Sister Mary Ange, "I am now very concerned, Sister. Too many priests are now involved in this issue. We don't know Father Brücklin well enough to be sure of what he might say about all of this and to whom. We'll have to see how this comes out."

Hearing that comment, Mother instantly felt the loss of Father Pierre Richard all over again.

Over the Christmas holidays Mother St. Andrew and her advisors decided, with the approval of Bishop Neraz, to send Sister Mary Florence and Sister Berthilde, who wanted to return to St. Jean-de-Bassel permanently, to Europe to recruit more subjects in Rhineland villages.

Their discussion of the New Braunfels problem led the advisors to ask Mother to call Sister Christine home to Castroville to review the situation with her directly. Soon after the holidays, Sister Mary Ange wrote to Sister Christine asking her to come to Castroville.

After talking with Sister Christine, Mother St. Andrew and Sister Mary Ange spoke honestly with each other. "Mother, I am afraid that Sister Christine is digging in her heels. The end result may be quite destructive. I have every reason to believe that she will speak with Father Kirch immediately upon her return to New Braunfels. She is very unhappy and will probably discredit us."

"We'll just have to wait and trust, Sister. Last year's deaths have wearied me. And this only further crushes my heart. We have so many concerns: opening new schools, forming our young members, increasing Texas vocations. I simply do not want to spend time on this matter!"

True to predictions, Sister Christine returned to New Braunfels in a very bad humor. She wrote to Father Kirch all that she believed she had been told in Castroville. He forwarded the letter to the Bishop.

Wanting to review progress on the academy buildings before Sister Florence departed for Germany, Mother St. Andrew visited St. Joseph's Academy in late spring. A candid conversation brought the situation related to New Braunfels into sharper focus.

"Mother," Sister Florence said, after they had walked through the newly-opened buildings at the Academy, "I am quite concerned. Are you aware that His Lordship has asked Father Pefferkorn to investigate the situation in New Braunfels?"

"I did hear that, Sister. Have you heard anything more specific?"

"One problem with this, Mother, is that Father Pefferkorn has intimated that your brother's incarceration in 1877 was basically your fault. He may not have all the facts straight since the incident happened years ago. I think Father may begin the investigation with prejudice. And he probably will be influenced by priests."

"Oh," was Mother's only comment. Her tone was flat.

Sister Florence continued. "I suggest that you be especially careful about what you say to the Sisters this summer. They will talk with their families; their families may speak with pastors. You may be misquoted." Sister Florence was quite prudent. Mother knew that she would miss her counsel this summer if anything went awry.

"That is of deep concern to me as well, Sister. I suppose all of us who hold positions of authority are at times misquoted and misunderstood. I shall be careful; but, let us not forget: Jesus too was misquoted and misunderstood, as was our dear Founder."

"Yes, Mother, but the consequences for both of them were dire," Sister Florence said with a heaviness in her voice. "Very dire," she repeated for emphasis. "I wish I were not leaving for the summer. Perhaps I should not go."

"Oh, no, Sister. We need new vocations. And you have been looking forward to visiting your family. Please convey my love to Mother Anna. I can hardly believe that Mother Constantine has gone to God. Her death is truly the end of an era. St. Jean-de-Bassel won't be the same without her."

"I didn't know her as well as you did, Mother. But I remember those first years when Lorraine and Alsace were absorbed into the Reich. Mother Constantine was so strong, so wise. Yes, she will be missed."

The next day as Mother St. Andrew waited for the train to La Coste with Sister Florence, she said, "May God go with you, my daughter.

We will miss you this summer. All is in the hands of Providence; all will be well."

On the short train ride to La Coste, Mother remembered the stories told about Father Moye to the novices at St. Jean-de-Bassel. Misrepresentations of his intentions about the project of the Little Sisters of the Poor, as they were known in those early days, led to the project being placed under interdict by the bishop. Opening new schools was stopped. However, in time, the project resumed and endured. Father Moye's words came to Mother's mind: ***"Abandon yourselves completely to God; put all your confidence in God and not in others. You will see from experience that those you rely on most will fail you in one way or another. But if you entrust yourselves to God, He will never fail you."****

I must hold these words in my mind and heart, Mother thought. I must believe that God will not fail me.

The summer of 1886 was memorable, to say the least. The Sisters, continuing their studies at the Castroville motherhouse, noted that their Superior and her consultors spent long hours in meetings. A school had been opened in Columbus the previous year, sending Sisters to serve a cluster of villages: Fayetteville, Frelsburg, Ellinger, Mentz, High Hill, Schulenburg, and Columbus. Mother St. Andrew's advisors also agreed to take the school in Clarksville, which had closed when the Sisters of the Holy Cross had abandoned the mission in 1883.

No one except the advisors knew of the mushrooming controversy over Father Pefferkorn's report to His Lordship about Mother St. Andrew.

On July 23ʳᵈ a messenger delivered a summons to Mother St. Andrew from Bishop Neraz:

> ***I have received a report from Father Pefferkorn on the New Braunfels incident. I have asked***

---

*   **The Directory, p. 224.**

Father Richard Maloney, Father George Feith, and Father Henry Pefferkorn to question you personally in regard to accusations from Father Kirch. Come to my house at 9:00 in the morning on Tuesday, July 27, 1886.

Mother immediately called a meeting of her advisors.

Her hand trembled as she handed the missive to Sister Angelique who read it silently and then passed it to Sister Mary Agnes. One by one, the consultors read the note and passed it on. They sat in silence.

Finally, Mother spoke. "At least we can have our annual celebration of the Feast of St. Anne," she said with a tight smile.

"Mother," Sister Angelique began, "I don't know what to say."

"There's nothing to say, Sister. This could have lasting and ponderous effects. We must all pray and trust our Provident God."

"Who among us shall go with you, Mother?" Sister Mary Ange asked. She was near tears, realizing that if she had taken different actions with Sister Christine, there might have been a different result.

"You yourself are most thoroughly acquainted with Sister Christine's case. Will you accompany me?"

"Of course, Mother. Of course."

The Sisters at Providence House gathered for St. Anne's Day Mass and a special dinner on Monday, July 26, having no idea that Mother St. Andrew and her consultors were in turmoil. After dinner, Mother and Sister Mary Ange left Providence House for San Antonio where they spent the night at St. Joseph's Convent.

Upon arriving at the bishop's house at nine o'clock precisely the next day, Mother was ushered into a parlor filled with priests while Sister Mary Ange waited in an anteroom.

Father Pefferkorn began the interrogation.

"Mother, I have a set of questions that we have been given by His Lordship Bishop Neraz who wants the answers to be written. I am the secretary and I will write your answers. When we have finished, I will require your affirmation that what I have written is accurate. Do you understand?"

"Yes, Father, I do."

"Then, the first question: Have you in private or in public spoken badly of the priests 1. in front of your sisters 2. novices 3. persons from the outside?"*

Mother replied: "I did not speak of priests, neither in private nor in public, neither before the sisters, novices, nor persons outside."

Father Pefferkorn continued. "Have you in private or in public said to the sisters or novices to distrust these priests and that without exception?"

Mother answered, "I did not tell the sisters or novices to beware of priests at any time."

Father Pefferkorn: "Have you consulted your Council, as your rule requires in all important matters?"

Mother: "I have."

Father Pefferkorn: "Did you conform to the opinion of the majority of the Council?"

Mother: "I did."

Father Pefferkorn: "Have you said that you were not afraid of any court, even ecclesiastical, even if the Pope were there?"

Mother: "In a conversation with Father Brücklin, I remember saying that I was not afraid of defending my cause before an ecclesiastical court, even if the Pope were present. The occasion was when Sister Mary Ange and I went to him to ask him to review a letter we had received from Sister Barbara. She told us in the letter

---

* **The questions listed are phrased and punctuated exactly as the English translation of the original French reads. Question 14 has been omitted; the reason for the omission of Question 14 is in the Endnotes to this chapter. Mother St. Andrew's answers are basically those recorded during the interview. The material has been translated from the French which Father Pefferkorn recorded as he interrogated Mother St. Andrew. The answers in Pefferkorn's report are not verbatim. [Archives of the Sisters of Divine Providence and the Archdiocese of San Antonio.]**

that Father Kirch had informed the Bishop of our admonishments of Sister Christine. That is all."

Father Pefferkorn: "Have you made the remark that some sisters stayed a long time in the confessional and when they came out their faces were red?"

Mother responded, "I did say that of one sister."

Father Pefferkorn: "Have you said that Father Japes had seduced a sister in the confessional?"

Mother: "I said that Father Japes has no other place to seduce a sister except in the confessional."

Father Pefferkorn: "Have you spoken badly of Father Kirch?"

Mother. "I admit to speaking badly of Father Kirch in my attempt to discipline Sister Christine."

Father Pefferkorn: "Have you accused a sister or some sisters of being intimate with Father Kirch?"

Mother: "With good reason, I have regularly cautioned Sister Christine that friendly behaviors can lead to worse behaviors. Yes. But I did not accuse Father Kirch of improprieties."

Father Pefferkorn: "Have you threatened to dismiss from your congregation a sister because of her intimacy with Father Kirch?"

Mother: "Sister Mary Ange and I both cautioned Sister Christine that her foolhardy actions could lead to her being changed from New Braunfels or her dismissal from the Congregation. She does not have permanent vows."

Father Pefferkorn:" Have you said or written that Father Kirch tormented the Sisters from 8 Miles (Solms) and that in order to please a miserable sister like Sister Christine?"

Mother: "I do remember doing that."

Father Pefferkorn: "Have you said that Sister Aloysia is more worthy of receiving Communion without confession than Father Kirch with confession?"

Mother: "I did say that. I was quite angry with Sister Christine."

Father Pefferkorn: "Have you said to one of your sisters, 'Sr. Christine, aren't you ashamed to let yourself be courted by a priest'?"

Mother: "I did not say that."

Father Pefferkorn: "Have you said that Father Kirch and Sister Christine was a story that they had together like Martin Luther and the Catherine*?"

Mother: "New Braunfels has a significant Lutheran population. I recounted for Sister Christine the story of Martin Luther in hopes that she would see the error of her ways."

Father Pefferkorn: "Have you said that if Father Kirch wants a woman that he go look for her in the world, but that he leave the sisters where they are?"

Mother: "In anger, I probably said that to Sister Christine."

Father Pefferkorn: "Have you said or written that if these visits of the Fathers to the sisters did not stop, you have nothing new or good to await from New Braunfels?"

Mother: "I said that."

Father Pefferkorn: "Did you not suspect a sister from D'Hanis to have been a victim of Father Japes? Did you speak of it to anyone?"

Mother: "I have not."

Father Pefferkorn: "Have you demanded that the stable in New Braunfels be moved to another place in order to avoid familiarities already too intimate?"

Mother: "Yes, I said that."

Father Pefferkorn: "Of which familiarities do you want to speak and what do you understand by this word?"

Mother: "I was speaking of the frequent visits that Father Kirch made to the Sisters."

Father Pefferkorn: "Have you said that we would become Lutherans in New Braunfels because of the conduct of Father Kirch?"

Mother: "I know nothing of anything like that."

---

*   **Martin Luther left the Augustinian monks and married a woman named Catherine.**

With the last of His Lordship's questions asked, Father Pefferkorn looked at his confreres and asked, "Do any of you have other questions to put to Mother St. Andrew?"

Though Mother had remained composed during the interrogation, there was no mistaking the toll the procedure had taken on her. The other two men shook their heads in reply to Pefferkorn's question.

"That being the case, Mother," Father Pefferkorn concluded, "thank you for your cooperation. We will make our report and recommendations to His Lordship by the end of the week." With that Mother was escorted to the small parlor where Sister Mary Ange waited and they were both taken to the rectory front door.

Once on Alameda Street, Sister Mary Ange said, "Oh, Mother, you look as though you've seen a ghost! Are you all right?" Her strained voice underscored her anxiety about her Superior General.

"Let's just walk to St. Joseph's, Sister. Once we're there, I'll confide everything to you. I'll be all right after I get some air."

True to her word, once they had reached the new convent at St. Joseph's Academy, Mother entrusted her encounter with the priests to her long-time friend.

So little could be said. Mother had not been given a copy of the questions. She had no knowledge of Father Pefferkorn's initial report which had led to the interrogation.

"I have done my best to be forthright. However," Mother said in a tight voice, "I will not be surprised at anything that may happen from this point on."

"What shall we tell the others tomorrow, Mother?"

"I'm going to review the encounter with them, just as I have with you. The questions revealed that there is some concern that I do not consult with my advisors on matters of importance. I must give no impression that I have concealed these proceedings from the council."

"I agree, Mother. And you know you have our confidence—and loyalty." With these last words, Sister Mary Ange placed her hand on her Superior's, a gesture of both compassion and support.

"Thank you," Mother St. Andrew said sincerely. "Let's see if we can find something to eat. And then we'll take the afternoon train back to La Coste. I just want to go home. When we get back to Castroville, will you please send a cable to St. Jean asking Sister Florence to return to Castroville at her earliest convenience?"

"Of course, Mother. In fact, I'll take care of that this afternoon before we take the train." For Mother St. Andrew to go to the expense of a cable, Sister Mary Ange thought, gave evidence of impending doom.

The priests' advisory council to Bishop Neraz met on August 16, giving him a full report of all that had transpired in June and July of 1886. On August 17, Mother received a message from His Lordship:

> *Please be advised that I am asking for a new General Chapter of the Congregation to be called on August 26, 1886. I will be in Castroville for the Feast of St. Louis on August 25 and will remain to supervise an election of a new superior. My priests have advised me that:*
>
> 1. *your Congregation must elect another superior;*
> 2. *any future difficulties between priests and religious must be submitted to my personal arbitration;*
> 3. *any accusation against a priest or religious must be accompanied by solid proofs and given only to myself;*
> 4. *that these types of accusations be confided to no one except myself.*

> *Those priests who are pastors in towns where your Sisters have the schools are adamant that your resignation is imperative for the future spiritual well-being of your Sisters. They are unwilling to continue supporting your schools if you continue as Superior and they refuse to hear your Sisters' confessions if you do not step down as they feel that their reputations in the con-fessional are in peril. This dictum comes from Fathers Pefferkorn, Walk, Tarrillion and Kirch.*
>
> *I will comply with their request. Please tender your resignation to me on August 26 in the morning and plan for an election to be held at 10:00.*

After Mother shared the bishop's message with her Council, a pall of sadness settled over Providence House.

The ten days until August 26 passed too quickly—and too slowly. Sister Angelique took over the operations of the Congregation, conducting the appointments with Sisters who were being changed and finishing preparations for renewing promises.

At exactly 10:00 in the morning on August 26, 1886, His Lordship knocked at the Paris Street door of Providence House. The young Sister who greeted him told him that the Sisters were awaiting him in the chapel. After escorting him to the assembled Electors, she joined all the other young Sisters, Novices, and Candidates who were gathered in silence on the south veranda.

Once again Sister Mary Agnes had been given charge of the election proceedings. A process similar to the one used in 1884 began with Sister Mary Ange and Sister Angelique again ready to count the ballots.

Sister Mary Agnes announced the results of the first ballot: "Mother St. Andrew has been elected our Superior."

Bishop Neraz sat in stunned amazement. "Vote again," he said.

The second ballot's results were again announced by Sister Mary Agnes: "Mother St. Andrew has been elected our Superior."

This time the Bishop stood, faced the Electors and glowered. "If you do not elect another Superior," he said, "I will bring a Sister from Santa Rosa here to take over as Superior. Vote again."

Now the Electors appeared dismayed.

Mother St. Andrew stood, and looking around at her daughters, gave a pleading look at Sister Angelique and Sister Mary Ange. One after the other, the two senior members of the community said sorrowfully, "Sisters, I ask that you do not consider me. I am too old and would rather not serve."

The seconds ticked by, turning into minutes as the Electors sat silently in the chapel. The presence of Bishop Neraz loomed over them. The future of their Congregation rested in their hands.

Finally, Mother stood again and said in a low tone, "Vote for Sister Florence." She then turned and walked out of the chapel and onto the veranda.

"Children," she began, "I can no longer be your mother." At this her voice broke and she went quietly back into the house.

In the chapel, the Electors balloted. Sister Mary Agnes announced the results: "Sister Mary Florence, 23 votes; Sister Angelique, 3 votes; Sister Regina, 1 vote; Sister Mary Ange, 1 vote; Sister Arsene, 1 vote."

"Thank you, Sisters. Please kneel now for my blessing," Bishop Neraz said, concluding the business. After imparting his blessing, the bishop departed for San Antonio.

The next day, Bishop Neraz and Father Pefferkorn met the train from Galveston into San Antonio to convey to Sister Florence the news of her new position in the Congregation. Upon her arrival in La Coste, a stunned Sister Florence was met by a number of wagons to take her and her recruits to Providence House.

The entourage arrived late into the night, and Mother St. Andrew met them at the door, warmly welcoming the young girls. "Girls,"

**Mother Florence Walter,
Second Superior General,
Sisters of Divine Providence
of Texas; circa 1900.
(Courtesy, Congregational
Archives)**

she said smiling, "I'm afraid I've misplaced my glasses! I can't tell one of you from the other, but I will sort you out in the morning when I can see. Please know that you are most welcome!"

After the young girls were dispatched into the care of seasoned Candidates, Mother St. Andrew and their newly elected Superior General walked arm-in arm to Mother St. Andrew's office.

Embracing her Superior and mentor, Sister Florence said, "Mother, I am so sorry. I don't know what to say." The tears on Mother St. Andrew's cheeks, the first she had shed since the day before, mingled with those of her new Superior's as they fell sadly into one another's arms.

CHAPTER XVI

ESTRANGED

Sister St. Andrew and Mother Florence spent a long night sorting out what had happened at Providence House the few days before Mother Florence returned from Europe. When she heard first-hand Mother's account of her interrogation by Fathers Pefferkorn, Maloney, and Feith, Mother Florence was aghast.

"I knew that Father Pefferkorn was upset by Father Kirch's account of what happened with Sister Christine in New Braunfels; but, Mother, I simply had no idea things would go that far! How did you manage?" Mother Florence's heart went out to her beloved superior who had gone alone into the "lion's den."

"Sister Mary Ange accompanied me into San Antonio. She was well aware of the intricacies of the situation in New Braunfels, and I knew that I could trust her implicitly. The priests never questioned her, however. And, I must say, the questions, which had been provided by Bishop Neraz, were grueling. His Lordship questioned my way of administering the Congregation, my advice in general to our Sisters about priests, and my specific admonitions to Sister Christine regarding her familiarities with Father Kirch. I felt simply wrung-out by the event. Though I answered each question honestly, I was certain that the end result was decided beforehand; it would not rely on what I said at all. Of course, that is exactly what happened. The priests rallied around Kirch, demanding of the bishop my resignation. He acted upon their demand and required that we hold an election. You know the result."

462

"I never should have gone to Europe. I should have been here. Perhaps I could have prevailed upon Father Pefferkorn to be more sensible about Father Kirch's accusations. Do you have a copy of the questions asked?" Mother Florence's voice revealed how shaken she was by what she had just heard.

"No, they did not give me a copy of the questions," Mother answered frankly.

"Tell me about the election, Mother. Exactly how did I get elected?" Mother Florence continued. She still did not believe what had transpired.

Mother recounted that the Bishop rejected the first two ballots because they had supported Mother St. Andrew's re-election. She then recalled how the other Sisters with perpetual vows declined to be considered. "Even though you don't have perpetual vows, you were the best choice, Sister. Regardless of how you were elected, I know that you have the abilities to lead and, more importantly, that His Lordship will work with you. The future of our congregation here in Texas is in jeopardy, and I believe that you have the temperament to deal with His Lordship in a positive way. He simply maneuvered the situation so that he would never again have to work with me." Sister St. Andrew had tried to couch her telling of all that had happened in a way that would encourage Mother Florence in her new work, as well as not derail Mother Florence's future relationship with Bishop Neraz. The events of the summer of 1886 had taught Mother St. Andrew that this Bishop would not deal with them as Bishops Dubuis and Pellicer had; she knew that the Sisters of Divine Providence would need to be cautious with their ecclesiastical superior.

"When His Lordship met our train in San Antonio, he gave me this." She handed Sister St. Andrew an envelope.

The enclosed letter, dated August 27, 1886, noted that Mother Florence must plan to make her perpetual profession "as soon as possible," and that she was not to name her Council and secretary until he had returned to the Motherhouse after September 3. He also indicated that he would be at Castroville the next day, Saturday, August 28, to preside over the new Superior's installation.

"So, he's coming back tomorrow?" Sister St. Andrew said with surprise. "He is certainly in a hurry to finalize your position."

Both nuns, one exhausted from months of travel and one exhausted from emotional travail, sat silently for some time. Finally, Sister St. Andrew said, "My dear, it is after midnight. There is nothing more that we can do. I will help you in any way that I can. Tomorrow this office will be yours. I will happily acquaint you with what we have on file. For now, let's go to bed."

Beginning to feel the great burden of the mantle of leadership, the young Superior nodded tearfully. "Very well, Mother" were the only words she could utter.

Upon his arrival just after noon the next day, the bishop asked that all the Sisters assemble in the chapel. Almost everyone was there—about 100 or so—counting the postulants, novices, and newly admitted candidates; a few Sisters had remained at their missions.

The bishop opened with the *Veni Creator Spiritus*, the traditional prayer of the Church calling upon the grace and guidance of the Holy Spirit. He then formally introduced Mother Florence as the new Superior General and said, "Sisters, I ask each of you now to give your pledge of obedience to Mother Florence. She has been properly elected. The sign that you render to her your obedience will be your coming forth, one by one, to kiss her hand. Should you choose not to acknowledge this election, I will take the Blessed Sacrament from your house and do away with your convent. It is that simple."[*]

Solemnly, each Sister came forward. The young Mother Florence extended a trembling hand which each one took and, bending forward, kissed ever so gently. The tender looks that fell on the new Superior pledged much more to her than religious obedience. The last one to come forward was Sister St. Andrew. Nearly fifty-six

---

[*]   **This account of what happened is based on the memoirs of Sister Leonille Hartnagel, CDP, who came with Mother Florence from Europe in August 1886.**

years old, her shoulders were still square under the broad *guimpe* and her back was straight. Choosing to ignore the presence of the bishop, Mother kept her eyes on her successor, pausing momentarily before the woman whom she had brought to Texas in 1880. Mother Florence extended her hand which Sister St. Andrew took and reverently kissed. Then, without a word, the outgoing superior embraced the young nun and kissed her on both cheeks. Tears filled the eyes of those gathered in this makeshift chapel. They would seldom speak of this day, but it was forever etched on the heart of the shaken Congregation.

After tho ɔhoi l installation ceremony, the Bishop led Mother Florence alone into the superior's office. After explaining to her how he intended to conduct the business of the Congregation, he took a few minutes to go through the papers that Mother St. Andrew had neatly filed, taking out Mother St. Andrew's correspondence and the minutes of various meetings of her council. Mother Florence stood speechless as she watched the history of her community being crammed into the Bishop's valise.^ᐯ And then he was gone.

In the next days, without an installed Council with which to consult, Mother Florence met with the consultors whom Mother St. Andrew had relied upon: Sisters Mary Agnes Wolf, Angelique Decker, Mary Ange Huvar, Mary Paul Keller, and Arsene Schaff. They agreed to help her maintain the Congregation on an even keel and pledged her their support. They further advised her to consult

---

ᐯ   **The lore of the Sisters of Divine Providence of Texas includes a story of Bishop Neraz burning their records on the front lawn of the Castroville Motherhouse after Mother Florence's installation. Neither Callahan nor Neeb carry an account of this. However, there are no extant records of Mother St. Andrew's correspondence with Mother Constantine; there are no extant records of any of Mother St. Andrew's correspondence; there are no minutes of General Council meetings before August 1886. The Congregation of Divine Providence cannot account for the missing documents.**

with Sister St. Andrew who had knowledge and understanding of the intricacies of Congregational administration that they did not. Sister Mary Ange agreed to continue to serve as Mistress of Novices and began to interview each newly admitted European candidate to determine each one's educational background and understanding of religious life.

A sense of uncertainty and trepidation settled over the Castroville Motherhouse. The air would not clear until His Lordship had returned to affirm a Council. And perhaps not even then.

In one of their many conversations, Sister St. Andrew and Mother Florence discussed the status of the Texas Congregation in terms of St. Jean-de-Bassel. "I believe that His Lordship has now completed our separation from St. Jean-de-Bassel. We shall never know what correspondence he continued with Mother Constantine since his visit to St. Jean in 1883 and now that she is gone ... well, we shall never know," Sister St. Andrew said with sadness.

"I found Mother Anna very welcoming," the new Superior General said. "I was not treated as a guest at the Motherhouse. I felt that I was at home. Mother Anna was eager to hear of our progress in Texas and was very encouraging. I know that my visit with her was not an official one—like one she would have had with you; but, nevertheless, she was more than cordial. And, of course, she allowed me to talk to the girls at St. Jean with the full understanding that I was intending to recruit them for Texas. I had the girls from the villages meet at St. Jean-de-Bassel as we prepared to leave for Texas. There seemed to be no problem with that. In my mind, I was at our Motherhouse talking with our Superior General," Mother Florence said with a puzzled look. "I don't know what to make of all of this."

"Be circumspect and be careful, Sister," Sister St. Andrew advised. "His Lordship could disband us and place us with other local Congregations."

Mother Florence chose not to tell her former superior that His Lordship had mentioned that possibility in his conversation with her after her installation. "Do you wish a role in the new Council?" Mother Florence asked innocently, still not quite comprehending Bishop Neraz's disdain for Sister St. Andrew.

"Oh, daughter! His Lordship would never tolerate that. I'm certain that he wants me to go far away! I will take whatever assignment you wish to give me. Just remember that I am growing old," she said, trying to inject humor into a humorless situation.

"Wherever you wish to go, Mother, we will send you. You think it over and let me know." Now beginning to understand how alone she would be, Mother Florence, had tears in her brown eyes.

"Now, now, dear. No tears. There may be much bigger things to cry about in the future. Save your tears for later." Sister St. Andrew had no idea how prophetic her words were.

Bishop Neraz returned to Castroville on September 4 and, with Mother Florence, named a new council: Sister Arsene Schaff, Sister Stanislas Kostka Piwonka, Sister Angelique Decker, Sister Agnes Wolf, Sister Mary Pierre Hetzel, and Sister Mary Paul Keller.

In a private conversation with Mother Florence, the bishop crystallized his intentions, making her situation very clear.

"Now, Mother. There are a few things we need to clarify. First, I will happily receive your perpetual vows in the near future. You and your council may determine a few possible dates, and then I will choose one depending on my availability. Secondly, you are quite young and inexperienced. I will lend you my understanding of the subtleties of a position such as yours and will expect you to consult with me regularly and frequently. For a while, it would be quite imprudent for you to make decisions without my advice and consent. The priests of this diocese expect us to cooperate. Thirdly, my first advice is that you send Sister St. Andrew somewhere where she might have the least possible influence on the workings of the Congregation and on the lives of the Sisters. I leave that to your discretion; but should she remain near Castroville, the priests will believe that you are not to be trusted. Is that clear?"

"Yes, Your Lordship. I now understand," was Mother Florence's terse reply. But she instinctively knew that her voice must carry a sense of both propriety and warmth. She needed his confidence for the sake of the Congregation.

"Now, I must leave, but I will return in a week or so to see how things are going." The bishop picked up his valise, adding, "And, Mother, I will expect to review any correspondence that you receive. Sister St. Andrew seldom shared correspondence with me, but I do not plan to maintain the same distance from your operations that your predecessor preferred." His curt tone revealed his feelings for Sister St. Andrew. Mother Florence wisely said nothing as he left her office for the front door where his buggy awaited him.

That night Sister St. Andrew had a long visit with Sister Arsene. Having made vows together at St. Jean-de-Bassel in 1855, they had maintained a respectful and enduring friendship. Now they were perfectly honest with each other.

"I don't like any of this," Sister Arsene began. "We are under siege and I dare say that Mother Florence has no idea what is really happening!"

"Now, Sister, let's try to remain calm. Mother Florence is young, but she is smart. After she figures out His Lordship's way, I believe that she will eventually learn to deal with him in a way that will save the Congregation from being dispersed. We have reached a precipice. Only Providence can save us."

"But, Mother, you always said, 'Help yourself and Heaven will help you.'* What shall we do to help ourselves in this predicament? We simply cannot sit back and let His Lordship prevail!"

"I have a few thoughts; but first, we must take some time to pray. I want to be certain that I am seeing all of this as God sees it. For me, the worst calamity is that we are now canonically separated from St. Jean-de-Bassel. I am trying to imagine a way to repair that breech.

---

*   **This proverb is found in Mother St. Andrew's October 27, 1886, letter to Bishop Neraz.**

After we have had time to pray, I will talk over my thoughts with you," Sister St. Andrew said with a thoughtful look in her eyes.

Both Sisters took the disturbances in their hearts to prayer and then found each other again the next day.

"Soon I must tell Mother Florence where I wish to be sent. I believe that I will ask to be sent to St. Joseph's in Galveston," Sister St. Andrew said.

"What a wonderful idea. I have so loved Galveston. But, Mother, the climate there may not be good for your arthritis. Have you thought of that?" Sister Arsene recalled that when Mother St. Andrew was in Galveston she ached all over whenever a storm brewed.

"I know. But I really have some other ideas that I want to discuss with you. Do you remember when I came to Galveston about five years ago—before Bishop Dubuis retired—and we set down on paper that the convent in Frelsburg was to be considered a branch novitiate?"

"Yes, of course. Bishop Dubuis was so pleased to think that we would open a novitiate of ours in his diocese. He spoke of it several times with us before he left for France," Sister Arsene said.

"I have been thinking. Since Frelsburg is not in the Diocese of San Antonio, perhaps a novitiate there could be considered separate from Castroville; as such, it could be connected to St. Jean-de-Bassel. I wish I knew canon law more explicitly. But I have no one to ask because whichever priest I ask will certainly convey my question to Bishop Neraz. Perhaps after I get to Galveston, I can find counsel with Bishop Gallagher. What do you think?" Sister St. Andrew had begun to sound hopeful. She went on, not waiting for a reply from Sister Arsene. "Even if Frelsburg becomes separate from Castroville, I will always work supportively with Mother Florence. Both houses can be mutually cooperative. Much like St. Jean-de-Bassel and Portieux were in our earliest days. But everything will depend on Bishop Gallagher. What do you think he will say?"

"I believe that he will be positive toward the arrangement. In truth, we are only separating the few Sisters at St. Joseph's, Frelsburg,

Ellinger, and Columbus—those in the Diocese of Galveston. The great majority of Sisters will remain with Castroville. It just might work," Sister Arsene replied thoughtfully.

"Good. Then I will ask to be sent to Galveston. And I will write to Mother Anna tonight. I suspect that she has no idea what has transpired here in the last two weeks. However, since I am not the Superior General, my correspondence will not be considered official; and I dare say that Mother Florence should not write to Mother Anna. If Bishop Neraz ever learned that our young Superior had begun a correspondence with Germany, dire consequences could ensue."

"I couldn't agree more. I will not discuss with Mother Florence anything that we have shared. We must not compromise her relationship with Bishop Neraz. He has threatened to disband us, and I believe he'll do it if he does not get his way."

Sister St. Andrew went to Galveston where she began negotiations with Bishop Gallagher to activate the Frelsburg novitiate. Though the Bishop of Galveston was most amenable to establishing a novitiate of the Sisters of Divine Providence in his diocese, he knew that, as a courtesy, he needed the approval of Bishop Neraz and urged Sister St. Andrew to write to Bishop Neraz asking for his support.

In the meantime, Sister Arsene found her work on the Council in Castroville limiting and lacking in vitality. Meetings were irregular and could only be official if Bishop Neraz were present. Within the first two weeks of September, she spoke frankly with Mother Florence, indicating that she would appreciate being able to return to Galveston to continue her teaching there, returning to Castroville again at Christmas as councilors had done during Sister St. Andrew's tenure. Mother Florence reluctantly allowed Sister Arsene to leave Castroville, but noted that Sister Arsene's decision to return to Galveston could not be approved since Bishop Neraz was not available to confirm it.

Once His Lordship learned that Sister Arsene had returned to Galveston, assuming that Sister St. Andrew would have undue influence on his Congregation's First Assistant, Neraz required Mother Florence to call her back to her duties on the Council in Castroville. Sister Arsene remained in Galveston.

Realizing that not all the Sisters in Galveston supported her plan, Sister St. Andrew spoke to them about future possibilities. "Sisters," Sister St. Andrew said to the Sisters at St. Joseph, arguing her case, "if we establish a new novitiate here in the Galveston diocese, then we can remain connected to St. Jean-de-Bassel and continue as we have in the past. We will always support Mother Florence, but the Castroville motherhouse is now a diocesan congregation under Bishop Neraz."

The Sisters at St. Joseph's School in Galveston wrote to Bishop Neraz, believing that clarity of their relationship with the Castroville Congregation was imperative. The September 24, 1886, letter noted that the writers were resigning their membership in the Castroville group, asking pardon for any trouble His Lordship had endured due to their actions, and asking Bishop Neraz to support the establishment of a new novitiate near the St. Joseph School property in Galveston.

With the exception of Sister Arsene, all of the other Sisters at St. Joseph had annual vows and had not been in Castroville at the time of the election. They were unaware of the causes and the consequences of the election of August 26. Since not all the Sisters at St. Joseph were willing to sign the letter to Bishop Neraz, a general signature was applied to the letter in order to maintain the integrity of the Galveston community should the San Antonio bishop refuse his support.

Bishop Neraz refused his consent to the establishment of a Galveston novitiate and Bishop Gallagher withdrew his hospitality.

"Now I have no idea what to do," Sister St. Andrew admitted to Sister Arsene. By withholding his approval, I fear that Bishop Neraz has indicted me, and now Bishop Gallagher will be suspect of my intentions. I have no idea what the two may have said in correspondence. But I know what the Bishop of San Antonio thinks of me. Priests in both dioceses will now consider me a pariah!"

"That thinking is quite extreme, Mother, but I won't argue with you. You'll have to stay here in Galveston, I suppose. Can you manage?"

"My aching bones tell me 'no'; there must be a hurricane brewing. The pain in my head is almost nauseating, but our dear Savior suffered so much worse. I'll unite my sufferings with His for the good of our Congregation. I can do no less."

However, within a few days, Sister St. Andrew and Sister Arsene, having resigned from the Castroville Congregation, decided to try one more option.

While Superior General, Sister St. Andrew had received a letter from Father Peter Stöters, pastor of St. Boniface Church in Anaheim, California. The small village of Anaheim was settled in the 1850's by immigrant German vintners from Westphalia, and by the 1880's its commerce relied heavily on its famous vineyards. Extending over all of Orange County, St. Boniface Parish had been officially established in 1875. Upon his coming to St. Boniface Parish in early 1886, Father Stöters began to consider the needs of his growing parish and decided to write to a number of religious orders of Sisters hoping to entice some group to begin a school in his parish. His letter to Mother St. Andrew had painted an attractive picture of a bustling parish: a new wood-frame church, German immigrants hungry for faith development, lots of children who needed preparation for the sacraments as well as a secular education, and families with whom Sisters could live until a convent could be prepared. He had no money to offer, but pledged his support.

Perhaps California would offer hope for the future of the Sisters of Divine Providence of St. Jean-de-Bassel in America. Though all the Sisters at St. Joseph could not support a new Congregation sepa-

St. Boniface Church, Anaheim, CA, c. 1885.
(Courtesy, Most Rev. Donald Montrose.)

rate from Castroville, their hearts went out to their former Superior General who seemed to be "without a country." Trying to help, they loaned the two nuns the money for train tickets. On October 11, 1886, Sister St. Andrew and Sister Arsene boarded the Southern Pacific railroad in Houston and made their way to southern California.

After meeting them at the depot in Anaheim, Father Stöters escorted the two nuns to the home of Peter and Mary Stoeffel who had offered the nuns hospitality in their small house on Center Street near St. Boniface Church. The Stoeffels had moved to Anaheim from Iowa, but were originally from Luxembourg, Germany. The two Alsatians felt immediately at home with their host-family and had a lively exchange of news about their families in Germany. Mary especially was excited about nuns with a German background coming to Anaheim. She and Peter had a growing family, and they had been urging Father Stöters to find some nuns who could open a Catholic school.

It didn't take Sister St. Andrew and Sister Arsene long to realize that Anaheim would be a perfect place for a school for the Sisters of Divine Providence of St. Jean-de-Bassel. The needs were great; the people were open to their coming; German-speakers would be well received; and the climate was ideal. After only a few days in southern California, Sister St. Andrew felt invigorated without any aches or pains. Surrounded by acres of vineyards, the residential area of Anaheim reminded Sister St. Andrew of her early days in

Heiligenberg where small plots of vines were interlaced among the village houses. The few lemon and walnut groves provided variety. Yes, Sister St. Andrew thought, this location is ideal!

By October 24 Sister Arsene and Sister St. Andrew had returned to Castroville where they asked for hospitality and a conference with Mother Florence to ask for candidates who would help begin a school in Anaheim. St. Jean-de-Bassel had always been generous with vocations for the Texas mission. Sister St. Andrew just assumed that Castroville would assist a St. Jean-de-Bassel foundation in California.

With Mother Florence away on visitation, Sister Mary Ange was hesitant about handling the unique situation alone. Bishop Neraz's way of dealing with congregational business left little room for independent decisions. The Mistress of Novices informed her former Superior General and fellow council member that both were considered to be "disobedient" and had been placed under an edict of excommunication.* In her opinion, she said, their best recourse was to write to Bishop Neraz as soon as possible asking for his pardon. The two nuns were shocked to realize that their resignation from the Castroville Congregation had not been accepted. Not wanting to jeopardize the well-being of the Castroville Congregation, they complied with Sister Mary Ange's directive. They wrote Bishop Neraz asking for hospitality at the Castroville Motherhouse and for a lifting of the edict of excommunication in time for them to receive the sacraments on the Feast of All Saints and All Souls on November 1 and 2.

After penning the letter of apology, the two Sisters talked over their situation. Without Bishop Neraz's approval, they realized that the pastor of St. Boniface would not accept them.

---

*   **Excommunication is a censure of a Catholic handed down by a bishop which prohibits the excommunicated individual from receiving Holy Communion (and usually the Sacrament of Reconciliation [confession]) at any time. Only the bishop who hands down the censure can reinstate the excommunicated person.**

"I feel quite uneasy about our predicament. I had no idea that the Bishop would do something as drastic as excommunication, although he is within his canonical rights," Sister Arsene said nervously. "Is there something more we should do?"

Realizing that their immortal souls were in jeopardy, Sister St. Andrew replied, "I will write another letter. I will try to explain why we went to California, how I have no confidence that priests will accept me in any of the schools in either the Diocese of Galveston or the Diocese of San Antonio. I can do nothing more than to throw myself on the mercy of His Lordship and trust in Providence. Should Bishop Neraz fail us, either we will have to return to Germany or humbly ask for re-admittance to this Congregation, taking whatever assignment Mother Florence will give us—if she will have us." The tremor in her soft voice indicated that her fear for their future was quite real.

Bishop Neraz extended the hospitality of the Castroville convent to the two nuns. But he refused to lift the edict of excommunication without assurance from Mother Florence that they had repaid the money that he believed they had stolen from the Congregation to buy their train tickets to California. Obedience to Mother Florence in all matters was required as well.

Upon her return to Castroville during the first week of November 1886, Mother Florence was surprised to find Sister St. Andrew and Sister Arsene at the convent. She immediately set about trying to understand how they had decided to travel to California. All agreed that their best recourse was to re-establish Sister St. Andrew's and Sister Arsene's membership in the Texas Congregation. The Sisters also agreed that a number of actions would be needed to assure Bishop Neraz that Sister St. Andrew and Sister Arsene were in compliance with his wishes.

Within a few days, the bishop came personally to Castroville to interview the two Sisters—whom he considered to be disobedient—to determine if they were deserving of his approbation. He accepted their apology and agreed that they could be re-instated in the Congregation and re-admitted to the Table of the Lord if they would agree to obey Mother Florence in all things and return the money they had taken from the Congregation for their travel costs to California. He further instructed Sister St. Andrew to write to the Diocese of Los Angeles explaining that Sisters of Divine Providence would not be sending Sisters to that diocese at this time. Mother Florence had prevailed upon her ecclesiastical superior to "leave the door open" so that in the future Sisters might be welcomed in southern California.

Thus a series of letters were posted from Castroville.

On November 6, Sister St. Andrew wrote to California indicating that Bishop Neraz was not prepared to send Sisters to Anaheim at this time, but that *"it would be better to prepare us for the next school session."**

On November 7, Mother Florence wrote to Bishop Neraz:

> *Sister St. Andrew fulfilled all the conditions proposed to her by His Lordship viz: She gave back to the Mother House all the objects she had in possession, and she will return the money as soon as possible; further is she ready to leave the Convent Wednesday the 10th inst for Clarksville. This being signed by*
>
> *Sr Mary Florence*
> *Gen. Sup.* *

Bishop Neraz wrote a note to Mother Florence on November 8 indicating that he would not rescind the edict of excommunication until she had assured him that all monies had been repaid.

On November 10, Mother wrote to Neraz:

---

* **Actual letter**

*Sister St. Andrew has reimbursed the money,
viz., four hundred and five dollars the ninth
of this current month to the treasury of the
Congregation.*

*Sr Mary Florence
Sup Gen* *

On that same Wednesday, November 10, 1886, Sister St. Andrew
left Castroville for Clarksville, Texas, and Sister Arsene was sent to
nearby Haby's Settlement.

Clarksville, Texas, in the far northeastern corner of Texas near
the Red River, was in the Diocese of Galveston in 1886. Begun by
a Sister of the Holy Cross of Notre Dame, IN, in 1879, St. Joseph's
School in Clarksville had remained small and the Holy Cross Sisters
under Father Edward Sorin, CSC, eventually decided to close the
school in 1883. Without Sisters the parish was unable to keep their
school going and the Sisters of Divine Providence were approached
to staff the school in 1885.

Sisters Regina Becker, Patrick Morrissey, Evangelist Kiernan and
Helena Kaiser who re-opened the school in September 1885, found
the first months to be a struggle. The school building was in disrepair; the convent was lacking in necessities. The school was the farthest distance from Castroville—about 450 miles—of any school the
Sisters served at the time.

When she joined the Sisters at St. Joseph's in Clarksville in
November 1886, Sister St. Andrew experienced a difficult transition.
Confined to a classroom in a challenging school in a village far from
Castroville and Galveston, Sister St. Andrew did not adjust well.
The children in her classroom seemed unruly. She found the other
two Sisters to be welcoming; but since she had been their Superior
General during their entire time in the Congregation, their relation-

* **Actual letter**

ship was guarded and distant. By the beginning of December 1886, Sister St. Andrew wrote to Bishop Neraz asking him to identify her options.

His Lordship's return letter outlined her plight. She could remain in Clarksville, return to St. Jean-de-Bassel, or leave the Congregation altogether.

Over the next months Sister St. Andrew's prayer centered on the meaning of her limited possibilities. Father Moye's life and the early experiences of the founding Sisters inspired her to remain hopeful and his advice directed her thoughts. She remembered Marie Morel's[V] story: the many humiliations and contradictions that laced her life and the way her zeal and courage in spreading the gospel everywhere allowed her to overcome all obstacles.[∞] However, it was Father Moye's experience with his bishop that sustained her darkest hour. *"The bishop ... forbade me to open new schools ... I was reduced to a sort of agony ..."*[▲]

Yes, she thought in prayer, this is an agony. I cannot go forward; I cannot go backward. And then she remembered: it was while under duress just as this that Father Moye had achieved some of his finest and most creative work.

Still believing that California would be a haven for her, Sister St. Andrew sent Father Stöters a Christmas letter intending to encourage his continued openness to the service of the Sisters of Divine Providence in his parish. His response received after the new year kindled her hope.

In January and February the situation in Clarksville only seemed more difficult. Never having known their ex-Superior General as a fellow Sister, the other four Sisters were at a loss as to how to console her. She seemed so bereft! Not wishing to slander their ecclesiastical superior, Sister St. Andrew said nothing to her community com-

---

V   **First Superior of the Sisters of Providence (late 18th century France)**

∞   The Directory, p. 350

▲   The Directory, p. 341

panions about Bishop Neraz and the edict of excommunication he had imposed upon her. It would not be good to expose these younger members of the Congregation to the inner turmoil that she was suffering. She tried desperately to follow Father Moye's advice: *"Love your enemies sincerely, pray for them, do good to them; hold no resentment against them and speak only well of them."* *

Every road open to her seemed terrifying. Remaining in Clarksville for the rest of the school year and returning to Castroville in June might place both herself and Mother Florence in an untenable situation. Sisters might rally around her in a way that could threaten Mother Florence's authority. Leaving Clarksville and going alone to California would surely disappoint Mother Florence and might create an irreparable breech in their relationship.

If she decided to return to California, however, Sister St. Andrew promised herself that she would not entice anyone to accompany her. If she decided to take this drastic step, she would take it alone.

Finally, Sister St. Andrew admitted to herself in prayer that she was afraid of Bishop Neraz. Her recent experience of excommunication told her how he would wield his power. There was simply no good path.

With summer approaching, Sister St. Andrew felt compelled to act soon. The welfare of the Congregation, she reasoned, would be more secure if she did not return to Castroville for the summer homecoming and retreat. Perhaps it would be less jarring if she simply left Clarksville quietly in the spring.

As Ash Wednesday drew near, Sister St. Andrew's prayer became more intense. I will storm heaven during the Lenten Season, she promised herself. Surely, God will give me an answer. I realize more each day that I cannot continue this charade forever. I must be a daughter of Father Moye. I must be courageous. I must depend upon Providence alone.

The Sisters who lived with her knew that she was under tremendous stress and they talked with one another about how they might

---

* **The Directory,** p. 210.

comfort their former Superior General. No one could have been a better superior, they agreed. Though she had a bit of a temper and was strict with them in terms of living the Rule, still she was always fair and wanted only what was best for the Congregation. "Mother Florence has a great deal to live up to," they whispered to each other as they watched Sister St. Andrew suffer silently.

True to her promise, Sister St. Andrew prayed arduously. Each day of Lent she spent not less than an hour with the Blessed Sacrament. The deprivation that she experienced while she was under the edict of excommunication gave her a renewed sense of love and awe for the presence of Jesus in the Eucharist. She received communion each day that they were allowed to approach the communion railing; she went to confession weekly. Deep within her wounded heart, she knew that only the grace of God could sustain her, regardless of which path God would call her to take.

By the middle of Lent, she had made her decision. It would be better to return to California where Father Stöters had so many needs in his parish. She felt that she was following explicitly Father Moye's directive: ***"Abandon yourselves completely to God; put all your confidence in God and not in others."*** [v] But still she was very afraid. Objectively, going to California would be a direct act of disobedience. In her heart of hearts, however, she no longer truly belonged to the Castroville Congregation. While the Congregation was under Bishop Neraz, Mother Florence would have no recourse except to send her to faraway villages like Clarksville. Perhaps if she were as far away as California, Bishop Neraz would release her and she could start over there as a Sister of Divine Providence of St. Jean-de-Bassel. Following this path would take a depth of abandonment to Divine Providence that she was not certain she possessed.

Remembering the terror that she experienced when Sister Clemens disappeared from Solms in 1883, she wrote to Sister Arsene explaining her plans and telling her to inform Mother Florence "when it is convenient." When she had left Castroville, the Christilles family

---

∇   **The Directory, p. 178.**

had given her a little money as a going away gift. Father Stöters had agreed to send her a ticket if she would come. She had lived on less in the past; she would manage. The pastor of St. Boniface had written that his parishioners were insistent that he find some Sisters to come and he wanted to assure Sister St. Andrew that she was welcome at any time.

Once she was in Anaheim, Father Stöters helped Sister St. Andrew to get settled with the Stoeffels. Mary was expecting another child; and, if Sister didn't mind helping a bit with laundry and housework, they would happily give her room and board until permanent arrangements could be made.

Father had been holding catechism classes for twenty twelve-year-olds who were almost ready for their First Communion. He happily turned over their final preparations to Sister St. Andrew who seemed to know exactly how to proceed. Sister also volunteered to direct the decorating of St. Boniface Church for Holy Thursday and Easter. Though there were many ladies who belonged to the Altar Society, they needed guidance. This was Father Stöters' first Easter at St. Boniface, and he was at a loss on how to get everything ready. Instructing them on exactly how much starch to use and how to iron the fabrics to meet canonical requirements, Sister St. Andrew distributed the various altar clothes and linens to the volunteers.

Then she spoke candidly with Father Stöters. "Father, I am so happy to be here, but I am here under false pretenses. I suspect that you believe my Superior General has sent me. That is not true. I have informed her that I have come here, but I do not have her permission. The Bishop of San Antonio will not support my coming here, and Mother Florence is completely dependent on his advice and consent for all Congregational decisions. She must do everything he says."

"This is serious, Sister. I am pleased with your work and I need you here. But this situation is outside my jurisdiction." In his first pastorate, Father Stöters found himself over his head with the situation which the Alsatian nun had outlined. "What do you propose?"

"I want to write to Sister Arsene to ask her if she would be willing to join me here. I know that she won't come without Mother Florence's permission. If she comes, it could mean that Mother Florence has given tacit approval. Are you willing to support this and purchase a train ticket for Sister Arsene?" Sister St. Andrew's voice revealed her own lack of confidence in her idea.

More desperate for help than confident in Sister St Andrew's plan, the pastor agreed. "Very well, Sister. Sister Arsene is welcome. Write your letter."

When Sister Arsene received her invitation to join Sister St. Andrew in Anaheim, she went immediately to Mother Florence to ask her permission.

"I don't know, Sister," Mother Florence said cautiously. "I wish Sister St. Andrew had not gone to Anaheim, although there is no doubt that she will never be sent anywhere other than Clarksville. Bishop Neraz is adamant about that. He insisted that she be sent as far away as possible—but never to California."

"But Mother," Sister Arsene said pleadingly to her young Superior, "Sister St. Andrew should not be alone in California. In a way she no longer considers herself to be a member of this Congregation, but she may not be clear herself on how to respond to the designs of Providence. She will trust me."

"I agree. Someone should be with her. However, Bishop Neraz no longer trusts you either, Sister. If you go, perhaps you should leave behind your profession ring and rosary. I can then assure His Lordship that you are no longer affiliated with us."

"Do you mean I will not have vows?" Sister Arsene was shocked. "I could never consent to that!"

"No, no. I'm really not certain at all about that, and I confess I do not know whom to ask. To ask His Lordship only exposes us to his ire. If His Lordship withdraws his trust from me, he will definitely place us under a Sister from Santa Rosa Hospital. I will do everything in my power to keep that from happening. I need you to help me." Mother Florence sounded desperate.

"I'll do everything you say, Mother. But I remain loyal to Sister St. Andrew." Sister Arsene felt caught. Her vow of obedience required allegiance to Mother Florence and Bishop Neraz; her heart, however, would never turn away from her former Superior and lifelong companion in religious life.

With Mother Florence's unspoken support, Sister Arsene took the train from La Coste to Anaheim to join Sister St. Andrew in parish work at St. Boniface, leaving her profession ring and rosary with her Superior as requested.

Peter and Mary Stoeffels welcomed a second German Sister into their small bungalow home on Center Street. The Sisters took turns cooking their favorite cultural dishes. With plates of sausages, pork chops, sauerkraut, and boiled potatoes frequenting the Stoeffels' table, Peter Stoeffels looked forward to coming home from the vineyards each night. Mary was in the earliest months of her pregnancy and often felt ill. She and Peter were grateful for the two German nuns who seemed to have unbounded energy as they provided catechism lessons for the parish children on Saturdays, took care of flowers in the church, helped with washing and ironing in the Stoeffels home, and even found time to bake an occasional *kugelhopf*. The real almonds and raisins that could be obtained in California provided their Alsatian dessert cake with an authenticity that was impossible in Texas.

After Easter, Father Stöters called the two Sisters to the rectory. His demeanor was serious.

"Sisters, I am so grateful to you both. But the time has come to set things straight. Father Adam, our vicar-general, suggests that we need to be certain of your bishop's approval before our own bishop returns from Rome. Father Adam has received a letter from Bishop Gallagher in Galveston and Gallagher's letter seems to indicate that there is a problem with you, Sister St. Andrew." Stöters was trying to be kind, but he knew that he had to be honest.

"I knew that this could not last. You have been very gracious, Father. We don't want to cause you any trouble. What do you suggest?" Sister St. Andrew appreciated this priest and was sincere in her remarks.

"I think that your Superior in Castroville should write Father Adam explaining your situation."

"I will write to her, Father, asking that she explain who we are and why we are here," volunteered Sister Arsene.

The letter that Mother Florence wrote to Father Adam only created more disparity. In her brief letter, written after consulting Bishop Neraz, she outlined that Sister St. Andrew's actions had severed her relationship with the Congregation and that "Miss Barbara Schaff" no longer belonged to the Congregation either. In her second paragraph, Mother Florence indicated that the Sisters of Divine Providence were still interested in supplying Sisters for schools in the Diocese of Los Angeles.

Once the contents of the letter had been conveyed to Father Stöters, he informed the two religious of their situation. They were no longer considered to be members of the Sisters of Divine Providence of Castroville. The bishop of Los Angeles would never approve of their work in his diocese if they were not in good stead with a religious congregation.

"What shall we do, Father," Sister St. Andrew said, close to tears.

"You yourself can write to Father Adam, I suppose. It's worth a try." Father Stöters actually had little hope, but was unwilling to send the nuns away without looking into every possible way to keep them.

Sister St. Andrew wrote the letter to Father Adam asking him to reconsider his order that she and Sister Arsene leave the Diocese of Los Angeles.

As First Communion Day at St. Boniface approached, Father Stöters had become hopeful that the vicar general was planning on allowing the Sisters to remain. Sister St. Andrew and Sister Arsene had done a superior job in preparing his parish children. When he quizzed the first communicants on their catechism before First Communion Day, the pastor was very pleased with how much the children knew. The Altar Society, under the direction of the Sisters, had decorated the church tastefully. Never had the parents of first communicants been prouder than they were on Ascension Thursday in 1887 as they filled the pews of St. Boniface's new church. Dressed in white and carrying white candles recalling the day of their baptisms, the twenty children processed down the main aisle and knelt reverently in the front pews. All were attentive and prayerful as Sister St. Andrew knelt at the end of the first pew and Sister Arsene at the end of the second pew. Parents and parishioners thanked the Sisters profusely for the work they were doing at St. Boniface.

But June brought only bad news.

Father Stöters received a letter from the vicar-general rescinding his faculties to hear the confessions of the two "disobedient" women from Castroville, Texas. No attempt at negotiating their position changed the fact that the two nuns were expected to leave Anaheim as soon as possible.

At the end of July 1887, both nuns wrote to Bishop Neraz in a last attempt to get his approval to establish the Sisters of Divine Providence in Anaheim. They received no answer, and by August 4 they were back in Castroville.

Mother Florence, unable to offer the two Sisters a haven in the community, assisted Sister Arsene to make arrangements for her return to St. Jean-de-Bassel.

Sister St. Andrew decided to remain in Castroville, estranged from the Texas Congregation she had founded. Several parishioners, including her friend Otilia Christilles, now married to Bill Cooner, invited her to their homes, but Sister St. Andrew felt that if she lived with a parishioner, she might cause a division in St. Louis Parish. She moved in with her brother Louis, his wife Theresa, and their seven children.

If the past months had been difficult for Sister St. Andrew, the next two years were nearly impossible. Father Moye's advice was never more needed: ***"You will expect everything from God: food,*** *clothing, health and strength, talents, and in a word, everything.*" * She had no source of income; no possibility of employment; and short of returning permanently to St. Jean-de-Bassel, no way to rectify her status: she was a nun without a Congregation.

Upon arriving on the doorstep of Louis' poor home, Sister St. Andrew sat down heavily in a rocking chair. Three-year-old James climbed up into his aunt's lap demanding her attention. Theresa held baby Julia who was a handful at eighteen months.

"Get down, James," Louis said to his youngest son, gently. "Auntie doesn't want to be bothered with you now."

"I don't mind, Louis, really. Holding James is somehow comforting to me. Leave him be," Sister St. Andrew said. "He's all right."

Louis had never seen his sister so shaken. Taking his pipe, he sat down at the kitchen table. The story he and Theresa would hear would be nearly unbelievable.

She recounted to Louis a summary of what had transpired during the previous ten months since she had told them good-bye as she left for Clarksville. He was astounded. Not sure where his sympathies should lie, he said without judgment: "I wish you had just come home to us, Sister. We would have managed to help you somehow."

"I simply could not. I had to try every possible means to continue my vocation as a Sister and to continue missionary work here in the United States."

"Now what are you going to do?" asked Theresa, pushing a strand of blonde hair out of her blue eyes and jostling baby Julia who had begun to whimper.

"I don't know. I cannot return to St. Jean. Mother Anna could never have confidence in me again. Besides, I cannot support the winters in Germany. Based on all that Mother Constantine told me over the years, I doubt that I could ever get a teaching certificate under the Reich."

"Do you want to stay here in Castroville?" Louis was trying to be gentle but he was not especially happy about his eldest sister's situ-

* **The Directory**, p. 78.

ation. However, both Sister St. Andrew and their brother Nicolas had made it possible for Louis to come to Texas, find work, and start a family. He owed her for that, and he knew it. But he was poor and his family took every penny he made. "You can stay here with us, but I have no money," he finally offered.

"I'm going to talk to Otilia Christilles—Otilia Cooner. Tillie thinks she might be able help me. I will appreciate being able to stay with you until I can make other arrangements." The stress of the last year had taken its toll, and Sister St. Andrew was close to tears.

That night Louis and Theresa spoke of Sister St. Andrew's plight. They both agreed that she had aged ten years in the year past—and her face looked strained.

The Feltin family had next to nothing. They lived in a poor house west of Providence House up near St. Louis Cemetery. During her days with them and having nothing else to do, Sister St. Andrew helped Theresa with her housework and the care of the children. Louis was working on a millwork project for St. Louis Church, but as usual lasting work was hard to come by. When he wasn't working, he spent his days fishing on the Medina River. At least his efforts at fishing usually brought food for the family's dinner.

Sister St. Andrew was unaccustomed to such stark furnishings. She had often lived in meager circumstances, but she tried to make her surroundings pleasant. The windows of the house didn't even have curtains; so, with Tillie's help Sister St. Andrew found flour sacks and taught Mary Teresa, now age fourteen, how to make window coverings. Little by little, with Sister St. Andrew's attention, the rustic little house began to look warm and homey.

True to their friendship, Tillie Cooner, who had gone to school at Haby Settlement and then boarded at Providence Academy at the Castroville Motherhouse, found Sister St. Andrew a stone house that had been recently abandoned. "I can get Bill and my brothers to patch it up—and it needs a new privy. But they can build one. I think we can have it livable by the middle of September." The help she received from Tillie and Bill Cooner and the Christilles boys brought a spark of new hope to Sister St. Andrew. While her house was being readied, she and Tillie enjoyed sitting in Tillie's kitchen talking over the happenings in Castroville and the possibilities for Sister St. Andrew's future.

"Are you going to wear that habit forever, Sister?" Tillie had asked simply one day. The people in the village wondered who Sister St. Andrew was now, though they continued to speak about her with respect. Only Tillie and Louis knew the full story. Everyone else conjectured about what could have happened, but they were careful never to speak ill of Sister St. Andrew. She had done so much for Castroville and for their children.

"I'm going to wear it until it wears out. Do you think I should do something else?" Sister St. Andrew had not even thought of what she would wear. Having worn her habit for more than thirty years, she shuddered to think that she might have to dress differently. She found herself haunted by Tillie's unvoiced question: Who was she now? Sister St. Andrew had much to pray about.

Alone in her little stone house, Sister St. Andrew had lots of time to pray. Each day she walked the six blocks to St. Louis Church to sit in the holy dark space where the Lord welcomed her. The hardest part of her situation was the reimposition of the edict of excommunication. Without being able to receive communion, the presence of the Lord in the Blessed Sacrament was even more sustaining.

The warmer days of Indian summer yielded to the winter months. Though Tillie's husband, Bill Cooner, and a few other men of the village had valiantly tried to fill the chinks in her house, the north wind blew through her kitchen without restraint. Sister St. Andrew had no money for food, but she never went hungry. Villagers whom she had taught as children brought her eggs, milk, butter, and home-canned vegetables and fruit. She depended on the generosity of Wilhelm Tondre who insisted that she take what she needed from his store. So many people were so good to her. Father Moye's words

were true: ***"Be assured that the more you abandon yourselves
without anxiety to God, the more He will take care of you."*** *

In her prayer she mused that if one abandoned oneself to God,
even <u>*with anxiety*</u>, God, would provide generously all that is needed.

Conversing with Tillie after Christmas, Sister St. Andrew voiced
her decision: "Tillie, I cannot remain here like this forever. I'm not old
enough to die; I'm too old to return to St. Jean. I've decided to write
our Ecclesiastical Superior at St. Jean—his name is *Abbé* Michel
and he actually lives in Metz. I'm going to explain my circumstances
and ask him for a new 'Letter of Obedience.' For us that is a teaching certificate that also indicates that we are in good stead with the
Congregation. I have my old one, but I am not certain of my status.
With a new 'Letter of Obedience,' I can accept Bishop Fink's invitation to come to the Diocese of Leavenworth, Kansas, to start schools
for him as we have done here in Texas. I can still do that."

"How do you know Bishop Fink?" Tillie asked curiously.

"Actually, I think it is Providence! His letter was with the mail that
Alton Tschirhart brought me last week. The Bishop does not know
that we have a different Superior, so the invitation was addressed
me. After I read the letter, I sent it on to Mother Florence. I'm certain, however, that she won't plan to send Sisters to Kansas. It's
simply too far away. But with a 'Letter of Obedience' from St. Jean-
de-Bassel, I myself can go. I've written to Bishop Fink telling him of
my circumstances. He wrote back that he is willing to accept me if I
have permission from St. Jean-de-Bassel. He says that he has many
areas that need schools, especially in the southeastern part of the
state. I know nothing about Kansas—but then, I knew nothing of
Texas twenty years ago!" As she spoke a sparkle returned to Sister
St. Andrew's eyes. Kansas could be a new start.

The first of March 1888 Sister St. Andrew wrote to *Abbé* Michel.
It had taken her more than a month to decide what to put in her letter and in the end she decided to describe her situation with stark
honesty.

---

* **The Directory, p. 225.**

I am all alone in a little house, ... without confession and communion, and no one dares do anything for me, under pain of excommunication; and neither mercy nor pardon is to be hoped for from the Bishop neither from Mother Florence or Angelique ...

From you I look for not only pardon, but help. ... With a good certificate from you, I shall go into another state, Leavenworth, Kansas, where there is a German bishop, and much good remains to be done there. ... Your kindness will not refuse a few good subjects to come and do good among the Indians, because we shall be quite close to the Indian Territory. My dear Father, do not pay attention to the disgrace which weighs on me at this time; consider rather the immense good which has been done and continues in Texas; you know that every good work passes through suffering; and that the demon strikes me is not astonishing, for many souls are snatched from him by our schools. Do not let me sit here in idleness while I could be useful elsewhere ...

I would have written to you sooner, but I had hope that reconciliation would be made; now I see that matters are growing worse; it would be better therefore for me to go away. But I am received no where without a certificate ... And as the Bishop of San Antonio has relieved me of my vows, it is all the easier for me ... A good idea tells me to throw myself at your feet and beg you to receive me again in the number of your daughters ... *

---

*   **Excerpts from the actual March 2, 1888, letter from Sister St. Andrew to *L'abbé* Nicolas Michel.**

No one could imagine the disbelief that Sister St. Andrew experienced after reading the letter postmarked Fenetrange, the post office that processed mail to and from St. Jean-de-Bassel.

Her hand shook as she read and re-read the short note:

> *I have the regret of not being able to do what you ask of me in your letter because I would commit a falsity, which I have never done.*
>
> 1. *We cannot give you another name in religion, since you no longer are a part of the congregation, having left it freely in 1866*
> 2. *Having neither the authority nor the desire to judge the scandal of Texas it is impossible for us to receive you again as a member of the Congregation.*
> 3. *We cannot have the hope that the Congregation will authorize or promise help to join you to begin again a work as that of Texas.*
>
> *All that I can do is to send you a copy of the certificate of 1866, omitting writing the name of Texas or the name you bore when you were a member of the Congregation. I regret to tell you that we cannot enter into your views of sending you help for the purpose of beginning a new work.*
>
> *Receive, my dear Sister Andre, with my regrets, my best sentiments.*
>
> *Michel*
Canon [V]

[V] **Exact text of the letter of *L'Abbé* Michel to Sister St. Andrew, March 21, 1888.**

Another letter posted from Fenetrange was delivered by Postmaster Tschirhart at the beginning of July 1888. *Sœur* Arsene—Camille—her dear friend who had returned to St. Jean-de-Basel, was writing to inform her that *L'Abbé* Michel had died suddenly in Metz. Although the Motherhouse had had a new chaplain since January, everyone was in mourning. Mother Anna was at a loss since she had leaned so heavily on her ecclesiastical superior in these early years of her administration. No one would even speculate about who might replace *L'Abbé* Michel. In her short letter, *Sœur* Camille pledged her undying friendship.

> ***I have no idea what has really happened in Texas. Rumors abound here, but no official word is given to us. I believe we are destined to remain in the dark. I suspect that you are suffering; all I can do is pray.***

Sister St. Andrew knew that the death of L'Abbé Michel closed the door forever on any further aspirations she had of leaving Castroville as a Sister of Divine Providence and finding new missionary work elsewhere in the United States. She now was doomed to her lonely life in Castroville until her death. And that, she thought, could not come too soon.

Over the next weeks, while the Church celebrated the Resurrection of the Lord, Sister St. Andrew remained in a private Lent. Her days were routine: three mornings a week she went to Theresa's house to help her with the children, do her washing and ironing, and help her with housekeeping.

By the winter, Theresa, now expecting another child, became despondent. Louis was usually unemployed; the children were growing up but had to do without so many things. Sister St. Andrew hoped that her eldest niece Mary Teresa, now nearly fifteen, could attend Providence Academy* at the Castroville Motherhouse when it opened, but there was no money for that. Lacking the ambition to learn a trade, John Isidore, almost seventeen, took any odd job that he could find.

Empty days followed empty days for Sister St. Andrew. Letters from Marie-Anne in La Walck assured her of her sister's prayers and love and occasionally she would receive a letter from Sister Arsene, now known as Sister Camille, who was at St. Jean-de-Bassel.

But the nights were agony. Often she would simply remain awake all night, praying the rosary on her *prie-dieu*. It did not seem to matter if she slept or not. Nothing required her energy until Lizotte was born in July 1889, and Theresa could not manage her household. Sister St. Andrew spent most days at the Feltin house where she did everything necessary to care for the neglected family. Theresa stayed in bed the greater part of most days and, since she had no milk, Sister St. Andrew had to feed Lizette warm goat's milk by the spoonful. Now, sleep came easily by the time she went to bed each night. She was exhausted. Nearly sixty years old, she found herself doing the hardest work of her life.

Theresa remained depressed throughout the winter of 1889-90, depending on her sister-in-law to take care of her home and children.

By February, Sister St. Andrew could leave the baby in her older sister's care every other day or so and take some time for herself in her crude house.

On the feast of St. Valentine, 1890, Tillie's carriage came rumbling up to Sister St. Andrew's gate.

"Come quick," Tillie shouted. "It's Theresa!"

Sister St. Andrew came running from her house. "Come with me right now. We must hurry," Tillie insisted. "There's no time!"

By the time they reached the Feltin house, the children were all huddled together in the yard trying to keep warm. Upon entering

---

* **Providence Academy opened on February 3, 1890, at the Castroville Motherhouse.**

the house, Sister St. Andrew saw the worst sight she had ever seen. The thin, limp body of her sister-in-law lay on the kitchen table, her purplish face and staring eyes evidenced that her soul was gone.

The next month was a jumble of events. Tillie convinced Sister St. Andrew that she really had to have some secular clothes and gave her a dress. Suspecting that major changes were in the offing for the Feltin family, Sister St. Andrew, wearing Tillie's dress, took the train into San Antonio to have her photograph made. If they moved away from Castroville as Louis was now planning, she would take off her habit and pack it in her trunk. She would leave Castroville as Louise Feltin.

Inconsolable, Louis decided within the month to take his children to California. Castroville held nothing but sorrow and bad luck for the Feltins.

Sister St. Andrew wrote to Marie-Anne telling her of their impending move to San Jose. Just before she sealed the envelope, she put a copy of her photograph in the letter.

"Who is that person," Sister St. Andrew thought, pondering the photograph once more. "Is that I?"

San Jose had been a haven from the beginning. Louis found work immediately as the city was growing and millwrights were in short supply. The house he eventually found on the north edge of town on Empire Street was large, providing ample space for his four daughters and three sons who had come with him. Only the absence of John Isidore marred the happiness of the little family as they started over in the place where dreams still came true.

Hardly a day went by that Louis didn't remember to thank his sister for coming with him to care for his children.

But Sister St. Andrew—Louise Feltin to her neighbors in San Jose—knew that God's own Providence had re-gifted her with a life that had purpose. Never could she have imagined that the tragic death of her sister-in-law would be God's instrument to restore meaning in her life. Each day that she sat in the rocking chair singing Lizette to sleep, each time that she brushed the tears from Julia's eyes when the little girl tripped and scraped her knee, each time that she ruffled Joe's thick brown hair encouraging him to keep after his homework, each time that she held Mary Teresa when she had nightmares about finding her dead mother hanging in the barn, each time that she went to confession at St. Patrick's, each Sunday as she knelt at the communion railing to receive her dear Lord in the Blessed Sacrament, she knew that this was a new life. After a Lent that had lasted for nearly four years, Easter had finally dawned.

CHAPTER XVII

HOMECOMING

Louise Feltin gazed off toward the mountains in the east. Since the children were playing with friends on this August Sunday afternoon, she had time to sit on the front porch of their home in San Jose and reflect. Yesterday had been the feast of St. Louis. She let her mind wander to Castroville and in her mind's eye she could imagine the parish festivities. The Sisters never attended the picnic at the Koenig Park, but the good parishioners always brought them pans full of their homemade Alsatian sausage. Next year she would be enjoying that sausage at home once again, God willing.

Her reverie took her to the days of her girlhood in 1849 as she prepared to enter the postulate at St. Jean-de-Bassel. During her four years of teaching with the Sisters in Krautergersheim, young Louise had proven to be a promising vocation and the Sisters there had encouraged her entrance into the postulate. Her mother had helped her pack a small truck with the items required: two white nightgowns, two chemises, four pair of black stockings, two towels, one black skirt, two black blouses. One of LaWalck's best-known cobblers, *Monsieur* Seiter, had made her a new pair of black shoes.

Even now at nearly seventy years old, Louise remembered the butterflies in her stomach as she and her father had traveled together from LaWalck to Bouxwiller and then on to Phalsbourg and Sarrebourg. Though she and her father had made the two-day journey each summer for four years, somehow that last journey in November of 1849 had been different. Her father had said very little, his mood seeming to match the rolling terrain in the foothills of the

Vosges which had taken on the brown of winter. Trees were bare and fields were empty after the harvest. A biting wind blew through the stagecoach and the passengers could see their breath.

That was the last journey she had made with her father. Before he had helped her into Jean-Pierre's wagon that day, Jean-Claude Feltin had placed his finger under his daughter's chin, gently lifting her face. His last look was a study of her countenance. Her heavy brows and brown eyes were striking, he thought to himself. Had she stayed in LaWalck, she could have married well.

No words were needed for this goodbye. After a quick embrace, the father helped his eldest daughter, his second child to leave home to serve God, into the wagon and waved her off as Jean-Pierre guided the horses east toward the tiny village of St. Jean-de-Bassel.

Now, fifty years later, here she was preparing her trunk to go to the convent once again. The butterflies were the same, but this time it was the parent leaving her children behind. How ironic! She had found that, like her father, she had begun to study the faces of Lou-Lou, Jule and little Lizette, etching their features on her heart. She often used her father's gesture, especially with the youngest two, lifting their little chins to take a close look into their eyes.

One evening, Lizette had complained, "Why are you always look-ing at me, *ma tante Maman*? Is my face dirty?"

"Why, no, child. I think you have a lovely face. Your little face gives my tired old eyes such pleasure." And with that, she had drawn Lizette into her lap.

"I am too old to be rocked, *ma tante*!" Lizette had protested.

"*Liebchen*, you are never too old for me to hold you." Realizing that she would not be released, the little girl relaxed against the only mother she had ever known and let her aunt hold her on her lap in the rocker.

Louise had talked everything over with Mamie and Joe and her brother Louis. None of them wanted to see her leave them, and Louise had seen a look of terror in Mamie's eyes as the conversa-tion turned to practical matters. Mamie would never be strong, but the younger girls would be able to manage. Lou-Lou's good business instincts would take care of the store; both Jule and Lizette were willing to help and would be at home for years while they finished their education. Lizette was already talking about being a teacher and working hard at her piano lessons. Jule had the personality to get a good paying job anywhere. The older two children had agreed with their aunt that it would be best to say nothing to the younger children until closer to the time when their aunt would leave. Even a talk with Lou-Lou would be postponed until just before Louise's departure.

Very little needed to be done. The lease on the house was now in Joe's name, and the one on the store was in Lou-Lou's name. Louise had one last thing to prepare, but she would wait to do that until closer to the time of her departure.

She drew Mother Florence's second letter of the summer from her apron pocket. Its arrival just the week before had stirred the butterflies already nesting in Louise's stomach. Perhaps Mother Florence had changed her mind. Perhaps the Sisters didn't want her to return. Louise had waited until evening when she could open the letter in private. But the letter warmed her heart. At the end of the annual retreat, Mother Florence had explained to the Sisters gathered at Our Lady of the Lake for summer normal school and retreat that she had received a letter from Sister St. Andrew. Mother Florence wanted Louise to know the Sisters' thoughts about her coming home:

> *While we were gathered in the dining room for the noon meal after the retreat was over, I told the Sisters that you had written asking to return home. There was a moment of stunned silence and then the Sisters began to smile and clap. Tears filled many eyes, especially those of the Sisters whom you know well. I had already gone out to Castroville to talk with Sister Angelique*

***and Sister Mary Ange. They, too, are happy that
you are, at last, coming home.***

Not having kept up a correspondence with anyone in Castroville, Louise was still afraid of what would face her in the village. During the two and a half years that she lived alone there, she had been well cared for by so many. Villagers brought her firewood, milk, eggs, and meat; a near neighbor shared his well water with her. Ten years is a long time, however, and things change. People change. She didn't even know who the pastor of St. Louis Parish was now. She had left everything behind on that day in May in 1890 when she horded the smaller boys onto the Southern Pacific and helped little Julia climb the steep steps into the coach.

Louise let her mind drift to prayer: God our Provider, help me to rely on You totally in the days ahead. I trust in Your mercy and care for me.

A second paragraph of Mother Florence's letter had set her mind at ease over another troubling concern.

"I want you to know," she had written, "that we now operate in accordance with a decree that came from Rome in 1890. No one may question a religious Sister on matters of conscience; and Sisters may receive communion according to their own consciences without asking permission of anyone. As you return to Divine Providence House in Castroville, I think you will find this information helpful."

Louise was struck by Mother Florence's discretion as she wrote of the 1890 decree. A discussion on the state of her soul with the chaplain at Divine Providence House or the parish priest would not be necessary! Just re-reading those few lines brought a sigh from her lips. God provides; God provides.

That night, after the young girls were in bed and the boys had gone out on the streets to meet their pals, Joe and his aunt Louise sat together over a cup of coffee at the kitchen table.

"So, you're really going to leave us, Auntie?" Joe said with disbelief. "I still can't believe it. Maybe I just don't want to believe it."

"Why, Joe, that is a very nice thing to say. We've been all through this, Joe; I must go. And, according to Mother Florence's last letter, the Sisters want me to come home."

"You're not going to like that sleepy old Castroville after you've lived the fast life here in San Jose. Why, they probably don't even have electricity!" Joe was always a tease. Louise would miss that.

"I'm certain they don't have electricity. That town voted against being on the Southern Pacific route. So most likely they've voted against having electricity, too!" Louise's smile revealed her love for her quaint village. "I will enjoy sitting on the veranda at Divine Providence House and looking at the stars in the clear Texas sky."

"When do you think you'll leave us?" Joe asked with a catch in his voice. He had come to truly love his aunt who had given her life to them after the tragic death of their mother.

"I believe I'll go in late October. The searing heat of the Texas summer will be over by then. The fall harvest will be gathered in and school will be underway. It will be a good time to return." Then she continued in a more solemn tone. "Joe, you know that I really don't have faith that Mamie can keep the store going. She will have to rely on Lou-Lou—but Lou-Lou is young. Your father said that I could have some of the money we've saved. I'm going to take $700. My plan is to give it to Mother Florence for safekeeping in case you children need it. Joe, all you'll have to do is write to me if there is an emergency and you need money. Do you understand?"

"*Oui, ma tante*," Joe said, reverting to the intimacy of the familiar French. Tears filled his eyes as he suddenly felt the weight of the family on his young shoulders. "I'll do my best."

The month of September flew by. Lou-Lou learned more each day in the store. She rotated the stock, paid invoices on time, and worked well with customers who owed them money. Most days Louise stayed at the house to prepare the noon meal, leaving Lou-Lou to take care of the store alone. Mamie gave her sister all the help she could, but she was often distracted and was sharp with the women who came in just to gossip.

Jule had adjusted well to high school and Lizette, in her last year of grammar school, had become a good pianist for her young age. Her piano teacher was both encouraging and challenging.

On their walk back from Sunday Mass on the first Sunday of October, Louis had broached the subject of Louise's leaving.

"Have you decided when you're leaving, Louise?"

"I want to leave on the Wednesday morning train on the 24th of this month. That will get me to Hondo on Saturday, October 27. Will that be all right?"

"Yes, if that's what you want." Louis, a man of few words, had never recovered from his wife's shocking death. He went on haltingly "Louise, I can never tell you how much your help has meant to me. I know that I could never have managed the children without you. You left everything behind to come here to San Jose and to mother these orphans. I'll never forget that."

"That's all right, Louis. When my life as a Sister of Divine Providence went awry, I begged God to give me a new purpose. I thought that continuing missionary work in Kansas would be that purpose, but God had other plans. I see now how all of His designs work together for good."

"Are you going to tell Jule and Lizette soon?"

"I don't know how to tell them. They are like my own daughters, and they've already lost one mother. Losing another mother may destroy something in them. Perhaps it would be best if I tell them I'm going to Castroville for a visit. I'll let them think that I will be back. Would that be kinder?"

"Maybe," was all that Louis could say, knowing that he would be no help.

The next day Louis bought his sister a one-way ticket to Hondo, Texas, on the Southern Pacific Railway.

The following Saturday the girls were all busy in the store. Louise, not feeling well, had stayed at home. She decided that she needed to do the one last chore that she had been putting off. Her trunk had taken up the middle of her small bedroom since July when Joe had brought it down from the attic. Every day she had walked around it to get into bed. Now she had to deal with one final thing.

She lifted the trunk's lid and removed the tray. The odor of mothballs wafted from the interior of the aged luggage. The contents on top were her few possessions that she planned to take with her to Texas: her woolen winter robe, her black shawl, a few small handmade gifts the children had given her over the years, a folder of the youngest girls' best compositions from school.

After everything had been placed on the bed, Louise bent over, removing the last item from the very bottom of the trunk: a bulky package wrapped in brown paper and tied with string. She untied the string and slowly opened the paper. There it was. She had not looked at the contents of the package in over ten years. Removing the protective tissue paper, she picked up each piece as though she were handling sacred objects: the black voile veil with its starched white wings, two coifs, two starched bandeaux, the collar and *guimpe*, the cape of black serge, the black serge waist with the wide sleeves attached to the black serge skirt. Tears ran down her face. Her dear habit. As she inspected it carefully, shaking out the wrinkles, she hoped that there weren't any moth holes. Only two or three! They could be easily mended.

She put the dress on a hanger to let the wrinkles begin to fall out, hoping that the smell of mothballs would fade in the next two weeks. The cape had been carefully folded along the creases and would need little ironing and the veil seemed to need only a light pressing. The clock in the hallway struck 9:00. Plenty of time to get the iron hot and do the needed ironing before the children came home for dinner. Then she would hang everything in her closet. She would pack her habit in the valise she intended to carry on the train so that she could change into it on her way to Hondo. The children would not be alarmed. The youngest two had never seen her in her habit, though they knew it was in her trunk. Lou-Lou might remember as she had been six when they had come west.

Then she thought: maybe I'd better try on the dress; it may not fit and I may need to adjust it!

She took off her flowered housedress and slipped the habit dress over her head. The location of all the hooks and eyes and snaps returned instantly to her memory and she quickly had the dress secured. It fit fine. In fact, it was loose at the waist. Ever since the doctor said that she had diabetes, she had tried to eat fewer sweets. What a cross! But perhaps it has made a difference, she thought. The weight of the habit on her shoulders was striking. She had forgotten how heavy the serge was. But I'll get used to that again, she thought.

Louise would not try on the headcoverings. There was no doubt in her mind that she remembered how to wear the *coif* and *bandeau*, and the starched linen piece on the veil seemed to be all right.

She put the rest of the habit in the top drawer of her dresser, now empty as she had packed everything in her trunk. Taking her habit dress into the kitchen, she found the hot iron on the stove ready to press the wrinkles from the wool serge skirt. Her fingers caressed the folds in the badly worn skirt. During her two years alone in Castroville this skirt had become so worn at the hem that she had had to take the waist off and turn it upside down. This habit would get her to Hondo, but she would need a new one soon.

By mid-morning, this last chore was finished. Louise took a cup of coffee out to the front porch for a little rest. Everything tired her so now and she was short of breath.

Oh, how I will miss these mountains, she thought. "You have given me so much comfort in the past decade," she said directly to her old friends. "You have continually reminded me of God's powerful care of us. I thank you."

In the ten years that the Feltins had lived on Empire Street on the northern edge of San Jose, they had watched the neighborhood grow, and now Victorian-style houses of all sizes and colors surrounded them. They had good neighbors, but Louise had never acquired the habit of going to their homes or inviting them to hers. In fact, Louise had had little social life to speak of while in San Jose. The French immigrants to San Jose were vintners and had a very exclusive social registry; the Germans were nearly as distant. There would be no one except Father McGuire to bid her *adieu*. Louise had planned to go to confession on Saturday as usual and then speak to Father before returning home. He probably wouldn't be surprised; she had been very forthright with him since Bishop Neraz's death. Over the last six years, Father McGuire had urged her regularly to consider returning to her religious community.

On Tuesday, October 23, Louise awoke early. Today the older children must be told while they were all at home for dinner. Even the boys would be home since they were between picking seasons and had found odd jobs working the late shifts at nearby canneries.

As though a bell had summoned them, the family gathered in the kitchen just at noon. "James, I'd like you to run next door to the store and ask Mamie and Lou-Lou to close the store for the noon hour. We won't miss any customers. I want to tell you all something," Aunt Louise said.

James jumped up, doing as his aunt had asked, and within a few minutes all of the older children were seated with their father around the table. Jule and Lizette who did not come home for lunch were at school.

After they said grace, their aunt began. "I have something to tell you all. I have decided to make a visit to Castroville. I want to go before all my old friends die and before I am too old to travel."

With the exception of Mamie, Joe, and their father, the others were shocked. "No, you can't go, *ma tante*," they chorused.

"Yes, I can; I must. I am leaving on the train tomorrow and will arrive in Castroville on Saturday."

"Where will you stay?" Nick asked.

"I'm going to stay at Divine Providence House, the convent. You probably don't remember the convent, Nick, since you were so young when we left Castroville. Mother Florence has invited me to stay there."

"When are you coming back?" Nick asked.

"I'm not certain."

"You're not coming back, are you?" Lou-Lou asked with a look of fear in her eyes.

"I don't know, Lou-Lou. I wouldn't go at all if I thought you weren't up to handling the store here. Everything runs perfectly without me. You are doing a fine job. It doesn't matter how long I'm gone. You will do a good job!"

Realizing that her aunt had made up her mind, the young grocer was silent. The rest of the family grew quiet as well. Usually the conversation at meals sparked with a lively review of what was going on in the orchards and fruit-packing plants. Today no one had much to say.

Finally, Aunt Louise added, "Tonight I'll speak to the girls."

By 4:00 in the afternoon Jule was working on her homework at the parlor desk while Lizette practiced her piano. The two girls were more than sisters. Their mother's death had left them to care for each other, and now they were seldom separated. Jule was the only one who willingly tolerated Lizette's piano practicing. Everyone else found occupations outside the house while Lizette practiced for two hours before supper each evening.

After supper their aunt took both girls by the shoulders to steer them out to the front porch. Twilight cast a purple hue over the mountains and Louise found herself gazing to the west as though mesmerized.

"What do you want, *ma tante*?" Jule began. "I'm not quite finished with my homework."

"Oh, I'm sorry, Jule, dear. I guess I am distracted. I want to tell you girls something important." With that she told the two youngest girls her plans.

"You're leaving tomorrow, *ma tante*? When are you coming back?" Lizette asked, on the verge of tears.

"I'm not certain when I'll return. I need to go to see Mother Florence and my other friends. You understand, don't you, *liebchen*?"

Their aunt's voice was tender; she knew that her going would orphan these girls again. "Now, now, we mustn't cry. Everything will be all right. Lou-Lou is running the store; Joe has a good job; the boys work the orchards and in the canneries. Jule, you'll go on through high school. I want you to become a lovely young lady and find a good man to marry. Lizette, I want you to practice your piano every day while I'm gone, and you will be busy preparing for your confirmation in the spring. You must study hard, too. You could be a fine teacher one day."

The girls didn't know how to take their aunt's advice. Was she going for good? Her leaving was frightening for them and they really did not want to know if she were not returning so they didn't ask any more questions.

The train trip from San Jose to Hondo was less chaotic this time than it had been in 1890. Without a crying baby to hold, a two-year old to entertain, and seven children to feed, Louise found these hours to be restful and reflective. Ten years ago she had barely noticed the broad valley between San Jose and San Fernando. This time she was struck by its beauty.

While the train stopped at Los Angeles, Louise thought of nearby Anaheim. How different her life would have been if the Bishop of Los Angeles had accepted her and Sister Arsene to work at St. Boniface Parish in that little German village! She wondered what had happened to the Stoeffels and other families when the blight hit the vineyards. Father Stöters had kept up a correspondence with her for a year or so; but after he wrote about the blight destroying every vine in every vineyard, his letters had dwindled.

While the train chugged through the Arizona desert the next day, Louise was captivated by the miles of cactus on either side of the tracks. This terrain had not changed at all in ten years. The Indian villages that dotted the countryside brought the same questions to mind: Had they camped there just yesterday or had they been there for decades? How did they eke out an existence in this barren land?

The hot, dusty day in the desert put most passengers to sleep as they dealt with the inclement weather by withdrawing into their dreams. Louise found herself entertained by some small children in a family seated near her chair. The boy and girl were about the ages of James and Nick ten years ago when the Feltins had come west. During that journey Louise had known nothing of caring for children. Though she had helped Theresa before and after Lizette was born, having full responsibility as she had had on that train ride in 1890 was different. Spending most of the three-day trip in the lounge car, Louis had left her and Mamie to deal with the little ones. Unlike this trip, the one ten years ago had held no time for an afternoon nap.

By the time the train pulled into Tuscon, Louise was beginning to be stiff from sitting so long. She was ready to get off the train and walk around the depot, but she was eager now to get to Castroville and welcomed the "All aboard" signal from the conductor.

The scenery became less interesting as the train snaked through the mountain pass at El Paso and entered the barren Texas flatlands. The occasional prairie dog village was a diversion, but the miles and miles of endless sandy plains on either side of the tracks soon became hypnotic. Only the frequent stops at small towns along the way to let off passengers and to take on freight or water broke the monotony.

Early Saturday morning, October 27, just as the train left Fort Stockton on the last leg of her journey, Louise changed into her habit and was just re-adjusting to the chafe of the coif and the tightness of the collar when the train pulled into the Hondo depot on Saturday afternoon. She had gathered up her belongings after Uvalde and was ready to disembark as soon as the train stopped. Making her way to the steps, Sister St. Andrew hoped that someone might be there to help her down.

Tears welled in her eyes when she saw George Christilles looking up and down the car. When the elderly man saw her, he let out a Texas whoop and virtually lifted her down from the coach. Her face was a little more wrinkled; she walked more slowly; there was a slight hump on her back; but there she was—their beloved *Mère* André. Just looking at her in her black habit took him back twenty years to when, as a young man beginning his family, George Christilles had helped with additions to the Castroville convent where she was the Superior.

Christilles got her trunk and settled her in his buggy for the ride to Castroville.

"Do the Sisters expect me?" Sister St. Andrew asked hesitantly.

George Christilles smiled and said, "Oh, I think they expect you."

The twenty-mile trip from Hondo to Castroville took two hours giving the driver plenty of time to tell his passenger all that had happened in Castroville since she had left. The story of his daughter Tillie's death brought tears to their eyes.

"But, Tillie's little girl is real cute and she's a student at the Convent," the grandfather said proudly.

"Who is your pastor at St. Louis now, George?" Sister St. Andrew asked with curiosity.

"His name is Father Kirch—came to us from New Braunfels, I think," George said innocently.

"Father John Kirch?" Sister St. Andrew asked.

"Yes, that's his name. Can't say much for him. He's changed a lot of things in the church but the people don't really like him, Mother."

"Oh, I see," was her only reply. Another irony: Father John Kirch now the pastor at St. Louis. Will God ever be finished testing me, Sister St. Andrew thought as they rode along the bumpy road in silence.

By the time the buggy stopped in front of the Convent on Paris Street, it was after sundown. The house was ablaze with light from candles in every window on both the first and second floors. As George Christilles helped Sister St. Andrew down from the buggy, the front door of the Convent opened; Mother Florence followed by Sister Angelique and Sister Mary Ange came to the front steps and down the path to the gate followed by another dozen nuns.

Rev. John Kirch
(Courtesy, Archdiocese of San
Antonio, Texas.)

"Welcome home, Mother," was their simple greeting repeated over and over again as they surrounded their long-lost Sister.

Mother Florence herself took the small valise that now held only the simple housedress of a woman who no longer existed.

Mother St. Andrew had come home.

The next days were spent in hours of visiting and catching up with all that had happened in the previous ten years. Sister Angelique, now in her fifty-fifth year of religious life, was frail but her mind was sharp. Sister Mary Ange, too, enjoyed reviewing with her old friend all that had gone right—and all that had gone wrong—in their years together since 1878.

For Sister St. Andrew the conversations with the companions who had weathered innumerable storms with her for twenty years were a balm for her heart. The burden of guilt and misgivings that she had carried alone for the last decade began to fall away.

The orchard on the south side of the convent had grown, and this year's apple crop promised a good harvest. The summer garden, now empty, was ready for the planting of winter squash and cabbage. Mother decided that she could sit on the veranda enjoying the Texas sunshine forever.

Mercifully, the fall weather remained cool but not damp. Now that she had to walk farther distances than she did in San Jose, Mother St. Andrew began to rely on a cane to ease the arthritic pain in her legs and to steady her when she went on her daily walks.

Hearing that their beloved *Mère* André had come home, the people of Castroville invited her onto their porches for coffee as she made her way through the village each day.

The convent was filled with the voices of girls of all ages who boarded at Divine Providence Academy while they studied a regular curriculum in addition to music lessons, lace making, culinary arts, and home management. The exuberance of the little girls seemed to brighten the days of the elderly Sisters in residence. As the retired Sisters gathered in the community room each evening, little stories of the antics of the youngest boarders laced their recollections of days gone by.

After supper one evening a few days after Mother had arrived, Sister Hilary, one of the Sister-prefects* of the boarders, said to one of the youngest girls, "Aren't you Otilia Christilles' daughter?"

"Yes, Sister," little Marie answered. "But now my name is Marie Marty."

"I know, child. I think there's someone you should meet," Sister Hilary continued. "Come with me."

The Sister-prefect took the little girl by the hand[v] and guided her into the Sisters' community room where several old Sisters sat knitting, crocheting, or reading. The girls were told time and again not to bother the old Sisters, so little Marie Marty, afraid that she was going to get into trouble, scooted behind Sister Hilary's skirt as they walked across the room. Sister Hilary spoke to one of the nuns.

"Mother St. Andrew," she began.

"Yes, Sister. How may I help you?"

"Do you know who I have here?"

Mother St. Andrew drew the little girl close to her and looked at her face carefully. "No, who is this child?"

---

*   A "prefect" is a person who supervises youngsters in a boarding school.

[v]   This story is from a memoir about Mother St. Andrew Feltin written by Sister Alma Marty, CDP, in 1936. Sister Alma Marty was Marie (Cooner) Marty. It is held in the Congregational Archives in San Antonio, TX.

"This is Tillie's little girl," Sister Hilary replied.

"So you are Tillie's little girl," Mother St. Andrew said slowly. "What is your name?"

"My name is Mary, but my uncles call me Marie, and the old Sisters call me *Marichen*."

The Sisters in the community room laughed as they watched Mother St. Andrew and listened to the exchange.

Mother St. Andrew, not knowing what the child understood about her mother, asked, "Where is mama?"

"In heaven," Marie said, "she is in heaven."

"Yes, they're all in heaven," Mother St. Andrew said, beginning to cry. Seeing their old superior's distress, the Sisters gathered around her with comforting words while Sister Hilary took the little girl away.

"So many of the people I left behind have died. I thought I had cried all my tears. When George Christilles picked me up in Hondo, he told me of Tillie's death. I shouldn't have cried in front of that dear child. Do you think she was frightened?" Mother St. Andrew asked gently. "I wouldn't want the child to be afraid of us."

Sister Mary Ange replied, "Oh, Marie Marty isn't afraid of anything, Mother. You above all couldn't scare her!" With that all the Sisters laughed again and the moment of sadness passed.

The next day, Mother St. Andrew, Sister Angelique, and Sister Mary Ange were sitting on the veranda in the morning sun.

"How are you doing, Mother? Are you finding your way around?" Sister Angelique asked gently. Secretly, Mother Florence had asked Sister Angelique to look after Mother St. Andrew until she herself had time for a long visit. "See to all of her needs," Mother Florence had said. "But she won't want you to hover over her!"

Mother Florence had been right. Mother St. Andrew was quite independent and had developed a personal schedule of helping in the kitchen, praying, and walking in the village.

"I'm doing fine, Sister Angelique. But, I haven't yet written the children. I suppose I'm putting it off. I don't quite know what to say.

I told the little girls that I was leaving only the night before I left. I didn't really tell them that I would not be back. I just couldn't bring myself to break their hearts—and mine."

"Why, Mother, you must write to them right away. They are mere children. You must write to them often. You are the only mother they have known!" Sister Mary Ange's strident tone indicated how important she thought these letters would be to the motherless children.

"Very well, Sisters, I will write next week."

"In the meantime, you heard that we have an invitation to go to Our Lady of the Lake for Thanksgiving. We did the same thing last year. We will take the train from LaCoste to San Antonio and then someone meets us at the depot and takes us to Our Lady of the Lake. I know that sometimes you don't feel well, but we hope you will decide to go with us," Sister Angelique said.

"Are you both going?" Mother St. Andrew asked.

"I may be old, but I never miss an opportunity to go to Our Lady of the Lake. After all, it is our motherhouse! And I love to see all the progress and improvements. They have more girls each year in both the high school and the normal school. Most of them will be gone during the Thanksgiving holidays and it will be peaceful. Please come. It will be a wonderful opportunity for you to see our motherhouse." Sister Angelique was very persuasive; she knew that Mother Florence would be very disappointed if Mother St. Andrew did not come.

"Very well. I will go with you."

"Tomorrow is the feast of All Saints. I think the children here have a special Halloween program prepared for us after supper," Sister Mary Ange reminded them. "And the Feast Day Mass is at 9:00 in the morning instead of at 7:00."

Mother St. Andrew's eyes filled with tears.

"My goodness, Mother," Sister Angelique asked, "whatever is the matter?"

"The Feast of All Saints. I was denied communion for the first time in my life on that Feast Day in 1886. I was right here in this house. That experience tore out a piece of my heart. Perhaps I shall always bear the grief of being deprived of the Sacraments of the Church," Mother replied in a choked voice.

Remembering that pain-filled day, Sister Mary Ange hung her head. Mother St. Andrew's old friends knew that no words could assuage the depth of pain that Mother carried. Their silent presence was their best response.

About a dozen of the retired Sisters at Castroville who were able to travel took the train into San Antonio on the Wednesday before Thanksgiving Day with plans to remain at Our Lady of the Lake until Saturday morning. A beautifully-prepared traditional Thanksgiving meal of turkey, ham, sweet potatoes, and vegetables would grace the tables of the Sisters at Our Lady of the Lake as they enjoyed a few days without their students.

Main Building, Our Lady of the Lake University, circa 1895.
(Congregational Archives, San Antonio, TX)

Upon their arrival at Our Lady of the Lake, Mother Florence took Mother St. Andrew's arm, helping her up the steps into the Main Building.

"I am so glad you came, Mother. Welcome to Our Lady of the Lake!" Mother Florence was effusive in her greeting, revealing her pride in the new Motherhouse.

"What a lovely building, Mother! How long did it take to build it?" Mother St. Andrew asked, remembering that the construction of the Castroville motherhouse had taken several years because of their dependence on volunteer labor and donated materials.

"We broke ground in August of 1895 and dedicated the building the following July. Actually, it went up in record time. I told the contractor that since Mayor Elmendorf was giving us this property if we could put $75,000 worth of buildings on it in ten years, that I don't have time to waste. He laughed at me; but, as you can see, we've started to honor our pledge to His Honor. The second building, St. Ann's Hall, went up last year; our next building will be just to the north. All the buildings will be connected. Just like they are at the Motherhouse at St. Jean-de-Bassel!"

"What a fine idea!" Mother St. Andrew affirmed.

By now they were in the entryway of Main Building where Mother Florence pointed out the lovely front parlors and the broad staircase leading to the second floor.

Mother St. Andrew's fingers traced the grooves in the dark wainscoting. "I love this," she said in a near-whisper. "It's not exactly like the wainscoting at St. Jean, but I always loved that touch to a hallway. Did you know that I began my religious life dusting the wainscoting at St. Jean? And this is so clean! Who does all the dusting here?"

"The postulants and novices, of course. Just like always!" Mother Florence laughed at Mother St. Andrew's interest in the detail of the building. "Come, now, let me show you the rest of this building. Here is a dining room that the priests use," Mother Florence said, taking her former superior into a room behind the staircase and then the dining room that the students use is next to this one, through those folding doors. The architect designed this building so that we could add on here," she said, touching the north wall along the hallway outside the dining rooms. "Then, you see, through the girls' dining room, you can go into St. Ann's Hall where the novices and postulants sleep."

Mother St. Andrew looked through the long windows in the dining room out into a small courtyard. "The courtyard reminds me of the one at St. Jean-de-Bassel, too, Mother. I like this."

Pointing southward, Mother Florence said, "Now, you will have to use your imagination: right there will be the chapel one day. You know how they reserved the space at St. Jean for years before they built St. Anne's Chapel in 1870. I have no idea when we will be able to build a chapel, but I will reserve that space for as long as it takes."

The two nuns who had done their training for religious life in their beloved Motherhouse in Lorraine, France, walked arm in arm throughout the new Texas Motherhouse. Mother Florence pointed out offices and classrooms, the library on the second floor and a dining room for the Sisters behind the library. The second floor had a large auditorium-style classroom that could be used for many purposes.

"Do you feel like climbing stairs to the third floor? I won't make you climb to the fourth. That floor is a dormitory for the Sisters."

"If we go slowly, I can manage it," Mother St. Andrew said.

After the two nuns had made their way to the third floor, Mother Florence said, "This is a study room for the girls who live here and a dormitory room at that end," she said pointing to the north end. "Down that hallway are more bedrooms. Let me show you these rooms," Mother Florence said as she took Mother St. Andrew's arm again and walked her over to one of the turret rooms. "Our contractor was very proud of being able to get usable space out of these turrets. The Sister-prefects who have these rooms are the envy of all of us," Mother Florence said smiling. "Of course, no one envies their job of prefecting high school and college girls!"

"You have done well, Mother. I am so glad to finally see all of this. Indeed, you have done very well." Mother St. Andrew's comment was genuine. Her voice held no envy of this young Superior who had been her own choice for her replacement fourteen years ago.

"Do you need to sit down, Mother?" Mother Florence asked, noticing that Mother St. Andrew was leaning heavily on her cane. "Most of the girls are gone. Perhaps we could sit up here awhile where none of the Sisters will find us."

Mother St. Andrew knew that this conversation was long overdue. The butterflies now stirring in her stomach reminded her that it might not be an easy one.

"Yes, I do need to sit down," Mother St. Andrew said, acknowledging that her nearly seventy years were taking their toll. "And there is much that we each have to say."

As they sat down, drawing the comfortable chairs next to each other, Mother St. Andrew began. "Mother, let me begin. First, I am uncomfortable that the Sisters call me 'Mother.' That title is reserved for you."

"No, Mother," Mother Florence interrupted. "It is the custom that a Superior General would retain the title of 'Mother' for life. None of our Superiors in Germany lived long enough to continue using the title; but, here in the United States, that is the custom, and we will follow it." Her dark eyes spoke with the authority that she had acquired over her tenure as Superior General.

"Very well, Mother, I will not disobey you—ever again." With that, Mother St. Andrew began her apology for all that she had done fourteen years ago that had not been in accord with her vow of obedience. As the words tumbled out, their sorrow over what had happened caused tears to stream down the cheeks of both women. Finally running out of words, Mother St. Andrew leaned back in her chair, exhausted.

"Mother, I, too, owe you an apology. If I had been then who I am now, perhaps I would have known how to protect you from Bishop Neraz. I realize that you had no advocate and that His Lordship simply could not abide your presence. I was desperately afraid for our Congregation. I truly believe that he would have carried through with his threats to disband us or to meld us with the Sisters of the Incarnate Word. Truthfully, I was afraid of him. When he came into your office and took your papers on the day I was installed, I knew that we had no recourse. I thought of writing to Mother Anna at St. Jean-de-Bassel, but I was uncertain about our relationship with St. Jean. His Lordship had said they didn't want us anymore. So, I felt that I simply had to go on according to his wishes."

Mother St. Andrew extended her hand, placing it on the sleeve of the younger nun's habit. "You need not say another word, Mother. I think now that God wants us to put all of this behind us. I am now too old to hold onto the storms of the past. My heart is no good; my legs are weak. I will spend the rest of my years atoning for the past. You must spend the rest of your years making a future which will last for our dear Congregation."

For the rest of the afternoon, the two nuns who had been through a tempest together sat comfortably with each other, sharing their experiences of the past decade and their hopes for their Congregation's future.

"One of the options that I am working on, Mother," Mother Florence shared, "is finding a way to have Rome declare us to be a pontifical congregation. I have to admit that I don't know who we are at this point. If we are separate from St. Jean-de-Bassel, we have no documentation of that. St. Jean-de-Bassel has established a house in Kentucky and I have corresponded with the superior there as well as Sister Camille. I hope to visit them someday, though they seem distant. I presume that they think of us as 'lost.' The little correspondence that I have with Sisters in Germany leads me to think that re-connecting with them is probably not feasible. However, I will continue to examine all possibilities. I am hoping that Bishop Forest will appoint an ecclesiastical superior for us who will help me."

"We were separated from St. Jean-de-Bassel by Bishop Neraz; of that I am certain." Mother St. Andrew spoke adamantly but without rancor. "Perhaps that, too, has been in the designs of Providence."

Upon her return to Castroville after Thanksgiving, Mother St. Andrew received a letter from Lizette and decided to write immediately to her daughters in San Jose. She now knew that she would remain at Divine Providence House for as many days as God would give her, and she must reassure her dear daughters that she was well. In a fine, strong script, she wrote:*

> *I am glad to tell you that I am getting along very well here, I had not once Heart ake since I am here and feel very well. It seems to me you pray much for me, as I do for you. We have a very nice fine statue of the Immaculate Conception of the Blessed Virgin here and every day about 4 clock I kneel before the Mother of God and pray for you my dear little Angelä ...*
>
> *Your letter was so nice that I give to read it to those good ladies here and one Angelique of the name give me this St. Elisabeth to send to you. We have so many little girls here to learn music, some play very nice, but I think not as nice as you do, my darling ... I hope Santa Clause will not forget you and Mamie will make lots of nice cakes for Santa Clause. Many many tousand kisses and good wishes to you my dear Baby Write to me soon a great big long.*
>
> *Your most devoted and loving Maman Auntie*

The days of one year melted into the days of the next. Letters to Mother St Andrew from Lizette and Julia softened the loneliness that settles into every old heart that knows that true peace will come only with the end of its final journey. In her letters to her daughters, Mother recounted a bout of malaria during the fall of 1902, assuring

---

* **Excerpts (unedited) from actual letters written by Mother St. Andrew to Lizette in late 1900 through early 1903.**

the children that once she "no more drink cistern water," she seemed to be cured.

Driven by his own restlessness and hoping to find work in Castroville or San Antonio, Louis Feltin returned to Texas in the fall of 1902. Mother St. Andrew's New Year's letter to Lizette on January 1, 1903, noted that their father could not find work and "I think he will come soon back to you again as he can not get work here." From a distance she continued to shape her nieces through her letters:

> *Be always good my dear child, keep your Heart pure, love God, pray to God who will reward you with eternal happyness. Oh my dear Baby! how glad I am to see you advance in virtue as in age like the Divine Infant Jesus. Our life in this world is very short, Eternity last for ever. So let us be good and serve and love God to gain that Eternal happiness.* *

In 1903, Sister Angelique Decker died. The afternoon of her funeral, Sister Mary Ange and Mother St. Andrew sat on the south veranda with Mother Florence who had come to Castroville for the burial.

"Her death is the end of an era," Mother Florence mused. "I remember when Sister Angelique left St. Jean-de-Bassel with you, Mother, in 1878. Actually, many of us thought she would be coming back within the year. We did not think she had what it takes to be a missionary in a primitive land. She had always been the *econome* at the Motherhouse. I'm not certain that she ever experienced mission life outside St. Jean-de-Bassel! But she proved us wrong, didn't she!"

"I suspect the Sisters at St. Jean-de-Bassel thought I would not last in Texas either," Sister Mary Ange said. "I wasn't young, you

---

* **Excerpts (unedited) from actual letters written by Mother St. Andrew to Lizette in late 1900 through early 1903.**

know. Mother Constantine had such hope for this mission. Mother, when you asked her for help, she was delighted. She never wanted to interfere with your ways here since she didn't know how things really were. But she always wanted to find a way to help you. She was so glad that you asked for us. I volunteered immediately and have never regretted it. Mother Constantine admired you very much, Mother," she added, turning to Mother St. Andrew.

"I think now that when you and Sister Angelique volunteered for Texas, I was inspired to come myself," Mother Florence said to Sister Mary Ange. The group of us who came in 1880 didn't know you at all, Mother, but stories of your ventures filled the hallways at St. Jean. The situation under the Reich was becoming unbearable. For me, Texas was an escape."

"For me, all of you who came were the evidence that Providence wanted us to survive," responded Mother St. Andrew. "I thought we might not be able to continue; and then I swallowed my pride and asked Mother Constantine for assistance. She was so gracious. I miss her still." Mother St. Andrew, Sister Angelique, and Sister Mary Ange had reflected often on the early days, but it was a special treat to be joined by Mother Florence. "Mother, are you very busy these days?" Mother St. Andrew asked her Superior.

"Yes, we are busy. I simply cannot keep up with requests from pastors for schools. Our schools in Louisiana are doing well; and the one in Antlers, Oklahoma that we opened in the fall seems to be a success. I worry about them, however; they seem so far away! I also have requests from the pastor in Vinita, Oklahoma—wherever that is—and Tulsa. The Tulsa school is at Holy Family Church and was opened by another community just a few years ago. But they have not been able to maintain it. The pastor has heard about our other missions and wants us to come. We hope to open those two schools this coming fall. With your prayers, I hope to be able to promise the pastors of three more schools in Oklahoma and two more in Texas that we will open their schools in 1904."

"We probably don't tell you enough, Mother," Mother St. Andrew began, "but we are very proud of you and all that you have done for the Congregation. The Sisters out here speak of you all the time. You are doing a very fine work." Sister Mary Ange nodded in agreement.

"Thank you, Sisters, I do my best," Mother Florence said simply.

The Sisters in retirement in Castroville spent long hours in prayer for the sixty-six missions of the Congregation and in the fall of 1903 Mother Florence gave them a report on six schools that she hoped to open in September 1904. She also asked them for special prayers for Our Lady of the Lake College which she hoped one day would be accredited through the University of Texas system.

On February 2, 1904, Mother St. Andrew sat next to the wooden coffin of her life-long friend Sister Mary Ange. When George Christilles had come to the "laying out room" on the west end of the convent to pay his last respects, he found Mother St. Andrew keeping watch over her friend who had died during the night.

"Mother," George said in a low voice, "will you be going to the cemetery after the Mass tomorrow morning? If you want to go, I'd be honored to take you."

Mother hesitated. "I don't know, George. Perhaps I shouldn't. I haven't been feeling well." Then, after a pause, she added, "Yes, I think I will. Sister Mary Ange and I made our vows together in 1855; I must accompany her to her end. Thank you, George. I'll see you after the Mass."

After the coffin was lowered into the ground, those who had come to the cemetery began to disperse. Mother St. Andrew turned to George who was at her elbow. "George, do you have time to wait for me?"

"Of course, Mother. Take your time," George replied. He would have done anything for this little old nun.

This was the first time Mother had been in St. Louis Cemetery since she had returned to Castroville and she wanted to say some final goodbyes. She doubted if she would come again until she too was laid to rest here.

She walked among the graves of her Sisters who had gone to God. *Sister Mary Agnes*—such a stalwart nun, steady and true. *Sister Victoria.* She could still see her at the reins behind her team of horses. *Sister Sacred Heart.* Oh, those Irish girls, she thought. *Sister Theresa.* Little Anna Schultz who wanted to become a nun "like you." Another stalwart vocation snuffed out by disease at such a young age. *Sister Gabriel.* She had so wanted to come to Texas but was not certain she could "contribute." Mother could still taste her wonderful *kugelhopf!* My, she thought, a lot of the Irish girls are here. Perhaps they were too young when they came. Tears began to slide down her cheeks.

George said nothing as he came to assist her as she moved away from the Sisters' graves toward the front gate of the cemetery. On the way to the grave she wanted to see, a marker caught her eye. *Bader.* Here lay the mother and father of Sister Mary Pierre, the first Sister of Divine Providence of Texas to die. The encounter between Mother St. Andrew and Sister Mary Pierre's mother at the time of their daughter's death was emblazoned on Mother's mind. Now mother and daughter were united in Heaven. I will join them soon, she thought.

"There's one more, George," Mother St. Andrew said. "Please help me."

George held her arm and she leaned on her cane as she walked up the incline to the small stone on the north side of the path. *"Feltin"* was all it said. The memories of that Valentine's Day in 1890 flooded over her and she reeled. George steadied her while she simply stood in silent prayer for her poor sister-in-law.

"We can go now, George," Mother St. Andrew said.

George helped her down the incline and through the gates to his waiting buggy. With effort, she climbed into the cab of the buggy and

George took his place next to her. The fifteen-minute ride down the hill to the convent on Parish Street was made in silence.

In the late spring of 1904 Mother St. Andrew received a disturbing letter from Joe and Mamie. Doctor bills and "business reversals" threatened their savings, and bills from vendors for the grocery store were in arrears. Lou-Lou, they wrote, was frantic and had begged them to write asking for money.

Immediately, Mother St. Andrew wrote[*] to Mother Florence:

> *Please be kind enough and send to me the money due to my children. Please have the check made out to San Jose Safe deposit Bank. I have lately so hard spells of heart ake, that I am anxious to have settled every thing in peace, before my last hour; and moreover the children need it at this moment very bad. On account of Mamie's sickness and her failure in business they are out of resource, and begged me to help now with what belongs to them.*
>
> *Expecting from your kind Motherly heart this my request. I remain your thankful and obedient child*
>
> *Sister St. Andrew.*

Before sending her letter, she looked it over. Her handwriting was still firm and clear. I wish I had learned to write better in English, she thought. Lizette would probably get an "F" if she turned this in. I know there are many mistakes. She looked once more at her signature: *Sister St. Andrew.* She simply could not bring herself to sign "Mother" to letters she wrote to her Superior. Setting aside her

---

[*]   **Letter of Mother St. Andrew to Mother Florence, May 1904.**

embarrassment at her poorly-written letter, Mother St. Andrew humbly tucked it into an envelope and addressed to it Mother Florence.

In the fall of 1904 Mother St. Andrew began to have chest pain regularly and was admitted to the infirmary on the second floor of Divine Providence House where she could receive proper care.

She was no better by Christmas; Doctor FitzSimon came weekly to attend her.

"Mother," he said on one of his visits after Christmas, "I can't do any more for you. One day soon your heart will stop."

"I know, Doctor. I'm ready."

"I can give you laudanum for the pain, if you wish," the doctor offered.

"No. Our founder, Father Moye, told us: *'Rejoice in pain and distress; it is the doctrine of Jesus Christ, of the apostles, and of the saints.'** I don't pretend to be a saint," she added with a slight smile, "but I do know that I'll never become one if I don't suffer for my sins."

"As you wish, Mother. Let me know if you change your mind. I'll see you next week, but have someone come for me if you need me."

"Thank you, Doctor."

January 1905 was especially cold and damp. During some of the nights Mother St. Andrew thought that she might never be warm again. Part of her longed for the milder weather of San Jose, but she knew that coming home had been the right decision.

Her chest ached all the time now. She prayed rosary after rosary in hopes that the prayer would calm her, relieving the pressure on her heart. Father Quinn had anointed her and now brought her communion every day. He heard her confession each week, listening to her confess her disobedience and obstinacy each time. Shaking his head, he had said more than once, "Mother, I forgave those same sins

---

*   **The Directory, p. 182.**

last week. You simply must believe that God in His merciful love has forgiven you. But I will give you absolution one more time."

On January 30 the Sisters began to sit with Mother St. Andrew through the night. Each breath came with more difficulty than the one before; the pain in her chest was more intense.

Just before midnight on January 31, the Sister in charge of the infirmary decided to send for Dr. FitzSimon who lived about four blocks away. He came immediately, arriving shortly after 1:00 in the morning.

The doctor, trying to get a pulse, said to Mother, "Your pulse is too weak, Mother. I can't tell what it is." As he listened to her chest, all he heard was the rattle of fluid building up in her lungs. "Not good, Mother. Not good," was all he would say. "Are you certain you don't want something. The pain must be excruciating."

"It can't be as bad as the sufferings of Jesus," Mother said in a hoarse whisper.

Through the night, the Sisters at Divine Providence House came into Mother's cubicle in the infirmary and began to pray the rosary aloud.

Mother St. Andrew lifted a hand, gesturing to the Sister-Infirmarian to come to her side. "Can you help me out of bed? I wish to die on the floor," Mother said quietly.*

"Oh, Mother, I can't do that," the Sister protested.

"Then I will get up by myself. The wood upon which our Savior died was a thousand times more painful than our clean wood floor will be for me."

Given no choice, the Sister-Infirmarian assisted the former Superior General out of bed and helped her to the floor. The Sisters who had gathered to say the rosary stopped in the middle of a Hail Mary as they realized what was happening. Once Mother was on the floor, they took up their prayer again.

---

* **In 1936 Sister Alma Marty (then age 43) wrote her memories about Mother St. Andrew. The story of her death is from this work. Sister was a twelve-year old boarding student at Divine Providence Academy in Castroville when Mother died.**

At 5:00, with Doctor FitzSimon, Father Quinn, and the Sisters of the house surrounding her, the little Alsatian nun gasped one last breath and journeyed home to her Provident God. Her old heart had worn out.

Doctor FitzSimon knelt and placed the bell of his stethoscope on her chest. Nothing.

"She is gone to God," he said simply as the nuns began to sing the familiar Gregorian chant softly: "*Salve Regina, mater misericordia* ... Hail Queen, mother of mercy ...*"

Without a word, the priest and the doctor picked up the small lifeless body, placing Mother back onto her bed. Before dispersing, the Sisters said the *"De Profundis* ... Out of the depths I cry to thee," each one of them remembering the extraordinary "depths" in the life of their Superior who was now in her eternal home.

The morning sun of February 1 brought a flutter of activity to the Castroville convent. Word was sent to Mother Florence; the coffin was brought from Tondre Funeral Home across the street; the girls in the Academy were told to prepare their white dresses as they would form an honor procession at the funeral.

Mother Florence arrived at Divine Providence Convent on the afternoon of February 1. Once they heard that their beloved *Mère* André was gone, the parishioners from St. Louis Church barraged Father Kirch, practically demanding that he allow her funeral Mass to be in their parish church. He brought his request to Mother Florence. Upon realizing that their small Convent chapel would never accommodate those who wished to attend, she agreed. She told Father Kirch that Father Quinn would say the first Requiem Mass at the Convent and then a second Mass could be in St. Louis Church. The girls from the Academy would accompany the body to the Church.

George Christilles had come to his pastor on the morning of February 1. "I have contacted *Mère* André's students. We will bear the coffin," he said firmly. Father Kirch asked Mother Florence who, having no other plans, acquiesced.

St. Louis Catholic Church, Castroville, TX
(Courtesy: Castroville Chamber of Commerce)

Crowds of parishioners spilled out of St. Louis Church into Houston Square—all mourning the passing of the Alsatian nun who had taught and ministered to so many of them. The members of the St. Louis Society formed an honor guard; St. Ann's Society led the rosary before the Mass.

After the last blessing of the remains at the church, George Christilles and Mother's "boys" carried the coffin down the main aisle and out to the waiting hearse. Pulled by Tondre's best black-plumed horses, the glass-sided hearse carrying the small coffin drew slowly away from the Church to lead the procession to St. Louis Cemetery. The six pallbearers led by George Christilles walked beside the hearse, three on each side, as it rumbled south on Amelia Street to London Street. The procession turned westward onto London Street in front of St. Louis School and the Motherhouse that Mother had built so long ago. The big bell, which had been baptized "St. Louis" by Father Richard in 1871, tolled as Mother Florence and her Council led the hundreds of mourners in the cortege.

With everyone gathered at the gravesite, Father Quinn said the traditional prayers of burial. Then George Christilles and his fellow pallbearers took up their shovels and filled in the grave.

The nuns in attendance sang one last *Salve Regina*, sending their former Superior General home to their Provident God in heaven where her tattered heart could be properly mended at last.

Louis Feltin, the youngest brother of Mother St. Andrew, born in LaWalck, Bas-Rihn, Alsace, France, in 1843[2], emigrated to Texas sometime before August 1869.[3] On December 29, 1870, he married Theresa Fruth of Austin at St. Mary's Catholic Church with his brother-priest, Father Nicolas Feltin, a priest of the Diocese of Galveston, officiating.[4] The Louis Feltins lived in Austin through 1878. During that time Louis worked in construction on a school building for St. Mary's Parish and a convent for Sister St. Joseph Rice, CDP, who was teaching in Austin at the time. While in Austin, the Feltins had four children. The eldest, John Isidore (b. Feb. 4, 1872/d. Mar. 2, 1959) who returned to Austin when the Feltins moved from Castroville to California, never married, but remained close to his aunt, Elizabeth Fruth Moore and her husband Joseph Moore. He is buried in Mt. Calvary Cemetery in Austin, Texas, in their family section. Of the older children born in Austin, three traveled with their father and Aunt Louise (Mother St. Andrew) to San Jose in 1890: 1) Mary Teresa [Mamie] (b. Nov. 15, 1873/d. Sept. 1944); 2) Louis Nicolas (b. Aug. 31, 1876/d. Dec. 16, 1916); and 3) Peter Joseph [Joe] (b. Nov. 20, 1878/d. March 1922).[5]

Sometime after 1878, the Louis Feltins moved to Castroville, Texas, where Louis worked on additions to the Divine Providence

---

2   Various records note the birth year of Louis Feltin as 1840 (Strebler, p. 39), as 1855 (1910 US Census) and 1843 (California Death Certificate). All agree on August 3. The date of 1843 is the one accepted by this writer.

3   Records of Marriage of St. Mary's Church at the Texas Catholic Archives, located at the Catholic Chancery Office in Austin, Texas, indicate that Louis Feltin witnessed two marriages on August 24, 1869. His brother Nicholas Feltin was the officiating priest.

4   Texas Catholic Archives.

5   Baptismal Records, St. Mary's Church, Texas Catholic Archives. Records at Calvary Cemetery, San Jose, California.

Motherhouse and did carpentry work for St. Louis Parish.[6] While in Castroville, the Feltins had five more children: 1) George (b. Dec. 23, 1880/death date and place of burial unknown)[7]; 2) Louise Briget (b. Mar. 20,1882/d. 1910)[8]; 3) Francis James [known as James or Frank] (b. April 27, 1884/d. Dec. 21, 1910)[9]; 4) Julia [Mrs. Otto] Hellwig (b. Feb. 3, 1886/d. 1963)[10]; and 5) Elizabeth [Lizette] (Mrs. Emile) Sarrail (b. July 24, 1889/d. May 28, 1966)[11].[12]

On February 14, 1890, Theresa Fruth Feltin committed suicide by hanging herself at her house in Castroville, [13] and was buried from St. Louis Catholic Church in the St. Louis Church Cemetery.[14] In

6   Ms. Connie Tschirhart Balmos told the author that the old pulpit that was pulled out of St. Louis Church when it was renovated in 1972 had the name "Louis Feltin" carved into it. She believed that that indicated that he constructed the pulpit. CDP Archival records and the History of the Sisters of Divine Providence by Sister Generosa Callahan, CDP, indicate that Feltin worked on the Castroville Motherhouse.

7   Date of birth and date of baptism are in the Baptismal Records of St. Louis Parish held in the Archdiocesan Archives, San Antonio, Texas. Since there is no indication that George accompanied the family to San Jose (His name never appears in the San Jose City The Directory.), one might assume that he died in infancy or in childhood in Castroville.

8   In a January 26, 1950 interview, Mrs. Elizabeth Feltin Sarrail indicated that her sister Louise had died in San Jose in 1910. No other verification of this date was found.

9   According to an article in the San Jose Evening News of December 23, 1910, "James Frank Feltin" died of Hodgkins Disease at the O'Connor Sanitarium in San Jose, California. Various City Directories of San Jose indicate that he was known as "Frank J." as well.

10   Records at Calvary Cemetery in San Jose, California

11   Death date of Elizabeth Feltin Sarrail from the San Francisco Chronicle, May 30, 1966.

12   Birthdates of the Feltin children born in Castroville are located in the Baptismal Records of St. Louis Catholic Church of Castroville, Texas, which are housed in the archives of the Archdiocese of San Antonio, Texas, in San Antonio.

13   CDP Archives

14   St. Louis Church Records now held in the Archdiocese of San Antonio Archives, San Antonio, Texas.

a 1972 letter to Sister Theresa Joseph Powers, Sister Alma Marty, whose family (the Christilles) befriended Mother St. Andrew during her estrangement from the Congregation between 1888 and 1890,[15] wrote about Theresa Feltin:

> *... she was—all my relatives said—a gentle, loving angel trying to be good to him (Louis) and the children, but she was so frail and exhausted. When she couldn't feed the baby [Lizette], she grew despondent and in despair one early morning tied a little rope around her thin, worn neck and swung her tired, limp body from a rafter in the barn. Neighbors took her [Mother St.Andrew] to her brother's house. She helped dress (wash, etc.) her sister-in-law, laid her out, etc. Neighbors helped. The priest agreed to bury her in the parish cemetery.[16]*

Two months later, April 21, 1890, the Feltin Family (with the exception of John Isidore as noted above) and Mother St. Andrew left for California.[17]

In the same letter referenced above, Sister Alma Marty indicated that they went to Anaheim, California, where Mother St. Andrew "had a few friends."[18] However, James A. Sarrail, Mother St. Andrew's great-grandnephew, says he doesn't know anything about his family

15 Callahan, History of the Congregation of Divine Providence, p. 154
16 Murphy, Sister Angelina, ed., Chronicle of Mother St. Andrew's Life, Letter of Sister Alma Marty to Sister Theresa Joseph Powers, 1972, in CDP Archives. This "Chronicle" is a compendium of mostly primary material compiled by Sister Angelina. Hereinafter, it will be referred to as "Chronicle." In addition, St. Louis Parish records, now in the Archives of the Archdiocese of San Antonio, carry the notation of her burial.
17 The Anvil (Hondo, TX), Vol. 4, April 19, 1890.
18 Marty Letter, Murphy, "Chronicle"

ever living in southern California. To his knowledge the Feltins had always been in San Jose.[19] *San Jose City Directories* dating back to 1890 confirm this.[20]

Relying on her memory of her father's grocery store in LaWalck, Alsace, Mother St. Andrew (Miss Louise Feltin) opened a grocery store in a one-story building next door to their home at 418 Empire in San Jose.[21] Her name as proprietor appears in the *San Jose City Directories* between 1893 and 1900.[22]

By 1900, with her own health failing and recognizing that her nieces and nephews were able to care for themselves, Mother St. Andrew wrote to Mother Florence Walter, Superior General of the Congregation of Divine Providence of San Antonio, Texas, asking permission to return to the Congregation. With Bishop Neraz's death in 1894 and Father Henry Pefferkorn's (former pastor at St. Joseph's Church, Downtown San Antonio, who had instigated the proceedings against Mother St. Andrew in 1886 that led to her estrangement from the Congregation) retirement to his family home in Lorraine, Germany, the climate in the Diocese of San Antonio allowed for Mother St. Andrew's return.

Though the Motherhouse had been moved from Castroville to San Antonio in 1895, Mother St. Andrew returned to Castroville where she was warmly received.

She lived her last five years at Castroville, praying, reading, writing to her nieces, and visiting with the townspeople who had loved her and cared for her. On February 1, 1905, diabetes and heart disease eventually took her life. She was 74 years old. She was bur-

---

19 E-mail of James A. Sarrail to Sister Diane Langford, November 2005.
20 San Jose City Directories housed at History San Jose, San Jose, California
21 Callahan, p. 154. It should be noted here that Sister Alma Marty's recollections are that the Feltins moved to Anaheim, not San Jose, and established a grocery store there. [Marty Letter, Murphy, "Chronicle"]
22 San Jose City Directories housed at History San Jose, San Jose, California

ied from St. Louis Church in Castroville and buried with other Sisters in the St. Louis parish cemetery.[23] When the Congregation of Divine Providence moved the remains of its early members from the St. Louis Cemetery to Providence Cemetery at Our Lady of the Lake Convent in San Antonio, Texas, in 1918, her remains were re-interred there.

ENDNOTES   *CHAPTER II*   *OLD FRIENDS*

When Mother Adrienne Frache, Superior of the Sisters of Divine Providence of St. Jean-de-Bassel, Lorraine, France, from 1864-1867[24], missioned Sisters St. André Feltin and Alphonse Boëgler to Texas in 1866, the Congregation in Europe was under the Bishop of Nancy[25] and *Abbé* Nicolas Michel[26] was its ecclesiastical superior. Nothing in the history of the Congregation in Europe[27] nor in Texas[28] indicates that the formal authority for the Congregational mission in Texas had been transferred to Bishop Claude Marie Dubuis (Bishop of Galveston, 1862-1882). The biographer of Bishop Dubuis, L. V.

23 Callahan, p. 154-155.
24 Letter to Mother Philothea Thiry from Mother Maria Houlné, October 8, 1928. [Copy, CDP Archives]
25 Wilhelm, Abbé J., La Congregation des Sœurs de la Divine Providence de Saint-Jean-de-Bassel (Moselle). *Imprimerie Saint-Paul,* Bar-le-Duc: 1927, p. 76. [Note: In 1874, new episcopal boundaries were drawn to coincide with the new political boundaries following the Franco-Prussian War. St. Jean-de-Bassel fell in the Diocese of Metz in the new designations and remains there today.]
26 Wilhelm, Abbé J., p. 58.
27 Gruber, Marie-Josée, La Congrégation de la Divine Providence Saint-Jean-de-Bassel, 1827-1918. I.C.F.P., 1982. (This book, in the main, was written by Sister Pierre Gruber in 1976 as partial requirement of her doctorate at the University of Metz. She died in 1980 and the Congregation published it posthumously.)
28 Callahan, Sister Generosa, The History of the Sisters of Divine Providence, San Antonio, Texas. Milwaukee: Catholic Life Publications, Bruce Press, 1955.

Jacks, barely mentions the Sisters of Divine Providence;[29] and in her history of the Congregation, Callahan describes a generous paternal relationship between Bishop Dubuis and the Sisters of Divine Providence, which included the Bishop providing them with property in Castroville on which to build their motherhouse, but not an ecclesial relationship comparable to that of "founder" in the United States.[30]

A letter to Mother Philothea Thiry of the Sisters of Divine Providence of San Antonio, Texas, in 1928 from Mother Maria Houlné of the Congregation of Divine Providence of St. Jean-de-Bassel, however, offers another point of view. She wrote "... it seems that Sister Andrew and Sister Alphonse from the beginning considered themselves independent of the Congregation of St. Jean-de-Bassel." According to that same letter, "ear-witnesses" note that Mother St. Andrew's 1878 visit to Germany was preceded by her letter—the first since she had left France for Texas.[31]

Bishop Dubuis may have considered himself to be the ecclesiastical superior of a Congregation which did not have pontifical approbation, but, unlike the documents establishing the Sisters of Charity of the Incarnate Word (CCVI) in San Antonio[32], no such document exists for the Sisters of Divine Providence.

In 1868, Father Peter Richard, the pastor at St. Louis Parish in Castroville was appointed ecclesiastical superior of the fledgling community by Bishop Dubuis, but there is still no evidence that this

29 Jacks, L.V., Claude Dubuis, Bishop of Galveston. St. Louis, MO: Herder Book Co., 1946, p. 210 and 224.

30 Callahan, p. 56.

31 Letter, Houlné, October 8, 1928. Note: The reader will recall that when Mother St. Andrew left St. Jean-de-Bassel, the Department of Lorraine was in France; by 1878, both Lorraine and Alsace were in Germany. Further, the reader will note that the analysis in the 1928 Houlné letter (written many years after the fact) is admittedly based on hearsay. No records of these relationships are in any archives.

32 Hegarty, Sister Mary Loyola, CCVI, Serving with Gladness-The Origin and History of the Sisters of Charity of the Incarnate Word, Milwaukee: Bruce Publishing Co., 1967, p. 288

action separated the Texas Sisters from their general motherhouse in France.

During her twenty years as superior, Mother St. Andrew made four trips back to Germany[33] (June 1878,[34] 1880, 1882, and 1883) to make reports to Mother Constantine Eck (Superior General from 1867 to1885) and to invite both professed members and postulants and novices at the Motherhouse to return with her to Texas. Each time Mother Constantine missioned seasoned professed Sisters and/ or numerous postulants and novices to Texas, suggesting her contin-

---

33 Alsace and Lorraine are two departments (states) in France which are renowned for their agricultural production. Alsace is home to numerous vineyards and wine producers; Lorraine produces wheat, beef, and cheese. These two departments were primary prizes for the winner of various wars throughout history. In 1871, the Franco-Prussian War ended in the defeat of France and Alsace and Lorraine were taken over by Germany. They continued as part of Germany through World War I. In 1918, they reverted back to France. (Michelin Travel Publications, The Green Guide-Alsace, Lorraine, Champagne. Herts, UK: Hannay House, 2004.) Thus, Mother St. Andrew and Sister Alphonse came to Texas from France, but when Mother went back to Europe to report to Mother Constantine Eck and acquire new recruits for the mission effort, she returned to Germany.

34 Though it may seem strange that the first visit to Europe occurred nearly twelve years after coming to Texas, several things need to be remembered: 1) the Texas mission was permanently established in Castroville only in 1868; 2) in 1868 the French motherhouse opened a mission in Algiers and Sisters at St. Jean-de-Bassel were encouraged to go there; 3) in 1870-1871 there was a war between France and Germany which was, no doubt, disruptive to travel, and created enormous stress on the German motherhouse, eventually requiring a complete change of curriculum for teacher certification; 4) building the Motherhouse in Castroville and a number of internal crises in Texas surely kept Mother St. Andrew focused; 5) various projects (building a chapel, improvements to the Sisters educational curriculum, transitioning to a German political regime) occupied Mother Constantine. (Wilhelm, Abbé J., p. 58-66 and Callahan, p. 82 ff.)

ued confidence in Mother St. Andrew as well as her support of the Texas mission.[35]

In 1883, unbeknown to Mother St. Andrew, Bishop Jean-Claude Neraz, Bishop of San Antonio from 1881 until his death in 1894[36],

---

35 Unfortunately, neither the archives at St. Jean-de-Bassel nor the archives at Our Lady of the Lake Convent hold any correspondence between Mother St. Andrew and Mother Constantine. Further, neither archives indicates why such correspondence is missing, although Mother Maria Houlné's 1928 letter to Mother Philothea Thiry says that the papers of Reverend Superior Nicolas Michel, superior of the European Congregation from 1862 until his death in 1888 were lost after his death. This leaves a gap in the history of the European Congregation. Only a letter from Sister St. Andrew to Abbé Michel and his response, written just before his death in 1888, are extant. [Original in SJB Archives, copy in CDP Archives]. This author would like to suggest another possibility. When Bishop Jean-Claude Neraz, Bishop of San Antonio from 1881 to 1894, visited Mother Constantine in 1883, he might have asked her to transfer the formal ecclesiastical superiorship of the Texas Sisters to himself and asked for archival materials from Mother Constantine's records to establish the history of the Congregation in Texas. Mother Constantine was in ill health and because of expenses incurred at the St. Jean-de-Bassel Motherhouse for improvements to their farm in order to secure the health of the Sisters, it is plausible that Mother Constantine might have released the Texas Congregation to the Bishop of San Antonio with the intent of better insuring their future. The alleged destruction of CDP records in Castroville in the summer of 1886 and subsequently during the tenure of Mother Florence Walter would account for the lack of correspondence in the Texas archives. Further, the Archives of the Archdiocese of San Antonio, do not have any materials in Bishop Neraz's file that would shed light on this issue. (Brother Edward Loch, SM, Archivist for the Archdiocese, noted to the author [September 2005] that Archbishop Robert Lucey "cleaned out" the archives to make room for his own papers.)

36 Finck, Sister Helena. The Congregation of the Sisters of Charity of the Incarnate Word of San Antonio, Texas (doctoral dissertation). Washington, DC: Catholic University of America, 1925, p. 60; Jacks, p. 215-216.
    Author's note: In 1874 the Diocese of San Antonio was established with Bishop Dominic Pellicer as its first Bishop. Pellicer died in 1880. Bishop Dubuis continued to serve as Bishop of Galveston until he retired in

made a visit to the St. Jean-de-Bassel Motherhouse. Though exactly what transpired in his conversations with Mother Constantine is unknown, Mother Maria Houlné's 1928 letter to Mother Philothea says:

> *Considering the great distance and consequently the difficulty of a regular supervision, the Superiors judged it prudent to decline all responsibility for a Foundation which had remained for them, up to then, a closed book. From that day on, theCongregation in Texas was no longer a part of the Mother Congregation in Europe. This decision was communicated to Mother St. Andrew.[37]*

If this communication took place in 1883, a written documentation of it is no longer extant and no other extant correspondence between Mother St. Andrew and Bishop Neraz mentions it.

In a letter of August 16, 1886, following a conflict between Mother St. Andrew and several diocesan priests over relationships between Sisters and their pastors, Bishop Neraz demanded that the Sisters hold an election to select another Superior. On August 26, 1886, Neraz came out to the Motherhouse in Castroville to supervise this election.[39] Some thirty professed Sisters, home for their summer studies and retreat, assembled. There is no evidence that Neraz told them that their Congregation was at that time, nor would be at any

---

1882. Bishop N. A. Gallagher was consecrated Bishop of Galveston in 1882. (from Wangler, <u>1874-1974—Archdiocese of San Antonio</u>, p. 13.)

37 Houlné Letter, October 8, 1928 [Copy, CDP Archives]

38 Strebler, Joseph, *Alsaciens au Texas*. Culture Alsacienne, Strasbourg: 1975, p. 66. [Unfortunately, Father Strebler does not designate specifically his sources for his book, though he lists "Documents and Works Consulted" at the end of the Chapter. Among works he consulted were Callahan, <u>The History of the Sisters of Divine Providence</u> (cited earlier) and several letters, but he does not attach his cited works to specific items in his text.]

time in the future be separated from their European Motherhouse. However, in 1960, in his short history of Alsatian émigrés to Texas, Archbishop Joseph Strebler of Togo (Africa) holds that it was Bishop Neraz' intention to separate the Texas branch and place them under his own ecclesiastical authority. Strebler also notes that since 1883 Mother St. Andrew had vigorously opposed his attempts at separation.[39] Since over half of the Texas Congregation was from Germany[40], a legal or ecclesial separation would have been very significant for them.

Mother St. Andrew received a majority of the votes on the first ballot, but Bishop Neraz rejected her election and called for a second ballot and then a third. On the third ballot, for the well-being of her beloved community, Mother St. Andrew directed the electors to vote for Sister Florence Walter. At that instant Sister Florence was en route to San Antonio by train having just returned with new candidates from Europe.[41]

In September of 1886, Sister St. Andrew was missioned to St. Joseph's School in Galveston, Texas, at her own request. Sister Arsene Schaff, who had been named First Assistant to the newly-elected Mother Florence, allowed her loyalties to remain with Mother St. Andrew and soon followed her to Galveston where Sister Arsene had been missioned before her present appointment and had "lived in continual peace and harmony for the [previous] eight years."[42] She attempted to resign her administrative position in Castroville in a letter to Bishop Neraz, but the Bishop refused the resignation. In a September 26, 1886, letter to Bishop Neraz, Mother St. Andrew resigned from the Congregation with the intention of establishing a separate novitiate at Frelsburg, Texas, under

---

39 Strebler, p. 66.
40 Lists of Sisters, CDP Archives
41 Callahan, p. 143-144.
42 Callahan, p. 145.

Bishop Gallagher of Galveston.[43] [The Frelsburg property had been acquired in 1881 by the Congregation while Bishop Dubuis was the Ordinary of Galveston, though the Frelsburg, Texas, mission dates from 1871[44]. Plans for another novitiate at Frelsburg had been discussed by Mother St. Andrew and Bishop Dubuis prior to the erection of the Diocese of San Antonio. Another novitiate at Frelsburg did not materialize before Bishop Dubuis retired to France.] Bishop Gallagher agreed to accept Mother St. Andrew; however, after hearing from Bishop Neraz, he changed his mind.[45]

In October 1886, at an apparent impasse with Bishop Neraz, Sister St. Andrew and Sister Arsene "procured some tickets and some money"[46] and went to St. Boniface Parish in Anaheim, California, without his permission.[47] There are no records that indicate why they chose this destination. The pastor at St. Boniface Parish was very positive toward having them establish a parish school and hoped that Bishop Neraz would send them back to California to begin a mission.

Upon their return to Castroville, however, Neraz excommunicated the two nuns. Mother St. Andrew immediately wrote the Bishop asking his pardon for going to California without permission and begging him to allow her to go to confession and receive Holy Communion. In his responding letter of October 26, 1886, Neraz gave Sister St. Andrew permission to remain in Castroville, but continued her excommunication until Mother Florence, who was away visiting other missions, would return to Castroville and all could be regularized with her. The excommunication lasted nearly a month.

When Mother Florence returned to Castroville, Sister St. Andrew repaid her the money that she had "procured" for the trip to California

---

43 Author's note: Callahan, on page 145-146, quotes a letter from Sister St. Andrew to Bishop Neraz. A separate house in Frelsburg seems intended.

44 Data from CDP Archives

45 Callahan, p. 146.

46 Callahan, p. 147.

47 Callahan, p. 146.

and promised to be obedient to her. She accepted Mother Florence's directive to go to Clarksville, Texas, as a teacher. Sister Arsene was sent to help at Haby's Settlement, a school some five miles outside Castroville down the Rio Medina road.

In March of 1887, however, apparently frustrated with her situation, Sister St. Andrew, again without permission, set out for Anaheim, California, in the Diocese of Los Angeles, where she reestablished herself at St. Boniface Parish pastored by Father P. Stöters. She immediately set to work teaching the children and preparing them for their sacraments. Recognizing how much there was to be done, she wrote to Sister Arsene, who was unhappily living at Haby's Settlement, inviting her to join her. With the permission of Mother Florence, but without the knowledge of Bishop Neraz (at the suggestion of Mother Florence) Sister Arsene went to California.[48] Callahan, in her history of the Congregation, says, "From this incident it seems that Mother Florence wanted Mother St. Andrew to work in a place where she would be happy; in fact, she tried to help her."[49]

Correspondence between the Bishop of Los Angeles, the Bishop of San Antonio, and the Pastor of St. Boniface indicates that the Bishop of San Antonio led the Bishop of Los Angeles to distrust the Sisters. The Bishop of Los Angeles subsequently directed the pastor of St. Boniface Parish to dismiss the Sisters. At the end of July 1887, the two Sisters returned once again to Castroville.[50]

This time Bishop Neraz instructed Mother Florence to dismiss them from the Congregation. Sister Arsene returned to St. Jean-

---

48 Letter, Sister Arsene Schaff to Bishop Neraz, July 30, 1887. CDP Archives.

49 Callahan, p. 150.

50 Letter from Bishop Jean-Claude Neraz to V. Rev. J. Adam, V.G., Diocese of Los Angeles, March 29, 1887. Letter from Bishop Gallagher, Diocese of Galveston to V. Rev. J. Adam, Diocese of Los Angeles, May 9, 1887. CDP Archives. Letter from Sister St. Andrew Feltin to V. Rev. J. Adam, Vicar General, Diocese of Los Angeles, May 24, 1887. CDP Archives. Letters from Rev. P. Stöters, Pastor of St. Boniface to V. Rev. J. Adam, Diocese of Los Angeles, June 12, 13, 1887. CDP Archives.

de-Bassel in Germany on August 8, 1887,[51] and Sister St. Andrew went to her brother Louis' Castroville home until a house of her own could be acquired. Sister St. Andrew continued to wear the habit of a Sister of Divine Providence and remained faithful to her religious vows.[52]

Little is known of this two-year experience of living alone in Castroville. Remembrances of Sister Alma Marty indicate that Sister St. Andrew was cared for by the people of Castroville who loved her very much.[53]

In March of 1888, Sister St. Andrew wrote a letter to *Abbé* Nicolas Michel, the ecclesiastical superior of the Sisters of Divine Providence at St. Jean-de-Bassel in Germany. Her letter offers a description of her situation: living in a "little house for negroes (sic), without confession or communion, and no one here dares do anything for me, under pain of excommunication ..." In the letter she asks *Abbé* Michel to give her a "certificate" which will authenticate her membership in the St. Jean-de-Bassel Congregation so that she can go to the Diocese of Leavenworth, Kansas, to work for the German bishop there. She begs Michel to remember her good works and "not to judge me according to the blame that is made against me ..." The letter also states that Bishop Neraz had "relieved [her] of [her] vows", and

51 Material from Sister Camille Schaff's file, Archives, St. Anne's Convent, Melbourne, KY.

52 Callahan, p 144-154. Sister Generosa offers a fuller explanation of this experience in the pages indicated. Copies of some of the letters referenced are in the Archives of the Congregation of Divine Providence. However, letters noted as from the Archives of the Archdiocese of San Antonio that were not copied at the time of her research in the early 1950's are no longer extant, due to the actions of Archbishop Lucey noted above. Much was lost by this action.

53 Murphy (ed.), <u>Chronicles.</u> "Names You Know—Mother St. Andrew Feltin, 1830-1905, Firsts (sic) Superior General in Texas," As Remembered and Written by Sister M. Alma Marty in 1936. CDP Archives.

she asks Michel to give her another name in religion, basically so that she can start over.[54]

In his response of March 21, 1888, *Abbé* Michel simply says he cannot do as Sister St. Andrew asks. Since she is no longer a member of the Congregation, he cannot give her another name in religion; he has determined that she cannot be received back into the German Congregation; she will not be authorized to begin any other work in the United States under the auspices of St. Jean-de-Bassel. He did offer to send her a copy of an 1866 certificate on file at the time that evidently indicated her original membership in the St. Jean-de-Bassel Congregation, "omitting the name of Texas or the name you bore when you were a member of the [German] Congregation."[55] This last concession seems to suggest that the Congregational leadership in Germany, saddened by all that had happened, and, perhaps, grieving the loss of their Sisters in the United States, were offering what they deemed possible to their estranged daughter.

For two years Mother St. Andrew lived alone in Castroville before accompanying her brother Louis and his children to California.

During this same period of time, Sister Arsene was at St. Jean-de-Bassel. Upon her return to Germany from Texas in August of 1887, she re-entered the novitiate and received a new religious name: Sister Camille.[56]

Mother Anna Houlné, the Superior General who succeeded Mother Constantine Eck, was continuing to struggle against mounting tensions that resulted from increased controls over educational standards by the German government. After taking counsel with her administration, Mother Anna began to actively seek other missionary possibilities for her Sisters in the United States. According

---

54 Letter to Abbé Nicolas Michel from Sister St. André Feltin, March 2, 1888. Held in the Archives of St. Jean-de-Bassel; copy in the CDP Archives. Translated from the French.

55 Letter to Sister St. Andrew from Abbé Nicolas Michel and Mother Anna Houlné, March 21,1888.Held in the Archive of St. Jean-de-Bassel; copy in the CDP Archives. Translated from the French.

56 Record in the Archives at St. Anne's Convent, Melbourne, KY.

to the history of the Kentucky province, when Mother Anna opened "a Catholic Directory at random, she saw at first glance the name Camillus Paul Maes, Bishop of Covington, Kentucky, and, taking this as an answer to prayer, she wrote "... [a] letter to the Bishop on May 19, 1888," offering to send Sisters to his diocese. This initial risk led to the eventual founding of the United States Province of the Sisters of Divine Providence of St. Jean-de-Bassel in August 1889. Sister Camille Schaff was one of the three Sisters sent to Kentucky to begin this venture.[57]

Sister Camille, baptized Barbara Schaff, was born to Louis and Catherine Petit Schaff on October 17, 1850, in Lambach, Lorraine, France. She entered St. Jean de-Bassel in 1866, and volunteered for Texas in 1878, where she served at St. Joseph's School in Galveston, and Haby's Settlement, near Castroville.[58] Upon her election as Superior General in 1886, Mother Florence Walter named Sister Arsene to be her First Assistant. As noted earlier, Sister Arsene's loyalty to Mother St. Andrew compelled her to resign her administrative position and follow Mother St. Andrew to Galveston, accompany her on her first trip to California, and then ask Mother Florence to send her to be with Mother St. Andrew on her second trip to California. When the mission in Anaheim, California, was not approved by Bishop Neraz, Sister St. Andrew and Sister Arsene returned to Castroville. Sister Arsene then chose to return to St. Jean-de-Bassel.

Sister Camille (Arsene) came to Kentucky in August of 1889, nearly two years to the day since she had left Texas. She opened a school at Ludlow, KY, in September 1890, and then opened another school in West Covington, KY, in 1891. Mother Anna Houlné visited Kentucky in 1892-93 and while the Superior General was in the US, Sister Camille asked to pronounce her perpetual vows. On the Feast

---

57 Humbert, Sister Agnes Margaret, CDP, A History of the American Province of the Congregation of Divine Providence of St. Jean-de-Bassel. Privately published by the American Province in celebration of the Province's centenary, 1989. Pages xi ff.

58 Archives, Sisters of Divine Providence, Melbourne, KY, and Archives, Sisters of Divine Providence, San Antonio, TX.

of St. Anne in 1893, Sister Camille made her perpetual profession and then on August 1, she, along with eight other Sisters, assumed charge of Caldwell Hall, a student residence at the Catholic University of America in Washington, DC.[59]

Sister Camille remained at Caldwell Hall until 1911 when she returned to St. Anne's Convent, Melbourne, KY. She lived there in retirement until her death at age 75 on December 27, 1925. She is buried in the Convent Cemetery at St. Anne's.[60]

Addendum to Endnotes

I. In a letter to the very Reverend J. B. C. Audet, Vicar General of the Diocese of San Antonio, dated September 11, 1901, Mother Florence is responding to an inquiry from Msgr. Audet, about the ecclesiastical status of the Sisters of Divine Providence. The full text of the letter follows here.

> *I beg [I] have to apologize for not replying to your kind communication earlier. Absence from home occasioned the delay. I[n] accordance to your request I answer the following:*
> *I. Our Mother House is situated @ St. Jean de Bassel Lorraine from which the first Sisters of Div. Providence came to Texas*
> *II. Our Congregation has only Episcopal approbation.*
> *III.At the request of Rt. Rev. Dubuis two Sisters of Div. Providence left St. Jean-de-Bassel Lorraine for Galveston Aug. 1866 accompa-*

---

59 The Catholic University of America had opened on November 3, 1889. The Kentucky CDPs served in various positions of domestic service there through 1986. [Humbert, footnote, p. 45.]

60 Humbert, p.13, 28, 45-46,

nied by the worth[y] prelate. The diocese of
San Antonio did not exist then.
Hoping the above statement to be satisfac-
tory, I beg to remain

Yours very respectfully
Mother M. Florence
Sup. Genl[61]

(This is a faithful copy of the letter [with the exception of the
inserted "I"in the first sentence, "n" in the third sentence, and
"y" in part III] which appears to be written by Mother Florence
personally, not a secretary. Specific abbreviations have been
retained. It would appear from this 1901 document that Mother
Florence believed that her Congregation was still connected to
the European Motherhouse.)

II. Though not germane to this work, readers may be interested to
know that in 1907 Mother Florence Walter and Sister Flavienne
Braun who had come to Texas from St. Jean de Bassel in 1882,[62]
visited Mt. St. Martin, the provincialate of the Sisters of Divine
Providence of St. Jean-de-Bassel, Germany, located in Newport,
Kentucky. They arrived on May 7, 1907, and remained until May
16, 1907. The purpose of this visit is unknown, but a General
Chapter of the Sisters of Divine Providence was held at St. Jean-
de-Bassel in September 1907, and Mother Maria Houlné (not
Mother Anna Houlné, but her blood sister), provincial superior
of the Kentucky province and Mother Ambroise, her assistant,
left for that meeting in July of that year.[63] It is plausible, even
likely, that various possibilities for the future relationship of the

61 Letter to Very Rev. J. B C. Audet, VG from Mother Florence Walter,
    Sept. 11, 1901. Held in the Archives of the Archdiocese of San Antonio.
62 Neeb, Sr. Joseph, Memoirs of the Congregation of the Sisters of Divine
    Providence. San Antonio, Texas: Nic Tengg, 1916, p. 37.
63 Humbert, p. 107-108.

San Antonio Sisters of Divine Providence to the Motherhouse at St. Jean-de-Bassel were discussed. A few years after this visit, in 1912, the Congregation of Divine Providence of San Antonio, Texas, received pontifical approbation making it canonically independent of St. Jean-de-Bassel and no longer a diocesan congregation under the supervision of the Bishop of San Antonio.

III. A thorough reading of the history of the Kentucky CDPs reveals that the loss of the Texas branch of the Sisters of Divine Providence greatly impacted the Motherhouse in Germany. The style of supervision by Europe of the fledgling Kentucky community, Mother Anna Houlné's early visit in 1892-93, the request of the Superior General at St. Jean that the three missionaries who established the Kentucky foundation make an "oath of allegiance to the Congregation,"[64] having Sisters travel somewhat frequently back to the German Motherhouse, and close contact with Provincial Superiors (all of whom were European until 1937) suggest that the Superiors in Europe were not going to allow what happened in Texas in 1886 to reoccur.

CHAPTER III   ROOTS   ENDNOTES

Jean-Claude Feltin and Marie-Louise Seiter were married in her home parish, Sts. Peter and Paul, in Pfaffenhoffen, Alsace, on the south bank of the River Moder, on July 25, 1825.[65] Jean-Claude, born in Fontaine, France, on October 20, 1786, was a lieutenant in the

---

64 This information is in a draft of Chapter I of Humbert's history, but is not in the final work. She further notes that an oath of allegiance was not actually required, but Sister Chantal Arth, named Superior for the new venture, Sister Camille Schaff, and Sister St. Lucie Damidio were asked to renew their vows before leaving St. Jean-de-Bassel. They were asked to include the phrase "In this Congregation of Sisters of Providence ..." in the formula, a phrase which has been retained. [Draft of Humbert's History, Archives, St. Anne Convent, Melbourne, Kentucky 41059]

65 Sts. Peter and Paul Parish Records, Pfaffenhofen, Alsace, France

customs service (*Lieutenant d'Ordre des Douanes*) of France and nearly twenty years older than his bride, Marie-Louise, daughter of Joseph Seiter, who had been born in LaWalck on April 18, 1805.[66] It is likely that Lt. Feltin was stationed in Mertzwiller at the time he courted Marie-Louise and made her his bride. Though their first child, Pierre-Isidore, was born in Marie-Louise's home village of LaWalck (November 1825[67]), the Lieutenant must have soon moved his wife and baby to Mertzwiller, about four miles away. Two more sons were born there: François-Joseph, born on August 30, 1827[68], and Nicolas, born in 1829[69].

Sometime in 1830, Lt. Feltin was transferred to the Strasbourg area, some 35 miles farther east on the Rhine River. He settled his family in a home on *Rue des Moines*[70] in the small village of Geispolsheim near Fort Lefebvre. Louise Feltin, their first daughter, was born there two days after Christmas in 1830.[71]. Three more children were born in Geispolsheim: a son, Celestin, in 1834; a daughter, Marie-Anne, in 1836; and another daughter, Rosalie, in 1837 (died in infancy in 1838).[72]

The Feltins lived on *Rue des Moines* (Street of the Monks) during Lt. Feltin's tenure of at least ten years in Geispolsheim, a rather large town of over 2,000 people. The village has existed before the Roman invasion and is on an ancient road from Strasbourg to Entzenheim which is about ten miles further south of Geispolsheim. Since the town was surrounded by good farming land, the people at

66 City records in Mayor's Office, LaWalck, Alsace, France.

67 Sts. Peter and Paul Parish Records, Pfaffenhoffen, France.

68 Bastien Family Record, handwritten copy given to Sr. Angelina Murphy by Rev. Bernard Bastian in March 2000. Copy held in CDP Archives.

69 Strebler, p. 39. Baptismal records in the parish in Mertzwiller show that Nicholas was baptized on May 17, 1829. (CDP Archives)

70 Geispolsheim—Entre Tradition et Modernisme, p. 194.

71 City records in Mayor's Office, Geispolsheim, France.

72 City records in Mayor's Office, Geispolsheim, Alsace, France and family record of Rev. Bernard Bastian, Strasbourg, the great-great grandson of Marie-Anne Feltin and her husband Isidore Seiter. (CDP Archives)

the time the Feltins lived there were not tied to raising animals and thus were "more cultured." Ste. Marguerite Church, built in the late 1700's, no doubt the center of the town's life, burned in 1833; but because Catholicism permeated the very fiber of the people's lives, this tragedy would not have disrupted worship. Religious processions abounded and religious symbols adorned public buildings and houses.[73]

It was in Geispolsheim that Louise Feltin began school. Smaller French villages often had a school for boys conducted by priests or a trained schoolteacher, but usually there was not a similar school for girls. Geispolsheim had a boys' school and in 1836, the Sisters of Divine Providence, whose Motherhouse is in Ribeauvillé, opened a school for girls.[74] These Sisters were founded by *L'Père* Louis Krempp who felt confident that he could shepherd the ministerial work of his sisters, but who told the fledgling group to "look to *le père* (Jean-Martin) Moye for spiritual guidance."[75]

Sometime around 1840, Lt. Feltin, then in his middle fifties, resigned his commission in *L'Ordre des Douanes* and moved his family back to Marie-Louise's home village of LaWalck. There he acquired a grocery store and Marie-Louise gave birth to two more children: their youngest son, Louis, in 1843 and their youngest daughter, Christine, 1846.[76]

---

73 Geisplosheim—Entre Tradition et Modernisme, pgs. 40 ff.
74 Geispolsheim—Entre Tradition et Modernisme, pg. 243-244
75 Personal conversations with Sisters of Divine Providence at their motherhouse in Ribeauville, France, June 2000 and presentation by their Superior General at the International Meeting of the Daughters of Father Moye, June 2000, Campion, Belgium. The Sisters of Ribeauvillé have consistently followed The Directory of Fr. Moye since their founding in 1783. In 2000 they were received as one of the "daughter" congregations, joining six other communities who trace their heritage to the 18th century French priest-founder.
76 Strebler, Alsaciens au Texas, p. 39 and Louis Feltin's Death Record, Santa Clara County Records, San Jose, CA.

It can be presumed that the children grew up working in the family grocery store. Isidore Jean-Claude Feltin died at age 69 in 1855; Marie-Louise Seiter Feltin died in 1871 at age 66.[77]

By the time Jean-Claude and Marie-Louise had died, four of their seven living children had immigrated to the United States. Nicolas, trained to be a priest at the diocesan seminary in Strasbourg (1849-1852), in 1852 was invited by Bishop Jean-Marie Odin, the Bishop of Texas to serve in his needy diocese. A subdeacon when he sailed to Texas with Bishop Odin, Nicolas was ordained a priest in Houston in 1853 following training for the missions and studies in the English language at St. Mary-of-the-Barrens in Perryville, Missouri. He served at St. Vincent de Paul Parish in Houston from 1853-1864; as pastor of St. Mary's Parish in Austin, Texas, from 1864 to 1874; and as pastor of St. Joseph's German Parish in San Antonio, Texas, for four years until his untimely death there in 1878 at age 49.[78] Nicolas made at least two trips back to his homeland.

Celestin followed Nicolas to Houston and died there of yellow fever in 1857 at age 23. He is buried at St. Vincent de Paul Cemetery there.[79]

Louise (Mother St. Andrew) Feltin came to Texas, also at the invitation of the Bishop of Galveston, then Claude-Marie Dubuis, in October 1866. She made four trips to her motherhouse, St. Jean-de-Bassel, Lorraine, Germany, before dying at Castroville, Texas in 1905 at age 74.

Louis Feltin came to Texas in 1868 and lived in the United States, never returning to his homeland, until his death in San Jose,

---

77 City records in Mayor's Office, LaWalck, Alsace, France.
78 Strebler, <u>Alsaciens du Texas</u>, p. 40-41; Certificate, Diocese of Strasbourg (CDP Archives); Records taken from Catholic Directories 1854-1878 (CDP Archives).
79 St. Vincent de Paul Church, Houston, records and note by Sr. Mary Paul Valdez, CDP, dated June 10, 1998. (CDP Archives)

California, in 1927 at age 84.[80] More about Louis Feltin can be found in the Endnotes to Chapter I.

The eldest son, Pierre, married Eva Berback and they had two children: Marie, born in LaWalck in 1864, and Pierre Isidore who died in infancy at age seven months in 1866. Pierre served his town as mayor but died at the early age of 42 in 1867.[81]

Marie-Anne Feltin married Isidore Seiter and they had five children. It is presumed that she lived her entire life in LaWalck, dying there on November 18, 1906.[82] Christine worked as a teacher in the United States (location unknown) but returned to LaWalck where she died on January 5, 1939.[83]

Unfortunately, nothing is known of Francois-Joseph.

Author's Note: The basis for the information in Chapter III is, in addition to specific references citied in the Endnotes, *Geispolsheim— Entre Tradition et Modernisme*, published by Edition Copru, in Strasbourg, 1999; and the author's own experiences of visiting Strasbourg, LaWalck, Pfaffenhoffen, and Geispolsheim in 2000 and 2007.

ENDNOTES   CHAPTER IV   A NEW LIFE

Father Jean-Martin Moye (1730-1793), a priest of the Catholic Diocese of Metz, France, was a curate at St. Victor Parish in Metz

---

80 Church records, St. Mary's Parish, Austin, TX, held at Texas Catholic Archives, Austin; Death Certificate, Santa Clara County Records, San Jose, CA.

81 City records, Mayor's Office, LaWalck, Alsace, France.

82 Bastian Family Records cited earlier (CDP Archives)

83 City Records, LaWalck, Alsace, France. And a notation on the back of a photo of Christine which is in the archives at St. Jean-de-Bassel indicates that she was a teacher. There is some indication in that notation that she "replaced Sr. Andrew when she rejoined her Congregation ..." There is no information about what happened to Christine while in America. The Bastian Family Record (handwritten by Remy Bastian in 2000) indicates that she returned to LaWalck and died there.

when he launched a project which was destined to bring forward seven congregations of religious women, familiarly known among

themselves as "The Daughters of Father Moye."[84] In their earliest years, these Sisters would specialize in opening and staffing schools in small, rural villages, first in France and then in the United States, Poland, Belgium, Italy, and various countries on the continents of Africa and Latin America. Moye's first "daughter" was Marguerite Lecomte, a Metz factory worker who taught herself to read while she convalesced from a broken leg. In 1762, he sent her to the hamlet of Befey/St. Hubert, about ten miles north of Metz, where she, at his direction, began a school and lived the spiritual and corporal works of mercy among the villagers. This small beginning eventually attracted other women who saw an opportunity to make a difference with their lives. As the numbers of women drawn to this apostolic work grew, an organized structure was needed. Madame Marie Morel was named by Father Moye to be the first superior of the fledgling group and a novitiate was established in Haut-Clocher in Lorraine, France, in 1768. Since Lorraine was one of the two states (the other being Alsace) along the French-German border, candidates were both German- and French-speaking. Schools multiplied as more and more pastors and mayors asked these women to begin schools for their parishes. Though Moye had

Blessed Jean-Martin Moye, Founder of the Sisters of Providence (1730-1793)

---

*   **At the 2006 International Meeting of the Daughters of Father Moye, participants learned of "The Sisters of Father Moye," a government-recognized Congregation of Women Religious in China. Little is known of them. In addition, Father Moye founded the "Chinese Virgins" while he was in China and it is believed that they still exist underground.**

84 See schematic in the front of the book.

used the names "Sisters of the Infant Jesus" or "Sisters of Christian Schools," the people of the villages called these pioneer educators "Sisters of Providence." And that name held.

In 1771, Father Moye felt called to be a missionary in China, leaving the now successful project in the hands of Father Antoine François Raulin. Another priest, Father Dominic Lacombe had also been involved from the outset. By the time Father Moye returned to France twelve years later in 1783 there were four novitiates, or training centers, for the Sisters of Providence: one at Cutting, Father Moye's home village in Lorraine; one in Siersthal; one in St.-Dié; and another in Essegney. Though these early training centers were chiefly oriented to teacher formation, Father Moye insisted that his "daughters" develop four virtues that he considered fundamental to their apostolic lives: simplicity, poverty, abandonment to the Providence of God, and charity. The formation at the training centers included in-depth work on an understanding of their life as religious and a general knowledge of Catholic teaching as well as secular subjects and pedagogy.

Fewer than thirty years after the opening of the first school in 1762, the secularizing effects of the French Revolution and its aftermath (1789-early 1800's) precipitated the dispersal of the Sisters. They either stayed in the villages where they maintained the schools and worked as laywomen or they returned to their home villages for safety. Moye himself and a few Sisters fled to Trier, Germany where, while ministering to refugees, he contracted yellow fever and died on May 4, 1793.

After the initial terrors of the French Revolution calmed, the Sisters regrouped, novitiates were re-opened, and the work and training of the Sisters resumed. In 1806 a novitiate was opened in Portieux, which eventually housed the French-speaking motherhouse of the re-established group. The German-speaking motherhouse-novitiate was re-opened by Father Pierre Lacombe in Cutting in 1801 and moved to Hommarting by Father Jean Decker upon Pierre Lacombe's death in 1812. Father Dominic Lacombe (Pierre

LaCombe's brother) had re-opened the novitiate at Siersthal in 1801, and at his death in 1815 it was merged with the novitiate at Hommarting. Thus, by 1815 there were two remaining novitiates of the Congregation, both in the Diocese of Nancy in Lorraine: Portieux, French-speaking, and Hommarting, German-speaking. The civil approbation of this Congregation, which came in 1816, united both principal houses into one Congregation. The two houses, Portieux and Hommarting, however, remained independent of each other in all but civil matters.

Ecclesial developments in the early 1800's led to the two houses becoming canonically independent of each other. Sister Generosa Callahan described this development in her book, *The History of the Sisters of Divine Providence*:

> In 1822, the Diocese of Saint-Dié, which included theDepartment of the Vosges with Portieux, was detached from Nancy. The Bishop of Nancy did not want to be deprived [by not having] the principal house of the Sisters of Providence (Portieux) in his diocese—the place in which it had been legally set up. Consequently, he began negotiations to make the Sisters of Providence [at Hommarting] in his diocese, ecclesiastically independent of the house at Portieux. But it was not until December 13, 1838, that the bishop obtained Church-approved independence.[85]

In the meantime, in 1827, the location of the German-speaking house was moved from Hommarting to the tiny village of St. Jean-de-Bassel near Sarrebourg (still in Lorraine) when Father Jean Decker acquired St. Jean Hall, an estate that had once housed the

---

85 Callahan, <u>The History of the Sisters of Divine Providence</u>, p. 29 for the quotation. In effect the entire first section of these endnotes is dependent upon Callahan's work, page 20 and following.

Knights of Malta and that offered more room for growth.[86] St. Jean-de-Bassel achieved canonical independence in 1838, but it would become civilly independent from Portieux only in 1852.[87]

Increases in vocations and the needed upgrading of the buildings led to expanded living quarters in 1834 when two stories were added to St. Anne's Hall, one of the original buildings. In 1847, St. Mary's Hall (*Maison Ste. Marie*) was built and additional lands for gardens and grazing cattle were acquired.

Ecclesiastically, the Congregation based at St. Jean-de-Bassel was a diocesan congregation and various priests appointed by the bishop served as fathers-superior. The first such superior was *Abbé* Jean Decker who had shepherded Moye's daughters from 1802 until his death in 1844. He was followed by Pierre Grusy who was appointed pastor of Danne-et-Quatre-Vents in 1850 and replaced by *Abbé** Christophe Larvette. *Abbé* Larvette continued as ecclesiastical superior until 1864 when *Abbé* Nicolas Michel was appointed to that position. Following the Franco-Prussian War (1870), newly drawn borders moved Alsace and Lorraine from France to Germany. St. Jean-de-Bassel, now in Germany, came under the Diocese of Metz.[88] *Abbé* Michel was appointed a "titular canon" for the Diocese and moved to Metz in 1882, but remained the ecclesiastical superior for St. Jean-de-Bassel until his death in 1888[89].

The ecclesial superior of the Sisters of Divine Providence of St. Jean-de-Bassel when Louise Feltin entered was *Abbé* Pierre Grusy. One of his most significant accomplishments as superior was the building (in 1847-48) of *Maison Ste. Marie,* a new building to house the young women in formation. He was intent on obtaining more

---

86 Callahan, p. 30.

87 Gruber, page 27.

*   *Abbé* is the normative form of address for French priests in the 19th century. The formal form of address is Monseigneur.

88 Gruber, p. 16–27.

89 Letter to Reverend Mother Philothea Thiry, Congregation of Divine Providence, Texas, from Sister Anna Marie Houlne, Superior General, St. Jean-de-Bassel, 1928. CDP Archives.

land for the convent so that the Congregation could be more self-sufficient, but his true legacy was instilling in the Sisters a love of solitude, an appreciation for silence, devotion to prayer, and a trust in God.[90]

His successor, *Abbé* Chrisophe Larvette, continued Grusy's focus on developing the young Sisters in their religious education, but placed less emphasis on their secular education. Larvette asked them to focus on humility and a spirit of faith, their four fundamental virtues and prayer. During his tenure, the Sisters were not as well prepared academically and were limited to proficiency in primary education only. Larvette was remembered for his fatherly concern for the Sisters, especially those farthest from the motherhouse. He spent a great deal of time visiting communities throughout Alsace and Lorraine, driving his small carriage pulled by a white horse. On his visitations, he took time to recruit new candidates in the villages.[91]

At the time Louise Feltin entered, the Superior General was Reverend Mother Basilisse Gand. Mother Basilisse had a delicate constitution and was remembered as a quiet, intensive soul.[92] Prior to the official separation from Portieux, Mother Basilisse was titled *econome* or treasurer of the St. Jean-de-Bassel community. When the civil separation took place in 1852, she was elected general superior.[93] She served in that position until 1864 when she stepped aside due to ill health.

She was succeeded by Mother Adrienne Frache who served as Superior for only three years until her death in 1867. Mother Adrienne was succeeded by Mother Constantine Eck who had served on the General Council under both Mother Basilisse and Mother

---

90 Gruber, p. 117
91 Wilhelm, p. 57-58
92 Wilhelm, p.56.
93 Wilhelm, p. 56.

Adrienne as well as having served as the Director of Novices.[94] Mother Constantine served as Superior General until her death in the spring of 1885 at age fifty-nine.[95]

During the first sixty[*] years of its existence the Sisters of Providence of St. Jean-de-Bassel flourished. A new novitiate building, *La Maison Ste. Marie,* replaced cramped quarters above the refectory in St. Anne's Hall in order to accommodate growing numbers of new vocations. In 1864, another new building, *Ste. Famille* (Holy Family), was constructed to provide classrooms, meeting rooms, and more dormitory space. And, in April of 1872, a new chapel was dedicated by the Bishop of Nancy.[96]

At the time Louise Feltin entered in 1849, as many as forty or fifty candidates were received annually and the Sisters of Providence of St. Jean-de-Bassel had a very young membership. The average age of the 151 Sister-teachers who staffed schools in the Departments of Meurthe, Moselle, and Bas-Rhin in 1845 was a youthful thirty-two and a half, while the oldest sister teaching was sixty-five.[97]

At St. Jean-de-Bassel in the 1840's and 1850's, the year of novitiate did not have the same character that it has today in religious life. It included both secular and religious studies and a great deal of manual labor. The novices at St. Jean-de-Bassel actually provided labor assistance to the building of *Maison Ste. Marie* in 1847 and they did much of the farm work. The novitiate year initiated the young girl into a laborious, spartan life that valued intellectual and spiritual development. Novices were prepared so that they could persevere in their vocation while they served God's People alone in poor French villages where secular teachers did not want to go, where living arrangements were austere, and where equipment for schools was non-existent.

---

94 Wilhelm, p. 56-58.
95 CDP St. Jean-de-Bassel Archives
*   **1816-1875**
96 Wilhelm, p. 67.
97 Gruber, page 126.

During the year of novitiate, the novice was examined in every possible way in order to insure that she would be not only a credit to her profession as an instructor, but also a positive reflection on the entire Congregation of Providence. Her family background, her generosity, her character, and her health were scrutinized carefully. All novices studied the writings of Father Jean Decker and the Congregation's Holy Rule of 1846, which had many admonitions from Father Moye. A strictly structured prayer life was woven within the hours set aside for study and labor. According to the educational custom of the time, almost everything was committed to memory.[98]

It should be noted that there is some confusion as to the exact dates that Sœur St. André Feltin left the novitiate and went to Epfig, her first teaching assignment. The data in both the Archives of the Congregation of Divine Providence of Texas and those of the Congregation of Divine Providence of St. Jean-de-Bassel agree on the following: Louise Feltin entered the postulate at St. Jean-de-Bassel on November 8, 1849; she received the habit on September 20, 1851. However, the Archives at St. Jean also indicate that Sœur St. André arrived in Epfig in 1850 and remained there until 1853.

Presuming that the year of canonical novitiate[99] was from September 20, 1851, until September 21, 1852, the date of 1850 for arrival in Epfig does not seem to coordinate. The discrepancy having been noted, this author has decided to follow this data:

1845-1849—Louise Feltin taught as a Candidate with the Sisters of Providence in the village of Krautergsheim in Alsace[100]

---

98 Gruber, pages 33-48.

99 The "canonical novitiate," a one-year time period, takes on formal directives under Canon Law today. However, the author acknowledges that the same formality may not have been in operation in the 1850's. Gruber gives an indication that this period of spiritual formation was a year-long and was fairly structured.

100 'Community Annals, Heiligenberg,' written after 1900. Archives of the Congregation of Divine Providence, St. Jean-de-Bassel, France.

November 8, 1849—Louise Feltin entered St. Jean-de-Bassel as a
  Postulant

September 20, 1851—Louise Feltin entered the novitiate and
  received the name "*Sœur St. André*"

September 1852 (presumed)—S. St. André went to Epfig

1855—Sœur St. André made her religious profession

The author is making this presumption as it agrees with the general plan of formation outlined in Gruber's work on the early history of the Congregation of St. Jean-de-Bassel.[101]

This is the religious congregation that Louise Feltin entered in 1849. Since Sisters of Providence* of St. Jean-de-Bassel did not begin a school in LaWalck until 1871,[102] we do not know why she chose this religious congregation. Perhaps the motherhouse of the Sisters of Divine Providence of Ribeauvillé who had taught her in Geispolsheim was simply too far away. Perhaps her pastor guided her to an order that he knew. We do know that in her heart of hearts she was always a Sister of Divine Providence of St. Jean-de-Bassel with warm ties to her motherhouse her whole life long.

ENDNOTES   CHAPTER V   EARLY MISSIONS

At the end of their novitiate studies of one year (thus, after three preparatory years in the Congregation), the Sisters at St. Jean-de-Bassel made formal public promises to be obedient to superiors and to remain poor and chaste. These are the traditional vows

---

101 Gruber, p. 41.

*   **The Sisters of Providence of St. Jean-de-Bassel only adopted "Divine" into their title after the Franco-Prussian War when the defeat of France led to the transfer of Alsace and Lorraine to Germany (Prussia). Since the Germans did not have an understanding of "Providence" as a characteristic of the Divinity, the Sisters added "Divine" into their title for clarity.**

102 CDP St. Jean-de-Bassel Archives

*   **In 1850/60, one franc = about $2.00 in US money in 2006**

that have been taken by religious for centuries. In the Sisters of Providence, these promises would be renewed annually; after three years of annual renewal the young sisters were encouraged to take the Vow of Chastity, which would be renewed triennially. This was designated as "Profession." At this time in the history of the Sisters of Providence of St. Jean-de-Bassel, Sisters did not take perpetual vows. From the novitiate, those who were going to be teachers were sent to village schools where an experienced teacher served as educational and spiritual mentor.

By 1849 some two hundred Sisters of Providence of St. Jean-de-Bassel taught in 190 schools in Lorraine and Alsace. Most of these schools, usually for girls and numbering between 40 and 100 students, were in small villages of some 1000 or fewer inhabitants. Instructors were paid, on average, 110 francs* annually with only a few Sisters earning 200 francs annually or more.[103] Generally, schools had only one Sister instructor.[104]

In addition to their salary, Sisters received wood for heating as well as vegetables and other groceries from the townspeople. In most places, the Sister-instructor took care of the church sacristy, washing the altar linens, preparing the altar breads, and ringing the bell for services. In remote places without a resident priest, the Sister would provide direct pastoral services such as leading the rosary in the chapel. For these types of services to the parish, the Sister might be paid an additional twelve francs per year.[105]

Lodging provided for the Sisters varied. In some villages the Sister lived in a one-room house with neither cellar nor attic. Sometimes the Sister lived in a room above the sacristy where she would live, cook, and teach school. In other villages, the Sister might live with a parishioner, share a house with a public school teacher, or board with a Jewish family. One account indicates that a Sister lived above

---

103 Wilhelm, p. 53 and Gruber, pages 68-77.
104 Gruber, p. 68-70.
105 Wilhelm, p. 53.

a dance hall! Once in a while the dwellings were new or in good shape, but usually they were dilapidated and ill kempt.[106]

Younger, less experienced members were sent with older, more experienced members to staff schools. After a probationary period of three or four years, the younger sisters were then sent to staff a school alone.[107] Expensive projects at the motherhouse (purchasing additional property to expand the farm, new buildings, repairs, etc.) meant that no Congregational monies were spent on Sisters' dwellings on the missions and thus each Sister lived her promise of poverty at a profound depth.

The educational training at St. Jean-de-Bassel, conducted in both French and German, was shaped by the expectations of the French government, which emphasized reading, writing, basic math, history, geography, and the religious sciences.[108] Sisters who taught were required to obtain a Letter of Obedience (the teaching certificate) from the French government, a license which carried their family name and their given name. In the 1840's the Letter of Obedience required a testimony of teaching ability by the Superior General,[109] but requirements for this license grew more and more strict as years passed. By 1850,[110] a government official came to the Motherhouse to supervise the qualifying examination. Eventually, the Congregation erected a new building, *Maison Ste. Famille* (Holy Family Hall) in 1864, and opened a normal school at the Motherhouse (1867) in order to prepare Sisters to sit for the licensure examination, which was administered by a government official.[111] If a Sister were going to be teaching in Lorraine, her studies would include two years of French. She might also be sent to Epfig, a large French-speaking Alsatian village with a larger community of Sisters, to improve her language

---

106 Wilhelm, p. 54.

107 Gruber, pages 68-77.

108 Gruber, p. 143.

109 Wilhelm, p. 70.

110 Wilhelm, p. 73.

111 Wilhelm. p. 67.

skills.[112] All teachers were bi-lingual[113] in French and German, and those who were native Alsatians were tri-lingual.

Sister St. André Feltin served in three villages—all in the Department of Bas-Rhin in the region of Alsace—before being mis sioned to Tonau. the parish school at St. Georges Parish in Epfig from 1852 to 1853, the parish school at St. Vincent Parish in Heiligenberg from 1853 to1859, and the parish school of St. Abrogast Parish in Batzendorf from 1859 to 1866. At Epfig she was with Sister Catherine Eschenlaub, Sister Marie Alphonse Boëgler, and Sister Marie-Octavie Reibel. In Heiligenberg, Sister St. André served alone from 1853 until 1859 when she was replaced by Sister Léonille Zerr In Batzendorf, her term of service overlapped with Sister Polycarpe Hiltenbrand from 1859 to 1861; she served alone from 1861 to 1864; she was joined by Sister Amarathe Fischer from 1864 to 1866.[114]

High up in the Vosges Mountains, Epfig was a large village of 2,962 people in 1851. Over 90% of the inhabitants were Catholics and about five percent were Jews.[115] A large baroque/Romanesque church, the Church of St. Georges, stands in the middle of the village. A painting of St. Georges on horseback dominates the sanctuary of the dark church today and the post-Vatican II sanctuary does not have a high altar, though there might have been one prior to liturgical changes since the Second Vatican Council.

The houses in Epfig are typical of Alsatian design: brown or salmon-colored stucco with exposed wooden traces. On the edge of Alsatian wine country, the village is surrounded by vineyards and cornfields.[116]

Heiligenberg was a much smaller village in 1853 with a population of only 500 or so.[117] Located on the east slope of the Vosges

---

112 Gruber, p. 25.

113 Gruber, p. 143

114 CDP St. Jean-de-Bassel Archives

115 Internet site @ www.rootsweb.com/~fraalac/alsaceaz/alsaceh.htm

116 Author's personal observation in 2000.

117 Internet site @ www.rootsweb.com/~fraalac/alsaceaz/alsaceh.htm

Mountains, the village is quite far from St. Jean-de-Bassel. In the center of the town, the parish church, St. Vincent's, is built in a Gothic style of pink-hued sandstone from the Vosges Mountains. Its tall spire casts a long shadow in the small village. The gothic-style altar of dark wood is balanced by a beautiful rose window over the main door. The depictions of the Stations of the Cross are now captioned in German, though this might be a result of the nearly fifty years of German possession of Alsace between 1870 and 1918. The typical Gothic pulpit of dark wood matches the altar and towers over the body of the church. The homilist who chooses to speak from there has a bird's eye view of his congregation![118] A plaque on the back wall of the church honors the memory of six Sisters from St. Jean-de-Bassel who served the parish in the school's early years. Sister St. André's name is listed first, suggesting that she began the school there where she served alone for six years. It is to be noted that some of the information on Sister St. André on this plaque is inaccurate.[119]

ENDNOTES   *CHAPTER VI*   *CHANGES*

Batzendorf, the third and last assignment (1859-1866) of Sister St. André in France, is a small village. In 1851,with a population of 908 inhabitants, Batzendorf in Bas-Rihn (northern Alsace) was predominately (+/- 92%) Catholic with a significant (+/- 7%) Jewish population.[120] Situated about ten miles southwest of Haguenau, the region's largest town, Batzendorf would have been at least a day's travel from Strasbourg in 1866. Since Batzendorf is not far (about 15 miles) from LaWalck, perhaps we can presume that Sister St. André was able to visit her family while she was stationed there.

In the spring of 1860, during the first year Sister St. André was in Batzendorf, her brother Nicolas, a priest of the Diocese of Texas since

---

118 Author's personal observation in 2000.
119 Author's personal observation in 2000.
120 Internet site: www.rootsweb.com/~fraalac/alsaceaz/alsaceh.htm

1853, returned home to visit family.[121] It seems likely that Nicolas could have visited his sister at her mission, inviting her to consider missionary work in Texas where needs were so dramatic. During the years Sister St. André served in Batzendorf, a friend, Sister André Keller, was stationed in Keffendorf, a nearby village. According to Sister André Keller's memoirs, Nicolas wrote to his sister often, begging her to come to America where he believed she could do much good.[122] Sister St. André, alone in Batzendorf for three years from 1861 through 1864, must have envisioned herself leaving France to do missionary work in Texas. According to Sister André Keller, Sister St. André went to the Motherhouse at St. Jean-de-Bassel and "placed the matter before her Superiors." The memoirs indicate that both Sisters were hoping to be sent to America. At that time the superiors denied their requests.

While in France with John Odin, the Archbishop of New Orleans, Claude-Marie Dubuis, a native of Lyon, France, was appointed Bishop of Texas. His consecration took place at St. Irenaeus Seminary in Lyon on November 23, 1862.[123] Following his episcopal ordination, Dubuis evidently traveled throughout France recruiting seminarians for Texas and begging for money, materials, and personnel to help his poor diocese.

According to the memoirs of Sister André Keller, at some point during her years alone in Batzendorf, Bishop Dubuis wrote to Sister St. André Feltin and those same memoirs recall a subsequent visit that Sister St. André made to Bishop Dubuis while he was in Strasbourg. Both Sister St. André and Sister André Keller were interested in

---

121 Strebler, p. 43.
122 Memoirs of Sister André Keller, CDP. Copy in Congregation of Divine Providence, San Antonio, Archives.
123 Jacks, p. 145-147.

missionary work in Texas, and Bishop Dubuis was hopeful that one or both of these Sisters would come to his diocese.[124]

In 1864, Mother Basilisse Gand, who had been the Superior General of the Sisters of Providence of St. Jean-de-Bassel since 1845, stepped aside as Superior due to illness. Mother Adrienne Frache succeeded her with Mother Basilisse remaining on the General Council as First Assistant. When Mother Adrienne died on March 30, 1867, Mother Basilisse served one month as Superior General until her own death on May 1, 1867. Following Mother Basilisse's death, Mother Constantine Eck was elected Superior General. During the time both Mother Adrienne and Mother Basilisse were in poor health, it is likely that much of the detail work of administering the Congregation could have fallen to Sister Constantine Eck, a member of the Council and Mistress of Novices*.

In 1863, *Abbé* Christophe Larvette, the ecclesiastical superior, was re-assigned to a parish, and *Abbé* Nicolas Michel was appointed to serve as the Congregation's ecclesiastical superior, a position that he held until his death in 1888.[125]

The decision to send Sisters to America in 1866 rested in the hands of these leaders of the Congregation.

Since Callahan gives credit to Mother Constantine Eck for the decision to send Sisters to America, a short description of her temperament is warranted.

Described by Sister Pierre (Marie-Josée) Gruber as "a woman with a big heart," Mother Constantine Eck was an Alsatian by birth. Sincere, sensitive, and devoted to her daughters, she would do everything possible to empower her sisters to grow in character and prayer. Gruber says that "those who were awkward or backward or

---

124 Memoirs of Sister Andre Keller, CDP

* **Sister Callahan says that Mother Constantine Eck was the *eco-nome* (treasurer), but the materials from the Archives of St. Jean-de-Bassel do not indicate that she held that position.**

125 Wilhelm, p. 58-61

closed were not her type" and she felt compelled to try to open them up.[126]

Mother Constantine's administration published the biography of Father Jean-Martin Moye in 1872, giving her Sisters a firmer foundation in their Founder's spirituality. Mother Constantine also adapted the Constitution of the Congregation twice in an effort to promote spiritual growth and a better community spirit. Under her leadership, the Sisters' religious habit was changed and formalized.

Always supportive, sweet yet firm, Mother Constantne provided strong leadership. She was only twenty-five years old when she assumed the position of Mistress of Novices and began her service of leadership. Though a crippling accident when she was a young girl left her with "bad legs," limiting her ability to travel, her expansive spirit motivated her to try new ventures.

During her tenure of office (1867-1885), the Congregation was plagued by the results of the disastrous impact of the defeat of France in the Franco-Prussian War. The germanization of Alsace and Lorraine presented the Congregation with an on-going challenge to upgrade the education of the Sisters in order to keep pace with ever-changing criteria for teacher certification set in place by German authorities. In addition, improvements to the convent farmlands (A significant portion of their farmland was a swamp that had to be drained to prevent the breeding of mosquitoes.) became imperative in order to offset typhoid and cholera, which took their toll on the Sisters. Also, the building of a chapel occupied both the energy of the leadership and the resources of the community.

Mother Constantine was elected to four terms as Superior General. Following a failed treatment of her legs in the summer of 1885, she died on September 18, 1885. She left behind a strong congregation with 700 members.[127]

---

126 Gruber p. 159-160.
127 Gruber, p. 159-160; 208.

ENDNOTES   *CHAPTER VII*   *EMIGRÉS*

In 1866, with the Civil War in the United States over, Bishop Dubuis faced anew the tremendous needs of his diocese, which encompassed the entire state of Texas. He made a recruiting trip to France in the spring of 1866 with the intention of attracting more seminarians who would accept the call to the mission fields that he had found so personally exhilarating. He also sought women religious who would be able to staff hospitals, orphanages, and rural schools, and, of course, funding for his many projects.

With the population of the State of Texas now exceeding half a million, the major cities were no longer small towns. In 1863, the Catholic Church of Texas had increased to 40,000 members, but the priests ministering in the diocese numbered fewer than fifty and the Bishop had only semi-cloistered nuns: Ursulines in Galveston and San Antonio, and Sisters of the Incarnate Word and Blessed Sacrament in Brownsville. Both of these communities of women religious operated boarding and day schools for girls. The population of the twenty-year-old State also had shifted, and by the second half of the nineteenth century, it included more Americans than Mexicans with German, Polish, and Czech immigrants flooding the empty expanse of the Texas wilderness.[128]

A letter to Archbishop Jean-Marie Odin written from New York on April 30, 1866, gives us the time frame for Bishop Dubuis' 1866 journey to France.[129] It seems plausible to think that Bishop Dubuis fully intended to be back in the United States for the opening of the Second Plenary Council of Baltimore on October 7, 1866, but due to circumstances surrounding his attempt to find non-cloistered religious women who would operate hospitals and orphanages in his diocese, his sailing from LeHavre to New York on September 25, 1866, made him late for the Council.[130]

---

128 Jacks, p. 156-163.
129 Letter held in Incarnate Word Archives, San Antonio, TX.
130 Jacks, p. 169.

It was during this visit to France that Bishop Dubuis visited the St. Jean-de-Bassel motherhouse. A letter from Dubuis to Odin written on August 2, 1866, recounts Dubuis' return to France from Rome in mid-July, his trip at the end of July to Vichy with Father Rousselon, and a stay at the seminary in Strasbourg where Dubuis recruited more seminarians for Texas. During these travels, he also visited St. Jean-de-Bassel, asking for Sisters for his parish schools.[131]

Given the reticence on the part of the leadership at St. Jean-de-Bassel to send Sisters to America earlier in the decade, we might suppose that Dubuis' visit would have been preceded by at least one letter introducing his cause and begging for teaching Sisters who could handle schools in small villages. Further, since it was the custom of the Sisters of Providence at that time to listen to missionaries speak on behalf of their missions, it is likely that Bishop Dubuis would have spoken to the entire congregation gathered for their annual summer convocation.[132]

Records do not exist which explain why and how Sisters St. André Feltin and Alphonse Boëgler were chosen to go to Texas. Neither the archives at St. Jean-de-Bassel nor those at the Sisters of Divine Providence at San Antonio, Texas, contain any primary sources (letters, minutes of Council meetings, etc.) that would offer background information on how the decision to send Sisters outside France came about and what criteria were used to send Sisters St. André and Alphonse. Callahan indicates that the August 1866 letter from Dubuis to Odin notes that three Sisters had been chosen for this historic mission, but only Sister St. André and Sister Alphonse actually sailed with Bishop Dubuis.[133] No explanation for the change in number is found in either primary or secondary sources.

The Sisters of Providence at St. Jean-de-Bassel attempted one other foreign mission in the 1860's: a mission to Algiers was begun in 1868 at the behest of the Bishop of Nancy who was the titular

---

131 Callahan, p. 37.
132 Gruber, p. 29-30.
133 Callahan, p. 35.

Archbishop of Algiers. This endeavor lasted only two years. When the Franco-Prussian War (1870) ended in the defeat of France, Alsace and Lorraine were transferred to the Second Reich (Prussia). Algiers remained a French colony and the political strain of the now-German congregation supporting a mission in French territory was too much.[134]

There are no archival materials that chronicle Sister St. André's last months in France in 1866. One can presume that her meeting in Strasbourg with Bishop Claude Dubuis led the two of them to believe that she was a good candidate for missionary work in Texas. Callahan notes that three Sisters of Providence were being considered for the missionary work in Texas, but archival materials do not indicate the name of the third possibility.[135] Perhaps it was Sister André Keller, Sister St. André's friend from Keffendorf. However, by her own admission, her health was in question, even by Bishop Dubuis.[136]

Sister Alphonse Boëgler, born Rufine Pauline Boëgler on January 22, 1830, in Offendorf, Germany, was the Sister of Providence sent with Sister St André to Texas. She had entered the Sisters of Providence at St. Jean-de-Bassel on November 10, 1848, one year previous to Sister St. André's entry. She received the habit on September 17, 1850, and taught in the villages of Epfig (1850-1859), Wolxheim (1859-1862) and Mittlebronn (1862-1866) before being assigned to Texas. None of the archives consulted (Sisters of Divine Providence, St. Jean-de-Bassel; Sisters of Divine Providence, San Antonio, Texas; Catholic Archives of Texas, Austin, Texas; Sisters of the Incarnate Word and Blessed Sacrament, Victoria, Texas) held any information on why Sister Alphonse had been assigned to Texas.

---

134 Gruber, p. 232-238.

135 Callahan, p. 35.

136 Memoirs of Sister Andre Keller, Congregation of Divine Providence Archives, San Antonio, TX

Perhaps her long-standing relationship with Sister St. André was a motivating factor.[137]

Bishop Dubuis had originally planned to sail to America in late August (according to his August 2, 1866, letter to Archbishop Odin) but complications with obtaining Sisters for hospitals changed his proposed schedule.[138]

Dubuis had intended to begin his hospitals with the Sisters of the Incarnate Word and Blessed Sacrament from Lyons whom he knew very well and whose work in education in Brownsville he greatly appreciated. However, since this Congregation was semi-cloistered, its Superior was unwilling to release Sisters to America to function in hospitals as that ministry, unlike their boarding academy, was deemed too public and would require Sisters to leave their convent. Callahan notes the solution to the problem in her work:

> … Dubuis was resolved not to return to Texas without hospital sisters. Therefore, after securing permission of Cardinal de Bonald, he wrote to Mother Angelique [Superior of the Sisters of the Incarnate Word and Blessed Sacrament at Lyons] asking if she would give to three young women, who had volunteered for hospital work in Texas, the Rules of the Incarnate Word and Blessed Sacrament Congregation. On September 23, [1866] these three received the habit and were given the Rules and Constitutions of the Sisters of the Incarnate Word and Blessed Sacrament but were to be known as the Sisters of Charity of the Incarnate

---

137 Information gleaned from Sisters of Divine Providence Archives, St. Jean-de-Bassel; the Archives of the Sisters of the Incarnate Word and Blessed Sacrament, Victoria, Texas; Catholic Archives of Texas, Austin, Texas.

138 Callahan, p. 37.

Word. Two days later they sailed with Bishop Dubuis
to begin their hospital work in Texas.[139]

The travel arrangements for Sister St. André Feltin and Sister
Alphonse Boëgler from St. Jean-de-Bassel in Lorraine to the sea-
port city of LeHavre on the west coast of France are unknown.
The three newly-received Sisters of Charity of the Incarnate Word;
Sister Regis Chavassieux, a novice in the Sisters of the Incarnate
Word and Blessed Sacrament in Lyons,[140] destined for their new
monastery being constructed in Victoria, Texas; and four Ursulines
from the Ursuline convent in Beaujeu (Diocese of Lyons) traveled to
LeHavre with Bishop Dubuis from Lyons.[141] Perhaps the two Sisters
of Providence traveled to Lyons and made the westward journey
across France with Dubuis and his troop of missionaries. On this
voyage were seventeen priests and seminarians, also destined for
the mission fields of the Diocese of Texas, in addition to other missionaries traveling to other locations in America. This band sailed
from LeHavre on *The Europa* on September 29, 1866, arriving in
New York on October 11, 1866.[142]

In New York, Bishop Dubuis assisted his missionaries to transfer
to the *S. S. Tybee* which was bound for Texas, a sailing that would
require two to three more weeks. After he had seen to the welfare of
his new missionaries, Dubuis proceeded on to Baltimore to attend
the remainder of the Second Plenary Council of Baltimore that had
convened on October 7th.

---

139 Callahan, p. 37. Her citation for this material is Sister Mary Helena
   Finck, *The Congregation of the Sisters of Charity of the Incarnate Word
   of San Antonio, Texas* (Washington, D.C.: The Catholic University of
   America, 1925), pp. 33-35.
140 *Extending the Incarnation into the Third Millenium*, p. 16. Archives
   of the Sister of the Incarnate Word and Blessed Sacrament, Victoria,
   Texas.
141 Callahan, p. 38
142 Callahan, p. 40.

Having approached the port at Galveston on October 23, 1866, the landing of the *Tybee* was delayed until October 25 due to a hurricane in the Gulf of Mexico. Once landed, the party of Sister-missionaries was given hospitality by the Ursuline nuns at their Galveston convent.[143]

The Bishop did not tarry after the Baltimore Council which adjourned on October 29, 1866, returning to Galveston by November 1, when he ordained six seminarians to the diaconate and, within the next few days, four others to the priesthood. After settling his new priests in various parishes near San Antonio, Texas, he again returned to Galveston for the celebration of his ordination to the episcopate on November 23. In the next weeks Dubuis attended to the future of the Sisters of Providence whom he intended to establish in Austin at St. Mary's Parish with Sister St. André's brother, Father Nicolas Feltin.

ENDNOTES   CHAPTER VIII   GALVESTON

In 1840, Father John Odin, a French Vincentian priest, was sent to Texas by the Archbishop of New Orleans to re-organize the Catholic Church in the Republic of Texas, then designated by the Vatican as a "vicariate-apostolic." Before his ordination to the episcopate in 1842, Odin had been overseeing a sprawling wilderness that stretched from the Rio Grande on the south and west to Wyoming Territory in the north and to Louisiana in the east—a nation with few Catholic churches, fewer priests, and no Catholic schools.

---

143 Callahan, p. 38-41.

* **To be "secularized" means that the pastoral responsibility for the parish in question is transferred from a religious order (Franciscans, Dominicans, etc.) to a diocesan priest. All parishes in a diocese, regardless of who the pastor is, are under the diocesan bishop, but when a religious order has responsibility for the parish, the Superior of the religious order decides who will be sent to serve the parish. Once that assignment is made, the bishop may approve or reject the religious priest assigned.**

Prior to Odin's leadership, the Church that eventually became the Diocese of Galveston had fallen on dark times. The outstanding Franciscan mission system established along the San Antonio River, in what is now the city of San Antonio, and in East Texas, had been secularized* in 1794 and turned over to the authority of the See of Monterrey, Mexico, which had no bishop at the time. A further disruption in ecclesiastical administration had occurred in 1810 when Mexico became independent from Spain. Once the Spaniards had withdrawn, the ecclesial resources of Mexico were extremely limited and did not stretch to the territory north of the Rio Grande known as Texas. In 1836 the defeat of Santa Ana at the Battle of San Jacinto ushered in an era of further complication for the Catholic Church as Mexican clergy returned to Mexico leaving Texas to the Texians.

In hopes of populating his expansive nation, President Sam Houston offered *empresarios* vast land grants which they in turn sold to immigrants from France, Germany, and Poland, thus bringing a predominately Catholic population to Texas.

As he rode from village to village in the nation under his ecclesial jurisdiction, Odin found few priests and poorly maintained churches. "San Fernando [Church in San Antonio], though still usable, had not been repaired after a fire in 1828; the San Antonio de Valero mission (the Alamo) had not been repaired since the fall of the Alamo [in 1836]." The three other missions along the San Antonio River were in complete ruin.[144]

In 1842, Odin undertook a journey of 2,000 miles to inspect the "vicariate-apostolic" and confirmed some 11,000 Catholics! There is no record that his travels took him into the northern or westernmost areas of the vast diocese inhabited by Native Americans.[145]

---

144 Wangler, Rev. Msgr. Alexander C., ed., <u>The Archdiocese of San Antonio, 1874-1974</u>. (Place and date of publication unknown.), p. 7-8.

145 Wangler, p. 10-11.

After being ordained as a bishop, Odin began to recruit priest-missionaries in his native France and in Germany in hopes of providing support for the faith of those coming to Texas in search of a peaceful future. Castroville and Fredericksburg, then one parish, were placed under the pastorate of Father Claude Marie Dubuis in 1847; Father Edward Clarke had followed Kentuckians to Texas and settled with them in Lavaca County; San Antonio was pastored by Vincentian priests as were Refugio and Victoria.[146]

In 1847, when Rome elevated the "vicariate-apostolic" of Texas to the Diocese of Galveston, it "may well have been the world's largest diocese from a territorial point of view," as it encompassed the entirety of the State of Texas, including all territories east of the Rio Grande, reaching as far north as Wyoming, and taking in parts of what are now Colorado, New Mexico, Kansas, and Oklahoma. In the years between 1840 and 1842, Odin had established priests in Victoria, Castroville, San Antonio, Laredo, Brownsville, Corpus Christi, New Braunfels, and Lavaca, but huge parts of his new diocese were either uninhabited or unreachable."[147]

The establishment of the Ursulines in Galveston in 1847 was Odin's first venture toward bringing in nuns who could begin a Catholic educational system in his fledgling diocese. [148] At the arrival of the Sisters of Providence, the Superior of St. Ursula's-by-the-Sea was Mother St. Pierre Harrington who had succeeded the founding Superior, Mother Arsene Blin.

Successful recruiting trips to France yielded Oblates of Mary Immaculate from Marseilles, Incarnate Word and Blessed Sacrament Sisters from Lyon, Brothers of Mary (Marianists), more Ursuline Sisters, and numerous French seminarians. German and Polish priests and seminarians came as well.

---

146 Wangler, p. 7-9.

147 Wangler, p. 10-11.

148 Wangler, p. 9.

When Odin was appointed Archbishop of New Orleans in 1860, the See of Galveston was vacant until Claude Marie Dubuis succeeded him as the second Bishop of Galveston in 1862.

Founded in 1836 by Michel Menard, Galveston City was a busy port, sending Texas cotton to textile centers in New England and Europe and receiving farming implements and supplies as well as thousands of immigrants who intended to carve farms and ranches out of the Texas wilderness.

During the Civil War, the Ursuline Sisters of Galveston, under Mother St. Pierre Harrington, Superior,[149] had transformed their academy into the city's only hospital, nursing both Union and Confederate soldiers who suffered from battle wounds and disease. Though little permanent damage had been incurred in the city, Bishop Dubuis' letters tell of St. Mary's Cathedral being "riddled with bullets" and "only on dry days [could he] say Mass within its walls."[150] When the Civil War ended, Galveston was quick to recover; and by the time Mother St. Andrew and Sister Alphonse (St. Claude) arrived in there in 1866, its population of 12,000 made Galveston City the largest in Texas,[151] boasting two Catholic Churches: St. Mary's Cathedral, built in 1847 and repaired after the Civil War, and St. Joseph's German Church, built in 1860.

Bishop Dubuis' prompt return to Galveston from the Second Plenary Council of Baltimore, which had closed on October 21,

---

149 Archives of the Ursuline Sisters, 4537 West Pine Blvd., St. Louis, Missouri 63108. Further note: The Ursulines in Galveston had come from convents in France, New Orleans, Boston, Germany, and Quebec. Only one Sister was a native of Galveston. The archives indicate that in 1866 there were 12 Sisters at the Galveston Convent. Sister St. Joseph Holly was the assistant to the Superior at the time and Sister Paul Kauffman was the treasurer.

150 Internet site: www.wikipedia.org The Roman Catholic Archdiocese of Galveston-Houston

151 Internet site: www.diogh.org The Archdiocese of Galveston-Houston.

1866,[152] indicated the urgency he must have felt to settle his latest recruits in the missions of his diocese.

On November 1, 1866, "he conferred the subdiaconate on six seminarians"; two days later he ordained them as deacons; and on November 4, 1866, he ordained them to the priesthood. "One more ordination followed on November 5th" and then Bishop Dubuis took his newest priests to San Antonio to settle them in the western part of the diocese. [153]

Following the celebration of the fourth anniversary of his episcopal ordination on November 23, Bishop Dubuis turned his attention to the Sisters of Providence whom he had brought from France for the purpose of beginning a parish-based system of Catholic education for his diocese.

Prior to returning from his recruiting trip in France, Dubuis had evidently arranged with Father John Gonnard of Corpus Christi to receive Mrs. Caroline Spann Rice into the Sisters of Providence in exchange for a Sister to manage the parish school in Corpus Christi. The immediate acceptance of Mrs. Rice into the novitiate of the Sisters of Providence would seem jarring in today's understanding of religious life, but given the circumstances of the three Lyonnaise women who became the first Sisters of Charity of the Incarnate Word in a basically overnight experience, it seemed to be in the character of Bishop Dubuis to "strike while the iron was hot."

Caroline Spann Rice, the first American Sister of Providence, was born in Charleston, South Carolina, to Charles and Eleanor Crowley Spann, and married William Rice, a Charleston widower with one son. After the death of Caroline's father sometime before 1840, her mother, Mrs. Eleanor Spann, and family moved to Galveston. When Rice died in 1840, Mrs. Carolyn Rice and her stepson followed her family to the Galveston area. While living in Galveston, Mrs. Rice became acquainted with Father John Gonnard, a priest from Corpus Christi, who became her spiritual director. Mrs. Rice had relatives in

152 Internet site: www.wikipedia.org Plenary Council of Baltimore
153 Callahan, p. 41.

Corpus Christi and she occasionally visited Father Gonnard there. It was Father Gonnard who saw a religious vocation in Mrs. Rice and invited her to teach in his parish school in Corpus Christi. Gonnard was so certain of Mrs. Rice's calling that he made an agreement with Bishop Dubuis—evidently before Bishop Dubuis ever went to France in the spring of 1866—to have her accepted into a religious community.

Once professed, Mrs. Rice could then be sent wherever her Superior wished if the community would send a Sister to Corpus Christi to take Mrs. Rice's place in Father Gonnard's school. And, thus, a ready-made novice greeted Sister St. Andrew and Sister Alphonse in Galveston.

On November 27, 1866, at a public ceremony in the sanctuary of St. Mary's Cathedral, Caroline Spann Rice received the habit of the Sisters of Providence, a cincture, a black rosary, the Constitution, and a cross "bearing a silver symbol of Divine Providence instead of the corpus of the Crucified" and a white bonnet that resembled the bonnets worn by the thousands of pioneer women who brought civilization to the plains and valleys of the United States. "At this ceremony, she received the name 'Sister St. Joseph.'"[154]

At the pontifical high Mass which followed Caroline Spann Rice's entrance into the novitiate of the Sisters of Providence, Sister St. Andrew and Sister Alphonse "pronounced their perpetual vows of poverty, chastity, and obedience." The Sisters of Providence of St. Jean-de-Bassel did not have the practice of professing perpetual vows until their Constitution was revised in 1867. Thus the two Sisters who emigrated from France to Texas had not made perpetual profession, though temporary vows of poverty, chastity, and obedience were professed annually. Only with the change in the Constitution of the Congregation in 1867, did the Sisters of Providence in France begin to profess perpetual vows. The archives of St. Jean-de-Bassel indicate that the group of Sisters who had entered the Convent with

154 Callahan, p. 43.

Sister St. André made their perpetual vows in 1867.[155] However, it seems that Bishop Dubuis must have required the perpetual profession, perhaps believing that their permanent commitment would lend stability to the Sisters' mission.

For an unknown reason, at the ceremony of profession, Sister Alphonse changed her name to Sister St. Claude.[156] And at the same ceremony, the Sisters of Providence "addressed the bishop as their superior, and in clear, loud, and soul-stirring voices made the required promises to him," as their ecclesiastical superior.[157] This ecclesial relationship established with Bishop Dubuis, however, did not separate the Sisters of Providence from their mother-community in France and no archival records exist that indicate such a separation. Unlike the Sisters of Charity of the Incarnate Word, who from their beginning were not connected (except for a shared Rule) to the Sisters of the Incarnate Word and Blessed Sacrament of Lyon, France, and who related to Bishop Dubuis as Superior and Founder, the Sisters of Providence never considered the Bishop to be a "founder-personality" for them.

It also seems that from late 1866 on, Sister St. André was known as Mother St. Andrew, though her signature on any number of letters, if she were writing in French, remained Mother St. André.

Following the investiture and vow ceremony on November 27, 1866, Sister St. Joseph, Mother St. Andrew, and Sister St. Claude (Alphonse) set out for Austin by train and by stagecoach where they were to begin a school for St. Mary's Parish.[158]

---

155 Callahan, p. 41-44.

156 Callahan, p. 44.

157 Callahan, p. 44 (taken from the Memoirs of Sister St. Claude Boëgler, Archives of the Sisters of the Incarnate Word and Blessed Sacrament, Victoria, Texas.

158 Callahan, p. 44-45.

Note: About Sister St. Joseph Holly, OSU

Sister St. Joseph Holly, OSU, was brought to St. Ursula's-by-the-Sea in 1853 by Father Nicolas Feltin, the pastor at St. Vincent de Paul Church in Houston. At the height of a yellow fever epidemic (the same one in which his brother Celestin died), Father Feltin, while carrying for the sick and dying of his parish, found three children whose parents were both deceased. He personally took the two little girls, Teresa, aged eleven, and Katie, aged six, to St. Ursula-by-the-Sea. He placed their brother in a Houston orphanage. At the time, Sr. Ursula's-by-the-Sea was not an orphanage. The chronicler of the early history of the Ursulines in Galveston, S. M. (Sister Francis, OSU) Johnston writes:

> One evening there was a great knocking at the convent door, and when it was opened there stood Father Felton (sic),the herculean missionary priest who worked in Houston. Beside him, each clinging to one of his huge tanned hands, were two pretty black-eyed childen. The older, a girl of about eleven, was pale and serious. The younger, a chubby little miss of six, smiled at the nuns and gazed around her with delight. Father Felton (sic) coughed nervously, "I was making the daily rounds of the sick, as usual, in my parish," he explained, "when suddenly I felt drawn by some unaccountable attraction, I do not know what! Glancing up, I saw these two children staring at me from the open window of a little white cottage. A new place it was. I hadn't even known any of our faith were residing there. When I went into the house, I found these two and a smaller brother alone, except for their mother, who was already in the last stages of the plague. The father had been dead for some time. When I asked the good lady why she hadn't sent for

me, she whispered that they were strangers in town—
immigrants from Austria. The youngest child, little
Katie Holly"—the priest gave a good-natured tug at
the small youngster's hand—"was born on shipboard.
After their arrival in this country, the family lived
elsewhere for a few years and then moved to Houston,
just in time to be almost wiped out."

He paused and drew the more timid child forward.
"This," he said cherrily, "is little Teresa Holly, an admirable little girl and a very brave one. All alone, she
nursed her mother to the end, at the same time caring
for her younger brother and little sister Katie. And
now, Reverend Mother, can't you give the poor children
a home? Tonight I must return in a hurry, for tomorrow I will take their brother to a good Catholic family
near Houston. Besides, I must be there to care for my
sick." His keen light-blue eyes regarded the Superior.
Reverend Mother Saint Chantal smiled kindly. "I am
sure that in time of stress Saint Ursula's-by-the-Sea
will never fail the people." Then, holding out her arms,
she drew the little girls to her.[159]

Theresa Holly entered the Ursuline Community at Galveston
in 1856, receiving the name Sister St. Joseph. At the arrival of the
Sisters of Providence in 1866, she was the Assistant to the Superior
at St. Ursula's-by-the-Sea. In 1874, she was sent to Dallas to open a
new monastery. Mother St. Joseph died in Dallas, Texas, in 1884.[160]

---

159 Johnston, S. M., <u>Builders by the Sea—History of the Ursuline
Community of Galveston, Texas</u>. New York: Exposition Press, 1971, p.
73.
160 Johnston, p. 92, p. 145

ENDNOTES   CHAPTER IX   AUSTIN

Austin, Texas, named for Stephen F. Austin, the founder of Anglo-American Texas,[161] was a stop on the northern stagecoach route from Alleyton, Texas, the railhead where all passengers on the westbound Buffalo Bayou, Brazos, and Colorado Railroad from Houston disembarked in order to catch northbound or westbound stagecoaches.[162] The town had been established on the banks of the Colorado River in 1839 to serve as the capitol of the very young Republic of Texas. This choice of location for the capitol of Texas was disputed by many because of Austin's remoteness from the population centers of Galveston and Houston. Subsequent attempts to remove the Republic's archival papers and bring them to Houston for "safekeeping" were abated by Austinites who believed that this gesture was an attempt to reestablish the capitol in Houston. Though President Sam Houston actually did relocate the government of the Republic, first to Houston and then to Washington-on-the Brazos, Austin was eventually named the capitol of the State of Texas after Texas joined the United States in 1845. Austin grew slowly during its first decade as state capitol, but "by 1860, the population had climbed to 3,546."[163]

Beginning in 1844, due to economic turmoil and revolutionary unrest in their native land, European immigrants, many of them Germans, began to pour into Texas, landing at both Galveston and Indianola. Whole families left their declining villages to seek their fortune in the New World,[164] lured to Texas by the many books circulating in Germany which publicized a "beautiful topography, the availability of large plots of fertile land, ... the plethora of wild

---

161 "The Handbook of Texas Online" @ www.tsha.utexas/edu

162 "Traveller's (sic) Map of the State of Texas, 1867" @ www.uta.edu/library/ccon (Virtual Maps)

163 "The Handbook of Texas Online" @ www. tsha.utexas.edu

164 "The Handbook of Texas Online" @ www.tsha.utexas.edu

game to hunt,"[165] and the promise of the protection of societies such as the Society for the Protection of German Immigrants in Texas (*Adelsverein*).[166] Immigrants who traveled through the *Adelsverien* were expected to pay $470 (US) per family or $300 (US) for a single person for travel expenses (train fare to the port of sailing, passage on a ship sailing for Texas, expenses during their wait in Galveston or Indianola for passage to their fifteen acres) and wood enough to build a house. Noting that the annual income of craftsmen in Germany in the 1840's was about $80 annually, only the well-to-do could even consider the venture.[167]

Over time, the societies formed to channel the immigration process from Germany to Texas failed as land purchases for immigrant farms did not always materialize. Notwithstanding the failures, the societies were responsible for fostering and supporting the emigration of over 5,000 Germans who settled in various parts of Texas. Germans built farms throughout central Texas and the settlements of Bastrop, New Braunfels, Fredericksburg, Frelsburg, Rockne, and Sandy Creek were among the many villages and towns established by the hundreds of families who were no longer able to make a living in their native Germany[168].

Under the Second Reich, Prussia frequently focused on engaging in wars that would expand its territory. The Franco-Prussian War of 1870, typical of these types of conflict, gave impetus to another wave of immigration from Germany. Thus, Germans, looking for a peaceful environment to raise their families and make a living, emigrated to Texas in even larger numbers in the post-Civil War

---

165 Oommen, Sheena, "Hin' nach Texas!" "Off to Texas!" @ www.houston-culture.org

166 Oommen, Sheena, "Hin' nach Texas!" "Off to Texas!" @ www.houston-culture.org

167 Balthus, Anna, <u>Rockne Region Germans, Immigrants from Würges, 1846-1883,</u> (Donald C. Goertz, translator), Austin, TX, Metekesis Books, 2004, p. 41-43.

168 "The Handbook of Texas Online" @ <u>www.tsha.utexas.edu</u> and "The German Texans" @ <u>www.texancultres.utsa.edu</u>

era. It is no wonder that Bishop Dubuis mined the seminaries of Alsace, especially the one at Strasbourg, for help. Missionaries with an Alsatian background such as Mother St. Andrew and her brother Father Nicolas, who were fluent in both French and German, were an enormous benefit to a frontier diocese with a growing population of German-speaking Catholics.

At its founding in the early 1850's and then known as St. Patrick's[V], St. Mary's Parish in Austin had been predominately Irish-Catholic, but trends in immigration in Texas changed the Catholic complexion to German with roots in Bavaria.

Conflicting data set the beginning of the pastorate of Father Nicolas Feltin at St. Mary's in Austin at either February 14, 1864, or the spring of 1866.[169]

Though the parish had not grown under the leadership of the previous Irish pastors, Father Feltin's energetic attention to the needs of the parish had a positive effect.

> His (Father Feltin's) records and books show that he had formed sodalities for the ladies, several parish societies, and a parochial library. To the poor and especially to the sick, that physician of souls gave unstinting attention. Oftentimes he would walk miles on a sick-call and if necessity demanded it he would remain all night administering medicine to the patient. When

---

∇   **Father Feltin changed the name of St. Patrick's Parish to St. Mary of the Immaculate Conception. Whether or not the declaration of the Doctrine of the Immaculate Conception by Pope Pius IX in 1859 precipitated this change is unknown.**

169 The Official Catholic The Directory of St. Mary's Parish (Catholic Archives of Texas, Austin, TX) says that Feltin's pastorate began in 1864 (p. 18); "A Short Biography of Rev. Nicolas Feltin", taken from St. Joseph's (San Antonio, TX) Parish Book (unpublished, Archives, Archdiocese of San Antonio) (p. 82) says that "before his (Dubuis') departure (for France in 1866), he made Father Feltin administrator of St. Mary's Parish in Austin." This author believes that the data from St. Mary's Parish is more accurate.

death came he wowuld [sic] lay out the body for burial.
Father Feltin was energetic in the physical make-up
of his parish. He built a rock school-house on East
Tenth where St. Mary's parochial school now stands
and he himself handled the shovel and spade, carried
mortar, and lent other physical aid in the construction
of the school.[170]

Anticipating his sister's arrival in the late fall of 1866, Father
Feltin began a building near the church, which would serve as both
school and convent. Mother St. Andrew Feltin, Sister St. Claude
Boëgler, and Sister St. Joseph Rice, having left Galveston on the
Galveston-Henderson Railroad on November 27, 1866, arrived by
stagecoach in Austin on December 2, 1866. Though the school and
convent were not finished when Bishop Dubuis visited Austin in
January 1867, he was pleased with the progress.[171]

St. Mary's first convent-school building was completed by
February of 1867; and according to Callahan, "by April, it is certain
that St. Mary's parish school was an actuality".[172] Sister St. Joseph
Rice, with a solid background in education from her teaching experience in Corpus Christi, was no doubt a tremendous asset to the
first venture of the Sisters of Providence in Texas. Though many of
St. Mary's parishioners were German-speaking, Mother St. Andrew
must have relied heavily on Sister St. Joseph since her own English
was limited and her knowledge of managing on the Texas frontier
non-existent.

Evidently, in his January visit, the Bishop reviewed his plan to
send a Sister to Corpus Christi for Father Gonnard's school, but "it
was March 7, 1867, before Mother St. Andrew sent Sister St. Claude

---

170 Official Catholic The Directory of St. Mary's Parish, p. 18. (Catholic
   Archives of Texas, Austin, TX)
171 Callahan, p. 51.
172 Callahan, p. 51-52.

to take charge of Gonnard's school,"[173] leaving St. Mary's School in Austin in the hands of Mother St. Andrew and Sister St. Joseph.

Callahan describes the Corpus Christi school for girls as a "two-story adobe building on the northwest corner of Tancahua and Lipan Streets."[174] Following the custom of the Sisters of Providence in France, Sister St. Claude lived alone in this school where she seemed to experience much unhappiness under trying circumstances: the great distance from Austin, the loneliness of a solitary life, the rowdy environment of a city that served as a military installation, and having to contend with disease, a foreign culture, and a climate drastically different from the one she left in France.

Yellow fever took its toll; and in August of 1867, only five months after Sister St. Claude arrived in Corpus Christi, the parish suffered the loss of three priests who succumbed to the disease: Father John Gonnard, the pastor; his associate, Father Antoine Miconleau; and a priest from San Patricio, Father Charles Padey, who had come to help them with the sick and the dying. These deaths no doubt had a tremendously jarring effect on Sister St. Claude. She remained in Corpus Christi only part of those two years between 1867 and 1869. Callahan notes that "it is ... probable ... that after Dubuis baptized Mary Atwood [presumably in Corpus Christi, though Callahan is not clear] on August 14, 1868, he took Sister St. Claude back to Austin so that she and Sister St. Joseph would be at the parish school when he took Mother St. Andrew at the end of the month to open the school in Castroville."[175]

Memoirs of Fifty Years, an informal history of the first fifty years (1866-1916) of the Congregation of Divine Providence, by Sister Joseph Neeb, CDP, notes that two postulants were received during the first and second year in Austin: Sister Mary Joseph and Sister Mary Agnes Wolf. However, this author believes that the "Sister

---

173 Callahan, p. 52.
174 Callahan, p. 52.
175 Callahan, p. 53.

Mary Joseph" referenced by Neeb is actually Sister St. Joseph Rice who had been received in Galveston.[176]

The second young woman to be received into the fledgling community of Sisters in Austin, Phillipina Wolf, the fourth of the seven children of Johannes and Catharina Bermbach Wolf, was born on January 19, 1845, in Würges, Germany, a town about thirty miles from Frankfort. Phillipina emigrated to Bastrop County, Texas, at the age of ten with her family. Her father, Johannes Wolf, was a blacksmith in Würges, Germany, where his family roots dated back to the late seventeent century. In Texas, the Wolf family carved out a farm along Walnut Creek on virgin land that lay adjacent to the farms of Phillip Goertz (aka Görz in Balthaus's book[177]) and Johann Hartmanns, Goertz' brother-in-law. These three Catholic families formed the nucleus for what would become the town of Rockne, Texas. Wolf both farmed and provided blacksmith services for himself and his neighbors.[178]

Catholic Masses for this fledgling community were occasionally held in the Goertz home; but, for the most part, these pioneer Catholic families went to the Meuth Hill Church at Sandy Creek, which was usually served by the priest from Sts. Peter and Paul Church in Frelsburg, about 70 miles south of present-day Rockne.

The Rt. Rev. Monsignor J. B. Leissner, then serving in Bryan Texas, acknowledged the Diamond Jubilee of the Sisters of Divine Providence (1941), in a letter to *The Southern Messenger*[*] on August 15, 1941. In his letter he recalled Sister Mary Agnes Wolf to whom he had ministered as she lay dying. He noted that the first Sisters Sister Mary Agnes had ever seen were the Sisters of Providence in

---

176 Callahan, p. 53.

177 Balthaus, p. 105.

178 Goertz, Rev. Alois, <u>Rockne-Sacred Heart Parish-Bastrop County, Texas, 1876-1976</u>. Privately published in 1996 by the Rockne Historical Association, Bastrop, Texas, p. 23-27; 535-550.

Austin. According to Leissner, Phillipina remarked to her mother: "I want to be one of them."[179]

Sister Generosa Callahan describes Bishop Dubuis' travels through the Walnut Creek area in early 1866 prior to his European trip later that year. It may have been during the Bishop's visits that Phillipina got the idea that she might be interested in joining a religious order. Since Father Feltin also served the Catholics in the Bastrop area, he may have spoken with Phillipina about his sister's Congregation.[180] Perhaps with these invitations, once Phillipina learned of the Sisters of Providence, there is no doubt the Providence of God led her to join this small community while Mother St Andrew was still in Austin sometime in 1868.

According to Sister Joseph Neeb,[181] Phillipina was received into the novitiate of the Sisters of Providence with Father Feltin acting as agent for the Bishop in the ceremony.

Though Bishop Dubuis had intended that Austin would be the site of the new motherhouse of the Sisters of Providence, circumstances dictated a change in venue. Austin, as it turned out, did not become the center for German immigrants that Dubuis at first believed it would. Dubuis' firsthand knowledge of Castroville, on the other hand, led him to think that that location would be a better place for the Sisters of Providence to settle—a locale that would offer the Congregation new vocations.[182] The Alsatian heritage shared by Mother St. Andrew and the Castrovillians, he believed, would create an immediate bond that could enable the people of the Parish of St. Louis in Castroville to trust the Sisters and encourage their daughters to become Sisters of Providence with them.

---

* **The Southern Messenger** predated **Today's Catholic**, **the Catholic newspaper of the Archdiocese of San Antonio, Texas.**

179 Copy of Monsignor Leissner's letter held in the Archives of the Sisters of Divine Providence of San Antonio, Texas.

180 Callahan, p. 6.

181 Neeb, p. 8

182 Callahan, p. 55.

Little is known about the nearly two years that Mother St. Andrew spent in Austin. When she and Sister Mary Agnes traveled to Castroville on September 2, 1868, she left behind a growing school in a "large stone building"[183] which served as both school and convent, and land that had been purchased with Sister Mary Agnes Wolf's patrimony upon which Father Nicolas would build a convent.[184] Sister St. Claude remained in Austin until 1871; Sister St. Joseph Rice remained there until 1874.[185]

ENDNOTES   *CHAPTER X*   *CASTROVILLE*

The growth of the population of Texas during the years of the Republic was primarily the result of an influx of immigrants from France and Germany. Two parallel efforts promoted immigration from Europe: a settlement plan that was engineered by Prussian noblemen who bought large tracts of Texas land, advertised in Germany, and sold segments of that land to German immigrants; and the efforts of the presidents of the Republic of Texas, who offered land grants to *empresarios* who promised to recruit settlers who were sold a portion of the land grant for farming or ranching.

Henri Castro, Portuguese by birth but an American citizen with economic ties to France, was such an *empresario*. President Sam Houston granted him a colonization contract on February 15, 1842. In exchange for bringing 600 single men or families to the Republic of Texas by 1845, Castro received an area of land west of San Antonio, which included what is now Medina County and beyond. Upon the building of a livable cabin, each single man over seventeen or head of a household was to receive 340 acres of land. In addition to land

183 Callahan, p. 51.

184 Callahan, p. 56.

185 Archives, Congregation of Divine Providence, San Antonio, TX; Archives, Sisters of the Incarnate Word and Blessed Sacrament, Victoria, Texas; Archives, Sisters of the Incarnate Word and Blessed Sacrament, Corpus Christi, Texas.

that he could sell to farmers, the *empresario* was expected to select certain land within his grant for townships.

Though Castro had intended to create a French colony, difficulties with the French government stalled his recruiting progress in France. In addition to his focus in Alsace, a northeast French province which lay along the Rhine River, he turned his recruiting plans to Germany. Alsatians and Germans, he thought, hardy and stubborn and of independent spirit, would make ideal settlers who would stay on the land despite any hardship.

Over a two-year period, from 1842 through 1844, Castro recruited and resettled 700 immigrants, mostly Alsatians, who established themselves in what became Medina County, Texas. He had focused his attention on recruiting solid farmers who had enough means and equipment to start a farm and sustain themselves and their families until crops would come in.

Early in his negotiations, Castro, though a Jew, began a relationship with Bishop Jean Odin of Galveston in the hope that the Church would see his venture as worthy of its support and would provide clerics for his immigrants. Thus, on September 12, 1844, only three days after the arrival of the first settlers, "even before the women and children had joined their husbands and fathers, there took place the solemn 'laying of the cornerstone of the church,' which was to be built and dedicated to St. Louis."[186]

Thus, the village of Castroville, set along the banks of the Medina River about thirty miles west of San Antonio, was laid out by Castro who named the village for himself and named the streets for favorite cities, family members, and friends. In addition to a tract of land for the Church, land was provided for a school, and for other church uses.

The first church, a one-room stone and cypress building, was built on land that was a short block off the town square, but the entire section of church-owned land was over six blocks square in the center of the village with other acreage farther out.

---

186 Callahan, p. 58-67.

This fledgling community's first permanent priest was Claude M. Dubuis who would later become the second bishop of Galveston.[187]

Upon his arrival, Dubuis found the 1844 St. Louis Church to be hopelessly small for the growing colony and set about to plan for a new church. With Father Emmanuel Domenech, his assistant who designed the building, Dubuis and his parishioners constructed the new building. This second church, finished for Easter of 1850, was built in the center of the block across the street from the town square.[188]

The old (first) church then became the schoolhouse.

Dubuis left Castroville in 1852 and during the sixteen years which followed his pastorate (1852-1868), St. Louis Parish was served primarily by Franciscan Fathers from Schonau near Wurzburg in southern Germany[189] and the Benedictine Fathers from St. Vincent's Abbey in Pennsylvania.[190] The tenure of these monks was not a happy time for the parish of Castroville, due in part to the Civil War. A deacon, Emile Fleury, replaced the last Benedictine in the parish in October of 1867. But it was the advent (February 1868) of a young French priest, Father Pierre Richard, "a builder, organizer, and administrator," that would again stabilize the Parish of St. Louis which grew from less than 100 families to 225 families in the first year of Richard's pastorate.[191]

---

187 Other priests who served Castroville prior to Dubuis: Rev. John Gregory Pfanner of Alsace who came with early settlers in 1844 and whose legal entanglements led to his departure in 1845; Rev. Jean Roesch, also of Alsace, who came with immigrants in 1845; and a Rev. Lienhard who came with Pfanner. None of these three priests stayed with the colony. Upon his arrival in 1847, Dubuis found the 1844 St. Louis Church. From Gittinger, Ted, Connie Rihn, Roberta Haby, and Charlene Snavely, St. Louis Church-Castroville, Graphic Arts of San Antonio, TX, 1973, p. 7-9.

188 Gittinger, et. al., p. 12-17.

189 Moore, James Talmadge, Through Fire and Blood, Texas A & M Press, College Station, TX. 1992, p.103.

190 Gittinger, p. 22-23.

191 Gittinger, et al., p. 21-27.

Richard, a native of Loire, France, had been recruited by Bishop Dubuis in 1863 and was ordained in New Orleans. After serving in Victoria, Texas, (1864-1866) and Coleto, Texas, (1866-1868), he was appointed to Castroville, a parish which included the surrounding villages of Quihi, Vandenberg, and D'Hanis.[192]

Following in the footsteps of Dubuis who saw a bright future for Castroville, Richard believed that the 1850 church was too small for his congregation. Planning and preparations for a third church had begun sometime in 1867, but loss of their pastor (Benedictine Father Eberhard Gahr) in the fall of that year slowed progress. Bringing new energy to the parish, the newly-appointed pastor, re-started the building project and in July 1868 a cornerstone for the new (third) church was laid by Bishop Dubuis.

On September 2, 1868, Mother St. Andrew Feltin and Sister Mary Agnes Wolf left Austin for Castroville. The stagecoach trip would have taken not less than four days, but a week of heavy rains, swelling the Medina River, caused the missionaries to remain in San Antonio for a few days delaying their arrival in Castroville. While staying in San Antonio, they depended once again on the hospitality of the Ursuline Sisters.

While they were at the Ursuline Convent-Academy, Bishop Dubuis who was in San Antonio for confirmation and the laying of the cornerstone for the new San Fernando Church, took that opportunity to legalize Mother St. Andrew's ownership of land in Castroville where the school stood as well as land for schools in other German and Alsatian parishes in central Texas: D'Hanis, Fredericksburg, New Braunfels, Martines, Panna-Maria, Frelsburg, and Bernard. It was this contract (full text follows), which officially launched the parochial school system of Texas that the Sisters of Providence were to supervise.

"Regulations concerning the convent of the Sisters of Providence in the city of Castroville

---

192 Callahan, p. 80.

in the Diocese of Galveston. In the year of Our Lord one thousand eight hundred and sixty-eight, on the eighth of the month of September, the following regulations or contracts, as it were, were made, and in fact, according to the civil laws of the State of Texas and the Republic of North America.

Let it be known: I, Claude Marie Dubuis, Bishop of Galveston, as one party, have granted, with the obligation upon my successors in office, to Mother Andrew, Mother Superior of the Sisters of Providence:

1st. The square of land, where the convent of these same Sisters stand in the city of Castroville in the State of Texas in the Republic of North America, also the school houses of other parishes approved by us and erected in the parishes commonly called D'Hanis, Fredericksburg, New Braunfels, Martines, Panna-Maria, Frelsburg, Bernard.

2nd. The usufruct and administration of this same property, which belongs to them, and never will it be permitted to deprive these same nuns of the possession of their property.

As the second party, Mother Andrew, the Mother Superior, has assumed through these letters, clearly made known before both parties confirmed them, the strict obligation of teaching parochial schools according to the statutes of Canon Law and of removing nothing from these possessions without our episcopal permission and that of my successors in office.

592 The Tattered Heart

> **Given in the city of San Antonio, in the State,**
> **year, month and day above written.**
> **C. M. Dubuis, Bishop of Galveston**
> **Sr. Andre Marie, Superior General, Div.**
> **Providence"**[193]

During her time at Ursuline Academy in San Antonio, Mother St. Andrew addressed the school girls on the life of non-cloistered religious and the service they could offer to the Church in Texas, meeting two future vocations: Anna Schulz and Barbara Keller. Three months after Mother St. Andrew and Sister Mary Agnes arrived in Castroville Anna Schultz, the daughter of German immigrants in San Antonio, joined the Congregation in December 1868. Anna, known in religious life as Sister Mary Theresa Schultz, was the third vocation.[194]

Mother St. Andrew and Sister Mary Agnes arrived in Castroville on September 9, 1868, twenty-four years after (almost to the day!) Bishop Odin had laid the cornerstone for the village's first church.[195]

It took the two pioneer educators a month to organize the school and on the first Monday of October, October 6, 1868, they opened the school in the first church with thirty-six students.[196] This was not the first school for the village as former pastors had provided rudimentary classes, but this establishment solidified the Catholic school in Castroville for the next one hundred years.[197]

---

193 Callahan, p. 56. (Original document in the Archives of the Congregation of Divine Providence, San Antonio, Texas)

194 Callahan, p. 83.

195 Callahan, p. 80; p. 67.

196 Callahan, p. 81 and Gittinger, p. 29.

197 Gittinger, p. 62-63. [St. Louis School closed in 1968, ending 100 years of Catholic school education in Castroville under the Sisters of Divine Providence. However, in 1992, the elementary school was re-opened and continues. A Sister of Divine Providence, Sister Marie Elise VanDijk,

The small first church barely accommodated the new school and it seems that work on the new church was put on hold while the parishioners built a two-story structure on the same block which served as both the initial convent and a larger school.

In residence at the Castroville school on London Street, according to the census of June 1870, were Sister Mary Andrew (age 39, profession: teacher, born in France); Sister Mary Agnes (age 24, profession: teacher, born in Germany), and Sister Mary Theresa (age 19, profession: teacher, born in Germany). The postulants (Barbara Keller of San Antonio [from the Ursuline Academy], Isabelle Zimmermann of Castroville, Mary Merian of Castroville, and Amalia Bader (of Bader Settlement) who must have been in residence were not counted at that address.[198] Gittinger, however, notes that on August 25, 1870, the feast of the parish's patron saint, St. Louis of France, the third church had been completed enough for services and, included in the liturgical festivities at this inaugural Mass in the new church, "four novices of the Sisters of Divine Providence [who] pronounced, solemnly and distinctly, their annual vows."[199]

These four new vocations, all from Castroville, were known in religious life as Sister Mary Louis Zimmerman, Sister Mary Paul Keller, Sister Mary Joseph Merian, and Sister Mary Pierre Bader. The number of members of the American contingent of the Sisters of Providence of St. Jean-de-Bassel had grown to nine in just under four years!

Special Notes:

A. Though Bishop Dubuis' sincerity about the advantages of moving the headquarters of the Congregation of Divine Providence cannot be disputed, other factors have been noted as motivating his

served as principal from 1998 until 2006 and at this printing, Sister Esther Haberman, CDP, serves on the faculty.]

198 Census Records located in County Courthouse, Hondo, TX

199 Gittinger, p. 30, quoting from Wahrheitsfreund (sic), September 7, 1870. [Copy in the St. Louis Parish Archives]

decision to move Mother St. Andrew to Castroville. Correspondence (1867) between Odin and Dubuis referenced by Callahan[200] speak of a year-long negotiation between Dubuis and Father Edward Sorin, CSC, superior of the Holy Cross Fathers at Notre Dame College in South Bend, Indiana. Desperate for priests and Catholic educators, Dubuis wanted Sorin to send priests to Texas to take over his seminary that had languished in Galveston. Sorin made bold promises but reneged on them as he himself did not have adequate personnel for his current commitments. Sorin eventually agreed to send priests to the Galveston seminary, but that venture did not endure.

During their crossing of the Atlantic in 1869 as they both traveled to the First Vatican Council, Dubuis and Sorin evidently came to an arrangement: "The diocese offered to donate two thousand acres of land in Bee County that the order could then sell to support its work in Texas."[201]

In further negotiations in 1872,[202] Dubuis extended the arrangement to include a large tract of land outside Austin that were to be willed to the church by Mrs. Mary Doyle, a parishioner of St. Mary's Parish in Austin. Sorin, however, would not agree to establish a school at that location unless the Holy Cross Fathers also had St. Mary's Parish in Austin which, at that time (1872), was pastored by Father Feltin. In addition to the pastorate of St. Mary's Parish, the Holy Cross Sisters were to receive St. Mary's School, where, at the time (1872), Sister St. Joseph Rice was teaching.[203]

B. In 1868, the same year that Mother St. Andrew moved the Texas headquarters to Castroville, Mother Constantine Eck (Superior General: 1868-1885) accepted an invitation from Bishop Lavigerie, Bishop of Nancy, France, and also the Archbishop of Algiers, who had become the canonical superior of the Congregation, to send Sisters to

200 Callahan, p. 55.
201 Moore, p. 162.
202 Moore, p. 163.
203 Moore, p. 163; Callahan, p. 55-56.

his diocese in North Africa. Six Sisters were sent to Algiers and two communities were established there. This establishment, however, was not to endure. Political changes following the defeat of France by Germany in 1870 transferred Alsace and Lorraine (the location of St. Jean-de-Bassel) to Germany thus leaving the now "German" congregation with a mission in French Algiers. Believing the situation to be politically untenable, and faced with growing financial strain at the St. Jean-de-Bassel motherhouse, Mother Constantine called the Sisters home in the summer of 1870.[204]

ENDNOTES   CHAPTER XI   EXPANSIONS

In the fall of 1870, following the pattern of expansion developed by the Sisters of Providence in France early in their beginnings, Mother St. Andrew remained in Castroville to supervise the school, welcome postulants, teach the novices, and provide administrative leadership for the Congregation. Meanwhile, Sister Mary Agnes and Sister Mary Paul went on to D'Hanis, Texas, opening St. Dominic School, while Sister Theresa Schultz and Sister Louis Zimmerman opened a school at St. Mary's Parish in Fredericksburg, Texas.[205]

Novices who received the habit from Bishop Dubuis in 1871, all German-speaking, revealed a ripe harvest of new vocations from the small villages where schools had been opened the year before. Three entrants came from Fredericksburg: Sister M. Virginia Koehler, Sister Mary Angela Koehler, and Sister M. Odilia Fritz. Castroville gave two more of its daughters: Sister Regina Becker and Sister Mary Rose Bader,[206] the aunt of Sister Mary Pierre Bader while

---

204 Wilhelm, p. 62; Gruber, p. 152, 232-238.

205 Neeb, p. 14-15.

206 Emma Bader, the aunt of Sister Mary Pierre Bader, entered the Sisters of Divine Providence at the age of 14 and was professed at the age of 17 in 1875. She served in the following schools: Frelsburg, New Braunfels, Fredericksburg, Haby Settlement, Bernard, High Hill, Honey Creek, Muenster, Cameron, Westphalia, St. John's, Pilot Point, Ellinger, String Prairie, D'Hanis, and Devine (all in Texas) and in Cloutierville and

Sister Philomena Bretner "may have been from Austin or a nearby district."[207]

Three more novices were added in 1872: Sister Mary Josephine Krust of Casroville, Sister Mary Christina Zurcher[208] of D'Hanis, and Sister Mary John Campbell of San Antonio.[209]

After about a year of education and training in the religious life, the young novices, like their predecessors in France, accompanied more seasoned nuns who were sent to open schools in central Texas. Thus by the end of 1872, schools operated by the Sisters of Divine Providence[210] were in Austin (1866), Castroville (1868), Fredericksburg (1870), D'Hanis (1870), Frelsburg (1871), New Braunfels (1871), Danville [also known as Solms] (1872), Panna Maria (1872), and St. Hedwig (1872), Bernardo Prairie (1872), and Mentz (1872).

Campti in Louisiana. She died in 1944 at the age of 86. The account of Emma Bader's entrance into the Sisters of Divine Providence in Chapter IX is found in her memoirs, date of compilation unrecorded. [CDP Archives, San Antonio, TX and "Bader" by Rev. Gerald Boehme, p. 6.]

207 Callahan, p. 88.

208 Callahan indicates that Sister Christina's last name was Zurcher (p. 90); Neeb says it was Buercher (p. 12). The name "Zurcher" is noted in Gittenger, et al, St. Louis Church-Castroville (Appendix B: Census of Catholics in Castroville, Texas, 1854), p. 129. The author tends to agree with this name.

209 Neeb, p. 12 and Callahan, p. 90.

210 From the outset of its history, the Congregation founded by Father Jean-Martin Moye was named the Sisters of Providence. However, when the Franco-Prussian War (1870) ended with the ceding of Alsace and Lorraine to Germany, the branch of the Congregation based at St. Jean-de-Bassel in Lorraine, changed its name to "Sisters of Divine Providence" because the German understanding of "providence" did not embrace its divine characteristic. The author will (beginning in Chapter XI) designate the Congregation as the "Sisters of Divine Providence", presuming that Mother Constantine Eck would have informed Mother St. Andrew of this change when it occurred. Branches of the Congregation which remained in France (Portieux, and eventually Gap, and their branches) continue to be called Sisters of Providence.

Though not all of the above early missions endured, three of the schools were maintained by the Sisters of Divine Providence for more than 100 years: St. Louis in Castroville, St. Mary's in Fredericksburg, and Sts. Peter and Paul in New Braunfels.

St. Mary's School in Fredericksburg, opened in 1870, and Sts. Peter and Paul School in New Braunfels, opened in 1871, were established in small towns which had been carved out of the Texas hill country by German settlers brought into Texas by the *Adelsverein²¹¹*. The village of Fredericksburg, founded in 1845 by Count Otfried Hans von Meusebach (naturalized under the name John O. Meusebach) of the Society for the Protection of German Immigrants, had been named for Prince Frederick of Prussia."²¹² Each married man in the original group of 120 received ten acres of farmland and a town lot. Skilled craftsmen, builders, merchants, farmers, and professionals, these newest Texans, were anxious to create a village that would mirror the ones they had left behind in Germany.

For the most part, this community was Lutheran in their religious persuasion, but the tiny Catholic group remained very loyal to their Church. In their earliest years, the Catholic Church of Fredericksburg was served by Rev. Claude-Marie Dubuis, the pastor of Castroville of which Fredericksburg was a mission.

John Leydendecker, a well-educated layman who had immigrated with the other settlers led prayers at Sunday services in the town (attended by both Lutherans and Catholics) and also provided a school for the village children in the village church, *Vereins Kirche* (old church). During the earliest years of the settlement, school attendance was poor; textbooks were non-existent. Within the first year however, Leydendecker abandoned teaching and took up farming. It was another ten years before a stable school situation

211 The *Adelsverein* was a German-based society which promoted immigration from Germany and Bavaria to Texas and offered immigrants protection and support.
212 "Fredericksburg," at the Internet Site www.texascapes.com and Balthaus, Anna, Rockne Region Germans-Immigrants from Wurges, 1846-1883 (Trans. by Donald C. Goertz, PhD.), p. 41.

emerged when in 1856 Franz Stein opened the first Catholic school with a beginning enrollment of seven students. Over the next two years, the Catholics bought lots surrounding their Church and built cabins that would be used for school buildings. "By January 1857, the enrollment reached forty-seven."[213] Between 1856 and 1870 several different people taught in the school, holding it together for the parishioners.

Rev. Peter Tarrillion initiated the invitation to the Sisters of Divine Providence of Castroville to send Sisters to stabilize his parish school. Though the people of Fredericksburg, ever dependent on the land and the weather for their livelihood, were struggling financially during these early decades of the town's history, the townspeople were always generous toward the Sisters. Tuition payments were usually in food and fuel for the Sisters.[214]

In addition to serving in Fredericksburg, Sister Theresa Schultz also served in St. Joseph's German Parish School in Galveston. She died in 1884 at the age of thirty-four. Sister Louis Zimmermann was transferred to St. Hedwig in 1874, but did not remain with the Sisters of Divine Providence.[215]

In April 1845, just one month before the founding of Fredericksburg, the village of New Braunfels, Texas, on the stagecoach route from the capitol city, Austin, to San Antonio, was founded under the auspices of one of the *Adelsverein*, protective societies formed to initiate German emigration to Texas. One year earlier, 1844, Prince Carl von Solms-Braunfels was commissioned to re-organize a floundering enterprise since the first attempts to settle German immigrants on land in Texas had failed miserably. Upon his arrival at the port of Indianola, Texas, Solms-Braunfels found "439 Germans waiting in the harbor" for placement upon land they had purchased.

213 "History of St. Mary's School-Fredericksburg, Texas," compiled by Sister Mary Angelita Fritz, CDP, and Sister Martha Anne Hunter, CDP, in September of 1966, p. 118-119. (Evidently part of a larger document, unpublished). Catholic Archives of Texas, Austin, Texas.

214 "History of St. Mary's School-Fredericksburg, Texas," p. 118-119.

215 Archives of the Congregation of Divine Providence, San Antonio, TX.

Due to fraud, no land had been purchased for distribution and so Solms-Braunfels acquired land in the Indianola area as a temporary camp for the bedraggled immigrants until land for permanent placement could be obtained. He then "acquired several thousand acres along the road from San Antonio to Austin, where the smallest settlement" could be initially founded. From that first launching point (New Braunfels), Solms-Braunfels intended to continue with the settling of a larger piece of land located farther to the north and west between the Llano and Colorado Rivers. This western piece of land would include the town of Fredericksburg, founded by von Meusebach a month later.[216]

The New Braunfels settlement on the banks of the Guadalupe River "was so small that each settler received only 3.75 hectares (1 hectar=2.471 acres)." In addition, no treaty had been established with the Native Americans who used all the area in question as hunting lands. Within the month (May 1845) Solms-Braunfels returned to Germany "leaving large debts behind in Texas. He was replaced by Count Otfried von Meusebach who managed to conclude a treaty with the Indians and bring security to the settlements." It was Meusebach who actually oversaw the transport of the German immigrants camped in Indianola to their destinations in New Braunfels and Fredericksburg.[217]

Due to its location, New Braunfels soon became a "commercial center of a growing agricultural area. ... Within a decade of its founding New Braunfels had emerged as a manufacturing center supplying wagons, farm implements, leather goods, furniture, and clothing for pioneers settling the hills of Central Texas. Its markets supplied places as close as Bastrop and Victoria (Texas) and as far away as New Orleans, New York, and the Nassau province of

---

216 Balthaus, p. 41.
217 Balthaus, p. 41.

Germany," where so many of the settlers had originated. By 1850, New Braunfels was one of the four largest towns in Texas.[218]

Catholics in New Braunfels established a school system parallel to the public system that emerged in the late 1850's. Beginning in 1871, the Sisters of Divine Providence staffed Sts. Peter and Paul School until its closing in 1984.

Frelsburg, called by the earliest German settlers "Kraewinkel" or "Crow's Nest," was the oldest of the three settlements that received Sisters of Divine Providence in the early 1870's. "The site of one of the oldest parishes in the Diocese of Austin, [Frelsburg] was founded [in the late 1830's] by German Catholics from the Rhineland" who were blacksmiths, leatherworkers, and essential tradesmen.[219] Although Catholic services date back to the mid 1840's, it was during the pastorate of Rev. Peter V. Gury (appointed in 1854) that Sts. Peter and Paul Parish experienced rapid development. During his tenure, a theological seminary for the diocese was established, and Bishop Dubuis and Mother St. Andrew actually planned to open a novitiate there. However, Bishop Dubuis' retirement to France in 1881 interrupted those plans.

The Sisters of Divine Providence established St. Joseph School in Sts. Peter and Paul Parish in 1871, believing that the small town of Frelsburg would grow. By 1876, the small town had a population of 250 people, and financial growth continued into the end of the nineteenth century with cotton being the major agricultural crop.[220] The Sisters of Divine Providence withdrew from the school in Frelsburg in 1915 after nearly forty-five years of educational service there.

---

218 Green, Daniel P., "New Braunfels," The Handbook of Texas Online, The Texas State Historical Association, 1997-2002; at the Internet site www.utexas.edu/handbook/online/articles/NN/hen2.html

219 "Frelsburg, Texas," at the Internet Site www.texascapes.com "1998-2006, Texas Escapes—Blueprints for Travel."

220 Frelsburg Historical Society, The History of Frelsburg—Kraewinkel [Crow's Nest], New Ulm Enterprise Print, 1986, p. 1-7.

*   See Special Notes in the Chapter XII Endnotes.

No specific reasons are given in Callahan's history regarding Sister St. Claude Boëgler's departure from Corpus Christi. Callahan notes that Bishop Dubuis brought Sister St. Claude back to Austin on or after August 28, 1868. Though no record remains of her experience at St. Mary's School there, perhaps the intensifying negotiations between Bishop Dubuis and Father Edward Sorin, CSC,* American Superior of the Holy Cross Fathers and Sisters from Notre Dame which would conclude with the Holy Cross Fathers and Sisters taking the St. Mary's Parish and School in Austin provided her with future transitions that she felt unable to manage. Callahan indicates that Sister St. Claude left Austin for the Incarnate Word and Blessed Sacrament Convent in Victoria, Texas "in the fall of 1871,"[221] while the archives of the Sisters of the Incarnate Word and Blessed Sacrament ((IWBS) note that Sister St. Claude entered their community on October 29, 1871, received their habit on May 2, 1872, and professed her vows in their community in June 1873.[222] There are no indications that she ever went to Castroville. Perhaps Mother St. Andrew visited her in Austin before her departure.

Sister St. Claude Boëgler had been born in 1830 in Offendorf, Germany, and entered the Sisters of Providence at St. Jean-de-Bassel in 1848. The archival record of her life with the Incarnate Word and Blessed Sacrament Sisters (IWBS) of Victoria, Texas, indicates that her dependence on Providence endured throughout her life as she is portrayed as a person of sound judgment, great devotedness to duty, and for many years she rendered important service to the [IWBS] community. No one who was taught by Sister Claude forgets her admirable training. 'There is a right way to do things and things should be done that way,' was [Sister's] motto.

> During the last years of her life she suffered very much, but with edifying patience. Her unbounded

---

221 Callahan, p. 94.
222 Archives, Sisters of the Incarnate Word and Blessed Sacrament, Victoria, Texas.

confidence in God was the admiration of all, and her peaceful death [June 19, 1911, the age of 81] showed that those who trust in Him shall never be confounded.[223]

The reader will remember that Sister Regis Chavassieux, IWBS, a pioneer founder of the Victoria monastery, was a novice from Lyons, France, who traveled on the *Europa* with Mother St. Andrew and Sister St. Claude. Sister Regis evidently went from the Ursuline Convent in Galveston to join Mother St. Claire Valentine who had come from the IWBS monastery in Brownsville to establish the Victoria convent and academy in 1866.[224] Perhaps the relationship between Sister St. Claude and Sister Regis, begun while they were en route to Galveston from France, was the motivation for Sister St. Claude's transfer to the IWBS community in Victoria.

Among the Incarnate Word Sisters, Sister St. Claude was known as "*Sœur* Marie St. Claude." Their archival material indicates that *Sœur* Marie St. Claude served as a teacher of German and sewing between 1873 and 1885. In her elder years (1881-1902) she served as a gardener in the very expansive convent garden.

It should further be noted that in 1877, Sister Joseph Merian, received into the CDP novitiate in 1870, also transferred to the Incarnate Word and Blessed Sacrament Sisters in Victoria when the "Blue Sisters" at Panna Maria dissolved in 1879.[225]

NB. The negotiations between Bishop Claude Dubuis and Father Edward Sorin, CSC, regarding the future of St. Mary's Parish in Austin began in 1869 but the Holy Cross Fathers did not take pos-

---

223 Archives, Sisters of the Incarnate Word and Blessed Sacrament, Victoria, Texas.

224 Extending the Incarnation into the Third Millennium [a privately published history of the Sisters of the Incarnate Word and Blessed Sacrament], p. 16. Archives, Sisters of the Incarnate Word and Blessed Sacrament, Victoria, TX.

225 CDP Archives.

session of the parish until the spring of 1874. However, since specific correspondence[226] from Mother St. Andrew to Father Sorin relating to the Congregation's claims on the school property was written in 1872, it seems logical to include that aspect of the development of the loss of Austin in this chapter. The letter written by Mother St. Andrew to Father Edward Sorin, CSC, on July 21, 1872, in Chapter XI is the actual text. Only minor insertions have been made for clarity. The reader is directed to the Endnotes of Chapter XII for a full explanation of this concern.

ENDNOTES   *CHAPTER XII*   *UPS AND DOWNS*

In 1869, Pius IX called the plenary meeting of the world's bishops and male superiors of religious congregations which is now known as the First Vatican Council in the history of the Catholic Church. This meeting occasioned the encounter between Rev. Edward Sorin, CSC, the American Superior of the Holy Cross Fathers and Sisters, headquartered at Notre Dame, Indiana, and Bishop Claude-Marie Dubuis, Bishop of Galveston. Both prelates sailed from New York for Italy on the *Peirera* about November 1, 1869.

Though this might have been (according to the stories in Holy Cross lore) the first meeting of these two pioneer French missionaries, records indicate that Dubuis and Sorin had corresponded earlier about the possibility of opening various types of Holy Cross missions in Texas.[227]

Concerned about the future of St. Mary's College[228] in Galveston which was without permanent staffing and not under the direction

226 Callahan, p. 94-95.

227 Dunn, CSC, William, Saint Edward's University—A Centennial History, St. Edward's University Press, Austin, 1866, p. 1-15.

228 This college, when Bishop Jean Odin started it in 1852, had at first been staffed by the Oblates of Mary Immaculate. Other administrators followed including the Brothers of the Christian Brothers who staffed the College for seven years. In 1869, a diocesan priest with a lay staff oversaw the school. [from Clancy, CSC, Rev. Raymond J., The Congregation

of a religious congregation, Dubuis invited Sorin to take over the college which would include ownership of the land and buildings.[229]

While they were both in Rome for the Council, Dubuis enlarged the offer beyond the Galveston college to include a large tract of church-owned land in Bee County. Dubuis believed that Sorin could sell the Bee County land, using the money for the college Sorin hoped to establish or other Texas enterprises.

In 1870, the Chapter* at Notre Dame, Indiana, accepted the proposal and agreed to send Rev. Daniel Spillard, CSC, and four Holy Cross Brothers to Texas. At this time, the Holy Cross Congregation seemed to be overextended and a Brother Boniface Muher actually led the group to Galveston to take over the college.

Brother Boniface loved Texas, especially Galveston, and worked diligently to develop the small college. By Christmas of 1870 he had eighty-four boys at St. Mary's in Galveston.

In some way, information from Father Nicolas Feltin, pastor of St. Mary's Parish in Austin, became part of the conversation between the two clergymen. Mrs. Mary Doyle, an Austin widow known to Feltin, had a large acreage south of Austin which she was planning to will to the Diocese of Galveston as long as it would be used to serve Catholic education in the Austin area.[230] Bishop Dubuis put this land on the table.

---

of the Holy Cross Comes to the Diocese of Galveston, an unpublished paper written at St. Edward's University, Austin, Texas, February 21, 1946, and presently housed in the Archives at the University of Notre Dame, Notre Dame, Indiana.]

229 Dunn cites an August 26, 1869, letter to Sorin from Chambodut, the Chancellor of the Galveston Diocese to Sorin.

* A "chapter" is a formal meeting of the members of a religious congregation which ordinarily has final decision-making authority. At this time, there were three components to the Congregation of the Holy Cross: the Holy Cross Fathers, the

Brothers of the Holy Cross, and the Sisters of the Holy Cross (known at first in France as the Sister Marianites of Holy Cross). The Holy Cross foundation began in France in 1840 under Rev.

In the fall of 1870, Bishop Dubuis again enlarged his offer to include St. Joseph College in Brownsville, a parish and school in Houston, and a school in Laredo. Mission San Jose in San Antonio was still included; and in March of 1871, Father Sorin traveled to Texas to meet with Bishop Dubuis to solidify the future of the Holy Cross Congregation in Dubuis' diocese.

In the spring of 1872, Sorin made another trip to Texas accompanied by Holy Cross Sisters Mother Angela Gillespie and Sister Raymond Sullivan. So that Mrs. Doyle would recognize that he was in earnest in his pledge to develop a college on her Austin property, Sorin actually bought another 123 acres that abutted the Doyle farm from a Colonel Robards. Sorin paid $5,189 for the Robards property with the understanding from Mrs. Doyle that he could begin building his college on her 398 acres, allowing her to live on the farm until her death when Holy Cross would actually inherit the Doyle property.[231] In addition to changing her will so that Holy Cross and not the Diocese of Galveston would inherit the Doyle farm as well as "certain city lots," Mrs. Doyle's will also forgave Sorin the $ 995 that she had asked to be paid to her before construction on her property would begin. The transaction was completed April 8, 1872.[232]

Basil Anthony Moreau who served as its Superior until his retirement from that position in 1866. Upon his resignation, the American group began to discern reconfiguration and by 1869, the Sisters of the Holy Cross had elected a new superior from among themselves—Mother Mary Angela Gillespie. However, "the Sisters continued to refer to and address Sorin as 'Father General,' the same title used by the Holy Cross men." (Dunn) In 1869, in America, Sorin was the Superior of all three of these groups.

230 Several unanswered questions arise at this time. Did Father Feltin intend for the Diocese of Galveston or his parish of St. Mary's to receive this gift from Mrs. Doyle's estate? Had Father Feltin worked on the arrangement with Mrs. Doyle himself and did he see his own school (St. Mary's, operated by the Congregation of Divine Providence) as the intended beneficiary?

231 Callahan, p. 97.

232 Dunn, p. 10-11.

In his book, <u>St. Edward's University—A Centennial History</u>, William Dunn, CSC, references a letter that Sorin wrote to Dubuis two days after the transaction had been completed, April 10, 1872. In the letter, Sorin "said that in his opinion the Austin affair was one of the most important of the bishop's episcopate."[233] Though Sorin profiled the Austin project as a high priority, unnamed circumstances delayed the actual implementation of the college. Dunn seems to suggest a lack of clarity between Dubuis and Sorin, leading Sorin to believe that he would be given St. Mary's Parish in Austin first and then he would begin to build the college. But, the transfer of the parish from Father Nicolas Feltin to the Holy Cross Fathers did not happen in 1872 or 1873.[v]

Dubuis, on the other hand, may not have placed the Austin project at the same priority as did Sorin. Since he did not have a firm date of accession from Sorin, Dubuis would have necessarily been slow at reassigning Feltin. And, if as his letter of December 14, 1872, to Sorin[234] indicates, Feltin seemed to be contemplating joining Holy Cross in order to remain in Austin. Dubuis may have been taking his time in order to see what Feltin really planned to do. In addition to this project, Bishop Dubuis was working on support for his fledgling hospital Sisters in Galveston, finding monies for his various projects, setting up new parishes, and advancing the organizational plan of his diocese which would lead to the creation of three Texas dioceses by Rome by 1874.

Sorin may have simply overextended his personnel and did not have priests and brothers to send to Austin. Or various governmental restructuring within the American branch of the Holy Cross Congregation after the resignation of the Congregation's French founder, Father Moreau in 1866 may well have been the cause of the slow start on the Austin college.

Dunn notes that before her death Mrs. Doyle herself was questioning the order of events as she seemed to expect the building

---

233 Dunn, p. 10.
v   See Special Notes on pages 593-594
234 Callahan, p. 99.

of the college to have started, at least by end of the year 1872. In November 1872, three months before she died, she wrote Sorin asking him why the college was not progressing. Dunn further states, "In the same letter Mrs. Doyle mentioned that the Catholic congregation of Austin had outgrown its old church. Now Father Feltin was building a new one with his own hands," which was "located where the parish school had formerly stood."[235] It seems that frustrations as to "progress" in Austin abounded!

Delay in the development possibly could be traced to some of these circumstances:

a) it took letters as long as two weeks to travel from Notre Dame, Indiana, to Texas and correspondence often crossed in the mail;

b) a shortage of priests and other resources in both Holy Cross and the Diocese of Galveston would have strained the abilities of both Sorin and Dubuis;

c) changes in the governmental structure of the Holy Cross Fathers, Brothers, and Sisters placed an enormous burden on Father Sorin, the Congregation's Superior;

d) because of the pressures of the debt on his church and his need to sell properties to avoid foreclosures, Nicolas Feltin, may have exaggerated the situation in correspondence to Sorin;

e) Feltin may have been waiting to see how the impending re-configuring of the Diocese of Galveston would place Austin; and

f) Mother St. Andrew may not have been informed fully as to various developments.

Confusion of all parties over the Austin transaction was likely, and documents that are extant may not explicate the situation fully.

In any case, the transfer of St. Mary's Parish to the Holy Cross Fathers took place only in April of 1874. The records of St. Mary's Parish, held at the Catholic Archives of Texas in Austin, note that Feltin "officiated at St. Mary's for the last time on May 3, [1874]."[236]

---

235 Dunn, p. 11.
236 Dunn, p. 13 and Record of Baptisms for St. Mary's Parish, Catholic Archives of Texas, Austin, Texas.

Final arrangements moved quickly. Bishop Dubuis "wrote Sorin, instructing him to buy the pastor's [Feltin's] schoolhouse. Dubuis added that he had a gift of $8,000 from Mrs. Doyle's legacy in favor of the school. Probably he meant that Sorin could draw on the money to meet Feltin's claims. [See below] At any rate, both the bishop and Sorin apparently came to Austin in April 1874 to formalize the transfer of the parish."[237] No extant records indicate whether this money was paid, to whom it was paid, or what happened to it.

Father Nicolas Feltin remained a parish priest in the newly formed Diocese of San Antonio. In 1874, Feltin accepted the assignment to St. Joseph's German Church in San Antonio, Texas, where he served as pastor until his death in 1878.

At the time of the transfer of the St. Mary's parish school to the Sisters of the Holy Cross, Sister St. Joseph, having no ties to Castroville, left the Sisters of Divine Providence and returned to her relatives in Galveston and Corpus Christi. While visiting the Buckley family in Corpus Christi, Sister St. Joseph heard about the Sisters of the Incarnate Word andBlessed Sacrament who had opened a Monastery and school in Corpus Christi in 1871. She entered this Order on February 2, 1875 ... On October 7, 1875, she received the Incarnate Word habit and the same religious name, Sister St. Joseph ... She made her profession on April 14, 1877.

> Again, Sister St. Joseph ministered as a teacher and again she was recognized as a very efficient and devoted teacher. She was appointed principal of the English school, and in hertenure as principal, through her efforts, Incarnate Word Academy of Corpus Christi received state recognition through an Act of the Texas Legislature, and was authorized to confer academic honors. Within the community, Sister St. Joseph served as a councilor. However her religious life as a Sister of the Incarnate Word and Blessed

---

237 Dunn, p. 13.

Sacrament lasted only twelve years. Sister St. Joseph died in Corpus Christi on October 7, 1889. She is buried in the Calvary Section of Rose Hill Memorial Park, Corpus Christi.[238]

Special Notes: Regarding Extant Correspondence

Another enigma occurred in 1872. In July of 1872, Mother St. Andrew wrote Father Sorin a quite firm, but polite, letter speaking of her own dismay at losing the school in Austin and her displeasure at not being reimbursed for the property on which the school building stood. She had purchased that land using Sister Mary Agnes Wolf's patrimony. [See Chapter IX] A translation of the letter (she writes in French) reads in part:

> *It is six years that I have been in Texas. With the approbation of my venerable Superiors and the desire of Monseigneur Dubuis, Bishop of Galveston, I founded the house of Providence, in this diocese, at Austin, the capitol of Texas ...*
> *... this House was founded at the cost of great sacrifices. After two years of assiduous work, Lordship [Dubuis] thought it fit to send me to Castroville to spread good work; in consequence, the House at Castroville became the Mother House, and Austin remained continued the work begun up until the present time. One of our good Sisters, Sister Mary Agnes, gave her patrimony, for the purchase of the lot on which the convent is built.*

The letter goes on to say that Mother St. Andrew had made a recent visit to Austin (July 1872) which led her to understand that

---

238 Unpublished materials. Archives of the Sisters of the Incarnate Word and Blessed Sacrament, Corpus Christi, Texas

the people of Austin were very satisfied with the work of the Sisters of Divine Providence at their school and did not want to change to the Sisters of the Holy Cross, as planned by Sorin. She admits that she had no official papers to verify her Congregation's ownership of the land in question, but she would depend upon Providence to vindicate her rights. She signs the letter

Your very humble and very respectful servant,
Sister M. André
Superior of the Sisters of Divine Providence[239]

She succinctly makes a point of owning the property upon which the school building in Austin stood. When all was said and done in final transactions in April 1874, Bishop Dubuis, evidently supportive of Mother St. Andrew's claim, required Rev. Edward Sorin to pay for the "schoolhouse."[240]

Another letter, penned on December 14, 1872, from Father Nicolas Feltin to Father Edward Sorin illustrates the Sorin-Nicolas Feltin relationship as Feltin saw it. Feltin begins by referencing correspondence between the two from the spring of 1872, which must have been a source of disagreement. He outlines his thinking on the arrangements between the Diocese of Galveston and Father Sorin, noting the Bishop's right to appoint whomever he wished to the pastorate in Austin. He further indicates his willingness to sell to Sorin various lots with improvements) which he had purchased in Austin. Though Feltin is not specific about this property, it is appears that he is including the land upon which the school-convent was built that Mother St. Andrew had bought in 1868. Interestingly, Feltin also says that "whenever a college shall be built, and be in operation, I may ask for admittance into your order, if it may suit me." Feltin

---

239 The letter and its translation is housed in the Archives of the Congregation of Divine Providence in San Antonio, Texas.
240 Dunn, p. 13. However, no record of that transaction exists.

understands that his service to the parish in Austin is at the pleasure of Father Sorin, as the "charge of the congregation of Austin was to be considered as having been transferred to yourself for the benefit of your order."

Though the letter reveals that already in 1872 Bishop Dubuis had offered Feltin the pastorate of the "German congregation" (St. Joseph's German Parish) in San Antonio, Feltin reiterates his interest in remaining in Austin and, perhaps, joining the Holy Cross order. The pastor of St. Mary's is clearly torn and is not anxious to disengage from his parish.

Final sentences in the letter describe the properties of the parish· the new school which Feltin is willing to sell to Sorin for $3025.45 (cost of building and improvements), another lot (with itemized improvements) for $658, and two other lots (recently purchased) which he thinks he will have to sell before the note on them is due in February (1873). Feltin offers all of the described property to the "Sisters of the Holy Cross, or any other religious Order, of nuns or brothers, or the Bishop or the congregation [the parish of St. Mary], or anybody welcome to buy from me ... at the price I paid for them."[241]

The tone of this letter is very conciliatory, suggesting that it is meant to mend a relationship that earlier letters might have injured.

Another letter, also written in December of 1872 (after the Nicolas Feltin letter) over the supposed signature of Mother St. Andrew

---

241 The letter, in its entirety, is in Callahan's book, The History of the Sisters of Divine Providence, p. 99-100. However, the original location of the letter is not clear. The text of the letter is followed by "ACSC.P" and, though in the "Key to Footnote Abbreviations" (p. xv), "ASCS" references "Archives of the Congregation of the Holy Cross," the letter "P" is not explicated.

Feltin,[242] is an abject apology for a letter that she supposedly (according to the letter of apology) wrote to Sorin in August of 1872.[243]

These letters reveal the complexity of the arrangements related to the transference of St. Mary's Parish in Austin to the Holy Cross Fathers, the mixed emotions of Father Nicolas Feltin at the loss of a parish that he had built up from next to nothing, and the great sense of loss felt by Mother St. Andrew as her first school is being taken over by religious of another congregation.

A final note: In March 1873, Father Feltin deeded to Sorin two lots (# 7 and # 8 on Block 112) which he himself had purchased. Sorin paid Feltin $2200 for the property. There are no records that indicate that the "schoolhouse" property was ever paid for by the Holy Cross Fathers; and, in addition, no records exist indicating that Mother St. Andrew ever received money for her land in Austin.[244]

---

242 The Archives of the Congregation of the Sisters of Divine Providence of Texas hold both a copy in French and the English translation of this December 20, 1872, letter supposedly written by Mother St. Andrew to Father Edward Sorin. This author presumes that these are copies of originals held in the Archives of Notre Dame University. Sister Generosa Callahan's private notes in the files of research for her book suggest that the signature of this letter is not that of Mother St. Andrew. The formal signature of Mother St. Andrew can be seen above (p. 3) as it appeared on the July 31, 1872, letter to Sorin. The signature on the December 20, 1872, letter is "Sister Andrew Mary," with the designation "Sup." underneath the name. It seems unlikely to this author that Mother St. Andrew would have written a letter in French to Father Sorin and then signed her name in English. The author offers the following as a plausible consideration. Perhaps, in her frustration at not receiving remuneration for property that she owned, Mother St. Andrew did send a firmer letter to Sorin than the one written July 21, 1872, which Sorin found jarring. Given his on-going hopes that he would be able to get Sorin to buy the properties at St. Mary's that "he" owned, Nicolas Feltin himself might have written the December 20, 1872, letter to Sorin to further assuage a deteriorated relationship.

243 This letter of August 1872 referenced in the December 20, 1872, letter is not in the CDP Archives.

244 This deed is housed in the University of Notre Dame Archives. Copy of the deed is in the Archives of the Congregation of Divine Providence in San Antonio, Texas.

"In 1872 Bishop Dubuis, in order to facilitate administrative matters in his vast diocese and in anticipation of future divisions of the Diocese of Galveston, created four districts, namely, Galveston, San Antonio, Laredo, and Brownsville."[245] In 1874, the Diocese of Galveston was divided into three new dioceses: the Diocese of Galveston, the Diocese of San Antonio, and the Diocese of Dallas. Bishop Dubuis retained the See at Galveston and "on September 8, 1874, Pope Pius IX named Father Anthony Dominic Pellicer, vicar general of the Diocese of Mobile, as the first bishop of the new diocese [of San Antonio]."[246]

At the time of Pellicer's consecration, the Sisters of Divine Providence had schools in Castroville, Haby's Settlement, D'Hanis, Fredericksburg, New Braunfels, Panna Maria, and St. Hedwig in the Diocese of San Antonio; and also Frelsburg in the Diocese of Galveston.

Mother St. Andrew's original contract with Bishop Dubuis had included schools for the two Polish missions south of San Antonio: Panna Maria and St. Hedwig. In 1872, Sister M. Louis Zimmerman, accompanied by Mother St. Andrew, was sent to Panna Maria and Sister M. Joseph Merian opened the school in St. Hedwig.[247]

The pastor of these two parishes, Polish Resurrectionist priest Father Felix Zwiardowski readily promoted vocations to the Sisters of Divine Providence and he and Mother St. Andrew worked together to assist the German-speaking Sisters to learn Polish and to teach the Polish girls who entered the Sisters of Divine Providence to learn English. Several girls from the Polish settlements entered the Castroville convent in 1873 and 1874, the first two being Cecilia Felix (Sister Casimir) and Albina Musiol (Sister Stanislas Kostka). Once

245 Wangler, Rev. Msgr. Alexander C., editor, <u>Archdiocese of San Antonio, 1874-1974</u>, p. 13.

246 Wangler, p. 14.

247 Neeb, p. 19. Callahan (p. 103) says "three German-speaking Sisters of Divine Providence," but she does not name the third. Perhaps Mother St. Andrew went with Sister Louis to assist in beginning the schools there.

the two Sisters mentioned above had been received and habited, Mother St. Andrew planned to send them back to their hometown and move the two German-speaking Sisters who had begun the schools in Panna Maria and St. Hedwig to other Congregational missions. Father Zwiardowski was willing to welcome his two Polish vocations back to their hometown settlements, but he refused to allow Mother to remove Sisters Louis and Joseph.

In the summer of 1874, Father Zwiardowski refused to allow the four Sisters teaching at his parishes to return to Castroville for their summer program and retreat. Upon the consecration of Bishop Pellicer, Zwiardowski appealed to the new and under-informed Bishop to allow him to begin a new religious congregation. In 1875, the Polish priest, having received the confidence of the new bishop invested seven young women with the habit of the Sisters of the Immaculate Conception, a community of women religious with roots in Poland. Six of those seven women had been trained to be Sisters of Divine Providence at Castroville. But, in the end, Mother St. Andrew lost eleven subjects to Zwiardowski's project since the priest had instructed the parents of five other girls in training in Castroville to bring their daughters home to his new Congregation.[248]

The Blue Sisters, as the new Congregation was known, disbanded in 1879; and, realizing that he had acted with insufficient knowledge about Zwiardowski's plans, Bishop Pellicer lost confidence in the Polish priest.[249]

Sister Louis Zimmerman never returned to the Sisters of Divine Providence; Sister M. Joseph Merian entered the Sisters of the Incarnate Word and Blessed Sacrament of Victoria, Texas, in 1877, where she was known as Sister Mary Magdalen Merian.[250]

---

248 Callahan, p. 105-106.
249 Callahan, p. 107-108.
250 Archives of the Sisters of the Incarnate Word and Blessed Sacrament, Victoria, Texas.

ENDNOTES   *CHAPTER XIII*   *GRAY DAYS*

On Tuesday, January 26, 1875,[251] Father Nicolas Feltin accepted his assignment to St. Joseph's, the "German" parish in downtown San Antonio. One of his first actions as pastor was to ask Mother St. Andrew for Sisters to begin a school for his parish. The parish was heavily in debt; but in March 1875, Bishop Anthony Pellicer purchased property for the school, which he then sold to Mother St. Andrew. Sisters Mary Clare Schorp, Odilia Fritz, Virginia Koehler, and Ursula Krust opened St. Joseph's Academy in September 1875. The three buildings existing on the property when Mother St. Andrew purchased it served as a school building, a residence for the Sisters, and a kitchen. With 150 students at its opening, the school was large and grew steadily.[252]

St. Joseph's Academy opened at a time when Mother St. Andrew's personnel resources were limited. The loss of the eleven vocations to the "Blue Sisters" at Panna Maria had left inadequate numbers to staff schools with mature vocations who were seasoned educators. In fact, since Sisters Virginia and Odilia had been at D'Hanis, it is possible that in order to open St. Joseph's School in San Antonio, Mother might have had to assign new novices to St. Dominic's in D'Hanis.

St. Joseph's Academy had a shaky beginning. During the school's first year (1875-1876), Sister Ursula Kurst* left the convent and was replaced by Sister Clotilde. The next year, 1876, Sister Odilia Fritz was replaced by Sister Catherine Kraus.[253]

---

251 "A Short Biography of Rev. Father Nicolas Feltin," taken from St. Joseph Parish Book, unpublished, p. 83 (2). Material held in Archdiocese of San Antonio Archives.

252 Callahan, p. 108-109.

* **Her sister, Sister Josephine Kurst, sent to teach in the Polish schools in Panna Maria/St. Hedwig, had been separated from the Sisters of Divine Providence by Father Zwiardowski.**

253 Callahan, p. 109.

Callahan notes, however, that the most profound challenge to Mother St.Andrew's administration during these years between 1874 and 1879 began with a quarrel between the Koehler Sisters, Sister Virginia and Sister Angela. During their visit to their Fredericksburg home in the summer of 1877, the two Koehler Sisters evidently had a serious disagreement. Upon their return to Castroville, the conflict continued. Upon the advice of Sister Angela,$^\nabla$ Mother St. Andrew decided to remove Sister Virginia, Sister Angela's sister, from St. Joseph's Academy where she had served for two years. Dismayed that his school and church would lose Sister Virginia who also served as the director of his parish choir, Father Nicolas Feltin, pastor of St. Joseph's, disputed the change.

Believing that Father Nicolas had suspect intentions toward his daughter Sister Virginia, the father of the two Koehler Sisters entered the fray. While visiting St. Joseph's Academy in San Antonio, Koehler accused Feltin of poisoning him and Feltin was arrested for attempted murder. Newspaper reports accused Mother St. Andrew of causing her brother-priest's arrest. Though the case was dismissed by the San Antonio court for lack of evidence, Feltin's arrest damaged the reputations of all concerned and even Bishop Pellicer became involved.

Bishop Pellicer learned from his earlier experience with Father Zwiardowski. This time he interviewed all parties concerned and found that a petty quarrel between Sisters Virginia and Angela Koehler had precipitated the catastrophe. In the end, Sisters Virginia and Angela left the Sisters of Divine Providence, returning to their Fredericksburg home.[254]

One might ask how this rather insignificant occurrence exacerbated into such a momentous event. The materials from St. Joseph

---

∇ **Sister Angela was serving at Haby's Settlement, thus coming back to the Castroville Motherhouse each weekend. Mother St. Andrew would have known her better than she knew her sister, Sister Virginia. Why Sister Angela sought her sister's change from St. Joseph's Academy is unknown.**

254 Callahan, p. 109-110; Neeb, p. 22-23.

Parish Book (cited in footnotes) indicate that this period of San Antonio history was dominated by post-Civil War reconstruction discontent. Feelings against German-Texans ran high as the German immigrants, for the most part, had sided with the Union. The Ku Klux Klan was especially vicious and fueled a "yellow press" which was anti-Catholic and anti-German. This atmosphere no doubt contributed to the turn of events which occurred, victimizing Father Feltin in particular and the Catholic Church in general.[255]

The jarring event prompted Mother St. Andrew to realize that, if success in Texas were possible, more mature vocations were required. Though she had sought to be as self-reliant as possible, Mother St. Andrew must have come to the conclusion that she would have to return to Germany to ask for more Sisters.

Between 1872 and 1878, other schools were opened at St. Roch's Parish in Mentz, Texas (1872), at St. Joseph's German parish in Galveston, Texas (1876), and the parish in Bernardo (also known as Bernardo Prairie), Texas (1877), fulfilling, for the most part, the contract made between Bishop Claude Dubuis and Mother St. Andrew in September 1868. From Congregational records it would appear that no school was ever opened in Martinez, Texas, a small village ten miles east of San Antonio on the railroad line.[256]

In the spring of 1878 Mother St. Andrew returned to St. Jean-de-Bassel. She found her Congregation, under the able leadership of Mother Constantine Eck, to be struggling with the effects of "germanization," the transitioning of the French culture to the German culture in Alsace and Lorraine. With the end of the Franco-Prussian War in 1870, Prussia, now aligned with the German States, acquired the highly prized French territory of Alsace and parts of Lorraine. In effect this political change threatened all religious con-

---

255 "A Short Biography of Rev. Father Nicolas Feltin," p. 83 (2).

256 Archives, Congregation of Divine Providence, San Antonio, Texas. Information about Martinez, Texas from www.tsha.utexas.edu/handbook/online: "Martinez, Texas" by Christopher Long.

gregations in those two departments. In 1872 and 1873 the Jesuits, Lazarists, Redemptorists, and Holy Ghost Fathers were all expelled from German territories. In an effort to destroy the Catholic school system, in 1875 Bismarck dissolved all religious congregations not devoted to the care of the sick. Mother Constantine was able to safeguard the Sisters of Divine Providence only because Father Moye had noted care of the sick as one of the primary duties of the Sisters. But as layer upon layer of bureaucratic requirements were piled on educators, the Sisters of Divine Providence struggled under the burden. Examinations for renewal of the Letters of Obedience (documents from the Superior General citing the Sisters' teaching credentials) were to be proctored by German inspectors. By the end of 1873 all religious had to possess a German certificate; French certificates would no longer be honored. And all teaching had to be done in German. Finally, the German authorities required that all primary teachers teach both boys and girls.[257]

At this time, the Sisters of Divine Providence of St. Jean-de-Bassel directed 317 primary schools in the Alsace-Lorraine area with some 400 Sisters teaching in these schools. The impact of this disruption in educational endeavors was no doubt very challenging for the now-German Sisters of Divine Providence.

Other endeavors also required Mother Constantine's attention. By the time Mother St. Andrew returned to St. Jean-de-Bassel after her twelve-year absence, a new chapel had been built. Begun in 1868, the chapel was in pure Gothic style and is patterned on the small chapel of Pont-a-Mousson. The sanctuary arch bears the coat of arms of both the Knights of Malta (who used St. Jean's Hall, the main Motherhouse building, for their headquarters in the early 1800's) and the Bishop of Nancy who dedicated the chapel to St. Anne in 1872. The sanctuary windows honor Blessed Jean-Martin Moye, the Congregation's founder; Father Jean Decker; and Father Dominique LaCombe. The left transcept contains the altar of St.

---

257 Callahan, p. 115-117.

Anne, patroness of the Congregation, and serves as a reliquary for the bones of St. Dafnida, a third-century Roman martyr.

Besides building the chapel and grappling with the transition of the Congregation from its French roots to the German political structures, Mother Constantine revised the Constitution of the institute (1867) during the twelve years that Mother St. Andrew was in Texas. Also Mother Constantine herself designed a new habit* that was adopted while Mother St. Andrew was at the European Motherhouse. The new habit of 1878 included a short, rounded white *guimpe* (larger than the previous *guimpe*) and a black veil which replaced the traditional bonnet.[258] The black cross worn by the annually professed Sisters had a Eye of Providence in silver on the wood. Perpetually professed Sisters received a black cross with a silver Corpus on the front and the silver Eye of Providence on the back.[259]

Mother St. Andrew must have experienced Mother Constantine to be very supportive of the Texas missions. Perhaps Mother Constantine believed that the future of the Congregation, given the uncertainties of dealing with the dictatorial Prussian regime, might lay outside Alsace and Lorraine.

Accompanying Mother St. Andrew and Sister Theresa Schultz on their return to Texas in August 1878 were five well-trained Sister-educators. Hoping to provide Mother St. Andrew with more internal stability, Mother Constantine also missioned the German

---

*   **Bismarck insisted that religious women wear a more stylized habit similar to habits worn by nuns in cloisters to set them apart from other women in the small villages. The reader will remember that up to this point, the headpiece of the Sisters of Divine Providence of St. Jean-de-Bassel was an Alsatian-style peasant's bonnet worn over linen headcoverings. The new habit would provide both identity and security for the Sisters, especially those alone, in small villages.**

258 Information on the evolution of the habit from the archives of the Sisters of Divine Providence of St. Jean-de-Bassel, France.

259 From information on file at the Catholic Archives of Texas, Austin, Texas.

Congregation's general treasurer, Sister Mary Angelique Decker, and its Mistress of Novices, Sister Mary Ange Huver, to Texas. The professed educators who volunteered for the Texas missions were Sisters Mary Pierre Hetzel, Sigisbert Megel, André Reisdorf, Arsene Schaf, and Donate Claude. Sister Gabriel Stephan volunteered for household work.

The band of ten retraced the same journey that Mother St. Andrew and Sister St. Claude Boëgler had made twelve years earlier: sailing from LeHavre on August 13, 1878, landing in New York, and then taking a steamship to Galveston. In Galveston, they rested at St. Joseph's School before continuing on by train to San Antonio.[260]

With this infusion of new Sisters, Mother St. Andrew was able to increase the number of teachers at St. Joseph's School for the 1878-79 term. The novitiate was placed in the able hands of Sister Mary Ange Huver who, in addition to providing classes for the novices, also translated the 1867 Constitution from French into English.[261]

The Sisters of Divine Providence staffed twelve schools in the 1878-79 school year: Castroville, Fredericksburg, Frelsburg, New Braunfels, Solms (Danville), St. Joseph's in Galveston, St. Joseph's in San Antonio, Haby's Settlement, D'Hanis, Ellinger (near Frelsburg), Mentz (near Frelsburg), and Bernardo Prairie. Callahan writes that there were thirteen schools in operation at that time, but archival records do not corroborate this. Though some records indicate that St. Dominic's School in D'Hanis closed in 1880, it is possible that due to diminished personnel, that St. Dominic's may have closed earlier.*

ENDNOTES   CHAPTER XIV   RETURN TO HOPE

Upon their return from Germany, the new missionaries no doubt began their orientation to Texas. Sister Mary Ange Huver, who had

---

260 Callahan, p. 117-118.
261 Callahan, p. 119.

been a novitiate companion[262] of Mother St. Andrew's in 1850-51, was the Mistress of Novices at St. Jean-de-Bassel. She immediately took over the novitiate and also began the task of translating the revised (1867) Rule into English. In Germany, the Congregation had also recently changed the daily prayer said in common. From earliest days, the Sisters in France had prayed "The Little Office of the Immaculate Conception," a compilation of prayers and psalms prayed in French or German. This same prayer was said in Texas. But by the time Mother St. Andrew returned to Europe in 1878, the Motherhouse had changed their prayer form, adopting the "Office of the Blessed Virgin Mary" which was prayed in Latin. No doubt Sister Mary Ange Huver was also busy instructing her English- and German-speaking novices how to chant the Latin prayers.

Eventually the other new missionaries were sent to schools where they were needed: Sister Marie Pierre went to Bernardo where a school had been opened the year before; Sister Arsene went to Galveston; Sister Mary Andrew (André) was sent to St. Joseph's Academy in San Antonio. Sister Angelique Decker, taking the position of General Assistant, and Sister Gabriel Stephen, housekeeper, remained at the Castroville Motherhouse.[263]

The year 1878 ended on a sad note for Mother St. Andrew. Her brother-priest, Father Nicolas Feltin, as pastor of St. Joseph Church in downtown San Antonio, lived in an upstairs sacristy room. The residence was drafty: hot in the summer and cold in the winter. Several days following Sunday, November 24, 1878, Father Feltin succumbed to a bronchial infection and rapidly worsened. Mother St. Andrew was brought to San Antonio where she joined Bishop

---

* **St. Dominic School in D'Hanis was re-opened by the Sisters of Divine Providence in 1883. Congregational records indicate that the reason for the first closing was that the Sisters serving in D'Hanis were not able to attend Mass on a regular basis during the week.**

262 Congregational records, Congregation de la Divine Providence, St. Jean-de-Bassel, France.

263 Neeb, p. 25-27.

Pellicer and several priests around his deathbed. Father Feltin died early in the morning of Saturday, November 30, 1878, at the young age of forty-nine. His funeral Mass was held at St. Joseph Church on December 2, 1878, with Bishop Pellicer presiding and nine other priests in attendance. The *San Antonio Daily Express* (December 4, 1878) reported an attendance of nearly 2,000 people at his funeral at St. Joseph Church with 1,200 accompanying the body to its final resting place in German Catholic Cemetery Number 1, about one mile east of the Church.[264]

Though Father Feltin's most colorful experience at St. Joseph Parish may have been his arrest and trial for the alleged poisoning of Sisters Virginia and Angela Koehler's father (who did not die!), he is remembered for loftier reasons.

In the 1870's the population of San Antonio grew from 12,000 to 31,000 and fully one-third of San Antonians were German-speaking. Under Nicolas Feltin, St. Joseph's Parish grew as well. Feltin is remembered as being wise and far-sighted. He enhanced the sanctuary of the Church and obtained two large church bells. Leading a spartan life in his debt-laden parish, he lived simply, taking his meals at the home of Mrs. William Menger, a widow living on nearby Bonham Street who owned the Menger Hotel and Brewery. He supported the Sisters of Divine Providence in starting a school for the parish, providing a Catholic school for those who could not afford to send their children to Ursuline Academy or the Marianists' College. Chronicles of Feltin's life indicate that his greatest accomplishment as pastor of St. Joseph Church was the purchase of the first parish cemetery grounds, "the Old German Cemetery," where he himself is buried, a mile and a half east of the Church.[265]

This tireless French missionary, remembered as "intelligent, pious ... [and] full of zeal," served the Catholic Church of Texas for a quarter of a century, pastoring three parishes: St. Vincent de Paul

---

264 Callahan, p. 120.
265 From materials on file in the Catholic Archives of Texas, Austin, TX.

in Houston, St. Mary's in Austin, and St. Joseph's in San Antonio.[266] Father Nicolas Feltin preached the word of God, celebrated the sacraments, tended the sick and dying, found homes for orphans, leaving behind a legacy of faith that has lasted to this day in the parishes and missions he served.

With her great burden considerably lessened by the assistance of Sister Angelique and Sister Mary Ange, Mother St. Andrew was able to devote her time to the Congregational administration and visiting the various missions outside the immediate Castroville area. Letters from priests asking for Sister-teachers continued to flood her desk. In response, Mother St. Andrew sent Sister Angelique Decker to begin a school at High Hill, Texas (near Schulenburg) in 1880; and in the next two years, the young Congregation opened schools at St. Rose of Lima Parish (St. John's School) in Schulenburg (1881), and St. Joseph's Parish near Schulenburg (1882).[267]

Bishop Anthony Dominic Pellicer died on April 14, 1880, after suffering from a long illness. Few visitors were allowed during his last days; but, upon hearing that Mother St. Andrew had come to see him, the Bishop asked that she be admitted. During that final encounter, the Bishop who had caused the loss of eleven members of the Sisters for the Sisters of Divine Providence gave one of his last episcopal blessings to their Superior and her Sisters. With his death, the ecclesial jurisdiction over the Sisters of Divine Providence passed to the vicar-general of the Diocese of San Antonio, Father John Neraz.

The Congregation remained under the direct supervision of Father Pierre Richard, pastor of St. Louis Parish in Castroville for less than a month after the death of Bishop Pellicer. In late April 1880, suffering from exhaustion and declining health, Father Pierre returned home to Loire (near Lyon), France, where he died on December 8, 1880, after only a few months with his mother and father. "Mother St.

---

266 From materials on file in the Catholic Archives of Texas, Austin, TX.
267 Records, Archives of the Congregation of Divine Providence, San Antonio, TX.

Andrew with a companion [had] accompanied him [to Loire] because his physical condition was such that he could not travel alone."[268]

From Loire, France, Mother St. Andrew traveled to St. Jean-de-Bassel in Germany where she obtained additional Sisters who had agreed to be sent to Texas. Continuing to be very supportive of the Texas venture, Mother Constantine gave Mother St. Andrew four Sisters: Sisters Mary Florence Walter, Mary Berthilde Thiel, Mary Luca Denniger, and Mary Rosine Vonderscher; and four novices: Sister Anna Ehrismann, Mary Beuchler, Augusta Rudloff, and Florida Seyler.[269]

On May 8, 1881, Jean-Claude Neraz, another Frenchman from Lyons, France, was the first bishop for the Diocese of San Antonio to be consecrated in San Fernando Cathedral. He was ordained to the episcopate by Bishop Edward Fitzgerald of Little Rock, Arkansas, with Bishop Claude Dubuis of Galveston and Bishop Dominic Manucy of Brownsville as co-consecrators.[270]

Recruited for Texas as a seminarian in Lyons, France, by Bishop Jean Odin in 1852, Neraz had been ordained a priest in Galveston in 1853. Neraz had spent his entire priestly life in the Diocese of Galveston; and when the Diocese of San Antonio was created in 1874, he was appointed vicar-general of the new diocese under Bishop Pellicer. His pastoral assignments in Texas included Nacogdoches, San Antonio, and Laredo, where he built St. Augustine Church.

As Bishop of San Antonio, he continued to serve as the pastor at San Fernando Cathedral, as well as the chaplain for the Sisters* at Santa Rosa Infirmary and at St. Joseph Orphanage.[271] After Father Pierre's departure to France, Neraz maintained the role of ecclesi-

---

268 Callahan, p. 121.
269 Callahan, p. 122.
270 Wangler, p. 18.
*   **These were the Sisters of Charity of the Incarnate Word founded in Lyons, France, and Galveston by Bishop Dubuis in 1866. Dubuis sent Sisters to San Antonio from Galveston in 1869 to open a hospital and an orphanage, establishing there a**

astical superior of the Sisters of Divine Providence, providing direct oversight. For instance, Callahan notes that for "untold reasons the bishop of San Antonio (Neraz) had forbidden her (Mother St. Andrew) to make the (spring of 1883) trip (to Germany); but some of the older members of the Congregation went to him with the plea of numerous schools asking for sisters who could speak English, German, and Czech." Only after this intervention by unnamed "older sisters" did Neraz permit Mother St. Andrew to make her fourth and final trip to Europe[V].

Other than this disagreement over the 1883 recruiting trip to Europe, Callahan indicates that there was no reason to believe that the relationship between Bishop Neraz and Mother St. Andrew in these first years of his episcopate was anything other than amicable.[272]

One other venture during this time period is worthy of note. During his episcopate, Bishop Dubuis of Galveston, and Mother St. Andrew discussed the possibility of a branch novitiate in Frelsburg and contracted for its establishment. Though the seminary that Dubuis had opened in Frelsburg in the late 1860's had not been continued, the buildings and grounds were still usable. In those days, the town of

---

foundation of the Sisters of Charity of the Incarnate Word independent of the Houston-based Congregation.

271 Wangler, p. 18.

V **Readers will note that Bishop Neraz also made a trip to Europe in 1883 and, unknown to Mother St. Andrew, visited St. Jean-de-Bassel in September 1883. This is further discussed in the Endnotes to Chapter XV.**

272 Callahan, p. 131.

∞ **Bishop Claude Dubuis continued ministering in France in the Lyons area helping confer the Sacrament of Confirmation and other pastoral duties. On June 6, 1894, Bishop Dubuis celebrated fifty years of priesthood, receiving written congratulatory remarks from those whose lives he had touched so deeply and gently, including the Sisters of Divine Providence of Texas. On May 25, 1896 (some sources indicate that the date of death was May 21, 1895), Bishop Claude-Marie Dubuis died. He is buried in his home parish at Coutouvre, France.**

Frelsburg had promise and both Bishop Dubuis of Galveston and Mother St. Andrew believed that a novitiate house in the Galveston diocese would attract vocations to the Sisters of Divine Providence.

However, in July 1881, experiencing declining health, Bishop Dubuis[x] formally resigned his episcopate in Galveston. Almost a year later, on April 30, 1882, Father Nicholas Gallagher, who had been serving as vicar-general of the Diocese of Galveston, was ordained its bishop. The branch novitiate was never established in Frelsburg. There is no doubt that the resignation of Bishop Dubuis was a distinct personal loss for Mother St. Andrew.

ENDNOTES   CHAPTER XV   UNRAVELINGS

According to the records of the Sisters of Divine Providence of San Antonio, the summer of 1881 saw the second death in the Congregation of Divine Providence in Texas; Sister Victoria Rothenfluch died of typhoid fever on July 21, 1881.[273]

In the fall of 1881, Sister Mary Florence Walter was sent to St. Joseph's Academy in San Antonio. According to Sister Joseph Neeb, little had been done to improve the buildings since the opening of the Academy in 1876, and Sister Florence's first tasks were to build up enrollment and solidify the support of parents. In 1884 work was begun on a new academy building which included new living quarters for the Sisters.[274]

Born in Surbourg, France, near Haguenau in the Bas-Rhin region of Alsace in 1858, Françoise Walter left her family home in 1872 at

273 Neeb, p. 32. The author notes a discrepancy. Two different Sisters remembered Sister Victoria in their memoirs: Sister Rosine Vonderscher recalled her as the driver of the buggy that took her to the train for Ellinger in the late fall of 1881; and Sister Seraphine Stecker who came to Texas from Germany in 1883 remembered Sister Victoria helping with the large convent garden in the fall of 1883. These memoirs are held in the Archives of the Congregation of Divine Providence, San Antonio, TX. For the sake of the story, Chapter XV will not carry the death of Sister Victoria as happening in the summer of 1881.
274 Neeb, p. 32-33.

age fourteen to enter the Sisters of Divine Providence at St. Jean-de-Bassel. Three years later, in September 1875, Françoise received the habit of the Sisters of Divine Providence at St. Jean-de-Bassel and was given the religious name Sister Mary Florence. After profession of vows in 1878, she had taught in German schools before volunteering for service in Texas in 1880.[275] Sister Mary Florence was only twenty-three when Mother St. Andrew, no doubt recognizing her leadership capabilities, sent her to take over the direction of St. Joseph's Academy in San Antonio.

Under her direction St. Joseph's Academy, the first semi-parochial school in San Antonio, grew to 259 students by 1885.[276] The Academy continued to educate San Antonians until it was closed in 1951 when the five high schools operated by the Sisters of Divine Providence in San Antonio (St. Joseph's Academy, St. Mary's High School, St. Michael's High School, St. Henry's High School, and San Fernando School) were consolidated into one new high school for girls: Providence High School. This school is still in operation today.

In 1882 and 1883, presumably at the invitation of Mother Constantine, Mother St. Andrew made two more trips to Germany to recruit volunteers. In 1882 seven professed Sisters and two novices* volunteered, and Mother St. Andrew was able to recruit thirteen candidates from German villages. In 1883, though no professed Sisters volunteered, a number of novices and candidates* from St. Jean-de-Bassel returned to Texas with Mother St. Andrew, along with a large number of young girls whom Mother herself recruited by going from village to village in Germany and Poland.[277]

Both the 1882 and 1883 voyages included side trips to Ireland for English-speaking recruits.

The story of why and how Mother St. Andrew recruited in Ireland is found in Sister Angelina Murphy's "Chronicles" where she records

---

275 Murphy, CDP, Sr. Angelina, <u>Mother Florence: A Biographical History</u>, p. 13

276 Callahan, p. 128.

277 Callahan, p. 122-123.

an interview with Sister Hubert Lavin, CDP, who received the information from Sister Ignatius (Johanna) Sheehan in 1935 while they were both stationed in Perry, Oklahoma.

Sister Ignatius was one of the first five girls to come to Texas from Ireland in 1882. Sister Ignatius recounted that the apparition of Our Lady of Knock had occurred on August 21, 1879, and that Mother St. Andrew had traveled from Germany to Knock, Ireland, to pray to Our Lady of Knock for the Texas missions and their concerns. While at Knock, Mother St. Andrew met Mother Francis Clare Cusack, the "Nun of Kenmare," who had recently left the Sisters of St. Clare and was founding the St. Joseph's Sisters of Peace of the Immaculate Conception, now known as the Congregation of St. Joseph of Peace.[278] According to Sister Ignatius, Mother Francis Clare had just received six young women and did not have room in her house for others who had applied. Mother Francis Clare gave Mother St. Andrew the names of five girls who had expressed interest in being religious and Mother St. Andrew sent word to them that she would interview them for entrance into the Sisters of Divine Providence in Texas, and they responded immediately, but because Sister Ignatius' dressmaker was longer than was expected in finishing her traveling dress, they were delayed in reaching Knock, and Mother Andrew had already left when they arrived because she had to meet another group who were waiting for her in France. However, she left a message: "If the Irish girls want to come to Texas with me, they will have to meet me in France."[279]

Five girls* from Ireland joined the Texas Congregation in 1882 and another eighteen Irish girls[V] joined in 1883.[280] One might surmise

---

278 This community now has three provinces: Sacred Heart Province (England, Scotland, Ireland); St. Joseph's Province (New Jersey); Our Lady Province (Oregon, Washington, Alaska) [from www.csjp.org]

279 Murphy, "Chronicle."

* **Candidates who came in 1882 became Sisters Eugenia Kaiser, Helena Kaiser, Antoinette Loth, Odilia Loth, Stanislas Kostka Keuchly, Blandina Schaeffer, Usula Rudloff, Regis Neil, Angela**

that Mother St. Andrew maintained contact with Mother Francis Clare, gleaning from the names of more girls who wanted to be missionaries in Texas. Evidently made in the summer, based on the date of the signing of the Articles of Incorporation (May 19, 1883) and the date of entrance of new German and Irish candidates (August, September, October 1883), the 1883 trip was Mother St. Andrew's last visit to her beloved Motherhouse at St. Jean-de-Bassel.

Though we have no extant records regarding the visits to the German Motherhouse, the numbers of vocations supplied by Mother Constantine seem to indicate her continued support for Mother St. Andrew and the Texas project.

Drouy, Pauline Hettig, Joseph Braun, and two others who did not remain.
From Ireland: Sisters Ignatius Sheehan, Xavier Sheehan, Francis de Sales Sheehan, Margaret Mary Keating, Patrick Morrisey.
Sisters and Novices who came in 1882 from St. Jean-de-Bassel: Sisters Flavienne Braun, Emil Joseph Pinck, Mary Reine Hickel, Matthias Braun, Clemence Guebel, Madeleine Sheltiene, Pelagie Biegel; Novices Gonzaga Moser, Aurelia Seyler.
∇ **Novices, and Candidates who came in 1883 From Lorraine, Alsace, and other parts of Germany: Sisters Philothea Thiry, Melanie Gerard, Felicite Bastian, Dosithee Riederer, Euphemia Geoffray, Adelaide Meyer, Constantine Braun, Seraphine Stecher, Adeline Jonas, Liguori Huber, Dionysia Kesseler, Stephanie Marquis, Genevieve Matthis, Liboria Theiman, Monica Kollner, Jodoca Stiehl, Alexis Lummer, Agatha Breyman, Basilisse Dastilling, Gertrude Ehrisman, Aloysia Schaeffer, Emily Asselburg, Margaret Zimmerman, Victoria Linneman, and six others who did not remain.**
From Poland: Sisters Dominica Radowski, Hedwig Dragan, Casimir Garus.
From Ireland: Sisters Benedict Fenelon, Bernard Connellan, St. John Walsh, Evangelist Kiernan, Philomena Hayes, Fidelis Hennebry, Joachim Sweeny, Borgia Sheehan, Lucia Sheehan, Bernardine Cassidy, Bridget Sheehan, Columba Brennan, Mary of the Sacred Heart Sullivan.
281 Callahan, p. 122-123.

However, Mother St. Andrew's return journey in August of 1883 is available, recorded in detail by both Neeb and Callahan. Having just left the port of LeHavre on August 25, 1883, the *St. Germain* ran into a freighter-in-tow and nearly sank. Badly damaged, the *St. Germain* returned to harbor at Plymouth, England, where Mother and her fifty-two charges spent a week lodged in army barracks awaiting another ship. The group sailed from Plymouth on the *St. Laurent** but met a dangerous storm en route to New York. Callahan writes: "all the passengers felt this time that they were really doomed to a death at sea ..."

Finally after a safe arrival in New York, the band of missionaries stayed with Franciscan Sisters and in a hotel. Another episode, this time leaking gas in the hotel room, could have claimed lives, but all were spared.

After a smooth sailing from New York to Galveston, the group landed in Galveston only after another minor maritime problem in the Galveston harbor. In Galveston, Mother St. Andrew and her new candidates spent a few days with the Sisters at St. Joseph's Convent, and then boarded the train for Castroville.[281]

Callahan notes that in these years when the Congregation was receiving Sisters, novices, and candidates from Ireland and Europe, native vocations were also growing. "Whenever a new place was opened, subjects usually came from that place during the year of its opening. Other parishes every now and then sent a candidate to Castroville. There were several vocations during these years from Frelsburg, where Sister Mary Agnes Wolf was superior; others came from D'Hanis, High Hill, New Braunfels, Fayetteville, and San Antonio."[282]

---

*   **Neeb writes that the name of the French liner was the *St. Laurent*; Callahan says that it was *Amerique*. Neeb (1816) is closer to the telling of the tale; Callahan probably did extensive research. Callahan says that the return trip from Europe in 1880 was made on the *St. Laurent*.**

281 Neeb, p. 43-44.
282 Callahan, p. 124.

During the years 1881 to 1886, eight new schools were opened in Texas: St. John's near Schulenberg (1882); St. Mary's Academy in Palestine (1883); St.Dominic's in D'Hanis (re-opened in 1883); St. John in Fayetteville (1884); St. Edward in Dubina (1884); Sacred Heart in Marienfield (1884); St. Mary in Columbus (1885); St. Mary in Clarksville (reopened by the Sisters of Divine Providence in 1886 after the Sisters of the Holy Cross had left the school in 1883). These openings indicate that the European vocations were essential both to schools in existence and to providing schools for pastors who wanted Catholic schools in their villages.[283]

During those same years, in addition to the death of Sister Mary Victoria Rothenfluch in 1881 (?), several other Sisters succumbed to the ravages of disease, usually typhoid fever: in 1884, Sisters Sacred Heart Sullivan, Mary Theresa Schultz, and Mary Felicite Bastian; in 1885, Sisters Gabriel Stephan, Mary Columba Brennan, Mary Regis Neil, Xavier Sheehan, and Mary Vincentia Wipff.[284]

The tragic death of Sister Mary Clemens Guebel in 1883, however, was unusual and was no doubt quite disturbing to Mother St. Andrew and the entire community of Sisters. Sister Mary Clemens Guebel had come to Texas in 1882 at the age of thirty-one. Though not perpetually professed when she came and given her age, she probably would have made a perpetual profession soon after coming to Texas. She was sent to New Braunfels; but because of her difficulties with English and homesickness for St. Jean-de-Bassel, Sister Clemens was changed to Danville (Solms), a smaller school, in 1883. But she did not adjust and "begged Mother St. Andrew to take her back to Europe."[285] Before the return trip could be made, however, in her melancholy the distraught Sister asked her superior in Danville (Solms) if she could return to New Braunfels. Since it was the middle of the week, the superior suggested that Sister Clemens wait until Friday when they could both go

---

283 Records, Archives, Sisters of Divine Providence of San Antonio, TX
284 Records, Archives, Sisters of Divine Providence of San Antonio, TX
285 Callahan, p. 125.

to their neighbor-Sisters. Sister Clemens, however, did not heed her superior and left for New Braunfels on foot, a journey of about eight miles. When she was finally missed in Danville and did not arrive in New Braunfels, a search of the area was made, but the distraught nun was not found. Some months later, a boy found her skeleton in the woods; her habit was intact.[286]

Other developments in the life of the Congregation during this time are worth noting. In 1883, the Congregation was incorporated in the State of Texas with Mother St. Andrew named as president; Sister Theresa Schultz as vice-president; Sister Mary Ange Huvar as secretary; Sister Angelique Decker as treasurer.[287] At the signing of the Articles of Incorporation, the Congregation owned land and buildings in Castroville and San Antonio valued at $20,000. Though the original contract drawn up between Bishop Dubuis and Mother St. Andrew in September 1868 indicated that school buildings and furnishings in those schools would belong to the Sisters of Divine Providence, it is not particularly clear what other properties in Texas were actually owned by the Congregation at the time of 1883 incorporation.

When the Diocese of Galveston was divided in 1875, this effectively placed a Congregation[288] with a German motherhouse, operating under the official ecclesiastical approval of the Bishop of Metz, Germany, in two different Texas dioceses: Galveston and San

286 Although the Congregational records in the Archives of the Sisters of Divine Providence at San Antonio carry the date of Sister Clemens death as June 29, 1883, the account in Callahan suggests that the death took place during the school year. This author is following Callahan's story. Neeb, p. 38-39; Callahan, p. 124-125.

287 Callahan, p. 127.

288 Readers may want to recall that these years were very precarious for the Sisters of Divine Providence of St. Jean-de-Bassel: Bismarck's system of education categorically excluded the Catholic school; Bismarck had expelled a number of French-based Congregations, both men and women, from the Alsace-Lorraine area; the Congregation of Divine Providence's very existence was threatened by the political policies being inaugurated by the Reich.

Antonio. Perhaps wishing to maintain some type of direct relationship with the Congregation, which he had brought to Texas, Bishop Dubuis of Galveston, contracted with Mother St. Andrew in January 1881 (during the months when there was no bishop of San Antonio due to the death of Bishop Pellicer) to establish a "branch motherhouse" in Frelsburg in the Diocese of Galveston.[289] The exact reasons for establishing this second motherhouse are unknown and there are no extant records of its activities.

Several events occurred between 1883 and 1886 that had life-changing impacts on Mother St. Andrew.

First was a dispute with Bishop Neraz who did not want Mother St. Andrew to make the 1883 journey to Germany to recruit more candidates. One can only surmise that the bishop was already contemplating the separation of the Texas branch from their German motherhouse. After "older members" of the Congregation approached the Bishop for the needed permission, he relented and allowed Mother St. Andrew to return to Germany. Neraz himself, unbeknown to Mother St. Andrew, likewise made a trip to Europe and visited St. Jean-de-Bassel in September 1883,[290] meeting with Mother Constantine and, supposedly, effecting the separation of the Texas Sisters from the German motherhouse.[291]

An election of Superior General was held in August of 1884 (see footnote # 35). Records of who called this election do not exist. Did

---

[289] Callahan, p.128-129; and materials in the Catholic Archives of Texas at Austin, TX. It should be noted that Bishop Dubuis resigned his position as Bishop of Galveston in July 1881. This would not have abrogated the described arrangement.

[290] This visit by Bishop Neraz to Mother Constantine Eck is related in a letter from Sister Marie to Mother St. Andrew, September 26, 1883. This Sister, from the tone of the letter a good friend of Mother St. Andrew's, was present at a meeting between Mother Constantine and Bishop Neraz on the future relationship between the St. Jean-de-Bassel Congregation and its Texas branch. The letter does not indicate that the Texas branch was separated from the German motherhouse during Neraz' visit. The letter does, however, note that Neraz believed that "you ought to hold an election in your convent." [Copy of letter in English in CDP Archives, San Antonio, Texas]

[291] Callahan, p. 133.

Neraz call for this election after he returned from his visit to St. Jean-de-Bassel? Did Mother Constantine ask Mother St. Andrew to call an election? Was the "election" actually called to confirm or reject Mother St. Andrew's leadership? Where is the basis for thinking that Mother St. Andrew or the Sisters of the Congregation understood themselves to be separated from St. Jean-de-Bassel? Did the election mean one thing to Neraz and another to the Sisters? At any rate, a source, "A Brief History of the Congregation of the Sisters of Divine Providence of San Antonio," says:

> The first Superior was Sister Andrew Feltin, who was elected August 24, 1884. A new chapter was convened in August 1886 and in the presence of Rt. Rev. J. C. Neraz, an election took place, and the choice fell to Sister Mary Florence. She was Superior General until 1925. In that year Sister Mary Philothea was elected and retained the post until some time after 1931.[292]

Neraz did not challenge the results of the 1884 election.

Special Notes: The Separation of the Texas Branch from Germany

This author is inclined to believe (based on the writings of Sister Generosa Callahan) that

1) Mother St. Andrew and the other Sisters in Texas were not aware of Bishop Neraz's intentions to separate the Texas branch from St. Jean-de-Bassel in 1883—or they chose to ignore his posture;

---

292 "A Brief History of the Congregation of the Sisters of Divine Providence of San Antonio," CAT Files Duplicate, p. 4. Material held in the Catholic Archives of Texas, Austin, Texas. It should be noted that no other reference to this 1884 "election" seems to exist and Callahan does not reference it.

2) Bishop Neraz did not clearly represent his plans for a complete separation to Mother Constantine in his 1883 visit to St. Jean-de-Bassel;[293]

3) Bishop Neraz's communications to Mother Florence (1886-1892) relative to the supposed separation are inconsistent and lacking in clarity;

4) The large numbers of Sisters, Novices, and Postulants sent to Texas by Mother Constantine over a period of five years seem to confirm Mother Constantine's confidence in Mother St. Andrew's leadership ability.[294]

There are no administrative records in the archives of the Sisters of Divine Providence of San Antonio of the tenure of Mother St. Andrew's years as Superior General. Also there are no records of Mother St. Andrew's visits to St. Jean-de-Bassel in their archives. Sister Gabrielle Metzinger, CDP, the Congregational archivist at St. Jean-de-Bassel, could not locate the letters and/or papers of the administration of Mother Constantine Eck, Superior General.[295] The specifics of exactly why and how the Sisters of Divine Providence of Texas became separated from the Sisters of Divine Providence of St. Jean-de-Bassel are convoluted.

Special Notes: The Deposing of Mother St. Andrew

---

293 Based on a reading of Sister Ann Margaret Humbert, CDP, History of the Sisters of Divine Providence of Kentucky 1889-1989 (Privately printed) and on a letter to Mother St. Andrew from Sister Marie at St. Jean-de-Bassel dated September 26, 1883.

294 Callahan, p. 132-135.

295 Sister Diane Langford, CDP, visited St. Jean-de-Bassel in March 2007, to speak at length with Sister Gabrielle Metzinger, Congregational archivist. A search of the archives for the letters and papers of the administration of Mother Constantine was made during this visit. Nothing was located, much to the frustration of Sister Gabrielle who pledged that she would "keep looking."

In August 1886, a second election of Superior General was held at Castroville, this time at the request of Bishop Neraz. Neraz refused to allow the re-election of Mother St. Andrew; and at Mother St. Andrew's direction, the Sister-electors voted for Sister Mary Florence Walter who was not in attendance.[296]

The following information, taken from materials in the archives of the Sisters of Divine Providence of San Antonio and Sister Generosa Callahan's *History,* is offered to enlighten the reader as to how the deposition of Mother St. Andrew at the 1886 election happened.

The first problem Mother St. Andrew encountered as Superior General occurred in the scholastic year 1885-86. Reports came to Castroville from Sister Barbara, the Superior in New Braunfels, that the pastor of there, Father John Kirch, made frequent visits to the convent, presumably to see Sister Christine. Since Sister Christine was still in annual vows, Mother St. Andrew turned the matter over to Sister Mary Ange Huvar, Mistress of Novices. Evidently, Sister Mary Ange wrote to Sister Christine admonishing her relationship with the priest. Sister Christine took the letter to Father Kirch who in turn took the concern to Bishop Neraz claiming that his reputation had been called into question. Kirch asked for a formal investigation of Mother St. Andrew. Bishop Neraz made a further investigation with Sister Barbara, but came to no conclusions.

Sister Christine went to Castroville to make her explanations of the situation and, upon her return to New Braunfels, she related to Father Kirch in a letter all that Mother St. Andrew had told her. The letter was sent to Bishop Neraz.[297]

In the summer of 1886, at the request of Bishop Neraz, Father Henry Pefferkorn, pastor of St. Joseph's Parish, San Antonio, investigated the situation because Kirch accused Mother St. Andrew of slandering him with other priests.

Pefferkorn's report to Neraz on July 17, 1886, included his findings relative to the situation in New Braunfels. In addition to investigat-

296 Callahan, p. 143.
297 Callahan, p. 137-138

ing the problem at hand, Pefferkorn reviewed the conflict between Father Nicolas Feltin and the father of Sister Virginia Koehler, which had happened almost ten years earlier. Pefferkorn's personal opinion on that issue was: "It would not be difficult to prove that [Mother St. Andrew] ran from house to house to incite the people to take her part."[298]

His report also cited three other alleged misdeeds of Mother St. Andrew: 1) holding conferences with the sisters and the novices in which she warned them to beware of all priests; 2) changing Sisters from their schools without the advice and consent of pastors; 3) maligning the character of Father Henry Japes, pastor of St. Louis Church in Castroville (1881-1886).

In conclusion, Pefferkorn's report to Neraz asked that the superior (Mother St. Andrew) write nothing to the sisters that might be harmful to the pastors, to which he added that if among all the sisters in Castroville there was "not a single one capable of directing the convent in a manner not disastrous to the reputation of the priests, then let the convent be razed."[299]

Following Pefferkorn's report, Neraz called a committee of priests into service to examine the question. Fathers Richard J. Maloney, OMI; George Feith, SM; and Henry Pefferkorn were asked to conduct a formal investigation and Neraz gave them a list of twenty-one questions to put to Mother St. Andrew. Chapter XV contains a faithful description of the "trial."[300]

---

298 Callahan, p. 136.

299 Callahan, p. 139.

300 Of the twenty-one questions that Neraz provided in French to the committee of priests (written in his hand and held in the Archives of the Archdiocese of San Antonio) one question, No. 14, carries two German words [*Gehocks* and *Geschlepps*] which do not translate in a way that fits within the context of the document. The author consulted several people who spoke French, German, and Alsatian and is unable to determine the meaning of the phrase. This question is omitted in the account in Chapter XVI.

In addition, Chapter XV holds an accurate account of the July 29, 1886, request by Fathers Pefferkorn, Kirch, Wack, and Tarrillion, pastors of parishes with schools conducted by the Sisters of Divine Providence, who took it upon themselves to ask that another Superior be elected by the Sisters.[301]

Finally, Chapter XV includes the four conditions, which Bishop Neraz required of the Sisters of Divine Providence on August 16, 1886. With the four conditions, Neraz set an election date of August 26, 1886.[302]

Though the Sisters, almost all of whom were in Castroville for the annual retreat, did not want to hold an election, Neraz said that if they chose to support Mother St. Andrew as their Superior, he would "bring in a member of another community to be their superior."[303]

ENDNOTES   *CHAPTER XVI*   *ESTRANGED*

On September 4, 1886, Bishop Neraz returned to Castroville to supervise the selection of Sister-councilors. Sister Arsene Schaff who had been the Superior at St. Joseph's School in Galveston was named first assistant. Sister Angelique Decker was named as *econome* (treasurer) and Sister St. Stanislas Kostka Piwonka as secretary. Three other Councilors were Sister Agnes Wolf, Sister Marie

---

301 Material in Callahan, p. 140-141.

302 Material in Callahan, p. 141-142.

303 Callahan, p. 143. In addition to the Callahan reference, an account of an interview with Sister Imelda Heyd who came to Texas in August 1886 with Sister Mary Florence, which was written by Sister Gonzaga Menger some time prior to Sister Imelda's death in 1954 at age 80. The account reads: "On her [Mother Florence's 1886] return trip an election was held. Mother Andrew was reelected but Bishop Neraz said if they do not elect some [one] else he would put some Sister in from S. R." The author believes that "S.R." is "Santa Rosa," meaning the Sisters of Charity of the Incarnate Word who were a diocesan congregation under Neraz at the time. Interview account is in the Archives of the Sisters of Divine Providence of San Antonio, Texas.

Pierre Hetzel, and Sister Mary Paul Keller.[304] Given her choice of mission assignment, Mother St. Andrew chose to go to St. Joseph's School in Galveston. Within a fortnight, Sister Arsene followed her former superior to Galveston.[305]

In September 1886, Mother St. Andrew, referring to the agreement that she and Bishop Dubuis had contracted in January 1881, tried to get Bishop N. A. Gallagher of Galveston to approve the activation of the Frelsburg motherhouse. Various letters suggest that the Frelsburg house could be identified as a branch of the Castroville motherhouse, or it could be construed as totally independent, a new foundation. Gallagher, thinking that Galveston would be a better location, suggested opening the motherhouse there.

Callahan notes: "On that day [September 24, 1886] she [Mother St. Andrew] submitted to the bishop [Neraz] the resignation which she said she should have tendered when it was asked of her, and she begged pardon for all the trouble she had caused." A closer look at the full text of the September 24 letter brings confusion to its reader as to its origin. This author suggests that an unnamed group of Sisters[306] at St. Joseph's in Galveston is writing the September 24, 1886, letter to Bishop Neraz.

---

304 Archives, Congregation of Divine Providence, San Antonio, TX.

305 General Council Minutes, September 13, 1886, Archives, Congregation of Divine Providence, San Antonio, TX

306 Sister Scholastica Schorp recalled in her memoirs written on February 27, 1927: "[Mother St. Andrew] came to Galveston. Her plan was to form an independent community; fortunately this did not materialize. Plans of separation were drawn up and submitted to the Sisters in the Galveston community for signature. The local Superior, Sister Arsene, was the only one willing to accede to her wishes. The Bishop of Galveston discouraged the project and Mother St. Andrew and Sister Arsene left Galveston, saying that they had a place and property on which to open a school in Liberty, Texas." [From the Archives of the Sisters of Divine Providence of San Antonio, Texas]

* **The signature is in the plural; the first line is in the singular. Perhaps a poor command of English accounts for the difference. The letter is not in Mother St. Andrew's handwriting.**

The writers of the letter say: "Through these few lines I* hand the resignation which I should have done when asked of me and humbly ask pardon for all the trouble caused through me."

Aspects of this letter are interesting. It is signed "Sisters of Divine Providence" and it refers to Mother St. Andrew in the third person: "Now there is another request, your Lordship will probably recollect that Mother St. Andrew spoke last year about a place being for sale adjoining our school [Galveston] ..."∞ Though the tone suggests that the writers believe they have a positive relationship with the San Antonio bishop, what is "requested" of Bishop Neraz is very unclear. It should be noted that though this letter is comparable to other correspondence of the 19th century, for the 21st century reader the message is both unclear and confusing.

This author wonders: a) Did the bishop of Galveston indicate that he needed clarity from the bishop of San Antonio before he could endorse and support a motherhouse of the Sisters of Divine Providence in his diocese? b) Did the unnamed writers intend to completely resign from the Sisters of Divine Providence of Castroville in order to re-establish themselves as the Sisters of Divine Providence of St. Jean-de-Bassel at Frelsburg (or Galveston) with Mother St. Andrew as their Superior? The answers to these and many other questions are lost to history.

Since the Sisters of Divine Providence were a diocesan congregation under the Bishop of San Antonio, establishing a second foundation in Galveston would have required the consent of both bishops. Neraz refused to consent and Gallagher withdrew his approval.[307]

∞   This letter references a request that they (the Galveston Sisters) be supported in buying the property as it had come down in price. Clarity is lacking. The writers do not seem to be asking for permission or for the money to buy the property. The letter is quoted verbatim.

307 Callahan, p. 146.

∇   From this point on Mother St. Andrew will be referred to as "Sister." Her correspondence is signed "Sister St. André" and she is referred to as "Sister" in other correspondence. Today,

The chronicle of the remainder of the 1886-1887 experiences of Sister^V St. Andrew is found in Callahan's *History*, numerous letters, and references in the "General Council Minutes, 1886-1903," of the Sisters of Divine Providence. For the sake of simplicity, a summary of these documents follows:

- October 11, 1886: Sister St. Andrew and Sister Arsene Schaff made a trip to Anaheim, California, to investigate the possibility of starting a school for St. Boniface Parish.[308]

- October 26, 1886: Mother St. Andrew, having returned from Anaheim and now in Castroville, wrote to Bishop Neraz asking that she and Sister Arsene be allowed to remain in the Castroville convent and to receive the Sacraments on the Feasts of All Saints and All Souls.[309]

- October 27, 1886: Neraz answered Mother's October 26 letter giving the two Sisters permission to remain at Providence House in Castroville until Mother Florence returns, but refusing them permission to receive the Sacraments.[*310]

---

however, the Sisters of Divine Providence consistently refer to her as "Mother."

308 Callahan, p. 146; General Council Minutes, November 8, 1886, Archives, Congregation of Divine Providence, San Antonio, TX. The material on Anaheim in Chapter XVI is primarily dependent on Father David Montrose's (now Bishop Montrose) The Story of a Parish, published in Anaheim, CA by St. Boniface Parish in 1961.

309 Letter: Mother St. Andrew to Bishop John C. Neraz, October 26, 1886. Copy in the Archives of the Congregation of Divine Providence, San Antonio, TX.

* **Excommunication is a censure of a Catholic handed down by a bishop which prohibits the excommunicated individual from receiving Holy Communion (and usually the Sacrament of Reconciliation [confession]) at any time. Only the bishop who hands down the censure can reinstate the excommunicated person.**

310 Letter: Neraz to Mother St. Andrew, October 26, 1886. Copy in the Archives of the Congregation of Divine Providence, San Antonio, TX..

- October 27, 1886: Mother St. Andrew wrote another letter to Neraz. She explains that she has no intentions of disturbing the well-being of the Castroville Motherhouse with her actions. She further notes her belief that she was *persona non grata* in both the Diocese of Galveston and the Diocese of San Antonio. She says how and why she went to Anaheim, asking Neraz's permission for the Sisters of Divine Providence to open a school in Anaheim where she could be missioned along with some of the novices and candidates presently in Castroville. She asks his pardon for her disobedience.[311]

- November 6, 1886: Sister St. Andrew wrote to Father J. Adams, Vicar-General for the Diocese of Los Angeles, explaining that Bishop Neraz said that at present a school in Anaheim could not be opened but that Neraz thought that a school might be opened in the next school year (1887-1888).[312]

- November 7, 1886: Mother Florence wrote to Bishop Neraz explaining that Sister St. Andrew had "fulfilled all the conditions proposed to her by His Lordship *viz*: She gave back to the Mother House all the objects she had in [her] possession, and also she will return the money as soon as possible-further is she (sic) ready to leave the Convent Wednesday the 10th inst for Clarksville …"[313]

- November 8, 1886: Sister St. Andrew spoke to Bishop Neraz, submitting to all of his conditions for re-establishing her relationship with the Sisters of Divine Providence

---

311 Letter: Mother St. Andrew to Neraz, October 27, 1886. Copy in the Archives of the Congregation of Divine Providence, San Antonio, TX.

312 Letter: Mother St. Andrew to Father Adam, November 6, 1886. Copy in Archives of the Congregation of Divine Providence, San Antonio, TX.

313 Letter: Mother Florence to Neraz, November 7, 1886. Copy in Archives, Congregation of Divine Providence, San Antonio, TX.

in Castroville. Sister Arsene was also readmitted with the Bishop's permission.[314]

- November 8, 1886: Bishop Neraz wrote to Mother Florence that he was withholding permission for Mother St. Andrew to receive communion until all monies had been returned.

- November 10, 1886: Mother Florence wrote to Bishop Neraz that the money had been returned.

- November 10, 1886: Sister St. Andrew was sent to Clarksville, Texas.[315]

- November 15, 1886: Father J. Adam wrote Sister St. Andrew acknowledging her November 6 letter. He continued to be hopeful that the Sisters of Divine Providence could come to the Diocese of Los Angeles in the future.[316]

- March 1887: Sister St. Andrew left Clarksville toward the end of March without the permission of either Bishop Neraz or Mother Florence. Other than planning to work in Anaheim, Sister St. Andrew's intentions are unclear. Sister Arsene followed her. According to General Council Minutes Sister St. Andrew and Sister Arsene are no longer considered members of the Congregation.[317]

- March 29, 1887: Bishop Neraz wrote to Very Reverend J. Adam, Vicar-General of the Diocese of Los Angeles regarding Sister St. Andrew: "She has given trouble to my predecessor [Bishop Pellicer], and as she was a power among the people

---

314 General Council Minutes, November 8, 1886. Archives, Congregation of Divine Providence, San Antonio, TX.

315 General Council Minutes, November 10, 1886. Archives, Congregation of Divine Providence, San Antonio, TX.

316 Letter: Father J. Adam to Sister St. Andrew, November 15, 1886. Copy in Archives, Congregation of Divine Providence, San Antonio, TX.

317 General Council Minutes, March 30, 1887. Archives, Congregation of Divine Proivdence, San Antonio, TX.

at Castroville, she had her way. but (sic) this time she could not succeed ...[318]

- Letter on "Monday" (date unknown, but perhaps early May 1887) from Father Stöters, Pastor at St. Boniface Church, Anaheim, to Father Adam suggesting that Adam write to the Bishop of Galveston for more specific information about Mother St. Andrew. Stöters says the two Sisters will remain in Anaheim until he hears from Adam.[319]

- May 9, 1887: Letter to Father Adam (Diocese of Los Angeles) from Bishop Gallagher of Galveston in reply to Adam's May 5, 1887 which we do not have. The reply letter outlines briefly the history of Sister St. Andrew in the last few years. The letter affirms the position that Neraz took with her and states: "I cannot recommend her as a Religious." Gallagher notes that Sister St. Andrew "has worked hard and zealously to build up her Community ... but I think she ought never to have charge of any community."[320]

- May 16, 1887: In a letter from Mother Florence to Vicar-General Adam Mother Florence presents a review of recent months in the life of "Ex. Mother St. Andrew" and "Miss Barbara Schaff." She also indicates that Sisters of Divine Providence can be sent to the Diocese of Los Angeles but "Be it well understood that in no way we will receive Sr. St. Andrew." In the letter Mother Florence clearly states that she is writing only after consultation with Bishop Neraz.[321]

---

318 Letter: Neraz to Adam, March 30, 1887. Copy in Archives, Congregation of Divine Providence, San Antonio, TX.

319 Letter: Father Peter Stöters to Father J. Adam (date unknown, but perhaps before May 5, 1887)

320 Letter: Gallagher to Adam, May 9, 1887. Copy in Archives, Congregation of Divine Providence, San Antonio, TX. (The underlining is in the original letter.)

321 Letter: Mother Florence to Vicar-General Adam, May 16, 1887. Copy in Archives, Congregation of Divine Providence, San Antonio, TX.

A close reading suggests that re-admitting Sister St. Andrew into the Castroville Congregation might have been a request of someone in the Diocese of Los Angeles. The exact meaning of the correspondence is not clear.

- May 24, 1887: Letter from Sister St. Andrew to Father Adam in reply to a May 23, 1887 letter (not available) which he wrote evidently withdrawing his bishop's support of Mother St. Andrew and Sister Arsene asking them to leave the Diocese of Los Angeles. Sister St. Andrew pleads her case and asks for reconsideration so that she can remain in the Diocese of Los Angeles at St. Boniface Parish in Anaheim.[322]

- June 12, 1887 (Sunday): Father Peter Stöters, pastor of St. Boniface Parish in Anaheim, wrote to Father Adam asking for faculties* in order to be able to hear the confessions of Sister St. Andrew and Sister Arsene. He praises their conduct, indicating that "they conduct themselves very well, do much for me to beautify the Church and teach the children catechism."[323]

- June 13, 1887 (Monday): In a second letter Stöters is asking Adams to receive the Sisters who wish to put their cause before him. Stöters affirms that he would like to keep the two Sisters in his parish and would like to receive more Sisters of Divine Providence but acknowledges he cannot pay them. His final notation is "They are coming Tuesday."[324]

---

322 Letter: Mother St. Andrew to Vicar-General J. Adam, May 24, 1887. Copy in Archives, Congregation of Divine Providence, San Antonio, TX.

* **At this time in Church history (19th and most of the 20th centuries), priests had to be given special "faculties" or permission by the bishop to hear the confessions of religious women.**

323 Letter: Father Peter Stöters to Father J. Adam, June 12, 1887. Copy in Archives, Congregation of Divine Providence, San Antonio, TX.

324 Letter: Father Peter Stöters to Father J. Adam, June 13, 1887. Copy in Archives, Congregation of Divine Providence, San Antonio, TX.

- July 30, 1887: Sister St. Andrew wrote Bishop Neraz from Anaheim to ask him to approve her establishing the Sisters of Divine Providence in Anaheim since the Bishop of Los Angeles is willing to receive them pending Neraz's approval. The letter indicates a) that Sister St. Andrew understands that returning to work in Texas is out of the question; b) that though Neraz had said at Christmas (1886) that he would assist her to return to St. Jean-de-Bassel, she says she doesn't know what she can do there and acknowledges that she "can no longer bear the cold of winter" in Germany; c) that she remains astonished that Neraz could "have acted that way towards me who bore for [you] for so long so much esteem and regard." She indicates that she will return to Castroville on July 31, 1887.[325]

- July 30, 1887: Sister Arsene wrote Bishop Neraz a letter clarifying "the whole truth" to the bishop. She asserts that Mother Florence, upon learning that "Mother Andre wrote to me where she is (California), she sent for me at Haby Settlement." According to Sister Arsene, Mother Florence left her "free to join Mother Andre if you want," and Mother Florence further agreed to send other Sisters to California to join them. Sister Arsene writes, "I then answered her, 'If you leave me free, and you know that I don't want to leave against you [Mother Florence's] will, I decide to go to California, but if we cannot continue there, I will return to Castroville. She gave me her benediction before leaving with the promise that she would pray and ask others to pray for our mission in California." Sister Arsene says that at that time (March 1887) she had wanted to go to see Neraz before leaving for California but "Mother Florence told me it was best not to go and see your Highness because he would ask where Mother Andre was and he would write against her. I never gave up my habit, but to please my superior, I left my

---

325 Letter from Sister St. Andrew to Bishop Neraz, July 30, 1887. Copy in Archives, Congregation of Divine Providence, San Antonio, TX.

cross, my ring, my rosary, and some little things so that she [Mother Florence] would be out of trouble." Sister Arsene references an earlier letter which she says Mother Florence had told her to write asking for release from her vows, but that tells Neraz that she does not "want to be unfaithful to my vows."[326]

- August 4, 1887: Both Sister St. Andrew and Sister Arsene returned to Castroville, Texas.[327]

- August 8, 1887: Sister Arsene returned to St. Jean-de-Bassel where she was required to spend another year in the novitiate. Her religious name was changed to Sister Camille and in 1889 Mother Anna Houlné sent her and two other Sisters to open a house in Kentucky.[328] This foundation continues to be a province of the Sisters of Divine Providence of St. Jean-de-Bassel, France.

  Sister St. Andrew, "still clothed in her religious habit, went to live with her brother Lewis (sic) ... The next year, Mother St. Andrew was given a small stone house on the corner lot of the same block and lived there alone. The people of Castroville provided for her needs, for they loved her."[329]

During the spring of 1888 Sister St. Andrew wrote to *L'abbé* Nicolas Michel,[330] Ecclesiastical Superior of the Sisters of Divine Providence

326 Letter from Sister Arsene Schaff to Bishop Neraz, July 30, 1887. Copy in Archives, Congregation of Divine Providence, San Antonio, TX.

327 General Council Minutes, August 25, 1887. Archives, Congregation of Divine Providence, San Antonio, TX.

328 See Endnotes to Chapter II, Old Friends.

329 Callahan, p. 154.

330 In 1875 after ecclesiastical jurisdictions were re-arranged to match governmental jurisdictions following the annexation of Alsace and Lorraine by Prussia, Michel moved to Metz where he served the Bishop of Metz as titular canon. He remained the ecclesiastical superior of the Sisters at St. Jean-de-Bassel, however. [From Wilhelm, p. 76, 77, 79.] A conversation with the Archivist at St. Jean-de-Bassel leads the writer to believe that since Michel lived in Metz during these crucial years of the history of the Sisters of Divine Providence in Texas, records of the

at St. Jean-de-Bassel. The letter described her living situation in Castroville and asked for a "good certificate*." With a new certificate she plans to go to Leavenworth, Kansas, where "there is a German bishop" and where she can "do good among the Indians."[331] The tone of the Sister St. Andrew's letter suggests that she considers herself to be a member of the St. Jean-de-Bassel congregation. She pledges that the Kansas mission will be "under your jurisdiction and that of Reverend Mother." The response from *L'abbé* Michel states:

1) that Sister St. Andrew cannot receive a new certificate because she is no longer a member of the congregation, "having left it freely in 1866;"

2) she cannot be received again into the St. Jean-de-Bassel congregation;

3) the St. Jean-de-Bassel congregation cannot "authorize or promise help to join you to begin again a work as that of Texas."

4) Michel said he could send her a "copy of the certificate of 1866, omitting writing the name of Texas or the name you bore when you were a member of the Congregation."[332]

---

development of the Texas mission may have been destroyed with his papers that were not kept after his death. The reader is reminded that the Archivist at St. Jean-de-Bassel cannot locate the correspondence of Mother Constantine.

* **This "certificate" is the "Letter of Obedience" which contained the name of the Sister and the data related to her teaching credential. For the most part, it was a document of the state.**

331 Letter: Sister St. Andrew to *L'abbé* Nicolas Michel, March 2, 1888. Archives, Sisters of Divine Providence, St. Jean-de-Bassel; Copy: Archives, Sisters of Divine Providence, San Antonio, TX.

The material in Chapter XVI related to the Diocese of Leavenworth, Kansas, is from Graves, W. W., History of Neosho County. St. Paul, Kansas: Journal Press, 1949, p. 222 ff.

332 Letter: *Abbé* Nicolas Michel to Sister St. Andrew, March 21, 1888. Archives, Sisters of Divine Providence, St. Jean-de-Bassel. Copy: Archives, Sisters of Divine Providence, San Antonio, TX.

A few comments about the contents of *L'abbé* Michel's letter seem warranted. (The reader is referred to the entirety of the letter in Chapter XVI.)

First, Michel notes that Sister St. Andrew *"quittée librement en 1866."* This phrase means "left freely in 1866." Given that Mother Constantine seemed so supportive of the Texas mission, sending various Sisters, novices, and postulants to Texas in 1878, 1880, 1882, and 1883, the year noted (1866) seems strange. Did *L'abbé* Michel err in noting the year? Did he mean to say 1886?

In the "Registry of Vows" at St. Jean-de-Bassel under Sister St. André's signature which she penned in 1855 when she made vows, it notes *"quittée Texas 1866"* ("left for Texas 1866). Could this notation have been added to the registry sometime between 1883 and 1888 and Michel was referencing that notation in his own letter? The same notation (*quittée Texas*) is found under the signatures of other Sisters who left St. Jean-de-Bassel for Texas in 1878, 1880, and 1882. This writer is inclined to think that *L'abbé* Michel who was living in Metz, wrote to St. Jean-de-Bassel for information about Sister St. Andrew, and the information returned to him included the notation under her signature as described above.

Second, the state of *Abbé* Michel's health at the time of the writing of the letter is unknown, but he died one month later on April 22, 1888.[333]

Third, Mother Anna Houlné, Superior General at this time (1888), may not have been fully aware of the relationship between St. Jean-de-Bassel and Texas, though she probably met Mother St. Andrew during the summer months of 1878, 1880, 1882, or 1883, while she was in Germany. Since we do not know what Bishop Neraz may have communicated to St. Jean-de-Bassel, we are left to wonder what the Superior at St. Jean-de-Bassel really knew and understood about the situation in Texas.

The reader is left to ponder the circumstances in which Sister St. Andrew found herself in 1888.

---

333 Wilhelm, p. 76, 79, 80.

From August of 1887 to the spring of 1890, Sister St. Andrew lived alone in Castroville. The suicide death of Theresa Fruth Feltin, Louis Feltin's wife, in February 1890, precipitated Sister St. Andrew's move to San Jose, California, where she lived for ten years with her brother and his family.[334] John Isidore, Louis' eldest son, moved to Austin to live with his mother's sister and her husband.

Some specifics about Sister St. Andrew's experience in Castroville between August 1887 and spring 1890 remain unclear.

- Her March 2, 1888, letter to *Abbé* Michel indicates that she remained under an edict of excommunication by Bishop Neraz and that she no longer had vows. This letter is our only documentation of this fact.

- It is not known if she was ever formally dismissed from the Congregation, though it seems that a legal dispensation from her vows was never acquired. [At this time in church history, particular decisions about these types of legalities in diocesan congregations seem to be completely dependent upon the desires of the bishop of the diocese.] When Sister St. Andrew returned in 1900, she supposedly "pronounced again her perpetual vows."[335] However, there is no record of this in the General Council Minutes of the Congregation of Divine Providence which note her return.[336]

---

334 Callahan, p. 154.

335 Callahan, p. 155.

336 General Council Minutes, 1886-1903, p. 13. [The date of the entry is November 10, 1887, but the section referring to Sister St. Andrew's return has been inserted from a later date, presumably 1900.]

* **The reader will recall a letter that Mother St. Andrew received from Sister Marie in the fall of 1883 after Bishop Neraz's surprise visit to the St. Jean-de-Bassel Motherhouse in September 1883. See Endnotes to Chapter XV and the chapter itself.**

- It is not known what support she received from Providence House in Castroville. Her letter to *L'abbé* Michel indicates that she received nothing.

Other Noteworthy Correspondence

November 12, <u>1892</u>: Bishop Neraz wrote Mother Florence:

> As to the separate house of Castroville, I am not the one who asked for it and established it. When I was in St. Jean de Bassel I asked the Mother Sup. if she could help Castroville by furnishing some subjects and in reconising (sic) your house a branch of the Mother House and the superior answered me that it was impossible for her to do so, on account of the distance,* but I understood well that her refusal was on account of Mother St. Andrew, so I did the best I could to keep up your house, and thanks to God I succeeded … I think you have the same rule as they have at St. Jean de Bassel; …[337]

A Final Note

Interested readers may enjoy a biography of Mother Florence Walter, *Mother Florence Walter, A Biographical History*, by Sister Angelina Murphy, CDP. Written in 1980, this book illuminates some of the material in Chapter XVI and XVII of *The Tattered Heart* from the point of view of Mother Florence's life. The book is out-of-print, but copies are available from the Archives of the Congregation of Divine Providence in San Antonio, Texas.

---

337 Letter: Bishop Neraz to Mother Florence, November 12, 1892. Copy in Archives, Congregation of Divine Providence, San Antonio, TX.

ENDNOTES   *CHAPTER XVII*   *HOMECOMING*

The death of San Antonio Bishop John C. Neraz on November 15, 1894, at age sixty,[338] and Father Henry Pefferkorn's retiring to France sometime before 1900,[339] changed the ecclesial climate in the Diocese of San Antonio for the Sisters of Divine Providence. According to Sister Louis Joseph Lefevre's memoirs, "When Bishop Neraz died, a priest told Mother Andrew in California, but she did not come home immediately. She raised the children first and then wrote to ask if she could come home."[340]

By 1900 Mary Teresa, Louis Feltin's eldest daughter, was almost twenty-seven years old, and Lizette, the youngest, had just turned eleven. Mother St. Andrew believed that the children would be able to manage the household and the store without her. She wrote to Mother Florence asking for re-admittance to the Sisters of Divine Providence. Callahan wrote:

> When Mother St. Andrew's note came to the convent of Divine Providence, Mother Florence read it to the sisters, then home for the summer retreat, and great was the joy that filled every heart. She who had done so much for the Congregation would be made to feel how greatly appreciated was their first mother.[341]

---

338 Wangler, p. 20.

339 Wangler, p. 21. (Note: Callahan [p. 155] says that Pefferkorn returned to France in the spring of 1895 but Wangler quotes the *Official Catholic The Directory* which says "for 1896 ... [the San Antonio] Bishop's Council [was] composed of ... Fathers Buffard, Henry Pefferkorn and Christopher J. Smith." A September 2, 1898 article in the Castroville *Anvil Herald* in reference to St. Louis Day festivities in Castroville notes that "Father John Kirch was assisted [at Mass] by Rev. Henry Pefferkorn, of Our Lady of the Lake of San Antonio ..."

340 Memoirs held in Archives of the Congregation of Divine Providence, San Antonio, Texas

341 Callahan, p. 155.

In addition to the fact that the children had grown up, Mother St. Andrew's health reversals (heart problems, diabetes, and a very painful surgery at O'Connor Sanitorium) were no doubt part of the reason that she decided to return to Castroville in 1900.

Her ten years in San Jose had been both positive and productive. As Louise Feltin, Mother St. Andrew had provided Louis and his children with a good, prayer-filled, goal-oriented home. She had opened and operated a successful neighborhood grocery store. The two older girls worked in the grocery store and all the boys were employed. Louis himself had held a job during most of the decade that his family had been in San Jose.[342]

During the years that Sister St. Andrew was estranged (1887 to 1900), Mother Florence led the Sisters of Divine Providence through a period of extraordinary expansion. The Congregation received many vocations, 148 of whom became perpetually professed. Vocations continued to come from Germany, Poland, and Ireland; and the small villages of Texas began to yield more vocations as well.

Forty-four schools were opened between 1887 and 1900. Though two schools (St. Henry's and Our Lady of the Lake High School) were opened in San Antonio, most of the thirty-one schools opened in Texas served small rural towns with immigrant populations from Poland, Czechoslovakia, and Germany. Twelve schools were opened in Louisiana. In addition to the schools opened for white children, the Sisters of Divine Providence also opened several schools for African-American children who by law were excluded from attending school with white children.

St. Joseph Academy, begun in 1900 in Perry, Oklahoma Indian Territory, opened the way for five more schools which the Sisters of Divine Providence began in Indian Territory before Mother St. Andrew's death in 1905.

During the years that Bishop Neraz was the ecclesiastical superior of the diocesan congregation, Mother Florence supervised the translation of the *Book of Constitutions* (1887) and the implementa-

342 Inferred from information in the San Jose City Directories, 1890-1900.

tion of an 1890 decree from the Sacred Congregation of Bishops and Regulars (Rome) forbidding superiors to require Sisters to reveal their consciences to them. The decree also gave Sisters permission to receive Holy Communion without first asking their superiors.[343] Believing that the decree from Rome would have far-reaching impact on the lives of her Sisters, Mother Florence had the *Book of Constitution* reprinted in 1891 with the decree included in the binding.

At the time of this 1891 printing, Mother Florence decided to send the *Constitution* to Rome "in order to be examined and approved,"[344] but before doing so, she wrote to Neraz asking for his support as was her custom in all matters.[345] In his November 12, 1892, letter, Neraz told Mother Florence:

> I think you have the same rule as they have at St. Jean de Bassel; in that case there is nothing to be done as Rome will not examine them [rules] if they have been examined before. If there are some changes, which I do not think or remember, then it is only since I acted on the words of Mother superior (sic) at St. Jean de Bassel.[346]

Though Neraz's reply does not specifically use the term "pontifical," Callahan asserts that "Bishop Neraz did not commend the idea of their [the Sisters of Divine Providence of Texas] attempting to become pontifical in his reply to Mother Florence's letter (November

---

343 Callahan, p. 160.

344 Callahan, p. 161.

345 Callahan, p. 158-159.

346 Letter: Neraz to Mother Florence, November 12, 1892. Originally written in French; English translation in Archives of Congregation of Divine Providence, San Antonio, Texas.

9, 1892)."³⁴⁷ In other words, since the rule of the Castroville community was the same as the Sisters at St. Jean-de-Bassel, Neraz
indicated that Rome would not review the Rule in order to establish the Castroville community in a pontifical right.* The changes
in religious life ordered by the 1890 decree were not imbedded into
the *Book of Constitution* of the Sisters of Divine Providence of San
Antonio until 1901.

Callahan's assessment bears repeating: "When Mother Florence
became mother general in 1886, circumstances under Bishop Neraz
required that she should function in the Congregation independently of the councilors who with her formed the generalate.ᵛ It was
the bishop and the bishop alone who guided and directed her."³⁴⁸

Perhaps the decision that changed the congregation most significantly related to re-locating the Motherhouse. Mother Florence and
her Council (Sister Angelique Decker, Sister Mary Gonzaga Mosser,
and Sister Mary Flavienne Braun) moved the Motherhouse to sixteen acres three miles west of downtown San Antonio on property
donated by Mayor (of San Antonio) Elmendorf. The first building of

---

347 Callahan, p. 161.
* **Congregations of Religious Women and Men fall into two
canonical categories at this writing: congregations with pontifical approbation (approved by the Sacred Congregation of
Religious in Rome) which can send their members anywhere in
the world; congregations with diocesan approbation (approved
as a congregation by a local bishop) whose members minister
only in the diocese of the approving bishop. Women and men
with private vows (known as "consecrated virgins") who do not
live in community make their vows under a specific bishop.
At the end of the nineteenth century most congregations were
diocesan. Consecrated virgins as a category of religious life did
not exist in the late nineteenth century.**
ᵛ **generalate: the customary designation of the general officers of
a Congregation of Women or Men Religious.**
349 Callahan, p. 192.
* **The Congregation of Divine Providence became a congregation
of pontifical right in 1912.**

Divine Providence Convent at Our Lady of the Lake was begun in August 1895 and dedicated on July 9, 1896.

The academic program at Providence Academy at Castroville was moved into the San Antonio site and opened as Our Lady of the Lake High School. In 1900 the additions to the Main Building at Our Lady of the Lake Convent allowed for all active members of the Congregation, novices, and postulants to live at the San Antonio motherhouse. At Castroville, in addition to operating St. Louis School, the Sisters of Divine Providence used the convent building as a residence for retired Sisters and, as a boarding school for girls during the school year.

Bishop John Anthony Forest (Bishop of San Antonio from 1895 to 1911) did not wish to have the same oversight of the Congregation as had his predecessor, Bishop Neraz. Beginning in 1895 Mother Florence began a more independent leadership style. By the early part of the twentieth century, Mother Florence decided to secure Rome's approval* of the Texas Congregation and needed a priest-guide who would assist her toward this goal. Early in his episcopate, Bishop Forest gave the Oblate Fathers of the Southwest the charge of providing chaplains for Our Lady of the Lake Convent. At a meeting which Bishop Forest attended in 1903, Mother Florence and her General Council, proposed that Father Henry Constantineau, then pastor at St. Mary's Parish in downtown San Antonio, be named ecclesiastical superior of the diocesan congregation. With Forest's approval and the approval of the Superior of the Oblates of Mary Immaculate, Constantineau became the second ecclesiastical superior of the Sisters of Divine Providence in Texas. In addition to serving as ecclesiastical superior, Constantineau also continued to serve as pastor of St. Mary's Church and later as provincial superior of the newly created Southwest Province of the Oblates of Mary Immaculate.[349]

---

349 Callahan, p.198-201. The reader may wish to read Chapter VII in Callahan. It reviews a very interesting conflict between Forest and some of his priests who were protesting as invalid the 1903 election of Mother Florence under the Superiorship of Constantineau.

During the nearly fourteen years that Mother St. Andrew was estranged from the Congregation, thirty-seven Sisters, including Sister Mary Paul Keller and Sister Mary Agnes Wolf, were called to their eternal home. During her four years at the Castroville convent, twelve more Sisters died including Sister Angelique Decker and Sister Mary Ange Huver, both of whom had served on her own councils.

According to the minutes of General Council, Sister St. Andrew returned to Castroville, Texas, on October 27, 1900. The minutes further note that

> on entering, she handed to the Rev. Mother M. Florence, Sup. Gen'l, the sum of seven hundred dollars—$700.00 on condition that if the children of her brother, Louis Feltin, at present residing in San Jose, California, should claim a part of said money, $350 should be paid to them: viz: fifty dollars ($50.00) to each of his seven children.[350]

Letters written by Mother St. Andrew to her nieces in 1902-03 indicate that Louis Feltin visited her in Castroville. There is no indication that she saw other members of Louis' family after she returned to Castroville in 1900, though it is possible and likely that John Isidore who lived in Austin may have visited his aunt sometime between 1900 and her death.

Little is known of the four years that Mother St. Andrew spent in Castroville after her return from California. This part of Chapter XVII is based on two main sources: the memoirs of Sister Alma Marty and the letters that Mother St. Andrew wrote to her young

350 Minutes of the General Council, November 10, 1887. Archives, Congregation of Divine Providence, San Antonio, Texas. [This part of the minutes was added at a date later than the 1887 date. Actual date of addition is unknown.]

nieces. Sister Alma Marty (born Marie Cooner) was the daughter of Otilia (Tillie) Christilles Cooner (d. 1896 of typhoid fever) and William Cooner. Upon the death of his wife, William Cooner "went back North" and his daughter Marie, born on April 2, 1893, was shuffled between a foster home in San Antonio and uncles and aunts in Castroville (Christilles and Martys) until she was six years old. At that age she was accepted as a boarding student at Divine Providence Academy at the convent in Castroville. A girl of seven when Mother St. Andrew returned to Castroville in 1900, Sister Alma Marty recorded her vivid memories of Mother St. Andrew's several times during her own lifetime. Marie Marty was twelve when Mother died.[351]

Mother St. Andrew Feltin died from heart failure at the Castroville convent on February 1, 1900, at 5:00 in the morning. She was attended by Dr. John T. FitzSimon[352] and Father James H. Quinn, OMI, convent chaplain. Father Quinn said a requiem Mass for her in the convent chapel; and then, at the request of Father John Kirch, pastor of St. Louis Parish, her body was taken to the parish church where a second Mass was said. Her own former students bore her body to St. Louis Cemetery where she was interred with the other Sisters of Divine Providence who had preceded her in death.

The *Castroville Anvil-Herald* of Saturday, February 11, 1905, carried the following:

> Mother M. Andrew, first Sister of Divine Providence
> in Texas died at Castroville last Wednesday morning
> ... the hardships, trials, and humiliations she encoun-

---

351 "Names You Know: Mother St. Andrew Feltin, 1830-1905," *CDP Newsletter*, November 20, 1975. This memoir was written by Sister Alma Marty in 1936.

"Names You know: Sister Mary Alma Marty, 1993-," *CDP Newsletter*, Vol. III, No. 3, October 27, 1975.

Letter from Sister Alma Marty to Sister Florence Marie Kubis, May 12, 1965.

352 County Death Records, Hondo, TX.

tered are known to Him alone for whose sake they were born so generously. She was a woman of strong character, imbued with a true missionary spirit, that no obstacles, however great, could crush ...[353]

In 1918, the remains of the Sisters of Divine Providence who had been interred in St. Louis Cemetery were transferred to Providence Cemetery on the grounds of Our Lady of the Lake Convent in San Antonio, Texas. Mother St. Andrew's remains rest there now in the shadow of the cross of Jesus which she bore throughout her entire life.

---

353 *The Anvil-Herald*, Vol 19, No. 26, Saturday, February 11, 1905, p. 3.

APPENDIX

THE FELTIN FAMILY

The following presents a summary of what happened to Louis Feltin and his children after their 1890 move to San Jose, California.[354] It also notes the living descondants of Marie-Anne Feltin Seiter, Mother St. Andrew's sister.

Louis Feltin (1843[355]-1927) was fifty-seven years old when his sister Louise (Mother St. Andrew) returned to Castroville, Texas. The family lived at 180 N. 7ᵗʰ St. in San Jose when they first arrived in 1890 but within the first two years they had moved to 9ᵗʰ and Empire, where the family lived for twenty years. During the years that he lived in San Jose, Louis worked as a carpenter but the City Directories never list an employer. On May 12, 1922, three months after the death of his son Joseph Peter, Louis was admitted to Agnews State Hospital (San Jose) for unknown reasons. Feltin died on December 2, 1927 of "Exhaustion from Senility." He was interred

---

354 The records which follow are based on 1) City Directories of San Jose, CA; 2) US Census Records found on file at the Church of Jesus Christ of the Latter Day Saints; 3) information given to the writer by James A. Sarrail; 4) cemetery records of Calvary Cemetery in San Jose, CA, held at the cemetery; 5) cemetery records of Calvary Cemetery, Austin, TX, held in the Catholic Archives of Texas in Austin, TX; 6) California Death Records in Santa Clara County.

355 Various records note the birth year of Louis Feltin as 1840 (Strebler, p. 39), as 1855 (1910 US Census) and 1843 (California Death Certificate). All agree on August 3. The date of 1843 is the one accepted by this writer.

at Calvary Cemetery in San Jose, California, in the same section as his son James Frank.

John Isidore Feltin (1872—1959) did not move to San Jose, California, with his father Louis and brothers and sisters. He moved to Austin, Texas, where he lived with his aunt Elizabeth Fruth Moore and her husband Joseph Moore. He witnessed their marriage on October 2, 1889. John Isidore lived in Austin his entire life. The 1900 census record indicates that he was working as a "dairy assistant." John Isidore Feltin died on March 2, 1959, and is buried with his aunt and uncle in Calvary Cemetery in Austin, Texas.

Mary Teresa (Mamie) Feltin (1873—1944) was nearly seventeen when she moved with her father to San Jose, California. Though Callahan asserts that she became a teacher, San Jose Normal School (now San Jose State University) has no record of her attendance there. The *City Directories* of 1892, 1893, 1899, 1904, 1907-08 all show her living at 418 Empire or "se corner Empire and 9." A letter from Mother St. Andrew to Mother Florence written on May 16, 1904, asks Mother Florence to send the money Mother St. Andrew had been holding for the children because "on account of Mamie's sickness and her failure in business they are out of resource, and begged me to help now with what belongs to them." The 1907-08 record shows her occupation as "groceries." *San Jose City Directories* published after 1908 do not carry Mary Teresa as one of the Feltins living at 418 Empire. Mary Teresa was interred in Calvary Cemetery on September 16, 1944, in the same location as other family members, although none of those graves have markers. Since a death certificate is not on file with the State of California, no specific information about how or where she died is available.

Louis Nicolas Feltin (1876—1916) was not quite fourteen when the family moved to San Jose, California. His name appears in the *San Jose City The Directory* in 1892, 1899, 1904, 1913-14, and 1915 at the 418 Empire address. The directories note that he worked as a laborer. Louis Nicolas died on December 22, 1916, and was interred in Calvary Cemetery in San Jose on December 23, 1916. Cause of death is unknown.

Peter Joseph (aka Joseph Peter) Feltin (1878—1922) was eleven when Louis Feltin moved his family to San Jose, California. His name first appears in the *1899 San Jose City The Directory* and his occupation is noted as "lab" or laborer. He is listed in the 1904, 1913-14, 1915, 1918, 1920, and 1922 *Directories.* Most of the time his address is noted as 418 Empire; however, in 1913 his residence is listed (with his wife Henrietta) at 146 Santa Toroca. The cemetery records at Calvary Cemetery in San Jose show that Henrietta Feltin, the wife of Joseph P. Feltin, was interred there on December 9, 1914. St. Patrick's Church records do not show that they married there, though they might have married at either St. Joseph's Church or St. Mary's Church or in a civil ceremony.

On September 12, 1918, at age thirty-eight, Joseph registered for the draft. The address on his draft registration was Oakland, California, and he listed his father, living at 418 Empire, San Jose, CA, as his next of kin. The draft registration describes him as a machinist helper with Bethlehem Steel Works in Alameda, CA. His date of birth is noted as November 30, 1878; however, the baptismal registry of St. Mary's Parish in Austin, TX, carries the date of birth as November 20, 1878. The draft record describes him as tall, medium build, with brown hair and brown eyes. It further states that his "right eye not good." There is no evidence that Joseph was ever called into service. *The City Directory* records in San Jose show that Joe lived with his father at 418 Empire while working as a foreman at the Golden Gate Packing Company from 1918 until his death in March 1922. He was interred at Calvary Cemetery in San Jose on March 23, 1922.

Louise Brigit Feltin (1882–1910) was just eight when the family moved to San Jose, California. Her name is carried in the *San Jose City The Directory of 1899*, where she is noted to be 17 years old and a student. She is also in the 1904 and 1907-08 directories but no occupation is given in either one.

An interview with Elizabeth Feltin Sarrail on January 27, 1950, which is in the Archives of the Congregation of Divine Providence of San Antonio, Texas, notes: "My sister Louise who died in 1910, must have known more than the smaller children" about their aunt, Louise Feltin (Mother St. Andrew). No specific information about Louise Brigit's death other than this reference is available. Calvary Cemetery records do not show a Louise Feltin to be buried there. The sacramental records at St. Patrick's Church indicate that she was confirmed in 1895 but the sacramental records do not indicate that she married. [NB: The secretary at St. Patrick's was not able to locate all sacramental and funeral records from that time period when the writer visited there in January 2005.]

James Frank Feltin (1884—1910), age six when the family moved to San Jose, California, was confirmed at St. Patrick's Church in San Jose in 1895. According to the San Jose City The Directory of 1904, he was employed by "J Stock and Sons." Three years later he is listed in the 1907-08 The Directory as an "appr" or apprentice. The San *Jose Evening News and Record* carried the following headline and article:

> **SON OF WELL KNOWN FAMILY DIES SUDDENLY**—James Feltin, plumber by occupation and but 25 years old, died at the O'Connor Sanitorium this morning after a short illness from stomach trouble. Feltin resided with his father and several brothers and sisters at the family home Nine and Empire streets in this city. The funeral will take place from the

family home Friday afternoon, thence to St. Patrick's
church with interment in Calvary cemetary (sic).

Santa Clara County records show that James Frank Feltin died
of Hodgkins Disease. A second newspaper article reads:

FELTIN FUNERAL TOMORROW—The funeral
of James Frank Feltin will be held from the family
residence at the corner of Empire andNinth street at
9 o'clock Friday morning. A high mass will be celebrated at St. Patricks (sic) church and interment will
take place at Calvary Cemetery. The date of death was
December 21, 1910; the funeral and interment were
on December 23, 1910.

He is buried in the St. Helen Section of the cemetery as is his
father Louis Feltin. The other Feltins are buried in the St. Francis
Section.

Julia Feltin Hellwig (1886-1963) was barely four years old when
the family moved to San Jose, CA. She was confirmed at St. Patrick's
Church in 1899. City directories note her residence as 418 Empire
through 1914 when she was twenty-seven years old. Her occupation, according to the *1914 The Directory* was "steno" (stenographer).
In the 1920 US Census, she is listed as "Julia Hellwig, age 26" and
married to Otto Hellwig, an ironworker. She and Otto were married
until her death in 1963 although they did not reside at the same
address for most of their married life. [Hellwig lived in a downtown
San Jose hotel; Julia lived at 1900 The Alameda St.] Hellwig and
his brother Richard owned Hellwig Iron Works at 407 Vine in San
Jose. Julia Hellwig corresponded at times with Sister Alma Marty
and two of her letters are held in the Archives of the Congregation
of Divine Providence in San Antonio, Texas. According to the Santa

Clara County Death Records, Julia Feltin Hellwig died on October 28,1963.

Elizabeth Feltin Sarrail (1889-1966) was eight months old when Louis Feltin moved his family to San Jose, California. Lizette (Elizabeth) was confirmed at St. Patrick's Church on April 5, 1901. The <u>Catalogue of the State Normal School at San Jose, California for the Forty-seventh School Year Ending June 30, 1910</u>, shows that Lizette Feltin was enrolled as a student there. Other records do not indicate that she graduated, although her wedding announcement in the Sunday, November 26, 1911, edition of the *Mercury and Herald* (San Jose, CA), reports that:

> Last Sunday at Santa Cruz, in the Holy Cross Church, Mr. Emil Sarrail and Miss Lizette Felton (sic), were quietly united in marriage. The Very Rev. Monsignor P. J Fisher officiated at the ceremony. The bride is a very amiable and accomplished young lady, having graduated from the San Jose High School and the June '10 class of the San Jose State Normal, since which time, she has successfully taught school in Yolo County [CA]. She is also a talented musician and popular among the younger set. The groom, Emil Sarrail, formerly of San Jose, but for the last few years of Santa Cruz, is an esteemed young man of sterling qualities. He is at present engaged in business in Santa Cruz where the young pair will reside. Their many friends, bothin this city and Santa Cruz, will receive their marriage as a pleasant surprise.

Lizette and Emil Sarrail had one son, Jean-Albert (1917-1999), whograduated fromCreighton University in Omaha to become a renowned eye surgeon with offices in San Francisco. Jean-Albert and Marjorie Houser Sarrail (d. 1995) had three sons: James Albert (b.1943); Robert Samuel (b.1947); John Houser (b.1950). All three are married and live in the San Francisco bay area at the time of this writing.

Lizette Feltin Sarrail died in San Francisco on May 28, 1966. Her funeral was held at St. Brendan's Church and she is buried at Holy Cross Mausoleum in San Francisco. The writer is in touch regularly with James A. Sarrail, an attorney in the San Francisco bay area.

About the Family of Marie-Anne Feltin Seiter, Mother St. Andrew's Sister

Marie-Anne Feltin (1836-1906), Mother St. Andrew's sister married Isidore Seiter in LaWalck where they lived throughout the rest of their lives. They had one son, Joseph Seiter, who also had only one child, Anne-Marie Seiter who married Emile Bastian. They had three sons. Their middle son, Laurent Louis Bastian, Mother St. Andrew's great-grand nephew, was born in 1924 and still lives in the family home in LaWalck. He and his wife Louise Hemmerter Bastian (d. 1994) have four children: Laurence Bastian, Remy Bastian, Bernard Bastian, and Patrick Bastian. Monsieur Laurent Bastian and his sons Bernard and Remy were most helpful in the research of this book. Rev. Bernard Bastian, Mother St. Andrew's great-great-grand-nephew is a priest of the Diocese of Strasbourg and the leader of a Catholic Charismatic Community called "La Communauté du Puits de Jacob" (The Community of the Well of Jacob), based in the village of Plobsheim near Strasbourg, France. In addition to their retreat ministry at their community house in Plobsheim, they support a mission in Togo, Africa. The community now numbers over 200 members. The writer is in touch with Father Bastian regularly by e-mail.

ACKNOWLEDGEMENTS

My deepest gratitude goes to:

The Sisters of Divine Providence of San Antonio, Texas, for their prayers and support during the writing of this book

Sister Jane Coles, CDP, and Sister Margaret Riché, CDP, whose editing and critique greatly facilitated the process of writing and enhanced the product

Sister Alma Rose Booty,CDP, Sister Charlene Wedelich, CDP, and Ms. Janie Groves, readers of initial drafts, for their constant encouragement

My mother, Mrs. Alison Langford, for her prayers and encouragement; my sister Regina Decker who crafted "The Tattered, But Holy, Pioneer" quilt, inspiring the title

Marie-Jose Moss, Associate of the Congregation of Divine Providence for translating French materials and for reading the manuscript for accuracy of the French

Mr and Mrs. Osama [Barbara Tondre] El-Zorkani of Austin, TX, for on-going support of this writing project

Sr. Charlotte Kitowski, CDP, Archivist, and Sister Margeta Krchnak, CDP, Assistant to the Archivist, Congregation of Divine Providence, Our Lady of the Lake Convent Center, San Antonio, TX

Sr. Generosa Callahan, CDP (deceased: 1994) for her diligence in providing detailed information on Mother St. Andrew Feltin in her book *The History of the Sisters of Divine Providence* (copyright 1955, Sisters of Divine Providence)

Sr. Mary Joseph Neeb, CDP (deceased: 1916) for capturing the earliest years of the history of the Congregation of Divine Providence in her *Memoirs*

Sr. Angelina Murphy, CDP, for her work in compiling an informal chronicle on Mother St. Andrew Feltin and for her biography of Mother Florence Walter, CDP

Sr. James Aloysius Landry, CDP, (deceased) who assisted Sr. Generosa Callahan with the research and whose translation work makes research today so much easier

Sr. Ann Linda Bell, CDP, whose translation of primary sources (French) facilitates today's research

Congregation des Sœurs de la Divine Providence, St. Jean-de-Bassel, France, for their hospitality and assistance with research in their archives, and *Sœur* Gabrielle Metzinger, Archivist, for her assistance

Andrew Garrett Cross for his work on the cover design

Sr. Mary Joan Dolhan, Congregation of Divine Providence, St. Anne's Convent, Melbourne, KY, Congregational Archivist

Sr. Amata Hollas, IWBS of Victoria, TX, for her assistance in gaining access to archival material in the Incarnate Word and Blessed Sacrament Sisters archives at their motherhouse in Victoria

Brother Edward Loch, SM, Archivist, Archdiocese of San Antonio, TX

Mrs. Minnie Bartsch, Curator of Bastrop County Museum, Rockne, Texas

Ms. Susan Eason, Archivist, Catholic Archives of Texas, Austin, TX

Staff at the History Room, Anaheim Public Library, Anaheim, California

James Reed, Archivist, History San Jose, San Jose, California

Sister Dorothy Anhaiser, Archivist for the Sisters of the Incarnate Word and Blessed Sacrament of Corpus Christi, Texas

Sister Rosemary Meimans, Archivist, Ursuline Sisters, St. Louis, Missouri

Sr. Francesca, CCVI, Archivist, Sisters of Charity of the Incarnate Word in San Antonio, TX

Mr. James A. Sarrail of San Mateo, CA, the great grandnephew of Mother St. Andrew who supplied valuable materials on the Feltin family in California

Mr. Laurent Bastian of LaWalck, Alsace, France, great grand nephew of Mother St. Andrew and his sons Rev. Bernard Bastian, Strasbourg, France, and Remy Bastian of Schiltigheim, Alsace, France, who were invaluable sources of information on the history Feltin family

Drew E. Guion, Graphic Designer, Our Lady of the Lake University, San Antonio, Texas, for help with graphics

Catherine T. Maule, Graphic Designer, Our Lady of the Lake University, San Antonio, Texas, for help with graphics

Anne Gomez, Department of Communications and Marketing, Our Lady of the Lake University, San Antonio, Texas, for help with graphics

And to those who helped through their prayers and words of encouragement.

SELECTED BIBLIOGRAPHY

Internet Sites

"About Bastrop County" Internet Site www.cr.nps.gov

Block, W. T., "German Immigrants to Texas" (2006) Internet Site: www.texasescapes.com

"Congregation of the Sisters of St. Joseph" Internet Site: www.csjp. org

"Fredericksburg," Texas Escapes Online, 2006, Internet Site www.texasescapes.com

"High Hill, Texas," Internet Site: www.tsha.texas.edu

"Handbook of Texas," Internet Site: texas.edu/

Jett, Robin, "Clarksville," Texas Escapes Online 2003 Internet Site: www.texasescapes.com

Long, Christopher, "Martinez, Texas" Internet Site: www.tsha.utexas. edu/handbook/online

"Mary Frances Cusack" Internet Site: en.wikipedia.org/wiki/

McComb, David G., The Handbook of Texas Online, 2001. Internet Site: www.tsha.texas.edu

Oommen, Sheena, Cultural Crossroads, "Hin' nach Texas! Off to Texas" Internet Site www.houstonculture.org

"Schulenburg, Texas," Internet Site: www.tsha.edu

"Sisters of St. Joseph" Internet Site: http://allexperts.com

"The German Texans" Internet Site: www.texancultures.ut

"Site Internet de Douane" (A French Internet Site)

The Columbia Encyclopedia, Sixth Edition, 2001-2005, Internet Site: www.bartleby.com"

"The History of Galveston Island," Internet Site: www.galveston.com/h

The Library of Congress, ed, *Digital History of America, 1876-1900*, "German Immigrants in Texas," Internet Site www.digitalhistory.uh.edu

"The Texas Almanac, 2000-2001" Internet Site www.angelfire.com

Thorsen, Steffen, "1860 Calendar" Internet Site www.timeanddate.com

Books

"A Short Biography of Rev. Father Nicolas Feltin," *History of St. Joseph's Parish*. Unpublished. Held in the Archives of the Archdiocese of San Antonio, Texas, San Antonio, Texas.

Boehme, SM, Rev. Gerald, *Joseph Bader—Co-Founder of a Texas Family*. Castroville, 1963. (Privately printed; located in Castroville Public Library, Castroville, Texas)

Callahan, CDP, Sr. Generosa, *The History of the Sisters of Divine Providence*. Milwaukee, WI: Bruce Publishing Company, 1955.

Costin, CSC, M. Georgia, *Priceless Spirit-A History of the Sisters of Notre Dame, 1841-1893*. Notre Dame, IN: University of Notre Press, 1994.

Fialka, John J., *Sisters—Catholic Nuns and the Making of America*. New York: St. Martin's Press, 2003.

Finck, CCVI, Sr. Mary Helena, *The Congregation of the Sisters of Charity of the Incarnate Word*. Washington, DC: The Catholic University of America Press, 1925

Geispolsheim—Entre Tradition et Modernisme. Strasbourg: Editions Coprur, 1999

Gittinger, Ted, Connie Rihn, Roberta Haby, and Charlene Snavely, *St. Louis Church, Castroville*. San Antonio, TX: Graphic Arts, 1973.

Graves, W.W., *History of Neosho County*. St. Paul, Kansas: Journal Press, 1949.

Gruber, CDP, Marie-Jose (Sr. Pierre), *La Congregation de la Divine Providence—1827-1918.* ICFP, 1982.

Heck, Michele-Caroline, *All Alsace.* Firezze, Italy: Cora Editrice, 1984.

Hegarty, CCVI, Sr. Mary Loyola, *Serving with Gladness*, Milwaukee, WI: The Bruce PublishingCompany, 1967.

Humbert, CDP, Sr. Agnes Margaret, *A History of the American Province of the Congregation of Divine Providence of St. Jean-de-Bassel*, France, Melbourne, KY, 1989. (Privately published.)

Jacks, L. V., *Claude (Marie) Dubuis, Bishop of Galveston*, New York: B. Herder Book Co., 1946.

Klein, Rev. Peter (ed.), *Catholic Source Book*, Worthington, MN: The Printers, 1980.

Landregan, Steve, *Catholic Texans: Our Family Album*, China: The Catholic Diocese of Dallas, 2003.

Larsen, Erik, *Isaac's Storm*, New York: Crown Publishers, 1999.

Lawler, Ruth, *The Story of Castroville.*

Ludwig, Yvonne Chandler, *Three Pioneer Families, Castroville*, Texas 1844-1899. Lick Enterprises: San Antonio, TX, 2003.

Michelin Travel Publications, eds., *The Green Guide—Alsace, Lorraine, Champagne.* Hannay House: Herts, UK, 2004.

Moore, James Talmadge, *Through Fire and Flood—The Catholic Church in Frontier Texas*,College Station, TX: Texas A & M Press, 1002.

Morkovsky, CDP, Sr. Mary Christine, "The Challenge of Catholic Evangelization in Texas," *The Journal of Texas Catholics* (online)

Montrose, Donald (Rev.), <u>The Story of a Parish—Its Priests and Its People</u>. Anaheim, CA: St. Boniface Parish, 1961.

Murphy, CDP, Sister Angelina, "Chronicles." [Unpublished collection of materials held in the Archives of the Congregation of Divine Providence, San Antonio, TX]

Neeb, CDP, Sister Mary Joseph, *Memoirs of Fifty Years—Congregation of the Sisters of DivineProvidence.* Nic Tengg: San Antonio: 1916.

Perrichon, Abbe Jean (Mme Hectorine Piercey, ed.), *The Life Of Bishop Dubuis, Apostle of Texas*, Lyons, 1900. [unpublished]

Rios, J. A., Guedas, *Recuerdos—The Hispanic Heritage of Medina County*. 1985. [Unpublished, Castroville Public Library]

Sisters of the Incarnate Word and Blessed Sacrament, ed., *Extending the Incarnation into the Twentieth Century*. Victoria, TX: IWBS, 1998. [Privately printed]

Strebler, Msgr. Joseph, *Alsaciens au Texas*, Strasbourg, France: L'Asatique de Poche, 1975.

Wangler, Msgr. Alexander C., Editor, *Archdiocese of San Antonio, 1874-1974*, San Antonio, Texas: Archdiocese of San Antonio, 1974.

Waugh, Julia Nott, and J. A. Guedes, ed., *Castroville and Henry Castro Empresario*, Austin, TX: Nortex Press, 1986.

Weaver, Bobby D., *Castro's Colony*, College Station, TX: Texas A & M University Press,1985.

Wilhelm, Abbe J.,*La Congregation des Soeurs de la Divine Providence de St. Jean-de-Bassel*. Bar-le-Duc: St. Paul Imprimerie, 1927.

Winks, Robin W. and Joan Neuberger, *Europe and the Making of Modernity*. New York/Oxford: Oxford University Press, 2005.

Wootens, Dudley G., *A Comprehensive History of Texas*. Dallas, TX, 1898 [Castroville Public Library]

SISTERS OF DIVINE
PROVIDENCE TODAY

We Sisters of Divine Providence of Texas are a community of women religious rooted in our confidence that God is provident. We participate in the mission of Jesus by responding to the needs of the time through ministry and service.

Founded by Blessed John Martin Moye in Alsace-Lorraine, France in 1762, and established in Texas by Mother St. Andrew Feltin in 1866, we have always had education as our traditional ministry. Little did Mother St. Andrew know that her zeal for education would animate us in our ministries for more than 130 years, that her words would kindle the fire of faith and trust in a provident God in the lives of so many.

Formal school structures begun by Mother St. Andrew and our pioneer Sisters are no longer the only means we Sisters of Divine Providence see as providing education for those in need. Today, in the Catholic Church's post Vatican Council II era, many of our Sisters have opted to continue educational ministries as pastoral and campus ministers, as counselors and family therapists, as hospice and hospital chaplains, as spiritual directors, as researchers and writers, as advocates for justice and peace. Wherever there are opportunities to call forth our potential and that of others we Sisters of Divine Providence are continuing the legacy of our Texas foundress.

Impelled by the spirit of Mother St. Andrew, we continue "to find creative ways to educate, to evangelize" (CDP Constitution # 51), to live out our spirituality, our total trust in a loving provident God. Giving direction to our lives in prayer and ministry in a world community of the 21st century, we have proclaimed:

677

In response to the pervasive violence in our society and our universe, we commit ourselves to work for peace and non-violence in all that we do.

In response to the spiritual hunger of our world, we commit ourselves to delve into God's love as contemplatives in action.

In this way our lives and our actions will witness hope in God's providential love for all creation.

(General Chapter Statement 2004)

All proceeds from the sale of this book assist the Congregation of Divine Providence of San Antonio, Texas, to provide for the care of their aged and infirm members.

978-0-595-43639-2
0-595-43639-0

Printed in the United States
124657LV00001B/123/A

9 780595 436392